CONTENTS

Title Page
ACKNOWLEDGMENTS
PART ONE: CRASH AND RUN

CHAPTER ONE	1
CHAPTER TWO	10
CHAPTER THREE	22
CHAPTER FOUR	35
CHAPTER FIVE	42
CHAPTER SIX	59
CHAPTER SEVEN	66
CHAPTER EIGHT	77
CHAPTER NINE	84
CHAPTER TEN	93
CHAPTER ELEVEN	102
CHAPTER TWELVE	108
CHAPTER THIRTEEN	120
CHAPTER FOURTEEN	132
CHAPTER FIFTEEN	139
CHAPTER SIXTEEN	149
CHAPTER SEVENTEEN	165
CHAPTER EIGHTEEN	177

CHAPTER NINETEEN	185
CHAPTER TWENTY	197
CHAPTER TWENTY-ONE	203
CHAPTER TWENTY-TWO	212
CHAPTER TWENTY-THREE	222
CHAPTER TWENTY-FOUR	237
PART TWO: REFINED BY FIRE	251
CHAPTER TWENTY-FIVE	252
CHAPTER TWENTY-SIX	263
CHAPTER TWENTY-SEVEN	275
CHAPTER TWENTY-EIGHT	293
CHAPTER TWENTY-NINE	301
CHAPTER THIRTY	309
CHAPTER THIRTY-ONE	319
CHAPTER THIRTY-TWO	333
CHAPTER THIRTY-THREE	354
CHAPTER THIRTY-FOUR	360
CHAPTER THIRTY-FIVE	377
CHAPTER THIRTY-SIX	395
CHAPTER THIRTY-SEVEN	411
CHAPTER THIRTY-EIGHT	422
CHAPTER THIRTY-NINE	431
CHAPTER FORTY	439
CHAPTER FORTY-ONE	453
CHAPTER FORTY-TWO	471
CHAPTER FORTY-THREE	488
CHAPTER FORTY-FOUR	504
CHAPTER FORTY-FIVE	518

CHAPTER FORTY-SIX	529
CHAPTER FORTY-SEVEN	539
CHAPTER FORTY-EIGHT	546
CHAPTER FORTY-NINE	558
CHAPTER FIFTY	573
CHAPTER FIFTY-ONE	581
CAST OF CHARACTERS	591
GLOSSARY OF TERMS	596
APPENDIX A - SUNSHINE LAKE RESIDENTS (BY CABIN)	605
APPENDIX B - MAJOR REX'S FIELD SURGEON BAG	606
ABOUT THE AUTHOR	608

TURN RED TOMORROW

By Michael Zargona

Enjoy!

MZ

ACKNOWLEDGMENTS

Turn Red Tomorrow is over 20 years in the making, so there are plenty of people to thank.

First and foremost, I thank my wife for all the evenings lost actually writing the book.

Thank you to Jess Molly Brown for her professional editing of my rough draft, advice on what to do next, and patience with my late-night random questions.

Thanks to B.G., a retired U.S. Army field surgeon, for his help with the medical and injury material in the book.

Thanks to D.F., a U.S. Marine Corps CBRN Officer, for his help with the CBRN material and suggestions that helped build one of the main characters.

Thanks to my beta readers, J.M. and D.C., for having the diligence to finish this weighty tome, especially considering it was about 10% longer before necessary trimming took place.

Thanks to Grace June for her help with the cover layout.

And finally, a thank you to my late father for providing encouragement for my writing throughout our lives together.

PART ONE: CRASH AND RUN

CHAPTER ONE
Early October

As was his Sunday morning habit, John carefully wheeled his motorhome into the parking lot of a church he had never attended before.

Some Sundays he felt all of his nearly seven and half decades of life in his bones, his joints, and his level of enthusiasm. On such days he sought out a small, quiet church where he could safely sit in the back and garner no attention.

On other days John woke, felt that figurative poke to the chest and looked for a large church, one with a parking lot full of new cars and SUVs and an electric billboard that scrolled upcoming events in bright LEDs along with the time and the temperature. Today was one of those days.

It had been easy to seek out this particular church as the small Missouri town he had hitched to for the last few days had only one street of consequence. In a month John would likely be in Louisiana—and clear to Florida by December. While his legal residence was in Ohio, his motorhome had served for several years as his year-round retirement home. The thirty-two foot long Mirada had a long list of amenities but "great place to spend a cold winter" was not among them.

As he walked to the glass double doors of the church he took note of the vehicles he passed. Very few were less than four or five years old and most had dings, dents, and damage that in years past would have been repaired in short order. This was not a new phenomenon for John, just another reminder of the thin gilding of American success starting to wear away, exposing the dull lead of economic reality. Two younger men in dark polo shirts and khakis, with radios clipped to their belts, roamed the parking lot; ostensibly to help the elderly or infirm but more likely to keep brazen daylight car prowlers away.

    The door greeters—a middle-aged man and woman dressed in business attire—both gave him a careful nod and a forced smile. John was quite aware that he didn't fit the mold of "perfect potential church member." He looked, appropriately, like a washed-up, hirsute arena rocker and had been recently described as an "anorexic Santa Claus" by a group of teenagers. The dirty, well-worn denim jacket, blue jeans, and laced leather roper boots he wore did not help bolster his image to the polished Ivory Tower church crowd.

    A paper was taped to the center glass between the doors. In bold purple letters, it read:

DUE TO RISK OF INFECTION LSCC STAFF AND GREETERS WILL REFRAIN FROM SHAKING HANDS AND OTHER PHYSICAL CONTACT UNTIL FURTHER NOTICE. THANKS FOR UNDERSTANDING!

    Perhaps the greeters' aloof attitude stemmed from the scare. John nodded back, entered, and found a seat near the back of the broad, well-lit sanctuary. As the service started he merely hummed along with the songs ably performed by their team. He knew them well, but too many years of booze, hard drugs, and late nights had wiped out the mediocre singing ability God had given him. While he hummed he looked around and confirmed his suspicions regarding this church body. There were very few children and teenagers, and no college-age adults whatsoever. Some large churches divided their services or classes by age, but John had noticed the disparity as soon as he had walked in the door. Even the young children seemed mostly in the care of grandparents or couples who had adopted well into their later years.

John had attended hundreds of churches across the country in the span of thirty years. Some congregations were vibrant and full of young adults and families. Others careened headlong, whether by commission or omission, into total senescence which invariably either led to the end of that particular church or a much-needed revival. John had made a point to revisit certain churches years later and it was a troubling trend he had witnessed grow and propagate firsthand. While his high-school hero Kerouac traveled in search of God, John liked to think that he traveled to see if others remembered Him. All churches changed over time; it was the direction that mattered.

Eventually the pastor (definitely of the Midwestern small town mold with cemented hair, a dark suit, and tie) took the stage behind the podium. Unlike the woman playing with her phone next to him, John intended to listen to the man's every word. Since he wasn't here for the community, coffee, or drinking fountain gossip, a good message was the only thing John truly locked in on.

In his experience churches tended to preach with three different models: different themes that changed every month or so, a "Bible study" where the Word was taught systematically from the pulpit, and the "current events" model that focused on making sense of earthly affairs via the Bible. This small town church clearly used that last model. Normally John believed it to be inferior to the first two but times being what they were, there was plenty of strife to focus on.

The pastor paused and continued, "If you have faith, do not worry yourself about these rumors of disease, the financial troubles we've been hearing about for weeks! *Nahum 1:7* says, 'The Lord is good, a refuge in times of trouble. He cares for those who trust in Him'."

Hmm, John thought, opening his Bible, *but the following two verses read, "But with an overwhelming flood He will make an end of Nineveh; He will pursue his foes into the realm of darkness. Whatever they plot against the Lord He will bring to an end; trouble will not come a second time."*

Going on, the pastor said, "The Bible makes it clear to us that if we just ask, if we just pray, we will receive if we have faith and we truly believe our prayers will be answered. One of my favorite verses is James 4:2 which says, 'You do not have because you do not ask God.' This goes hand in hand with Matthew 7:7, 'Ask and it *will* be given to you.' Can I get an amen to that?" About half of those present murmured in response.

John shook his head slowly and muttered under this breath, which was enough to break Phone Lady's concentration and earn him a glare. Nearing noon, John noticed some congregants begin to fidget, check the time, and generally make it known that the end was nigh. Football, potlucks, and barbeques awaited. At the close of the service John picked up the worn Gideon Bible he had tucked into his suitcase almost forty years before and headed for the door.

"Excuse me sir," John heard from behind, "but I wanted to welcome you to our church, I don't believe I've seen you here before." It was the pastor. "Apologize for not shaking your hand, but with the outbreak...."

John was feisty, opinionated, and often lacked tact, but he wasn't mean. He wasn't going to point out the dissonance between those words and what the man had just said not ten minutes before. "I won't hold it against you, and yes I'm new here. I'm retired—a snowbird if you will—and I'm hopping my way south at the moment."

"Well, in that case I hope you enjoyed the message today."

John cleared his throat. "I don't mean to sound rude, but, frankly, I didn't agree with it at all."

The pastor's expertly-trimmed eyebrows went up a notch. John knew well that the pastor had been mentally gliding after having preached two services already today and John had him at a bit of a disadvantage. Having been on stage and in front of a crowd for most of his life, John knew the taxed feeling and lack of wit that lingered for hours or even days afterward.

"Sir, I'm sorry you feel that way. What didn't you agree with?" A small crowd had gathered though not to hear the brewing discussion. Merely the usual group of people that needed a bit of a pastor's time after a service.

"I don't claim to know the mind of God, but I do know that He is *not* a system that can be gamed for earthly benefit. What you preached today falls in line with *faith theology*—the belief that if you just have enough faith everything will be fine and that a person's troubles in life suggest a lack of faith. I've found that in both the Word of God and my personal experience, sometimes times are toughest when you're closest to God. Just look at the apostle Paul, for instance. He seemed pretty close to his Creator while in a Roman jail cell."

The sets of eyes that had been fixed on the pastor, waiting for him to conclude his greeting of this odd old man to their church, had snapped over to John and now back to the pastor, waiting his response to a clear challenge. "Ah," the pastor stammered, "I've heard of 'faith theology' or the 'name it and claim it' belief system, but it's something those powder blue suit televangelists use to suck money out of the pockets of widows and the weak willed. We don't teach that here." The pastor paused, then his eyes lit up and the smile returned. "Even so, didn't Jesus tell his followers that faith the size of a mustard seed could move mountains, and that nothing would be impossible?"

John listened to the rebuttal but didn't form a counterpoint; if the pastor didn't believe he taught it, John knew he wouldn't convince him otherwise in a minute or two—

and it wasn't his intent to do so. "Yes, of course, but how did that play out in the lives of others that encountered Jesus? When Jesus spoke of the 'mustard seed faith,' the disciples had just tried to cast out a demon but could not. Later, in the book of Acts they could. What do you believe changed?"

The pastor thought for a moment, then answered, "They had more faith. They had seen Christ resurrected. They knew the truth."

"But, do we read that they prayed for their own well-being? Any of the early church leaders? Tell me, *were they in it for themselves at all?*"

"I don't suppose so, no," replied the pastor, looking away.

John read the body language and knew the impromptu debate would soon be over. "Sir, we are both brothers in Christ, I have no anger or condemnation for you or your flock here. I am no prophet, but I have felt it in my soul to continue to spread the message that the current state of affairs won't last forever. Hard times *will* come and faith *will* be tested. It is already harder to be an authentic follower of Christ than it was twenty or thirty years ago. Soon none of us will be able to live like the Laodicean church as described in Revelation. Lukewarm will not be an option. I fear that the Fair Weather Christian attitude will be extinguished and many will turn away from their faith. We need all the strong brothers and sisters we can get. I'll be praying for this church."

His mini sermon hadn't connected, or perhaps he'd taken his point too far. John found that was all too common at this point in his life, but he felt time was too short for anything less than straight talk. John saw the pastor shift back into glide mode as he put on a forced smile. "Thank you for coming today, sir, and while I'll agree to disagree with you, I hope you'll come back when you pass through in the future."

As he headed toward the exits, a striking older woman with short white hair, a blue pantsuit, and a multicolored brooch on her left lapel stepped in front of him. "I really don't like to admit it, but I agree with what you said to Pastor Dunlap just now."

"Oh?"

"Yes. My late husband led this church for almost thirty years, and things were different then. Not perfect, but better. My name is Kathy, by the way. When my husband Lonnie passed, we did a formal search and here we are, five years and three pastors later. This church body is half the size it was ten years ago. I'd leave myself, but I fear that so many of people here, people that were close to my husband, would follow me out the door and this church would be done for."

"I'm sorry to hear of your loss, Kathy. Why so many church leaders?"

Kathy sighed. "Well, the elders and members originally felt that we needed to get younger. It wasn't a bad idea. I'm sure you can tell we're not exactly boiling over with young people here." She chuckled humorlessly. "So we brought in a young man right out of seminary, and the worst of both worlds happened. We lost many of our older members, but almost no young people showed up."

"Why not?" He was genuinely interested.

"The messages, services, songs—everything really—are controlled by the elders, people our age, of course. It ended up being a young man preaching an old man's message, which didn't resonate with anyone. So, an elder, a respected businessman stepped up and offered to lead the church. That didn't work either. He couldn't devote the time necessary and ended up using canned sermons that no one liked.

"Pastor Dunlap seemed like a godsend at first. He had led a very successful church in East Memphis but had wanted to semi-retire to a one-service church like ours used to be, you know, one out in the country. We didn't do our homework very well though. The church he left was as country club as they come—valet parking, silver punch bowls, you know what I mean. Now he's trying to recreate that here, but most people in this town are on assistance and don't have two nickels to rub together after they cash their check, buy groceries, and pay their bills. I don't like how we all just pretend everything is okay with our lives. We should be helping one another, not hiding our problems."

"Kathy, I appreciate you confiding in me. I've been to hundreds of churches in the last thirty or so years, many as a guest speaker but mostly just sitting in the pews getting fed. Your fears are well-founded. The old 'social club' churches are dying on the vine. That old rule, especially in small towns, that you had to be in the right church to be seen as successful no longer applies. I actually see what is happening as a *good* thing. People that 'did church' just to be seen in a better light by others are like the chaff John the Baptist described. I've been in thriving churches where millionaires sit right next to teenagers and hold their hands high in the same way. Because they realize it's not about your earthly accomplishments, all the straw they've built up over their lives."

"Yes, exactly."

"Kathy, I doubt I will be back here to find out, but please promise to do one thing."

"What's that?"

John looked her in the eye. "When tough times come, and I'm sure they're coming, do what you can to make sure the people here are taken care of. It's my experience that people who pin their faith to their circumstances will turn away when times get really bad. I'm not talking about, 'chuck instead of top sirloin' hardship, I'm thinking it will be more like, 'I don't know where my next meal is coming from.' Congregations that are about a nice building and an hour on Sundays will simply dissolve away, but those that are about people helping one another through will survive. I can't say when it will happen, I don't know that, but I believe it in my heart that it's very soon."

"I feel it too, John. Best of luck to you, and God bless.

You're brave to do what you do, coming to churches and, well, ruffling a few feathers."

John chuckled. "Brave? I'm not brave at all. If I was brave, I'd pick a church and stick around to do the actual hard work of making it better. But I haven't stayed in the same spot for more than a month since nineteen sixty-eight. It's in my blood to ramble on, so I will. Thank you for your time, and as I told Pastor Dunlap I'll be praying for you all."

John left with the feeling that he had served His purpose there that day.

CHAPTER TWO
Monday, Late October

Matthew Flanigan carefully wrapped the shoulder strap of his carry-on bag around his left leg and settled down to catch a quick nap before his flight. A laptop case that had embarrassingly disappeared a few years before had been a hard lesson he wasn't going to repeat. Matt was thankful this was only a three day trip, which allowed him to just take the one bag through careful packing. He was also thankful he'd found an actual seat and not been left with the floor like so many waiting for Monday morning business flights. Seattle-Tacoma hadn't seen the dip in traffic experienced by most other airports in the country and remained the gateway to Asia and beyond. Fortunately his flight was only to Bob Hope in Burbank for the twice-yearly sales meeting at their regional HQ. While he'd miss home and his wife of three years, Desirée, he definitely looked forward to leaving the Seattle area's gloom in April and October for some much-needed Southern California sunshine.

Closing his eyes, he heard the television overhead blurt out, "Breaking news has just come in. The New York Stock Exchange has enacted a trading curb for the day to ease the decline that began in overseas markets and elsewhere over the weekend. While we're still gathering facts, there has been no announcement of a bank holiday or other measures in effect. We'll keep you updated as more information becomes available." Matt's eyes snapped back open and he saw the coiffed blonde anchorwoman turn to her male counterpart. "Ben, do you think this a repeat of last year?"

"Too early to tell, Jen. If it hadn't happened before, I'd say there would be nothing to worry about. Let's just hope people keep their heads and don't overwhelm the system. I mean, of course, create a run on the banks. Even with the controls in place, millions of people overreacting could still create a lot of havoc."

Heaven forbid people 'overwhelm the system' by wanting their own money. Neither previous holiday had affected Matt, but it did cause him and Des to keep extra cash on hand at home. Unfortunately for Matt, he only carried a single emergency $100 bill in his wallet, which was more than most.

Matt watched as several people just shrugged off the news and went back to what they'd been doing, playing on phones or managing unruly children, mostly. This type of announcement was just not a huge shock to anyone anymore. For two plus years, countries in Europe had been dumping the Euro and reverting to their old currencies. Saber-rattling in the Middle East between Israel and several Muslim nations in the Middle East was rising to a fever pitch, which had caused swings in the price of oil and by consequence everything else that relied on transport. Terrorist attacks on the European continent and Britain had become regular news, barely even making the front page of most big city newspapers. The stock market crash last fall, and the subsequent three day bank holiday, had played a major factor in the Presidential election. The new President had already been running on a platform that included the reigning in of the financial sector, and the disruption highlighted that need for many voters. With inflation ratcheting upward and the accompanying cash controls, there had been constant buzz in the news and online about the total nationalization of the American financial sector. People figured, 'if taxpayers have to foot the bill when things fail, why don't we call the shots?' It was overly simplistic but made for great headlines.

Fortunately for Matt, he worked for Dynamix Medical, a key supplier to major hospital groups in the United States and Canada. No matter the downswings or upswings in the economy, there were always people who needed medical care. Matt had literally started on the ground floor after leaving the Army almost ten years ago, packing boxes in the company's warehouse in Fontana, CA. From there he had become a CSR—customer service representative—and had waited for his turn to apply for the handful of positions close to his childhood home of Dupont, Washington, a small, upper middle class community about fifty miles south of Seattle. He'd been in his current role of territory sales rep for five years and was the sole survivor out of an original group of six. All of his cohorts had been near the end of careers that had begun around the company's founding in the late 1980s, and all had been eased out of their positions into unwelcome early retirement. While terms like "ageism" and "exorbitant health benefit costs" had been muttered darkly in the lunchroom, the real culprit had been client consolidation. Thirty years ago, it had been enough for people in Matt's position to work with local purchasing agents, bring them donuts, and take them to a baseball game now and again to create a good book of accounts. Now, there were just a few gigantic healthcare groups that made up 85 percent of the company's clients, and one determined, energetic, and professional rep could handle the workload.

Matt made no apologies. Things just shook out differently for different folks. The last generation had enjoyed constant business growth and job security for a long, long time, something Matt couldn't take for granted. He knew he looked older than his true age of thirty-one and used it to his advantage. In high-level business negotiations, most of the people on the other side of the table were near his parents' age and wanted to work with someone they looked at as a peer and not a punk kid. With prominent crow's feet around his blue-gray eyes, an olive complexion courtesy of his Italian grandmother, and prematurely graying mustache and well-kept beard, most figured him closer to forty. The key was to look older, but actually have youthful energy to cope with the 'road warrior' schedule and not be forced to simply recuperate during the weekend. Matt had to cover all of Washington, Oregon, Idaho, Western Montana, and Alaska —the largest territory in the company—and physically keep up without burning out.

His brother Kyle, an entrepreneur, had turned him onto a news site a few years ago that Matt brought up on his phone. The main television news networks did a decent job of reporting the "what" but never devoted any time to "how" and "why" things happened. The very first headline was, "THE MOTHER OF ALL STOCK MARKET CRASHES IN PROGRESS, MORE TO COME." Matt clicked on it, but the article failed to load. It was clear their servers were swamped.

The first three days of the meeting, unsurprisingly, had been strained and unproductive. Out of the seven company reps from west of the Mississippi, five, including Matt, had flown in and were all anxious to wrap everything up and get home. Discussions of sales numbers, margin improvement strategies, and current account penetration took a back seat in Matt's mind when compared to the safety of his wife and uncertainty for the future.

That very morning, the feared bank holiday had become official, though it had been a *fait accompli* as anonymous bank executives had leaked the information through blogs, social media, and print the night before. This would have been more earth-shattering if not for the ongoing economic disintegration everyone had been already living with. The proverbial boy had already cried wolf quite enough already.

Rigid controls had been put in place that made it very difficult for anyone to withdraw physical cash, ostensibly an effort to control inflation. Only $100 at a time, a day, per account, was the legal limit. And that was only held to by the better banks; many forbade it for personal accounts even though the legality of such policies was questionable at best. Cash deposits, on the other hand, were welcomed without restriction. Moving money overseas, strictly controlled for years, had become almost impossible in anything but token amounts. Most stores, particularly the big chains, had finally moved away from accepting cash entirely. It didn't matter much. People were hoarding cash under their mattresses, not spending it at the local supermarket for groceries. The old adage applied: If something became artificially scarce, but was still legal to attain, it was probably worth the trouble to get more of it.

Valuable durables and precious metals had gone through the roof. People didn't trust the banks any longer, and anything people could physically hold in their hand instantly rose in value. It did stimulate the economy in that people had been burning through their savings to get tangibles.

Last night, the company had been nice enough to break open the little-used petty cash box to pay for a meal out at a local Mexican restaurant. Their waiter had literally begged for a generous cash tip.

"What's taking Ed so long?" asked Jim Thomas in his Texas drawl. Jim had been the company's South Midwest rep for several years.

"I'm not sure," Matt replied, completely honest. "Haven't given it much thought. I really just want to wrap this up and get back to the hotel."

"Back to the hotel? Heck, what we need is to get on *planes* and get the hell out of California. I live way out in the sticks, Matt. I'll betcha my door's getting knocked on *right now* by a friend or relative from the city looking to hole up with my wife and kids until this all blows over."

Matt raised an eyebrow. "After only two days? Seriously?"

"You bet your sweet buns! Last year there were food riots by now, and no one in their right mind is gonna stick around and wait for that to come to them. Even money that I-35 and I-20 out of Dallas are parking lots right now. I had my folks, my brother and his two kids, and his neighbors all crammed into my place for *four days*. 'Bout as welcome as a skunk at a barbeque. They ate every scrap of food I had in the house. Heck, I ended up buying a bunch of canned food just in case it happened again. Tore up my toy budget real quick. And, Lord have mercy, here we are once again!"

Matt nodded. "I did too, the canned food thing I mean. My brother runs a company that sells that sort of stuff, survival food and gear, and he did a ton of business after the scare."

"No kidding? Well, I bet he's sold out by now for sure."

"I don't know about that. His business is all via the Web or phone-in orders with a credit card or bank draft. Since neither of those are working, I don't know how he'd sell anything."

"That's right! If cards aren't working, that means EBT isn't working. Those food riots are right around the corner—just like last year. Betcha."

Ed Vasquez, their regional VP of sales, entered the room with a strained look on his face. Matt had never seen him lose his cool in the five years he'd worked for him. Ed looked like a late middle age Latino soap star, clean shaven with wavy salt-and-pepper hair. Unless it was an important meeting that required a suit, Ed almost always wore a muted golf polo and khakis; today the polo was maroon with dark blue horizontal stripes.

"Gents," Ed began, "while I had a long list of things to accomplish tomorrow, I've decided to cut this short a day.

Unfortunately, we haven't been able to reach anyone at the airlines to move your flights up to tonight. The recordings all suggest getting down to the airport in person ASAP to resolve any issues. Let's cut it short here so you all can check out of your hotels and get down to Bob Hope."

Jim, along with several others at the table, groaned and reached for their phones.

"Just be glad none of you have to make your way down to LAX, it's completely backed up all the way south. If you run into problems, give me a call directly."

Matt looked at Jim, gave him a nod, and headed for the parking lot.

- - - - -

When Matt reached the lobby, it was filled with nervous, agitated people waiting for the airport shuttle. Most were trying desperately to make calls or work on their smartphones. Retreating to his room on the second floor, Matt packed up and checked out via the room's television.

He got out his own phone and texted Des. *Ed letting us go early. Flights are a mess but I'll try to get one tonight. I'll keep you posted.* Matt watched the text spin and spin, not sending. He hovered over the call button when he heard footsteps coming up from behind.

"Hey!"

Matt turned and saw a tall, well-tanned blonde woman, a bit older than he, and her preteen daughter. Both were pulling heavy wheeled suitcases behind them. "You have a car? Are you going to the airport?"

"I am, but not heading straight there. Just taking the shuttle would be faster I'm sure."

They stopped in unison. "The shuttle is *super* slow right now, the roads are jugged up, everyone who can is trying to get out of the city. It's all on the news, all over. We have flights at six to get back to Denver. That's only two hours!"

Matt pressed the unlock button on the remote and the car flashed its lights. "I'd like to help, I have the room, but I have to drop the car off first and then take a shuttle myself. The line is probably really long to drop off the car. I just doubt it's the fastest method right now."

She stared at him. "Yeah, but *we* don't need to wait in that line, right? We could just get out and go. Can't you help us, please?"

"True, I didn't think of that. Hop in."

"Thank you *so* much! My name is Jessica, this," pointing to her daughter, "is Veronica."

Matt extended his hand to each of them in turn. "I'm Matt."

They filled the nondescript hybrid to capacity, the largest of their bags taking the remaining spot in the back seat. From the hotel, they had a short drive to the northwest which, unfortunately, corresponded with both everyday commuter traffic and the new throng of people trying desperately to leave the Los Angeles Basin from the south. What would have been a twenty minute drive stretched into fifty. Matt and his companions saw several trucks loaded to capacity with hastily-packed boxes and other effects, their leaf springs groaning under the weight.

"Getting out of Dodge," Matt said, breaking a long silence.

"What's that mean?" said Veronica from the back seat.

"It's something my brother says. It means getting out of town when things get bad. Trying to get some space around you."

"I wonder where they are all going," Jessica said.

Matt shrugged. "Who knows, really. Going north, maybe east, away from L.A. Away from the teeming millions. They probably don't have much of a plan beyond that."

Jessica frowned. "There's nothing but dusty hills and McMansions out there. I grew up in Northridge, not far from here. If they think they'll all just head to Castaic and camp out until this blows over, they're crazy. Head the other direction to the Mojave and die of thirst."

Matt thought for a second. "I don't know. Better to get out and hunker down for a few days than to stick around and wait for something to happen. What if this goes on for a while? What's to say this time it won't be two weeks? Or a month?"

Jessica and Veronica both stared at him, mouths agape. "There's *no way* it would last that long," Jessica shot back. "I mean, someone, the government, would step in eventually and get it fixed, right? A lot of people lost money last year, with the bail-in, but things got back to normal. Everything will turn out fine. Right?" Now she didn't sound quite as convinced by her own argument.

"I really don't know. But I'd rather think about, prepare for it, and be wrong than the other way around."

Jessica snorted. "I . . . I don't mean to sound rude, but are you one of those *survivalist types*? My uncle fell into that noise all those years ago . . . with Y2K. Bought a bunch of stuff, buckets of food, paid way too much, then five years later he decided he'd rather have a fishing boat and sold it all for way less than what he paid for it."

"Do I *look* like a survivalist?"

Jessica chuckled. "No . . . not really. I mean, you did fly to L.A. during a stock crash. I can tell from that bag that you've only been here a day or two. If you were one of those types, you'd have canceled your flight and headed down into your bunker to clean your guns and what not."

Matt let the stereotypical knocks go for the sake of peace. "Well, we're just about to pull in here. It was nice to meet both of you. Good luck getting back to Denver."

Jessica smiled. "We'll be okay. I figure we will be cutting it real close at this point, but if nothing else we'll catch the next one."

Matt parked in the check-in line, which wasn't as

busy as he would have imagined. He helped his two passengers with their bags and waved goodbye as they made their way to the shuttle stop.

He saw one of the attendants and waved him over. "Hey, seems pretty light. Isn't everyone checking in their car and leaving?"

"No no," the attendant said, waving his hands in front of his chest. "There's a ... *problem* ... at the airport. Flights are delayed, canceled. Don't go unless you have to. Wait 'till tomorrow."

Matt thought for a second. He did have the car for another day but had already checked out of the hotel. At this point, he couldn't depend on anything working the way it was supposed to. The hotel could already be shut down for new guests. In any case, if his credit cards didn't work he had no way to pay for a room.

"Can I get the car fueled up here, on the corporate account?" Matt asked.

The attendant frowned. "We've been told not to fuel the cars. The gas truck didn't show up this morning."

"I have some cash," Matt said, producing his wallet. "I don't need much, I think I'm at two-thirds of a tank which means maybe ... four or five gallons?"

The attendant put his thumb and forefinger to his chin. "Okay. Cash is good. Ten dollars a gallon."

Matt grimaced but it was definitely a seller's market right now. "That's fine, if you can break a hundred."

The man nodded and pulled his car around. Returning a few minutes later, Matt saw that the gauge read full and there were five $10 bills on the passenger seat. Before stepping back into the car, he looked back at the shuttle stop, but Jessica and Veronica were nowhere in sight.

He punched Ed's number on his smartphone. The call took at least twenty seconds to connect. "Ed? This is Matt."

"Is ... is everything okay?"

Matt exhaled. "No, not really. I checked out of the

hotel, but at the rental lot they're telling me that the airport is pretty much shut down. I could go there and wait, but there's no guarantee I'm getting a flight anytime soon. If I check in the car, I might get stuck down here."

"Yeah, it's on the news. LAX and Long Beach shut down completely a couple of hours ago. They're trying to put people up in hotels for the time being. I guess Burbank is next. How can I help?"

"Well, I had hoped I could pop up your way for the night. Being shuffled around by airport people to hotels doesn't sound all that great."

There was a short pause. "Sure, Matt, come on up. I'll text you the address. We're just up in the hills, in Valencia. It's not far from the airport."

Matt hung up and immediately dialed his wife, noting that his earlier text had failed to send.

"Hey Des. How's it going at home, sweetheart?"

"Pretty crazy, babe. Are you okay down there?"

"Yes and no. I'm fine, but remember my text about flying out early? I don't think that's happening. The airport is a total mess. I'm headed up to my boss Ed's place for the night and we'll figure out how I can get home tomorrow."

"Okay, honey. Just be safe. I'll be fine here."

"You sure? No problems so far?"

"Umm . . . I wasn't sure whether I should tell you, but there was a shooting a few blocks away last night. There were police running all over the place."

Matt closed his eyes and rubbed his face with his other hand. "Des, if things get really crazy, pack up and head to the family cabin, all right? Our key is on the hook inside the hall closet, with the green plastic cover. Take everything you can. Kyle and Amber might already be up there."

"No, he called about an hour ago to check in. He was pretty bummed when I told him you're still down in L.A. Kyle and his people are totally swamped trying to get all of their orders out. Package carriers are still working, for now. He figures everything will shut down completely by the weekend unless the banks and markets open back up. His words."

"Yeah that sounds like him. You have enough to eat? Water still running?"

"Yes Matt, it's all normal except for the banks and credit cards."

"Okay. Sweetie, I better get on the road. I love you and I'll see you soon."

"I love you too, honey. Be safe!"

CHAPTER THREE

Tuesday, Late October

Sergei Kostadinov pressed his card up to the reader, heard the lab door unlock with a click, and turned the brushed metal handle.

Two of his three project partners were already there; Avi was fiddling with a tablet while Val was picking at one of their motors with a small screwdriver.

"Val, where's Chase? I didn't see him in class or around the campus today."

"Sergei," Val began, "I've said it many times, call me 'Bane.' No one calls me Val here. Val sounds too much like a girl's name in English. Chase left last night. I caught him carrying a couple of bags out to his car. His parents asked him to come home right away. I think they are down south, near the border."

"Yes, they're ranchers of some sort down there. You shouldn't be ashamed of your name, *Valentin*. Just because Americans don't understand our names doesn't mean we need to change them. Do you know how many jokes I've heard made of my name, how it sounds in English?"

"You're so serious about being some true Russian patriot, Sergei, lighten up. Plus, Bane is an awesome name. Girls here *love* it." Val had chosen his nickname from how the first four letters of Valentin appeared in Cyrillic: Вале. His family, back in Russia, was wealthy and connected. Not rich enough to get him into an American Ivy League school or its European equivalent, but well above Sergei's family back home.

Val had a point. Sergei had a tough time fitting in with his classmates. Mainly, the age gap. The University of New Mexico engineering program had some foreign students, but none were close to thirty. Also, his military bearing and disinclination to spend his free time binge-drinking and partying had made him a bit of a social pariah on campus. He was the weird, old, stereotypically humorless Russian guy.

Sergei didn't mind. He had enjoyed his time here, for what it was, but he never forgot that it was penance, exile, for the accident.

Val put down the screwdriver and leaned toward Sergei. "Do you suppose Chase has the right idea? I mean, we were all here last year when this happened. The cafeteria was locked down, there were some break-ins, but nothing much went wrong. Right?"

"I'd rather not be here, and be wrong about it, than be stuck here if it gets bad." Neither of them had their own car. Or a place to go, outside Albuquerque.

"Things will open up soon enough," Avi added, looking up from his tablet. Avi, too, was a foreign student, from Israel. "But this isn't social studies. Back to the project. We have a real problem with the drones."

Sergei had seen the problems coming with this project for a while but didn't see a great solution, so he'd kept his mouth shut. The concept was sound: a group of drones that would hold station and automatically swap out, sort of a changing of the guard, periodically to maintain full coverage, all day and night. Their audio and video feed would go straight to a receiver, probably a laptop or mobile phone. They thought it might be useful in applications where installing permanent cameras was impractical, like temporary locations or in the wilderness. The drones worked, but sucked so much power that their dwell time was only about four hours. Having to lug around six fairly heavy and expensive drones made the system less than useful.

Sergei nodded. "We can't get them any smaller and still carry observation equipment, GPS, all the controls, and a battery. If we shrink the battery, they won't be airborne long enough to be useful. Shrink the controls, and they will be too sluggish to battle breezes and such. Cut the camera and voice pickup and the drones are useless. No GPS and RF beacon, they can't get back to the charging station."

"Well, so what do we do? Go to Professor Douglass and say, 'We tried, but the drones suck?'" Val said.

"No. I don't want to go and throw up our hands. If we want a good grade for this, we need to do it ourselves."

"That's great, Sergei, but we're at the end here. It's due Monday. We don't have any more bright ideas and there's not enough time for a clean slate redesign," Val said.

"I could ask a friend back home," said Avi. "He's an engineering genius. He's my age but he's already doing graduate level work at Technion. That's sort of the Israeli MIT or CalTech. I think he's been in college since he was thirteen. I'm sure he's done work like this before. He helped me a bunch last year on a project."

"Okay. It's one in the afternoon here. What time is it in Israel?" Sergei asked.

"Pretty late, nine or ten at night I think. I'll ping him right now and see if he has some time."

Avi tapped his tablet a few times, then entered into what looked to be a text conversation.

"So, what's the deal?" Val asked after a minute.

"He's up and working right now. I sent him the overview and some of the specs. He's going to look them over for a couple of minutes. Then we'll do a video chat. He wants to see what we have on the table, too."

Not wanting to sit and wait, Sergei got up, went for the coffee machine across the lab, but saw with dismay that it was empty. Someone had taken the public tub of preground coffee. He then headed for the soda machine in the hall and was pleasantly surprised to see it still worked fine with paper money and change. Returning with his drink, he saw that Avi and Val were waiting for the video chat to connect.

Sergei saw a handsome face appear, boyish but with the beginnings of a faint dark brown mustache and beard. Behind him was a brightly lit work area. "Can you see me?" he said in excellent English. Unaccented, unlike Avi's.

"We can see you, David. These are my project-mates, Sergei and Bane. They're from Russia."

"Good to meet you both." "He looked down, then up again. "I looked over your notes and you're right: using off the shelf parts you're not going to see any dramatic improvements. You don't have enough time to fab and test anything new. You're just trying to rearrange existing technology in a better way, which is fine, but mini-drones aren't all that novel, sorry. Lots of people, R&D types, have been beating at these for a couple of decades."

"Thanks for the *good news*, David," said Avi.

"It's too bad that I can't send some stuff I have here. You could make a great drone with these parts. Dwell time measured in days, cut the size in half."

All three of them perked up. "What 'stuff' are you talking about?" asked Val. "Don't tease us like that. Is it something we can fab? Send us the specs."

David shook his head. "No, no. If the university doesn't get angry, I'm sure the Israeli government would. You're right, I shouldn't have brought it up."

"Even if you can't share the particulars, the general points might help," Sergei said.

David exhaled heavily through his nose. "Sure. Well, so you're using low voltage for everything. Controls, camera, voice pickup. What if you could go extremely high voltage, still DC, for the motors and controls? Cut current way down, wire sizes, everything."

"Okay...," Avi replied, "but I don't think we can cram

a high voltage transformer into the drone. Whatever we'd save in weight on the other parts would be totally negated."

"Don't use a transformer. The power source is already at the correct voltage."

"There are power supplies that are small, but I'm not aware of any high voltage tiny rechargeable battery packs, David." Avi pointed out.

"Don't use a battery."

"What are you talking about?" Val said. "A tethered system? No way. That's off the table."

"Not tethered. A new kind of power source, not technically a battery, that provides DC at over seven hundred thousand volts with no line loss via a pressurized fullerene cable."

Avi snorted. "Carbon sixty is superconductive at what, thirty degrees above absolute zero? Not going to work."

David shook his head. "I wouldn't have mentioned it if we hadn't figured it out. No, it's completely room temperature. Cutting edge process. I can't go into the particulars, but in twenty-five years we'll all look back at power generation and storage from this time, now, like it's a different age. This will eventually change the whole world from AC to lossless high voltage DC power. It took one hundred and thirty years, but it looks like Edison is going to have the last laugh!"

"Why can't you talk about that?" Val asked. "From what you just said, it will be out and available pretty soon anyway."

"There are certain, ah, *military* applications that the Israeli government would like a head start on. We're aware of a handful of labs in Europe, America, and Asia working toward this as well. For all I know, one or more of them are there already but have kept it secret. If not, we don't want to give them any free help."

"So, where does that leave us? All you've told us about

our project is what we already knew. It's too heavy and tries to do too much," Sergei said.

David rolled his eyes to the left, nodding slightly, looking contemplative. "I think I can help you guys out. It won't be the bleeding edge like I just mentioned, but I can two day air a pair of setups to you guys. Batteries, piezo transformers, wiring, that will definitely be lighter and more powerful than what you're using. They should keep your drone up for over twelve hours, so you'd only need two, the minimum to maintain continuous coverage, right?"

"Great, that would be a big help, David. I'll text you the address right now," said Avi.

"No problem. By the way, how are things there? We're keeping a pretty close eye on the bank closure. It's definitely rattled the markets here. American made stuff has disappeared off the shelves. People figure they won't get more for a while."

"Not too worried," replied Avi. "I mean, this happened last year, and we're all still here, right?"

David signed off, and Avi started tapping away again, most likely texting the address to the lab.

"I'll see you guys tomorrow," Sergei said as he headed for the door.

Sergei was three quarters of the way back to his small apartment when he heard someone running up to him. It was Val, who stopped in front of him, huffing, and grabbed at his knees.

"What are you doing?" Sergei asked, genuinely confused.

"I . . . I got a text on my way back to my dorm. You need to see it." Val held his gold iPhone out and Sergei took it.

Valentin you need to get out of America. If you do not

leave immediately you will be trapped there. There will be a car to pick you up tonight at seven thirty. Be ready for it.

"Who sent this? Your family?"

"Yes, it's from my father. He must know something peculiar is up. Something different. He didn't act like this last year."

"So why are you showing me this? All that running just to tell me you're leaving tonight? You could have just texted the group. We'll manage, especially once Avi's friend's parts get here."

Val recoiled slightly. "Sergei? Think about it. You need to go as well. I doubt my father would mind if you hitched a ride, a fellow Muscovite no less. If things really do crash and burn here, where are you going to go?"

Sergei didn't like it—it hurt his pride a bit—but Val was right. He didn't have anywhere to go, and really didn't know anyone well enough to take him in. On the weekends, he'd been working at a local big box store, but wasn't close with any of his coworkers. He'd picked up a few ex-girlfriends in his year and a half in Albuquerque, but none that would look forward to him showing up on their doorstep.

"Okay. I just hope the car coming for you isn't a two seater."

Sergei made his way to his very humble apartment about a mile from campus. The building was mostly filled with students like him or locals living paycheck to paycheck. Anyone who could do better, did. It wasn't a place one would pick to weather a financial disaster.

First, he called his boss. "Yes? This is Sergei."

"The Russian guy?"

"Yes. The Russian guy. I probably won't be in this weekend. I might be leaving town."

"You and everyone else," the shift manager replied,

sounding drained. "Keep in mind, any temporary employees that don't show up for work will be terminated. That includes you."

"Noted," Sergei replied and hung up.

Next, he went to pack, which was a depressingly quick process as he had very little of value. Sergei had been that classic poor bachelor, with one dinner plate, one good glass, a futon, and a refrigerator full of condiments and beer but no actual food. His passport—very important—and other identification were essential but beyond that he only needed to take a few changes of clothes, a toiletry bag, his laptop, and his phone.

"Ah, the beer!" Sergei cracked open a dark brown bottle of Negra Modelo. Its golden foil wrapper prevented the bottle cap from falling away and hit him lightly in the nose as he took a swig.

Close to six P.M., Sergei made his way back to campus and the cafeteria, still a bit groggy from the five beers he'd made disappear earlier in the afternoon. It was far more sparsely populated than usual for dinnertime, and several campus police had the exits covered.

"Is there something wrong?" he asked the closest of them.

"No, son," the officer replied. "Jest tryin' to keep the students from carrying off all the food, that's all."

Sergei could feel the hushed nervousness of those in line, the normally boisterous cafeteria damped down by the events of the last two days. He sniffed derisively at the signs indicating calorie counts, the presence of gluten, or whether or not the particular menu item was vegan.

In two weeks, if this continues, you all will eat anything put in front of you. He then frowned, realizing he'd already grown smug with the thought that he'd be back in Moscow in less than twenty-four hours. The other students here, munching away at their gluten free tofu wraps and piles of plain white rice—or sausage pizza, fries, and a tall Coke—might be blissfully complacent, but that didn't mean Sergei somehow stood above them. For all he knew, the American crash would eventually tumble Russian markets and banks as well.

At just after seven, Sergei cleared his tray, grabbed his bag, and headed for Val's dorm on the other side of the campus.

At seven twenty-eight, a glossy black Lincoln sedan with its headlights on pulled up to the building and stopped in front of them. Val had come down just a couple of minutes before, wearing an orange mountaineering pack and dragging a large green suitcase, and had been pleased to find Sergei waiting for him.

A middle aged man stepped out, balding with a neatly trimmed goatee. He wore a dark tailored suit and black leather driving gloves. "What's this?" he said sharply, in perfect Russian. "I was told one young man. Which one of you is Valentin?"

"I am," Val replied, also in Russian. "This is Sergei Kostadinov, another student here. He needs to get home as well."

"*Ochen priyatna,*" Sergei said. *Pleased to meet you.*

"Well, doesn't matter to me. I have the room in the car. But, Sergei, if the people we work for don't let you on the plane, you'll be stranded in a very bad place."

"What bad place?" Val asked. "Aren't you just taking us to the airport? It's a ten minute drive from here."

"Oh no. Airport, yes, but not *that* airport. You'll see."

The sunlight that had accompanied them out of Albuquerque had long faded as the trio approached El Paso.

Sergei and Val had learned that their driver, Yuri, was employed by one of Val's father's associates and had been in the U.S. for about seven months, living up in Santa Fe. Yuri said he was a butler, but to Sergei he carried himself more like a bodyguard.

"So, Sergei," Yuri said, angling his head toward the back seat, "you're from Moscow, yes? You have family waiting there? Anxious to see them again, hmm?"

"Yes, some family. But once I get back, I'll report to my command first."

"You're military?" Val spouted. "I mean, still *in* the military?"

"Military exchange. An officer, then?" Yuri asked.

Sergei nodded. "Yes. Senior Lieutenant in the Russian Air Force. Pilot."

Yuri looked at Val, then glanced back to Sergei. "Usually, you go to college, *then* become a pilot. Not the other way around."

Sergei sighed. "This is true. But, the easiest way to put it..."

"Yes?" Yuri prodded.

"There was a flight accident. A big air show. I lost control of a top-of-the-line fighter, an Su-35, during an acrobatic maneuver. The aircraft failed to respond so I ejected at low altitude. Three people died when the plane crashed. A few more were very badly hurt. I was immediately taken off the active flying roster. My command didn't know what to do with me. But ... there was the student exchange program. Some people must have figured it was a good way to get rid of me for a while."

"Wait, a big air show? You mean *MAKS*? That was *you*? Two years ago? You're a Russian Knight pilot?" Val asked, agog. The Russian Knights were roughly the equivalent to the U.S. Air Force Thunderbirds or their Navy's Blue Angels.

Sergei nodded. "I was, sort of. I was an alternate. I wasn't even supposed to be part of the show that day. None of that matters, now. I don't know what I'll be when I get back."

About fifteen minutes later, they stopped at a gas station about a mile off of the freeway.

"Stay in the car," Yuri said. It wasn't a suggestion.

He spoke with the attendant, there all alone, which struck Sergei as not particularly safe given the times. The two men exchanged something, Yuri filled the big sedan with gas, and they were on their way.

"Where are we headed? El Paso's airport?" Val asked.

Yuri chuckled. "No. Where you are headed, an American airport would be a problem. If this weren't so, you would have left from Albuquerque."

Sergei filled in the blanks. If it wasn't an American airport, they were headed to *Mexico*. That meant they were probably flying someplace that didn't allow, or made very difficult any flights directly from the United States. Like, say, Cuba. Filing a flight plan from, say, El Paso to Miami, and angling south to Havana would never go unnoticed.

Confirming his suspicions, they proceeded south, then angled off the interstate on a series of back roads, then, after a pause to pull some fuses, over the border sans lights in the dead of night on a dirt road. After about thirty minutes of driving, they came to a small airfield somewhere in the Chihuahua desert, and Yuri stopped the sedan short of a small prop-driven plane. One that was far too small to take them directly to Cuba, much less to Europe and on to Moscow.

The three of them stepped out of the car and were met by an older, bearded man in a leather brimmed hat, distressed brown leather jacket, and a tan flight suit. He was backlit by the aircraft's landing lights, but the engines were silent.

"I'm expecting one young man and a few personal effects. You're him?" he asked Val in a folksy American accent Sergei couldn't place.

"Yes, but my friend here, he needs to come along as well."

The pilot—Sergei knew he couldn't be anything else—looked down at his boots and kicked at a couple of rocks. "Well that's really nice," he began, sounding sardonic, "but this isn't the free city bus down to the soup kitchen. I have received and confirmed payment for *one* passenger."

"I'll pay," Val blurted. "I mean, my father will pay."

"Fantastic," the pilot replied, folding his arms across his chest. "But I don't work on advance. Give him a call and get it worked out. Should be waking hours back home."

Val went to pull out his phone and the pilot held up his hand. "Unless you have a really *special* phone, it won't do jack out here. Since you're working hard to make me more money, use mine. Sat phone."

Val dialed directly and, after a short, heated conversation, hung up. It still wasn't clear to Sergei if he'd said yes or no.

"It is done. My father increased your payment by fifty percent."

"Fifty? I don't know where he learned arithmetic, but one plus one is two, not one-point-five."

"He determined that would not be warranted, since most of the fixed cost of the trip has already been paid for."

Val didn't add, "Take it or leave it," but that was the implication, Sergei realized. If the pilot said no, Sergei was not only not going home while things crumbled in America, he might be stuck in the Mexican desert miles from anywhere. Sergei was reasonably sure Yuri was returning north to the States but the man was clearly under no obligation to take Sergei with him. And although Yuri seemed like the sort who could handle himself in a crisis, Sergei didn't want to be stuck hanging off his coat tails. Sergei didn't want to be in Val's father's debt either. No wealthy and influential men in Russia were squeaky clean in their dealings, and repaying favors usually meant becoming involved in something with which they didn't want to personally soil themselves. But the risk was preferable to being stuck here.

"Very well," the pilot decided after a few moments. "Deal."

"If you don't mind me asking, where are we headed? This aircraft won't get us very far. Not across the Atlantic, certainly," Sergei said to the pilot.

"What are you, an expert on aircraft?"

"Actually, I am. Fighter pilot. Russian Air Force."

"Well then, fighter pilot. How far do you think we can get, in your *expert* opinion?"

"A few hundred miles. I think we're going to fly to somewhere near the ocean, the Gulf I mean, refuel, then stop in the Yucatán, then Cuba, then maybe a big airliner to Europe. It's the only route that makes sense to me."

The pilot clapped once and grinned. "Exactamundo! Give the man a cigar. Now load up and we'll get in the air."

CHAPTER FOUR
Wednesday, Late October

While he wanted to get to the Vasquez house as soon as possible, Matt desperately wanted to score some supplies with his remaining cash. He envisioned two likely scenarios: one where things returned to normal in the next couple of days and he wouldn't need his emergency cash, or a true disaster situation in which even cash wouldn't do him any good—there would be nothing to buy.

The supermarkets and big box stores were a no-go by now. By Monday evening they would have been pretty much cleaned out; he was way too late at this stage. Matt saw a gas station/convenience store on his side of the street and turned in. Already there was a large plywood sign posted, lettered in black spray paint.

NO GAS—DEISEL 5 GALON LIMIT $50
ALL STORE ITEMS X2 PRICE
CASH ONLY

"I guess ten bucks a gallon really is the market rate right now," Matt muttered as he entered. The grocery-type items like canned food and boxed crackers were all gone along with first aid supplies, bottled water, diapers, formula, etc. All of the alcoholic beverages were sold out. Matt chuckled under his breath. Clearly a lot of people were riding this unplanned vacation out in their own way.

Not much was left but some oddly-flavored pork jerky, unpopular soft drinks, hot pickled sausages, and candy. Matt bought some jerky—both the garlic wasabi ginger and the honey jalapeño varieties, a couple of 32oz sports drinks, and even a couple of the plastic-encased sausages, mentally adding up the prices in his head as he shopped.

Another twenty minutes of driving brought him to the Vasquez residence, a well-manicured two story Neo-Mediterranean with a view of the nearby golf course and the rest of Santa Clarita to the south. Matt parked behind Ed's black Mercedes coupe. The house lights were on, it was quiet, and everything seemed to be completely normal here in Outer Suburbia. So far.

Ed opened the door as Matt stepped onto the porch, his wife behind him. "Matt, glad you made it here safely. You remember Samantha?"

Matt did recall meeting her a couple of years back, during a company golf event attended by some of the more local family members. Samantha was probably fifty but looked ten years younger, with auburn hair and an ever-smiling disposition that caused her to look as though she had a permanent squint.

She extended her hand and Matt took it gently. "Nice to see you again, Samantha."

She waved with her other hand. "Oh, please, just call me Sam. Come on in. The guest room is ready for you. Dinner's in about forty-five minutes."

"Are you sure I'm not imposing? I brought some food I picked up. It's not much but I should be good for a day or so." he added, holding up a plastic sack. "The stores are pretty much cleaned out. It's the best I could do."

Ed looked at the small bag and smiled. "I think we'll be okay. I took stock. I think we have about two weeks' worth of food, give or take."

Matt set his bag down by their shiny brown leather sofa. While the outside of the house was pure Spanish villa, the inside was done up in an Asian theme, with dark woods, bamboo jutting from cloisonné vases, and colorful, framed embroideries of exotic animals, dragons, and Chinese warriors. A large dining table was just visible from the entryway, and the bronze-colored living room, while on the small side, was packed with dark brown leather furniture, and a deep red entertainment center done up like a pagoda. The moderate-sized television was flanked by two faux-ivory Chinese wise men holding ebony staves. The home smelled faintly of peppermint and eucalyptus.

Matt followed Sam down the hallway and the décor changed abruptly to "standard suburban American" with off-white paint and family photos spaced randomly along its length. The guest room was last, across from a half bathroom. "Here you go," she said. "This used to be my daughter's room, but she's in grad school, back east at Columbia."

"Hmm, well, I hope she's all right. That's in New York City?"

"Yes, Upper Manhattan. We spoke yesterday and so far everything is fine there. Classes have been canceled, of course. She's in her apartment with her roommates waiting it all out. Stores and restaurants have shut down, lots of sirens, but according to her it's been pretty orderly."

"What about here?" Matt asked as Ed came down the hallway to meet them. "Lots of police running around? Gun shots?"

Sam thought for a moment. "I don't think so. We've slept pretty deep these last two nights, surprisingly enough."

"This is a pretty nice neighborhood. Is there a security service?"

"No," Ed replied, "but we do have a neighborhood watch."

Matt frowned. "I saw those signs as I drove up. I don't

think that's quite the deterrent as a twenty-four-seven security service though. What about defending the house? Do you own any *guns*?"

Matt caught Sam's look of shock and revulsion, as if he had asked if they ate human flesh or shot up heroin in their spare time. "Are you kidding, no! Never! I hate guns!"

Matt glanced at Ed, who just looked away.

Dinner that evening was pleasant. They discussed their families over a meal of chicken covered in mushroom gravy piled on white rice, with steamed broccoli on the side. Matt had suggested Sam conserve the rice and eat perishables, but she had just waved him off. "This is how I've always made this meal."

The television had been looping through the same stories of major riots and shootings all day, none particularly close to their part of Southern California. Supermarkets and gas stations had been hit hard. Police had taken over the remaining functioning fuel stations under the guise of protection, but Matt suspected this was just back door fuel sequestration. There had been no formal announcements made by the federal government, but clearly local authorities were taking matters into their own hands. It was also crystal clear that the airports were shut down—they couldn't take off without crew or fuel—and Matt wasn't going anywhere today. Likely not tomorrow, either.

Ed spoke. "Have you seen enough of this, Sam? Matt?" Sam nodded.

Matt had definitely had his fill. "I'm fine. What do you have in mind?"

Ed turned off the TV. "Matt, you seem to be taking this pretty seriously. I mean, we all went through the stock 'correction' and bank shutdown last year. And, you were probably pretty young, but the country pretty much shut down after the 9/11 attacks. My point is, there are blips here and there but we seem to always be just fine soon afterward. No doubt, it takes some people a while to put their lives back together, but most of us just got along with what we had been doing before. You seem to be, well, obsessed with this end-of-the-world scenario. Why?"

"I guess I'm just wired that way. A year in Afghanistan, and being around my brother, who—trust me—is far more of a 'doom and gloom' pessimist than I am, I suppose that makes me expect the worst and be pleasantly surprised by good results. I actually consider myself a realist."

"You were in the war?" Sam asked.

"Yes, I was in the Army for four years. An MP. Military policeman."

"I have to admit, I don't know much about what we were doing in Afghanistan, other than what I saw on CNN. I guess it looked scary ... but what would I know, right?" Sam said.

What would you know, indeed. Matt, in his tired state almost blurted it out, and felt a tinge of shame. This was his boss's wife and he was a guest in their home. It wasn't as if she was pretending to understand, a legitimate offense. "It definitely was. Scary, I mean. I left a few months before Bin Laden was killed in Pakistan. It was ... not a great place to be."

Both Sam and Ed caught the hint that this was a sensitive topic for Matt and moved on. "So, what do you think will happen if things don't get back on track soon?" Ed asked. "You've obviously given this some thought."

"I don't know exactly, but I think I can give a general outline. If this really is the mother of all crashes, we're going to see huge riots once all the food runs out down in L.A. People are going to get organized to find food or just take it from others. Eventually those huge food warehouses are either going to be discovered by civilians and looted, or commandeered by the police, military, whatever. Gas might already be all gone. Sooner or later, the power will go out, either from the source or damage to the system by things like fires. With it will go running water and sewage. I bet there will be some attempt by the government to keep order, but try to imagine the number of police and troops it would take to clamp down on eleven or twelve million people. Not going to happen."

"My God," Sam said. "That sounds awful. Like that hurricane in New Orleans—what was it called? Katrina, right? Or the one in Houston a few years ago. But here in L.A. All over the country, really."

Ed nodded. "I think that's pretty spot on, if it goes on for a while. I just don't think it will get to that stage. It's not like there's been a real disaster like an earthquake or, what Sam and I were scared of as kids, nuclear war. How could things just ... fall apart?"

Matt treated the question as a rhetorical one. "You're in a good place here," he said, "but is there somewhere you could both go if it gets really bad?"

Ed and Sam thought for a few seconds. "Well, there is the Peterson's cabin up by Big Bear Lake," Sam said. "We've stayed there a few times on mini vacations. We even have a key. They're old family friends."

"Would they be expecting you to show up?" Matt asked pointedly.

"I seriously doubt it," said Ed, eyebrows tight. "They live down in Anaheim but they could be up there already. It's a small cabin. Only one bedroom."

"Is there any food stored up there? There's not much in the way of hunting and gathering in those mountains. I've been to Big Bear in the winter, back when I lived down here, and it gets pretty dang cold. Any way to stay warm?"

"I think there is a fireplace," Sam answered. "As for food ... I don't think so. Spices in the cabinets, utensils, but we always brought our own food up there."

"It sounds like a last resort to me." Matt rubbed his

eyes with his right thumb and index finger. *They are doomed if this doesn't clear up in a couple of weeks. They have no backup plan whatsoever.*

Come to think of it, neither do I.

Ed looked at him. "You asked us about our fallback. When you get home, what's yours?"

Matt thought for a second. "If I were back home, I'd probably head to the family cabin near Hood Canal."

"Hood Canal? Where's that?" Sam asked.

"It's an inlet west of Seattle. The Olympic Mountains run right up to the water." He noticed their blank looks. "It's touristy, but not real well known outside the state. The cabin is along a lake right in the foothills. It's pretty remote."

Matt looked over to Ed and Sam. They were quiet for a moment, then Sam spoke. "Matt, you're welcome to stay here until flights resume. Or, until there's gas to buy for your rental. Either way."

Ed nodded. "Absolutely. We'll all ride this out here until something changes."

CHAPTER FIVE
Last Monday in October

Kyle Flanigan arrived at the warehouse early, unlocked the front office, turned on the lights, and prepared to give away more of his company's inventory.

Four years ago, after coming to the conclusion that he just wasn't cut out to be an obedient employee, he'd started up Bene Praepara Supply—BPS for short. Kyle's revelation hadn't been a surprise to his mother, who had always said he was wired just like his grandfather, Arthur "Artie" Overberg, the family patriarch. BPS really had its roots in what Grandpa Artie had begun after WWII. He had been a post-Normandy addition to an Army infantry unit and had fought in The Battle of the Bulge. After returning home, he'd finished his accounting degree and had married Kyle's grandmother, Isabella, a waitress at his favorite Italian restaurant in Chicago. A few years later, he'd seized upon the opportunity to buy a financially profitable but poorly managed chain of three drug stores in central Illinois.

By the early 1980s, he'd grown the business to thirteen locations spread across the central Midwest. On the advice of Kyle's uncle Rich, a then-recent MBA grad from the University of Chicago, Artie had sold the business to a large national chain. It had proved to be excellent timing as they were able to hit the wave of national consolidation early and get top value from the sale.

Uncle Rich, despite being a verifiable financial guru, had been less successful in managing the new family trust fund. He had lost about a third of the fund's value in the wake of the dot com bubble bursting, coincidentally just after Grandpa Artie's passing. Kyle's mother, Susan, and his other uncle, Rob, had elected to take their portions of the diminished fund elsewhere. While their nest egg certainly wasn't enough to make them filthy rich, it had meant they had been able to live 'The American Dream' without taking on debt and allowed them peace of mind and flexibility not shared by most of their peers. After all those strained years —Uncle Rich had taken their decision very personally, and his siblings had never quite forgiven him for 'wasting Dad's money'—he became very interested in Kyle's idea for BPS, had provided some initial capital, and also served as Kyle's best source of high-end clients.

Bene Praepara—Latin for "Prepare Well"—catered to the top end of the market and, unique in the business, only sold large, complete preparedness packages. The five basic packages started at around $5,000 and moved up incrementally to over $50,000. This was their key selling point: they took the research and guesswork out of people's hands and only provided the very best food and gear plus essential spare parts, batteries, et cetera. Kyle personally knew how frustrating it could be to buy cheap and buy twice. In a real survival situation there was no option to return an inferior piece of equipment or rotten can of food. Kyle made a point to source from U.S. manufacturers and suppliers whenever he could, although for some items he sourced from companies in Europe, Japan, and South Korea. Other sources were a last resort, and Kyle made every effort to uncover shady suppliers that stated their products were "Made in the U.S.A." when 95% of the actual work was conducted elsewhere.

It was a statement against foreign, state sponsored anti-competitive measures, human rights abuses, unchecked pollution, and quality issues. It was also good marketing to truthfully state active support of other American businesses. Kyle didn't really market in the traditional sense. The headlines and simple word of mouth did most of the work.

The patterns in BPS's client base fell into three general buckets. In Bucket One were those people that had either just personally experienced one of those disasters or were reacting to them—they almost always ordered the least expensive packages. Often times these were paid for with high limit credit cards, which Kyle wasn't thrilled with —going into usurious debt had its own set of survival problems—but at least they were doing something positive with their money.

Bucket #2 was filled with retirees who had large cash accounts they could access, or inheritors of those types of accounts who had always wanted to prepare for uncertainties but never before had had the money to take it seriously. These customers usually opted for the middle packages.

Bucket Three contributed the most to their top line but were smallest in number. These were often his Uncle Rich's referrals or people they drew in through word of mouth. Kyle admitted he had let a lot of disdain for this particular group of clients creep into his mind lately. They were most often men like his uncle: late middle age or early retirement age, very successful financially, but overweight and on chronic medications. These were people who threw money at problems to make them go away, men who hired experts so they could have more leisure time or opportunities to make more money.

It seemed like a contradiction, but Kyle believed that what he sold via BPS—food, water (bottled and purification systems), power generation (mainly solar panels), outdoor gear, tools, etc. were of limited usefulness in a true *long term* disaster scenario. Short term—yes. But over the long haul, eventually you'd just flat run out of the necessities of life. No one could realistically store decades of food, water, and gear.

In short, Kyle didn't give nearly as much weight to the old "Three **B**s" mantra; **B**eans (food), **B**ullets (firearms and ammunition), and **B**and-Aids (medical supplies) as most in the preparedness community. Kyle liked the less catchy but more substantive acronym of **SFP**: **S**kills (what do you actually know how to do, right now, not what you're planning to learn *after* a disaster hits), **F**riends (people who complement your skills and can watch your back), and **P**roperty (a place to go that's actually yours; the ability to grow food, hunt, trap, fish, and hide from others). It didn't mean that the Three B's *weren't* important ... but starting and stopping there just limited your odds over the long term. Eventually the storage food ran out. One man with ten guns was a lot less effective than ten men with a gun apiece. And medical supplies were great ... until you were forced to treat yourself out of a textbook.

A few months ago, a preparedness blog had asked Kyle to write a guest post on a topic of his choice. He didn't think he was much of a writer but reasoned the free publicity and marketing couldn't hurt. He'd ended up causing quite a controversy with the topic he'd chosen and the conclusion he'd reached. Kyle had interviewed one of his big money clients who lived out near Chicago, a finance whiz like his uncle, and then he had asked the same set of hypotheticals to the owner of his favorite Vietnamese restaurant, a gentleman who had come of age during the tail end of the war in Victnam and escaped to the U.S. in the late 1970s, settling down along with thousands of other refugees in Washington State owing to an open arms policy by the then-governor. Both men were virtually the same age; less than a year separated their birthdays. The questions were fairly broad e.g. what would you do if the power went out for a week, or where would you go during an earthquake.

It had been so blatantly clear that Mr. Nguyen was far more prepared to weather a crisis than Mr. Brodowski that

Kyle hadn't dared to mention the latter's status as a client with Bene Praepara. Kyle's advice at the end of the post?

> *"If you really want to survive long term, go form some genuine friendships with folks from the Third World, people who have lived with that peculiar fear of not knowing where their next meal is coming from, or the fear that men with guns—official or not—could come for them at any time. People who know how to butcher an animal, any animal, and cook every edible part of it and make it taste delicious. People who are content with very little and can get by with almost nothing if need be. Because in order to make it, you're going to become just like them, and it's better to have someone patiently hold your hand than to learn on your own the hard way."*

Needless to say, Kyle hadn't garnered much new business from his post. The comments were a mix of people who thought he was out of his mind and those that, in principle if not execution, agreed with him wholeheartedly. So Kyle had found himself lately in a zone of cognitive dissonance; he ran a successful business that sold a product to people that gave them confidence, but given a disaster of sufficient length would be their undoing because they believed they were "well prepared" and had failed to actually prepare for the long term. BPS sold short term solutions to what could very well be a long term problem.

He wasn't glad for the current crisis, far from it, but it had served to break him out of his funk. He and his five employees—Dale Morton, his shipping and receiving guy; José Gomez and Markus Thomas, his warehouse schleppers who put the orders together; and Caleb Wan, his college intern who was here to complete his degree and soak up some business knowledge—had all worked like crazy last week to fill the orders that had come in the week before, nearly all of them from mid-level financial industry people who obviously had either insider knowledge of the crash or had correctly connected the dots and realized time was growing short. On Monday, Kyle had been forced to not take any additional orders except for local pickup—cash only—which surprisingly had garnered him one sale as not many people had several thousand dollars in cash on hand anymore. Kyle had suspected the buyer was a fellow business owner who had broken open the company safe and was (wisely) foregoing small details like the comingling of assets and paying bills for the time being.

 By Thursday morning, they had shipped all received orders but still had a third of a 60' by 60' warehouse full of preparedness gear and food. BPS, by its very nature, ran counter to the common business practice of running as little inventory as possible; the JIT or "just in time" methodology. There were two main reasons they kept so much on hand: the wavering nature of their business, which spiked right after an economic scare or natural disaster; and the fact that most survival gear, even the high-quality stuff, was still a drive to the bottom in terms of price. Often, the newer model was lower in price but also lower in overall quality. Kyle had a habit of buying up a supplier's stock of soon-to-be-discontinued but high-quality items. Being able to offer better gear than the competition was key to Kyle and BPS's business model.

 Kyle had made the executive decision late last week to dole out most of the food, medical supplies, and water purification systems to local churches. Kyle reasoned it was far more than he and his family could collectively take with them and store at home, and it was just simply the right thing to do. He didn't worry for a second about the business implications—if things magically went back to normal it would be the mother of all write-offs. In all, they had delivered to twelve churches so far and, not surprisingly, word had gotten around pretty fast about the guy giving away free survival food. He'd had eight voicemails waiting for him this morning from other area churches asking him for help.

Not long after turning the lights on, Dale arrived in his big silver diesel rig and parked it right next Kyle's newer tan Dodge Ram 2500 diesel quad cab. As Dale was shutting his engine down, the warehouse crew pulled in, carpooling in José's dark grey commuter sedan. Kyle knew not to expect his intern, who had, with more than a gentle nudge from Kyle, decided three days ago to head all the way home to Bellingham, a small city up near the Canadian border.

"Hey boss," called Dale as he entered the office. "What's on the agenda?"

Kyle took his hands from the keyboard, put them behind his head, and leaned back. "Well, I suppose we're going to give away more stuff, and when the warehouse is empty we'll lock up and go home until whenever. How was church yesterday for you and the girls?"

"We didn't go. No one could get a hold of the pastor, not since Thursday, so there was a big email and social media blast to everyone that service was canceled. Some of us went by the pastor's house to check in on him but it was just all locked up. No foul play there at least, but . . . no church service."

"That's a shame. If there was a time that people really need fellowship, it's right now. No one stepped in?"

"If someone did, no one told me. How was it for you? I take it your pastor didn't disappear into thin air."

"No, he was there for both services," Kyle replied with a chuckle. "I did get peppered with a lot of questions before and after though."

"People wanting to buy?"

"Some," Kyle answered. "One gentleman, I've known him for ten years, came up to me and said he had ten gold coins he would offer me. Maple Leafs, for anything I'd sell him at last Friday's spot price. Thing is, I've chatted with him before. The guy has bought loads of storage food over the last decade or so. He just wanted ... more."

"So ..."

Kyle shrugged. "So, I told him, 'No.' Man, was he surprised! But I gave him a short lesson in supply and demand."

Dale laughed expectantly as he took a seat. José and Markus walked in and stood by the doorway, listening in.

Kyle continued. "I said to him, 'Gold is just *money*. While it's a *great* form of money, that's all it is. You can't eat it, can't defend hearth and home with it, can't drink it, and it won't keep you warm at night.' You get the idea. 'Right now food is the most valuable commodity in America, and there are people that legitimately need it. I already have gold, and those people might have some too, but for right now I'm giving away my food to those that really need it. This church has received a lot of it and is going to be cooking meals once a day so no one nearby will go hungry for quite some time. I would rather do that than take your gold, which would just sit in my safe and do nothing. Plus, I know you and your family are already set for a while. When, I mean, *if* this all blows over, come talk with me and I'll be happy to take your gold in exchange for one of our preparedness packages.'"

"I bet he wasn't too happy about that," Dale said.

"Not one bit. But how much gold would the last spot on the last lifeboat on the Titanic have been worth? One of my favorite stories is about Colonel John Jacob Astor, a man worth about one hundred million dollars—in 1912 you could buy half the country with that kind of money. Astor went down with the Titanic because he gave up his spot on a lifeboat to a woman. Some say he was forced to because it was a strict 'women and children first' policy, but nowhere has it ever been credibly said that he tried to use his wealth and fame to get a spot. When it's life and death, money holds no power."

"I dunno, Kyle," Markus cut in. "There are a lot of

people, bank robbers and what not, that put money ahead of their own lives."

"They don't count on dying though, do they? If you knew ahead of time you were going to die doing it, would you rob that bank? No one can spend money from beyond the grave. People don't rob banks for charitable causes either."

"No, to finish my answer, Dale, most of the other people at church quizzed me on where to go and what to do. Some asked me if I knew where they could get a gun. I asked them, 'Do you know how to shoot?'" Kyle paused and went on. "Of course, none of them had shot much at all, all ones on the ten scale, meaning they sort of knew how to hold one from the movies. You can't wait until you've jumped out of the plane to decide on where to get a parachute. And how to use it properly."

Kyle's ad lib metaphor bought smiles from his crew. "So, let's load the two rigs, Dale's and mine, and deliver some supplies. I got voicemails from eight churches and emails from about ten more. Most are pretty close to other churches we've already helped out, so let's try to spread out the wealth a bit. I'll call the first four and then we can decide on the second group."

Kyle and José had finished dropping off at the first church, a small non-denominational group about ten miles from the warehouse. Their next stop was clear down in Eatonville, a hilly town fifteen miles to the south. Traffic had been very light, no doubt because the stations they'd passed were completely out of gasoline. Kyle had stopped and haggled with one gas station manager for some readily available diesel. Having a few hundred pounds of food and other supplies gave him a lot of bargaining power, and he ended up exchanging twelve #10 cans of rice, chicken TVP—

textured vegetable protein—or 'fake steak' as his daughter Isabella liked to call it, and freeze dried vegetables for a full tank of fuel.

"Did you see the guy in the store?" José asked as Kyle got back into the driver's seat.

Kyle nodded. There had been a serious-faced younger man holding a newer 'tactical' shotgun and sporting a big black handgun holstered on his hip inside. "Sure did. Manager said he was his son-in-law. He was watching us closely, too. Pucker factor needle is definitely moving to the right."

They promptly arrived at the next church. There to greet them was a man of perhaps fifty, balding with a pot belly, and a man with perfect teeth who looked to be about thirty. "Boy, we're glad to see you guys. I'm Doug, one of the elders here," said the older man with a wide grin, "and this is our pastor, Grady." Kyle and José took turns shaking each man's hand. "Some of our people have already run out of food." Doug continued. "One of our deacons got an elk last week so we've been busy smoking the meat and handing it out, but that's it for fresh food."

"None of mine is fresh, but it's high quality storage food, the kind that will last ten to thirty years or more. Not that I expect any of it to need to last *quite* that long."

"When I heard about you through the grapevine," Grady began, "I looked you up a little bit. You're some kind of survival expert?"

Kyle shook his head. "No, not really, not of the 'live off the land with a piece of flint and steel' mountain man survivalist type I think you're referring to. I run a business that sells preparedness packages, like this one here," he said, pointing to a large box that read "E-4 (H)" on the side in bold black lettering under the oval BPS logo. "The side of the box tells me it's from our bottom package, or 'E,' it's the fourth box out of six, and it's marketed specifically as 'healthy,' and all that means is it's lower in grains and higher in fruits and vegetables. Although it's just marketing, none of them are

51

unhealthy. Amber, my wife, takes care of that part."

"She's an expert too?" Doug asked.

"She's a dietitian, actually. She assembles the food portion of the packages for optimum nutritional and caloric value. I end up researching the other gear we sell," Kyle replied. Once, while they were dating, he had referred to her as a nutritionist, which was akin to calling a board certified medical doctor a 'health specialist.' One required a lot of school and accreditation, while the other was a title that anyone could bestow upon themselves unilaterally.

"Well, this truly is wonderful," said Grady with a smile. "I have to tell you, Kyle, you and what you brought really is an answer to prayer. A lot of prayers. I'm curious though, if things continue like this we're going to run out of everything before we know it. If anyone knows what will happen next, I suppose it's you."

"No, I've just given it a lot more consideration that most people. Even after the bank holidays and 'stock market fender-benders,' a lot of people have just assumed things would always remain that same normal we've had since just after World War Two—full supermarkets, a place to live, a car, available jobs, entertainment, et cetera. So they made no backup plan, or they figured that if things crashed all around them the government would step in and take care of them. That still might happen, but those people will become fully dependent on whatever new system is set up."

"People like us, you mean," said Doug.

Kyle looked at each of them in turn. "Please don't take this as condescension, but I can't turn back the clock and give you more than what you have. It's true that this stack of food, feeding a hundred people or more, will only last a few days. It's designed to feed a family of four for six months. I doubt I'll be back with another load of food. As you can imagine, the response to my offer of free food was pretty doggone strong and I'll be done handing it out by tomorrow at the latest. So, if this continues, you have prayer, the options that God gives you, and the mind to choose the best one—as you're led by the Holy Spirit—for you and your loved ones."

"I have a nice camper and a truck," said Doug. "If it really comes to it, I suppose I'd just head up farther into the mountains with the wife and scrounge and hunt what we can."

"Two things to think about. One, you won't be alone, there will be a ton of people doing the same thing. Two, it's going to get cold, and unless you're a lot luckier than me you won't be able to run the engine or a propane tank all winter to stay warm. So it might be tough sledding. Not to burst your bubble."

Doug nodded. "Hadn't thought about it that way. Thanks... I think."

Kyle extended his hand to Grady. "I'd love to stay and chat, but we have one more run we'd like to finish today, and I want to get back home before nightfall at all costs. Let's get these unloaded."

After a couple of minutes and another round of handshakes, Kyle and José were on their way back to the warehouse. All morning, they had listened to the news, and when the radio came back on the regular host had been replaced by a repeating message.

"Please stand by for an official announcement from the President of the United States. Thank you."

"Uh oh," Kyle muttered. "This can't be good."

"Why not?" said José. "It could be an end to the holiday."

"The President wouldn't announce that. Unless she's coming on the air to tell us she's nationalized all the banks over the weekend and the People's Revolution finally is complete."

When the station cut over to the national broadcast it was not the President as they had anticipated. It was a man's voice, deep and resonant.

Michael Zargona

"Good morning. My name is H. M. Donaldson, Director of the Department of Homeland Security. The President apologizes for not making these announcements, but she is presently in a secure location along with other key members of the federal government.

First off, thank you all for your perseverance and patience during these last several days. There have been those that have taken advantage of the situation for their own benefit, but by and large there have been very few major incidents across the country.

"Due to the nature of the market crash and bank closures, there is no indication that they will be ready to reopen by the end of the week. Contrary to what many are saying in the news and online, the federal government cannot force the banks and stock markets to reopen. We are working with their representatives and have full confidence that they will reopen next week. Our target is Monday.

"Until further notice, all flights, domestic and international, will be grounded. All border checkpoints will be sealed off. Those here in the United States on a temporary basis will be granted an indefinite extension until the current crisis is resolved. American citizens abroad will not be permitted to return until further notice."

There was a short pause of about five seconds. With the volume turned up over the rumbling diesel, Kyle could just make out some hushed whispering.

"Furthermore, from this point forward until further notice, a national curfew will be in effect to ensure order and safety. From nine in the evening until six in the morning, no persons may be on public property or roadways except those with a specific exemption; those exempted will include persons involved in critical infrastructure and safety roles such as firefighters, police, and utility workers. If you are unsure if you warrant an exemption to this curfew, contact your supervisor or visit the DHS website for further details. I want to emphasize that these *are simply continuity of government measures, not martial law. Habeas corpus is still in effect, and breaking the imposed curfew will be considered a felony. We do ask that everyone cooperate with the authorities and military personnel that will be working to keep order.*

"All operations of the federal government not deemed necessary to the security or critical operation of the United States will be suspended until further notice.

"Effective at 4:00pm Eastern Daylight Savings Time today, all media and communications, to include the Internet, radio, television, and cellular are to be nationalized by executive order. This is to coordinate actions, prevent misinformation from spreading, and to allow a consistent message to be broadcast to the American people.

"As for the matter of food distribution, we are coordinating with local authorities to provide central distribution stations within major cities and, as much as possible, will continue with smaller cities and outlying areas. This will be a free program, open to everyone.

"Gasoline and diesel distribution has been halted, and local authorities have been instructed to sequester any remaining fuel for emergency services use. These services will not include aiding and transporting those who have run out of fuel, so plan any curfew-compliant trips accordingly. We are asking that everyone not directly involved in maintaining order to stay home and keep calm until this situation is under control. Updates will be made in the very near future. Thank you."

"Can they really do all that?" asked José. "Just up and declare how it's going to be? Arrest me for walking my dog at five in the morning?"

"I'm pretty sure that the President has the authority to do all that and more. All those emergency powers that have been granted over the last few decades are finally being put to use. Plus, what does it matter? Do you, or I, or anyone we know have the power to change *any* of that? What are we going to do, get a lawyer and take them to court?"

Kyle continued his spirited discussion with José on the drive back, and parked beside Dale's truck by the loading dock.

"The phone has been ringing off the hook," Dale yelled from within the warehouse as Kyle shut the truck door. "Must be folks trying to beat this... phone blackout or whatever you wanna call it."

"You heard that too?" Kyle yelled back.

Dale came closer, wiping his hands on a towel. "Of course. It was on every station. TV, too. My wife has already called me to make sure I get home before this curfew. Kinda crazy, huh? Treating all of us like children who need to get home to mommy."

Kyle shrugged and held his palms up. "I really don't know what to tell you. That guy, the DHS head honcho, gave reasons for some of the points but not others." As much as he had hated the phrase since his time in the Marines, it was appropriate here. *"It is what it is."* Kyle paused, kicking at some rocks by the concrete/asphalt transition. "I suppose I better get in there and find out what these people want. We still have about a truckload apiece. Maybe a bit more."

Kyle listened to the seven voicemails in order. Predictably, they were churches they had not visited yet. He tore off the note with their info as he wanted to discuss these with the crew first.

Leaving the office, he looked through the lobby windows and saw a small blue SUV or wagon pull into the parking lot and around to the back. Not anyone he knew, and not Dale's wife's car either.

He snuck up to the hallway entrance to the warehouse, cracked it open, and saw six hands in the air above the stacked boxes.

"You don't have to do this, Bobby!" Markus said.

Bobby? The only Bobby they all knew was . . .

"*Shut up!*" a man yelled. "I know what you guys have! I need *everything*. You, load up my car. *Everything!*"

. . . the longtime delivery driver for their preferred carrier.

Three young, strong men would not surrender to just one man unless that man had a gun. Kyle slipped his right hand under his bright green Seattle Seahawks sweatshirt, drew a Smith & Wesson Shield 9mm pistol from its Kydex holster hidden in his waistband, and flicked the safety off. Kyle then quietly stepped through the door, turning the knob as he shut it.

"Bobby, put the gun away, *please*. You can have whatever you want," Dale said, voice even. "We've been giving it away for days. This isn't necessary, man."

"Shut up, Dale! I'm not an *idiot*. I put the gun away, you guys jump me."

Kyle tiptoed to the right and peeked around the corner. Bobby was bracketed in Kyle's vision by Markus and Dale, the current target of Bobby's small black revolver. José was at the back hatch of Bobby's vehicle, about to shove in a box.

"Put the gun away, Bobby," Kyle called as he emerged from behind stacked boxes, his Shield level with his eyes and pointed at Bobby's chest. Bobby tensed and started to shift to point his gun Kyle's way. "Don't do it. You point that at me, you get shot. You point it at my guys, you get shot. Believe it or not, I don't want to shoot you. Put your gun down, get in your car, and get out of here. José! Get away from Bobby's car. He's leaving."

Kyle could see the gears turning in Bobby's mind. The man had gambled . . . and lost. Bobby turned quickly, gun still in hand, and ran for his vehicle. The four of them watched as he raced out of the lot, barely making the left turn to avoid the ditch.

Kyle flicked the safety back on and holstered the

small pistol. "Okay then," he said, wiping his brow with his sleeve, shaking slightly. "With that, I'm declaring that Bene Praepara is officially closed for business until further notice. Let's load up the trucks and José's car as best we can. If we have to leave something, so be it. If Bobby, someone we've known and trusted for years, can flip his lid and do that, what's next?"

Kyle helped his crew load up each vehicle and gathered them together. "Guys, listen up. It might be a while until we see one another again. Let's pray about this, together, and then go our separate ways.

"LORD God, we don't know what the future holds, but we put it in Your hands. God, I ask that You protect us, our families, and friends during this time of trouble. Let it be an opportunity for us all to grow closer to and trust You more. In your Son Jesus' name, Amen."

"Amen," the other three echoed.

They said their goodbyes with tight handshakes and fierce man-hugs, and Kyle watched them drive off. He locked down the warehouse, opened the office safe, and took out what cash they had—just shy of six thousand dollars. Kyle then set the security code and locked up, feeling as if it might be for the last time.

All things on earth, good or bad, must come to an end. He hopped into his Dodge, detoured slightly to drop off the load of supplies intended for his church in nearby Buckley, and made his way home.

CHAPTER SIX
Tuesday, Last Week in October

It had simultaneously been one of the most exciting and most boring weeks Matt had ever experienced.

Ed and Matt were both active people by nature. Ed preferred golf and jogging while Matt liked hiking and mountain biking. Sam had done her best to keep them from going stir-crazy but had been only partially successful.

Even the television, oddly, had not given them much. The news networks were abuzz, of course, but the rest of the channels were on autopilot. The sports channels, which Matt preferred, were filled with those apoplectic over the postponement of the World Series, tied after four games, that was turning out to be one of the best in recent memory. No football, college or NFL, since the Monday before, and the start of the NBA season had been pushed back. Professional hockey was also on pause. Naturally, there was virtually nothing of substance for those networks to talk about.

Locally, there had been little news besides pictures of looted stores and police admonitions to keep inside and stay put. Sam had acted a bit vindicated by the news that no cannibal hordes had emerged on I-5 North to sweep them away.

Yet.

Once the big national pronouncement had come down yesterday though, things changed. Immediately after, local radio and TV had reported that power would be arbitrarily cut to residential and the majority of commercial customers during the curfew period. The back and forth cellphone updates with Des had come to an abrupt halt as well. She had been waiting for a clear indication to get out of the city. Matt hoped that the pronouncement would spur her to leave.

"Why do you think the government would want to stop cellphones? And email?" Sam asked as they gathered for a fine meal of stew made with most of the remaining food in the freezer—peas, a chuck steak, and beans, along with a can each of tomatoes and potatoes.

"Not sure," Matt replied. "Although, without power it doesn't really matter."

"I wish we had set up that solar array that sales guy pitched to us a couple of years ago," Ed grumbled. "It fed into batteries that would have kept us powered up throughout the night."

"Honey, it was very expensive. Tax break or no, it didn't seem like something we needed. Don't be hard on yourself."

Matt looked across the table. Both of his hosts had pronounced bags under their eyes. They had been up and alert until almost four a.m. Ed had a very nice pair of Swarovski binoculars for birdwatching, but last night they were pressed into service to view the dozen or so fires that were clearly visible down in the valley. There had been no media coverage of the fires or the sporadic gunfire they had heard off in the distance.

"Matt, do you think the news isn't reporting everything?" Sam asked. "I mean, if we're seeing all this in little old Santa Clarita, imagine what L.A. is like right now."

Matt shrugged. "I wish I knew. I'm not sure what they have to gain by not reporting what's going on. Bad news is their bread and butter and this has to be the motherlode right now."

"Do you figure though, if the government took over the phones, the Internet, maybe they took over media broadcasts too—the content I mean—and just didn't tell us?" Ed wondered aloud.

"Again I'll have to plead ignorance," Matt said. "It's possible, but I don't think it changes our situation."

Ed nodded slowly. "True. No news from the rest of the country, just the same requests that people stay home unless they're out to get food from the new distribution points."

"Yeah. Well, unless something changes dramatically in the next twenty-four hours, I think I'd better head north."

Sam furrowed her brow. "Matt, be sensible. It would take a miracle for you to get home safe right now."

"That may be. But when faced with two bad decisions that could kill you, you pick the one that doesn't take your friends with you," Matt said.

Ed broke into a wan smile. "Jeez, Matt, you're not *killing* us by staying here. Sure, we'll get short on food, but you saw the news. We'll just have to get in line for some of the FEMA handouts until this is over. The government's not going to let everyone just starve. You saw it when I did, that there will be a distro down in Van Nuys. We'll just hop in Sam's wagon and collect what we can."

"I'm not sure how long that's going to work. The government can't *miracle* food into existence. When things run dry, there's going to be an army of looters—or worse—heading up this way looking for what they can carry away. Once I'm gone, you both should head out to that cabin in Big Bear. Take what you can from here and go."

"Matt, you sound crazy right now," Sam responded. "You're worried about your wife, that's understandable, but don't make up a story just to make leaving sound like a good idea. I mean, this is America! What you're talking about sounds like, well, someplace else. Some Third World hellhole."

"I might be desperate, sure. But so will those millions

of people when things *don't* get put back together in a hurry."

"If you're going to leave, the least we can do is give you a few parting gifts," Ed said. "I have a few things in the garage that might come in handy. You might have a lot of walking in store."

They made their way out there and Matt saw a small pile of gear. "Wow, you're quite the psychic, Ed. I made my decision just after the morning announcements."

"I haven't exactly had much to do over the last few days. I wanted to take stock of what we had, plus I figured it was about fifty-fifty that it would eventually come to this. Now, we don't have much food to spare."

"Understood. Anything you have is appreciated." Matt saw what looked to be two sleeves of saltine crackers, two cans of black beans, and a can of stewed tomatoes.

"Here's a nice ski jacket and a down bag," Ed went on, showing the teal jacket and taut dark blue compression bag. "They're older, and you won't win any style points in Aspen with that coat, but they'll keep you warm if you end up hoofing it. I don't have a nice backpack, but here's a knapsack, it was probably my daughter's book bag in high school. I threw in some rope, a couple of books of matches, and an old folding knife too."

"I can't say thanks enough." Matt took stock of what he had. He had shared most of the over-flavored jerky with Ed but still had the rest of the gas station food. It still wasn't much, maybe three thousand calories total . . . not nearly enough to get him all the way to Washington State on foot. But better than nothing.

"I don't have any boots you'd want. Or would even fit into," Ed said.

"That's okay. I have my running shoes." It was a welcome stroke of good luck. Matt had considered leaving them home for this trip, but he worked better and thought more clearly when he did a short run in the morning as opposed to sucking down a few cups of coffee like most people.

Matt spent the next hour or so packing the rental Prius, checking fluids, and inflating the tires as far as he could with a hand pump.

After he came back inside for good, the three of them made their way to the second story deck. The sun was setting, and lights still sparkled across the valley—for another hour or so at least. They all sat there for several minutes, observing the handful of cars on the road and enjoying the quiet.

"I'm going to do the dishes while we still have hot water," Sam said as she went inside.

Ed stood. "I'll be right back. I want to get something."

He returned a couple of minutes later with two stemmed glasses and a bottle of red wine. *Brunollo . . . expensive stuff.* "Champagne is for celebrations. White is fine with dinner. But a good red, that's for when you just want to sit and think."

Ed sat, pulled a corkscrew from his pocket, opened the bottle, and poured them each half a glass. "So, honestly, what do you think? How is this going to pan out?"

Matt took the offered glass. "These new government regulations tell me we're in for a bumpy road. I'm being polite here. I don't think they would enact these measures if it was a short-term deal. To me, these are rules that don't just go away one day. I could be wrong. I *hope* I'm wrong. But I wouldn't plan for it."

"Well that's you these last few days, always expecting the worst. I'm coming around though. Nothing is getting better. Just bad news." Ed paused for a few seconds, took a sip of wine, and went on. "You know, when you asked if we had a gun the other day, it reminded me of something I haven't thought about in a long time. I actually owned a gun, briefly, after the Rodney King riots in ninety-two, back when I was living in L.A. proper. I suppose I was about your age. Nothing special happened in my neighborhood but . . . it woke a lot of us up. Woke *me* up to the fact that bad things can happen whether you want them to ... regardless of whether you believe they actually can or not. So I went into a local gun store and there was this shiny pistol with wood grips. It looked good, like something from an action movie. I remember now, it was a nine mil, engraved with 'TAURUS' on the side in bubble letters. I also remember how I felt holding it in my hand, knowing that with something like this I had to choose whether I was a good guy, or a bad guy. There was no middle ground anymore. Something like, if you had a gun in your hand you had to make that choice every minute." Ed glanced over to Matt, and he gave a knowing nod.

"I left with it and a couple of boxes of bullets," Ed continued. "I shot it a week later at a range downtown. That summer, I think at a Fourth of July get together with the family, I mentioned the gun to my father. He didn't seem a bit surprised. He just said to me, 'Ed, let's take Mikey,' Mikey being my little brother, 'and head up to the Mojave and do some shooting sometime. I'll bring mine.' I never recalled us having a gun at home growing up so I was bit surprised by this. Right then I thought that maybe he bought it after the kids had left home. Long story short, we did go out and shoot some soup cans later that year once the summer heat had passed. His pistol was an old revolver, a thirty-eight. I asked him when he had bought it since I didn't remember it. He looked me in the eye and said, 'Right after Watts, son. Nineteen sixty-five.' So that gun had been in our house my entire life and I never was the wiser."

"So where is it now? Assuming you didn't do what your dad did and hide it under the floorboards."

Ed cupped his wine glass in both hands and leaned forward a bit. "No, I wish. I met Sam the following year and we were married in late ninety-four. When she found out about the pistol, she put her foot down and refused to have the gun in our home." Ed pointed his now mostly-empty wine glass at Matt and added, "Now don't take that as me bad-mouthing Sam. I would never do that. In twenty-five plus years together I can count the ultimatums on one hand. No, I just decided this was not a battle I wanted at this point in our marriage, so I put it up on consignment in a pawn shop and it was gone in two weeks. I haven't held a gun since." Ed sat back in his chair and looked out into the sparsely lit valley below, pensive. "The really odd thing that occurred to me when I thought about this story is the timing. Dad bought his after a disturbance brought about by politics. Twenty-seven years later, I bought mine under similar circumstances. Now, here we are just over twenty-seven years down the road, it's still money and politics causing trouble. When this whole thing blows over, I'll reason with Sam and be right in line at the store to get a gun again. I think I'm ready to cash in those chips, to take that heat from her. I don't like this helpless feeling one bit."

The next morning, they were all up early for Matt's send-off. While they would have liked a real breakfast, without power, buttered bread and sliced apples was the best they could manage, and Matt wanted to hit the road right as the curfew lifted.

"Take care of yourself out there," Sam said, and leaned in to receive a hug, which Matt enthusiastically gave.

Ed extended his hand, and Matt shook it firmly. "Matt, I still don't know how you're going to get there, but I wish you a safe journey. Take care of yourself."

Matt smiled. "I'll find a way."

As Matt pulled out of their driveway, he felt in his heart that he would never see the Vasquezes ever again.

CHAPTER SEVEN
Wednesday, Last Week in October

Once Kyle related what had transpired down at BPS earlier, it didn't take any prodding to get Amber to agree to pull up stakes and head out to the family cabin.

Owing to her penchant for organization and efficient storage, they had existed in a continual state of being half-packed, even after living in their home for the past seven years. After last week's events they had packed everything they could with a load plan that would have made a military logistician proud. If they needed to get out in a hurry, there wouldn't be a lot of racing around.

Between work and packing, he'd done a fair bit of neighborhood watching since the financial bust. While Kyle considered his neighborhood the outer edge of the Seattle suburbs, most from the city viewed it as the middle of nowhere and therefore a safe haven. Heavily laden vehicles had started to arrive at surrounding homes only a couple of days into the crash. To Kyle, this area had far too many people to realistically support everyone through gardening, hunting, and fishing—not a desirable choice for a long-term survival spot.

Of course, he had watched for real trouble, too. Times like these were when people went off the deep end. The whole situation reminded him of a project he'd helped on a

Turn Red Tomorrow

couple of years ago. Someone in his church body had needed help with his house; it had serious foundation settling issues, a common problem in the soft, wet soils in Western Washington. The professional crew doing the tough work had put in some sort of hydraulic lift to prop the house up in order to allow for the fix. At first, there were a couple of small *pops*—not unusual at all. But this was followed by a tremendous *BOOM* with white smoke pouring out the windows and open doorways of the old farmhouse.

Everyone had scrambled thinking there was a fire. But it had turned out to be simply plaster dust. Over the last few decades, as the house had sagged, the series of owners had patched the cracks and painted over to match. Once there was a massive, sudden correction, all those cosmetic fixes had blown apart spectacularly.

That's what Kyle was seeing. The dust particles in the analogy were all those people who had made their lives in the plastered-over financial system—in effect, pretty much everyone who depended on the daily use of money to survive. Now that their "house" had been corrected, they'd been blown out the door. Some significant portion of those people had doubtless only held to the niceties of modern society because they had skin in the game. Now, who knew what they would do? Kyle was determined to leave before he found out the underlying motives of his neighbors, people he unfortunately did not know well enough to trust completely.

Last night, in the dying fall light, Kyle had mounted the fifth wheel trailer hitch to the bed of the Dodge and, with a little help from his wife, mated it up with their toy hauler: a black, red, and gray Keystone Raptor model Kyle had picked up four years ago, used and at a steep discount. It was a perfect fit as it was large and had great cargo capacity while being light enough for the Dodge to pull around safely, even fully loaded. He'd managed to add a couple of features, the most visible one being the photovoltaic array on the roof.

67

It was a system he'd had installed by another Pacific Northwest small business, an RV-specific solar power solution firm down in southern Oregon. He'd had the job done while at a weeklong rifle course at Thunder Ranch three summers ago. The setup included their top of the line array feeding up to 160 watts of clean DC power into a lithium ion battery stack where one of the trailer's closets used to be. The series-wired battery stack, using a pure sine wave inverter, fed standard 120v AC current into the trailer's electrical system with unusually high wattage for such an array, enough even to run the microwave or television.

Not visible were a half dozen hiding places that he and a handyman friend had added within the walls, roof, and undercarriage of the trailer. Four were pretty small, but two within the interior walls could each hide rifles or other bulky items.

One thing Kyle had put off was installing a real shortwave, or "Ham" radio in the trailer. Mostly it had to do with the fact that he was a bit intimidated by all the gear and expertise he'd have to invest in. His compromise was a couple of small handheld models that didn't have much power to transmit but cleared up more space for other gear. These covered the common FRS (Family Radio Service) and CB (Citizen's Band) along with the ham shortwave frequencies. He also had a "base station" that lacked shortwave transmission capability, but acted as a decent scanner and picked up AM/FM as well. Kyle's model had the ability to be hand-cranked to charge the internal lithium ion battery. On the bottom end, he had a couple of inexpensive FRS-only handhelds in a "tree" camo pattern that he used for hunting. He wasn't a big fan of these—not only were they weak radios, if you dropped one in the brush they were really difficult to find.

"I had hoped to get on the road right at six," Kyle called to Amber, who was packing items into the cab of the truck. For this trip, Kyle would run point in their other vehicle, a midnight blue Dodge Durango, while his wife and the kids followed in the truck and trailer. They would be using the handheld Ham radios to communicate on the way there using CB, old school style.

Over the last week, he and Amber had loaded up one of BPS's "A" packages—top of the line—into the cargo area of the trailer. It was enough food to last a family of four for a year. In the Durango they stuffed the smaller "E" set of boxes, which was much lighter on gear than an "A" but still had half the food—another six months. They supplemented all that with odds and ends from the pantry: canned soup, tuna fish, vacuum-sealed bags of homemade jerky or dried fruit, home-canned fruits and vegetables, et cetera. Kyle figured that even without hunting, fishing, and gathering they had over two years' worth of food with them.

All that was left to load were items Kyle had kept secure in the house: weapons, ammunition, and precious metals.

Kyle hefted the first hard gun case into the back of the Durango. Over the last fifteen years he'd managed to acquire thirteen firearms, which in some parts of the country would be classified as "a good start" but here in progressive Western Washington, where more people proudly carried latte stand punch cards than guns, it would probably brand him as "one of those alt-right gun nuts" and his collection as an "arsenal of destruction." When people naïvely asked him how many guns he owned—and it came often enough given his profession—Kyle always replied with, "More than one, less than a hundred, and not enough."

The case held the first rifle he'd bought with his own money, right after leaving the Marines nearly fifteen years ago, when he'd had a wad of cash burning a hole in his pocket. It was a civilian version of the military-standard M4 carbine, made by Bushmaster back before they sold out to a huge holding company. He'd broken the bank and had topped it with a Trijicon four-power ACOG. The other gun he'd bought that day, a Glock 17 9mm, rode in a shoulder holster under his blue nylon jacket. Amber would tote yesterday's hero, the much smaller Shield, from here on out.

Truth be told, he didn't care much for his Bushmaster AR. It was a quality rifle, but he had bought it for the wrong reasons. Kyle had served as a heavy machine gunner so he'd never got much time with the lightweight M4 before or after Iraq. To him, the handy carbine had seemed "just right" compared to his issued M16A2, an older version that was longer and heavier. Kyle had toted one of those around Iraq; his had ridden in a rack just left of the steering wheel of the fifty-caliber machine gun carrying Humvee he'd driven during the invasion.

In military application, the smaller M4 shone as it was easier to maneuver in buildings and was lighter and less fatiguing to carry around for long periods of time. In civilian application, Kyle felt it wasn't much to write home about. Gone from the civilian versions was the "fun switch"—either a three-round burst or fully automatic setting—and the probable scenarios in which one might use a rifle were different.

Long after buying the Bushmaster, he'd been turned onto a couple of seminal books on civilian riflecraft. About ten years ago, his Uncle Rob had given him a worn copy of Colonel Jeff Cooper's *The Art of the Rifle*. He'd called it "the best g**d*** book ever written on shooting" at the time. Then, later, a shooting buddy had "permanently loaned" him a copy of *Boston's Gun Bible*. Kyle didn't know who Boston was but he was pretty sure he wasn't the same guy who'd taught Kyle how to make a neat Manhattan in a chilled martini glass.

Both writers made it pretty clear that one could discard many military applications of a rifle in civilian use. Concepts like suppressive fire—pinning down an enemy so you could maneuver or drop something explosive on them, or recon by fire—let's shoot those bushes and see if there are any bad guys inside—were just not going to happen in the civilian world. The only realistic application of a rifle as a civilian was the most fundamental one: putting aimed shots on properly identified targets, whether they were game animals or people trying to kill you.

This *civilian rifleman* concept that Kyle had grown to respect demanded a weapon that could reach out a lot further than the little Bushmaster. In the Marines, Kyle had learned that if a target was beyond effective range for what you had on hand, you called up something that could get there: heavy machineguns, mortars, artillery, aircraft, et cetera. As a civilian, *you're it*—there's no one else to call—so whatever you brought along had to fill more niches and be more adaptable.

After this self-led crash course in how to be a civilian rifleman, it was clear to Kyle that every man (or woman, if they were inclined to fill that role) should have a rifle with which he could quickly and reliably score hits up to and beyond 500 meters—over a quarter of a mile away. Pistols and shotguns had their uses, but if you were going to have one gun, it needed to be a full-sized rifle. There was nothing quite as demoralizing as being unable to effectively return fire because one's foe was hopelessly out of range.

He had wanted to re-barrel the carbine in something a lot more terminally effective, but he'd simply never gotten around to it. Kyle had done what a lot of people do, he had just bought other guns that better met his criteria.

The next two cases held his main big game hunting rifles, a Tikka T3 Lite Stainless bolt action in .308 and a Marlin 1895 GSBL lever action in .45/70.

"Honey, I'm going to load a few of these into the trailer. Split them up a bit," Kyle called and made his way over to the open ramp door at the rear of the trailer. He grabbed the next couple of cases, which contained his two 12 gauge shotguns, a plain-jane Model 500 pump with a long barrel for bird hunting and spare short barrel for two legged critters, the other a decidedly more intimidating 930 SPX semi-auto seven-shot with a factory tan finish and ghost ring sights.

Kyle then pushed the last three cases into the trailer. The first held a Ruger 10/22 Takedown, while the other two cases held the oddest rifles in his small collection, both American-made versions of the Russian Vepr sporting rifle, a 7.62x54R carbine and a .308 standard barrel model.

Walking back to the Durango, he grabbed the olive green range bag containing the three handguns they weren't already wearing and placed it on the passenger seat. In the bag were three revolvers: a Ruger Single Ten .22, a stainless Smith & Wesson snub nose in .41 Magnum he'd bought from Uncle Rob a few years ago—Kyle's hiking gun—and a rare JM model Smith & Wesson 327 eight-shooter in .357 Magnum.

Nearly all of their ammunition was stored in metal cans and easily loaded right up into the vehicles. By design it was a lot more than the average person kept around. Too many gun owners foolishly bought a twenty round box or two and called it good, expecting stores to always have more.

Kyle said a short prayer under his breath for the people at his church that couldn't quite shake their adherence to Christian pacifism, people who genuinely believed they were more righteous by eschewing self-defense. He had participated in, and very rarely, ended debates with his brothers and sisters in Christ on the topic. Kyle had looked up and quoted Psalms and parts of the Gospels so often they'd stuck in his mind.

Rescue the weak and needy; Deliver them out of the hand of the wicked. - Psalm 82:4

Blessed be the LORD my strength, which teacheth my hands to war, and my fingers to fight. - Psalm 144:1

And He said to them, "When I sent you without money bag, knapsack, and sandals, did you lack anything?" So they said, "Nothing." Then He said to them, "But now, he who has a money bag, let him take it, and likewise a knapsack; and he who has no sword, let him sell his garment and buy one. – Luke 22:35-36

It was mindboggling to Kyle that many Christians, even accomplished Bible scholars, took this plain language to mean some loose allegory about simply trusting in God. *Of course you're supposed to trust in God!* But Jesus was plainly saying His followers would face future persecution and would need to prepare—in an earthly way—for these coming troubles. In the past, they had been among friends and were at worst minor troublemakers for the Pharisees and Romans of the time. But after His crucifixion they would all become dire enemies of both. They were most certainly *not* called to take up arms in revolt but merely for their own personal defense. While it was fine and proper to defend oneself, one's ultimate trust must still be in God. Even among his collection of guns and ammunition, Kyle aimed to not forget that fact.

"Daddy, where are we going?" asked his seven-year-old daughter Isabella—Bella for short, the half-scale carbon copy of her mother who tugged at Kyle's shirt sleeve. His four-year-old son, Cole, was following close behind.

"Sweetie, we're heading up to the cabin for a while."

Her little nose scrunched. "But, Daddy, it's almost *Halloween*! We *never* go up to the cabin this time of year. Or take so much... *stuff*."

"That's true. But this is a special trip. You need to stay strong and do what your mother and I tell you to do, okay? I don't want to scare you, but things could be pretty crazy for a while, and we might ask or tell you to do things that need to happen right away, no arguing. Can you promise to do that?"

"I promise, Dad."

"Good. Take your brother over to the truck and load up. I think we're about ready to head out. I just need to get a few more things."

Kyle entered the concrete floored storage room within his three car garage that, at this point, looked almost empty. The large gray gun safe swung open freely—he didn't want anyone to break it open and destroy it as it wasn't holding anything anyway. Kyle opened a very rarely touched footlocker that contained a more or less pristine set of old Interceptor body armor complete with civilian-style Level IV steel plates. Steel was considerably heavier than the standard ceramic but could also take more punishment before failing completely. The footlocker also contained two sheathed fighting knives, a very common Marine Corps KA-BAR and a rare and highly valuable Randall Model 14.

He set those aside for a moment and rocked an empty filing cabinet out of the way, exposing a combination floor safe built directly into the concrete. Kyle dialed in the numbers and popped the lid. Inside were two items: a large blue binder and an inexpensive Brazilian-made .38 Special revolver.

Kyle thumbed open the binder and smiled. There was page after page of different coins, what appeared to be quite a haul. But appearances could be deceiving.

He had purchased this particular model of safe through one of his Uncle Rich's clients, Daedalus Systems, which specialized in over-engineered and virtually unbreakable custom security systems. In reality, the binder and the gun were a fool's hoard. The "silver" coins were made of a zinc alloy that mimicked the look and heft of silver at a fraction of the price, while the "gold" coins were just plated lead. They would fool most criminals but would never pass with a pawn shop or real numismatist. The cheap revolver was just there for looks. It had been neutered, the firing stud on the hammer ground down so that it could not strike a primer and fire. Even so, the cartridges in its cylinder were dummies—no powder or primer to set off.

From the other side of the room Kyle grabbed a cardboard tube that held four innocuous thin metal rods, each about eight inches long with a different color painted on one end—yellow, red, green, blue. At the bottom of the safe were four small holes, each with one of the same colors painted around them, but this was a yet another trick. If the rods were placed into the matching color holes, the bottom safe, the real safe, would mechanically hard-lock for twenty-four hours. The only combination that opened the safe was to diagonally cross each color up. The rods each had a specific magnetic signature along their length, and once in correct alignment they locked into place and served as handles to pull out the rather heavy "plug" that contained the mechanism and acted as the safe's door.

Its genius was in the fact that very few people in the world had this particular type of safe, one of several different designs Daedalus used. Each was a word-of-mouth secret and, too, there were also variations on the basic designs. His uncle's safe in Florida was similar, but was opened by placing the rods clockwise one position from their matching color instead of Kyle's two positions. Even if a criminal were astronomically lucky enough to encounter more than one of these safes in his or her lifetime *and* managed to figure out the sequence, there was no guarantee the second would open in the same manner as the first.

The actual hoard was a binder, this one much smaller than the one in the fool's hoard and contained thirty one-ounce Canadian Maple Leaf gold coins with a number of fractional coins that amounted to nearly another ten troy ounces. Along with the gold were four hundred troy ounces of silver bullion in one ounce rounds contained in four cardboard boxes of one hundred rounds each, plus three $100 face value bags of pre-1965 dimes, each about seventy-two ounces of silver by weight. A week ago it all would have been worth around one hundred thousand dollars.

Kyle split the gold and silver evenly between both vehicles in case they had to quickly abandon one. It would hurt tremendously to lose either vehicle, especially the truck and trailer, but he knew not to place all his proverbial eggs in one basket. He then loaded up the armor and knives into the Durango and called Amber over.

"We should go over the trip again," Kyle said.

"Sure thing."

"Let's stick to channel twenty-seven on the radios, but we can pop over to another channel if we need to. Don't forget that it's completely in the clear, so no mentioning who we are or where we're headed."

She nodded. "Of course."

"As we talked about, I'll take the lead in the Durango. Just follow me and, by default, do what I do. I'll radio if we need to change anything."

"What about police? Or . . . if someone stops one of us?"

Kyle let out a breath. "Easy answer is we're cooperating with the police. Once the curfew is lifted for the day there's nothing illegal about driving down the freeway. If they are turning into highway robbers, which I suppose is possible, we deal with it as it comes. Now if it's real bad guys, setting up a roadblock or whatever, you get out of there with the kids. Make sure that wherever we are, you can turn around and boogie out of there."

"So . . . you're just going to sacrifice yourself? How *noble*." She smiled.

Kyle smiled back. "It is sort of that, yes. I'm not risking you and the kiddos in a real gunfight. Just let me take care of business. If I'm still standing afterward, I'll get to the cabin."

CHAPTER EIGHT
Wednesday, Last Week in October

Matt took the on-ramp to Interstate 5 North, pegged the cruise control at a sedate and fuel-maximizing forty-five miles an hour, and watched the scenery pass by as he climbed toward Castaic.

His strategy of fuel conservation and caution wasn't shared by many. At the tail end of a group of several smaller vehicles, an older motorhome had blown by him doing at least sixty, a round-faced, mop-headed boy giving him a raspberry from the back window.

He probably thinks this is the adventure of a lifetime. A few miles later, Matt passed an older couple on a red tandem road bike, black nylon panniers stuffed. He didn't dare sniff in disdain as it was very likely he'd gladly trade the Prius straight up for a bicycle in about eight hours. He had estimated the car would get him about five hundred and fifty miles, which the car's GPS informed him would be good enough to get just past Redding, CA if he stayed on the interstate.

But Matt had no intention of heading straight into the heart of the Siskiyou Mountains in late October and hoofing it into Oregon along that route. While they weren't all that impressive, elevation-wise, the Siskiyous were very rugged mountains that rose right out of the Pacific Ocean and climbed quickly to eight or nine thousand feet. If they weren't already covered with snow it would be coming soon enough. He had decided that the best route was to skirt the larger Californian cities and, once well north of the Bay Area, head west to the coast. The weather would be far milder and the terrain more forgiving if it really did come down to a long walk north.

There were still very few vehicles on the road and no commercial trucks of any kind, almost surreal for this major artery that fed into Southern California. The government announcement was clearly preventing the feared outpouring of people from urban areas into the country. A guarantee of free food that required people to stay put to receive it was proving to be pretty convincing.

Soon enough he reached the "Y" where he could choose to either stay on I-5 or head north on Highway 99 which cut right down the middle of the San Joaquin Valley. In good times, it was an easy decision to take 99: more places to stop, fuel up, and get a bite to eat. While the speed limit was lower, during the day one typically ended up going faster because 99's third lane was off-limits to the big trucks. Interstate 5 suffered from what Californians called "the I-5 dance" where the posted speed limit was much lower for trucks, and when they slowly passed one another it caused a see-saw effect that was immensely frustrating for car travelers.

Today, though, the roles were swapped. Highway 99's advantages—lots of towns, people, and places to stop—were exactly what Matt wanted to avoid, and with zero big rigs on the road it was clear sailing on I-5 all the way north to Stockton. Of course, even if there were any trucks headed north and going their speed limit—fifty-five—Matt wasn't going to catch up with them.

He wished he knew the shortcuts and side roads better here in the Valley. Matt would have to risk going through Stockton, one of the most depressed cities in California, where the Dream Had Died in the last decade, real unemployment had been close to 30%, and there were large sections of town that had been simply abandoned by people escaping bad home loans.

Matt spotted some fires in the distance, with dark smoke billowing off to the northeast. For the first time since leaving Santa Clarita, he saw people on foot along the freeway. Most were walking south, some with backpacks, while others pushed shopping carts. One man was even pulling a child's red wagon stuffed with goods and covered with a blue tarp. Out of the corner of his eye, he witnessed two people fighting over a heavily-laden blue plastic shopping cart.

As he passed through the middle of town, there were far more people on his side, northbound. Matt passed a caramel skinned woman with a boy of about ten. They both had their thumbs out, waving with the other hand. Matt sighed heavily. He really didn't want to pick anyone up when he was due to run out of gas in a couple of hours. Already the tank was just under a third full.

Next was a man with a cardboard sign held up with both hands that read, "EUGENE." Appropriately, he had a green Oregon Ducks hat on over his long brown hair. Again, Matt thought it didn't make much sense to pick up someone he couldn't really help. Taking the poor guy to the California coast wouldn't do him much good.

He was so engrossed with his mental musings regarding hitchhikers that he almost missed his exit, Highway 12 heading west. Matt went that way, then turned north on CA-113. Besides the slow turning of white wind turbines in the distance, it was as if he had this section of California all to himself. Next was a short piece of Interstate 80—the same I-80 that went clear to Chicago—and he was back on CA-113 heading into Woodland, a stretch with a sad, scrubby median and badly in need of resurfacing.

Woodland, too, was quiet, as he got off of 113 and headed west through town. Now Matt was among retail stores and what looked to be an industrial area out his passenger window. He passed by a gas station that had two different police cruisers out front, a black and white city department vehicle and an all-white sheriff's car. The officers, both dressed in the black-on-black that was pretty much standard in California, seemed to glare at him through sunglasses as he passed. Matt figured he looked pretty clean cut and was driving the most inoffensive car on the planet, so unless they had serious chips on their shoulders they should just leave him alone.

It wasn't long before he was out of the town and back into the small farms and country living spreads that were popular in this part of the state. Highway 16 would take him to 20, which joined with 101; Highway 101 led clear to Washington State along the Pacific coastline. Matt passed a small airport, then up ahead saw what looked to be a metallic green truck blocking the other lane. As he drew closer, he could see a county police cruiser pulled along the road on his side, lights off. It sat with its driver's door wide open. It looked as if a man . . . no . . . a police officer was sitting on the ground with his back against the inside of the open door, head slumped. Matt pulled up to a stop behind the cruiser and saw that there was another man, not an officer, laying on the ground face down in front of the older Ford F-150 blocking oncoming traffic.

The hairs went up on the back of his neck and his heart rate instantly shot up. Matt quickly scanned his surroundings to make sure this wasn't an ambush, a kill zone of some kind. While there were a few scrubby pines along the road, there really wasn't any good place to hide. He kept the car's engine running, opened the door, and approached the closest man, the one lying face down. A pool of blood had formed under him and a host of flies had gathered.

Dead.

Even with the slight breeze, Matt could smell the coppery tang of drying blood in the air. A John Deere baseball hat had popped off and lay in front of the man, who

Turn Red Tomorrow

looked to be around sixty with thin silver hair. A well-worn lever action rifle lay by his side and a spent case about six feet away glinted in the afternoon sun. Matt then walked over and peered in the truck. Among the crumpled, empty fast food bags and plastic tins of chewing tobacco laid a Colt .38 revolver with plenty of holster wear. Matt flipped out the cylinder and saw it was fully loaded.

Next, Matt approached the cruiser and could now hear the purr of the still-running engine. The smell of fresh blood mixed with the stench of bowels loosened by death was overpowering, and Matt gagged reflexively. The officer, a fit man about Matt's age, shaved bald with a deep tan, sat in his own pool of blood. Matt could see that he'd been shot through the left side of his chest. The name badge above his right breast pocket read "J. COLQUIST." A full-sized Glock pistol lay on the ground next to his slightly curled right hand and just outside the sticky puddle. Matt carefully put his right index finger to the side of the man's neck.

Also dead.

Looking into the cruiser, Matt saw the usual police setup; a screen and keyboard that dominated the center of the car, radio, camera, and light bar controls. In the passenger seat was a bulk store box of granola bars next to a black nylon patrol bag. The fuel gauge on the cruiser's dash read just over a half tank.

Matt quickly took stock of the situation and tried to deduce what might have happened. *No sane officer would pull up alongside to chat with man waving a rifle around.* It seemed much more likely, based on what he knew about law enforcement SOP, that the officer had been parked here along the side of the road and the older man had come alongside. Since the revolver was fully loaded, the older man must have shot Officer Colquist with the rifle, who had returned fire with his duty weapon. This too made sense since a pistol would not have penetrated the officer's soft body armor while a rifle would easily do so. Matt believed the officer had never even had a chance to radio for help; even with the crisis, his fellow officers, once notified, would have definitely made it here long before Matt had stumbled across the scene. Matt envisioned the officer being shot with the rifle, falling to the ground, then drawing and firing, striking the older man several times, then losing consciousness, all about two to four hours ago.

His first no-think instinct was to pick up the guns, get his bag, hop in the police cruiser, and head west on his original route. The cruiser had more gas than his hybrid and he'd no doubt make it a lot further. But he couldn't outrun a radio—if there was a BOLO for the cruiser now, or later, he'd be stopped well before he ran out of fuel. Getting caught behind the wheel of a stolen cruiser with a dead cop's gun tucked into his waistband wouldn't leave a whole lot of room for conjecture.

Siphoning the fuel was off the table. He knew that newer cars had an anti-rollover valve that prevented easy siphoning by hose. Plus, there was the small issue that he didn't have a hose in the first place. No, it was pretty clear that the best option was to take what he could from the scene and get going—quickly.

So that it, hmm, his inner voice cried. *You've stooped to robbing the dead.*

"No," Matt muttered out loud. "Just picking up what I find along the way."

First, he walked back to the older man's truck and did another quick scan, but there was absolutely nothing more of value. The rifle was a real beater that had seen decades of hard use. Matt shucked out the rounds into his left hand and, perhaps predictably, found it was one shy of fully loaded. There may have been more ammunition or other valuables in the man's pockets, but there Matt drew the line. The thought of reaching into a cold, bloody, and very dead man's blue jeans to root for a wallet or spare bullets made his stomach turn. He reloaded the rifle and placed it across the back seat of the rental.

Next, Matt walked back over to the cruiser. He unclicked the officer's duty belt which thankfully was not in the sticky pool of blood. Matt noted that the officer had set it up well, almost exactly as he had been taught as an Army MP—handcuffs, baton, Taser, OC spray, holster, spare magazines, and radio—for best access. He then slipped the Glock into its plastic retention holster, taking note that it was the .40 caliber version of the iconic polymer-framed handgun.

He then grabbed the box of granola bars and the patrol bag and made his way back to the rental; he'd inventory the bag later. Coming back, he popped the trunk as most cars had tools and other gear he might want to bring, even knowing he'd likely be hoofing it for a long, long time and the last thing he wanted was to weigh himself down.

"SWAT," Matt said under his breath as he saw the black rifle case and a set of similarly black body armor complete with full magazine pouches. Across the chest the armor read, "POLICE" in white block letters on a vinyl patch. He unzipped the case and pulled out an AR-pattern carbine topped with an Aimpoint red dot sight. As he ran his left hand along the railed handguard and up toward the barrel, the memories came flooding back.

CHAPTER NINE
Wednesday, Last Week in October

Leaving just after six in the morning, the Flanigan mini-convoy made good time heading west toward Tacoma, where they took the highway's final exit and continued on Interstate 5 south toward the state capital of Olympia.

While it was possible to avoid going through JBLM—Joint Base Lewis-McChord, a combined Army/Air Force installation and one of the largest concentrations of military personnel on the West Coast—it would have been a very long detour to the south. This would have also taken them along many, many lightly traveled back roads that could have their own dangers by now. Anything was possible, but Kyle felt that the Army wasn't in the business of stopping RVs leaving the city. Not yet, anyway.

His suspicion proved correct—the entrances to the base were closed off with hastily-erected Jersey barriers and manned by soldiers with rifles, backed up with new JLTVs with mounted fifties—but they had no interest in the traffic that whizzed by on the interstate. Traffic wasn't heavy, far from it, but it was almost all going their way, away from the teeming millions around Seattle and Tacoma.

"Let's hope it's all that smooth," he radioed to Amber.
"Roger that!"
"Ten-four, buddy!" Kyle joked back.

They dropped down into the Nisqually River valley, crossed the bridge, and then back up a grade.

"You see those lights back there?"

Kyle peeked into his driver's side mirror—the center mirror's view was completely obscured by boxes and gear—and saw the flashing lights of a state patrol car coming up behind them.

Fast.

"You think he's coming for us?"

Kyle keyed the handheld. "I don't see why he would be. Just stay calm."

Soon enough, the car passed them on the left and kept going. It slowed behind a full-sized red truck with a matching canopy and hit its siren.

What happened next was so quick Kyle almost missed it. Something poked out from the driver's side of the truck, there was a flash, and the cruiser immediately careened to the left, right into the broad median and came to a stop. The truck then quickly weaved over the two left lanes and stopped some two hundred yards ahead of the trooper's vehicle.

"Did you see that?"

"Yes . . . that truck shot the police car. Looked like a shotgun . . . probably hit the windshield. Keep moving, I'm going to speed back up." Indeed, Kyle had unconsciously coasted, not wanting to get too close, but now he wanted nothing more than to put plenty of asphalt between them and the mystery truck.

"Shouldn't we stop to help?"

"No, keep going." He would have to talk to her about it later. *Not enough information to pick sides.* He had a rough policy to trust the police, but not utterly—say ninety percent. Zero percent, and you were a criminal, totally opposed to law and order. Fifty-fifty didn't work either. Who could ride the fence and be intellectually honest? He had seen that sort of thinking among political protestors and such who, on any given day would rally against the police, spit on them, but would then also fully and completely expect them to respond when 911 was called. One hundred percent trust in police was bad as well. They were human and made mistakes, blindly followed bad policies, or simply caved to their weaknesses. Kyle had no idea what the state trooper was doing or whether it was lawful or not. It likely was —again the 90% rule—but Kyle couldn't say for sure well enough to interfere.

As long as there were perfectly legal police strategies such as civil forfeiture, quotas for ticketing and, by extension, harassing the local population, and the attitude of loyalty before integrity, where police departments routinely closed ranks around a fellow officer who was clearly in the wrong—the so-called "thin blue line"—Kyle would continue to believe as he did, though he knew it was something he struggled with spiritually.

About ten uneventful minutes went by and they approached the off-ramp onto Highway 101 which led north past Hood Canal. In normal times, there would have been a dozen police cars responding from the other direction by now, but besides the passage of a northbound car every twenty seconds or so, there was nothing.

"Kyle!" his radio squawked. "*That truck is coming up behind us! What do I do?*"

"Just keep driving. I'll drop back behind you. If they're coming after us because we witnessed what happened back there, they can try me out first. Just make sure you take the 101 exit. Hopefully they just keep going south on I-5." Kyle moved over a lane, braked slightly, and let their truck and trailer pass by.

"*We will. What if they start shooting?*"

"I'll shoot back. I won't even wait for that to happen. If I see a barrel, it's go time." Kyle wondered if that truck had a scanner and was listening in. *If they do, that's good. They'll know I'm serious . . . and armed.* He flicked the brass button open on his leather shoulder holster and removed the Glock with his right hand, steering with the left. Then, he opened his window and was greeted with a blast of cold morning air.

The red truck didn't pass them, but instead got behind Kyle to take the same exit. Getting on Highway 101, their pursuer maintained a six car length gap behind his Durango.

"Okay," Kyle called, "make sure you head to Shelton and not out to the coast. The interchange is just a few miles ahead."

"What if they follow us, clear to, ah, where we're headed?"

Kyle smiled, proud that Amber had remembered not to mention the lake or cabin. "We're not going to just lead them there. We'll figure it out as we head up there." He kept alternating his attention between the rearview mirror and the windshield. As Amber angled the Ram and trailer to the right to continue north, Kyle exhaled and did the same. The red truck continued west toward the coast and out of sight.

"Well there's a piece of good news! They're headed elsewhere. Thank God."

"Amen! Do you want to swap back, take the lead again?"

"With pleasure. Over and out."

The remainder of the trip went smoothly. The small towns along the Canal, quiet during normal times, were absolutely dead. Most had tried, and most had failed, over the last few decades to become tourist destinations. Before their turnoff just north of the tiny town of Lilliwaup that led to the lake, Kyle had counted a total of five vehicles headed the other direction—a station wagon, two fully-loaded trucks, and two motorcycles traveling together.

SUNSHINE LAKE – 3 MI

Kyle saw the familiar metal sign, brown to denote it was a recreation area complete with reflective icons for camping and fishing. No one really knew where the name

'Sunshine Lake' had originally come from. It was either a wry joke, as no lake in Western Washington surrounded by mountains would ever truthfully be known for its sunny weather, or was the work of some past glass-half-full optimist, who might have noted that while the imposing Olympic Mountains blocked the light from the north and west, the lake had a decent southern exposure as only low foothills lay to the east and south.

The small jellybean-shaped lake, maybe half a mile across, was considered a hidden gem by those that owned one of the twenty cabins along the southern shore, all built on the same floorplan during the 1960s, though #2 had burned down sometime in the early 1990s and had been rebuilt a bit larger than the rest. Like the much larger and more popular Lake Cushman to the south, Sunshine was wedged up against National Forest land on its western and northern edges; unlike Cushman, Sunshine did not quite border Olympic National Park. To the east it was quite marshy and dominated by stands of water-loving trees like aspens, cottonwoods, vine maples, and alders; elsewhere it was Douglas fir and Western red cedar with a few spruces and hemlocks mixed in.

Kyle hit the "T" in the road by the waterfront public park and turned left. The cabins were numbered right to left as one faced the water, with #1 through #7 to the right/east of the park and #8 to #20 to the left/west. The Flanigan cabin was #11. Even though they were almost seventy years old, they had been built comfortably for that era, with multiple rooms, power, plumbing, and fireplaces. Kyle's folks had purchased theirs back in the 1980s as an investment, renting it out most of the time, but as that sort of recreation began to decline in popularity during the "aughts" and the recession, it just became a full-time family cabin, great for spring and summer getaways and as a hunting lodge in the fall. Kyle had been here just three weeks ago for deer season.

He saw that there were vehicles parked next to all

but one cabin within sight. Most had two or three. In front of number eight, an elderly gentleman waved and smiled at Kyle as he crept by.

He pulled the Durango directly in front of the porch, hoping the actual parking area along the right side would be sufficient for the other rig. They had never had the trailer up here before as it would have been a bit redundant. Kyle got out as Amber began to pull in and guided her by hand signals. It proved to be a tight fit but was a success.

Kyle hugged his wife then his kids in turn. "Let's get everything unpacked. But remember . . . we need to stack everything high and leave plenty of elbow room. It might get crowded in here real quick."

He wasn't terribly surprised they were first to make it to the cabin even though the list of people with keys was pretty long. He knew from his last conversation with Des that Matt was stuck down in Southern California, and his sister-in-law wasn't leaving until it was absolutely necessary. Their BMW, no trailer of course, was just too small to tote everything Des considered valuable. It wasn't the same list as what Kyle might draw up, but she was free to make her own decisions.

His mother had been staying with friends in Chicago helping a nonprofit group there with some pro bono consulting work. She was a nonprofit "lifer" who couldn't quite stay retired.

Kyle hadn't spoken to his father, a retired Army lieutenant colonel living in western Michigan, in almost two years. Neither he nor Matt were particularly close to the man, who had seriously burned the proverbial bridge by finding a "honey"—while still bound by his vows to their mother—on unaccompanied deployment to South Korea over twenty years ago. He had been there, in full dress, for Kyle's Marine Corps boot camp graduation and made a repeat performance for Matt after his Army basic training. Those two, and Bella's birth, had been the only three times he'd seen his father since the split. Phone calls and emails were infrequent at best. The last Kyle had heard, the man was living on his VA checks and spending his time fishing and writing his memoirs. Though Kyle would have welcomed him, he hadn't had his own key since the divorce.

His uncles, Rich and Rob, as part-owners had access as well, but the chances of either of them showing up were very remote. Uncle Rich lived with his second wife, Dot, in the opposite corner of the country. The last Kyle had heard, Uncle Rob was out in Missouri living on a much bigger and well stocked lake than Sunshine. Uncle Rob had a lot of flaws and shortcomings, but being able to live off the land and water were not among them. It had been his uncle, not his father, who had taught Kyle to hunt and fish while he was a teenager.

Kyle had put out open invites to a couple of very close friends as well. They didn't have keys but were welcome to come during situations like this. One friend, Marshall, was still on active duty in the Marine Corps back east at Camp Lejeune, in North Carolina. The other, Brett, a high school bud and fellow Eagle Scout, last Kyle had heard he was backpacking/hosteling in Europe in the midst of a midlife crisis. Not too likely he would see either of them anytime soon.

Kyle stifled the urge to worry but instead vowed to continue to pray for each of them. There was nothing to gain by worrying when he had no earthly way to help any of them, save maybe his sister-in-law, but she was not someone you drove up on and barked orders to leave. Stubborn was too mild a term for Des.

"Shouldn't be a problem," Amber said. "The food will stack up fine. Where are you going to keep all of those guns? There's no safe or locking cabinet here. Maybe in the trailer?"

"We're in full readiness mode. They're going to be loaded and stowed where they can be reached in a hurry. I'm going to carry at all times and I'd appreciate it if you did the same. You and I will go through a refresher course on them over the next couple of days. Loading, failure drills, usage, tactics, you name it."

Amber frowned. "I'm a bit worried about the kids, Kyle. Bella is smart enough to not play with guns, but Cole, he's pretty curious. And, I might point out, a boy who wants to be like his daddy."

"I'll talk with him. We'll keep the weapons up high or on our bodies. Most of them we can leave with empty chambers which will be enough to stop a snooping four-year-old from doing anything dangerous. I understand your concern, sweetie, but we're on our own up here. You saw what I saw, no doubt. It's us and a bunch of retirees. Not going to be a lot of warning—or help—if trouble shows up."

"Who do you think will show up next? Not trouble... I mean family."

Kyle scratched his chin. "I'd have to say Des. I mean, she's the closest by a lot. Honestly though, I'm not sure we'll see anyone else before this crisis blows over. Matt seems to be fine holed up with his boss in California. Mom, Dad, my uncles, no chance, although I'd love it if Dad or Uncle Rob got here. Their military experience might come in handy even though they're no spring chickens. But, well, the personalities might be an issue."

Amber crossed her arms and cocked her head. "Umm, you think? I don't think your dad is showing up if there is any chance he might run into Susan. She'd probably kill him. Not joking. And what about your Uncle Rob? You always talk about him like he's some former super soldier. Wasn't he just a... whaddyacalit, a quartermaster sergeant? And, since we're being brutally honest here, an alcoholic? All I remember from family events is him drinking and arguing with everyone."

"Yes, you're right on all counts. Uncle Rob definitely has a hard edge and isn't exactly a 'people person,' but he's loyal as heck and a master outdoorsman. I have a strong feeling we're going to need people like him."

"And what about your buddies? I liked Marshall when he came by a few years back." She was referring to his friend's two day visit in transit to Okinawa. It was then that Kyle had extended the cabin invite and had given his old friend clear directions on how to get here. Included in those clear instructions was that it was only open to Marshall and any immediate family: wife, kids, et cetera. Last time he checked Marshall still rode solo. Despite their many differences—Kyle the white upper-middle class kid with a nerdy bent and an officer dad, Marshall the black lower-middle class kid from a tiny town in the Midwest—they had become close friends during and after the Iraq invasion. Marshall, with less to fall back on, had become a Marine lifer. A few months back Kyle had put a date on next year's calendar, sometime in the early summer, to head back to North Carolina to attend Marshall's retirement ceremony. Kyle assumed that was pretty much moot at this point.

Kyle nodded. "If he could make it up here, why, that would be fantastic. He's the real deal. Plus, his skills are a lot fresher than mine."

CHAPTER TEN
Middle of June
Several Years Ago

Fighting season was three months old, and Private First Class Matthew Flanigan, part of the squad-sized military police attachment to a company within the 10th Mountain Division, had been in country for two of those three months and already had experienced all the things his recruiter had specifically promised would never happen.

Before enlisting, his primary sources of military knowledge had been his estranged father, a retired Army officer, who had tried his best to talk him out of joining under any circumstances; his brother, who had served as a Marine infantryman and who naturally had tried to convince him to go that direction; and his uncle, a retired Army sergeant who was brief in his advice: go to college.

But Matt didn't want any regrets, and his family, clearly, had strong ties to the military and the Army in particular. His late grandfather had been in the Battle of the Bulge, toting a Garand and taking shots at Jerrys through the trees until the war ended. Matt had been pretty young at the time, but remembered Grandpa finally opening up a little to all of them once *Saving Private Ryan* had hit theaters. His stories, and later his brother's telling of his little part in the invasion of Iraq stuck with Matt. He didn't feel as if he'd walked into the recruiter's office two years ago with something to prove, but later Matt realized that's exactly what it was. He didn't want to be on the outside looking in, excepting his uncle Rich the lone male in the family who had never served.

When he'd walked into the nondescript recruiter's office in a local strip mall, Matt was set on becoming a paratrooper, maybe even a Ranger or Green Beret later down the road. He had been a three sport athlete in high school—tall, a decent sprinter, and could run a sub six minute mile. While he had suffered from a lack of focus, he had been bright enough to get A's and B's without much effort, so he'd figured there wasn't anything the Army could throw at him that he couldn't adapt to and handle.

The recruiter had wrapped all that up, saw that he had a clean juvenile record, hadn't tried drugs, and had told him to box up that Airborne dream and throw it out the window. Someone with his skills and background should be an MP—Military Police.

"A cop? Seriously?" Matt had replied, totally surprised.

"Absolutely. You get all the advantages of the infantry guys. You get to shoot guns, ride around in Hummers, get out in the field and get dirty. But you get to go home at night, and you have a job to do here in the States besides sit around and wait for the next deployment, and you actually build some skills of use in civilian life. What do you think?"

"I'm not sure . . . I mean, I never pictured myself as a police officer type."

The recruiter picked up some paperwork and tapped it on his desk. "Look, Matt. It ain't like the cop shows on TV. You're not busting drug dealers and making chalk outlines at murder scenes, that's not what MPs do. You get to do all the stuff you talked about, hang out with people with triple digit IQs, you just aren't going to jump out of working aircraft. Sound good?"

"What about in war? I know I'll get deployed at least

once. What do MPs do in...in combat?"

"The infantry does the fighting on the ground. MPs do stuff like guard prisoners, train locals to be police at academies, that sort of thing. Rear echelon stuff. You can always volunteer to get out there and mix it up—if you feel like it—but your real job is behind the fence."

Matt found himself in a small COP—combat outpost, the very opposite of rear echelon—walled with Hescos, an easily erected barrier originally designed as a temporary levee but worked fairly well at stopping bullets, RPGs, and fragments. It contained the squad of MPs he belonged to plus the infantry company and its other attachments, maybe one hundred and fifty soldiers total.

Not that Matt was any stranger to walking either. Their main mission here was to walk to nearby villages, some twenty miles away, and train local ANP—Afghan National Police—to try and act more like actual police and less like the Third World thugs they actually were. Little aspects of routine police work like, "Don't kill prisoners," and, "Don't point your rifle at people and demand bribes" still needed to be ingrained in these men. Matt was skeptical that would ever really happen.

While making their rounds, they were indistinguishable from a regular infantry patrol, complete with M4 carbines and their attached M203 or the newer M320 grenade launchers, Mk48 and M240 machineguns, disposable AT-4 and LAW rockets, grenades, and body armor. Most of their rifles and machineguns had ACOGs, a no-batteries-needed sight that worked well at the longer ranges one encountered here in 'Stan. A medic and RTO—Army-speak for radioman, but in reality just another grunt—were also attached to his squad.

Three weeks ago, he'd fired his first shots in anger at a couple of Taliban who sprayed at them at long range with AK fire, doing a mag dump each, and fled. They had all gone to the ground and returned fire, but with no clear targets it was a wasted effort. Bullets were small, and the large Afghan valleys provided innumerable places to hide.

Matt rubbed the last of the sleep from his eyes as he made his way over to his gear. It was well before sunrise, maybe four in the morning, and his squad leader had told him they were in for a long mission that day. They would be the assigned handlers, the go-betweens, for a combined ANA (Afghan National Army) and ANP force that was accompanying an infantry push to locate a person of interest.

"You awake, Flanigan?" called Cpl. Simmons, a short bulldog of a man with a blonde crew cut.

"Yeah, sure, Corporal. The usual. Could use a nice hot coffee right now."

"I'll get right on that. You want sprinkles too?" he cracked. "We're moving out in about ten minutes, so get squared away and form up."

Matt already had his basic uniform on, all Scorpion camouflage pattern—far superior to the gray, green, and light tan digital ACU which was standard for the rest of the Army outside of the combat theater. At combat distances, ACU tended to merge into a light green-gray blob that, outside of sagebrush really wasn't a color found in nature—anywhere. Camouflage patterns had been poo-pooed late in the Cold War with the rise of thermal and night vision sights that didn't care what color of uniform you had on. It had become way more important to launder your uniform without brighteners than worry about the specific pattern.

But the Afghans didn't have any of that high technology—they could only shoot what they could see with their bare eyeballs. Ergo, ACU standard uniform out, Scorpion in.

Matt quickly slung on the chest rig and plate carrier that were done up in the same pattern. To the surprise of his ex-military friends and family back home, his rifle's thirty round magazines were black plastic, not the metal that had been standard clear back to Vietnam.

It was a double-edged sword to be lucky enough

to only lug around an M4 carbine, the lightest weapon in their squad. To make up the weight disparity, Matt carried an extra belt for their Mk48 and M240 machineguns. He checked to make sure he was fully loaded up, had enough MREs and water, and formed up.

"All right, listen up," their squad leader, Sgt. Rodrigo began. "We're heading out with the full platoon, syncing up with the rest of the company plus ANA and ANP, and heading north ten clicks to a small village. We'll search there, then if needed we'll continue north until we reach the next checkpoint, another no-name village.

"All the standard ROEs apply, gents. Keep your head on your shoulders and don't do anything stupid. Those infantry guys are always watching and we know they love it when we screw up 'playing grunt.' If the Afghans do something dumb, they'll probably blame us for that too since we're supposed to keep them in check. Everything understood?"

In unison they bellowed, "Hooah!" and set out northward.

After five hours of walking in staggered file through the dusty valley, the sun was beating down hard on Matt's right shoulder. At twelve thousand feet, temperatures didn't climb as high as one would think in this part of the world, maybe eighty degrees, but the sun was strong and exposed skin would burn fast. It was hottest right by their feet here, and the temperature fluctuations created a constant breeze and occasional whirlwinds as well.

The patrol reached what looked like a fallow poppy field ringed with fruit trees, with several squad buildings in the distance—the village without a name.

"Okay," called Sgt. Rodrigo. "Orders are to wait here and let the brass figure out our approach with the village."

"Approach?" chided Cpl. Simmons. "Secure the perimeter. No one gets out. Kick down every door until we find the Afghani S.O.B."

Sgt. Rodrigo glared at his subordinate. "You, me, and everyone else here would do it like that. But the CO told us to hang tight. Feel free to offer up your plan to him though, he's right over there."

Simmons pursed his lips but didn't venture a comeback.

An hour dragged into two, then three. Matt's eyes snapped open. He had nodded off sitting up. He looked around, comforted—somewhat—that he wasn't the only one. Several of the nearby 10th Mountain soldiers had put their helmeted heads against a rock and were busy examining the insides of their eyelids. It was something few outside the military understood—the soul-crushing boredom of war.

Matt turned the other direction and saw a lazy plume of smoke, maybe fifty yards away, and got up to a knee to take a better look.

"It's a campfire, the ANA knuckleheads," called one of Matt's squad mates. "They built it about ten minutes ago. You racked out there for a bit, Flanigan. Hey, what the heck is *that*?"

Matt turned back and saw five of the Afghanis, ANA troopers, holding hands in a circle, chanting, and dancing like kids at recess. "Look, one of them is their commander!" Matt said. This caught the attention of some of the nearby American troops, who were transfixed by the absurd display.

"What are we even *doing* here? These are the stupidest people on Earth. I swear, put these dudes back home and they'd flunk *lunch*," Cpl. Simmons grumbled from a few yards away.

Matt just shrugged. While their culture and behaviors were utterly alien to American eyes, they Afghanis he'd seen were generally were just like everyone else on Earth. They wanted to be with their friends, raise their families, and manage their own affairs within their social confines.

BRRAPP! BRRRAP! PUMM PUMM PUMM! The air was

pierced by a couple of AKs and a DShK—a Russian heavy machinegun—which opened up on them from the village, some five hundred yards away. Matt hit the ground, now intimately aware of how open the field was, a perfect kill zone for machineguns and mortars.

To his left, one of the infantry guys began rattling off bursts from a belt fed machine gun, every fifth round a tracer showing a bright orange line right to the village. Matt shouldered his M4, flipped the selector up to "SEMI," and peered through its EoTech holographic sight. The reticle, a large orange circle with a small centered dot, wasn't really made for long shots like this, but it was what he had, so he squeezed off a couple aimed a couple of shots at a figure moving in a window, holding the dot about two feet high to account for the range.

From the right side of the village, a shoulder fired rocket—an RPG—roared and impacted a small berm to Matt's right where about ten of the Afghan troops had taken cover. The concussion shoved him slightly, and small bits of rock and dust pelted the side of his face and right arm. He looked up, and through the dust saw two of the Afghanis splayed out on their backs, the others running away from the cloud, coughing. The stink of the explosive mixed with the dust, causing Matt to sneeze.

For the next couple of minutes, Sgt. Rodrigo pointed out targets in the village, the enemy just out of range of his M203. The enemy fire slackened noticeably.

"Let's go!" called Sgt. Rodrigo from about twenty yards to Matt's left. "We're moving up to the wadi for cover!"

Matt pulled himself to his feet, and glanced over to Cpl. Simmons who was getting up as well. Even in the din and confusion, Matt knew better than to run in front of the man's rifle. The gunfight was now a physical *thing*, with the animal-like "rip-snarl" of massed small arms fire punctuated by explosions.

The wadi wasn't very far, maybe a little over a hundred yards, but it brought them closer to the village and the Taliban. Matt dove feet first into the dry creek bed that acted as a natural trench.

BRRRRUPPP! A machinegun blasted the trench from the hillside to the left, sending more fragments into Matt's face as he tried—too late—to shield himself with his left arm.

By advancing aggressively, they had walked right into a classic "L-shaped ambush"," which from above would look just like you'd imagine—shooters forming an "L" with the target on the inside, which kept you from shooting your own people but allowed flanking fire to any target within the zone.

"Get that PKM up on the hill!" Sgt. Rodrigo screamed over the renewed rattle of fire. Matt felt something hot tug at his right side, spinning him slightly as he tried to sight in on the hillside. He fired several quick shots at the gunner and the rifleman at his side.

Five yard in front of Matt, Cpl. Simmons went down in a heap. Matt staggered over, as did another soldier, Specialist Wu, their attached medic.

"Keep firing! I'll take care of him," the smaller man yelled. Matt slunk back to the edge of the wadi and resumed firing up the hillside at the winking machinegun barrel. His side began to sting fiercely, and a warm, wet sensation spread down his left hip and thigh.

"Flanigan! You're hit too!" Wu said.

"I—I'm okay!" He fired, saw the tracer that signified it was time to change magazines, and swapped them out, not bothering to stow the empty one.

A bright light and a deafening sound threw Matt to the hard ground, his rifle swiveling up to bash his lip, nose, and cheek. He lay there, stunned, deaf, and unable to open his eyes. Time lost meaning. When the swirling stopped he cracked his eyelids open to see Sgt. Rodrigo there.

"Flanigan? You there?"

"Yeah, I'm okay."

"You've been laying there for almost ten minutes. We've secured the village. The Haj bastard we're looking for is long gone. Someone tipped them off we were here, obviously, they were waiting for us all loaded up for bear."

Matt had acquired several cuts to his face plus a piece of his cheek gouged out by the front sight of his own rifle. His side, his love handle, had been shot through clean. He'd received a free trip back to the rear, to Bagram, and had been awarded his Purple Heart there as well. After his six week "vacation" he'd returned to the same COP, which was identical minus Cpl. Simmons, who had been evacuated to Germany. Simmons would live, but his left arm and shoulder would probably never work well for the rest of his life. Nine months later, Matt was back in the States for good, having experienced a few more scrapes but nothing quite like No Name Village.

CHAPTER ELEVEN
Wednesday, Last Week in October

Rob Overberg took a swig, nestled the half-empty can of light beer into the closest cup holder, and steered his small aluminum fishing boat farther out into the lake.

He had picked the rental house not for its own merits —Rob pictured himself as the type of man would could sleep anywhere and live on very little—but because it was right on one of the best crappie and bass fishing lakes in the state of Missouri, tucked up in the northwest corner of the state, and with its own private boat launch. Good game and bird hunting were close by. Rob wondered offhand what the bank crisis would do to the upcoming deer season. He had managed to take a buck in three of the past four years. If food distribution couldn't get back in order very soon, getting a deer (or two, or three) before winter set in would become a top priority.

Rob let out a long belch as he surveyed the water, looking for deadheads or other obstructions. Things were quiet along the shore, even with the boon of a sunny late October morning, with only a chill breeze to remind everyone that summer was long over and snow wasn't far away.

BOOM! Thump-thump-thump! Gunfire erupted from the opposite shore, the large RV park that was lately filled to the brim with city folk. He had seen their numbers build over the past week and a half and had smelled the smoke from their barbeques and late night campfires. *Thump! Thump-thump-thump! BOOM!*

Glass shattered and shouts echoed off of the lake's surface. *Sounds like a shotgun and a rifle working together.* It was enough to pique his curiosity. Rob guided the boat closer, sticking his hand in the right pocket of his surplus desert camo Gore-Tex jacket to wrap around the comforting wood grip of his .357, a Smith & Wesson snub nose.

More shouts, and several engines gunning, followed by the snarl of more gunfire. Through the first row of trailers Rob could see a young man with long brown hair, a red T-shirt, and blue jeans running, waving a cheap nickel-plated pump shotgun back and forth.

Unconsciously, Rob started to bring the tiller hard to port to get back into the middle of the lake. This wasn't his fight, or his friends. He knew he wasn't going to heroically stop several armed men with a six shooter and no reload. That was strictly pulp western fantasy.

Out of the corner of his right eye he saw three men standing in a triangle in front of a newer small Class A motorhome. Nearest to the vehicle was an older man, bearded like he, wearing a denim jacket. The other two had their backs to Rob but were clearly much younger. One, long haired like the first man Rob saw but wearing a forest green track suit, had a stubby rifle or shotgun; the other, shorter and darker skinned than his companion, with a black polo and khaki shorts, was holding a large matte black handgun.

Rob couldn't hear what was being said, but something clearly was exchanged as the old man interlaced his fingers behind his head and went down to his knees, staring at the ground.

Well, damn. I'm witnessing an execution.

Without further thought, he brought the boat to the muddy shore and cut the engine. As it slid into the clay, Rob popped out of the bow and climbed the bank, slipping slightly. He could now hear the exchange between the three.

"Show us what you have, old man! We don't have time to go through your stuff!" bellowed one of the young men.

"I... I don't have much," said the older man, sounding surprisingly calm. "Nothing you'd want. No money, no food. Please."

"Not good enough! You had better come up with somethin' I like pretty quick! You wanna die right now?"

At that moment, Rob cleared the slick drop-off, the small stainless steel wheelgun held straight out in his right hand, hammer back. *"Hey!"*

The long-haired youth to the left started to raise his weapon.

You can't outdraw a gun pointed right at you, Rob thought as he lined up the orange front sight on that man's chest and pulled the trigger.

The thug fell heavily to the right, dropping his weapon with a tortured scream as a dark blotch emerged on the right side of his chest. Rob immediately swung the muzzle over to the shorter man, who was staring dumbfounded at his weapon while yanking at the trigger. Rob's eyes weren't as crisp as they used to be, but the perp's pistol looked like an old Colt 1911 with either the safety on or the hammer forward; either one would render it unable to fire.

Rob took aim, but the young man looked up wide-eyed and instantly dashed to the right and into the jumble of trailers, likely saving his own life in the process.

"You all right?" Rob called to the old man, but it was Rob that was shaking.

"I'm fine," the man replied in a gravelly voice with a faint Southern accent, and stood to his feet. "Whom do I have to thank, sir?"

"Name's Rob. I'm staying across the lake from here. Out fishing and heard the gunfire."

"Hard to miss, that. I'm John."

Several feet away, the mortally wounded man gurgled, groaned, and tried unsuccessfully to roll over. Rob casually picked up what he now recognized as a sawn-off shotgun, noting that camouflage duct tape had been purposelessly wrapped around what was once a decent walnut stock. The ends of the barrels looked like a thirty-second hacksaw job. "Shame. This ugly P-O-S used to be pretty nice." He opened the action, confirmed both chambers were loaded, and snapped it shut again. "I've been by here a few times. I'm pretty sure there's only the one road in and out of here, and you can bet these guys have it blocked off tight. If it's all the same to you, I suggest coming along with me."

John nodded. "This motorhome holds everything I own. Granted, I won't die for any of it, but it's all I have."

Rob heard shouting in the distance, and they both turned, breaking their respite.

"Hey! He's over here!"

"Well-p, time to go," Rob said. "Lock it up, hope they don't kick the door in, and we'll come back when they're gone. Tonight, hopefully."

For an older man, John moved pretty well as they stumbled down the bank to the boat. "Get in by the stern, the back. No weight in the bow. I wanna move!" he barked. The excited shouts were getting louder as the raiders—that's what Rob thought of them as— caught up to the scene up above. Rob pushed off as hard as he could, and with cool lake water slopping up to his knees he hopped into the boat.

Gunshots rang out and made that distinctive 'BANG-whizz-zzzip' noise as they impacted the water to Rob's right, just short of the boat. Rob threw himself to the back of the boat, fired up the small gas outboard, and looked up to see one of their pursuers taking aim with an AK-47 type rifle, easy to distinguish with its curved "banana" magazine. Rob pulled the tiller all the way to the right, punched the throttle, and straightened out quickly, making certain ensuring they weren't in a direct line with—and an easier target—for the shooter.

Once halfway across the lake, Rob throttled down and handed the junker shotgun to John.

John frowned, but took the weapon, cradling it. "Why did you do it?"

"What? Give you that gun? Every gun I own is ten times better than that tur—"

"No, why did you ... why did you get involved. I thank God that you did, but—"

"But ... I could have just thought to myself, 'Well, darn it all, that guy is sure gonna have a bad day?' I don't think I can explain it with words, John. Maybe I'm just a selfish sonofagun who didn't want to see your brains blown out and wake up in the middle of the night for a few years with that stuck in my mind. It just seemed ... *right* ... at the time."

"And now?"

"No regrets here. No extra holes in me." Rob joked, patting down at the Gore-Tex jacket and his grease stained woodland camouflage trousers with his free hand.

They pulled up to the launch. John hopped out of the bow and surprised Rob with how quickly he pulled the boat up. "You're pretty strong for an old guy."

"Old guy? I suppose you're right. Turned seventy-four this last August. But the muscles, I got those a long time ago."

"Got me beat by almost fifteen years. Veteran?"

"Military? No sir. Just ornery."

Rob chuckled, which helped fend off the adrenaline crash blues. "We still do have a problem, though."

"My RV? It can wait for a while."

"No, it's those dirtbags. I figure I poked the hornet's nest pretty good there. What's to say they don't just have their way with the trailer park, then come around the lake and clean out every house? Ten, a dozen of those clowns, that's way too many to have showing up at my door. I think it's time to get a little *proactive*." Rob started toward the house and unlocked the porch door facing the lake with John following right behind. He entered the one car garage which held a medium-sized gray gun safe along the back wall. Rob punched the code, swung the door open, and pulled out two rifles: his old-school Mark V bolt action in .300 Weatherby with a Shepherd scope, and his Alexander Arms AR carbine in .50 Beowulf—his custom-made hog hunting gun—topped with a very pricey but extremely effective thermal sight. With it he could detect targets by body heat alone, day or night. It didn't have much range, maybe 150, 200 yards max, but it hit like a freight train.

Rob grabbed his hunting belt, which had a leather pouch containing 20 of the long, high velocity .300 Weatherby cartridges. He then put on his camouflage hydration pack, pockets stuffed full of ten-round Beowulf magazines and additional Weatherby ammo, then slung the short but heavy AR cross-body and pulled it tight.

"Oh, almost forgot," he murmured, opening yet another box of ammo. He then pulled out his .357, flipped open the cylinder, and loaded the one empty chamber.

"If I don't come back in four hours, pack up and get as far from here as you can," Rob said. "If that one short punk comes by and remembers you, it'll be a bad deal. Actually, if those guys come by period, no bueno. I'll leave you with the combo to the safe. There are a few big, heavy boxes in the garage, it's all survival stuff I got from my nephew. Food, solar panels, that sort of deal. I'll help you load it up in my truck now. It's all yours if I don't come back."

"What are you going to do?"

"Bucks to bagels these dirtballs have never taken accurate rifle fire from four hundred yards. Sit here and wait for them to show up? Can't do it."

CHAPTER TWELVE
Wednesday, Last Week in October

The Prius' gas engine died about ten miles south of Garberville, CA, well up into the mountains, just past a gas station and the self-proclaimed "world famous" One Log House. Both establishments were deserted, the station with a prominent plywood sign stating, "NO FUEL." The car's huge battery array alone got Matt about another two miles before the vehicle shut completely down, and he steered it to the edge of the road.

Matt sighed. *So . . . this is the end of the line.* He hadn't dared stop, half-seriously imagining a line of police cruisers in hot pursuit, *Blues Brothers* style, as he'd made his way west past beautiful and serene Clear Lake, met up with Highway 101, and turned north again.

He had begun to take inventory of the officer's patrol bag about then, briefly coming to tears when he found a worn photo of a smiling, bespectacled Officer Colquist with his raven-haired wife and three young children: a curly-haired girl and small identical twin boys. When would they find out they'd never see their husband or father alive again? *And what of my own raven-haired wife, a mere seven hundred miles away? What is going through her mind right now, not knowing?*

The more mundane items included several bandages, nitrile gloves, a trauma pack loaded with QuikClot coagulant, inexpensive eight power pocket binoculars, two spare Glock magazines filled with hollowpoints, a SureFire flashlight and spare batteries, an orange-handled Spyderco serrated folding knife, spare black socks, and even two unopened civilian MREs. He didn't see why he'd want to bring along the evidence tape, pens, notepads, and other non-survival type items, and separated them out.

Matt took the Jansport knapsack Ed had given him and began filling it with the granola bars, MREs, his spare clothes, spare dress shoes, and the tightly-cinched down sleeping bag. He tucked the .38 into the front pocket. Then, he wrapped the heavy jacket around the pack—even in the late afternoon in the coastal mountains it was too warm, especially with the SWAT body armor that Matt donned next. Then, the police belt, and finally he slung the patrol rifle across his body.

He didn't really know what to do with the beat up .30-30. He could justify carrying the weight of the .38, figuring it could be his ace in the hole if someone got the drop on him and stripped him of his visible weapons and, implausibly, left him alive. But the levergun, with only five shots and no sling with which to carry it, just didn't provide enough juice to justify the squeeze. Too, it was impractical to carry two rifles and the AR was far more capable. He left the old rifle along the back seat, loaded, for the next weary traveler to stumble across. Paying it forward.

Matt frowned, finally coming to grips with the stark reality of how difficult this journey was going to be. Unless he discovered a way to move over two hundred miles a day, he'd be out of food about the time he reached Eureka, CA. While in the Army, Matt had heard plenty about Ranger School, where they fed you a single MRE a day and ran you ragged for two months. He wasn't in peak condition anymore but figured that approach was his best shot to stretch out his food supplies. That might give him a week or so, Matt thought, a nice improvement from his three-day estimate, although he'd be ravenous the whole time. That still required about a hundred miles a day to get to Hood Canal, impossible on foot and about at his limit—for a day only—on his high-end titanium-framed touring bike, which inconveniently was back at his condo in Washington State. Even if he found a bike of that caliber, soon, he wouldn't be able to physically do that amount of riding for seven days straight, especially on reduced rations.

None of this took into account the possibility of catching Giardia or some equally nasty bug from drinking unpurified water along the trip, or simply dying of exposure during a heavy downpour, or catching pneumonia in said downpour. *Et cetera.*

Kyle, the ever-religious one, would probably have something pithy to say about the predicament, some flavor of "just trust in God." Matt was an agnostic keeping his options open until a moment of clarity—but figured if, in fact, he made it home alive, the slider would certainly head in the "God" direction.

Since moving off the road and through the redwoods and rocky hills ran a very real risk of turning an ankle—or worse—Matt made up his mind that after picking his way off-road today he'd stay awake, move at night along the road, hide when he saw headlights or heard a vehicle approaching, and sleep during the day.

Four nights and days had gone by, mostly without incident, though he'd had some close calls with the police moving up and down the highway. They constituted the majority of the traffic, and not only was Matt breaking the emergency curfew, there was the small matter of carrying a bunch of stolen police property. After a particularly close brush that involved a spotlight and a barking German Shepard, he'd contemplated ditching the cop gear altogether. But he felt what he needed was more gear, not less, and everything he'd taken with him served a purpose.

Matt had kicked himself for forgetting to ask the Vasquezes for one of the basic necessities of modern life: toilet paper. He would have gladly traded one of the handguns for a twelve pack of soft, brand name TP. Matt thought it was pretty remarkable how people often traded depending on their abundance and lack, not how intrinsically valuable something actually was. He'd ended up pressing one of his three dress shirts into service, slicing it into small chunks with the Spyderco to serve the same purpose.

That first night had been the most difficult. Out of shape from laying around for a week, Matt had to quit and find a place to hole up well before sunrise. He'd made it past the small mountain town of Garberville, waltzing right through downtown at about two in the morning, and onto a gradual descent that led all the way to Eureka and the Pacific coast.

He'd woken up, sore, about four hours before dark. Matt had tried to scout for game in the woods but had come up empty. Kyle was the hunter in the family, though Matt had tagged along about three years back when his brother had taken a deer. He'd watched the skinning and gutting process and felt he could at least not botch it too badly. Preserving the meat was a different story. Matt had zero experience in the curing department.

After another cycle of walking and sleeping, he did spot two deer, both does, but across the road—and at least eight hundred yards away. When he'd tried to close the gap to where he could realistically score a clean kill with the patrol rifle, they'd caught his scent and had bounded out of sight.

That night he had witnessed a convoy of sixteen military trucks on the opposite side of the road, heading south at a conservative pace at about one in the morning, but that had been the only event of note. By the very early morning of the third day on foot, Matt had been tired, hungry, and bored to tears. But he'd reached Eureka.

He had carefully skirted the downtown area; unlike tiny Garberville, Eureka had actual activity. There had been a few police cruisers on the move, but mostly it had been military vehicles that Matt could see with the binoculars—Humvees and 2-1/2 ton trucks, most still with desert paint schemes from past deployments. It was certainly more than what was needed to catch a few curfew breakers.

As Matt had passed through the widely-spaced houses to the east, dogs barked and porch lights came on. He had felt like an intruder, and almost certainly would have been treated as one if he'd ended up in the wrong place at the wrong time. He had found an old wooden hay shed well away from any other houses and had climbed in, figuring it was as good a place as any to rack out and keep out of sight.

Tonight, he pressed on north of Eureka, making good time under a waning gibbous moon and clear skies. His body had adjusted pretty well to all the walking, and he was no longer sore in his muscles though his feet were taking a beating. With dawn peeking over the low hills to the east, Matt knew it was time to start searching for a place to sleep. A light drizzle had begun to fall, and Matt grumbled, not for the first time, that he didn't have a poncho or umbrella. He couldn't really blame the Vasquezes for not giving him one, they did live in Southern California after all, but he had been surprised that Officer Colquist's bag hadn't contained one of those cheap plastic ponchos.

He crested a rise and saw, down about a quarter mile, the dim outline of a vehicle parked off the shoulder and almost into the tree line. It was an old four door sedan, an early 1990s Pontiac, dark blue with a lot of paint peeled away on the hood, roof, and trunk. Matt wondered if the vehicle had been run out of gas like the dozens of others he'd seen over the last few days, or if it had broken down just prior to the crisis. It didn't matter, and Matt would never know, as he saw through the driver's side window that there was no key in the ignition.

Matt tried the driver door, the rain increasing now, and figured the car was far from ideal as a hiding place—it was right next to the highway—but it would keep him dry and, once he was in the down bag, warm. Matt had been fanatical about keeping Ed's down sleeping bag dry as the feather filling would lose all of its wonderful insulating qualities once wet.

The inside of the car reeked of stale cigarettes. It didn't seem damp, so maybe it hadn't been sitting for long, but the car was a beater: headliner sagging, vinyl cracking, and gooey filth in every crack and crevice.

Beggars can't be choosers. Matt set the rifle in the passenger seat, took off the knapsack and body armor, set those alongside, and then crawled in the driver's seat. Out of habit, he wiped the rainwater off the rifle with what was left of his 'number two shirt,' ate a granola bar, swigged down some river water from one of his plastic bottles, put the seat all the way down, and prepared to bed down for the day.

As he crawled into the down bag, Matt looked out the dirty, rain streaked windshield and wondered, for the hundredth time, how things were going back home. Worry wouldn't change anything, but there had been a lot of time to think and very few good topics upon which to ruminate these last few days. For years, Matt had been in a state of constant stimulation—personal and work emails pinging his phone, social media, television, sports, Internet news, you name it. Des and Matt had enjoyed an active and reasonably exciting lifestyle, fueled by their DINK—Double Income, No Kids—status and Matt's success at work. Even when he had unplugged and went off into the woods, he had been with Des, or his family, or formal events through the Mountaineers, a Seattle-based organization focused on enjoying the outdoors. He had never been truly alone and off the grid for as long as he could remember.

Des didn't have the survivor mindset, but she was smart, tough, and would know when to pack up and get out. The Vasquezes, Matt wasn't so sure. He had spent so much energy with both of them, especially Sam, trying to convince them to leave their beautiful home and finely gilded neighborhood if things got bad.

Here he was, alone, a bit north of Eureka and a lot south of Crescent City, his stomach growling—the good food like the MREs and the canned food long gone, down to eating a dead man's club store box of granola bars—sitting in a smelly thirty-year-old clunker trying to catch some shuteye. Matt remembered a book he'd read in high school, the one about the guy who'd slept in an old mail truck and took a dead man's uniform. *The Postman.* But that book was set a couple of decades after everything fell apart. Here, not two weeks from the beginning, and Matt was already reduced to sleeping in strange cars to get out of the elements.

He'd been hungry like this before. A couple of years ago, he did the Wonderland Trail with a group of experienced hikers, a ninety mile trek around Mt. Rainier. Matt had realized on day seven he'd eaten through his food a bit too fast and had started to cut his rations slightly. By the last day, day nine, he'd been flat out of food save a few bits of trail mix and had been too proud/embarrassed to admit his mistake to his group. But then, he'd known that they'd eventually get back to their cars and hot, delicious restaurant food was less than an hour down the road.

His thoughts wandered to the vision of a huge roadhouse double cheeseburger, thick cut strips of pepper-encrusted bacon sticking out the sides with Matt's favorite—barbeque sauce—dripping down both patties and into the bottom bun. Not unexpectedly, his stomach gave a larger than normal growl as Matt fought to remove the unhelpful picture from his mind.

For what seemed like the millionth time, Matt racked his brain trying to remember a friend, acquaintance, *any-*

one he knew along the coast in southern Oregon, and came up empty. There just weren't that many people, period, through that area. Without somewhere to hole up and rest, he'd be continuously pushing north, digging for shellfish, trying to find fresh water, and not freezing to death.

One thing Matt was certain about, he wouldn't stoop to taking what he needed by force. He might not believe in the afterlife like his brother, but if it came down to dying or robbing others—others that were still alive, that is—Matt would choose death.

A high-pitched voice outside the window hissed. "Be careful, Kaleb, he's got a gun. See? In the other seat." Matt realized he had nodded off. He tensed a bit, carefully feeling for the finger release on the Glock holster. Every night, Matt had taken off the duty belt but had slid it alongside his right hip, just in case.

"Jeez. He's asleep, Abby." came another, different childlike voice. "Maybe we should just keep going. I mean, if the car worked, why would he stop here?"

Matt cracked his eyelids open just enough to see a couple of young faces peering in. The taller of the two—presumably Abby—looked to be about ten or eleven and had long, dirty blonde hair that partially obscured her freckled face. She wore a dark blue hooded coat. Next to her was a boy, younger, maybe about eight, also with a hooded coat. His was gray, and he had dark hair in a bowl cut with dark eyes. Matt thought he looked just like the kid from one of his niece's favorite movies, *The Neverending Story*, the one who was bullied all the time.

Matt slowly opened his eyes. Both of the kids jumped back a bit, eyes wide. "I'm okay. I'm not a bad guy," he said, he hoped loud enough so they could hear through the window.

"Who are you?" Kaleb asked.

"Can I open the door and talk?"

"I . . . I guess so," Abby squeaked. She looked as if she was trying to be brave for the boy but couldn't quite pull it off.

Matt crawled out of his bag, opened the door, and let his feet dangle, not wanting to get his socks wet in the ankle-high grass. About twenty feet behind the car he could see two bikes leaning on kickstands: a purple one with white and purple streamers, and a shorter blue and orange one. By each one was a fairly large framed pack. "I'm Matt. I'm from up near Seattle. I got trapped in California when the airports closed down. I've made my way up from near L.A. to here, it's been about a week since I left. I think."

"I'm Abigail and that's Kaleb. My brother." Her face took on a skeptical look. "L.A.? With a car you should have gotten a lot farther in a week than right here."

Matt smiled, he hoped it looked authentic to the two kids. "That's very true. But . . . this isn't my car. I've been walking from Garberville. That's where my car ran out of gas."

"And that gun? That's an army gun," Kaleb added.

"Well, actually," Matt began, "it belonged to a police officer. I came across, ah, the aftermath of a shootout. I figured it would be better to have with me than leave there."

When Matt mentioned the shootout, the two took a noticeable step back from Matt and the car. "Look, there's nothing to be scared of. I'm just a regular guy. Want to see a picture of my family?"

They nodded as Matt carefully pulled out his wallet. "See, there's my wife, Desirée, and in between us is my mom. There's my license. See? I live in Federal Way, up in Washington State. It's right by the airport near Seattle. So, you know where I'm headed. What about you two?"

Kaleb lowered his head as Abigail replied. "So, there was no more money, then no more food. Mom and Dad left one day and didn't come back. We waited for a few days, but I guess . . . they . . ." She turned her head, sniffling, then began crying silently. Kaleb joined in with his own soft blubbering.

"Hey now, it's okay. I'm sure they're fine, they probably just got held up somewhere," Matt said, trying to soothe as best he could.

Abigail's face turned red and her eyes narrowed. "Don't treat me like a little kid!" she barked. "I'm *eleven*. I'm old enough to know that if they were coming back they already would have. So we *had* to leave."

"So... you and your brother are just... *traveling north*? To what?"

"*No*," Abigail replied, still on edge. "We've only been in Eureka for a year, okay? And Grandma is in Medford, up in Oregon. She's the only other family we have. We don't know anyone really well in town. I stopped by my best friend's house, from school, but they had already packed up and left."

"You were going to just ride over the Siskiyou Mountains? In November? That's got to be two hundred miles or more from here."

Abigail canted her head to the left. "Well, do you have a better idea? I didn't want to stay home and just starve."

"To be honest, I left for the same reason. But you two shouldn't travel by yourselves. If you're really set on going to Medford, I propose I come along, if that's okay with you and your brother. Those mountains are pretty rugged and, well, I think you'll need some help."

Abigail and Kaleb looked at each other for a moment. Trying to nonverbally figure out why this grown man would offer to help them out. "I guess so," she replied, arms crossed. "If you're heading our way anyway, sure. We've just been pushing our bikes with the packs on top. You ready to go right now?"

"Well, I wouldn't mind getting a little rest first, I don't think I slept more than thirty minutes before you two came along. I've been traveling at night. It's easier to hide that way."

"Hide from who?" Abigail asked, narrow-eyed.

Matt frowned. "I'm carrying a ton of stuff that used to

belong to a dead police officer, okay? Having the police ask me where I got all this cop gear, now *that* would be a bad deal."

"We're not going to wait 'till night, and we need to get going, with or without you." Abigail said firmly.

Matt patted his knees with his palms. "I kind of figured that would be an issue. Well, obviously I can't walk around in daylight with all this stuff visible to the world. I can try to cram what I can into my knapsack, but it's not very big."

The two watched as Matt pushed in both takedown pins on the rifle, separated the two halves, and pushed the collapsible stock tight to the receiver. Placing both pieces into his now significantly lighter and roomier knapsack, he was dismayed that the top of the barrel wouldn't quite fit inside, an inch and a half of flash suppressor remaining exposed.

His untucked dress shirt did a decent job of covering up the police duty belt, but the SWAT plate carrier and magazine pouches would be a lot more difficult to hide. Trying to wear the ski jacket over it would be far too hot, even with the cool coastal breeze. So, Matt did what he felt was the next best thing, he wrapped the jacket around the bulky vest and used some of Ed Vasquez's thin blue nylon rope to secure it down to the top of the knapsack. The flimsy book bag wasn't really designed to have something that heavy on top of it, it didn't have a frame, and it would probably flop around a lot.

He hefted the ungainly load onto his back. "What do you think?"

"Terrible," Abigail chided. "I tell you what, if you're going to walk with us, maybe you can carry some of our stuff. It's pretty clear that you don't have much, and you're bigger and stronger than both of us shrimps put together. You can wear my dad's pack. It's next to my bike. We can rearrange everything so, you can carry our heavy stuff and your junk too. Deal?"

"Such a deal. But to put a real pack on my back, with an actual hip strap, that would be worth it. I just have one question for you kids. *Do you have any toilet paper?*"

CHAPTER THIRTEEN
Friday, Last Week in October

Susan Overberg had almost missed the meeting. She had awoken, lazily, saw the sun streaming through the east facing windows of her Bucktown rental condo, and had realized instantly that she had somehow slept through her alarm. Susan blamed the fact that her phone had served as her alarm clock for several years, and now, since it no longer worked for calls, texts, or Internet connectivity she had accidentally set it to silent. The only things it *did* provide were incessant alerts from the government, FEMA mostly, and nearly all of them were completely irrelevant to her.

Susan had shot out of bed, dressed quickly in warm garb, and took a quick look in the mirror—just to make sure she didn't actually look like she'd just woken up. At her recent *fiftieth* high school reunion—still hard for her to imagine it had been that long—most of her classmates had been shocked at how little she had aged over the years. Her dark brown hair did have a couple of gray streaks, and her light olive complexion had its fair share of laugh lines and crow's feet, but most people took her for a fit fifty-five than her real age of almost seventy.

Grabbing a stale muffin to munch on, Susan made her way down the four flights of stairs to the street. Even though the power was on, at least during the day, the elevator doors

Turn Red Tomorrow

had copy paper signs posted that read, "OUT OF SERVICE" on all four floors.

At least the walk to the national headquarters of SNA —Society for a New America, or simply "Snah" to the staff— was short. Susan had been temporarily contracting with the group she had once directed. Before the financial crisis hit, they had needed extra help with the election season and the pay had been tough to ignore. She had been uncomfortably tied to the ups and downs of the family fund and the pittance from Social Security since she'd semi-retired seven years ago and had moved to Washington State to be closer to her two sons and two grandchildren.

Now, the elections were on hold and she was trapped in Chicago with few friends and fewer options. She had heard through Kyle, before the big radio announcement and communication shutdown, that Matt faced similar circumstances down in California. Susan hoped that soon enough things would get back to normal and she could simply fly home.

As she opened the door to the conference room, she received a few smiles but also a few glares, which she took in stride as she was a few minutes late. Everyone appeared tired. They had all, Susan included, seen and done things over the last week that they would like to forget. At least their baggy eyes and worry lines were temporary, she thought. Other people in Chicago had problems of a more... *permanent*... variety.

On the day of the announcement, SNA had been contacted by a mid-level bureaucrat from the convoluted FEMA hierarchy to gauge their ability to assist with food distribution and other essential tasks. acute to the crisis and expected societal breakdown. For the last few days, at about noon, they had all been bussed over to the local food distribution point at Holstein Park—guarded at first by Chicago P.D. which, for the last three days, had been supplanted by the Illinois National Guard. Via idle chatter with the soldiers, Susan had been pleasantly surprised to learn they were a military police unit from Aurora, not far from where she had grown up. Yesterday, though, when they had returned for the day they learned that there would be a special meeting at nine A.M, mandatory, and would cover to address important changes in their work.

Susan noted a stranger standing at the head of the long oak conference table: a tall, professionally dressed caramel-skinned and dark-haired woman of middle age holding a dark grey tablet computer. In front of her on the table was a boxy device that looked like a small printer of some sort. In front of each of the Society staff members was a spiral-bound packet and a water glass; the glass carafes filled with ice water spaced evenly along its length had made condensation puddles. Susan smiled meekly at SNA's director, her protégé and friend Erin Young, and took the last seat.

"It looks like we're all here," the tall newcomer said in a pleasantly-accented but deep voice. "Good morning. I'm Shandra Williams, and I've been appointed as your Homeland Security liaison for the time being. Now, you all have been doing a great job here in your part of Chicago, but things are changing rapidly at the federal and even international level. To put it bluntly, the food distribution points will, starting today, be repurposed as federal processing and vaccination centers."

There was a murmur at the table as the staffers turned to one another, trying to gauge reactions. Susan looked toward Erin, but the younger woman glanced away.

"You will still give out food," Shandra continued, "but daily food handouts will only be accessible to those that complete the process Homeland Security has mandated. Everyone will also be required to get the vaccine for the latest strain of hemorrhagic fever. This is necessary to avoid a quarantine—Dallas, Houston, Charlotte, San Diego, L.A., and even right down the road in St. Louis all have quarantined zones right now."

Airborne Ebola, she thought with dread. Although there had been several reports off and on over the last few years, and especially within the last six months, Susan hadn't actually heard much about a real no-doubt outbreak that had claimed lives.

"The machine on the table," Shandra said, waving her free hand at the matte black plastic device, "is an identification card printer. You all will be setting up a dozen stations with these. We estimate that should be enough to process the number of people that have been visiting your *zock's* distribution point."

"Umm, excuse me, what's a zock?'" asked one of the younger female staffers near the head of the table. Susan wondered the same thing.

"Oh, I'm sorry," said Shandra with a tight smile. "It's an internal term we've started using, it stands for zone of control, or Z-O-C. Zock. I don't have the map for Chicago available at the moment, but we've established these zones in roughly five mile circles around each former distribution point—now processing centers—with overlapping borders. That way, all residents should be within realistic walking distance of one or more points, which, since they are at the center of each circle, we've taken to calling 'hubs.'

"As I was saying, we're creating these identification cards not only to remedy some of the problems we've seen with people attempting to 'double dip' at the hubs, but also because the federal government and international aid groups are going to start expanding into other services that will require tracking and reporting."

"Like what, Shandra?" Erin asked from across the table.

"Unfortunately the full list hasn't been made available to me, that's way above my head. But it's really rather unique, what we're doing. If you just think of the ramifications, this system will allow us to solve a number of past and current problems. The current level of control over food distribution will ensure complete fairness, and I know you experts can identify other aspects where this amount of oversight might be useful. Housing. Employment. Medical care. Educational opportunities. And more."

For the first time, there were some nods and smiles. The concept of social and economic equality appealed to almost everyone at SNA.

"Will people still be able to get food without getting a new card?" that same inquisitive young staffer asked.

"Absolutely not," Shandra replied, killing the nascent good mood in an instant. "Those who want their daily food ration to continue to be disbursed must show a valid form of photo identification and provide a valid Social Security number, or a listed alternative, to get started. Children and those without current photo I.D. can provide a birth certificate, but we are not creating cards at this time for children under the age of thirteen. Younger minors will be listed in the electronic records of their parents or guardians. Those details are all in the written packet and will also be on a file on the tablets we're providing for each station. As processing liaisons, you all will record the information on your tablet, take pictures of the identification documents, and take a current pictures of all four sides of the person's head—front, each side, and back. You will also, using a specific setting on the tablet, take retinal photos of each eye. Lastly, full fingerprinting of each hand via a touchscreen application. All of this information will be encrypted, fed into their card, and uploaded to a secure federal database.

"All subsequent visits or interactions with emergency services will require a scan of the card. Each one has an embedded RFID chip, pretty standard technology really. Announcements are going out in approximately two hours directing people to bring the necessary information when they go for food pickup."

"What about people with no I.D. at all? Like, people here illegally?" Erin asked. Others nodded.

"Ah, yes, of course, I neglected to mention that detail. For the purposes of the national I.D. system, there are no distinctions between citizens, legal visitors from other countries, or undocumented immigrants," Shandra answered, changing Erin's wording to the more politically correct term. "One of the fields is for country of citizenship, and citizens of a foreign country will go through the exact same process as everyone else."

Erin tilted her head to the side for a moment; Susan had seen this quirk before when Erin neither agreed or disagreed. "I don't know, but I think most of them will view this as some back-door deportation program. We've been working with the immigrant community for a long time, and as a whole they're not very trusting of the government."

Shandra cocked her head forward slightly and glared at Erin. "It's quite straightforward. If they want to eat, they will get a card. If not, they are on their own. You probably won't need to mention this, but so you all know, people won't have forever to wait to voluntarily get a card either. Hoarders, those people who are fat and happy right now, thinking they are independent, sooner or later will run out of food and the deadline will have passed. Since we don't expect they will just show up to register, we'll reach out to them via ... other means."

"I don't know if I'm comfortable forcing people to sign up for this," came a woman's voice. Susan's eyes went wide. She realized with shock the voice had been her own.

That earned Susan her very own searing glare from Shandra. "You're not forcing them to get the card. None of them will have guns to their head."

"But ... if it's starvation or an I.D. card and giving up all their privacy, people are understandably going to see it that way," Susan shot back.

"Susan's right," blurted a short, swarthy staffer dressed in a tan polo—George, Susan remembered—"I'm a volunteer here, all I signed up for was to gather signatures for the election, and I don't want any part of this program. This is nothing but herding up the desperate and unfortunate and making them register in your ... system ... or *starve*! This has absolutely nothing to do with helping people in need." He pushed his chair out and got up to leave. Susan wanted to crawl under the desk and hide. She didn't want to be remembered as the catalyst for this outburst.

"*Sir*," Shandra said, remaining calm, "before you leave here, there are a couple of things you need to see and know."

George paused, clearly caught off guard, and Shandra continued, pulling out a reddish-orange card that read "SAMPLE" in white letters across the front. "Can everyone see this? This is an example of the new national ID card that you'll be creating by the thousands over the next few weeks. Now, take a look at this." She pulled a cobalt blue card from her back pocket. "This is my card, made two days ago. It not just the color that's different. It's specifically for federal employees, and it's identical to the ones you all will have in about an hour."

There was a short pause. "But ... we're not a federal agency. We're a private non-profit," Erin pointed out.

Shandra nodded; perhaps in agreement, or perhaps acknowledging something else—it wasn't clear. "Actually, as of eight A.M. this morning, all organizations and their members—employees, volunteers, or otherwise—working directly with FEMA and the food distribution system have been converted to involuntary federal service status as authorized by Executive Order 13603."

The entire room erupted with noise. "That's ... that's absurd!" George bellowed. "Involuntary service? Are you saying we've all been *conscripted* by the government? Under what authority?"

Shandra raised a finger, bringing an end to the hubbub, and cleared her throat. "Under the authority of the President of the United States of America. Is that sufficient for everyone here? 'Conscripted' is not the word I would personally use, but it's essentially correct. The President and her designated agencies have the power to employ individual experts or whole organizations in times of national emergency."

"Employ!" George cried. "What you described is not employment, it's... it's slavery!"

"That's such an ugly term, sir. This isn't *slavery*," Shandra replied coolly.

George pointed his index finger at his face. "Look at me! I'm the great-great grandson of a sharecropper, descended from honest-to-God slaves. Don't think you can lecture me on what slavery is or is not. I'm out of here. You can keep your blue cards, red cards, whatever color cards, and phony 'executive orders.' This is all crazy."

Erin, sitting next to him, grabbed his forearm gently. "George, don't leave. I... I don't think we can, actually."

"She's right, George," Shandra said. "You're legally a part of the federal government now, like it or not. If you leave, I won't stop you. Just know, you'll lose *everything*. This nice blue card? Which, incidentally, opens a lot of doors, both literally and figuratively, will be gone, and by leaving you'll forfeit the chance to get one. You'll still get a standard I.D.—everyone will have to get one—but it will be recorded as 'involuntary issuance' in writing on the front and within the chip. You won't have access to anything but the most basic services, ever. You'll be in the same category as all the criminals getting their yellow cards made over the next few days. Do you really want to doom your future like this, George? I know you're angry right now, but be reasonable. This all is just the government trying to get the country through a crisis, nothing more."

Susan felt uncomfortable admitting that she felt the same kind of dread as George did, but in her mind she really had no other option. If not for SNA, she'd have no one to turn to, so whatever transpired with them, Susan felt like she was simply along for the ride.

She recalled how terrified her older brother, Richard, had been of the possibility of being drafted and sent off to Vietnam. Fortunately for him, the draft ended just as he was reaching eligibility, and the war soon after. Susan remembered the news showing people burning their draft cards and being arrested. But those draft dodgers didn't starve to death for their convictions.

George let out a heavy sigh and put his hands on his head, perhaps a subconscious surrender. "I . . . I don't know what to do. Until something changes, I'm here for my friends. Just know I don't agree with this. At all."

"Noted," Erin said. "This will all be over soon enough, and everything will be back to normal. Just hang in there."

True to Shandra's word, all fifteen staff members had their matte plastic blue cards in hand within an hour. While in line, their phones had all beeped and buzzed at the same moment, all with the same text message that included the basic details about the I.D. program, intended for anyone who wanted to get food from now on. Once finished, they were bussed out to the park as usual with Shandra in tow as their official supervisor. Waiting for them there were the dozen stations she'd mentioned. Their National Guard detail looked different but Susan couldn't quite place why.

"Weird. Same soldiers, different uniforms," Erin pointed out as they walked up to the makeshift kiosks, her breath condensing in the cold fall air. "I wonder why? They look more like police now."

Susan now realized their uniforms *were* different. The Army camouflage pattern, the new one that was mostly olive green, was gone, replaced with solid colors. With dull gray shirts and bottoms, and black or dark grey vests on, it certainly wasn't supposed to be camouflage anymore.

The crowd on the other side, the early birds in between them and the National Guardsmen, was much larger than it had been in the last few days. Susan saw a large white cardstock sign that read in red permanent marker:

Hell NO to ID!

"Uh oh," Susan muttered. Erin, seeing the same sign, and a few others like it, echoed her.

"Yeah, more people who think like George," Erin said, voice jaded. "You heard Shandra. If they want free food, they need to play along. That's the deal."

Susan stopped and stared at the younger woman. "Erin, I've known you for over fifteen years. Do you *really* think this card deal is going to be a good thing? Or is ever going to go away?"

"Well, no, of course not," Erin answered. "But look, I've just had more time to accept this. Shandra and I spoke yesterday and went over all these details on my cell. The whole federalization thing was a surprise, but I knew about the rest."

What? "You have a phone that actually *works*?"

"They all *work*, Susan. People like Shandra—FEMA people, Homeland Security—they can call, email, text anyone they want. It's just the little people like you and me and everyone outside the fence right now that can't. Our service is shut off because it's not critical to the emergency efforts.

"Believe me, I didn't sleep much last night, and it wasn't the sirens, gunshots, and my neighbors screaming that kept me awake. Honestly, Susan, I think we're all being used as a means to an end. I don't want to know what that 'end' is, really, but we're trapped by the flow of events. You're right, I joined SNA so I could help people and make a difference, all those noble goals. But now? I just want to get through this in one piece. No matter what it takes. Sounds selfish, sure, but what can you or I do about it? You're not going to mention this to anyone, right?"

Susan laughed, though she felt nervous . . . ill even. "Of course not. You're right. What are you going to do? Say no to the *government*? It's like saying, 'I don't agree with income taxes so I'm not going to pay them, or . . . I think I have the right to blow off dynamite in my backyard.' You act on it, and people with guns come to make sure you get back in line."

Susan looked up and saw a dozen people shuffling their way, holding bags and backpacks. "Oh look, they are starting to let them in. We better get ready."

"Don't do it, people!" a man's voice blurted through a megaphone. "They have suckered you in to registering yourself and your family into a world government system! They shut everything down just so they could put it back together, but with them on top and with all of you," he shouted, "under their heel!"

"Pfft. What a wacko," remarked the tall fortyish lady, the first person in Susan's line. She had on a blue, red, and white Chicago Cubs knit hat and a long ash gray peacoat. "I mean, the government was already in charge! Like anything is different. Let's get on with this. I'm ready to get my card and my food."

Susan had watched Shandra do it earlier, but still bumbled a bit through the process at first using the unfamiliar tablet. After about three minutes though, a card popped out with the woman's face forward picture in the lower left corner. The software was pretty slick, Susan had to admit. It had automatically cropped out the background of the park and surrounding buildings and replaced it with a blank white area.

"Don't believe the announcements!" the same man with the bullhorn bellowed. "We ARE under martial law. It's in place and turned on full blast. They shut down and controlled food distribution, communications, travel, and destroyed our currency. Next, they will take your gold, your silver, your guns, and if you're useful and do what you're told, they'll keep you alive. If not, you—"

There was a tremendous explosion in the direction of the gate, the concussion of the blast slapping Susan hard but not quite knocking her over. Immediately, people began screaming and running in all directions; almost as quickly Susan smelled the acrid stench of explosives and burnt clothing.

"Get the food! Get it!" a man yelled from near the gate. Susan recovered and watched as at least thirty or forty people rushed past the stunned Guardsmen. Some of them had blood splattered on their clothes.

A shot rang out to her right, then another, and one of the running men stumbled and fell to the grass.

Oh my God. This is like Kent State. Like Chicago when I was a kid... the riots.

"Stop!" one of the gray-garbed soldiers to her left yelled to no effect. More shots rang out, Susan wasn't sure if it was the soldiers or someone else. The shots made an odd sound as they echoed off the buildings, each a hard *SLAP* much like dropping lumber on concrete.

At that moment, Susan wondered if the soldiers were there to protect the staff, or the stuff—the food that was piled up on crates behind them. She didn't intend to find out.

Susan turned to run, but someone crashed into her back, sending her sprawling to the ground.

BOOOM! A second explosion, larger than the first, or just a lot closer. Susan's ears were ringing intensely as someone, or something, struck her head, and everything went black.

CHAPTER FOURTEEN
Friday, Last Week in October

"Where in the hell do you think you're going?" Chief Warrant Officer Marshall Cross yelled through his mask as the corporal he'd just gassed squeaked and ran off into the tree line.

He couldn't run after the knucklehead as the hot canister of CS—o-Chlorobenzylidene Malononitrile—which Cross had taped to a stick would run out quickly, and he still had several Marines that had to qualify this morning. There were very few instances where Marines subjected themselves to their own ordnance: pepper spray for the MP types and CS gas were the only two he could think of. Cross preferred the field qualification to the more well-known "gas chamber" since the former counted as an actual CBRN environment, checking off training in that environment as well. After he finished stuffing the stream of tiny irritant particles into each Marine's masked face in turn, he unmasked to see the young corporal walking back, mask in hand.

"What happened to you? Emergency head call?" Cross asked.

"No, sir! I took a deep breath when you gassed me and it shot straight into my lungs! I looked at the mask, the filter wasn't on right."

"Let me see that mask, Marine," he ordered, holding

his hand out. The young corporal handed over his mask and immediately Cross saw the issue. Earlier, he had specifically pointed out how to properly remove and reattach the filters, and the one on the left had not been seated correctly. One had to push down pretty hard and turn the filter with some authority, and this Marine had failed to do so. Cross rolled his eyes. *That's what training is for, after all.* "Here you go. Remember, next time, seat the filter and *test* it! Clear the mask and check the seal. Understood?"

The Marine nodded and returned to the circle. The recent crash had made it very difficult to get anyone to take what Cross did very seriously. He remembered the discomfort of MOPP Level 2, which consisted of an extremely hot, bulky, and uncomfortable suit plus black vinyl overboots, when he'd entered Iraq with 3/5 as a baby-faced lance corporal back in 2003. Then, there had been an actual risk of chemical attack—Saddam Hussein had had a well-established history of gassing his own people, and whether or not he actually had any, people had been scared into taking it as a genuine threat. That invasion, along with the earlier Gulf War fought when Cross was in grade school, were pretty much the only times in the last fifty years that anyone had cared one bit about CBRN—Chemical, Biological, Radiological, Nuclear—Defense, pronounced "See-Burn." As a warrant officer fresh from school in the States, he'd been assigned to another infantry unit in Afghanistan and had quickly wished he was a rifleman again. At least then he'd have a real job to do. No one had feared a Taliban chemical attack, ever, and nearly everyone had viewed their CBRN gear as a completely useless hindrance.

Now, all of Camp Lejeune was on edge with the financial crisis. Payday would be Monday, and even without an official announcement everyone feared that would be put on indefinite hold. All Marines had been ordered to remain on base, but it was well known that many had left—deserted—to take care of their families or to simply head to Mom and

Dad back home. It wasn't honorable, and it definitely wasn't authorized, but that's where some had their priorities.

Some smaller overseas units had already returned home early while others were reported to be on boats home. Something was clearly brewing if deployments were being canceled, nothing of the sort had happened the year before with the three day bank holiday. This was different though, almost two weeks now without an end in sight. Cross wasn't high enough on the totem pole to know all the details; a CWO-3 could usually pull some strings, but not with generals. He couldn't hit that altitude.

"Okay gents. This concludes your yearly qualification. Head back to your units, you're released. Be safe." He watched them pile into three Humvees, the soft topped cargo variety, painted in inappropriate-for-North Carolina desert tan.

"You ready, sir?" It was Corporal Dunn, his CBRN Defense Specialist, obviously anxious to get back and figure out what was going to roll downhill next. Cross opened the passenger door to their Humvee and the pair returned to mainside.

Cross had brought his field gear into his office when his phone, his hardline on his desk, rang. "Sixth Marine Regiment CBRN, Chief Warrant Officer Cross here."

It was the regimental adjutant, Captain Hartford. "There's a meeting in half an hour at the field house. All officers and staff NCOs."

"Sir, do I need anything? What's it about?" Cross asked.

"No to the first question, and I have no idea to the second. With the way things are going off-base, could be anything."

Thanks for filling in the blanks, brother! He shrugged his shoulders, washed his face off with cold water from the sink, and walked over.

\- - - - -

"Anyone have *any* doggone idea what the hell this is all about?" the large, thick-necked master sergeant to Cross's left asked no one in particular. They had been sitting in the second row of the field house's bleachers for almost forty-five minutes. Cross noticed with some surprise that the regimental commander and the rest of his staff sat along the front row to his right. Normally the colonel would be the one to take charge and provide some direction on what was happening and not be just another uniform in the crowd.

He also noticed several stations, eight in all, set up along the opposite side of the basketball court. There were placards by each, the one to the far left read "A-C," the second "D-F," and so on down the line. Behind each placard was a black boxy device and a dark gray tablet computer, and behind the row of tables and chairs were large cardboard boxes stacked up. Cross did quick math on the boxes, and the number of bodies in the room, and it appeared there would be just about a box per Marine present.

The opposite doors opened, and a very large, very tall man strode in, soon followed by about two dozen men and women, all in uniforms of a bland gray color that made them look like park rangers or rent-a-cops.

Cross could now get a better look at the first man, who sported a bullet-shaped head topped crew cut every bit as severe as a Marine Corps "high and tight" along with a thick brown walrus mustache. Cross imagined that if one did an image search for 'huge mean looking cop' this guy would be the first result.

"Hello everyone," he barked, "I'm Martin Fentwhistle, assistant regional director of the Department of Homeland Security." *Burly man, nerdy name.* "I won't waste time with niceties. Effective immediately, your unit has been disbanded by executive order. All personnel are to be placed under control and command of the Department of Homeland Security and the newly instituted Office of Peace Enforcement."

The crowd of Marines exploded with loud voices and commotion at the announcement. Obscenities flowed freely.

The regimental commander stood and instantly there was silence. No one dared talk over the colonel. "Listen up, Marines. I received my own brief at division HQ this morning. This is straight from the White House. Now, do your duty as Marines and follow Mr. Fentwhistle's orders. By order of the President, he's in charge now. That is all."

"Thank you, Colonel. When I give the order, line up behind the station corresponding to the first letter of your last name. You will give your current military identification card to the attendant who will issue your new one. You will also be given a new set of uniforms and equipment. You may examine them but please do not don them until directed. And, in case it isn't perfectly clear, no one will leave this building—for any reason—until ordered to do so. Line up now."

Direct and without niceties—the man certainly knows his audience. Cross headed for the far left station and was first in line. He handed over his light green military ID to the young lady in front of him. "Stay still, please," she asked, and took his photo with the tablet, then two more, slowly. She had him face right, then left, then around in turn.

"Place your right hand on the screen," she asked, and then motioned for the left. There was a whirring noise, and the small black box on the table spit out a light grey card. Other than the color, it was not much different than his military ID.

"Ma'am," Cross began, "you got my rank wrong. I'm a chief warrant officer, not a second lieutenant. See these two little red boxes?" he said, pointing to the insignia on his collar.

"Oh, there aren't any warrant officers in Peace Enforcement," she replied matter-of-factly. "All warrant grades one through three are being reassigned as second lieutenants, fours as first lieutenants and fives as captains."

The words hit Marshall Cross like a blow to the chest. On paper, he'd just been promoted—according to the official chart he'd just jumped a couple of rungs on the ladder—but in reality he'd just taken a huge step backward. Most second lieutenants were in their early to mid-twenties and still learning the proverbial ropes, while chief warrant officers were usually in their thirties or forties, experts in their respective fields, and generally considered more valuable in the grand scheme than a second lieutenant despite the difference in command authority. Lieutenants had more *potential*—they could eventually become the colonels and generals that led the Corps—but when breadth and depth of experience were needed, *right now*, Marines turned to those like Cross. It would also be a significant pay cut as well—if this "Peace Enforcement" followed the same pay scale.

Still stunned, he was handed one of the large cardboard boxes, on the side was a sticker that read "M. Cross" with a UPC code below it. Cross walked away from the row of tables, put the box down, and pulled the packing tape off the top with a quick jerk. On top was a gray long sleeve shirt, a thinner material than his current uniform and identical to those worn by the DHS staff. It was his size, had his last name above the right pocket, and in the middle of the chest was a small ironed-on patch of a brown bar.

"Jeez, they just had to copy the Army, didn't they," he criticized with a whisper, still stunned.

Below the three shirts were three pairs of trousers, same gray color, and below that was a black nylon tactical vest with permanently sewn-on pouches and loops—in direct contrast to the highly customizable MOLLE system that had been in use throughout most of his career. While there were sleeves for plates, they were empty. It felt cheap.

He had a moment of clarity and realized something

that made his blood run cold. He looked at the uniforms, gear, and then glanced up at the stations still working on the queued Marines.

There is no way in hell they put this all together in the last two weeks. Whatever this is, whatever we're supposed to be, it's been in the works for a long, long time.

CHAPTER FIFTEEN
Friday, Last Week in October

Desirée stood on the deck of their second story condo, gripping the white metal railing and watching the gentle waves. She missed the trundle of boats and ferries back and forth through the Puget Sound, the sun glinting off their windows and chrome. Even so, there were occasional reminders of normal life. Nearby, a loud motorcycle came to life and she listened as its engine noise trailed away to nothing.

It certainly doesn't feel like a massive crisis. So far, the last two weeks had simply felt like a vacation from work for her. Des never had been much for television or mindlessly surfing the Internet, so their loss didn't cause her any great grief. They still worked, of course, but the only content came from the government, the DHS and FEMA updates and news. It was like an endless stream of C-SPAN, seventeen hours a day. Seventeen hours of lights, hot water, and useless updates every day. Not ideal, but not a *disaster*. She had been just a baby for Hurricane Andrew but she'd heard the stories from her parents. Just before she'd gone into the eighth grade, Hurricane Charley had hit South Florida and while not close to her home, it had felt like a real disaster.

This is a piece of cake.

Desirée went back inside, slid the door shut and locked it. Here on the second story it seemed like a useless measure, but Matt had drilled it into her until it had become second nature. There in the middle of their white carpeted living room ringed with black leather furniture were fourteen heavy boxes stacked in three unequal columns: the preparedness kit that Kyle had given them for their first Christmas as a married couple. At the time, she had thought it a very strange choice even from a man who ran a company selling such things. In her family, each person made a wish list and received something from it; simple, predictable. Desirée would have never put steel cans full of dried potatoes or powdered nonfat milk on her Christmas list.

Later in the day on that Christmas three years ago, she had cornered her brother-in-law about the gift. "Why did you give us all . . . this?" she had asked. "We live in a condo. We don't have much space. There are four grocery stores within a ten minute bicycle ride of us. I know it's your living and all, but I don't know what in world we're going to do with all of these big boxes."

Kyle had just smiled. He had always been a tough one to figure out; always thinking, tough to catch flat-footed. A bit like the young, arrogant hot-shot attorneys she had to deal with every day. Desirée wondered if he was into disasters only because nothing short of that ever got his blood moving. "Just put them in a closet, or under the bed. Keep them dry though. A couple of the boxes are full of gear, I thought you and Matt might want to bring some things like the filtration straws and emergency signal mirrors along on hikes and your bike trips."

Even by that time, Desirée had been doing less and less of those excursions into the wilderness. She'd joined the Mountaineers on a coworker's recommendation; she'd described it as a good group to meet cute athletic guys, but Des lacked a lifelong love of the outdoors and the peculiar masochism of being wet, cold, and far from civilization. She'd broken her credit card at a high-end outdoor equipment retailer and signed up for just about every activity she could fit into her schedule. About three months later, she'd met Matt on a day hike up to Panorama Point, on the south slope of Mount Rainier, and they had hit it off more or less immediately.

She frowned, thinking of Matt, not sure what things were like down in California. Ever since the communications cutoff she'd been completely in the dark, and even before there wasn't much to gather beyond the big picture. The government news alerts had not helped sate her thirst for news on what might be happening to him; they were strictly local.

"But we have food. And we have lots of outdoor gear already. More than we need, really. So, again, why?"

"Anything could happen. Earthquake. Tsunami. Heck, a trucking strike that keeps food out of the stores. It doesn't take much."

Desirée had felt he was holding back. "And what else? Meteor strikes? Nuclear war? *Alien invasion?*"

"Well, not really banking on the last one, but the other two, why not? You don't prepare for just one crisis happening any more than you'd buy life insurance just for a heart attack. You cover all your bases. You'll always need to eat, right?" The kit has plenty of food to keep you alive, at least for a while. Call it six months for you and Matt together."

"Nuclear war? That's over. That's Cold War stuff. My parents told me about the drills, hiding under your desk as if it would stop a nuke from burning you to a crisp in an instant."

"As long as they're still around, nuclear weapons that is, it's possible," Kyle had replied. "Even more possible now, sad to say. The Soviets didn't risk it since we would have replied in kind. But what about a terrorist with no ties to a government? How would we respond to that? Blow up his homeland and kill millions of otherwise innocent people just because one clown got his hands on a loose nuclear device? Doesn't quite match up. And, just so you know, if you're not right in the blast radius, the actual nuclear strike probably won't kill you. What might get you is radiation poisoning, or the breakdown of society that will prevent those four grocery stores you mentioned from restocking their shelves. In one of the gear boxes are radiation detecting strips, some potassium iodide tablets—they keep your thyroid from collecting up radioactive iodine."

It still creeped her out, how Kyle had been able to chat so casually about that sort of thing. *Oh, gee, you'll have another six months while everyone around you dies, then you'll join them. Enjoy!* But they had taken the boxes home, stored them in a corner at the bottom of the walk-in closet, and over the years they had become just another thing to bump into. She had pulled them out a few days into the crisis, her refrigerator and cupboards starting to get bare, and wouldn't you know it—the next day, FEMA had set up a food distribution area over at the nearby elementary school, even closer than the grocery stores she had bragged about to Kyle. She hadn't enjoyed standing in line, waiting for a plastic sack full of odds and ends and some kind of plastic encased meal, but it got her out on her touring bike and relieved a bit of her cabin fever.

It had kept her from being forced to head to Matt's family cabin, a good thing in her mind. First, Matt wouldn't be there. With no gas, no overnight travel, and no flights, Desirée couldn't piece together a scenario in which her husband would be there waiting for her. Kyle and his family might already be there, but she'd feel like a guest, a third wheel. At least here, it was her house, and she took orders from no one.

She clicked on the television as she did every morning, hoping for some thin sliver of news that might point to an end to the crisis.

—quired to bring identification to your local food distribution point today. There a new national identification card will

be issued to all current residents over the age of twelve. The list of approved documents will be on your screen for thirty seconds. You may also access a list by going online to w-w-w dot FEMA dot gov. No food will be distributed to those who do not obtain a new identification card. Future emergency benefits will only be available to cardholders, and the opportunity to obtain a national identification card will expire at a later date. Thank you for your cooperation.

The message began to repeat in Spanish, her second language, then it went on to what sounded like Chinese, or maybe Korean, she wasn't really sure.

The documents were simple enough. Des imagined this wouldn't be any different than going and requesting a birth certificate or starting a new job.

That afternoon, she biked down to the school where there was a much larger crowd than usual. *Must be that, 'expire at a later date' lingo that's got everyone out of their house.*

When her turn in line came up, it was pretty simple, really. A friendly woman guided her through the steps and her card spit out of a machine in about ten seconds. Her card, like all the others given to the people in front of her, was a reddish-orange color, the same size as her driver's license, but a bit thicker and heavier. On the back was the expected magnetic stripe across the top and right below that was a white box full of tiny squares, much like a QR code but larger. The front contained her frontal shot, today's date, name, birthday, and physical characteristics pulled from her license.

The vaccination didn't take long, but the thick needle inserted in her left shoulder seemed unusual, different from vaccines she'd had in the past.

Next, she picked up her bag of food and was on her way home.

Something crashed, loud, and Desirée shot awake into pitch darkness.

"Hello?" she yelped.

A slam against a wall, near the front door. It seemed like it came from their neighbors in #202, home to a leggy blonde woman named Julie, pretty in a country truck stop waitress sort of way, maybe a couple of years older than her, and her boyfriend Tommy, a large, heavily tattooed and pierced man who was pushing forty. They had been polite enough when Des had run into them, but always kept to themselves.

"Where's Tommy?" a deep male voice yelled, clearly agitated even though his voice was muffled through the wall.

"I-I don't know, Bennie! He left this morning on his bike and didn't come back," came a trembling response.

Julie.

"Yeah, he helped himself to about fifty grand in product and took off! He didn't come back here?"

"No! I swear. He hasn't been back. Just leave! Please!"

"You sure he isn't here?" Bennie asked, suddenly without anger in his voice. Something different.

"No. I already told you. Now please just go!"

"Oh no," replied the man evenly. "Finally my chance to do something I've wanted to do for a long, *long* time."

There was another crash and Desirée heard the screams. She froze, listening—though she didn't want to—but her body simply wouldn't move.

Perhaps a minute had gone by—it was hard to tell—and her fear suddenly shifted to anger. To rage. Des wiped her eyes on her bedsheet, leapt to her feet, and ran to the kitchen.

The knife block sat on the small island in their kitchen, barely illuminated by the moonlight coming through the window above the sink. Matt had a couple military type knives stashed somewhere in the condo, but there was no time to search. Selecting the largest, thickest knife, she held it in her right hand with an ice pick grip, point down, and opened her front door.

Across the walkway, the door was halfway open and the cries that came forth were muted, smothered. Des peeked inside, shaking, and saw what she expected. The man —Bennie—was muttering something with each thrust. He still had on his motorcycle jacket; the red and gold patch across the back impossible to read in the dim light. One hand was against Julie's neck and the other held a pillow to her face. Stepping forward, Des raised the knife with both hands and brought it down swift and hard.

Bennie yelled volcanically as he shot to his feet, breaking her grip on the blade and launching Des back onto her haunches. She stood only to take a very large fist to her left eye which sent her sprawling into the door and onto the concrete walkway where she landed on her left elbow, hard. Her vision wavered and she blinked, finding her left eye wouldn't cooperate.

"You little bitch! *I'm gonna kill you!*" he screamed, shuffling forward. He favored his right leg.

Des slowly pulled herself to her feet, unsteady and dizzy. She felt her left wrist grabbed tight as sharp pain shot up her triceps and into her shoulder, causing her to yelp in agony.

Bennie stumbled and they fell in a heap on the concrete, Des landing flat on her back and smacking her head. Her vision swam again and she felt his hot, sour breath on her face.

"Now it's your turn!" he yelled, grabbing at her underwear with his right hand. He jerked it down, hard, tearing the fabric in two. She felt his bare flesh against hers for a moment.

She reacted by sinking her teeth into his left trapeze muscle.

It was Bennie's turn to howl in pain. He arched up, and as she released her bite Des brought her legs up to her chest and planted her bare feet on the big man's chest. Years of bicycling and aerobics gave her the explosive power in her glutes and thighs she needed to fling Bennie back and on to his back. She heard another yell, no doubt the knife plunging deeper in her assailant's back.

Des rolled to her feet and retreated back into her condo, grabbing another knife from the block, and turned to see Bennie lurch into her doorway, breathing heavily.

She held the smaller knife point forward. "Get out of my house, you son of a bitch! Now!"

There was a loud explosion and Bennie fell forward, flat on his face. A couple seconds passed and another figure blocked the weak light in her doorway.

Julie.

"Are . . . are you okay?" Julie mumbled, then coughed, as she stepped over Bennie's lifeless body and, pausing for a moment, spat on his back.

"Yeah," Des lied. A massive headache was beginning to settle in. "You?"

"I'll live." She walked closer and Des saw the weapon in her hands. It resembled a gun Matt and Kyle failed to get her to try a couple years back. Yes . . . a *shotgun*. She remembered thinking there was no way she was shooting anything that big. Des set the knife down, walked to the end of the counter, and picked up the LED flashlight she'd been keeping there since the power outages began.

"I . . . I need to be sure," Des said as she pressed the button on the base, lighting up the room. Bennie's eyes hung halfway open but did not react. The knife was still there in his back, a small rivulet of dark blood running down the black leather, but it was by far the smaller wound. Above it and right between the shoulders was a ragged hole as big as her fist; the blood flow had been significant but had ceased. Bennie was dead.

"I'll be right back," Julie stated. Des shone the light at her and could make out the red marks on her neck. Her lip was bloodied and she, well, looked like hell. Understandably so.

"You don't look so good yourself, honey," Julie quipped, perhaps reading the expression on Des's face. As Julie turned to leave, Des shone the light at herself and walked over to the mirror on the closet door. Her left eye was already deep red and would surely be purple in a few hours. Bringing her elbow up was difficult and she saw that it was scraped and bruised as well. Her sense of modesty kicked in and she donned a pair of yoga pants lying on the living room sofa.

Des heard footsteps behind her and turned. It was Julie, now similarly clothed from the waist down, with a lit cigarette between her lips and gun over one shoulder.

"What . . . what are you going to do now?" Des asked, voice wavering. It was odd; Julie seemed to be recovering from all this much better than she was.

Julie shrugged. "I don't know where to go, really. And how I'm going to get there. But I can't stay here. Someone will come looking for Bennie. Or Tommy. Doesn't matter which, same thing will happen. But before I go anywhere I *will* help you drag this piece of s**t out your doorway."

Des nodded. She felt the same way about leaving. If Julie wasn't around, maybe they'd come after her. Maybe someone here in the complex would tell these scumbags she helped kill Bennie.

It was then it really sunk in. She'd helped *kill a man*. Justified? Sure. But thinking about it sent chills up her spine.

"Hey," Julie said, breaking Des out of her mental track. "You gonna help me or what?"

They got to work, pulling the corpse on to the walkway and down the stairs, but it was slow going with Julie holding her gun in her right hand and Des with a useless left arm. Twilight broke as they got him to the stairs. There were three young men at ground level staring up at them, wide eyed. One had a pistol in his hand.

"Are you just going to stand there?" Julie snapped. The three nodded and pitched in, swearing in Spanish as they made their way over to the nearby dumpster that, after a heave-ho, became Bennie's final resting place.

Walking back, they spied a large black motorcycle parked along the side of the building.

"I think I know how you're getting out of here," Des said.

"Yeah," Julie replied, flicking her cigarette butt into the bushes.

CHAPTER SIXTEEN
Saturday, Last Week in October

"Honey, shouldn't the electricity have come back on by now? We need to make breakfast," Amber said to Kyle, who was getting ready to go out and split some dry fir rounds.

Kyle nodded and looked at his wristwatch, the one he'd had to dig out of a box since he'd previously only used it while hiking off the grid. It read *6:13*. "Yes, the curfew should be up. Maybe there's a problem with the service line coming from the highway. I'll go check it out."

He wasn't a lineman and wasn't about to go climbing poles and checking voltages, but in the case of something catastrophic it usually didn't take a trained eye to figure out what had gone wrong. A downed line or blown transformer would be easy enough to visually diagnose. Kyle hopped into the Durango and slowly crawled down the road, looking up at the power line. Even in the weak light thirty minutes before sunrise, he could see it was totally intact running all the way down to Highway 101.

Returning, he noticed a few of his neighbors out in their yards with confused looks on their faces. Obviously they'd picked up on the power issue as well.

And here I thought I would get bored to death.

Kyle looked out onto the lake and saw a couple of familiar boats with lines in the water already. It was probably more out of boredom than hunger; Sunshine Lake wasn't a great fishing spot. It was stocked but the trout tended to be on the small side, making it more of a recreational 'catch-and-release' lake. Even so, a day on the lake sounded fun and he was a little jealous. He had stuck close to the cabin, maybe being a little overprotective, but there was no guessing at who would come down the road at any time. The incident along the interstate with the truck and the state trooper still had him rattled a bit. What would happen if a group of vehicles full of men with bad intentions just rolled up to the lake? Kyle admitted that he alone wouldn't affect the outcome much, but he would rather be here to face it, out in front of his family, than out on the lake or somewhere chasing game.

    It was putting a serious damper on his fishing and hunting plan, the main way Kyle had planned to stretch out their food reserves during this crisis. While the cabin was best suited for short-term family vacations, Kyle had always justified it as a legitimate long-term survival retreat due to the large variety of game, fish, and fowl in the immediate area, along with a decent growing season for fruits and vegetables. He'd listened for years to so-called "survival experts" that had recommended some extremely remote and harsh places, especially throughout the Rocky Mountains and the short grass prairie regions—the High Plains— directly to their east. They met some important criteria, but there were good reasons why these areas were passed through by so many early settlers back in the pioneer days. Long, brutally cold winters, short growing seasons, difficulties in irrigation, and a relatively low density of wild game. Contrary to popular belief, the Rocky Mountains, especially the drier eastern half, were not teeming with large game animals. The deer and elk in those areas, while large, were exceedingly difficult to find and reach—fine if you're running a hunting guide business for adventure-seeking types, bad if you're trying to for consistently putting meat on the table. Those who wanted steady meat in that part of the country ran ranches.

Things wouldn't be too bad in that part of the country if you already had one of those real, genuine ranches—not the fake 'all hat and no cattle' kind favored by yuppies and celebrities—with plenty of meat on the hoof, clean running water, a stocked root cellar, and a solid house with plenty of firewood stacked up. It was the height of absurdity to believe that Joe Sixpack, his wife, and 2.5 kids could leave the city, plop down a trailer in a one of those remote parts of the country, and just start living off the land. People that pushed pencils all day for a living, made regular visits to a fast food drive-thru, and depended on all the conveniences that a modern consumerist culture could provide would be dead within a month during an average Eastern Montana or Wyoming winter. At least in Western Washington the climate was far milder and the wild food was a lot more accessible.

At Sunshine Lake, there were a few trout in the lake, sure, but three miles away was Hood Canal, one of the most biodiverse temperate water bodies in the world. There were gray sandy beaches loaded with shellfish; on most clamming trips Kyle could pull out one or two legal ones with every shovelful. Oysters were a bit harder to get but were also plentiful. The waters themselves were chock full of Dungeness and Red Rock crab—Kyle had circular nets that required a boat along with the more common boxy crab pots to catch them—plus cutthroat trout, shrimp, and several varieties of both salmon and bottom fish if you had a boat. Kyle didn't, and if this really was The Big One, he knew establishing a deal with someone or just buying a boat outright down off the Canal would be a high priority. He figured there would be plenty of guys willing to trade him a boat for one of his spare rifles or maybe even some gold. Protecting it from three miles away was another matter.

Michael Zargona

Several weeks ago, during the actual state hunting season, Kyle hadn't been able to find a legal buck out in the Olympic National Forest land north of the lake, but given the current situation he was pretty eager to get back out there, legal season or no. There were also sizeable herds of Roosevelt elk out there and it was just the right time of year to go find them. Additionally, the nearby Olympic National Park had been off-limits to hunting for over a century and was teeming with game—animals that were likely unafraid of humans. Kyle was all for wildlife refuges but saw nothing wrong with an occasional foray into areas of known deer and elk activity. He wasn't into wanton lawbreaking, but this was about survival.

All that available and relatively easy-to-attain protein was what made the lake cabin such a viable retreat. Supplemented by their own long term storage food, and future berry gathering and gardening, especially with high-density shade-tolerant plants like kale, chard, beans, and potatoes, Kyle believed they would be able to hold out for a long time. Several years if necessary.

There was still one major weakness with the cabin and lake area in general: security. It wasn't particularly far from civilization and there was absolutely nothing stopping a decent sized group from waltzing in with guns and taking over the place. While there was only the one paved road in from the east, there were a couple logging roads that met up with the western end of the cabin driveway, and nothing besides the lake itself to impede those on foot.

A major concern of Kyle's was that most of the residents here had brought very little food with them, certainly not enough to last through the month not to mention the entire winter. Things would begin to get just a little awkward at Sunshine Lake when the Flanigan clan was well-fed while their neighbors starved to death on Thanksgiving.

"Hey," he called to one of his neighbors as he drove past. It was the older gentleman in cabin eight again, garbed in a flannel robe and a straw hat to suit the foggy fall morning. "I'm Kyle Flanigan, I'm in eleven. Would you and your family come to a meeting, say in two hours at the park? We need to figure a few things out around here. I just checked the service line and nothing appears to be broken, so we might be shut off from way down the line. It might be a while until power is restored."

Or, never.

The man peered back at him. "Two hours you say? All right then, young man. My wife and I will be there. You need us to spread the word?"

"Sure. I'll do the same."

- - - - -

"Seventy-four, including us and the kids," Amber stated as she finished the headcount. Unlike many newer recreational developments, Sunshine Lake didn't have a resort, conference center, or large meeting hall; the covered picnic area would have to suffice. Most of the people were bundled against the damp morning chill.

"Wow," Kyle replied to his wife as he stepped up onto one of the green picnic tables. "Already stacked up pretty deep for twenty cabins. And I don't think number ten has anyone in it yet." He looked out at the crowd. Considering he'd come up here at least once during every year of his life, except for the four he'd served in the Marines, Kyle knew very few of the faces staring back at him.

With a frown, Kyle recognized four people he had secretly hoped weren't present. It seemed like every neighborhood had that one family that just caused trouble and believed they operated under a different set of rules, and at Sunshine Lake that was the Kleins. The patriarch, Bill, was a heavyset man of about fifty-five, bald with a white goatee and mustache, and had a perpetual ruddy, flushed complexion with lots of thread veins around his nose and cheeks. His son, Mike, was here as well, a chip off the old block but with a full head of brown hair. Their wives looked like clones twenty-five years apart in age, both with long blonde hair and too-tan skin that was starting to fade due to a lack of regular visits to the salon.

The Kleins were one of only a couple of families on the lake that would bring a genuine speedboat suitable for water skiing. Their blue and white craft was also quite suitable for interrupting swimming, relaxing, fishing, or any other normal lake activity. Kyle and Amber were far from the only people to have held shouting matches with the Kleins over the years, usually regarding their boating behaviors or their habit of getting dead drunk out on the water and shouting words they'd worked hard to shield Bella and Cole from.

The Kleins doubling up seemed to be the norm, not the exception. The typical cabin owner up here was about the same general age as Kyle's parents—Baby Boomers and Silent Generation folks, mostly middle class people who had been careful with their money. But just like the Overberg/Flanigan clan, the kids and grandkids considered the lake their getaway retreat as well.

Kyle could tell at a glance that many of the cabins were three generations deep at the moment.

A couple of the older ladies had brought their little toy dogs to the meeting. He wondered, perfectly serious, who would eat little Muffy or Poopsie first: a coyote or a human. He'd seen a couple of larger dogs wandering around. They wouldn't last long here on their own.

"Thanks for coming out everyone. I'm Kyle Flanigan," he began, and proceeded to tell them about his early morning check of the power situation. "So, since the power probably isn't coming on for a while, I don't see how we'll all be able to get by with just clinging to our own cabins and doing our own thing. We're going to need fires to cook, and if the pumps aren't running we won't have clean water or our own bathrooms either. I'm pretty sure we're going to need to work together from here on out."

"Who appointed you the boss?" a man blurted. Kyle suspected it was one of the Kleins but couldn't be sure.

"Some of you know me. I've been coming up here since I was a kid. I run a preparedness supply company out of Enunclaw called Bene Praepara. I've been in the disaster prep business for a few years and have been planning for and consulting on just this sort of scenario. Just to be clear, I'm not 'appointing' myself to anything. I *do* have some ideas we all might consider to make things easier around here.

"I'm going to lay it all on the table. I really, honestly, and truly believe this is probably the proverbial 'Big One,' the event to crash this country down and usher in a new government, probably a global government." There were a few snickers from the crowd. "Laugh if you like," Kyle continued, "but it's my conviction and it's going to flavor my thoughts and opinions. Some of you probably believe this will clear up by Thanksgiving and we can all return home, get a nice fat turkey with all the trimmings, and this can just be a neat story we can tell our kids and grandkids." That brought a few chuckles. "I pray to God that's *exactly* what happens. But the winds I see don't match that sort of weather. I seriously doubt the government would make announcements and go to the trouble to set up a food distribution network if this were only a short term problem. Yesterday, as some of you heard, the government issued the edict about a brand new national ID card, something that's been on their wish list for years. They've obviously used this crisis as their opportunity to green-light it. Now, the power is out for no good perceptible reason. Someone down the line turned it off, and my semi-educated guess says that the powers that be want everyone to gather in tighter to the cities, near the food distribution points, get their IDs, and wait patiently for whatever comes next, all the while totally dependent on government services.

"I'm not asking you to believe me. If it ends tomorrow, I'll be thrilled. But I don't think it's smart to assume that. I'm asking everyone here to bear with me, hear me out, and maybe we can figure out a way to make it through this, together."

Kyle surveyed the crowd. So far, they looked a lot more bored than inspired. A couple kids were playing with a small foam football off to the right.

"There are two approaches I see us taking, and I'll do my best to explain each of them. The first I'd simply call *charity*. We set up a system where we help one another out as needed, but everything we brought here remains our own. The other is the *commune* approach, where we pool everything together and dole it out as equally as possible. Having thrown that out there for consideration, it really doesn't matter what everyone decides on, or votes for, I won't go along with the commune approach."

There were a few murmurs from the crowd. "Why in the heck did he bring it up?" said one to a neighbor. "I kinda liked that idea," muttered another.

Kyle continued. "The reason why I won't do it, if you'll forgive me for channeling Ayn Rand's Hank Rearden, is because everything I brought up here belongs to me and my family. Yes, God *owns* it all, He always will, but as the steward of all of that stuff I've been provided, I have earthly authority over it. No one can vote me out of that. I don't recognize anyone else's authority here to decide to just take what I have, and Heaven help the person that thinks he can try. That type of thinking, where we feel it's our right to vote ourselves a piece of someone else's pie is *exactly* the attitude that got us into the mess we're in right now. So, forgive me the time spent with the lesson. I just wanted to make sure everyone is clear what I'm all about. It's no doubt true I brought a lot more food and supplies than anyone else up here. I'm neither ashamed nor proud of that fact, it's just that —a fact. In saying that, I'm pretty sure I'm going to end up giving away a lot of it. I spent most of the last couple weeks giving away my company's warehouse full of food because I pretty much figured I'd end up here and I couldn't take it all with me anyway. And, well, I felt it was just the right thing to do.

"So if it pains anyone to rely on charity, I don't know what to tell you. If everyone else here decides on the commune approach, that's fine, as I said I'm not in charge, but I won't take part."

"Well, what about the other problems?" asked an elderly lady who sat near Kyle. "Seems like we'll need to divvy up some chores around here. Won't we have to work together? Just like a commune?"

"Absolutely. But my point is, with charity our stuff remains our own. The problem with the commune approach, aside from morality, is that there has to be a power structure to decide who does what, who gets what. Kind of like Orwell's *Animal Farm*. Someone has to be the pigs, otherwise everyone just reaches into the pile and takes what they want. And in that model, the pigs always seem to have more and better goodies than everyone else."

A few people nodded knowingly, particularly the older residents. "Back to the charity model. I brought enough to feed my family for well over a year on storage food alone. That won't stretch very far with this many people, but I'll get to that in a bit. I brought water purification systems, both of the gravity variety and one using UV light that requires power. Speaking of power, I have two smaller solar systems in boxes and a larger setup on my trailer. Neither will power a cabin, but we can use them to purify water, charge portable radios, provide some lighting in common areas, et cetera. Which brings me to my next concern, security. We need a twenty-four-seven armed security detail set up as soon as possible."

"What for?" a younger, thickly bearded man asked. "Are you expecting trouble?"

"I'd rather us be proactive and ready rather than be surprised. Consider it like insurance. I'm betting that outside of federal installations like military bases and the 'zocks' things are pretty wild. If anything happens, we're on our own. Who here has police or military experience?"

A fiftyish man, tall, barrel-chested, and clean shaven wearing a safety-yellow jacket and blue jeans raised his hand. "I served as a Marine. Went to the Gulf, back in ninety-one." A couple of other hands went up, older men. "Army, Vietnam," said one. "Coast Guard," said another. Another hand went up, a petite but fit woman with short black hair heading to gray. "Police officer." Kyle suspected that in this crowd there were more veterans but couldn't blame them for not wanting to volunteer for long, boring shifts carrying a gun and a radio. Most of the people here obviously still considered this a weird, surreal vacation from their real lives and not a long term problem.

"A fellow Marine. Always nice to run into a brother. What's your name?" Kyle asked.

"Greg Samuels."

"Greg, would you be willing to head up that detail? I can make it worth your trouble."

"Ahh, sure, I'll take some of that charity you're talking about. You bring any steaks?" There were a couple of laughs from the group.

Kyle smiled, thankful for the change in mood.

"Greg, we'll get together later and put it into action. So that brings me to the volunteer system. No one here can force anyone to help with security or any other chore that needs to be done. Remember, no Orwellian pigs. It all must work on a volunteer system. That said, I'm going to be a lot more charitable with my stuff with those that are pulling their weight. If you don't pitch in and help, don't expect much from me. It's pretty cut and dry. If you're young and have a strong back, you're going to be needed for different chores and duties than the more, ah, *seasoned* among us here that might end up watching kids, cooking up chow, that sort of thing."

"All volunteers. This sounds like a church ministry," the same older lady remarked.

"I like that. That definitely fits," said Kyle, nodding. "I don't think it's going to be a big shock, but I foresee that most of our time will be spent staying fed. None of our plans matter much if we starve to death, or we're so weak a virus runs through here and takes us all out. I'm personally most eager to volunteer for and organize a hunting and fishing crew. Once I know things are secure here at the cabins, I'll feel a lot more comfortable going out and chasing game. An adult elk or a couple of good-sized deer could give everyone here a nice chunk of meat, and I plan on heading down to the Canal and loading up on shellfish as well. Kids that want to try can go for the trout in the lake or even get a goose with a twenty-two. Whatever we can't eat right away we can cure or smoke for the long term. If you're interested in helping me with any of that, please let me know. The next area of concern is clean water and along with it, cooking. My purification systems will help but we're still going to want to boil a fair amount of lake water in order to meet our needs. What I brought can't handle seventy-five people and I'm sure more will arrive in the next few weeks."

"What about that? More people, I mean. Who are we letting in?" someone asked from the back.

Kyle frowned, trying to think of a good answer. "Well, what makes sense to me is that anyone vouched for by a resident here can come in, and that family would be responsible for putting them up and taking care of them. Cabin owners, obviously, can come in but then those already in their cabin are their responsibility. As for refugees, we'll need to turn them away unless someone decides to take them in."

"But the park we're sitting in, and most of the area around the lake is public land," said a sad-eyed middle-aged woman to Kyle's left. "We own our cabins, sure, but we don't own the whole lake."

"That's true, but as long as we're holding to legalities, look at the sign behind us. See? 'No Overnight Camping.' So no, people can't come and just squat in the park. Maybe we're overstepping our bounds, but having strangers in tents right next to our cabins isn't going to fly. Those that come and camp on the north end of the lake, if they can find a spot in that marsh, are on their own. If they come and are peaceable I don't see a problem.

"So, back to some of the things I think we need to start doing. If we're going to boil water all day and cook hot food, we're going to need a lot more wood than the little piles most of us have stacked up next to our cabins. I brought a chainsaw and some two-stroke gas but I hope I wasn't the only one. There's a nice tight stand of skinny firs a little west of here. Most of them are snags and basically dry and ready to burn except for the very bottom cut. I don't mind doing cutting wood from time to time, but we'll need a few other strong backs to haul those logs down here. We'll also need some thinner lengths to build open latrines."

There were a few noses that scrunched up and groans went up from the crowd. Kyle went on. "I know it's distasteful and not very private, but without running water it's our only viable option. We can fill our toilets with lake water, but I don't even know where it heads from here, and the last thing we want is for *that* to back up into our cabins. If everyone is on board with this idea, I'll ask for some volunteers to build those."

Kyle took a deep breath. "So that covers food, water, cooking, sanitation, and security. Oh, do we have anyone here with advanced medical training? A doctor, nurse, or paramedic?" He paused for a second. "Anyone?"

No hands went up as the lake residents looked at one another. Kyle's heart sank a bit. *You've got to be kidding me.* Seventy-four people and no one who could do better than put a Band-Aid on straight. Kyle was pretty sure they would have medical problems sooner than later. Too many elderly people up here and certainly some had to be on chronic meds that would run out. He didn't even want to think about a tree falling on someone or an honest-to-God gunshot wound. Or infectious diseases. Or childbirth. "Am I really the most qualified here, with a Boy Scout first aid badge I earned twenty-five years ago?" Kyle whispered to his wife, incredulous. It was in half-jest, as the other vets and that female police officer would have had decent first responder type skills.

"I think you just might be," Amber whispered back.

"So, what's it looking like for security volunteers?" Kyle asked to kick off their informal meeting around his kitchen table.

Greg grunted. "It was a pain, lemme tell ya. Can't 'voluntell' people like the days when we wore green for a living, right? So far I got three teenage boys who pretty much just want a chance to put their booger hooks on guns, those two other vets that put their hands in the air earlier, and that lady who says she was a cop down in Houston back in the eighties and nineties."

"Hnnf," Kyle grunted. "That's pretty thin. I had hoped for about eight, not including you or me, as a minimum."

"It'll be tight but should work okay. We have three two-person crews and run six-hour shifts. That way it rotates around the clock and no one crew gets stuck with nothing but night shifts. We did it like that in the Gulf."

"By the way," Kyle asked, "what did you do in the Marines? Me, I was a machinegunner, oh-three-thirty-one. Mostly ran a fifty-cal in the Fleet."

"Grunt, huh? I was a total pogue, a field radio operator, oh-six-twenty-one. I got to play grunt during Desert Storm though. Lot of pogues did, right?"

"Yeah."

"I ended up door-kicking through Kuwait City with Force Recon, no joke, during the invasion. I felt safe as a baby in his mother's arms with those hard chargers around me. Never had to fire a shot but it was a blast."

Kyle nodded. "I ended up in the same spot as you, out in Iraq, just twelve years later. And, well, no offense, we got to finish the job you guys started in ninety-one."

"Yeah. Would have been too easy to just keep going when we were there. S'way it goes. Desert Storm was definitely not like Iraq when you were there. Most of those Iraqis had zero fight left in them by the time we went in."

"Yeah, it was a mess," Kyle remarked. "I was with Third Battalion, Fifth Marines. We were the first unit that officially entered Iraq for OIF. Took the oil fields over the border and pushed north all the way to Baghdad." Kyle stared off into space, and after a few moments noticed Greg looking at him curiously.

"So, comm guy huh?" Kyle said, breaking his spell. "I have two nice multiband radios that can pick up and send just about anything including shortwave, a CB base station that can be crank powered, and a couple of junky handhelds I use for hunting. I figure we'll use those two for security. I'd like to hang on to the better ones to listen in on the rest of the world. Unless you have some comm gear...?"

"Uh, me? No. I haven't touched more than a car stereo since I got out. I'm really not that technical, man. I went in open contract and ended up with the luck of the draw. I told my recruiter I liked engines, motorcycles, that sort of stuff but y'know how the Marines don't care about any of that. It's just some guy driving a desk, filling billets."

"Do any of these volunteers have weapons? Do you? I have some to spare but I'm not a gun store."

"Yeah, sure. The cop, her name is Jeanie Suarez by the way, she had a nice pistol she was packing when we talked. I don't know about the other guys. I got pretty well cleaned out in a divorce a few years back but I managed to hang on to a few of the better guns."

"You were a collector?"

"Naw, not really. My old man kind of was. He got hit by a city bus back in the nineties. No lie."

"Oh man, I'm sorry."

"No, no, it's okay . . . he lived. What I was trying to say is that he got a big settlement and spent it on whatever caught his eye. Not really a saver, y'know? Guns, a big truck, a fishing boat, Dad was that kind of guy. He passed about fifteen years ago. My brother got the boat, my sister got the truck, and I got the guns. Like I said, I had to sell most of them, but I kept a real deal German made HK91 rifle, a Coonan auto, and this," he said, raising his shirt. The handle of a wood-gripped 1911 pistol was buried in a leather holster inside his jeans. "A Kimber .45 compact. Dad had about ten other nice guns I had to dump and it hurt me to my core, man. Lawyers and ex-wives, parasites I tell ya. Watch out, because if I ever have to sell these last three guns, the kidneys are next!"

"So my next question," Kyle began, "is this: those are some great weapons, but can you *hit* anything with them?"

Greg smiled, wide with all his teeth. "C'mon man, I'm a *Marine*, brother! I haven't shot that HK in a couple of years but it's a solid rifle. My Coonan is a laser out to a hundred yards with hot .357s, and the Kimber, well, it's a great up close gun."

"The guns are accurate. Are you? Not trying to be rude but that's the question. We seem to be very short on people who know to put the fat end of a rifle against the shoulder versus the skinny one. A bunch of ones on the ten scale. Range shooting is fine, but I'm talking point and shoot, unknown distances, putting lead on target in a hurry and under stress."

Greg nodded. "Sure thing. That 91 is heavy but I can snap it to my shoulder and bang 'em out pretty good. I haven't forgotten how to get prone and lay down fire. We're good, Kyle."

Kyle went on. "For the security detail, I'll loan out a shotgun and my AR. It's your show but I think it'd be wise to keep those teenagers separate and pair them with the older volunteers." Greg nodded. "Let's draw up a schedule and let everyone know."

Just then, Kyle heard a vehicle pull up and looked over to Greg, who had instinctively clutched his pistol. Kyle drew his Glock from its shoulder holster and peeked out the window.

"It's my brother's BMW!" The big wagon/crossover was loaded so full the wheel wells were almost scraping the tires. Two bikes, Matt's yellow and dark gray one and Des' purple one, were perched vertically on the black car's roof.

The driver's door swung open and Des got out of the driver's side. Kyle could now see that the passenger side was packed full with two black garbage bags. His heart sank. He had truly hoped and prayed that his little brother had found a way to return home after all.

"You made it!" Kyle said as he opened the cabin's door, genuinely happy despite his disappointment. He could instantly see that his sister-in-law was distraught. And hurt. Her left eye was bruised and swollen, the other red-rimmed and bloodshot, and the normally well-kept woman was disheveled, with no makeup and obvious bed-hair done up in a ponytail.

"I-I just had to get out of there. My neighbor ... she ... she was *raped* this morning and she ... *we* ... killed him!" She broke into fresh tears and hid her face with her hands. Amber and their kids, who had been off near the lake, came around the right side of the cabin. Amber ran over to Des, said nothing, and gave her a tight embrace.

CHAPTER SEVENTEEN

Monday, First Week in November

There was a knock at the Traylors' front door. "Yo, pause it," Dillon snapped.

"Okay, bro, chill. It's probably just Nick and Adam." Ryan, Dillon's longtime bud, sat to his left on the well-worn blue carpet.

Dillon walked to the front door of his family's single-wide trailer. He glanced through the peephole. One couldn't be too careful with all the weirdness going on. But it was only Nick and Adam, as Ryan had said.

The pair just kept showing up day after day like cockroaches. Nick's mom wouldn't let him smoke weed at his house, and Adam usually just blindly tagged along with the three of them. Adam, if left to his own ideas, would probably never think of a reason to leave his own house. But he conveniently acted as the fall guy, time and time again—really the only reason the three of them kept him around.

"Hey man, ready to get lit?" Nick predictably asked as he walked in and sat down on what was once a cream-colored microfiber sofa; it had gone brown with age, smoke, and dirt.

"I guess," Dillon replied, unenthused.

"What is this, 'I guess,' dude? You havin' issues or something?"

"Naw. It's just, that's all there is to do anymore. Can't drive anywhere. Can't buy anything."

"Huh. Like you bought stuff before," Adam cracked.

Dillon couldn't think of a comeback. It was pretty sad, getting one-upped by Adam.

"Whatchu been doin' all day?" Nick asked. "Catch the news this morning?" Nick asked.

Dillon shrugged. "Been playing all day. Kind of sucks, no multiplayer, no online play. I mean, it all *works*, right? The cable TV works fine."

Nick exhaled a cloud of dense smoke. "Bro, you can't change it, it is what it is. But the announcement, wow! Crazy."

Dillon and Ryan looked at him, expecting Nick to fill in the blanks. Adam had picked up a car magazine and was trying to read it.

"Oh, sorry man. The government, the DSH people—"

"DHS," Ryan corrected.

"Oh yeah, right, the DHS guys, they announced some kind of confish, umm..."

"Confiscation?" Ryan proposed.

"Yeah, that's it. Something about all bouillon? Which is weird, since isn't that those little salt cubes you use to make sou—"

"For real Nick, shut up," Ryan interrupted. "Bullion. Like gold bars. Silver. The kind of thing rich guys buy and put in their safes hidden behind old paintings and what not."

Dillon scratched his thin patch of stubble. He didn't know anyone who owned lots of gold. "How in the hell are they going to know who has gold?" Dillon asked. "It's not like there's a list."

"There prolly is a list of investors, or collectors," Ryan said. "I mean, if the government put a bunch of different lists together, they could figure it out. They might not know how much you have, but they'll know about most of the people who have it."

"Oh, and get this, they're bringing *money* back!" Nick continued. "There was some money guy from the government talking too. Only it's not dollars anymore. Something about 'the U.S. dollar is finished as a current sea.'"

Ryan groaned. Dillon slapped his palm to his forehead. Adam, completely oblivious, was reading about a sports car that none of them would *ever* be able to afford.

"Dude ... you're *way* too shortbus," Ryan teased.

"What?" Nick said, surprised. "I just said they're bringing money back, bro! Who cares what they call it. I think the TV dude said it was called a 'banker' though."

"'Banker?' That's stupid," Dillon said.

"Whatever," Nick shot back. "So, the money gets put on your ID card by the government and you can use it for stuff. They said you'd have to pay for food with these 'bankers.' No more just showing up every day and getting in line. You get new money every two weeks to get food. *Free money!* And get this—you get money for the, uh, bullion, too. If they confish ... uh, take it, you don't get anything, but if you turn it in on your own, you get *more money*."

"Mr. Weathers," Adam blurted from the recliner.

"What?" Dillon said.

Adam looked up at the three of them. "Mr. Weathers. The science teacher. He's big into coins and stuff. He brought a couple to class once."

"Yeah, I remember him," Ryan said, nodding slightly. All four of them had dropped out of high school at various points in time. Adam was the youngest of the four and had stayed in school the longest, probably the reason he remembered the man. Nick would barely remember yesterday—three years ago in science class would be a miracle.

Dillon remembered Mr. Weathers, but nothing specifically about gold coins. Maybe he'd missed that day or hadn't had that class. Mr. Weathers was a nerd, bow ties and suspenders, and he drove a little sissy red convertible. "So what? He has some coins. What are we going to do? Burn all the gas Ryan has left in his car, go over to his place and say, 'Hey Mr. Weathers, can we pretty-please have some coins so we can get some money? Oh, gee, you're going to keep them and get the money yourself? Aw, shucks.'"

"Dude, Dillion, I think Adam is sayin' we should go *roll him*," Nick posed, wide-eyed.

"I know where he lives," Adam said, smiling menacingly. "Across town."

Dillon tried his best not to look scared. All of them had gotten in trouble, either in school or with the cops at some point. Dillon had gotten probation and community service for vandalism four years earlier, when he was sixteen. He'd been kicked out of school a few times, and the last time he'd just never come back. He also knew Adam had been in some trouble with the cops but didn't think it had been anything violent. Dillon didn't like the look in the eighteen-year-old's eyes.

Ryan looked at each of them in turn, brow furrowed. "Seriously. You want to do this? I mean, I don't care about the dude or anything, but it's pretty cold to roll him just so we can get some more of that crappy food they're handing out."

"Oh no, bro," Nick replied, shaking his head. "It ain't just for food. It's *real money*. You can buy stuff. Gas, cars, season tickets, whatever. The power company leavin' the juice on? Yeah, for a while they have. Now you gotta pay, man. You gotta pay taxes, pay for your water, pay this, pay that. Just like before. But we all start with the same little tiny amount on our cards. And unless you got a job, workin' for the government, you're just gonna get a tiny little bit every two weeks, just enough to get some food. Near the end of the news deal, there was somethin' about 'work parties' for people to earn some extra cash. I mean, on their card. Not real cash. That's all gone. Over."

"So the only way to do better than not starving to death is to find something valuable. Like gold," Ryan said.

"What about all the money people had before?" Dillon asked. "I mean, not us. People with real bank accounts."

Nick shook his head, exhaling another noxious cloud of smoke. "I dunno, man. I guess they lost it all."

They met back up that evening at Ryan's place, a quarter mile bike ride distant. Dillon had changed into a black long sleeve shirt and black sweatpants. By agreement, they had scrounged up whatever tools they thought they would need. Dillon had put a crowbar and a framing hammer into a small knapsack and had slipped a cheap folding knife into his right front pocket. In the other was his wallet, containing only his new orange ID card.

The idea was to get in there quickly, keep Weathers quiet, and hope he hadn't already turned everything in already. If Weathers wasn't there, fine, they would just have to tear the place apart. If he had a safe, they would just have to load it into Ryan's truck somehow and figure out how to open it later. Or just pound on it with sledgehammer and a breaker bar. Enough time and muscle would do the trick. Dillon wasn't a burglar, but he'd picked up a few tricks talking with older guys he knew, guys who ran with one gang or another. Some of them had knocked over houses here and there, usually waiting for the residents to leave on vacation. People would post their trip on social media, get well-wishes from their friends, and one of Dillon's buds would just look up their address. Too easy. Even better were the idiots that put tough-guy signs in their yard like, "Protected by Smith & Wesson" or "Forget the Dog, Beware of Owner" with a picture of a hand holding a big gun. One of Dillon's break-in pals called them "get your free gun here" signs.

Nick and Adam were late, still riding down the long

street as Ryan opened his front door. "You all set?" Ryan asked.

"Sure."

Their two less bright buds pulled up and dropped their bikes. "Let's do this!" Nick said, too loud for Dillon's liking. "Hey, check *this* out!" Nick lifted his sweatshirt, and tucked into his waistband was a large, blocky pistol.

"Dude! You brought a *gun*?" Ryan said.

"Pfft," Nick sputtered. "We're not gonna to get caught. We'll get back before the curfew, no sweat. I just want it, in case the old fart tries to pull something. Y'know, his own gun, whatever."

Adam pulled out a large knife from a leather sheath. The blade was at least a foot long, and it gleamed in the late afternoon sun. "My dad's Bowie knife. Isn't it cool?"

Dillon looked at Ryan, who just shook his head, barely perceptible. It wasn't a good idea to tell two guys with guns and knives that they were definitely out of their freakin' minds.

They loaded up in Ryan's truck, Adam riding shotgun by default since he couldn't physically fit in the jump seats, and made the short drive across Sunnyside.

"Hey, park a couple of houses before his place. It's coming up on the left, a yellow house with a white roof," said Adam, voice calm in contrast to the spastic Nick. The houses here on the edge of town were pretty sparse, most on an acre or more. Dillon didn't see the point of parking so far away, but Ryan stopped well short of the yellow one-story down the street.

"So what do we do now?" Dillon asked. "Just go up, head to toe in black, and knock?"

Adam smiled. "Yeah. That sounds good," he replied, missing the sarcasm. "If he don't answer, we just get in somewhere. It's not like anyone can call the cops, right?"

They walked up in file, Adam surprising them by taking the lead. *Huh. Maybe he's been fooling us all these years.*

Adam went to knock but recoiled back.

"What's wrong?" Nick cried, hand under his sweatshirt.

"The door! It's been busted open already!" Adam swore several times, kicking the side of the house with his black leather boots.

"Beat to it," Ryan said.

"Gee, Sherlock, you think?" chided Adam. "What are we gonna do now?"

"We came all this way. Let's at least check it out," Dillon said.

Adam pushed the door open, and as Dillon passed, he could see the gouges in the doorframe where someone had bashed or pried it open.

"Place is trashed!" Adam shouted. Dillon came around the dividing wall to see for himself. There were papers strewn all over the floor, and two bookshelves along the far wall had been tipped over, books of all sizes lay askew all around. A flatscreen TV, an older black plastic framed LCD, laid face up with its screen beaten in. Framed pictures and artwork had been taken off the walls and thrown across the room. All of the furniture had been moved away from the walls.

"Someone looking for the same thing we came for," Ryan said.

Dillon just shook his head and kept walking deeper into the house. Beyond the living room, there was an open door leading to a small office. On the desk there were several large three ring binders, all open. Dillon looked more closely and saw they were meant to hold coins in plastic sleeves. All of them appeared to be empty.

"Hey guys, I found his office! With all of his coin collecting stuff!" Dillon yelled. His three cohorts came running.

"No kidding?" Nick shouted.

"Yeah, but it looks like everything is gone. Either the dudes who trashed the place took the goods, or Weathers did. It looks pretty nice and neat. Guessing he's been gone for a while, and whoever came here before us just busted up the house looking for anything he might have forgot."

"Wow Dillon, you shoulda been a cop or one of those investigator types, like on TV," Nick said.

Ryan frowned. "Came all this way for nothing then. Hey, what about that, in the corner?"

Dillon turned and saw a squat safe in the corner, about three feet high and painted black. He should have seen it when he'd walked in, but it was obscured from that angle by a couple of boxes that had been thrown down and emptied. "Yeah, he might have left something in there," Dillon said. He took off his pack and removed the heavy steel crowbar. "I know some real pro break-in guys," he began. "If it's a good safe, this won't be enough to get in. But we might be able to get it to the truck even if we can't open it here."

He could see that it was closed, but just to make sure Dillon tried to pull it open; it was locked tight. Then, he wedged the tip of the crowbar into the crack of the door and cranked back. The steel gave slightly, but not much, not nearly enough. Dillon knew that some of these were little better than sheet steel boxes that a crowbar would rip apart; this one appeared to be of the better, thicker fire safe variety. "Hmm, well we need to take this guy home. Let's see if we can pull it away from the wall."

"I dunno bro," Nick said. "You really think he left anything we'd want in there? I bet it's like, his tax records or whatever."

Adam crossed his arms. "Yeah. All the coins are gone, man. I say leave it."

Dillon looked at Ryan who nodded. They grabbed the safe from the back and tried to rock it, but it held fast. "This sucker is either bolted into the ground or it's really heavy," Dillon said. "Maybe this is just a wasted deal."

"Yeah, a waste," Adam said.

They walked through the destroyed living room and

out the front door into the twilight.

Dillon saw Adam flinch a split second before he heard a loud "*BOOOM!*" from across the street. The big kid gurgled as he pitched forward into the dirt walkway leading to the front porch and rolled over. Several dogs started barking.

"Get to the truck!" Ryan yelled as he started toward his Nissan. Another shot rang out and the driver's side of the windshield starred, then another shot and the truck lurched as one of its tires was shot through. Ryan stopped short, key in his right hand.

BOOM! Another shot from the direction of the other house rang out as Ryan fell to the ground and onto his left side. "My leg!" he screamed. "*Help me!*"

It had all happened so fast, Dillon had frozen with fear on the porch steps. "Get inside!" he yelled, pulling Nick by the back of his sweatshirt. They crashed through the doorway and rolled several feet before stopping by the entryway to the home's kitchen.

"I knew you would come back!" came a distant cry, an older man's voice. "My wife told me about you punks coming by earlier! Think you can just come trash our homes, do ya? You come out, you're gonna get shot too, y'hear?"

"*Help...*" came a feeble cry through the partially-open doorway. Ryan. "Dillon, I'm bl . . . bleeding! Don't just leave me here!"

There was another shot, and Dillon heard glass breaking. The shots made an odd whizzing sound, now that he could actually focus on listening to them.

"Dude. Do something. A, what do you call it, diversion," Nick whispered. "I'll go out the back and light that fool up."

Dillon tried to send signals but his muscles would not cooperate. The best he could do was nod slightly.

"All right, bro. I'll head out the back in a minute."

Dillon tried to gather some courage, but found he had very little to draw from. He was the opportunist, the guy who grabbed at what was easy, the low hanging fruit as it were. Facing a guy with a gun, who he couldn't see, while armed with a pocket knife, was at the opposite pole.

"Why don't you come out and show yourself?" Dillon blustered, too feeble sounding. He repeated it, more loudly this time. There was no response.

"Bro, you gotta do better than *that*," Nick whispered from the other room.

"What do you want me to do?" Dillon whined. "Stand at the door and yell, 'Come and get me?' That dude will kill me in one shot."

From the front yard, Dillon heard another painful cry, this one indistinct. He peeked through the narrow view left by the mostly closed door. Adam lay in a heap, not stirring, his back to the house. Dillon could see the glint of something wet on the ground. Ryan's truck wasn't visible, and trying to see it would line him up with the neighboring house. Bad idea.

"I'm gonna shoot you!" Dillon shouted. The bluff didn't work. Three shots quickly rang out and Mr. Weather's front door sprouted two fresh holes as the bullets buzzed angrily past him. After the third shot, Dillon heard a soft 'ping.'

"Nick! Go! I think he's empty!" Dillon heard shuffling behind him, a door opening, and footsteps running around the house. There were two quick *pops* from the other side of the house and the sound of glass shattering. *Nick.* Someone yelled something indistinct; Dillon couldn't tell if it was Nick or the shooter.

Dillon heard a faint 'snik-ca-ching' from across the street. A couple of seconds later, a single booming shot rang out. Then, not a thing, save the dogs barking and a faint cold breeze through the front door.

Dillon felt something in his ribs. He cracked his eyes

open. It was the barrel of a rifle, connected to a short, heavy-set police officer. He was wearing some kind of bulky black vest and wore a matching black helmet with some sort of thick, tinted goggles.

"Wake up kid. You live here?"

"Uh..." Dillon began to reply.

"Yeah, thought so. Stand up and keep your hands away from your body. Now!"

Dillon complied, still groggy.

"You have your ID on you? Your orange card?"

Dillon nodded.

"Well... Where's it at?"

"My front pocket."

"You have two pockets, a right and a left. Which one?"

"Right pocket."

The officer looked impatient. "My right, or your right?"

"My right."

"Here's the deal. You're going to reach in and take out your ID. If you pull out a weapon, I shoot you. This is not a taser or a beanbag gun, it's a rifle and it's aimed at the base of your neck. It *will* kill you. Do you understand?"

Dillon nodded again as he slowly reached in and produced his wallet. "Dillon Traylor. Says here you live across town. Were you going to lie to me and say you lived here?"

"No. No, sir."

"Umm hmm. So, my guess is you can... *enlighten*... me all about the three dead kids in the front yard. And why this house looks like a war zone. I have a theory, but I'm hoping you can set me straight."

Dillon heard footsteps on the porch and the door creaked open. It was another officer, a younger, taller man. "We taking this one with us, Sherman?"

"Yeah. Cuff this clown, will ya?"

"Uh, don't you have to read me my rights?" Dillon said.

Both officers smiled. "Oh, so you've done this before?" the rifle-wielding cop joked. "Actually, you can thank the President for suspending the Miranda requirement. Put your hands behind your back. *Now.*"

CHAPTER EIGHTEEN
Monday, First Week in November

There were five columns of black smoke rising off to the east, over the Anclote River and into Tarpon Springs proper, as Richard Overberg lifted a heavy cardboard box into the rear passenger seat of his silver Mercedes G550 SUV. Gunshots rang out, closer now than ever before.

"Ow!" he exclaimed as he felt his lower back crack. Rich reflexively dropped the box, spilling canned goods of all varieties. He dropped to one knee, scraping a hole in his khakis on the cement driveway. *Why did Kyle use such huge boxes?* "Dot! Come help!"

"What is it dearie?" his wife of twelve years, Dorothy, called from within their five thousand square foot waterfront home.

"It's my back! Bring my Percoset and some water, will ya?"

Rich stayed there on one knee, sweating from both the pain and his exertion this morning which had made his chest feel tight. Like everyone else in his neighborhood, they had stayed put over the last couple of weeks and had gone to the food distro across the river as needed. Richard, with his big five-seat Mercedes, had served as a taxi for both of their adjacent neighbors. The power had been on—at least during the day—water flowed out of the tap, and the toilets flushed.

While it wasn't great it was livable, and besides, where would they go?

Now events were forcing his hand. The power had not come back on and there was a gun battle raging upriver somewhere. It had started two hours ago, had slacked, and had started back up again with gusto twenty minutes ago. About ten minutes ago there had been a tremendous explosion; Rich had guessed it was one of those big propane tanks touching off. It had a rattled their windows and set off distant car alarms.

Rich cursed again and wondered why he hadn't devoted at least a little mental effort over the last two weeks to figure out a good place to fall back to. His best idea so far had been to head north and keep going until he and Dot stumbled across a place they could hole up for a while. Civilization started to thin out quickly as one headed north on Highway 19 and dropped off to wilderness after about sixty miles. Even with all the short food trips the Benz still had half a tank of gas.

He glanced into the garage at their other car, a near perfect midnight blue 1967 Corvette roadster with a factory original 427 cubic inch big block V8. Rich had dreamt of owning one since he was a teenager and had finally made the dream come true ten years ago, not long after coming to Florida from Chicago. Rich dreaded leaving it, even in a locked garage, but the car drank high octane like no tomorrow and, due to a lack of foresight on Rich's part, it had less than a quarter tank of gas. It would barely make it out of the county.

Offhand, Rich wondered how things were going back in Chicago, back with the financial consulting firm he'd been a part of, eventually as a key managing partner, for over thirty years. He'd cashed out in early 2008, definitely a prescient move as many of the firm's longtime clients had lost their shirts later that year. Rich had been wrong about the dot-com bust and had vowed to never get caught in a bursting bubble like that ever again. Unlike some of his friends, he hadn't lost anything with last year's bail-in involving some of the top banks. He'd salted it away in numerous spots, all relatively small slices of his overall pie, so that the loss of one or even a couple wouldn't doom him to poverty.

Now, it was *all gone*. Rich had seen national economies crash, zero out, from afar as sidebar material in the *Wall Street Journal* or fund management updates. But in the *United States*? It was . . . *unthinkable*. Even though Rich had been retired for over ten years, he'd kept up his craft and managed his own fortune—well. He seriously doubted whether, when everything was stood back up, there would be anything left of his substantial portfolio. Stocks, bonds, real estate ventures, and small stakes in several businesses including his nephew's company. The government had set itself up to essentially nationalize all necessities of life and it appeared that the fulfillment of needs, not wants, would be all that people could hope for in the near future, possibly for the next several years. Rich remembered how broke they were when he was a young boy. His father had been leveraged to the hilt, at least by 1950s standards, and had worked eighty hours a week or more just to get the drug stores back in the black. He eventually achieved middle class success, then true wealth with the sale of the family business. Rich could barely believe he'd come around full circle to poverty once again.

Rich heard the click-clacking of flip-flops and looked up to see Dot holding a small glass of water in one hand and two pills in the other. He took the pills greedily, gulped them down, and followed with the glass of tepid water. "Thanks. Can you help me inside, honey? I need to rest for . . . just a few minutes. Then we'll finish packing up and get out of here."

"Are you sure we need to leave?" Dot asked for the tenth time that day.

"No, I'm not sure. But whoever is causing those gunfights and that explosion we heard earlier is coming closer. And those fires concern me. We can always come back after things cool off."

Dot's brow furrowed. "Well, if you want to head all the way up the coast to Cedar Key we're going to pass right through all that trouble. I really don't know."

Rich shook his head as he stood up. "I don't know about Cedar Key. That's a long way from here, over a hundred miles. God knows what the roads are like. We might have to take some detours and I don't want to leave us flat out of fuel and a long way from home. That G-wagon sucks fuel pretty good so we'll have to be careful."

Dot shrugged. "Not nearly as bad as your 'Vette, sweetie. Come on in," she said, grasping his hand, "and lay down on the couch until you feel better."

That had been her best idea all day.

The pills had started to take effect when Rich heard another series of shots, rapid fire, these closest by far. "Dot! Are you okay? What's happening? Where did that come from?"

"My God!" she cried from the kitchen. "I think it's the Davidsons!" Only two houses down and across the street. Two more shots rang out, bang-bang, quick. Rich could hear the rumbling of engines from up the street.

"What's going on? Can you see anything?"

"Yes! Come look!"

Rich, still in some pain, rolled off the leather sofa and stumbled to the kitchen which had a bay window facing the street. He saw several strange vehicles parked on the opposite side of the waterfront drive with their engines running. Several men milled about. All were holding guns, and they definitely *weren't* police or soldiers.

He looked on, horrified, as one of the men lit a bottle

and threw it at the Davidsons' beautiful home. It shattered against the side of the house and instantly flames shot up into the awning.

"Molotov cocktail," he whispered.

"What are they doing, Rich?" Dot asked, her voice trembling.

For her sake he fought to keep his voice even. "They're burning their house down, honey. Did Mark shoot at these... people? Is it some kind of payback? Or just a gang that picked their house at random?"

"I wasn't looking out the window when the shooting started," Dot said, tears welling at the corners of her blue eyes. "Are they coming *here* next?"

He put his hand on her shoulder. "Dot, I don't know but I'm not waiting to find out. Take two minutes to get just the absolute essentials that aren't already in the car. I'll meet you downstairs. Okay?"

She nodded and headed up the thickly carpeted stairs. Three minutes passed, and she came down with a garment bag over her shoulder. *Are you kidding me?*

"Dot! You're worried about *clothes* when there is a *gang* less than a block away burning down the neighborhood?"

"Just some things I don't want to leave here. What? Let's go!" she replied, motioning to the door. They stepped outside and saw that their driveway was already blocked by a black sedan and a large white truck with a bed full of boxes and equipment, no doubt stolen. Three men, two in their late teens or twenties, and one quite a bit older, maybe forty or forty-five, stood outside the vehicles. The younger men had rifles—or shotguns, Rich couldn't honestly tell the difference, while the older man grasped a silvery pistol in his right hand.

"Afternoon!" said the older man in an almost friendly tone. "Glad you came out to greet us, friendly-like, unlike your neighbor there." He motioned to the Davidsons' home, which was now half-engulfed in orange flames. "They shot up one my boys. Stevie. Killed him right there on the porch. You can see where that got them. Now, you're not going to do anything stupid like shoot at me or my boys, are you?"

Rich shook his head and showed his open hands. Even if he had owned a gun, which he did not, he wouldn't think to square off against three armed men. A trickle of sweat ran down his left side. Dot, to his left, started blubbering.

"Now, check it out," the older man continued. "Your lady friend will stay out here, and we're going to take a walk through your house. I also need the keys to this fine ride you have here," he said, pointing to the Mercedes. "You do this right, cooperate, and you'll live. When the lights come back on and this is all over, all you gotta do is file a claim and presto! The top notch insurance company I just know you have will send you that big fat check and you can head down and get a new one. No hard feelings, right?"

In his heyday Rich had been a top negotiator, one of the best. Now, all he could do was nod, dazed with fear.

The man with the pistol, the talker, walked toward the house and nonchalantly pointed the deadly weapon at Rich, using it as a prod to get him inside. The thin sweet-talker veneer didn't quite cover up what was obviously an experienced armed robber. *And a murderer*, Rich realized, thinking of his neighbors.

"Okay," the intruder said as they got into the foyer, "remember how I said we're going to walk through the house? Forget I said that. I don't want a tour. You're going to take me to the good stuff. Gold. Silver. Guns. Watches. Jewelry. Right now. You follow me?"

Rich nodded once again, mind racing. All his considerable precious metal holdings had been on paper—metal stored in a vault somewhere. Not here. Dot had some nice jewelry, but they weren't into watches, and certainly not guns. His brother Rob, the millionaire hobo, was the gun nut of the family and had infected their nephew Kyle with the same bug. Rich had never seen the point. If you had money, you paid others to protect you, like their neighborhood security service.

But the security guards hadn't shown up for over a week now.

"Ahh, well, let's go to my office, it's upstairs," Rich said, hoping to buy some time. They ambled up, Rich in the lead.

"So, whatcha got, chief? I don't have time to screw around," said the gunman as they entered Rich's home office, voice growing more stern.

"I have some cash, maybe three grand." By now he was shaking and the sweating was intense.

The man shook his head. "You musta missed the news earlier, *a-mi-go*. Cash is dead! The world officially killed the dollar today. Only thing that matters now is gold and silver. *Those* I can turn in for the new money. Only reason I ask for guns and watches is because, well, I kinda like them. So, like I said before, show me something I want. *Quick*."

"I . . . I have a Rolex, in a box somewhere in here. It was a retirement present. I'll find it." Rich certainly did not own a Rolex, but figured digging through the boxes would give him some time to think. Or give time, hope beyond hope, for the police to show up. *Someone, anyone.*

"Rolexes are nice. I'll give you *one minute*," the man replied, waving his pistol about.

Rich began digging fruitlessly at the stacks of paperwork, ten-ream boxes full of odds and ends, fighting back tears. He worked with his right arm as his left went strangely numb.

"Time's up, *chief*."

"I . . . I know I can find it!"

The gunman sat in Rich's office chair, a large brown leather model. "C'mon now. You really think you can fool me? The car out front is nice, but I'll need a lot more than that to make me happy. Unlike these methhead punks runnin' around, I've been doing this a long, long time, way before the banks closed up. So, you can quit stalling and show me where it's all at and you'll live. If you think you can hide it from me and I'll just go away, you die. And if you don't have anything I want, you die. Starting to get clear now, old man?"

Rich went to his knees, sobbing now. "I don't have anything! Please, believe me!" he pleaded. "I'm a retired fund manager. I have stocks, bonds. It's all on paper. No gold. No guns. Please, take the Mercedes and go! Just go!" His chest, pained all morning, now felt enormously tight.

"Sorry bud, it don't work like that. You should have invested better!" Pistol level with his eyes, Rich stared down the barrel, tunnel vision.

Blinding light.

CHAPTER NINETEEN
Tuesday, First Week in November

Matt burrowed his face deeper into the hood of Ed Vasquez's old ski jacket, the cold early morning rain slanting into them from the Pacific, a classic "Pineapple Express" type storm.

They had not made very good time, partly due to the weather, but also due to Kaleb turning his ankle on their first day traveling together. The boy still hobbled a bit, but with his bike to support his weight he'd done surprisingly well. Even though Matt surmised that traveling on his own he'd be at least to Crescent City, if not into Oregon, he was glad for the company.

And the toilet paper.

Over the last three days he'd learned quite a bit about his two young traveling companions.

Both were smart, Kaleb in an "aw shucks" sort of way, downplaying it, while Abigail was sharp and was not shy about showing it off. Matt had embarrassingly walked into several of the girl's verbal traps over the last few days. Matt, thinking of his pride, had chalked it up to flipping his sleep schedule and a chronic lack of blood sugar.

That issue—food—was starting to come to a head. Neither of the kids had brought much—certainly not enough to walk to Medford—and combined with what little Matt had added up to about three, maybe four days' worth of food. Matt, to the protest of his stomach had divided up everything equally. He could handle hunger, but he wasn't sure about the two kids, especially Kaleb, who was a bit of a complainer.

"So tell me more about the Army," Kaleb prodded.

"I'm not sure there's much more to tell. I think I've recounted just about every event over those four years. Why don't I tell you about something else? Like my lovely wife waiting for me back home?"

The youngster shook his head. "Naw, c'mon. Lovey stuff? Get real."

Abigail glared back at her brother. "It's not lovey stuff, Kaleb. He said *lovely*. You know ... pretty." She turned to look at Matt. "And he wouldn't talk about *lovey* stuff with a couple kids, would you, Matt?"

"Uh, no. Hadn't planned on it. If your parents haven't ... never mind. So, like I was about to say, my wife—"

"Des. Desirée. You told us already, when we first met at that stinky broken down car, actually." Abigail said.

"Right. So, we met on a hike on Mount Rainier. You ever see pictures of Rainier?"

"Yeah sure," Abigail replied. "It's okay. But everyone knows that Shasta's prettier."

Matt rolled his eyes. "You, young lady, are entitled to your opinion, but I've seen both up close and there's no comparison. Shasta is kind of wide and stumpy compared to Rainier."

"You ever been up Rainier? Like, to the top?" Kaleb asked.

Matt shook his head. "Sadly, no, but I'd like to someday. Been as high as Camp Muir which is about as far as you can go without real equipment. Ten thousand feet."

The rain picked up for a few minutes, pounding hard and causing them to button up as best they could while still on the move.

"I'm still sooo bummed about Halloween," Kaleb said

as the rain abated somewhat. "I was going to be a ninja! It would have been so epic."

Abigail snorted. "Yeah, and I had to make you leave those stupid throwing stars and plastic sword at home! You wanted to carry them all the way to Grandma's!"

Matt heard a vehicle approaching from behind him, heading north. He turned and saw a teal, or maybe turquoise truck headed their way, water spraying from the tires. He stuck out his thumb and the kids did the same.

"Ohmigosh he's stopping!" Kaleb cried, giddy.

Matt heard the wet brakes squeal as the older full-sized truck pulled alongside them. It was pretty beat up. It looked like a well-used work truck and had one of those big separate fuel tanks across the bed against the cab. The passenger window slid down with a squeak. In the driver's seat was a middle-aged man, blond but balding, with a couple of days' worth of darker beard poking through. He wore a faded red tank top that showed off what looked to Matt to be an out-of-shape bodybuilder's physique and a pot belly.

"Where you guys headed?" He sounded friendly enough.

"They're trying to get to Medford," Matt answered. "Me, I need to get clear up to Washington State. Past Olympia a bit."

The driver took his right hand off the wheel and stroked his cleft chin for a few seconds. "Dang, Washington? That's a long ways. Medford isn't too far though."

"So ... you'll take us?" Matt asked.

The driver looked him in the eye. "Dude. I'm just heading to Crescent City, y'know? But hop in, maybe we can figure something out. You guys are a mess!"

Normally Matt would be wary of a spontaneous act of charity from a stranger, but remembered that for one, the Glock was right at hand under his coat, and two, *any port in a storm*. And this was a storm in every way.

They set the bikes and the packs in the bed and piled

into the single cab, Abigail in the middle and Kaleb on Matt's knee by the door. As he closed the door Matt realized that their Good Samaritan could have just hit the gas after they'd thrown all of their gear in the back and mentally kicked himself for his carelessness. Being dog tired and hungry for days had obviously taken its toll.

"Kevin. Kevin Biemal," the driver said, sticking out his callused hand. Matt shook it firmly and introduced himself and the kids. As the truck's very welcome heat hit their cold, wet bodies, it began to fog up the cab, and Kevin turned the defroster vent up all the way.

"So, why you all headed to different places?" Kevin asked over the din of the accelerating diesel engine and the roaring vents.

"Oh, the kids? I'm not their dad," Matt replied, putting two and two together. "They woke me up about three days ago. Blending our gear seemed to make a lot of sense, and I just couldn't let these two try to walk to Medford on their own. I actually started clear down near L.A."

"Medford, hmm. Summertime, no prob, y'know? But there could be two feet of snow on the road that heads up there. I don't think anyone is out plowing, right?"

Matt nodded. "So, why are you headed that way?"

"I work for the marina in Eureka. So, check it out. The cops came and, whadda-ya-call-it, seized all the fuel tanks there. But it's my job to make sure they're are full, right? And there are backup tanks, five hundred gallons each of gas and diesel that the cops didn't know about, or maybe no one told them. I've been getting in there and, y'know, taxiing people and stuff from there to Crescent City, down the coast, wherever."

"For free?" Kaleb asked.

"Naw," Kevin replied, chuckling. "See, people are paying me what they can. Plus I got a girl in Eureka, and one in Crescent City, and..." He trailed off, glancing at the kids. "So yeah, anyway, people just pay what they can. I got a whole pile of stuff at home now."

Matt looked at Kevin, trying to figure out if he really was what he seemed: an over-the-hill "chill dude" or if it was some sort of front, a con, to put them at ease. After all, the three of them were pretty much at his mercy. If Kevin drove them into some sort of trap, Matt could only do so much. However, worrying about it wouldn't solve anything so he decided to keep his eyes peeled and not worry about what he couldn't control.

"Well, what are you looking for?" Matt asked. "I mean, things are pretty strange right now. Stuff that people would have clawed over three weeks ago wouldn't even get a second look. I'm not sure we have much to offer."

"You're telling me! So you guys have been on the road, right? You didn't hear yesterday's announcement? What about on Friday, with the ID cards?"

The three of them shook their heads. "So, like, you have to get an ID card from the government to get food. And yesterday, I heard it on the radio on my way down to Eureka, they're bringing money back ... only it's not the dollar anymore. I was like, *fer real*? And then, check it out, if you have gold or silver, anything that's not jewelry, you have to turn it in at the food handout places, but you get some of the new money put on your card for it."

"I definitely don't have any gold or silver to give you," Matt said. "At the moment I'm a little wealthier in, ah, a different category."

Kevin perked up and turned to face him. "Hmm? What's that?"

"Don't panic, but there's a nice rifle in my pack back there. Lots of ammo, too. Definitely worth a ride home to me."

Kevin smiled. "Wow, I might have to check it out when we stop. A couple-a-people gave me guns for going around picking up their friends or what not but nothin' too special. Like this one here." He used his left thumb and forefinger to bring up the butt of a large chrome plated or stainless automatic hidden against the driver's side door. "Good to have around here y'know? Me and Mr. Colt .45. No one's tried to hijack me yet. You wanna know the truth, Matt? If you had been by yourself, without these two lil' scrubs, I probably would have just kept on rollin'. The loners out there right now, man, they scare me, and you look just like one of them."

Matt nodded, letting it sink in. He checked his face in the side mirror. He had a good start to a thick, dark beard and his hair was matted to his head with sweat, grime, and rain. Right now he thought he looked like one of those handout guys he'd often see at the overpasses on his way to the airport or up to Seattle.

Hell . . . except for the cardboard sign I am *one of those guys.*

"So we'll hit Crescent City pretty quick," Kevin said, breaking Matt out of his reverie. "You guys . . . well, Matt should really get a card and get some food. List these two as your kids or dependents or whatever and get them some grub too. I know one of the gals doin' the cards up there. I picked up what they call a week's worth yesterday. Used all the money they gave me. It ain't gonna last a week but I'll figure it out. Dude's got to eat."

At the mention of food Matt's stomach growled audibly. Something besides granola bars would be amazingly welcome.

"So, all ya got is your driver's license? Didn't you see or hear the announcement? You need two forms of ID," Gloria, Kevin's friend on the inside, said to Matt after he'd produced his wallet. The workers, and the first person in line enjoyed cover while everyone else simply got soaked in the downpour.

"'Fraid so. Our mutual friend Kevin seems to think it's pretty important to get one of these."

She smacked her gum. "He ain't lyin', sweetie. Well... there is an exemption for people *temporarily* separated from their identification documents. That's you, right?"

Matt nodded.

"Okay then. I can put it in for up to thirty days. You *are* going to be home by then, umm hmm?"

"Yes. If I'm not home by then, I'll have bigger things to worry about than ID."

Gloria shook her head. "Oh no honey, you *need* to fix this as soon as you can. You wait thirty-one days or more, and 'pow!' there go your bennies. The only people doin' anything now is the government, and if you can't get bennies, you're history! Now, put your right hand on the screen, fingers splayed out."

Matt finished the process and the machine spit out his card. He turned it over in his hand, wondering why getting these made seemed like such a huge priority for the federal government.

"Now, you won't be able to get weekly disbursements of necessities with that temporary status. Just day to day. And what about your kids here?"

Matt turned to Kaleb and Abigail, who were staring at the ground and kicking pebbles, trying to keep their faces out of the rain. The workers, and the first person in line enjoyed cover while everyone else simply got soaked. "Actually Gloria, they aren't mine. I'm helping them get to family up in Medford. But from what I understand, I can set them up as dependents for now."

"Well there are rules against running around claiming kids that aren't yours," Gloria stated. "People might try to abuse that, get more than their share."

Matt shook his head. "No, it's not like that at all."

"I'm just making sure you know, that's all. You won't be able to get a food ration for them, I can tell you that for sure, but you can turn them over to Peace Enforcement if you'd like. They'll get them home. It's part of their job."

"Peace Enforcement? What's that? Like . . . cops?" Matt asked, confused.

"Honey, they're like cops, FBI, and Homeland Security all rolled into one."

"I don't wanna go with the cops!" Kaleb cried. "I wanna go with you!"

Abigail looked terrified. Perhaps there had been some sort of incident in their past. "Matt, you can't make us go with the police! Right?"

Matt turned to them, whispering, "Don't worry, okay? You're with me, I'm not handing you over to anyone. Got it?"

They nodded in unison, visibly relieved.

"Where ya travelin' from anyway?" Gloria asked.

"Just north of L.A. The kids were walking from Eureka."

Gloria shook her head. "L.A.? There's a quarantine going down there. The whole county, Orange and Ventura too. Three days ago." She squinted, staring at him. "Airborne Ebola. I hear some of the big cities have the vaccine in stock, but not way out here in the middle of nowhere. 'Cept for workers like me of course, we got the shot already. Be real bad if you already have it without the vaccine, sugar. Won't help if you're already infected. When did ya leave?"

Matt thought for a moment. "Umm, six days ago now. Last Wednesday. And I don't have it. If I'd been infected I'd be showing signs by now for sure."

"Uh huh. You wouldn't-a gotten very far if you'd left Saturday," Gloria said. "Blocked off roads, freeways. Helicopters scannin' for people on foot. It's real bad times down there."

Matt let that sink in. His brother was always skeptical of the announced outbreaks as they never seemed to lead to the mass deaths that pundits swore would occur. It always just seemed like rabble-rousing. But real or imaginary, had Matt stuck around just a little longer, he'd have been trapped down there behind a quarantine wall.

"Kevin said something about free food?" Matt asked, turning back to Gloria. She pointed him to a set of lines, far longer than the short one for cards. After thirty minutes of shuffling, his brand new ID was scanned and his identity was confirmed with a thumbprint reader. Then, a man in a gray uniform handed over a small black plastic bag, not unlike the one he'd carried out of that Burbank convenience store over two weeks ago. Matt started to peek inside.

"Hey bud, there are people waiting behind you," the uniformed man snapped.

They made their back to where Kevin had dropped them off. Kevin had gone to check in with some locals for some undisclosed reason. While they all liked him and thus far he'd proven to be trustworthy, Kevin had understood when the trio had asked to hang on to their bikes and gear, which Matt carried and the kids pushed through the local high school's muddy baseball field.

Matt looked inside the flimsy sack. Inside was tan plastic package that, while it looked similar to the MREs he chowed down on back in the Army, was considerably smaller and thinner. Along with that were two packets of some kind of generic fruit drink and a small bag of dry white rice. Nothing more, but to Matt it looked like manna straight from heaven. He could barely wait to see what was in the MRE. As they stepped into the school's parking lot, Kevin's teal Ford pulled in and lurched to a stop in front of the trio.

"Didya get some grub?"

Matt held up the bag.

"Well let's go. We're gonna cook some soup up at my girl's place. She's not far from here."

They hopped into the truck once more and repeated the defogging process from the morning. "Her name's Sheila.

Don't bring up my girlfriend in Eureka, got it? That would, ah, cause me some problems, y'know? It's a little late to hit the road and beat that curfew thing, figure we'll stay there and head out tomorrow. That gonna work for you guys?"

"Sure thing," Matt answered.

After about ten minutes, they pulled into an expansive mobile home park, the large wooden sign at the entrance optimistically reading "Riverview Estates." A sure sign of a below average apartment, condo, or mobile home complex was a geographic feature in the name that wasn't actually part of or visible from the property. And there wasn't a river in sight. They drove in, slowly, hitting the overly tall speed bumps straight on. A lot of people milled about outside, some waving at the truck as it passed, most of them huddling over cooking fires that smoked mightily in the rain.

No lights were on. There had been traffic lights on in town. "What's up with the electricity?" Matt asked.

Kevin shrugged. "Dunno, man. It's like that in Eureka too. Works down around the food handout places, but it's turned off everywhere else." He pulled the big Ford into a spot next to a dark blue double wide with white trim. As he and shut the engine off, the front door opened. A curvy lady of perhaps forty-five, with dirty blonde hair done up in a sort of messy French braid and wearing a red flannel shirt and jeans, stepped out.

"So these are your friends?" she asked in a sweet voice. "Aw, they remind me of my two kiddos when they were little. Kevin told me all about how you two got left all alone down in Eureka. Poor babies!" She mussed Kaleb's hair affectionately.

Kevin and Sheila got a fire going and started adding things to the pot. His hosts had only asked for his rice ration. To it, they added canned beans, some elbow noodles, green onion, some bouillon, cubes, several freshly diced potatoes, a can of chunked chicken, a can of whole kernel sweet corn

—juice and all, and several smatterings of what Matt figured were herbs and spices. As they prepped the soup, Matt and the kids sat and dried off under a pop-up tent set up next to fire. It was pretty clear the soup would never appear on the menu at a fine restaurant, but after a week without food, Matt craved *any* hot meal.

"You guys seem to be taking all of this in stride," Matt remarked. "I figured a lot of people would be going crazy by now. This park seems pretty, well, orderly."

"Hon, look around. This ain't exactly Beverly Hills," Sheila said. "Rich people have dahlias and roses in their gardens. Poor folks like me have potatoes and beanpoles. We're used to making ends meet. Those bags of food we're getting from Uncle Sugar don't quite cut it. I don't know how they expect people to make it on a meal a day."

Matt heard a distinctive pop and saw Kevin offer up an open beer. "No thanks, Kevin. Empty stomach, tired, warm fire. I'd probably pass out after two sips. Maybe later."

"S'ok with me, man." The big man took a swig from the silver can.

The ad hoc soup was surprisingly good. *Hunger truly is the finest spice.* As Matt had seen them do over their days together, Abigail and Kaleb said a quiet prayer together before eating.

"So, show me this cool rifle you got," Kevin said as they finished with their bowls. Matt nodded, grabbed the pack from the truck, and headed back inside. He opened the top flap, frowning as he noticed a couple of dots of rust had formed on the flash hider, at the end of the barrel where it would have touched the damp nylon, and he wiped them away with his thumb.

Pulling out both halves he quickly connected them, retracted and locked the bolt back, and handed the former police rifle over.

"Dang man, this thing is pretty sweet. I saw one like this at a sports store out in Nevada a couple of years ago,"

Kevin said. "They don't sell them here in Cali, haven't for years, man. You seriously going to let this go?"

"You get me up to my cabin up past Olympia and it's yours."

Kevin's brow furrowed. "What about those kiddos? Their family. In Medford, right?"

"Of course. Them too. Your truck have enough diesel?"

Kevin smiled wide. "Shoot, Matt, with the refuel tank topped off that truck will go two thousand miles, maybe more. You're talking about, what, about a thousand, round-trip?"

"A rifle that was free to me for fuel that was free to you. Sound square?"

They shook hands and headed back outside to warm up by the fire.

CHAPTER TWENTY

Wednesday, First Week in November

Lewiston Riggs, heading back to Spokane, wanted to make a quick stop along the way. No . . . he *needed to. For Angel.*

He knew his memory was solid, but in an age where most people didn't clutter their brains with addresses—too easy to let GPS handle the work—Lew found himself cruising side streets, hoping to tease out a mental connection. He definitely didn't want to pick the wrong house. Not for what he had planned.

Lew couldn't really remember where he'd started with his old set. It had morphed from a bunch of kids in the same dirt poor neighborhood, hanging out every day, to getting into petty trouble: stealing energy drinks from the local convenience store, beating up a kid who mouthed off to them, that sort of thing. Later, one of their crew had hooked up with an old established set in Spokane, a group that had formed up way back in the 1980s in response to the L.A. gangs that were starting to branch out into Washington in a big way. Once Lew saw the kind of money his bud was drawing in, hanging on to a high school education by a thread no longer seemed all that important. He'd dropped out in the beginning of tenth grade. Already sixteen, held back a year in elementary school, the older guys in the set had put him to work *driving.*

Driving was a job for the kids, the minors, those not quite eighteen. Legal to take the wheel, but in no danger of serving long prison sentences if caught. Lew hadn't always known what he was carrying. Safer that way, but he had been smart enough to guess it was chiefly drugs, weapons, or cash. Later, after hanging it up, he'd confirmed his suspicions and learned more about the triangle trade. Among the sets those three were their *currency, each interchangeable for the other.*

He'd only had to walk away once, a clear setup. Lew was almost certain it had been a cash shipment—it was no secret cops preferred seizing cash. It was really difficult to buy a new patrol rig or pay out a new officer's salary in drugs or stolen guns. He'd avoided juvie—first time offender and all, got back out on the road, but a few months later his time was up. If he'd been caught with the same load of cash a day over eighteen, he'd still be locked up down in Walla Walla, for sure, these four years later. A sick system that made it easy, irresistible even, for seventeen-year-olds to commit felonies but upped the ante at that arbitrary line of adulthood. Some guys were stupid enough to do just that; the set didn't care, it's not like they went along to prison with you if you got caught. It was bad enough here on the outside. Lew didn't want to imagine what life was like in the State Pen right now.

There wasn't a retirement plan in the sets. No surprise. Some guys went off on their own, climbing up the ladder of violent crime as far as they pleased. Nearly all after five years were dead or in prison. Lew had made some extra cash straw buying some rifles and shotguns for the crew—still too young to buy the handguns they actually wanted—but after a few months he had went straight, gotten a job, a girlfriend, and had become just another uneducated kid with no connections scratching his way along.

About six months ago he'd been let go from yet another job. Lew could work hard, he didn't mind sweating to earn a buck, but this had been the third employer in a row that had demanded he work extra time off the card in order to keep his job. He'd refused. So, jobless with no prospects, he'd reached out to the old set once again. They'd told him there were two jobs available: driver, and someone who knew a lot about guns. Lew had assumed the latter meant a jackboy—an armed robber—or maybe a foot soldier type. He'd been surprised to learn they'd just needed someone to actually train the kids that were flooding their ranks. They'd lost the few ex-military types who normally filled that role; walk-aways or carry-aways, didn't really matter and Lew hadn't asked. The top dogs in the set knew guns left and right —they had to—but they had better things to do with their precious time than teach some sixteen-year-old how to put shells in a shotgun. They needed someone over twenty-one with a clean record to act like a local gun nut, buy ammo, "take a buddy shooting," that sort of thing. Lew had grown up around guns. His grandfather had taken him out hunting and didn't mind when he'd tagged along to the gravel pit to shoot cans and bottles. He knew it didn't make him an expert, but he was way ahead of the kids whose exposure to guns consisted of foam dart launchers and video games.

Gang weapons trainer didn't pay much but it allowed Lew to maintain a low profile, both within the set and with the cops—he never, ever brought home or carried a stolen weapon—and this had suited him just fine.

When the banks closed three weeks ago, and cash immediately ceased to be something of importance, that side of the triangle had become a mix of gold, silver, artwork, gems, tools—anything valuable. Some of the top dogs had weird and expensive tastes; not all of them wore thick gold chains and wifebeaters like in the movies. Food was valuable, sure, but gas even more so. His set, or one of the affiliates, had quite a stash of fuel somewhere. Lew guessed it was a couple gas stations they'd kept from the cops and the fed types.

The death of cash, the lack of easy gas, and the crazy

police presence meant that shipments *had to get through.* The unreliable teenage drivers got pulled from their cars and suddenly Lew found himself back in the role he'd always loved—and dreaded—the most.

"I think this is the place," Lew whispered, parking the nondescript dark grey sedan along the street. He didn't know the car's make or model nor did he particularly care. It was a misconception of people who did what he did that they were car guys. Beautiful muscle cars, foreign sports cars, they looked great in movies but didn't work well in real life. For one, no one would ever believe a scrubby half-Native American kid would own an expensive ride. Two, the whole point was to obey the law and posted speed limits—don't get pulled over—and that was a lot easier to accomplish in a regular car. Three, if you did get caught and you lost it all, better a cheap car you had no attachment to.

He stepped out, having to duck hard to get his lanky six-foot-four frame out of the vehicle, and patted his back just to make absolutely sure his Springfield XD .45 would be there if needed. Lew hoped it wouldn't come to that as the noise would attract unwanted attention. From the long black duffel bag in the back seat he removed a wooden baseball bat. In high school he'd drilled out the end, poured in about a pound of molten lead, and closed it off with a wooden plug held fast with gutter sealant. Lew called this his *goon stick.*

Lew walked up to the home's front door, holding the bat in his right hand and feeling perfectly calm. Years ago, he'd watched a program about angry people, abusers, and how there were two basic types. There were the volcano guys who got worked up and then, once they couldn't take it anymore, lashed out. Then, there were the *cobras. These people actually experienced their heart rate drop when they attacked.* Lew realized right then, watching the TV, that he was one of them. A cobra.

Lew reared back and delivered a stomp-kick with his

left boot where the deadbolt entered the doorframe. The metal door gave slightly and with another kick, just as hard, the door swung open and crashed into the wall. One of his buds had shown Lew this technique. He had never seriously considered the burglary trade; with his unusual height, distinctive sunken cheeks, and closely shaved head Lew figured he'd be way too easy to pick out in a lineup. Plus, people *shot at you when you broke in to their house.* Lew liked money as much as the next guy, but there were better, easier ways to get it.

"Donny! It's Lew!" he shouted. Silence. Lew advanced in the low-ceilinged home, goon stick in his left and right hand on the grip of the big .45.

A shorter man flashed around the corner, knife in hand, and lunged at Lew with the blade. Still a little stiff-legged from the drive, Lew barely avoided the tip as he brought his right hand around to the handle of the bat, stepped forward, and swung. With the reach advantage of both the bat and his long arms, Lew clipped his attacker in the left bicep, causing him to retreat.

"You knew I'd come to find you, right?! For what you did to my sister!"

The smaller man paused, knife still extended. "Who ... who the hell are *you?*"

"My sister. Angel. The girl you raped five years ago? Ring a bell?"

"No ... no man! I never raped no girl!"

"Not what she told me. I trust my flesh and blood, Donny. Cops wouldn't arrest you, but *I know.* She had to get an abortion because of you, Donny. She told me all about it before she died. She OD'd on heroin, Donny. You did that to her, man."

"I don't know what you're talking about, pal. Todd! Get down here!" he yelled down the hallway.

With that, Lew sprang forward, swinging low for the legs, and felt the bat hit home and crunch bone. Donny screamed as he toppled to the carpet, banging his head against the wall, his knife tumbling out of his hand. Lew collected himself, drawing the pistol from the small of his back.

"Nooo!" Donny cried, shielding his face with his arms.

"I'm not going to shoot you, Donny," Lew said, voice level. He'd drawn it just in case they really weren't alone. With his left hand, Lew snapped the heavy goon stick downward, striking Donny's temple. There was a distinct crack and the smaller man slumped to the floor, face down.

Lew scanned the hallway, gun arm extended, the pistol's night sights glowing faintly in the partial darkness. Satisfied that he was indeed alone, Lew left, closing the door behind him.

CHAPTER TWENTY-ONE

Wednesday, First Week in November

Matt awoke, feeling refreshed for the first time in a week. He was even clean: Kevin had insisted he "bust off the funk"—Kevin's colorful words for a soapy sponge bath—if Matt was going to travel in the cab of the truck the following day. Otherwise he'd be riding in the bed.

He glanced over at the kids still snuggled in their bags, Abigail in her purple one and Kaleb in a smaller bright blue bag with gold lining.

Matt sat up and reached for his toes. Without the slight paunch that had been forming over the last couple of years—too much restaurant food on business trips—Matt found he could easily grasp the bottoms of his feet with the tips of his fingers.

After his quick stretching session, Matt slipped his jacket over the duty belt to conceal its bulk. There was still a part of him that held back from trusting, not quite sure of Kevin's intentions.

Once they'd eaten a quick breakfast of instant oatmeal, they loaded up as Sheila hugged each one of them in turn. She pressed close enough to feel the concealed duty belt, and she cocked her head, raising an eyebrow, but didn't say a word. Matt smiled sheepishly. A couple of minutes later, they were headed up the winding highway that led up to Grants Pass and on to Medford.

Matt had been down this road on a trip back from Washington when he'd lived near L.A. It had been mid-summer and wonderful weather. Back then he'd had a beautiful yellow Honda roadster with the top down and in no hurry. He'd taken the scenic route, down 101 and Highway 1, hugging the California coast and testing the to test his nimble roadster's brakes and steering.

Today, headed in the opposite direction, conditions were far different. The drizzle started to change to sleet after about thirty minutes, then coalesced into driving snow as they climbed into the mountains.

"This rig have four wheel drive?" Matt asked Kevin over the squeaking wipers. They had slowed to about twenty-five miles an hour.

Kevin shook his head, face serious. "Naw, man. This is the marina's truck, y'know? Never snows down on the coast really."

Finally, they hit several days' worth of deeper snow and they started to fishtail slightly.

Matt's knuckles were white from grasping the door handle. "We need to turn back."

"Yeah . . . I'm pickin' up what you're layin' down, brother." Kevin muttered and started to slowly turn eased the truck to the left. The back end let loose a couple of times, causing Abigail and Kaleb to yelp, but they soon were headed back down to Crescent City.

"What *now*?" Abigail asked, a tear streaking down her freckled cheek.

"I promised you both that I wouldn't hand you over to anyone outside your family, remember?" Matt said, looking at each of them in turn. They both nodded, tears flowing freely now. "So, I'm going to take you two back north with me. Once this is all over, I'll work to get you two back home or to your grandma's. Or wherever you'd like. Sound okay?" Once again they nodded, Abigail wiping away her tears with the back of her hand.

Matt turned to Kevin. "How far do you think we can get before the curfew hits?"

Kevin shrugged. "Man, I dunno, really. I'd like to make Astoria. I mean, normally this is an eight hour drive, right? Clock in the truck says eight forty-eight, so you think, no prob. But we'll wanna go real slow. I know the road pretty well down south, but 101 up north of here? No friggin' clue what's up there, man. So I figure we'll get to Astoria at what, maybe seven at night? Curfew is at nine, and I gotta find this boat bum I used to know. No phone booths with white pages to find people anymore, y'know?"

"Taking it slow, yes. Definitely. You never know what or who you're going to run into."

Kevin hit a cutoff road and a couple of minutes later they could see the Pacific Ocean through the trees, which was gray thanks to the rain but relatively calm. They crossed into Oregon with little fanfare, enjoying the views which switched from deep woods to open views of the ocean. They even saw the tall white mainsail of a lone sailboat off in the distance.

The small beachside towns they passed through were quiet with a few people milling about or on bicycles. All stopped and stared at the noisy teal pickup. Matt guessed that civilian vehicles on the move had become a very rare sight.

Surreal ... as if the entire country hit a pause button and froze in place. This stretch of the Pacific coast was sparsely populated, but in normal times would have cars whizzing past every ten or twenty seconds, people flying kites down on the ocean, et cetera. Now, the only consistent signs of human habitation were the far-off wisps of wood smoke.

They rolled through Gold Beach at a steady twenty

miles an hour, ignoring stop signs. A lanky man in a green baseball cap, orange shell jacket, and jeans, holding hands with a young girl in black braids with a puffy pink jacket, both bronze-skinned, walked out of a storefront and waved them down. Kevin, grasped the big handgun stuck in the door pocket and looked over at Matt.

"Can't hurt to see what they want," Matt said. "If the guy starts anything funny, no need to shoot anyone, just floor it."

Kevin pulled alongside and stopped.

"Are you going north?" the man asked in a thick Spanish accent. "We need to get to Leen-cone City." *Lincoln City ... a long drive north from here.* "I come here to see my sister and brother-in-law. My car was stolen. My wife and son are there." He looked down at the girl, then back to Kevin and Matt. "Can you help us?"

Matt saw Kevin's mental gears turning. "Sure thing, we're headin' that way already," Kevin said after a few seconds. "You need to grab anything? Like, uh...."

"No, no! Thank you! I have what I need. *¡Muchas Gracias!*"

"Hey," Matt called, "your daughter can ride up here where it's dry. You and I can ride in the bed with the bikes and packs."

Their new companion nodded a couple of times. Matt got out as the man's daughter came around to the passenger side. Kaleb and Abigail switched spots so the girls could share the seat belt by the door.

Matt and the man hopped in the back. "Matt Flanigan," he said, shaking the newcomer's extended hand.

"Pedro Sanchez. My daughter ees Patricia."

Matt whacked the side of the truck twice with the palm of his hand and it crawled forward, Kevin going even more slowly with them in the back. Ordinarily it would have been difficult to carry on a conversation in the bed of a truck on the highway, but at thirty miles an hour it proved easy. Matt gave Pedro the quick version of his journey, purposely leaving out the gunfight.

"Much more, ah, *exciting* than my last two weeks," Pedro said. "My sister just, how do you say, re-marry? Couple months ago. I find a house for them, make sure it hokay, you know? My wife, Brisa, she work so I bring Patricia with me. I think then... it will be a quick trip and I be back in a couple days. I should have jus' gone back that night, you know? But the next day, my car ees gone, and my sister no have gas to get me home. The power went out a-couple-a days ago, and thas when we start just waiting out by the road."

Matt nodded. "I'm glad we could help you out, Pedro."

At about noon, the rain let up and the sun started to peek through the clouds. Not long after, a long convoy of matte battleship gray vehicles approached rapidly from the rear. It was a lot more uniform than the somewhat shabby convoy he'd seen in Eureka. The lead vehicle was unmarked, an armored vehicle of some sort with a machinegun turret mounted up top. Matt leaned over the truck's white steel bed tank to tap on the back glass.

Kevin slid open the window. "What's up, bud?"

"Military convoy coming up on us real fast. We can either speed up or get the heck out of their way. I vote for the latter."

Kevin pulled off on the next side road, went down the street a couple of blocks, and pulled a U-turn. Matt fiddled in the pocket of his ski jacket, producing the small binoculars that he'd taken from the patrol bag. A minute went by and the unmarked vehicles began streaming past at more than sixty miles an hour. First, the armored vehicle he'd seen, which vaguely resembled a U.S. Army Stryker, an eight wheeled armored personnel carrier. Then two Suburbans with tinted windows, then a large truck with several whip antennas and a small dish up top, and finally another armored eight-wheeler acting as rear security. Kevin idled, waiting for the vehicles to get well into the distance.

"You, ah, you *hide* from someone?" Pedro asked.

"Not the authorities. Just don't want to attract any attention. Who knows what those guys want?"

Pedro just shrugged.

Behind him and to his right, Matt heard a house door open and slam shut. A man ran out into the street, about a hundred yards behind the truck, gripping a long barreled gun in both hands.

"Kevin!" Matt yelled. "Floor it!" The truck lurched violently as the big diesel V8 roared. Matt saw Pedro slide into one of the kid's bikes and yelp as the rear derailleur gashed his right shin. Shifting his gaze back, Matt saw that the man on foot had brought his weapon to his shoulder and kept a steady aim on them as they accelerated away.

"You okay?" Matt asked Pedro, who was rubbing his leg with both hands. Kevin braked hard, taking a right turn back on to the highway.

"Yeah."

"Not too friendly around here, eh? Maybe he thought we were thieves."

"Th...what?" Pedro sputtered.

"Thieves. Um...*criminales. Chicos malos.*" Bad guys.

"*¿Hablas español?*" Pedro asked, perking up. *You speak Spanish?*

"*Sí, de vez en cuando.*" *Yes, every once in a while.* "Sorry...bad joke. Helped me when I met my wife. She's, ah, *puertorriqueña.*" *Puerto Rican.* "Probably helped more with her dad actually, when I asked him for his blessing. Old fashioned."

"*Oh, sí, claro,*" Pedro replied. *Yes, of course.* "*¿Eres latino también?*" *Are you Latino too?* Matt's olive complexion and thick dark hair had invariably led many to assume so.

"No, part Italian. *Italiano.*"

"Ah, *sí.*"

"With a truck full of stuff," Matt went on, "and a couple dudes in the back, I can see how people might think we're out stealing stuff. I'm just glad he didn't shoot."

It was just after sunset when they pulled up to Pedro's small home on the outskirts of Lincoln City. Brisa and what Matt assumed to be their preteen son emerged from the house, and in no time there were hugs and kisses all around. Pedro and Brisa briefly conversed in Spanish, far too fast for Matt to follow, and Pedro turned to the truck. "You all . . . stay here? Astoria . . . too far for tonight. Come, stay."

Matt, standing by the driver's side door, turned to Kevin. "What do you think? I can wait another day."

"Yeah, I guess, man. But . . . I didn't bring much to eat." Kevin said, concerned. "Kinda figured this would be a two day deal."

Matt soon learned that their hosts didn't have a lot of food either, but were more than willing to share. Unlike tiny Gold Beach, there had been a small FEMA distro set up in town so at least a little food had trickled their way. Brisa had been stuck walking into town and back—eight miles each way—while their son Esteban watched over the house armed only with an old single shot .22 rifle. There had been some violence in the first few days after the crash for sure, but the big news locally, as translated by Esteban, was that an armed gang of men had attacked the city police station and had briefly taken it over before a military unit of some sort had fought the gang for several hours before wiping them out. The police station was now an abandoned shell.

"Dang," Kevin whispered. "Makes me wonder what Crescent City will be like if, well, *something* happens at the prison. That sucker is maximum security . . . solitary for the worst of the worst. Bad muthas, lemme tell ya. Thousands of 'em. Maybe I oughta, y'know, avoid bein' around there for a while."

With no electricity and only candles to illuminate

the house they bedded down very early, well before nine. The next morning, Kevin, the kids, and Matt said their goodbyes and thank-yous to the Sanchezes and continued north.

"So, Pedro ended up being a pretty cool dude. Like I said before, the guys with kiddos are okay," Kevin commented after they'd passed through the locally famous town of Tillamook, breaking their observant silence. Now with an empty truck bed they had agreed to look out for more folks like Pedro and Patricia. Unfortunately, everyone they saw shuffling north had either been of the "lone wolf" variety that scared Kevin, or in groups of five or more. Most had big backpacks or were pushing carts, baby carriages, or bike trailers. They had even seen a man pulling along a motorcycle trailer by hand.

Not everyone was as badly off. A few minutes before, they had been passed by a bright yellow Porsche 911, an older air-cooled Turbo with the fat back end and whale-tail spoiler. The car had been doing about seventy, and once past the truck its engine had made that distinctive air-cooled Porsche snarl as it accelerated to at least one-twenty and disappeared over the next rise.

"Yeah. I'm glad you agreed to take them, good call," Matt answered. "I'm curious about something though. You never asked them for anything to pay for the trip."

Kevin smiled and shrugged. "Hey, y'know, my memory ain't so hot, but I never asked you for anything either, right? I do remember sayin' how people are payin' what they can, and you offered up that cool gun. Those two didn't have anything. What was I going to say, 'Nope, sorry Pedro, you need to pay to play?' I mean, heck, we were headin' his way anyway. And seein' as how we got a meal and a place to sleep for the night, I think we did okay."

"Just glad he was a good guy not a bad one," Matt said.

"Why? Back there in the bed of the truck, were you worried he might try somethin'? What would you've done?"

"Well," Matt answered, "his little girl was in the cab

with you guys. I don't think he picked up on the way I split them up but there was definitely a reason behind it. Plus, there's this." He unzipped the jacket the rest of the way and showed off the belt and Glock.

"Dang man, you were holdin' out!" Kevin said, much more surprised than angry.

"Man's got to be careful these days."

It was not quite eleven in the morning when they reached Astoria. "You want to look for this guy? Andy, right?" Matt asked.

Kevin shook his head. "Naw. I'll hook up with him on the way back if I need to. I just want a place to stay, that's all. I'd like to get you guys up to that cabin now. Four hours there and back will give me plenty of time to get back down here before the curfew."

"I'm sure you could stay with us tonight. Least I could do, really."

Matt looked up at the winding onramp to the Astoria Bridge, spanning the broad Columbia River. He recalled that, as a six-year old, he'd been scared of how high the bridge stood out over the water, and how Kyle, then thirteen, had teased him for crying.

Up above, there was some sort of shack erected as the bridge began, and Matt could just make out a man standing beside it with a rifle in his hands.

CHAPTER TWENTY-TWO

Wednesday, First Week in November

Rob, despite complaints from his back and elbows, maintained a solid prone position as he looked through his tripod-mounted Nikon spotting scope, cranked all the way up to forty-eight power, and observed current ... *developments* ... across the lake. The same gang of lowlifes—or one like it—had returned early in the morning and had begun a new round of robbing, killing, and mayhem.

No. Probably isn't the same group. Most of those schmucks had been stone dead for over a week now. After he'd saved John's hide, Rob had returned—loaded for bear—and had and set up a nice prone position behind a sturdy hickory tree up a bit from the lake shore. At over four hundred yards, he'd systematically picked off the bewildered marauders. At first, it had proved difficult to gauge the success of his efforts; the hard kicking rifle had made it impossible to observe the impacts, but after several minutes there simply weren't any bad guys left to shoot. They had either wisely hunkered down or were already dead. Rob had waited an hour, saw no further movement—good guys or bad—and had motored back home.

That evening, he'd ferried his guest back across to

fetch his motorhome. Aside from a couple of bullet holes and a broken rear window it was no worse for wear. Most of the residents had already pulled up stakes, unaware that they were safe—at least for now—thanks to Rob's work earlier that afternoon.

The last week, fairly quiet in most respects, had been an odd experience. He and John shared very little in common other than old age and reticence. Rob had spent his days out on the lake, cooking the catch that supplemented the survival chow, and the evenings he poured a glass of bourbon and caught up on the scant news of the day—nothing good or new with the economic crash— and turned in. Rob learned John was a complete teetotaler—not even beer or wine—so he continued to drink alone. He had reined in his normally salty tongue for John's sake. He'd also tried to get the mercurial John to play cards, darts, anything, but the man had patently refused, instead enjoying the solitude of his RV, now parked behind the house and away from the road. They had shared meals together, though 'shared' might be stretching the truth as they typically just eyed one another like a lion and a crocodile at the same watering hole.

The door to John's motorhome creaked open and John emerged from his RV, dressed in a maroon flannel shirt and jeans.

"Are you going after these men as well?" Gunshots, though faint, could be clearly heard. By now there were two dark gray columns of greasy smoke winding into the clear fall sky.

"No," Rob replied, taking his eye out of the scope and looking up. "Last time, I had a good reason for doing what I did. They'd seen my face and they knew I lived across the lake. *This* bunch," he said, tilting his head toward the carnage, "could be a threat but it's best to just watch and see. They bust out of there, heading around the end of the lake and up our way, we'll need to *di di mau*."

John shot him a confused look.

"*Di di mau*. Something all the crusty Vietnam vet sergeants would say. Means 'get out of here.'"

"Ah, I see. Well, let me know if I need to hit the road, or '*di di mau*'. I am not going to be much help in a gunfight."

Rob shrugged. "Even if they tear out of there, they'll hit the houses along the southern shore first. We'll have two, maybe three hours to get out."

"What if they just head straight here?"

"Not sure why they would. In that case, we'd have five minutes or less. Hmm. Stranger things have happened before. I suppose this means I should pack up my truck and hitch up the boat, just in case. You comfortable watching for a while?"

John hesitated. "I would rather not lie on the ground like that, but yes, I can take over."

"Don't sweat it. I'll get a folding table and a chair, hang on."

Rob had just finished packing up his black Dodge Ram 2500 Outdoorsman Edition and hitching up the fishing boat when he heard the distinctive chatter of fully automatic rifle fire off in the distance, followed by several single shots, then another long burst of full auto. John began hollering from the other side of the house and Rob jogged up.

"What's goin' on out there, pardner?" Rob asked, trying to sound nonchalant.

"It was quiet there for a while," John began, still squinting into the Nikon. "Then, some new vehicles showed up, and they attacked one of the houses on the lake, down on the south end."

"Same crew?"

John looked up and stared at Rob for a couple of seconds. "I believe so, since the ones in the park mounted up and are behind the newcomers."

"Let me see." John stood up and Rob took his place. He peered through the tube, adjusting it slightly as John had changed the focus, and saw the house in question. At forty-eight times magnification, the house, over three miles away, appeared to be right next door. A large vehicle was visible among a few smaller trucks and vans: boxy, painted black along the on top and along the bottom, and tan in the middle. There was a logo along the side, near the back, that Rob couldn't quite make out.

"Did you see the big one?" Rob asked. "An armored car. These clowns are pretty serious."

"Yes. Didn't know what it was, but there was a bigger car up front. Thought it might be a panel van of some kind."

Rob watched as two men approached the armored car, both holding either rifles or shotguns, and got in. The big vehicle pulled out along with two of the trucks, while the others stayed. Following the small convoy with the scope, he saw them pull up to the next house. Several shots popped off, likely from within the target house, but the armored car pulled up unscathed.

"I guess it's too much to ask for someone to have a fifty cal around here," Rob remarked.

"What's that?"

"Nothing, just wishing out loud. They're getting ready to hit the next house." Rob watched as the doors swung open and the raiders began shooting; he could see the muzzles flash but the reports were several seconds behind at this distance. Wisely, the bad guys hid behind the doors of the cash transporter, nearly completely protected. The passenger side gangster bore the full-auto gun, Rob saw, — an underfolder AK with a drum magazine. It wasn't the same rifle as the AK that had been used against him at the RV park, though it was externally similar.

Rob frowned. Contrary to what the ignorant press reported from time to time, it wasn't possible to head down to Moe's Gun Barn and pick up fully automatic weapons over the counter. And the feds made sure the models for sale could not be easily converted. Back in the Army, nearly forty years ago, he'd overheard a well-sauced sergeant brag he'd smuggled back from 'Nam a couple captured North Vietnamese Army AKs. He was certainly not the only one and there were plenty of similar stories from other wars. While it was possible the punk was wielding one of those 'Nam bringbacks, in reality, Rob knew, it was much more likely it had been brought in much more recently over the porous southern border.

"They're hitting the houses with the armored car and then leaving for the next target, letting the truck and van guys pick up the loot," Rob explained. "We'll have to move up our timeline a bit... their method is a lot faster than I originally figured."

"So. Where to go?"

Rob sighed. "I know of a few places. Top of the list is my sister's cabin way out in Washington State. But... with things the way they are I doubt we'd ever make it that far. We'd have a better chance wintering somewhere a lot closer."

"We? Perhaps it is time we part ways, Rob. You're not responsible to take care of me."

Rob looked the older man in the eye. "Listen. We've been dancing around this for a week now. You don't want to feel like you owe me any more favors, I get it. Guess what? You don't, okay? You *don't*. I wasn't looking to be a hero when I headed out to do some fishing the other day. I just didn't want to close my eyes that night and see the image of an old man's brains being blown out. It might not make us buddies, but in a way I *am* responsible. So, yeah, you're free to do what you want, but I feel like..."

"Like what?"

"Like, *damn it*, I didn't risk my neck to save yours just to have you drive off and die anyway. There. I said it. You've got no food, no clean water, nothing that'll keep you alive.

I hear your prayers, you know? But prayers don't put hot chow in your gut. Prayers don't keep you from freezing to death during a blizzard."

"I disagree. God provides what we need."

"I really got no time for platitudes, John. As I was saying, there's no chance of getting to Washington right now. Snow in the Rockies and no gas to buy. So, choice number two is our best bet as it's pretty close by. Problem is it might not actually be *available*. One of the places I used to live at, a rental house on a small lake in Kansas, that's our best bet, but if it's already occupied I'm not sure where to head next. That's where I'm headed, for better or worse. If, along the way, you decide to tail off and head in your own direction, I'll understand. Okay?"

John simply nodded.

With John's RV behind him, Rob got underway, first heading headed west over the Missouri River and briefly into Nebraska, then turned south on Highway 75. Wanting to avoid coming near Interstate 70 and the larger cities, Rob turned west once again, Highway 36, then cut south on Highway 81, almost to their destination. It was nearing dark and dusk. Rob flipped on his headlights.

Up ahead, he could make out some sort of obstruction in the road and took his speed down to twenty miles an hour. Two dark colored sedans each blocked a lane at a forty-five-degree angle. On each hood sat a man dressed head to toe in dark colors. Rob pulled up, still several car lengths away, lowered his side window and stuck his head out.

"Hey! Get the hell out of the road!"

"Stop your vehicle! We're Peace Enforcement Auxiliaries!" the one on the left cried back. "We're authorized by the federal government to search any and all vehicles, persons, and property at our discretion. Shut off your engine and step out of your vehicle!" The speaker hopped off the hood and began walking over. His companion did the same, walking toward the passenger side of the truck and past it, heading for John's RV.

Rob couldn't fail to notice the talker had a handgun in his right hand. He saw now that the pair were wearing card-style badges on lanyards around their necks that were difficult to see clearly in the dark. He killed the engine and stepped out of the truck.

"Look bud, I'm just trying to get home. It's been a long trip. Now, you wanna tell me what this is all about?"

"Keep your hands up where I can see them," the man replied, tone assertive. He looked to be about thirty, with a thin dark mustache and somewhat shaggy hair that touched his collar.

So much for the hair regs.

"I need to see your national ID card. Now."

Rob shrugged. "That? I heard the news about those. Don't have one though, sorry. Heck, where I was it's so remote we didn't have one of those food distribution places within twenty miles."

The man rolled his eyes. "Your state driver's license then. Once we're through here, I'll need to enter your information. After I do that, you'll be required to obtain ID within forty-eight hours, standard procedure."

Rob pulled out his wallet and produced his driver's license. "Who in the hell are you guys anyway? I know Kansas State Patrol and you guys ain't them."

"All you need to know," the uniformed man continued, "is that we're authorized to search for and seize all contraband. You can declare any and save us the time, and we won't rip open every box, bag, and briefcase you have."

Rob heard the door to John's RV creak open behind him. "What are you looking for? If there was an announcement we missed it. We've been without power for a few days now."

The younger man shot him a condescending smile. "It's a pretty short list. Hoarded food and fuel, weapons, ammunition, explosives, narcotics, and bullion. Have any of those?"

Rob's blood went cold. There was no way he was going to let these two take his guns and supplies, official representatives of the government or not. But with a pistol trained in his general direction, and another armed man somewhere behind him, he knew he'd have to wait for the right moment.

"Nothing here."

"*Sure.* Now, put your hands behind your head."

Rob complied, and the officer—Auxiliary?—came around behind him, obviously ready to perform a body search. If he didn't act immediately, Rob would lose the .357 in his coat pocket and with it any realistic chance of defending himself.

Rob lashed out with an elbow to the man's windpipe, striking home and staggering him backward. The brown clad officer raised his pistol, but Rob was already drawing down on him with his .357. Rob fired once, striking the man's stomach, and fired again, hitting him in the chest. Lanyard Man gurgled and crumpled like a rag doll to the asphalt.

Rob spun and saw the second uniformed man emerging from John's RV.

BANG! BANG! Two quick, unaimed shots from the man's pistol sailed completely over Rob's head. Rob brought his left hand up to form a two-handed grip, cocked the hammer, squeezed the trigger, and watched the second man stumble backward and crash into the front of John's vehicle. Rob walked up, still training his own gun on the fallen man, who he now saw had been struck near the heart. Frothy blood emerged from the entrance wound. Still conscious, the second man tried to raise his pistol up once again. Rob fired three more times, emptying his weapon and ending the threat.

A shot from behind whizzed past and to the left. Rob

spun and saw the first man staggering back to his vehicle, firing wildly as he stumbled.

Body armor. Must be. He shoved the empty revolver into his pocket, ran up to his rear driver's side door, and swung it open. Another shot discharged as the window beside Rob's head shattered.

Working quickly, aided by the truck's dome light, Rob unzipped the rifle case on top and slid out his AR. With a press of a button the thermal sight turned on.

Another two shots rang out to no effect. Rob shouldered the stubby rifle and snapped the optic into view. It showed his assailant clearly as a glowing white figure crouched behind the passenger door of his vehicle and shooting one-handed around its edge.

Rob centered the crosshairs on the door itself. The .50 Beowulf cartridge was designed for this sort of thing—extreme momentum and barrier penetration—and he had no doubt it would punch through the door and most likely whatever vest the wannabe cop was wearing. He clicked the selector to "FIRE", pulled the trigger once, grunted with the significant recoil, and to his satisfaction saw the man's arm drop away.

He kept the AR to his shoulder and approached the vehicle. Lanyard Man did not move. Rob went around to the driver's side, put the car in reverse, and watched it head into the far ditch. He repeated the process with the other vehicle and, nodding with satisfaction, approached John's RV.

John emerged, wide-eyed and pale as a ghost. "I . . . I'm starting to question my choice in company. Where you go . . . death . . . seems to follow. Killing police officers? Rob, I think you're mad. I truly think you enjoy this."

Rob looked at him, pained and panting for breath. "No, not at all. I don't enjoy this one bit. And, well, these guys *aren't* cops. I don't know what they are . . . some kind of new fed goons . . . but not cops. Not very professional . . . whatever they are. I wasn't going to let them just take my guns and who knows what else."

"Cold dead fingers, and all that, hmm?"

"Something like that, sure." Rob, involuntarily shaking, went down to a knee. "So, I guess that's it, then. I never said I was a good guy, John. I am going to do what it takes to keep myself alive. If it means doing some unpleasant things . . . so be it. Wouldn't be the first time. So, good luck out there, John. I get the feeling this where we go our own ways."

"I don't know, or want to know, why you did what you did. That's between you and God. I'm not your judge. I know that God put me in your path, and I am going to keep heading down this path until I feel the pull to do otherwise. Clear?"

Rob nodded and stood up, surprised by John's resolve. Rob would have thought he was crazy, too. "Fair enough. I know you're a churchgoing type, John. This . . . probably isn't something you're used to seeing."

"I've seen some pretty awful things in my time, sure. And yes, I am the churchgoing type as you say. Tell me this, though. Back at your lakeside house, I saw those two copies of the Word of God on your bookshelf. Are they there for appearances . . . or do you believe in Christ?"

Rob shook his head. "Those old Bibles belonged to my parents. I don't know why I hang onto them, honestly. Do I believe in those old stories? I've read 'em. Dad was Lutheran and Mom was Catholic. But no . . . to me they're just fairy tales, stories of people who didn't understand their world. No offense."

"None taken. I've been called to share the Good News, not force others to believe in it."

"Y'know, what stuck with me is that Jesus always talked about coming back 'soon.' Well, it's been two thousand years, any way you cut it that's not 'soon.' I get hung up on plenty more than that too, brother. John, if I ever become a Jesus freak, make sure you have warm socks on because Hell just froze over."

CHAPTER TWENTY-THREE

Wednesday, First Week in November

"Don't get on the onramp," Matt blurted.

"W-what? Why not? You wanna get home or not?" Kevin said.

Matt pointed with a finger. "See, up there? Some kind of checkpoint."

"I see it!" cried Abigail from the middle seat. "A guy with a gun. There's another one! Now one of em's looking down at us!"

Kevin kept on driving deeper into Astoria. "What was that about? What are they checking for, way up there?"

Matt shook his head. "I don't know. Maybe it's like that quarantine your friend Gloria mentioned. Or they're looking for someone in particular."

"Oh, you mean the Ebola thing, down in L.A.? I heard about that, on the radio before they all went off the air. Bad juju, man."

"Well, before we go up there we need some answers. Where's that Andy guy live?"

Kevin held up his palm. "No clue, man. I figured we'd just go down to the food handout place and ask around."

It was impossible to not know where to go: the

stream of people was proceeding in one direction, toward the squat hospital at on the eastern end of town.

"I should stay with the truck," Kevin said as they came to a stop. "I already got my whole week of food, back home, y'know?"

"Probably a good idea. The kids can stay here too. This Andy guy," Matt asked, "What did you say his last name is?"

"Peterson."

"Okay. I'll ask around. What's he look like?"

"Hmm. It's been a long time, but back then he had dark hair and a thick mustache. He's what, I dunno, maybe five ten? Pretty solidly built dude, too. My age, I suppose."

"Anything else? Tattoos? Peg leg? Hook hand?"

"Dude, c'mon. He's a *boat guy*, not a *pirate*."

Matt smiled as he headed toward the crowd.

"Attention! I need your attention!" blared a man's voice from up ahead, amplified by a megaphone. "There will be *no* food available for purchase today!"

Immediately shouts and cries rang out from the crowd. "*WHAT?*" screamed a young, dark skinned woman to Matt's left. "What are we supposed to do?"

"Unfortunately, our shipment coming from Portland was hijacked last night. My supervisor informed me this morning it was the work of a local right-wing conservative militia that overwhelmed the security detail and stole several tons of food and other supplies. Please! Keep your eyes open for anyone with a large supply of food! We do have fresh water available. Please line up at the water trailers for your daily ration of one half gallon per person.

A half gallon? That's hardly enough to survive.

"For those willing to make the trip, we will be taking buses to Portland where there is a supply of food for purchase by cardholders. You will be able to return tomorrow. Thank you for your consideration and patience." Boos and insults rippled through the tired, hungry crowd.

"Pfft," the same young woman sputtered. "Just as likely that guy had his buddies take the shipment. Conservative militia? Get real. More like a bunch of nearby rednecks they can blame."

Matt turned to the woman, who had swiveled around and looked as if she was leaving. "Hi, excuse me, I'm looking for a friend of a friend. Andy Peterson, you know him?"

"Huh? Oh, me? No, no one by that name. He live around here?"

"Yeah, last I heard. He's big into boats."

She shook her head. "Nope, doesn't ring a bell. Maybe try down at the marinas? There are two around here, at opposite ends of town. If he has a boat it'll be at one of them."

Matt was pretty much out of ideas. "Well, thanks anyway. Too bad about the food, huh?"

"Too *bad?* Seriously? They've been giving us, what, twelve hundred calories a day? Or less? It's way beyond the 'too bad' stage. Pretty soon, hungry people are gonna turn into dead people."

"What about the buses? Just head over to Portland and get something to eat."

"*That* doesn't make any sense. They can get buses here but not food? What's it take to feed all these people, maybe a couple tons of food? I don't know about you, but I can fit that into six or seven buses pretty easy. No, something's not right. I don't know what they're up to but it doesn't fit. Won't catch me on one of those buses." With that, the woman shook her head and walked away.

The crowd was now boiling away in all directions—toward the military "water buffaloes" stationed to the right side of the field, or the buses to the left along the dead-end street, or just walking away in disgust. Matt shrugged and went back to Kevin's truck.

"No dice on finding your friend," Matt said through the truck's passenger window as he walked up. "I would have asked more people, but there's nearly a riot going on down there."

"Yeah, what happened? Lots of people streamin' out in a hurry."

Matt told Kevin about the announcement. "Dang," Kevin said, deflated. "That's crazy. Conservative militia? What does that even mean, man? Is that even a thing?"

"No idea." Matt tried and failed to seriously envision Kyle and Amber—quite conservative in their political leanings—armed to the teeth and taking down an armed convoy. As the woman in the crowd had also realized, the excuse used by the official didn't fit. While Matt didn't run in those circles, Kyle had assured him in the past that most of those people were pretty much like him and Matt: responsible business owners or employees, no criminal record, married, kids, the typical mainstreamer type. But the main reason Matt couldn't see his brother and sister-in-law doing something like that was the simple fact they'd already accumulated a pile of food and other supplies. Kyle had told Matt in the past that while he was unusually well-prepared—he did *own a survival supply company* after all—most of the people Kyle knew that shared his political and socioeconomic views had *at least* a month or two of food stocked up, especially after the earlier bank hiccups. Why steal, with the risk of death on the line, what you already have in abundance?

"The one person I *did* talk to," Matt went on, "she said to just check the two marinas. You know where they are?"

"Sure, man. There's one right under the bridge." He winced. "Maybe we'll just skip that one for now. The other one's down the road a bit, maybe a half mile. Hop in."

"I'm going to ride in the back. Maybe I'm paranoid, but I'm worried that someone might try to steal the bikes or the packs right out of bed."

"Out of a moving truck?"

"I think things are falling apart around here. Desperate people do stupid things."

Michael Zargona

Luck shone upon them, for once. One of the marina staff, still working despite the crisis, knew Kevin's friend pretty well. Naturally, he was reticent about giving out many details to two nosy Joe Schmoes, showing up and asking questions, but had lightened up when Kevin had provided a solid description and a couple of old stories. It turned out that the guy lived a few miles east of town a few miles, off a side road of Highway 30 that ran along the Columbia River.

The house was a small one-story, yellow with white trim that was streaked brownish-green with old pollen and dirt. Moss covered maples circled the house along the ringed its back. A metallic blue Subaru station wagon was parked in front. Kevin pulled alongside it and killed the engine.

"I hope he's home," Kevin said as he walked up and knocked twice. Matt could just make out a muffled, "Who is it?" from inside.

"Andy! It's Kevin Biemal. Remember me? From Cali!"

The red front door swung open. Matt didn't think he looked much like Kevin had described. This man was clean shaven, gray haired, and thin. He looked the four of them over. If this was Andy, he didn't look particularly excited to get reacquainted. "I see how it is. Guy owes you money, hides for a decade or two, and suddenly pops back up when there's no such thing as money anymore. Your timing *sucks*, Kevin."

"Good to see you too, bro!" Kevin ignored Andy's jab or took it in stride, and embraced him.

"Ooh! Be careful! I'm, ah, a little more fragile than I used to be."

Kevin stepped back. "What's wrong?"

"Let's talk inside."

Matt and the kids followed Kevin into Andy's home. A petite Asian woman of maybe fifty stood in the chilly, unlit living room, decorated in Early Flat Broke American with a plethora of garage sale knick-knacks: a shelf adorned with dusty commemorative shot glasses, lava lamp, outdated entertainment center, and a mounted deer head. along the far wall. "Guests, meet my wife, Yuki." They all shook hands in turn as Matt introduced himself and his young companions.

They took a few minutes to settle in. Yuki broke out a few board games for the kids and they settled on checkers.

"I'd offer you a drink, or something to eat, but there's not much to choose from," Andy said. "River water of course, and we're down to crackers and canned soup. You bring anything with you?"

"Not really, no," Kevin answered.

"So . . . what brings you all out here?" Andy asked. "Kev, you're a long way from home."

"Yeah." Kevin proceeded to give Andy the abridged version of their encounters.

"I saw that roadblock up on the bridge when I went two days ago to get my food allotment," Andy said once Kevin had finished. "I asked one of the local cops about it. Word is, it's some new federal security service, another three-letter group, that's been given carte blanche to search anyone on public property."

"What are they looking for?" Matt asked. He saw Kevin muttering under his breath, looking distracted.

"That was the first thing I asked, too," Andy said. "Cop said that he'd heard they patted down some travelers and then searched their car. They had a gun . . . most people who move around these days have one, but those gray suited federal guys took it with no explanation. They did let them go of course, otherwise we'd have never heard about it. And there are boat patrols too. The guys on the Oregon end of the bridge have radios and act as lookouts."

Matt nodded. Good thing they hadn't risked the checkpoint earlier.

"So, the cops don't even know what these bridge and boat guys are really up to? Like, they're just on their own

227

program?" Kevin asked.

"'Fraid so, bud. Cops are too busy doing their regular jobs during this mayhem to get their shorts in a bunch over some jurisdictional deal. If there's been a public announcement, well, no one has electricity. I've looked down the river at night and it's freaking spooky, let me tell you. I've never seen it that pitch black along the Columbia before. I've heard there are a couple of radio stations broadcasting the government crap but if no one can hear it, who cares? Have you guys been trying to scan and listen in?"

"Naw, not really," Kevin replied. "Just listening to the wind mostly. These three aren't much into my old CDs, man."

"What if I want to get to Washington?" Matt asked Andy. "If the bridges are out, couldn't we just take a boat across? You have one down at the marina, right?"

Andy smiled. "Sure. But I trust my cop buddy and he says not to draw the notice of the guys on the bridge. The river is ten miles wide or more there, really no chance of making it across undetected, and I don't see how I could sneak *Pacific Grace*, that's my boat, this far upriver. And there's the little problem of docking. She's not a rowboat, you just can't run her up on the beach. But yeah, if you need to cross quickly and undetected, well, you'd have to go upriver a bit, and have the right kind of craft."

"So what about tonight? After dark but before the curfew," Matt said. "I don't mean to be rude, but the three of us haven't eaten more than a couple of good meals in several days. I . . . we really just want to get home." Just mentioning food made his stomach pang and groan. "Leave it to me figure out what we'll do from there. If we have to walk, so be it." Matt said it, but he knew that with almost no food left and a hundred miles or so to go, it would take some considerable good providence to get there. He'd already traveled too far with very little to eat, and while the recent respite had been very welcome, Matt could feel his physical and mental performance beginning to degrade.

"The kayaks," Yuki offered, shifting her gaze from the checker game. "We have two nice ones."

"Kayaks would work. I've gone kayaking before," Matt said. "You in one, guiding, and me in the other. Kids and gear riding on top somehow."

"I don't know about that," Andy said, "Ours are both decked singles. A little room for gear but that's about it. And the bikes I saw in the bed of your truck, those for sure aren't going to fit."

Matt frowned. Losing the bikes and their ability to carry gear would hurt their progress for sure. "I just want to get across, it doesn't have to be all that smooth as long as we get there. Lash the gear, put the kids on top, tell them to hang on, and take it slow."

Andy shrugged and looked over at his wife, who just smiled and nodded. "I guess that's worth a try. Let's head out to the shed."

The three men went out the back and Andy keyed the padlock, swinging the double doors wide. "I could use a hand loading up. Used to muscle these suckers on myself. Now, not so much."

"You okay?" Kevin asked. "Man, you used to be my size. You've lost fifty pounds, at least."

"Yeah, well that's what happens when you get your thyroid removed. Cancer, about six years ago. Been taking hormone replacements but I don't do well with them as you can see. The killer beach bod is long gone," Andy said, turning to Matt. "That's how I met this guy," Andy said, turning to Matt. "We were both young and dumb down near Venice Beach, late eighties early nineties timeframe. Bums, basically. Y'know, live out of a van, blaze, girls, surf, do odd jobs in order to eat and buy weed. I found a sugar momma and dropped out of that whole scene. Then, ten plus years later I ran into him at a boat show out in Portland, all straight and respectable. We hung out here and there for a couple of years.

At the time I was having some, ah, financial difficulties. One night, after a few too many I leaned on Kevin here pretty hard for the fifteen hundred he owed... *owes* me and that was that, never saw him again till today. Wasn't shocked, really. I probably would have done the same."

Kevin smiled. "Yeah. You were a good dude, but put some booze in ya, and well..."

They picked up the first kayak, a lime green model that read, "DAGGER" along the sides in white letters. "So, where are you all headed once you get across? Long Beach area?" Andy asked.

"No, quite a bit farther than that," Matt answered. "Hood Canal."

Andy's eyebrows raised slowly. "How much food and water do you have?"

"Virtually none."

"I'm pretty sure there's a distro point, or 'zock' or whatever they're calling them now out in Longview, up the river a ways. Still going to be quite a walk on an empty stomach. Your next spot after that is probably Chehalis. But Kevin said the distro in town here didn't have any food today so... who knows what the best route really is. Let's set this thing down," Andy said, referring to the kayak. "I need to dig out the roof rack. Haven't done this in a while."

"If there's no food it's going to put me in a tight spot with those kids tagging along," Matt remarked as they walked back to the shed. "Down in Cali they offered to let me turn them over to the police. Kaleb and Abigail didn't want to go, obviously, but if it's a choice between that and watching them starve, I'm going to have to cut them loose to the authorities."

After loading up the kayaks, Andy slipped Matt an address in Cathlamet, on the Washington side of the Columbia. "Old friend. Look him up when you get across. He might be able to get you a bit closer to where you're going. Or maybe suggest someone who can."

Matt's mouth watered as he watched Yuki slice cheese and summer sausage by candlelight. Their hosts had forgotten that they had one of the world famous dark red boxes full of meats, cheeses, and jarred condiments most often seen around the holidays; Andy had stumbled across it while digging around for a wetsuit that, to his dismay, was missing.

"So, Matt, we're gonna part ways here in a few," Kevin said after swallowing a cracker with a slice of dill Havarti cheese. "Can I get that gun from you?"

Matt, chewing, motioned with his index finger while he savored his last cracker and sausage covered in Dijon mustard. "Sure thing, Kevin Let me get it." They had brought the packs into the living room earlier, while the bikes had gone into the Peterson's shed and essentially constituted payment for helping them across the river. Matt dug out the rifle, pinned it together, and grabbed the six loaded magazines from the armored vest.

"Hey, that's quite a piece there," Andy said as Matt entered the kitchen. "Where'd ya get it?"

Matt took that as an opening to tell his travel story, starting with leaving the Vasquezes and ending with their encounter with Kevin along 101.

"Man," Andy said. "I can't imagine coming across a shootout scene like that."

"It wasn't the first time I've seen that sort of thing," Matt said. "But I really hope it's the last." He handed the rifle over and Kevin appraised it, aiming it up toward the ceiling and looking through the red dot sight. Kevin held the rifle out in both hands, gesturing for him to take it.

"Yeah, it's nice. Definitely fair payment for taxiing you up here," Andy said.

Kevin looked his old friend in the eyes. "You keep it,

bud. We're square now, okay?"

Matt's eyebrows shot up. *I did not expect that.*

"What?" Andy said, astonished. "I . . . I can't take this! This is worth a fortune right now!"

"We're good, Andy," Kevin said. "The money, fifteen odd years of interest, and part of the last decent meal you've got in your house. We're good."

"I-I don't even know what to do with something like this. This is a long way from the Red Ryder BB gun I had growing up."

Matt smiled. "I'll give you a quick class before we head out."

Twenty minutes later, Matt and the kids said their goodbyes to Kevin Biemal. Matt got the now-familiar feeling of permanent loss, knowing that he'd almost certainly never see him again.

"When this is all over, look me up," Kevin said to Matt as they broke their back-pounding, macho embrace.

"Yeah. I'll do that," Matt said, feigning confidence.

"Good luck out there, lil' scrubs." Kevin added, squeezing each kid in turn.

"Thanks, Kev. You too." Abigail said. Kaleb, the shy type, merely nodded.

They opened their respective doors on the Subaru. Matt peered down. Andy had the AR wedged between the center console and the front passenger seat. Matt furrowed his brow. "You're bringing the rifle?"

"Why not? You and I both know there are crazies about. I can slip it down by my legs in the kayak."

Matt shrugged. "Honestly, I'm not sure what good it will do in total darkness, but okay. It's your baby now, right?"

The drive was brief. "The crossing is really short. Maybe six, seven hundred yards," Andy explained.

"The river is that narrow? Heck, it's wider than that way upstream in eastern Washington."

Andy parked and turned off the engine. "It's because we're not crossing the whole thing. I'm taking you to Puget Island, right in the middle of the river. When we get there, you'll help me tie your kayak to mine so I can tow it back. Head north. There's a bridge into Washington. Don't forget to look up my friend Craig."

Matt frowned. "What if there's a checkpoint like up on the Astoria bridge?"

"I doubt they'll go to all that trouble just for the handful of folks on the island," Andy reasoned. "But if so, you're back in the same situation. Guess you'd have to locate a boat of some kind and wait for dark again."

- - - - -

They unloaded the kayaks and dragged them down near the river's edge. "Remember, you need to be quiet and do exactly what we tell you to do," Matt whispered as he finished snapping the buckles on Kaleb's too-big adult life vest. "Abby, you'll go with Andy, all right? Kaleb, you're with me."

In contrast with his cohorts, Matt had on the tactical vest. With its pair of heavy ceramic plates it was quite the opposite of a flotation device. However, wearing it made the backpack much lighter and easier to manage, and he wasn't particularly worried about the calm waters of the Columbia, even in the dark.

It became clear that there was no good way for the kids to straddle the kayaks without putting their legs calf-deep in the chilly water. Seasoned to foul conditions by now, both took it in stride. Each took off their shoes, rolled up their pant legs, and entered the river. Kaleb slipped his left leg over and hugged Matt as if a passenger on a motorcycle.

The gibbous moon, just now over the low hills to the northeast and under the thin cloud cover, bathed the river in just enough light to make out the far shore and the other kayak. The only sound other than the lapping of their paddles and the occasional dry rustle of a breeze through the mostly-denuded trees behind them was Andy's gulping for breath. Matt, unintentionally, had pulled ahead of his out-of-shape guide as the outline of the shore became visible. Trees grew almost right up against the edge of the water.

Off in the distance, downriver, Matt heard a boat rev hard.

"Something's up!" yelled Andy from about ten yards behind.

"Yeah!" Matt shouted back. "Paddle hard!"

The boat was heading their way. Matt's mind raced as his arms worked to shove the kayak forward. Was there someone spotting on the shore up ahead? *No. Too coincidental.*

Their lime green craft hit the shore with a thud. "Let's go!" Matt yelled to Kaleb as he popped out and unclipped the pack from the rear deck's bungees. Twenty yards downriver, Matt saw the other kayak jerk to a stop by the base of a tall fir tree.

"Stop!" boomed a man's voice through a bullhorn. "Federal Peace Enforcement! Stop and submit to a search!" A spotlight stabbed out from downriver, about a hundred yards away, and quickly found them.

"Run!" Matt yelled, starting for the stand of trees fifty yards inland with his left hand firmly around Kaleb's upper arm.

Two shots rang out, then three more. Matt stopped halfway and turned around only to see Andy outlined by the spotlight and hip-firing the rifle. Abigail was running full-tilt, no pack.

"Run, Andy! Abby, over here!" he cried. He watched as the older man turned to run. Three more shots rang out. Matt could see their muzzle flashes near the stern of the small craft. Andy staggered, went down to a knee, then to both elbows, crying out in pain.

Damn, Matt thought as he ran back toward the fallen

man. The boat would be near shore at any moment. Just outside the spotlight's beam, he drew the Glock and, with a two-handed grip, lined up the weapon's three glowing tritium dots and snapped off three quick shots toward the muzzle flashes on the boat. Return fire buzzed past him as the spotlight shifted.

Andy tried desperately to get to his feet and Matt hauled him upright with his free left hand. Andy mumbled something incoherent as they staggered away.

"You're okay, you hear me? Let's go! If they want us they'll have to come ashore and get us."

Just then, Andy stumbled and fell, the rifle slipping from his hands. Matt holstered the Glock and grabbed the AR from where it had fallen.

Okay, guys, my turn. Matt dropped to a prone position in the wet grass. He kept both eyes open as he peered through the Aimpoint—turned on and ready for use, put the dot on the center of the boat's spotlight, and pulled the trigger. The shot had no visible effect, so he took a more careful squeeze, fired, and was rewarded by the blinding white light blinking out with an audible pop. A muzzle flashed again from the stern, and Matt aimed a foot to the right of the signature and pulled the trigger.

The boat's engine revved and it made a hard turn to starboard, heading back downriver at full throttle. He placed the rifle on safe and looked to his left, toward Andy.

"You all right, Andy?" Matt called. There was no response. He got to his feet and looked down at the man, just a few feet away. He had turned over on to his back, breathing raggedly. Matt knelt down, ran his fingers down the older man's torso, and felt the warm stickiness of blood near his abdomen. In the moonlight, Matt grabbed the man's right hand with his own.

"You're going to be okay, Andy, understand?" Matt said, trying to hide the doubt in his voice. "Let's get up and find someplace to hole up until morning, okay?"

"I . . . I," Andy whispered.

Matt heard soft footsteps and jerked around. It was Abigail and Kaleb, eyes wide. "Don't sneak up on me like that!" Matt said, voice wavering.

"Is Andy . . . is he okay?" Abigail asked.

"He's okay," Matt lied, hiding his bloody hands from their view. "We just need to find some cover in case those guys come back. They don't have a spotlight anymore, but I'm betting they have NODs, or maybe thermals. Only way they could have seen us while we crossed."

"Huh?" Abigail asked.

"They're ways to see in the dark. I'll explain later. Where's my pack?"

"Uh, back there a ways," Kaleb mumbled.

"Andy, I'm going to pick you up, okay?" There was no response, and his breathing had fallen silent. Matt felt for a pulse at his neck; it was very weak. With the post-adrenal crash in effect, it took all of his strength to put the man in a fireman's carry.

"Kaleb, pick up the rifle, and keep your fingers away from the trigger," Matt ordered. "When we get to my pack, you need to carry it," he said to Abigail as they walked.

Once into the stand of trees several hundred yards from shore, Matt, gently as possible, set Andy down next to the trunk of a tall maple and again checked for a pulse. This time there was none.

CHAPTER TWENTY-FOUR

Thursday, First Week in November

Kyle saw the bull's head through his older but quite serviceable ten power Steiner binoculars, at least a four-point rack—by Western reckoning—and shouldered his rifle.

For today's hunt, due to the foul weather and low visibility he'd brought his Marlin. The stubby rifle, with its red dot and close-range hitting power afforded by the cigar-shaped .45/70 cartridge, was perfect for the types of shots he anticipated. If a longer shot was called for, his hunting partner, Timothy, carried Kyle's .308 Vepr clone. Timothy, who quite emphatically did not go by Tim, belonged to the Benson family in cabin #4. He had never hunted before, and two days ago Kyle had agreed to take him along and mentor the young man. Kyle knew he was about to appreciate the boy's strength once the bull was down. Three weeks ago, Timothy had been a senior and playing both sides of the ball, in the trenches, at a small high school outside Olympia. In contrast, God had given Kyle a classic ectomorph body type; great for endurance, but not physically powerful or explosive. Hauling around an adult bull elk required a lot of physical power.

Even though this herd had probably never been hunted extensively—by Kyle's estimation they were right on the edge of Olympic National Park—the animals were plenty smart enough to avoid strange two-legged critters chasing them. Since men on foot would never catch elk moving away from them, Kyle and the other team of two had worked together to get the herd within range.

His opinion of Bill and Mike Klein had improved over the last few days. They'd proven capable hunting partners and had taken a three point buck a few days before. Mike had made a tough 300 yard shot seem pretty easy. After hanging for a couple of days, the deer had been butchered and split up between the lake residents. Trading their former diet of cigarettes, beer, coffee, energy drinks, and fast food for lean meat and fresh water, along with walking up mountains all day meant that both Kleins were getting into some semblance of shape. They weren't nearly as fast cross-country as Kyle and Timothy, but their radio calls to "hold up a bit" had decreased significantly over the last couple of days.

Kyle took a breath, let it out, and with both eyes open put the red dot right at the base of the neck of the bull. It was still looking up, clearly trying to make sense of where exactly these humans were. It wasn't the ideal broadside shot, and if the bullet struck low it would hit right in the rear —a terrible and decidedly unsporting place to hit a game animal. In better times, Kyle might have waited for a better shot.

He slowly squeezed the trigger. The handy rifle bucked hard against his cheek and shoulder as the bullet headed downrange. There was no getting around physics, and the Marlin threw a fat, heavy projectile—twice as heavy as most game rifles, and almost as fast—out of a seven pound package. Kyle saw, to his satisfaction, the big elk go down immediately, falling forward with a soft crash. By reflex he worked the lever and chambered another round. Too many campfire stories told of well-shot animals getting right up and running away. Wordlessly, Kyle and Timothy walked the hundred and fifty yards to the fallen bull.

"I like to say a prayer after taking an animal," Kyle said.

"Seems appropriate."

"Keep your eyes open. Just in case." He paused and bowed his head. "Thank you, God, for the gift of this animal, Your creation, that it may feed us and sustain us. Let it be a blessing, let us never forget that we are Your stewards here on earth, and that it is our responsibility to take only what we need and no more. In Your Son's name, Amen."

"Amen."

"Spine shot," Kyle explained as he pointed to the ragged hole at the base of the bull's neck. "Best place to hit if you can. I won't lie, it was partly luck." Timothy simply nodded, taking it in. "While I want you to learn how to do this, to dress the elk, I really need you to keep watch. Once the Kleins get here you can swap off and I'll show you."

"What am I watching for? Bears and cougars?"

"Those, sure. But I'm more worried about two legged trouble." They were a lot better camouflaged than a regular rifle hunting season—no blaze orange—but the sound of the shot could have attracted unwanted attention. Kyle had known a couple of hunters in good times that had been relieved of their kill by armed thieves. He didn't think it was a stretch to assume this was a lot more prevalent now.

Kyle remembered he'd turned his radio off once spotting the bull and figured it was only polite to let the Kleins know the hard work was about to begin. "Foxtrot One to Kilo Two, come in."

"Uhh, this is Klei . . . Kilo Two. Was that you?" came Mike's reply.

"Sure was. Got the bull. Come on down."

"How big?"

"At least seven hundred on the hoof. Maybe four dressed."

"Got it. Dad's gonna go get the truck."

Bill had been complaining about a chronic bad back and always seemed to avoid the heavy task at hand. Kyle really wanted to give the man the benefit of the doubt, but found that his opinion of the man built and reinforced over the last two decades worked against that.

The bull was easily the second biggest Kyle had ever taken. In normal times, even this far into the hills, Kyle would *cape* the elk—dress it to save the hide for taxidermy—but right now pragmatism was in order. He prepared to debone the animal, taking just the meat and leaving the hide, bones, and offal. There actually was some nutritional value to the bones for soups and such, but that would require him to quarter the bull, and with three men to carry four very heavy pieces, the math didn't add up.

Even with the barely forty degree fall weather, Kyle knew he needed to work quickly or else the meat would start to turn sour and take on that unpleasant "gamey" flavor. He took out six large black garbage bags and with them made three double bags. Then, from his hunting pack he grabbed his folding saw and from his hip he drew his Benchmade skinner knife with a gut hook on the back. Thinking ahead, Kyle got out his ceramic knife sharpener. While the meat wouldn't dull his knife appreciably, the dirty hide certainly would. A few quick strokes with the sharpener here and there would save him a lot of time and aggravation in the long run.

Fortunately, the bull had fallen on his left side, saving Kyle some extra work. He dug right in with the knife, exposing the hindquarter. Next, Kyle cut away the large roast from the thigh, and then collected the lesser cuts; all got piled into the first bag. After twenty minutes of cutting, he moved to the backbone and the highly desirable backstrap meat, cutting along the bone much like fileting a fish. Next came the front quarters—the flank steak and neck meat—and then he turned to the time consuming work of removing carefully removed the meat between each rib without puncturing the gut. Last, for this side, came the heart, liver, and the hard to get to tenderloin under the backbone. Kyle turned the much lighter animal elk over and repeated the meat removal process for the other side. About halfway through, Mike huffed up in full camo, his rifle slung over his shoulder.

"You need some help?"

"No," Kyle replied, bloody up past his elbows. "Almost done. Where's your dad heading? To the end of the logging road, I hope."

"Yeah. I think so."

"Okay. Go and relieve Timothy, then keep watch."

Mike nodded and turned away. Dockworkers like him and his old man were used to simple, direct orders. Even so, sometimes he was too brusque. Kyle had found himself slipping back into his Marine NCO habits and parlance with just about everyone. There just wasn't much time for 'pretty please' with all the hard work to be done. Kyle welcomed the change after four years of polite sales calls and "gosh sorry sir/ma'am it'll ship out tomorrow" mollifying of his customers.

Once finished, he called the two younger men over. "Pick up a bag, carefully, and cradle it or carry it on your shoulder opposite your rifle. Don't throw it over and let it hang, or it will get caught on a branch or something and get torn open. Then you get the fun chore of carrying a pile of dirty, bloody meat in your arms. You'll want to cross-sling your rifles across your backs, nothing like having your rifle fall off your shoulder with your hands full. Muzzles down so the end of the barrel or your front sight doesn't tear the bag." Kyle followed his own advice, took out slack in the Marlin's sling, and put it over his left shoulder.

He'd made them even as possible, each bag holding over a hundred pounds of meat. Bearable for a short distance. "Now, let's hurry back to the lake so we can split this up." The lesser cuts from the ribs and neck would become stew meat or turned into jerky, while the roasts would either get sliced up and smoked or turned into steaks. The wonderful backstrap and tenderloin cuts would be grilled as rare as the lake residents could tolerate. They would all eat well for the next several days.

Especially since, as of yesterday, there were two fewer mouths to feed. The older couple, Rufus and his wife—her name escaped his memory—in cabin #8 had headed back to civilization. Rufus had let Kyle know that she had a heart condition and had been experiencing episodes of chest pain despite her medication. The older man felt their best bet was to head home and try to find a doctor. Kyle had wanted to urge him to reconsider, but the older man already had a pretty good idea of what he might find away from the lake and had weighed that against watching his wife of forty-seven years die while he did nothing. While Kyle didn't agree, he understood.

It was a quiet trudge to Bill's burnt orange Chevy long bed parked right where Kyle had hoped it would be, at the dead end of a logging road just past a two or three-year-old clear cut. They had been alternating trucks over the last several days, but fuel would soon be an issue even with their short jaunts. Kyle had brought six full five-gallon jugs of diesel to Sunshine from home, but was reluctant to start using that stash. If things turned for the worse at the lake, it was just common sense to have enough fuel to hitch up the fifth wheel and leave with their belongings.

Bill got out of the truck and helped his son put his plastic bundle in the bed as Timothy and Kyle did likewise.

"See anything on the road here? More tracks? Evidence of other hunters?" Kyle asked.

Bill shook his head and spat to the side. "No. Just wet dirt."

They made the half hour trek back to the lake along a series of dirt roads. With the heater blowing hard against his exhausted body, Kyle found it impossible to stay awake for the last few miles.

"Kyle, wake up! There's a Jeep parked out in front of your place! And a bunch of strangers!" Timothy yelled, shaking his shoulder.

Kyle shot awake and alert, grabbing for the Marlin. He peered through the windshield and sure enough, there was an old CJ-7 with off-road tires and a large winch up front, painted in safety orange with "RESCUE" in reflective silver decal block letters along both sides of the hood.

And his family—Amber, Isabella, and Cole—stood out by the road with two children he didn't recognize and an older, balding man with a pot belly. Kyle's sister-in-law, Des, was tightly hugging a tall bearded man.

"Matt," Kyle whispered, stunned. "*Matt!*" he yelled with joy as he sprung from the rear driver's side, not bothering to wait for the truck to crawl to a stop. He ran up as Matt and Des broke their embrace, Kyle crashing into his brother with arms wide open.

"You made it!" Kyle said with a wide grin.

"That I did. Just pulled up, actually."

Kyle gave a final slap to the back and stepped back. "Man, you look like, well, you look like *hell*, brother." It was true. Matt's eyes were bloodshot, his hair looked as if he'd worn a wool beanie for a week and pulled it off, and his beard, while not long, looked scraggly. "You've lost a good ten pounds."

"More like twenty," Des corrected.

"Well, let's get inside. We can fry up some grub and you can tell us all about your last few weeks," Kyle said.

Matt shook his head. "While I'm plenty hungry, I have some, ah, business I need to attend to. Kyle, everyone, this is Craig Huntington," he said, motioning to the balding man that Kyle figured owned the Jeep.

Kyle stepped forward and shook the taller man's hand, a firm grip. "Pleased to meet you. You brought my brother here from California?"

"No, just up from Cathlamet. I won't tell his story for him, it's a good one. Not to be rude, everyone, but I really need to hurry home and, ah, attend to a certain matter. Matt, shall we?"

Matt nodded and Kyle watched as they went back to the Jeep and took out two large hiking packs and a smaller bookbag. From the larger pack, Matt removed what was clearly the upper half of an AR-pattern rifle, followed by the lower half. Kyle walked up. "Where did you get *that*? Down in Cali?"

Matt nodded again. "Another long story. Craig, you sure you still want this, even after hearing my story?"

Craig nodded. "Yeah, it needs to go to Yuki. Maybe she can use it to trade for some food."

Kyle tried to get the gist of the discussion but came up blank. "I'm not sure who you're talking about exactly, but if it's food you want I'll trade you some right now for that rifle. We're a little short on high-end guns up here." It was true. Other than the small arsenal Kyle had brought and Greg's guns, there weren't enough. The Kleins had their hunting rifles, Jeanie had her 9mm, and he'd spotted a couple of other residents with handguns on their hips. That was about it. Not surprising, really. Gun ownership, particularly among the sort of white collar people that owned most of the cabins here, had been on the decline for years due to political and social pressure.

"Ahh, bro, you really don't. This rifle is bad luck," Matt said.

"I don't believe in *luck*. You know that. So, Craig, what do you need? Or would you rather have gold? I listen to the radio, I know they're taking in gold and loading up those new orange cards with 'world bucks' or 'bancors' or whatever they're calling them so you can buy more food."

Craig looked at Kyle. "Pfft. Extra food. They never have enough, and then you're just taking what could have gone to someone else. One can in the hand is worth more than two in the FEMA warehouse, I always say. What do you have?"

Kyle thought quickly. They had a few buckets of wheat and both his wife and daughter were sensitive to gluten, making them by far the most disposable of their stockpile. "How about four five-gallon buckets of hard red wheat, two number ten cans of powdered milk, one each of powdered eggs, beans, and mixed vegetables. Plus a fresh elk roast with a cooler to help you transport it back."

"Ahh, sounds like you're one of those survivalist types," Craig said, extending his hand and smiling. "Sounds like a wonderful deal. That's a month of food or more from the distros."

Kyle met his hand and sealed the deal. "I suppose 'survivalist type' is pretty accurate. I prefer 'preparedness-minded' but it's all semantics. You all are welcome to stay the night and head out in the morning, if you'd like."

Craig looked down at the ground. "As I said, I have something I need to see to. Matt can explain. And there's that damn curfew too."

Kyle, Amber, and Timothy brought out the buckets and cans from inside the cabin. "How are we going to do this?" Kyle asked, looking at Craig. "Not much room left with your kids and all."

"Oh, them? They're not mine, oh no. They're traveling with Matt. He's taking care of them."

"*What?*" Des said off to Kyle's left. Definitely her tone of "surprised as heck."

Matt smiled sheepishly. "Yes. I stumbled across them. Well, *actually*, they stumbled across me down in California. Another part of the story."

Kyle glanced over to Des, armed crossed, eyebrow raised. The glow Kyle had seen on the woman just a couple minutes ago had faded. She looked like she was taking this all in. It certainly hadn't fit her script.

Inside, Kyle, Matt, and Des sat at the small kitchen table, sipping purified lake water while Amber chopped and floured the enormous elk heart. The kids—Abigail and Kaleb, Kyle had learned—were being shown around the cabin by Isabella while Cole played with some blocks in the main room.

Kyle could hear his brother's stomach growling. "You sound a tad hungry, bro. Fresh elk heart. Just got him today."

"Sounds fantastic," Matt said. "I'd eat the north half of a southbound skunk right about now. Raw."

"Umm . . . right. I think we can do a bit better than that. Amber, what's on the rest of the menu?"

"I think we'll round out with a rice pilaf and a sprout salad," she said, continuing to slice. "Wish we had some fresh leafy stuff though. Too late to find miner's lettuce up in the hills and still waiting on the greenhouse to produce."

"Nice barricade you put together, Kyle. Took a couple of minutes to convince the old guy on guard that I belong here. I'm assuming that was your idea?"

He was clearly referring to the ad hoc gate they had made using a resident's diesel pickup blocking the main entrance, transmission left in park. The guard on duty had the key and would push the truck aside for legitimate guests.

"No, actually I can't claim that one. Fellow jarhead, Greg Samuels, came up with that idea. Works pretty well. You'll meet him pretty soon, I'm sure."

"You gave up too much for that rifle," Matt said. "A month's worth of food?"

"God brought you back safely, and through His provision I'm able to help those who helped you. It seemed just fine to me. I would have given more if I'd had to."

"Well then . . . thanks. You guys ready for the recap?"

"Let's hear it," Des said.

Matt started at the beginning, going through the trip

up to the Vasquez house and his rather uneventful stay there. Then, the trip in the rental.

"That's a strange scene," Kyle remarked about the description of the shootout.

Matt then went on to describe the walk north and the encounter with Abigail and Kaleb, then the journey with Kevin Biemal.

"I can see why you couldn't just leave them be," Des admitted. "They'd be dead or in police custody right now. But seriously, Matt, we need to find their parents as soon as possible. I'm sure they must be super worried. Plus, well, it's already very crowded here. Plenty of kids to deal with as it is."

"This Kevin character sounds like a real godsend," Kyle said, changing the topic for his brother's sake. Trying to be diplomatic, he did not bring up the fact that his sister-in-law was not exactly a *key contributor* to their ongoing survival efforts. The vulnerable, scared woman who'd arrived a week ago had morphed into an idealist who struggled to pitch in. In Kyle's opinion, she was coping with the assault at her condo by holding to the belief that everything would shortly be back to normal. This belief was preventing her from learning how to contribute and find a useful niche here. "You know, we've all been praying for you, bro. Maybe Kevin was the answer."

"Maybe," Matt replied, pursing his lips. "You ever meet someone who's just trusting and selfless like that? I mean, toward the end I felt like a jerk, hiding a loaded gun from him just in case he went all nightly news on us. It's really strange, but I feel closer to Kevin than a lot of people I've known for years. Y'know, now that I think about it, it's a lot like Afghanistan. There were guys I only knew for a few days there that I'd jump on a grenade for. Same feeling."

"The blood of the covenant is thicker than the water of the womb," Kyle quipped. After a pause, he continued. "That truck you described, with the spare tank, could have driven all the way to Alaska without refueling. Why didn't he drop you off instead of the orange jeep guy ... Craig?"

Matt described the checkpoint in Astoria and their ill-fated river crossing two nights before.

"So, Kevin's friend," Des started.

"Andy."

"Yes. Andy. He ... *died* ... right there? By that tree?"

"Honestly ... probably while I carried him up from the riverbank. It sucked, I didn't want to do it, but we had to leave him there and get moving right away. The three of us crossed the bridge the next morning and walked our way to Craig's place by about noon. We ended up waiting there until he returned from a food handout run out in Longview. Once I introduced myself and broke the news about Andy, we ended up heading out there, wrapped him up in a couple old bedsheets, and went back to Craig's place for the night. That's what he needs to get back there for. He's going to be the one to break the news to Andy's wife, Yuki." Matt lowered his eyes.

"Life is fragile," Kyle said. "We're not promised anything. Don't tear yourself up over what happened. He made the choice to help you out."

Matt shook his head, eyes welling. "I just don't get it! Why did they do that? The government, those police types? Why aren't they out *helping* people? They even stopped handing out food in Astoria, some B.S. about a highjacked shipment that didn't jive. What's going on out there?"

"Listen Matt," Kyle said. "When I'm not on guard, hunting, with my family, or asleep I've been in the trailer listening to the shortwave broadcasts. Some broadcasters are overseas but there are a few here in the States. I imagine they have to move around a lot to avoid the Feds. They're the only real, non-government-controlled mass communication that exists right now. Those guys with lanyard badges? They're part of what's being called the new Peace Enforcement Auxiliary. They're guys off the street who sign a contract to rat out and rob people while wielding the full and absolute power of the federal government. Anything goes as long as they get results. Then there are the guys in gray, Peace Enforcement, an unconstitutional mix of military and federal police glommed together into a domestic fighting force. They're the heavy hitters who come in and deal with the big issues or tough nuts that the Auxiliaries dig up. If they discovered us up here, they'd probably send a platoon of Peace Enforcers to root us up and put us on buses back to civilization—those *zones of control*. Aptly named."

"You're kidding," Matt said, clearly dumbfounded. By now Des had her hand up to her head, looking down at her lap. Kyle's words were a needed reality check to her as well.

"I wish I was. So much has changed in the last three weeks I'll have to dole it out in small chunks or else you won't really believe me. While you've been in Wonderland, dear Alice, a lot has changed in the real world. Welcome back."

PART TWO: REFINED BY FIRE

CHAPTER TWENTY-FIVE

Monday, Third Week in November

The sedan's tires crunched gravel as Lew drove up to the meet house. He'd been here before, five years ago, during his original stint as a driver. Back then, it had been a bigtime lab and waypoint for stolen goods. According to his contact, nothing had changed.

A tall chain link fence surrounded the two or three acre property, topped with shiny razor wire. He'd seen the same setup around sensitive military installations. And prisons. Lew pulled up to the gate, a ten foot high wrought iron affair topped with a bell-shaped wave of decorative —and functional—spear points, and stepped out, surveying the area. A faded plastic "NO TRESPASSING" sign hung from the chain link section directly to the left of the gate.

A small slip of paper tucked under the spare pistol mag in his front left pocket bore the code he'd received to open the gate's combination lock. However, he didn't need it. The gate was closed, the chain remained wrapped around it, but the lock had been neatly cut with something like a high-speed cutting wheel.

"Hmm . . ." Lew's sixth sense tickled. He crouched as he pulled the big .45 from its holster at the small of his

Turn Red Tomorrow

back. He scanned ahead but saw nothing out of the ordinary. The house and its large shed, Lew recalled, were around a wooded bend and out of view. He looked back at the car he'd left idling, considered getting back in and just driving up, and shook his head. If there really was something wrong at the house he'd drive right into it. Lew stepped around to the driver's side and took the key from the ignition.

He jogged up to a nearby cedar, pistol forward and hip-high. After a pause, Lew leapfrogged from tree to tree, making his way within view of the small white single-story house. An old, metallic gray Ford Taurus sedan, flat-tired and covered in a pollen and orange fir needles, rested out front. No other vehicles were in sight—another surprise.

Legit people had the comfort of insurance and filing a police report in the event their valuables were stolen. You couldn't exactly call the 5-0 when your trove of drugs, cash, and stolen property went missing. No one in Lew's circles left *anything* of value unattended. If they did, word would get around and they'd lose it in a heartbeat. Contrary to Hollywood, there existed no honor among thieves. If you were weak, you were toast. End of story.

He advanced to the house, slowly, his weapon extended straight out from his chest. Nothing moved but the occasional breeze rustling the nearby plants. The front door sat cracked open slightly. Lew felt goosebumps form on the back of his neck as blood pounded in his ears. His vision started to narrow, centered on the door.

Just leave...

No. He was here to make a delivery. If he left, and it turned out the guys had just gone into town for food or some fun, Lew would be branded a coward or worse. No set had use for a driver that chickened out at the first sign of something unusual.

Except there'd been about a half dozen signs.

He nudged the door open, keeping the big auto pointed straight ahead, finger on the trigger. The only illu-

253

mination came through curtained windows that barely let in the late fall Pacific Northwest sunlight, even weaker with dusk approaching. Lew's young eyes adapted quickly as he stepped left into the living room.

"Whoa," he whispered sharply, taking in a breath. Two men were sitting up on the couch, their heads flopped to the side. Both men had been shot at close range. Congealing blood covered the man on the right, the result of a neck shot, while the one on the left, a stocky man with a thick, dark beard, sported only a clean hole in the middle of his forehead.

Lew felt the bile rise in his throat and stifled a gag. Six years running with a brutal gang and he'd never seen a dead man face-to-face before. Well, except maybe for Donny, but that hadn't made him sick at all.

There was no sign of a gunfight. No brass or guns strewn about. Most places like this had guns in every nook and cranny and were very hard to take by complete surprise.

Inside job. Happened from time to time. Some disagreement? Or a calculated plan to take over. No, trusted insiders and customers wouldn't need to cut the lock. *Something doesn't add up.*

Gravel crunched and then Lew heard the back to back slam of two car doors. He peered through the crack between the grimy orange drapes. He couldn't see anything.

Two men came into view on the road, walking slowly, weapons at the ready. *Of course.* They would have encountered his car blocking the gate. The one on the right —tall, bushy-bearded, and barrel chested—wore mirrored aviator sunglasses and a brown shirt with camo sleeves and sewn-in elbow protectors, the kind Lew had seen the war vets wear from time to time. He scanned ahead using smooth, precise movements with a tan bullpup carbine against his shoulder. The man on the left, wearing a plaid jacket and walking a step or two behind his partner, was older with a beer belly, mustache, and sharp beard—sort of an unkempt Vandyke style. He carried a pump shotgun, waving it back and forth, a lazy, untrained facsimile of the younger man.

Time to go.

Lew rose and made his way to the back of the house, hoping there was a back door of some kind. He passed through the kitchen and slipped, just catching the edge of the countertop with his free left hand.

Blood. In the dim light, another man lay on the floor in a puddle. His left eye, gray-blue, stared up sightlessly.

A dirty sliding glass door led out to a small deck. Lew tugged hard but the door only moved an inch. An inch-thick wooden dowel—a *ghetto lock*—was blocking the track. Behind him, the front door creaked open and slow steps clicked on the linoleum entryway.

Lew grabbed the dowel, cast it aside, hurled the door to the side and leaped through. Someone shouted. He could *feel* the rifle sighting in on his back. Lew was no great athlete, but his long strides fueled by adrenaline got him out of the open backyard and into the trees in no time.

Someone fired twice, quickly, then twice again after a pause. One struck close; Lew heard the sharp snap of the bullet pass by his left ear as he crashed through the bushes. Up ahead was a tangle of blackberries and nettles. Lew planted his left foot to shift direction, took another long step, and felt his right foot catch an exposed root. He flew forward, hands extended, and crashed headfirst into a dark, spiky bush.

"Stop!" The angry yell was way too close for comfort. Lew collected himself and pulled away from the bush, its branches scraping his arms, face, and neck. His pistol was gone. He had neither time nor a flashlight to find it. Lew groaned and started pumping his legs again, hoping his heavily-laden pursuers would simply give up.

Lew ran alongside a barely visible river, as fast as he could manage, for twenty or thirty minutes, looking back

Michael Zargona

every so often for signs of pursuit. It was highly likely the men had given up and gone back for their vehicle by now. He needed a place to hide. Lungs burning and throat dry, he stumbled up to the nearest building in an industrial park, a long row of glass fronts and doors and approached the first one. Its door hung wide open to darkness within. The small metal sign above, just visible in the moonlight, read, "Bene Praepara Supply, Inc."

    Lew groaned as he awoke—stiff, sore, and enormously thirsty—into near complete darkness. He realized that he'd wandered into a warehouse of some kind, and light was coming in from underneath a big sliding door at the back of the room. Standing, Lew took stock of his situation. In his right front pocket, he had keys to a car that had, by now, either been roughly jerked out of the road with a winch or simply placed in neutral and pushed into the ditch. In his left pocket sat a fully loaded magazine to a handgun that currently resided in a bush a couple miles or more away. His back pocket, thankfully, still held his wallet, which contained his only item of real value: his new National ID card. Other than a few minor scratches and bruises, Lew was unharmed by yesterday's incident back at the meet house.

    He considered heading back toward the house to search for his weapon. Lew felt naked without the .45, and if he was going to get back to his guys, he'd have to take a car from someone. Everyone had a twitchy trigger finger these days. An unarmed thief would probably end up a dead thief pretty quick.

    He thought of his situation and groaned. Lew had lost a good car, whatever was in the trunk, and hadn't made the pickup. His relationship and standing within his set was already sketchy and they knew quite well he had only looked them up because he'd lacked any other options. To them, he was a bottom of the totem pole foot soldier, a know-nothing delivery boy who'd cast aside his loyalty and had made a failed attempt to go legit. AKA a retread, a loser. At best, they'd make him pay for yesterday. He'd have to get his account back to zero the hard way. At worst, he'd end up like those two on the couch as an example of what happens to people who don't get the job done.

Lew stumbled outside into gray light that barely penetrated the thick cloud cover. He had no idea where the local ZOC was, but he knew that north led back to trouble. So he headed south along the river. It wasn't long before he saw the telltale signs: bicycles, people pulling wagons, others pushing shopping carts, or simply on foot heading in the same direction. Lew nodded, thankful to no one in particular that he'd chosen well.

The distro point here was at a local high school next to a football field. The crowd was at least three or four thousand, bigger by far than any Lew had seen at a ZOC. Where yellow school buses would normally park to disgorge children there were several newer, sleeker white buses, similar to the ones used by tour groups, with heavily tinted Plexiglas windows. The new gray-suited cops were everywhere: on foot, standing in truck beds, and on the roof of the school.

His eyes caught something that he hadn't seen before. Along with the graysuits were several pairs of guys wandering around in regular clothes, but with highly visible brown badges dangling from their necks. They weren't carrying rifles or orange-stocked nonlethal shotguns like the graysuits. He watched as a pair of the brown badge guys roughly escorted an older man toward a group of graysuits, had a short conversation, and made their way back into the crowd, tucking their badges into their shirts. Lew checked the long lines for food and picked the one he hoped moved the fastest.

"I'm going to need you to report to Peace Enforcement," came a deep male voice. Lew had let his mind wan-

Michael Zargona

der, still dazed from the events of the last twenty-four hours. He looked around and realized that it was the FEMA employee speaking to the short, middle aged woman directly in front of Lew and first in line.

"W-what? Why?" she replied, clearly afraid.

"Says here you're a medical professional?" Lew gazed over the woman's shoulder, easy as he towered over her by a foot or more. The FEMA worker, bald and heavyset, was looking at his tablet and tapping at the screen with pudgy fingers.

"Yes, I'm a registered nurse. Or, at least, I *was*. Why? Is that important?"

"Ma'am, the federal government is authorized to employ civilians with needed skills during this crisis. As I'm sure you can imagine, we're desperately short of experienced medical personnel."

"But . . . I have a *family*. Are you saying I have to drop everything and go with those troopers there? Just like that?"

"I really can't go into much detail here, ma'am. There are people waiting behind you." At that moment, the FEMA worker raised his chins and pointed at the woman in front of Lew. Two men in regular clothes but with those hanging badges he'd seen earlier grabbed the woman who, by reflex, pulled back in surprise. They tightened their grip and led her away to Lew's right. Lew shrugged. He knew there was zero chance he'd be led away like that. He simply didn't have any skills the government would care about. They already seemed to have plenty of trigger pullers and guys who could work a steering wheel.

His small bag of food now in hand, Lew scanned the crowd for the two men who'd led the nurse away. They obviously had already turned her over as they stood side by side, scanning the assemblage.

Lew made his way over to them. He knew it was a risk, but he needed to sate his curiosity. "What are you guys supposed to be? Undercover?"

The taller of the pair turned and sized Lew up with a quick up-down-up glance. He wasn't unarmed as Lew had previously thought; a pistol was holstered on the man's hip. He had a large mole on his left cheek.

"You serious? Peace Enforcement Auxiliary. Where've you been?"

"You guys like, security muscle then? I saw you lead that woman away."

The shorter man, older than his partner, snorted. "Hell no! We've got the best job in America right now. Find the troublemakers or those under warrant to report for federal service, turn them in, get paid. Hoarders, people who refuse to get ID, curfew breakers, you name it."

"Get paid? Who cares? I've been to at least ten of these distro points. There's nothing to buy but rice and noodles."

Another snort. "Pfft. Maybe for everyone else." Mole Man furrowed his brow, staring at Lew. "You seem pretty keen on asking us a lot of questions. You trying to distract us?"

"Uh... no?"

"Sure. Why don't you step over here and put your hands along the hood of this car, hmm?"

Lew was stunned, but eying that pistol and the serious look on both men's faces, he swallowed his pride and complied. Not a second into the patdown and Mole Man recoiled back. "What you got in your pocket there?"

"Oh. That. It's a clip. Pistol's gone though. I lost it yesterday."

"Sure you did," the shorter man, Snorty, shot back. Lew now saw a small pistol in his hand. "Come with us. Someone I'd like you to talk with."

Lew shrugged. Other than death or torture, there wasn't much they could do to worsen his situation.

The pair led him up to a camouflage-painted Humvee, military style with a machinegun mounted up top and a young, bored-looking graysuit slumped behind it. Another graysuit was by the driver's door, wearing gold-rimmed sunglasses and picking his teeth with a toothpick. This one was older, maybe forty, with a thin black mustache cropped at the edges. A golden lump of some kind was sewn in the middle of his chest. Lew read the name tape above his right chest pocket: Nicoloro.

"This guy was asking us a lot of questions, and he'd got a pistol clip in his pocket, man," Snorty said.

"It's called a *magazine*, nimrod," said Nicoloro, shaking his head. "And . . . I know you guys have been doing this for, what, *a week*, but you will refer to me as *Major* or *Sir*. Not *man, dude,* or *bro*. Understood?" The younger pair nodded.

"So, did you do a complete search? See and confirm his ID? All that? Y'know, your jobs?"

"Uh, no . . . sir," Snorty replied. "We didn't know if he had a weapon or not."

"One of you *covers him* with your weapon," Nicoloro replied, pantomiming with his index finger pointed out, "while the other performs a *search*. You want to finish that little step for me?"

Snorty continued to train his pistol on Lew, who raised his arms above his head without prompting. "You got ID?"

"Yeah, sure. Back pocket."

Mole fished out Lew's wallet, then his orange ID. Lew watched out of the corner of his eye as the man swiped the ID across a small cellphone-like device.

"Put your thumb here," Mole ordered, pointing toward the screen. Lew once again complied and the screen lit up with a green bar across the top.

"Good to go," Mole said. "Now, pull out that, uh, *magazine*, and hand it over."

"It won't do any good," Lew said, handing it to Mole. "Gun's up in the woods somewhere. Lost it in the dark."

"Not interested in your story." Nicoloro raised his non-toothpick hand. "Transport of arms, ammunition, explosives, or other contraband is illegal until the cessation of the current national emergency. Gents, I believe simple confiscation is in order." Nicoloro reached into a pocket of his vest and produced a device that looked identical to the one that had scanned Lew's ID. He tapped on its screen for about fifteen seconds. "There. I've credited you both for this little event. Now . . . push off from my shore here and go fish some more."

Lew watched as the two walked away, back into the throng. "Uh, sir? What about me? Am I free to go?" Lew had played the game enough with cops. Eventually, unless they put you in handcuffs, they had to let you go on your way.

"What about you? Go get in line and get your food allotment. That's what you're here for, right?"

The food. Left it on the hood of the car. Almost certainly gone now. "Ah, yeah, sure. I mean . . . sir. What's the deal with those guys anyway? I mean, are they looking for more people? Hiring?"

Nicoloro chuckled. "They put their hands on you, take your stuff, and that makes you want to join their little brown badge club? You on drugs?"

Lew licked his dry lips. "No. Sir. It's just that, I'm, ah, a little short on options right now. Ya see –"

"Spare me. It's a pretty simple arrangement with those Auxiliary window licker clowns. Guys like me, Peace Enforcement," he explained, tapping a patch on his right shoulder, "we're federal employees. We get paid, we get fed, we get our boo boos fixed, no matter what. The Auxiliaries are contract workers. They're paid by commission and they have a quota to meet. Don't meet the quota, they lose their badge and revert to a regular schlub. Like you."

"Quota? For what?"

"They're authorized to search anyone, anytime, outside of their home. On foot, car, boat, airplane, Space Shuttle, doesn't matter. They find contraband and turn it in, they get credit. They find someone out and about without an

NID, they lead 'em to a ZOC and hand them over to us. They find someone holed up with a bunch of weapons, or hoarding food, that sort of thing, they call us and we take care of them."

"What's the badge get you? More food?"

"That, and you're authorized to be armed. No curfew—part of the job is to find curfew breakers. Access to fuel if you have a vehicle. Other perks that you'll find out along the way. Now, I've got things to do. If you want to join their merry band of morons, go chat with the guys by the truck over there."

Lew walked over.

CHAPTER TWENTY-SIX

Friday, Third Week in November

The canvas-topped truck lumbered south on MLK. Lieutenant Marshall Cross sniffed at the familiar mix of diesel exhaust, weapon lubricant, and that peculiar sweat-stink of exertion and fear. Except for the temperature—low 40s in Chicago today—it could have been Iraq during any of his three tours there.

He tugged at his M4 carbine's thirty round magazine, making certain it was secure and locked. This particular rifle had seen a lot of hard use in its life, none by Cross himself. The old days of a junior officer being issued only a pistol had clearly come to a close. It didn't provide enough firepower and just made the carrier stick out from the crowd. Any smart enemy marksman would look to plug the one waving a handgun and barking orders first.

Cross's Direct Action Team—the familiar term "platoon" was strictly *verboten*—was on its way for some payback and to recover stolen goods. The nearby ZOC had, until yesterday, been manned by a unit of Illinois National Guard converted to Peace Enforcers in the first wave, a pencil-pusher unit from the middle of the state somewhere. Cross had learned that Peace Enforcement units all wore the same gray but fell into three broad categories. First, there were the actual law enforcement types, generally former federal service people augmented by local yokel cops who didn't seem to mind squeezing their neighbors with *de facto* martial law. You didn't see them in mass concentrations much. Then, the glorified security guard units glommed together from reservists, retirees, and others who had no or very little police or combat training. They got tasked with protecting ZOCs, federal installations, and infrastructure locations like water purification facilities and nuclear power plants. Then came the hammers—the Direct Action Teams or DATs—assigned to supply military solutions to military problems and circumvent that whole pesky *Posse Comitatus* deal. Naturally these were comprised primarily of converted active duty Marine Corps and Army combat arms personnel.

That administrative unit turned security force had been forty strong, with two older hardback Humvees with M240 belt-fed machineguns mounted. Pretty standard for an urban ZOC. Three days ago, there had been a minor riot as the distro had run out of food early and several locals had been killed in the fray. Cross and DAT-63(A) had been pulled off a low-level sweep and clear detail to reinforce the ZOC security but had arrived too late to prevent the carnage.

He'd chatted with several of them as they cleared the area and tried to clean things up. They were good people, although way out of their element. A month ago they had been schoolteachers, construction workers, baristas, and file clerks who wore green one weekend a month and two weeks in the summer.

Most likely they were now all dead.

His mind turned to the briefing earlier that morning. After the food riot, a couple of local gangs had teamed up and returned two days later, just as the Peace Enforcement crew had shown up with the other federal workers. Eighty or ninety strong, they had taken out the machine gunners with surprisingly effective sniper fire from the surrounding buildings, then moved in on the flat-footed Enforcers, whose better weapons could not overcome their disadvantage in numbers and attitude. The gangbangers had stripped them of their weapons and carted off several prisoners; by eyewitness accounts the surviving female members of the crew. Inside an open fenced area devoid of hiding places, all other Peace Enforcers had been shot. The federal employees handling distribution and NIDs were spared but, as expected, the food stocks had been taken. The operation had been quick, vicious, and highly successful. Cross thought of it as nothing less than that, a well-planned and executed operation; he'd come across plenty of "former" gang members in his time in uniform, and it followed that many had linked back up and added Uncle Sam's training to the streets.

"I still can't believe it," came a voice to his left. "People dying to get MREs. Not even the real deal. Cheap FEMA lowest bidder crap."

"Yeah," answered another. "My old man was in Somalia. He said the skinnies there were killing one another over sacks of flour. I bet he never thought that would happen here."

Cross couldn't put names to the voices. They may have been Marines from his old regiment or another unit at Lejeune. Or Army from Fort Bragg or maybe Fort Campbell. His DAT and others had been formed from a common pool assembled at Fort Knox just over a week ago and sent off to their assignments. Cross and his men had drawn Chicago along with nineteen other DATs that all reported directly to a Department of Homeland Security regional director. To some, it sounded like a lot, but twenty DATs of twenty men each wasn't nearly enough to control a city of millions coming apart at the seams.

"Back when I was with, I . . ." began the first Enforcer, trailing off as the older, bearded man across from Cross glared.

Lieutenant Preston was their assigned DHS liaison.

Technically, Lieutenant Cross was in charge of the team, but in reality anything and everything could be overruled by Preston, a man with no military experience. They had all been specifically instructed by Preston to not discuss their prior service. Wiping the slate clean as it were. To Cross, he was no different from a political officer—a Soviet-style commissar—assigned to babysit his crew to ensure compliance with all directives.

Military units, Cross reasoned, were comprised of men more loyal to each other than to higher command, which scared the eggheads and planners. Established ones were unpredictable. Those made up of strangers, while far less effective in the field, were easier to manage from above. They had no competing loyalties and were a lot more likely to perform within SOPs—Standard Operating Procedures—because they didn't bring along their own way of doing things.

Cross was accustomed to having civilians around during combat operations. On his second tour in Iraq, there had been an embedded reporter with his platoon. But the reporter hadn't carried a weapon, nor did he ever imagine he had the power to countermand orders. So far, he and Preston had not butted heads, but Cross knew that time would inevitably come.

Today's mission was not to find all of yesterday's assailants. It was ludicrous to imagine that they would let Cross and his nineteen team members—he refused to count the tactically useless Preston—dictate a pitched battle on their own turf and duke it out toe-to-toe. The thugs had no ideology beyond their own skins and, whether by commission or by accident held quite well to the tenets of guerilla warfare. Seek out soft targets and run from the hard ones. And, while flawed, DAT-63(A) was pretty hard. Cross had arranged each of the two squads of nine more along Marine Corps lines, something Preston had frowned at on principle alone. Besides the squad leader, there were two fire teams comprised of a point man with an M4, a light machine gunner armed with a SAW, an assistant machine gunner who carried an M4 along with additional ammunition and spare barrel for the SAW, and a fire team leader with yet another M4—this one with a M320 grenade launcher attached underneath the barrel. Ordinarily, they carried a lot of 40mm tear gas grenades but today it was nearly all of the high explosive variety. In addition to the launchers, there were plenty of regular hand grenades. Each man wore soft ballistic armor augmented by hard plates across the chest, back, and sides, along with a four-point harness ballistic helmet bearing attachments for communications and night vision devices. Neither device was present nor available due to a chronic supply chain problem, which could prove problematic in unlit projects and dilapidated apartments. Hopefully, their tip from the Auxiliaries regarding the location of the stolen food would open up some new leads and allow them to send a message to the punks here on the South Side.

The truck lurched to a stop and Cross motioned for the men to pile out.

"I'll be here with the truck," said Preston. "Route anything through me."

Marshall nodded and turned away. Not having the ability to talk to higher command was a new experience for him. Other than a busy DHS director (who probably did not know Cross's name) he had no one to report to. Within the DAT, Cross alone had one of the precious new FEMA multiuse phones and the only number he had went to Preston. It used the old cellular network when available, and PTT trunked and encrypted VHF freqs when it wasn't. The phone also tracked his location and could ping for nearby NIDs using their embedded RFID chips. This was a roundabout way to keep track of his team since they didn't have comms of their own.

"Okay, listen up," Lieutenant Cross began, his small-town Oklahoma accent purposely slipping through. "You were all there for the briefing so this is just for y'all that struggle with short term memory loss." That garnered a couple of chuckles. "Squad leaders, stay with your number one fire teams. I'll be with First Squad's number two and Sergeant Abernathy will attach to Second Squad's." Abernathy was technically the "Assistant Team Leader" but Cross reflexively thought of him as a platoon sergeant. "Since the powers that be have elected to *not* give each of you a radio, stick close and make sure I know where you're at. You run down a rabbit hole and don't tell me, that's on you. Anyone not in PE gray in the building is someone we want to round up and take back. Remember your ROEs. No 'recon by fire.' Identify all targets and only pull the trigger if clearly hostile. Anything you put downrange, you own it. If you locate the FEMA rations and other stolen goods, just give a shout. The warehouse isn't that big, I'll hear you. If you do get lost, separated, or whatever, just get back to the truck. This is the rally point. Got it?"

The men started to split up and Cross locked onto Corporal Reyes, the fire team leader he'd be with. "Corporal! You ready to roll?"

"Yessir," Reyes replied, his eyes shifty.

"Man, this is wild," said Reyes' scout, a private whose name escaped Cross. With their nametapes covered up by their armor and vests, he struggled to remember the names of the troops he'd been leading for just over a week. "Pull up to some dirty old furniture warehouse, hop out, sweep for bad guys, get the package, extract. It's like one of those video game missions."

"Yeah, sure Cables," Reyes shot back. "'Cept when you take one through the brain bucket there's no reset button, *pendejo*."

"Naw, Corporal," Cables replied. "That's the *ultimate* reset button. Am I right or what?"

Reyes spat on the asphalt. "Whatever. So, sir . . . are you taking over my fire team for this one?"

"No, Corporal. I'll have plenty to do on my own. If something happens to me, make sure you grab that DHS phone, got it? You'll need to relay regular updates to *Lieutenant* Preston."

"Will do, sir."

Per the earlier briefing, a squad approached on either side of the unnervingly silent street. They hugged the walls of empty storefronts and warehouses similar to the one they were targeting. The destination building was old, with gray lead-based paint peeling in all directions along its front face. Two bay doors gaped open to the world. That gave Cross pause. If the bad guys were hiding valuables, he imagined they'd button up tight.

The street resembled far too many others in Chicago these days. On the left sat an abandoned shopping cart half-full of black plastic bags. On the right lay the remains of a sedan. Every bit of glass was smashed in and the body panels were all heavily dented. By the car lay a dead dog, a couple of weeks gone by the look of it.

Cross motioned for the first of the four fire teams to advance up to the door on the right, then pointed for the team ahead of him to take the door on the left. Both teams stacked by the door, the scouts peeking inside.

"Well?" Cross demanded.

"Nothing here, sir," said the scout on the left. The man on the right simply shook his head.

"Okay," Cross said in a low voice. "First squad, first fire team, you're up. Fan out and seek cover." He watched as they scooted into the building, weapons up and ready. Even if they lacked familiarity with one another they definitely looked the part. Cross nodded at the next team and repeated the process for the remaining two.

He peered down at his FEMA phone, set to ping the area for any NIDs not belonging to his team. It came up with nothing. "Shine some light out there." Several beams of light sprang into view as his men turned on their weapon mounted lights.

The warehouse did not contain any missing food stocks. It was empty except for the steel shelving units his men were hiding behind. Toward the other end was a more open area, but it too was bare. Cross frowned. Given the time lag—over a day—he never had high hopes they would find much, but to find absolutely nothing was... disappointing.

"Hey, sir, there's some stuff in the corner up there." It was Reyes, directly to his left. Cross peered ahead and saw a couple of tables, some boxes, four chairs, and two bundles of fabric or clothing.

"Listen up," Cross said, just loud enough for everyone to hear. "My fire team will investigate while you all keep an eye out. Sergeant Abernathy, you and your fire team watch our six. Got it?"

Abernathy's men nodded. Cross watched as they bounded ahead silently, their flashlight beams sweeping back and forth at the darkness.

Cross walked up to the tables. On the first one was a pile of NIDs, maybe a hundred or more, all neatly sliced about a third of the way in from the left side. Right through the RFID chip. Most were civilian orange but there were a few federal blue and Peace Enforcement gray pieces in the pile.

Corporal Reyes was right behind him. "Oh. Why would someone slice 'em up like that?"

Cross picked up the larger piece of an orange card with his free left hand. The name was truncated and read: "-la Denise Williams."

"Whoever did it knew what they were doing, cutting through the chip and all." Cross started to imagine where the owners of these cards were and stopped. It was not a good rabbit hole to follow, even hypothetically.

"Think some of them are the missing troops from the ZOC detail?" Reyes asked.

"Hey!" Cables shouted, much too loudly. "There's uniforms here in this box!"

Cross and Reyes walked over as Cables held up a gray shirt. On the right breast was the nametape: Rodderick, rank of private first class. Dried blood on the left shoulder had run down the sleeve to the elbow.

"Anyone by the name of Rodderick with that crew?" Reyes asked.

"I'll pull up the briefing on the phone, one second," Cross said. He read down the list of those still missing or unaccounted for from the ZOC detail:

1LT FELICIA R. SWENSON
2LT JAMIE A. MARRIOTA
SGT JENNIFER D. DENNING
SGT GWENDOLYN T. KATO
CPL MELISSA B. RODRIGUES
CPL TAMARA S. HESS
PFC CASSANDRA G. RODDERICK

"Yes, she's on the list. How about these others?" Cross showed the other men the screen. In less than three minutes, they found uniform shirts for all except Lt. Marriota.

Cross swung the flashlight to the chairs. All four had dried blood along the top edge and near the rear of the seat. He conjectured that people had been bound to each one but no ropes or bindings were present.

"This is messed up," Cables said in a disgusted tone. "Where in the hell are they? They stripped them down. Did they..." His voice trailed off, likely coming to the same conclusion Cross had a few minutes before.

Cross motioned toward the back of the building. "Let's not try and piece this together just yet. We need to check out what's beyond the back door."

The pair advanced, muzzles up. Reyes tried the door. "Locked, sir."

"Step back, Corporal." Cross took two quick steps forward and kicked the flimsy interior door just below the doorknob. It broke completely away from the knob and deadbolt, swinging open into darkness.

A short hallway ended in what looked like a metal exterior door. There were four interior doors, two on each side.

"Let's get to it." He opened the first three doors, which were empty. He tried the fourth and his breath caught in his throat.

A young woman, head slumped, hung from the ceiling by her wrists. She wore a white T-shirt and gray Enforcer trousers.

"What the—" Reyes blurted.

Cross put his left index finger to his lips. He walked over and felt her neck. It was warm and he could just feel a faint pulse. Putting his cheek up, he could just feel breath moving through her chapped and bloody lips. "Corporal, cut her loose. I'll hold her, make sure she doesn't fall."

The mood immediately changed with his team as they carried her out into the warehouse. The mission wasn't a complete bust.

"Let's have her sit down, maybe tell us what happened," Reyes suggested.

"No. That's not our job. Sergeant Abernathy! Still all clear?"

"Yes, sir!"

A faint whisper. "*Who...*"

"We're here to get you out of here," Cross said. "Don't exert yourself."

"*Water...*"

Now it did make more sense to have her sit down. They carefully set her into one of the metal chairs. Cross took off his own hydration pack, opened the valve, and put it to her lips. She sipped slowly for about a minute.

"Lieutenant Marriota?" Cross asked.

The woman finally opened her eyes, looked up, and nodded.

There was much he wanted to ask. But his train of

thought was interrupted by an eruption of gunfire outside. Several long bursts rattled off, some striking the walls of the warehouse. Abernathy and Second Squad returned fire.

Looks like I was wrong about the gangbangers . . . guess they do want to mix it up.

"Team! Fall back to the truck! First Squad, second fire team on me! Get her clear!"

Cables and Reyes helped the still extremely weak Marriota to her feet. Behind them, Cross heard the back door creak open.

Thunk. Something hit the concrete floor and rolled to a stop. A very familiar, sharp scent hit his nostrils.

"*Gas gas gas!*" Cross yelled, muscle memory causing him to slap at his left side for his M50 case.

Which wasn't there, since DATs weren't issued CBRN gear.

Marshall Cross had experienced tear gas in his eyes, throat, and lungs as much as any man alive. It was not something to which one could build a physical resistance, only mental coping techniques. His eyes began to water as he shouted, "Out out out!"

More gunfire rang out. Cross brought his M4 up and fired a pair of three round bursts into the broken back door.

Mouth closed and lungs empty, he watched as his men quickly carried Marriota out. Eyes burning, he searched for anyone on his team with the issued phone. Nothing. Satisfied and nearly out of oxygen, he dashed for the main doors.

As he reached the doorways and fresh air Cross inhaled deeply.

A cough to his left. "Over here, sir!" It was Reyes.

There was a *thump* followed immediately by an ear splitting explosion, then more automatic weapons fire.

"Will *someone* give me a doggone SITREP?" Cross called, still clearing his vision.

"Sir . . . it's the gangers! Well frickin' armed too," Sergeant Abernathy said.

"Well don't let 'em just pin us down. Second Squad! Bound to the corner! First Squad, cover!"

Their bound was hampered by their newest addition and the other fire team's scout, who was recovering from taking a round off his chest plate. Once in place, Second Squad started to lay down fire at anything that moved or flashed in front of them.

A blue car rounded the corner and sped their way. Up through the sunroof stood a man in a white T-shirt, shouldering a tube.

Rocket.

"Priority! Light that car up!" Cross called as he brought his rifle up. Tracers from their two SAWs converged, peppering the vehicle. It swerved to the right and slammed into a building on the far side of the street.

"Let's go, First Squad! Bound!"

They bounded back to the rendezvous truck, opposition melting away. A couple of potshots missed his men.

"Where's the truck?" one of the lead men yelled.

Cross looked back and forth. There was no sign of it.

"Lieutenant! Over here!"

Cross bounded toward the source of the shout. In the alley lay a bearded man in Forcer gray.

Preston.

"He alive?" Cross asked flatly.

"No, sir," said the man from First Squad kneeling by him.

"Well, damn. I'll hop on the phone and get us a ride back. Doubt we'll ever see that truck again."

CHAPTER TWENTY-SEVEN

Monday, Fourth Week in November

They attacked in the morning, around breakfast time. Loren Pearce heard the now-foreign growl of several engines followed soon after by gunshots just outside the double wide. Then, the screams.

She shared the small room at the end of the house with her infant nephew, Max. Loren, her sister Cassie, Mom, and Max had all escaped from nearby Bremerton—a working-class and military town across the Sound from Seattle—just after the collapse. There had been some riots in the first couple of days, but a zock had been created very quickly, a really big one, and made it really tough to get into the area with checkpoints and such. Loren figured it was because of the submarine base . . . she'd heard they had nukes there. But leaving was no big deal. Her aunt and uncle had brought them to the sticks near Hood Canal. In no time Mom had abandoned the family for a self-appointed neighborhood tough guy. Nearly full when they'd arrived, their forty-five unit complex now had less than fifteen occupied homes. The promise of free food from the distros in nearby Shelton and Olympia was tough to resist. There wasn't much lying around to eat here besides shellfish.

Loren peeked through the edge of the window between the wall and the drape. Even in the dull morning light, somewhat obscured by a light drizzle, she could see several unfamiliar vehicles and a gaggle of heavily armed men gathered on the street. Heavy bodied, too, which meant they had been eating well these last few weeks. About half the vehicles were big shiny motorcycles and the other half were full sized trucks. A couple of the trucks were piled high with jugs, cans, and boxes, all protected from the weather by brown or blue tarps.

There was a loud slam. *The front door ... knocked clear off its hinges.* She felt her heart begin to beat faster. Curiosity pulled at her. Loren cracked open the bedroom door and peered down the dim hallway. She couldn't see much; the front door wasn't visible from this angle, but she could see her Uncle Tom standing well away from the door with his shotgun in his hands, flanked by her aunt and sister a half step behind. His well-worn brass duck head cane was set against the wall.

"Get down on your face!" barked an unfamiliar voice. "Don't try anything stupid!"

Would Uncle Tom fight back? In the last few weeks he'd taught her a few things about weapons. How to hold them, how to aim. Before that, she'd never even held a real gun and—technically—she still hadn't shot one. Uncle Tom had also taught her the right way to stab with a knife and where it would do the most damage. But mostly, he taught her that if you can, you run. Uncle Tom had a bad knee. He couldn't run.

She saw the shiny shotgun barrel twitch. The boom and blast rattled the open door. Ears ringing, she immediately shut and locked it.

Loren let out a deep breath. *You can handle this. Don't panic.* She went over to the crib where Max was now crying. Moving quickly, she grabbed her small knapsack—a couple of sets of clothes and a few bathroom items, nearly all of her worldly possessions at this point—and then paused to stuff the remaining few diapers and cleaning wipes inside. She threw the bag onto her shoulders and cinched down the straps tight. Scanning the room, she saw her book of poems beside the loveseat she'd used for a bed these last few weeks and grabbed it, stuffing it into her coat pocket. Then came a scream and several more sharp shots. More screaming, a woman's scream. *Aunt Joan.*

Footsteps in the hall. Loren gently picked up her nephew in his green blanket, pushed the crib with her foot against the door, and in two strides was at the slider to the back deck.

Someone tried to turn the knob, hard, but the lock held. Loren knew that whoever it was would next kick the flimsy hollow door, which would give easily. She worked the lock to the slider, slid the door open with a jerk and heard the expected loud crash behind her as the door gave way.

She broke into a full sprint toward the water with Max in a football carry.

"Hey! Get her! Don't let her get away!"

Loren clenched her teeth, expecting to get shot in the back at any moment, but the shot never came. She broke into the wood line inside of twenty seconds, her legs beating away damp ferns and underbrush. More gunfire behind her.

Lungs burning, she slowed her pace and looked back. None of the homes were in view, though she could still hear a gunshot, shout, or pained scream every couple of seconds. She peeked down at Max, flipping aside a corner of fuzzy cloth to expose his face. A single blue-gray eye peered up at her and little fingers clenched and unclenched by his chin.

"Hey."

It was a whisper to her right. She spun, wide-eyed.

"Over here."

Loren scanned and just saw a hint of bright white shoelaces. Then a pale face surrounded by messy dark brown hair. She recognized him, a neighbor kid. A local. Always dressed in black, kind of emo, but with no weird piercings or tattoos like some of those kids. She'd heard his dad didn't want to leave and go get a new ID because he was wanted by the cops.

"I know you," Loren said through raspy breaths as she crept closer and hunkered down close. "You're down on Kelly Lane. The—the sage house. Big truck out front?" Maybe her age? She wasn't sure.

"Yup, you got it. Any idea what the hell just happened?"

Loren looked down at the ground. "Remember that old guy trying to peddle spices a couple of days ago? Bald. Sort of goofy. Said he was heading up to Port Angeles."

"I didn't get to meet him."

"Well anyway, one of the things he said is that there are these gangs roaming around looting, killing, and kidnapping. Said we need to either get serious about protecting ourselves or just call it quits and head for the zocks."

"So..."

"Are you an idiot? That back there is one of those looter gangs!"

"Hey now. Just making sure we're talkin' about the same thing here. What are you holding onto anyway? Is that a..." the boy replied, pointing toward the green bundle in her arms.

"Yes. *A baby*. Not mine. My nephew, Max."

His nose wrinkled in disgust. "You—you brought a *baby* with you? Seriously? What in the heck were you thinking?"

She glared at the boy. "I was thinking those murderers would probably kill him if I didn't get him out of there, okay? What was I supposed to do? And, wait—who are you to decide anyway?" Max stirred and grabbed at the outside of her coat, mewling. Loren realized, with a groan, she had no way to feed him. Her sister nursed him the old-fashioned way. There was no formula and he wasn't eating solid food yet.

"Okay, okay, chill," he shot back as he turned to look toward the complex. "I want to take a peek, see what's going on now. You coming?"

"No. I don't want to see ... whatever is going on back there. I'm following the river down to the Canal. If I have to walk to Shelton, I will. No one left to help me here. Maybe the government will. I don't know anymore." She turned away, tears forming at the edges of her eyes. The realization that her uncle, aunt, sister, and mother were probably dead began to sink in. She sobbed messily, drops falling onto Max's blanket.

"Hey. You're alive, okay? Let's get out of here. I live here, y'know? There's a trail up ahead." The boy stood and offered up his hand. She wondered how he was taking this all so well.

Loren looked up, eyes still cloudy. "Well, if we're traveling together I kinda need to know your name. I'm Loren."

"I know. I'm Malachi." She grabbed his hand and he jerked her to her feet, surprising her with such strength considering how skinny he was.

◆ ◆ ◆

Kyle and Max had already caught fifteen good size Dungeness crab and two nice coho salmon, both over ten pounds. It was a good start but Kyle wanted to triple that number before heading back for the day. He'd had the Kevlar composite fifteen foot boat only a week and this was his third time out. It had been tempting to simply commandeer a boat from the closest little inlet marina—most clearly had remote owners—but he didn't care to go down that path unless there was no other option. Accompanied by his constant shadow, Timothy, Kyle had asked around and found a legitimate owner, an older widow who had kept her husband's boat for sentimental reasons. She had agreed to lease him the boat in return for some of the catch.

The central part of Hood Canal, just south of Quatsap Point on the Olympic Peninsula side and west of Stavis Bay on the Kitsap Peninsula side, was quiet today. On earlier trips Kyle had spotted other boats but there were none today. Farther north, where the natural canal widened from about a mile to over four, it forked; to the left up Dabob Bay and to the right, out to meet the Puget Sound. Kyle painstakingly avoided heading northeast as this route would draw near to Bangor Trident Base—the home port to some of the Navy's nuclear submarines. Even in normal times, it was a good place to avoid. Kyle had known Marines tasked with guarding the nukes stored here and its sister base in Georgia. With everyone at full pucker, a small craft with two guys armed to the teeth, even with fish in the boat, would probably lead to trouble.

Today, his brother was his wingman. Both he and Matt wore boonie hats and excellent surplus rubberized nylon Swiss ponchos to stave off the wet. Under Kyle's left armpit rode his Glock 9mm while his Tikka .308, now swathed in camouflage wrap to cover its shiny stainless barrel, sat cased at his feet. Matt had, as usual, the ex-cop guns he'd brought back from California. Traveling anywhere not heavily armed seemed completely foreign now.

Even though they lived in the same small cabin, Kyle hadn't seen much of his brother in the two weeks since he'd arrived. After a couple of days of getting settled in and reacquainted with Des, Matt had taken Kyle's spot on the security detail which had freed Kyle up to hunt and fish that much more. Spending quality time with his brother was new territory for Kyle. Six years apart in age, they'd always seemed out of phase. When Kyle had been a kid, Matt had been the baby. When Kyle was in high school, Matt had been the little punk brother who, more often than not, got in the way. Then came Kyle's years in the Marines, marriage, and children. Matt had followed a similar path, just several years behind. As adults and equals, they had spent very little time with one another despite living only twenty miles apart for the past few years.

The situation at the lake was not getting easier. Some residents had opted to leave, most fearing they'd be left out of whatever structure the federal government was putting together from the ashes of the financial crash. People with only tenuous links to the actual residents had arrived to take their places. None had arrived with any appreciable food or supplies; for them Sunshine Lake was the final redoubt. Most chafed at the system in place. They wanted to be cared for. For those in real need, that was okay— it fell in line with Kyle's concept of charity—but if you could pitch in in some manner, you needed to.

The main problem, not surprisingly to Kyle, was the men. In the modern age, most men were good at their job —usually a New Economy position steeped in bureaucracy, technology, or both—good at watching TV, and sometimes good at a hobby or two. Even hobbies commonly deemed to be "manly" were of limited use in a survival scenario e.g. tinkering with old cars or Brazilian Jiu-Jutsu. Either might be called on in special circumstances but neither helped put food on the table or defended against real trouble. While there certainly were plenty of exceptions among women, especially in the big cities, they had simply not strayed as far from the skills used in "the old days." The only competent hunters and fishers at the lake were Kyle and the Klein men. Matt and Timothy were willing to learn but the other twenty-five or so men of the right age at Sunshine were all banking on the imminent end of the current crisis and a return to a semblance of their old lives. Why take the time to learn how to plow, hunt or gut fish when you're just going to return home tomorrow, turn on the boob tube, and throw a pizza in the microwave?

Matt was staring out into the drizzling gloom. "You

look glum, bro," Kyle said, breaking the long silence.

"Yeah."

"Des?"

"Yeah. Among other things."

His sister-in-law's attitude hadn't been great before Matt had returned, and Kyle had hoped that would change for the better once they'd reunited. This had not been the case. Now her knight was back and all could really return to normal. She had talked about heading back to their condo. But Matt had no intention of leaving the cabin and the lake. He'd seen, more than anyone up at Sunshine, how people were eking by everywhere else. How the promised food supplies often didn't arrive for distribution, or were just enough to maintain starvation levels. And then there was the matter of Abby and Kaleb. He'd made a pact that he'd only hand them off to their family and no one else. While she wasn't intentionally rude or mean to the pair, she hadn't embraced a caretaker role with them.

On the flip side, Abby and Kaleb had fit into their household as if by design. Abby had been a huge help watching the younger kids. She'd showed unusual wisdom and discernment for someone her age. And she was a fierce competitor at cribbage, UNO, Farkle, and most of the other games they played in the quiet evenings after dinner and cleanup. Kaleb had made a wonderful playmate for Isabella and Cole and was seriously unbeatable at hide-and-go seek—the boy was both double-jointed and loved cozy hidey holes.

"You want to talk about it?" Kyle prodded.

"Not sure there's much to talk about. Des still thinks everything is going to revert back to normal. Every day it's 'tomorrow.' The banks will reopen, the account with have money in it, gas trucks will roll up to every station and fill them back up. She refuses to believe this may be normal for a long time, maybe years."

Matt had listened to some of the same ham radio broadcasts in Kyle's fifth wheel, their makeshift TOC—tactical operations center.

Occasionally they heard from sources inside the States, but these were always at low power and seemed to be folks on the move, possibly in setups similar to the Raptor. Most of the best broadcasts had come in from outside North America, places like South Africa, Australia, and Eastern Europe. While not as dramatic, most of the rest of the world had crashed along with the United States, not unlike the 1929 stock crash. They told of plague outbreaks, border wars reigniting, massive food shortages in places that depended on American and Canadian suppliers.

No official media source could be trusted, so they primarily listened to scrappy ham operators pushing out low wattage broadcasts from the more remote corners of the world. The news was never good. Mainland China was reversing its capitalistic course and reverting back to the days of strict Mao-style Communism, and gearing up to take Taiwan and maybe more. With no fear of American intervention, most of the Middle East was re-igniting with violence and, as was typical of the region, it was impossible to tell the good guys from the bad. The Jordanian royal family, one of the few friendly to the West in the region, had reportedly escaped to the United Kingdom. North Korea had not moved to attack its southern neighbor, but most of that was probably weather related as most of NE Asia was locked into one of the worst early winters in memory.

It seemed to be a four-way race to fill the American power vacuum: the European Union, Russia, China, and a coalition of the remaining three of the BRICS—Brazil, South Africa, and India.

"Matt, I definitely don't have the magic solution for you," Kyle said. "If I did I would tell you. But this reminds me of something I read about once. There was a guy, a Vietnam POW named Admiral Stockdale."

"They captured an *admiral?*"

"No, I think he was a commander at the time. Don't

rabbit trail on me. Now, you know that I don't hold much regard for anchor yankers unless they wear a trident, caduceus, or pilot's wings. Stockdale was a pilot, like most naval officer POWs, I'm sure."

"Okay. So . . . what's this guy got to do with Des?"

"He wrote a ton about the conditions at the Hanoi Hilton. Stockdale made it really clear that the guys that survived did so because they had low expectations. The POWs that said or thought things like, 'It will be better tomorrow,' or 'I just need to make it to Christmas' ended up literally dying from disappointment. Stockdale made it almost *eight years* by just confronting the reality of the situation, but by also *never* giving up. Being a cautious realist isn't enough. You have to believe, to really know, that you're going to prevail in the end. That right there is the main reason me and mine are staying up here. Once we surrender our future to the government, it's over. What is there to prevail against?"

"I'm not sure this is helping. Des isn't like that. We're not going to turn her into a stoic warrior type overnight."

"What I'm saying is, Matt, she needs to be or she's going to crack. You're going to hear the engine of your Bimmer kick over one morning and find her gone. Or she'll just curl into an emotional ball and shut us all out. I don't know, I'm not a psychologist, but I've seen people crack before. When their illusion of reality is blown away by the real thing, weird stuff happens. Bad stuff."

"I hear you there. So . . . try and toughen her up?"

"I think you need a *Coming to Jesus Meeting*."

Matt rolled his eyes upward. "Ah. That."

"Yeah. Tell her that you're not leaving, you're not dumping Abby and Kaleb with the government goons, and that's final. Remind her that you're her devoted, loyal husband who wants the best for her, but there's no debate on those two points. Impart on her that we may be holed up out here for quite some time."

"About that," Matt said, clearly ready for a new topic.

"How long do you think we can hold out at the lake? A year?"

Kyle thought for a few seconds. "Quite a bit longer than that, if we have to. Maybe three or four. Past that, things will be really tough. Ammunition, grains, and clothing that fits the kids or hasn't worn out completely will be in short supply. This isn't taking into account I'm draining my stock of food more quickly than I had planned." A flock of Canada geese honked overhead and Kyle gazed skyward. He wished he'd brought a shotgun. A couple of fat geese would round out this trip nicely.

"Because of me, Des, and the kids?"

Kyle smiled. "Yeah, them and the other seventy people up at the lake. Hunting, fishing, and gardening the poor soil there won't be enough over the long haul. I think the area will support, maybe, thirty deeply committed, tough people including kids. So, six to eight families, tops."

"A tribe."

"Something like that. But I don't think we'll get the chance to hold out that long."

Matt raised an eyebrow. "No?"

"No way. Eventually the government will branch out from the big cities and suburbs. I doubt they're going to let us carry on under their noses. My guess is someone official will be paying us a visit by next summer at the latest."

"Tax collectors, probably. With guns."

"Well they're going to have a tough time getting any *bancors* from me. I don't have any," Kyle said. "More likely we'll get discovered by something like that convoy you told me about, the one in Oregon. I'm convinced they were out looking for rogue radio broadcasters."

"We're not doing any of that, though."

"No, but with our radios, we're transmitting in the clear. Family band doesn't go too far, not legally anyway, but if their equipment is top notch I imagine they just need to be moving down 101 to figure out we're up here."

"I don't know, Kyle. I'm way more worried about the

looter gangs we heard about the other night. Big enough to knock over most towns while small and agile enough to elude the feds. An armed gang like that would have no trouble with Sunshine Lake."

Kyle merely nodded. It was true. Their security detail was set up to prevent lone infiltrators, not a huge vehicle-borne gang bristling with firepower.

"But back to my original point," Matt said, "what are you going to do when the storage food dwindles away? There are still way too many mouths to feed."

"You weren't there for the original speech that kicked off the current state of things, but I think you've picked up the gist of it. Amber and I give because we want to, not because we have to, and we'll continue to help those God has put in our way. Even past a point where some people might say, 'Wait, I need to stop and take care of my own.'"

Matt rolled his eyes. This reaction wasn't exactly new to Kyle. Kyle knew when he made his decision to accept Christ in high school that it would drive a wedge between him and the rest of his family. Their father was at best an agnostic. Their mother, an Easter and Christmas Lutheran, would never commit to anything stronger than the irresolute, "I believe in God." Uncle Rich, the materialist who refused to let discussions of faith challenge his "biggest net worth wins" mantra formed from decades working in the Chicago Loop with the country club set. Uncle Rob, the angry, bitter old soldier who viewed faith in Jesus as a crutch no better or worse than a bottle of hooch.

"Look, I know you don't share my faith, but I'm not going to pull any punches on your account. God has made it clear that we're to be responsible with our assets, but very generous to those in need. I won't quote Scripture since it won't mean anything to you, but when we get back I'd be happy to tell you where to look."

Matt shrugged and they fished in silence for several minutes. "Do you personally believe this is 'it'? The biblical apocalypse? Christians flying up to heaven and all that?"

"I think we're going to see a global government take shape. America and the dollar had to die for that to happen. Some may call it tinfoil hat stuff but it's the truth. So, to answer your question... it sure looks like it to me. Don't get me wrong, if the end times haven't arrived, I sure as heck won't be disappointed. Just because a lot of signs line up doesn't mean this is it. Look at all the people during World War Two that believed they were living during the last days and Hitler was the Antichrist."

"Well that'd take care of your problems, right? Before things get really intense, you and the rest will just get whisked up to heaven to wait things out. That's what you believe. Right?"

"That's the most popular view, sure, but it's not necessarily how it would play out."

"Oh? So all those authors and movies are wrong?"

"There's only one Author, upper case. And He said Jesus could come back at any time. No one would know the date and time except God Himself."

"So he could be here now? Wait, what about all that Revelation stuff? I remember you telling me about all that years ago. Trumpets and seals and such. Doesn't that mean that certain things have to happen first?"

The same question had been raised over fifteen years ago, when Kyle was still a "baby Christian." Some of his questions were never answered, but Kyle had let them be and moved on to other concerns. "There's plenty here to debate. The consensus is that things will get bad, really bad, and the Antichrist and his False Prophet—his sidekick, as it were—come to the fore. They're to be given seven years to rule the world, and at the end of that time Jesus will defeat the counterfeit trinity of Satan, the Antichrist, and the False Prophet. That sums up the middle chapters of Revelation. As for when all believers are brought up to Heaven, that's *not* known. And I think that was absolutely intentional on God's part.

Like everything else. It could be at the beginning, like most Christ followers believe these days. Or in the middle, or at the end."

Matt shifted on his bench and adjusted his borrowed boonie. Drops fell from the brim. "Why would something like that be *unclear*? I mean, that sounds like a pretty important detail."

"I've given that a lot of thought. Christian bookstores have a whole section on end times prophecy. I figure it's unclear to force us to be ready for anything and anticipate nothing."

"That's what got you into preparedness? Trying to make sure you were set for whatever happens?"

"Partially. When I was single and church shopping after my enlistment, I saw that at least ninety-five percent of the people that had formed an opinion believed we'd all be swept up, or Raptured—that term isn't actually in the Bible though—before things got bad. I'm not saying it can't happen like that, but I saw the consequences of Christ followers deciding that was the only logical outcome, that God would never allow His flock to go through seven years of hell on earth. The people I ran into at church, for the most part, didn't physically prepare for hard times; by that I mean both in stuff stored up but their own bodies as well. Why bother getting in shape when you're just going to get a new, perfect body before everyone else? They had that, 'well, I got my ticket punched and everyone else has seven years to be here and figure it out for themselves' attitude. What happens if it *doesn't* pan out that way? I think they'll seriously doubt their faith.

"If anything, it's best to prepare to be here through the whole thing. Not a big surprise that I have that attitude, I get it. But it's like insurance. Better to spend some money and put out some effort just in case the worst happens than to ignore the possibility and get caught completely flatfooted. There are plenty of Christians standing in those food lines as we speak. If this really is the end, soon enough a requirement to be in those lines will be to denounce Jesus Christ and worship the Antichrist. They'll either end up physically dead or spiritually lost forever. The first one is obviously preferable from an eternal standpoint."

"If I'm hearing you right and connecting the dots," Matt said, "it's not crystal clear in the Bible so that people won't try and game a system . . . game God . . . and think they have it all figured out. They'll have to have faith and just let it all play out regardless of their preconceptions."

Kyle smiled. "A to-the-point explanation. Exactly."

Kyle saw Matt glance to the right, toward the western shore. Kyle followed and saw a beached pleasure boat, stern facing them, about a quarter mile south.

"You see that?" Matt said, continuing to gaze.
Kyle nodded, reached under the poncho and brought his Steiner binos up, removing the attached lens covers with his index fingers. "No one moving. Hasn't been here too long. I didn't see it two days ago when I went by here with Timothy."

"Okay."

Something tugged at Kyle a bit. He knew what it was and smiled. "Let's check it out. Just a hunch."

Matt's right eyebrow went up. "Look, Kyle, it's raining, I'm tired, and we've got a ton of mouths to feed. Let's just get on with it and get home. A beached boat can only be bad news."

Kyle stowed the binos under the poncho, took the oars, and started to row. His brother huffed, rolled his eyes, and began reeling in both poles. The slender, lightweight craft cut easily through the negligible chop. It wasn't long before they pulled up to shore about a hundred yards north of the beached craft.

"So, since we're obviously going to do this, how?" Matt asked. "You sending me in there and covering me with your rifle?"

"Not a chance. We're going up together." Kyle put his foot on the shore and drew his Glock, holding it in the alert position in both hands. The long barreled Tikka would be less than useless in the confines of a thirty-five-ish foot pleasure boat. He saw Matt slide his AR from the dry bag, tug on the magazine, and confirm the red dot was on. The rifle's stock was fully collapsed and his brother tucked it under his armpit, making a compact package. While not as easy to maneuver in tight spaces as his pistol, it hit a lot harder and had thirty shots on tap to Kyle's eighteen.

Stepping closer, he saw that the boat was a pretty standard design circa the late '70s or early '80s, white with lots of exposed wood trim and railings. Up above was a flybridge complete with a couple of bench seats and a table. A white fiberglass lifeboat hung at the stern. Along the starboard flank read "SUZANNE" in large Cooper Black font, light blue with faded brown borders. One of the three starboard windows was shattered and there were a couple of small ragged holes through the cabin.

"I'll go first," Kyle whispered, although he didn't relish walking in front of Matt's rifle blasting behind him. He hopped over the railing, scanning with the Glock. The hairs on the back of his neck stood up.

"You hear that?" Matt whispered behind him. Kyle strained but could hear nothing but the gentle lap of water against the hull and the white noise of the steady drizzle.

Ah. A high pitched pained cry, faint but distinct. Kyle opened the stern door and peered down. The galley was empty. A large brownish stain along the port side bulkhead, almost certainly blood, ran down to the deck. Most of the cabinets and drawers hung open.

That small cry issued from behind the closed door of the bow. There was an open door to the right side, likely a small berth along the hull, and the head was directly across to their left.

"What's cookin'?" Matt asked.

"Definitely foul play. Maybe the owner is up there and injured. Or... maybe it's a trap."

"Doubt it. Pretty far off the beaten path to set a trap." Kyle nodded.

Another cry was followed by a distinct "shush." *What in the world? That sounds like a baby.*

"Hey!" Kyle called out. "We're not here to hurt you. We're the good guys."

"What *are* you doing?" Matt said in a harsh whisper.

"Cool it. You don't think that sounds like a baby?"

The bow door cracked open, Kyle saw a dark eyeball for a moment, then it slammed shut.

Of course. We look like a couple of bandits. "Yes, we're armed. Even the good guys have to be careful. We were just out fishing. We live nearby. We'll put our guns down, okay?" Kyle nodded at his brother who, after shaking his head, set his rifle on the galley's small table. Kyle did likewise with his Glock.

The door cracked open again. A slender teenaged boy's dark wet hair dripped down his forehead from under a black hoodie with bright green pull cords.

The boy grimaced. "What do you want?"

"We don't want anything," Kyle replied, hands open in front of him. "We saw the boat here and thought we'd check it out. You thirsty? Hungry?" He paused. "Look. I get it, there are a lot of bad dudes around. We'll understand if you don't trust us. We're willing to help, but we're not going to drag you out of here. Your call." He now saw a thin girl with strawberry blonde hair sitting on the bed. Neither kid could have been more than seventeen. She too was soaked, and clutched a green blanket that wiggled slightly.

"You have anything to feed that baby?" Kyle asked calmly. The girl shook her head and looked away. "Where are you headed?"

"Away," said the boy, sounding defiant. "We . . . just needed to get out of the rain for a while.

"Where are you from?"

"We live ... *lived* up at Rembrandt Village."

"I've been by there." Rembrandt Village was only a few miles southeast of Sunshine Lake. It didn't quite qualify as a real town, just a gas station/grocery store and a dive bar along Highway 101 serving a 1960s-era low end housing development. That stretch of the Canal had a steep, rocky coastline—no good for beachside homes, which kept property values very low.

"It's gone now. Gang came in this morning and destroyed ... everything..."

"We didn't hear anything or see any smoke," Matt noted. Kyle looked at him and shook his head just enough for his brother to notice. Now wasn't the time to pump them for info.

"I'm going to be real with you both," Kyle said. "You have a thirty mile walk to the food distro in Shelton. Along the beach that's three days if you're really pushing it during daylight hours and don't get hurt. And that's with a full belly. That baby there," he said, pointing, "won't make it three days without food. You both already know all about the weather." Kyle was trying to think fast so he didn't make false promises. It wasn't as if they had any easy way to feed a baby back at the lake. "How old is it?"

"It ... he ... *Max* ... is four months old," the girl replied. Kyle tried to remember when his two kids started eating solid food. *About six months?*

"Here's my offer," Kyle began. "If you'd like, we'll bring you back to our little community, get you some food, do our best for your little Max there, and help get you along south if that's really where you want to go. In return, I ask that you give us some info on the men who attacked you. We're not far from here and they might look to hit us next. Deal?"

The boy looked back at the girl, who nodded. "Deal."

CHAPTER TWENTY-EIGHT

Monday, Fourth Week in November

A key in the door startled Amber. Kyle had said they would fish until dark and it was a three mile walk back. It was too early by at least two hours. Dull light still hung over the Olympia Mountains to the west. *The Gang of Four*—Isabella, Cole, Kaleb, and Abigail—were hanging out in the trailer with Greg Samuels along with a few other kids to enjoy a little juice and watch stored movies on a tablet, so she wasn't expecting them either.

Kyle entered, carrying his gear and the front handle of their giant red cooler, followed by Matt, a scowling teenage boy, and an exhausted teenage girl holding a green... baby blanket. *A baby?* As if reading her thoughts, it gave out a pained cry, then another.

Amber crossed her arms from the edge of the kitchen and raised her eyebrows. "Oh my word... you two caught a little something extra this time."

Kyle and Matt set down the cooler and her husband spread his hands wide, conciliatory. "Honey, we were fishing, we spotted a beached boat and I made the call to check it out and, well, they were trying to wait out the rain inside. They'd never make it to the Shelton ZOC. The baby, for sure."

Amber added it up in her head. Shelton was thirty miles to the south. The weather was unpleasant but not particularly life threatening. Neither teen looked like they had much in the way of gear for a three or four day walk. Kyle was right.

"You're not the mother, are you?" she asked the girl, who certainly didn't look like she'd been pregnant recently. "You don't have anything to feed the baby. It's pretty young, not even six months I take it?"

The girl sighed and nodded. "Max is four months old. Five on the fifth. You're exactly right, but there's a lot more to explain—"

"Which we will as soon as we settle in and you two go get dried off as best as you can," Kyle interrupted. "Amber, did we bring anything that might fit Loren here?"

Amber sized the girl up with a glance. Half her age, about the same height but a good thirty pounds lighter. "I suppose. It'll be baggy. I think the first priority should be figuring how something that baby—Max—can eat. Kyle, will you help me look?" She stared at Kyle, giving him the one finger come on.

In a lot of families, the mother wore the nutrition hat and was expected to know what growing kids needed to not only survive but to thrive. For Amber it was more than that: it was her life calling. As a child, it had become clear she had a moderate intolerance to both wheat gluten and lactose, the sugar naturally present in all dairy products like milk, cheese, and yogurt. She'd grown up staring at the food pyramid poster at school highlighting a loaf of bread, spaghetti noodles, a tall glass of milk, and a big wax-coated wheel of cheese. Amber had wondered if she'd get enough nutrition to grow as big and tall as her cheeseburger and pizza eating peers. It turned out she'd had nothing to worry about.

She had discovered, both in her personal experience and through her education, that the officially approved American diet was fundamentally imbalanced and unhealthy. It was not possible to be healthy by simply eating less of a diet heavy with processed sugars and starches, meat, seed-based oils, salt, and fruits and vegetables that had lost most or all of their nutrients through excessive hybridization or outright genetic modification. If it came in a wrapper or box, was slipped through a drive-thru window, or had its own TV commercial, it was almost certainly bad for you. She'd adopted a diet heavy in organic heirloom fruits and vegetables, expeller-pressed non-seed-based oils, and beans in all their varieties. Her starches tended to be rice, quinoa, or potato based. Meat was on the menu—with a game hunter in the family she'd learned how to best integrate it into their meal plans—but was usually as a supplement to the other foods, not the main source of calories.

Seeking out healthy alternatives to prepared foods had been what led her to formally study nutrition and become a licensed dietitian in the first place. Not long after finishing college and her internship, she'd met Kyle and Isabella had come along less than a year after they'd married. Amber had decided to forego a full-time position and had stayed at home to raise and homeschool their kids, though she did use her knowledge to provide educated nutritional advice to Kyle when he'd started Bene Praepara. Advice he'd been able to honestly (and legally) package as licensed dietitian approved meal plans to both the "normal" people and those with special dietary needs brought on by diabetes, Celiac disease, or allergies to foods like peanuts or eggs.

But she'd never had either a need or an opportunity to feed an infant *sans* breast milk or formula. Such a thing was just never a consideration in her line of work, not with government programs that gave away formula to just about anyone who asked for it. Giving a baby store-bought formula carried no risk—it had been completely sussed out by the maker already; while some would argue it wasn't ideal it certainly wasn't killing infants. Trying to make your own definitely carried a risk. Too much or too little of anything could matter a great deal. Too often she'd come across a story about parents of a newborn or infant trying to cut corners on formula, cutting it with too much water or some other substance, which resulted in killing or doing permanent harm to their child. Amber knew that too much water and not enough electrolytes would lead to death. Too much salt would damage a baby's kidneys. Not enough protein or fat could lead to stunted growth, both physically and mentally.

"We didn't exactly prepare for babies, Kyle," she asked as they entered their bedroom with the canned goods piled along the wall. Amber racked her brain, trying to think if any of the residents were either breastfeeding or had an infant. The Morrisons, down in #18 had a baby but she was almost a year old. That was the youngest child here at the lake that she could think of.

Kyle put on his 'acting dumb' face. "I-I didn't know what to do, sweetie. I couldn't just shrug and let them keep going once I saw that baby in her arms."

"I understand. How long are they going to be here?"

"Just a day or two until they get their strength back and we can get them south. It's not permanent. They've been through a lot today. Go easy on them. Go easy on me too, for that matter."

Amber grinned. "I'm not upset. I just don't want to make any promises I can't keep. What happened?"

Amber listened while Kyle took a couple of minutes to secondhand recount the attack on Rembrandt Village and hammer home his concern that Sunshine Lake might be their next stop. From the next room, she could hear Max cry with hunger and the girl—Loren?—ineffectively trying to shush him.

"So, any ideas on baby food?" Kyle asked. "Maybe we could grind up some rice flour and make some cereal."

"Yes, definitely, but that's just filler, just calories. He needs nutrients. He needs *milk*."

Kyle turned to the pile of food. "You know full well

we don't have much in the way of that. Some number ten cans of powdered nonfat. We've given a lot of that away though."

They definitely had, Amber realized. Powdered milk had been a standard item in all of BPS's packages. It just wasn't something she could consume with her dairy intolerance so it had become expendable to them, like the wheat they'd given to Matt's Jeep-driving friend a couple of weeks ago and others since.

"Maybe, if we added some fat and sugar," Amber explained. "Water it down a bit. Cow's milk is too heavy for an infant. Add some sugar. Didn't we bring a flat of evaporated milk?" She knew they had, but Kyle had unloaded the trailer and she didn't know where it had ended up.

"I'll get it."

In fifteen minutes Amber had whipped up her best approximation of baby formula* based on what they had lying around. It was part canned evaporated milk, part purified water courtesy of their Big Berkey, a little powdered milk, some refined sugar, and a little expeller-pressed organic coconut oil. Kyle had a fire going so they could warm the concoction to body temperature in a pot of water.

> *For legal and liability reasons, the author has chosen not to give a recipe for the ad-hoc baby formula described here. Do not attempt to make and use homemade baby formula!

Matt came in through the front door, huffing with exertion and clutching a plastic bottle. "Morrisons have three and kindly gave us this one. Cindy said the opening is a little too small for their little Emma, whatever that means. They were lucky enough to have brought several big tubs of formula although they're almost out now. I'm sure they'll be interested to hear about your homemade recipe."

Amber took the bottle and set it on the countertop. "Well, unless we can barter for a dairy cow or a few milking goats it's not going to last very long. Twenty-four cans of milk, six number tens of powdered, and that's it. He'll eat through all of that in no time. He'll be on baby food—here or wherever else—within a few weeks. I just hope his tummy can handle it when the time comes."

An hour later, little Max was sleeping soundly on Amber's lap. She'd taken over so Loren could towel off and change into the tightest shirt and jeans Amber owned. Even so, the clothes hung loosely off the girl. Amber was not fat—far from it, and what little she carried had disappeared since the crash—but no amount of diet and hard work would return her hips to where they were twenty years ago when she was built just like the teenage girl beside her on the sofa.

Loren, the full weight of the day's tragedy beginning to take its toll, was curled up under a light blue fleece blanket. She'd rebuffed Amber's entreaties to talk. Amber didn't press. It was obviously too raw, too fresh. Every couple of minutes, a tear would streak down Loren's face into her still-damp hair and she would emit a sniffle. Her companion, Malachi, sat on the other sofa with his hands clasped together on his knees and his head down. He hadn't been in a mood to chat either.

Matt had left about a half hour before for his six PM to midnight guard shift. Earlier today, Des had grown bored enough to help with some outdoor chores and had come back just to see her husband off. Amber's raven-haired sister-in-law, after a short explanation to bring her up to speed, had introduced herself to their guests and simply gone to bed.

Greg Samuels had come in for dinner, carting around the base station radio, followed by The Gang of Four. Abigail and Isabella had offered to whip something up and soon a pot of potato, Vienna sausage, and onion soup was warming over the fire.

"So, Kyle, what's next?" Amber asked. "If you really think we're in crosshairs of those . . . people." She couldn't think of a word she felt appropriate in front of the children.

Kyle showed his palms. "First, we need to get some eyeballs on that crew. I figure I'll head out at first light, maybe take Timothy along. We'll get some intel and figure out what to do from there."

"What about Cushman?" Greg added, referring to the much larger and well-known lake to the south.

"What about it? That's fifteen, twenty miles from here."

"What I'm getting at is, y'know, if one of us goes down there and checks out Cushman, that'll give us an idea of these guys' M.O.," Greg said. Amber had no idea what 'M.O.' meant but nodded anyway. "If they rolled up Cushman that's a bad deal. Lots of cabins and houses and what not down there."

Kyle frowned. "There weren't many cabins at the resort there, maybe ten or twelve, but lots of RV parking and tent spaces. Plus, I don't know, maybe fifty to a hundred private homes or cabins around the lake. There could be a thousand people or more around there right now."

"Malachi, how many . . . *people* . . . came to Rembrandt Village today?"

The boy looked up with bloodshot eyes. "Umm . . . it was hard to tell. They were all over the place and I was too busy running. I only saw about ten bikes—motorcycles I mean—and about that many trucks. I really dunno . . . how many people would that be?"

"Thirty or forty, probably," Kyle replied, face tight. "Enough to run us over if they came here. Even if we were ready for them."

Amber thought that bit of pessimism actually made sense. She had no military experience but could do simple math. An eight-person security detail, plus Kyle, Matt, the Kleins, and maybe three or four others that could safely use a weapon, versus double or triple that number, could not prevail. Besides the makeshift gate, there was nothing to slow down a group of vehicles. Motorcycles could ride right around it anyway, through the trees.

Kyle continued. "Hmm. Well, let's eat and rest up. Greg, can you take someone down with you to Lake Cushman tomorrow, maybe my brother if he feels up to it? You'll have to take the Forest Service roads since you'll pass right by these clowns if you take the hardtop. I'll head over to the Bensons' after chow and ask if I can borrow their son for the day."

"Kyle, if it's okay with you, I'd like to come along instead," Malachi said. "I want to see the guys that did . . . what they did."

CHAPTER TWENTY-NINE

Tuesday, Fourth Week in November

Kyle was confused. The world was fuzzy and dark. Explosions rung in his ears. He hunched over the hood of a tan truck, a rifle in his hands. He tried to focus and seek out a target but it was just too gray. Gray and . . . *confusing*.

"Kyle . . . help . . ." came a pained groan below him and to his right. Kyle looked down and saw his brother flat on his back, badly damaged rifle by his side. He was clutching a dark, shiny patch on his abdomen. *Blood.* Some of it pooled next to him on the asphalt.

Bullets snapped by Kyle's head, a couple smacking into the body of the pickup truck with dull thuds. He slumped behind the driver's side front wheel, hoping the steel would protect him. Glancing up, he saw two cabins on fire, the flames shooting out windows and soaring above their rooflines, black smoke heading skyward into the cloud cover. Kyle looked back down and saw a leather-vested and handlebar-mustachioed man on a huge black and chrome motorcycle, engine blatting, coming his way down the narrow road. The biker, clutching a flaming Molotov cocktail, paused slightly to throw it at an intact cabin. Kyle watched as the bottle shattered and spread flaming gasoline over the porch facing the road.

Finally... a target. Kyle quickly brought his rifle up to his left shoulder and fired three aimed shots. None seemed to have effect on the rider who appeared to accelerate, aiming the big cruiser right at Kyle. Now the biker produced a length of heavy chain, swinging it over his head like a flail.

Kyle lined up the sights and squeezed three more times, the bike only a hundred feet away. Astonishingly there still was no effect, and Kyle threw his body to the right just as the bike smashed into the hood of the truck with a loud crash.

Then, the shaking. The ground shook violently and Kyle's body tossed back and forth with a quick, but steady rhythm—

"Wake up!" came an agitated woman's voice.

Amber.

Kyle opened his eyes. He lay in bed, damp with cold sweat, the room completely dark save the green glow of the tritium dials on his outdoorsman's wristwatch. They showed it was just after four in the morning.

"Honey, are you all right? You were mumbling all kinds of nonsense and tossing around!"

Kyle wordlessly set his feet on the cold hardwood floor. "Just glad it was only a nightmare, sweetie. About time to get going anyway."

As the memory of it started to fade, he realized he should have known it wasn't real. The rifle he'd clutched wasn't his civilian-style Bushmaster, it had been his old and well-worn Marine Corps issue M16A2. The "tan truck" had been the hardback Humvee he'd piloted around southern Iraq almost twenty years ago. And the biker: D-Day from *Animal House*, one of his father's favorite movies.

He grabbed the wand lighter on the end table, lit a stubby red candle, and started to put on the "scout" outfit he'd laid out the night before. Wool socks, a black compression shirt, then his top and bottom set of surplus Swiss camouflage with their distinctive Alpenflage pattern. It had the typical greens and browns, but also small bits of red that nicely matched the fallen leaves and holly bushes commonly found in late fall in the Olympic Mountains. He slipped on the matching boonie hat, still slightly damp from the day before despite a few hours by the fireplace. He then slipped on and tied his Danner all-leather boots. Malachi would closely match him by putting on one of Kyle's Swiss ponchos over his regular clothes.

Kyle clipped on the shooter's belt that held his Glock 17 in a Kydex holster, two spare 17-round magazines stuffed full of hollowpoints, an LED flashlight, his Randall Model 14 knife in its original leather sheath, and two small pouches that each contained a five round spare magazine for his Tikka.

He hefted the small backpack, patterned in simple Coyote Tan, a medium brown that hid well just about anywhere in the world. Inside were his Steiner binoculars, Burris 20-60x spotting scope, one of the cheap FRS handheld radios, a weatherproof notepad and write-anywhere pencil, a compass, a whistle, his full Camelbak hydration bladder, a filtration straw, spare socks, and two of the precious military-grade MREs.

"You gonna give me a kiss goodbye?" a still-groggy Amber asked.

Kyle walked over to the other side of the bed. "Wouldn't dream of leaving without it," he whispered. He leaned over in the dim light and met her lips for a moment. "Pray for us out there, honey. No idea what we're going to run into."

"Of course I will."

They were halfway to Rembrandt Village, dawn beginning to transition the sky from black to midnight blue. Kyle was glad for the drizzle that occasionally turned into a full shower as it concealed their sounds and movement. The towering Douglas firs and cedars along the trail gave them reprieve from the worst of it and their ponchos stopped the rest.

"I still think you should give me a gun. Y'know, just in case? What if we get ambushed?" Malachi asked for the fifth or sixth time. It was beginning to get on Kyle's nerves.

Kyle reached into a dusty corner of his mind and pulled out the rarely used but still quite useful 'Marine NCO Voice.' "Like I said before, this is an intelligence gathering mission. If we get whacked, well, we screwed up. Or someone who was there in my living room is secretly an informant for this marauder gang." It had been an easy decision. The boy knew lots of facts and figures about firearms, but when Kyle had put the proverbial finger in his chest it became clear he'd only shot a .22 rifle a couple of times—definitely a one on the ol' ten scale in terms of ability. The vast majority of his knowledge had been gleaned from the first person shooter games he had filled his waking hours with before the economic crash.

Malachi scowled. "*You* have two guns. Or maybe more, hiding in your pack. And a huge knife. At least let me carry that Glock. Those are easy. No safety, just point and shoot. I've played with those before."

Kyle shook his head. "*Played* with one? This ain't a game with neat crosshairs dancing on the screen. If you don't know how to aim, you won't hit anything past a few yards or so. If there are bad guys closer than that, we have a *big* problem. If that happens, *you are running*. And not straight back to the lake, I'm talking about circles, loop-de-loops, hexagons, and whatever other shapes you can dream up before you get there. Understand? Now, to answer your question, I'm armed not because I'm looking for trouble—if that were the case I'd be loaded out a lot differently than I am—but because there are circumstances where I might need to defend myself, you, or just have a target of opportunity I can't pass up. That definitely *doesn't* mean I'm here to take all of them out. That can't be done, not by one man with a rifle."

Which was mostly true. A thoroughly trained and highly attuned two man sniper team, made up of a shooter and a spotter, could put a mighty hurt on thirty or forty men that lacked a means of escape and couldn't ID their location. Kyle's scoped Tikka was a fine rifle that shipped with a match grade Sako barrel; snipers in most Twentieth Century wars (and even a few more recent ones) would gladly trade him straight across. Kyle could hit a three-inch square Post-It note at two hundred yards, offhand, with boring consistency, and three hundred wasn't much tougher. But that was about the limit of the setup, far too close for an extended bout of sniping. Plus, his 'spotter' was a seventeen-year-old video game addict.

"So, no more on this subject, clear?"

"Uh, yes . . . yes sir."

It was another hour before they came to a ridge overlooking the Village. Hood Canal was behind it and to the east. Highway 101, never very busy this time of year, was completely devoid of traffic in either direction, no great surprise. It was just after sunrise and weak sunlight spilled over the horizon and just below the cloud cover.

Kyle set up the spotting scope, careful to shield its lenses against the rain, and settled in behind. He started on twenty power just to get his bearings, found the cluster of trailers and manufactured homes that he was looking for, and bumped the magnification to sixty with a twist.

"Thanksgiving is this week. Two days from now," Malachi whispered.

"That's very true," Kyle replied. He paused for a second, then continued. "What sparked that memory?"

"Oh, just . . . it feels weird. I mean, I'm thankful I'm alive, but there's nothing else really. Nothing else I'm thankful for, I mean. It feels, well . . . *selfish*, I guess, but it's true. My family and friends are all gone. All I have really are the clothes on my back."

Kyle put his eye back to the scope. "So, do you believe Thanksgiving is about that? The people in your life and the stuff you have?"

"Well . . . yeah. What else is there?"

"Would it surprise you if I told you that Thanksgiving is the most religious American holiday? I say 'American' because we can't exactly claim Christmas and Easter as our own. It's about giving thanks and praise to an Almighty Creator."

"Uh, yeah. Surprised, I mean. What in the world makes you think *that*?"

"I don't *think* it, Malachi, I *know* it. And it's not my opinion or what I'd like to be true because it makes me feel better. It's just historical truth. No less than George Washington and Abraham Lincoln both proclaimed it to be so. We've changed it over the years to be thankful for the things we have versus being thankful for what God has given to us. The two *sound* similar but trust me, they aren't. I look at you and you've been given a lot more than you think you have."

"Like what?"

"You're young, you have a whole life ahead of you, that's a gift. You're healthy, you're smart, and you are a part of an . . . *interesting* time in history."

"Pfft. You really expect me to be thankful for *this*? I just want things the way they were before."

Kyle shrugged. "Suit yourself. Just keep in mind that satisfaction's not about what you can touch, taste, and feel. You'll never be satisfied with life, you'll never have enough, if you stay at that level. Plus, things can't go back to what they were. They might improve someday, but they won't ever be the same." Kyle had scanned the remains of Rembrandt Village during their conversation. He could see that a couple houses had been burned out, but with the soggy conditions the fires had not spread. The distance made it hard to tell for certain, but Kyle thought he saw the lumps of bodies on the ground as well.

Nothing bigger than a squirrel moved. While there were some vehicles parked, they looked like they belonged there and had been motionless for quite some time. No motorcycles or big trucks loaded with loot were in evidence.

Could they have already packed up and headed out? Possibly ... to Sunshine Lake? Kyle felt a wave of sudden dread. *I would have heard those big bikes Malachi talked about*, he reassured himself, the vision of D-Day bearing down on him superimposed on the view through the scope.

So where are they?

"Well, I don't seem them," Kyle whispered.

"So ... that's it? They've just left?"

"I'm saying that they aren't *here*. That doesn't mean they aren't still a threat we need to assess. For all we know they're camping down at the Canal and roasting oysters on sticks. Or they took their show clear up to Port Angeles or Sequim. That's why we walked six miles in the dark, to figure this stuff out. Let's pack back up and get down closer to the highway."

The pair picked their way carefully through the underbrush, which was much thicker here than in the hills. The rain eased up but the ever-present fall cloud cover remained. After about forty-five minutes, they came to the last small ridge facing Highway 101. Kyle stopped and peered south, spying the old roadside bar and general store about a half mile away. Several large vehicles and motorcycles were parked out in front of both buildings. Something indistinct was sitting in the road directly across from the bar.

"I think we found 'em," Kyle whispered. "Let's set up here. I'll need you to scan around with my binoculars and make sure no one sneaks up on us. If your eyes get tired,

Michael Zargona

that's okay, just let me know when you need to take a break. Settle in, we're going to be here for a few hours."

CHAPTER THIRTY

Tuesday, Fourth Week in November

Matt awoke to daylight. Per the plan that Greg had laid out while Matt had manned the "truck" gate, he got dressed in the same clothes as the day before—now nearly dry by the fire—and strapped on the duty belt he'd carried up from California. He was pulling his boots on when Des awoke.

"Where are you going?" she asked. Matt had not woken her up last night to explain today's trip.

"Greg needs a partner to head over to Lake Cushman, to see if the people there know anything about the gang that attacked Rembrandt Village yesterday. Quick drive over, chat with them a bit, come back. Should be back by this afternoon."

"Don't you think you've done *enough*?" Des asked in a pained voice. "Your brother should be the one to go. Hell, you're still recovering from your trek up from L.A.!"

Matt shook his head. "Kyle can't be the one, sweetheart, he's going down to the Village to scout it out. He's probably already left, actually. And no, I'm not *recovering*. I walked less than a hundred miles and that was three weeks ago. I'm still skinny, sure, but until Sunshine Lake gets an all-you-can-eat steakhouse I'm probably going to hold steady."

Even that wasn't enough to get his wife of three years to crack a smile. "You've risked *enough*, Matt. This is it. No more running your brother's errands. Okay?"

"Des, you know I can't promise that. There are tough jobs that need doing and we have a shortage of people who can do them. All of us have been working hard to train up people here but occasionally the A-listers have to step in. I'll have Greg to watch my back." With that, he leaned forward, gave her a kiss on the forehead, and stepped out.

The living area looked like a refugee camp, a distended pile of sleeping bags, blankets, and pads. Matt noted that Abigail and Isabella had given up their prized sofas to the teenagers. The baby slept peacefully on a blanket in the corner of the room. "Where ya goin?" Kaleb asked, rubbing his eyes, from his foam pad on the floor as Matt cracked the door open.

"Running my brother's errands, lil' buddy," Matt replied with a smile.

It was a short walk over to Greg Samuels' cabin, #9. It was the quietest stretch of the Lake these days, as #10 still sat locked and empty, and the elderly couple in #8 had gone home a week or so ago. Greg had taken in only one person, Lenny, one of the Vietnam vets on the guard detail; most of the other cabins were filled up with four to ten people like the one he shared with Kyle, their wives, and four kids. Now, Matt remembered, two teenagers and a baby too, at least temporarily.

Greg was waiting out front in a yellow rain jacket, old-school woodland camouflage Gore-Tex pants and brown boots. He had on an Atlanta Braves baseball cap and rainbow-finish sunglasses.

"We takin' your truck?" Matt asked.

Greg shrugged. "We could, but I'm runnin' pretty low on gas, and I need to leave at least a little bit, just in case. I thought something else might work better. Come over here and check *this* out." Greg waved him over to the porch. On the left side sat something fairly large, shrouded by a light gray nylon cover. Matt had seen it in passing more than a few times but had never been curious enough to ask.

Greg slipped the cover off with a jerk.

A mass of lime green, aluminum, black plastic, and chromed steel. Matt whistled with appreciation. "Dang. Is that a..."

"Yeah. Kawasaki Ninja. 1990 ZX-11."

"Whoa."

"Yep. Fastest bike in the world back in its day. What can I say? I came back from Saudi with a zillion bucks burnin' a hole in my pocket. A sergeant I worked with had bought it new with his re-up bonus, but then he got orders to Diego Garcia."

Matt snorted. "Middle of the Indian Ocean."

"Rear end of the Earth really. Rather than store it for the length of his tour, he took it in the shorts and sold it to me for cheap. Don't ask me to count how many times I've thought about selling, I'll need to take off my boots to get up that high, but I just never could pull the trigger."

"Can't say I blame you."

"Man, for a while there I had the fastest thing on wheels in all of California, back when I was stationed at Two Nine, out there in the desert. I blew away Corvettes, Mustangs, other bikes, even a Ferrari or two. I've had her up to one-fifty out around Joshua Tree and wasn't even brushing the redline." Greg looked up at the cloud cover and frowned. "But, yeah, don't think we're gonna hit that today."

Matt chuckled. "No, don't think so." The bike was definitely a stellar specimen. It didn't look thirty years old. Other than a few scratches and tiny chips it looked brand new. "The Cushman people will definitely see—and hear—us coming on this."

"Yeah."

"You sure we can both fit on this sucker? You're, ah, not exactly..."

"Small? No, not the same size I used to be. The bike suit hides the gut pretty well, know what I mean? More than a few college girls have been surprised when I popped off the helmet and showed them my gray hairs. We'll be okay. Just hold on tight."

- - - - -

It had become clear in about five minutes that Greg's fuel saving idea was going to lead to some pretty serious, but thankfully temporary, soreness in places Matt held pretty dear. The bike's suspension was just not designed for poorly maintained gravel-and-dirt Forest Service roads.

Halfway to Cushman, a big bodied cow elk popped out of the woods to the left about fifty yards ahead of them. Greg braked, another cow appeared, then a tremendous old bull. All three took note of the idling sportbike and galloped into the tall firs on the other side of the road. Behind trailed two more cows, these smaller than the first pair.

"Don't tell Kyle," Matt said over the engine noise.

"Why not?"

"Because he'd be ticked that we didn't try to get one. Especially that bull."

"What are we gonna do? Carry an eight-hundred-pound elk back on a Kawasaki?"

"That sort of logic won't matter to my brother."

After another hour of picking their way along, stopping twice to check their maps and give their loins a break, they crested the last ridge, just east of Mt. Washington, which rose to over six thousand feet less than ten miles from Hood Canal—sea level.

They had to backtrack toward the Canal, then headed west again to Cushman at a steady twenty miles per hour.

Two men stepped out, one on each side of the road, the one on the right holding up his left hand. Both were dressed for the weather in commercial camo patterns and black Gore-Tex boonies. Both also had healthy six-week-old beards similar to Matt's. Despite the dreary conditions both wore mirrored sunglasses. The man with the outstretched arm had a pistol grip shotgun in his right while his partner pointed a compact magazine-fed rifle right at Greg's Ninja. Greg got the message loud and clear and came to a stop. Matt's teeth clenched. If these were raiders, they had the drop on them bigtime. He just hoped Greg would punch the throttle if warranted.

"State your business," shouted Shotgun Man over the idle of the bike's engine.

"We're from Sunshine Lake, up north of here," Matt replied. "Don't know if you've heard, but Rembrandt Village got taken out by a gang yesterday. We think we might be next. Came here to see if they've been by this way."

The two men exchanged a look, and Shotgun Man nodded. "I think you need to talk with Lawson at the resort lodge. You guys armed?"

Matt nodded. "Of course. It's like American Express. Don't leave home without a gun or two."

Shotgun Man cleared his throat and spat. "We'll call for someone to escort you in. You'll need to surrender any weapons before heading into the lodge. We're, ah, a bit on edge right now. You'll see."

It didn't take long for Matt to develop a dislike for Kent Lawson. The man, perhaps in his early sixties with neatly combed gray hair and a handsome, clean-shaven face, was affable enough, but his smile didn't reach his eyes. Matt had been in plenty of negotiations with people who made a living out of talking from both sides of their mouth. Lawson, making small talk, claimed to be a former city councilman from a mid-sized city outside of Minneapolis. He certainly fit the stereotype of a slick politician.

The inside of the lodge was warm owing to a well-fed central stone fireplace. Matt had been up here about fifteen years ago; he'd just gotten his driver's license and had snuck away during a weekend at the cabin to, well, cruise for girls. Back then it had been quite a bit more humble, full of 1960s-era cabins and structures much like the ones at Sunshine. Judging by the look of the lodge, someone with some cash burning a hole in their pocket had bought up the place and had thrown up some newer, fancier buildings. Exposed wood timbers, still golden, adorned the lodge along with burled tables and plenty of leather sofas.

Lawson clutched a mug of hot tea. "So, Lake Sunshine you say? I've *heard* of it but never been. How are things there right now?"

"As well as can be expected, I guess." Matt sipped his own tea, nothing special but it was pleasantly hot. "It's a pretty small group, and not a lot of people prepared for what's going on right now. How are things here? We guessed there might be several hundred people or more around Cushman."

Lawson shook his head. "No, not that many. I think we peaked around five hundred or so, but families started to run out of food and headed back to civilization. Mostly the campers and RV people. There might be two or three hundred left."

"If you don't mind me asking, what is your role here, Mr. Lawson?" Greg said with a politeness Matt didn't expect. "Do you own the resort?"

Lawson gave another of his inauthentic smiles. "Oh, no, not at all. I'm merely quarterbacking some details to make sure things get taken care of. My main focus is security. Don't you have someone like that at your lake?"

"That's me, the security part," Greg said. "Though Matt's brother, Kyle, came up with the framework we use up there."

Matt shook his head. "Eh. My brother has taken charge on a few things, but mainly he likes to take care of people.

just sharing some of what he brought along. It would be pretty accurate to say he was, well, *is*, one of those 'preppers.' Lately though he's just delegated people and spent his time hunting and fishing. He's pretty darn good at it. Leading a bunch of... civilians... is like herding cats."

"I don't know about that," Lawson argued. "In my experience the buck has to ultimately stop on one person's desk or things don't get done. Hierarchies exist for a reason. It's not just so people can have fancy plaques on their doors. If you can motivate people under you, great. If not, you'll get replaced."

The side door creaked open and a broad shouldered man dressed in soggy Multicam fatigues limped in. He looked to be mid-thirties, balding with a thick reddish-brown beard. In his right hand he clutched an older, brown-painted AR pattern rifle by its railed handguard.

"Speak of the devil," said Lawson. "Terry Graham, our head of security." Lawson stood and shook the big man's hand. "Glad you got the call." He introduced Matt and Greg and explained their presence. Matt then detailed what they knew about the raiders.

"And you think they might be heading your way," Graham said to Matt.

"That's the concern. My brother is down there at the Village now scoping things out."

Graham looked over at Lawson who nodded slowly, smile completely gone. "Well, based just on what you've just told us I'm about ninety nine percent sure this is the same group that hit us four days ago. They claimed to want to trade with us, but the road guards wouldn't let them in. They shot both of them, including my brother." Graham took about ten seconds to collect himself and continued. "Several of us heard the shots and got down here, down to the resort area proper. We had residents streaming in and taking pot shots at them left and right. The firefight lasted about ten minutes by my reckoning. I ran my rifle dry and had less than a mag left for my sidearm when they finally decided we were too big to tackle and turned tail. We scored ten kills and took out three bikes and two of their trucks. But we ended up with a dozen WIAs and nine KIAs on our side."

"I'm really sorry to hear that," Matt said. "Especially about your brother."

"It's done."

"What are these guys like?" Greg asked after another short pause. "I mean, weapons, tactics, you name it."

"Best guess is there are more or less thirty of them left. You already know they have several trucks and a bunch of big bikes. Nothing crazy in terms of weapons. No belt feds or grenades or else they would have used them on us. Be careful though. Check out what we found on the ones they left behind." Graham produced a plastic bag from one of his pockets.

Matt poured out a police officer's badge and two military IDs onto the wooded coffee table. One ID belonged to an Army staff sergeant, the other a Navy petty officer. "These guys deserters or something?"

"Some are, for sure," Graham answered. "Not all. Some of the bikers had beards way too long to be active military, even with a month to grow. But let's get down to brass tacks. I'm interested in hearing about how you're going to deal with these mothers. You guys planning on setting up a defensive position up at your lake? It's going to be tough to contain those motorcycles. Those bastards know how to ride."

Matt shook his head. "I know my brother. He's not big into digging foxholes. If they're still around he'll want to go down there and kick their teeth in."

"I like the sound of that. Your brother, he military?" Graham asked.

"Marine infantry. I'm an Army vet. Thirty-one bravo, Military Police."

"Marines," Greg added. "Comm guy, but hey, every

Marine is a rifleman."

"That's good to hear," Graham replied. "Army Ranger here."

Matt perked up a bit. Rangers were always good to have around in a gunfight. "Afghanistan?"

"Yeah, Iraq before that. You do some time in 'Stan?"

"Sure did." Matt paused and looked Graham in the eye. "I know it's not your fight anymore, but we sure could use your help. We might be able to scrounge up fifteen, maybe twenty effectives, most with no combat training or experience. Needless to say, the more guys who know how to shoot on our side, the better."

"Now, wait a second," Lawson interjected. "Let's not put blinders on here. That was one gang, there might be one just like it—or bigger and nastier—headed our way right now. Until the government restores order we have to assume we're on our own."

Graham grabbed at his left pant leg and lifted. Underneath was a prosthetic, metal with a black plastic molded calf, which formed an articulating joint where the knee once was. "As you can see I'm not really cut out for offensive maneuvers anymore."

Lawson stood and set his empty mug on the end table. "There. That settles it. We'd love to help you all up at, what was it? Sunbeam Lake?"

"Sunshine," Matt corrected.

"Sunshine. Yes. We have our own problems to deal with. You have your intel now. I wish you the best, but if you'll both excuse me I have some things I need to attend to."

Graham stood. "I'll walk you both out. Gentlemen?" He motioned, palm up, toward the main doors.

The trio stepped outside. Graham transferred his rifle to his left hand and extended his hand. "Have to apologize for Lawson. He's, well, true to himself."

Matt shook the bigger man's hand. "He certainly

seems to know how to pull the strings around here."

Graham shook his massive head. "You ever have one of those lieutenants that gladly takes on the dumb administrative stuff but is an empty suit in the field?"

Matt nodded with a grin. "Absolutely."

"He's kind of like that. He's treating this like a big chess game, but sometimes the pawns move on their own, know what I mean?"

Matt nodded again, smirking. "I have a list of freqs and a set of codes to leave with you. Can you monitor HF?"

"Can do," Graham replied as he took the tightly wrapped plastic sandwich bag that contained the small sheets of paper. "I'll keep my ears open. I want to get those mothers. It's personal. There are some other men here with scores to settle too. Let us know."

"Okay," Matt said. "We should have a plan by tomorrow at the latest. Those codes my brother and Greg here came up with should cover every relevant scenario."

"One more thing before you go," Graham said. "Those two kids with a baby you mentioned? It's a good thing you picked them up. The Shelton ZOC is gone. They bused the residents out to JBLM. There's a gigantic refu camp outside of the base's fence. I mean huge—bigger than anything I ever saw over in the Middle East."

"Seriously?"

"Yeah. Olympia, right around the capitol proper at least is still a ZOC but it's a closed-list deal now, pretty much just for government staff and their families. To get anything you'd have to keep moving up the interstate another fifteen miles. From where you found them that's a good sixty miles total. Those three would have never made it that far on empty stomachs."

CHAPTER THIRTY-ONE

Tuesday, Fourth Week in November

K yle and Malachi walked back along a slightly different route, making an effort to be quieter than they had been earlier that morning. They bypassed the 'gate' this time and were headed back to Kyle's cabin when they heard the growl of a motorcycle from the rear. Kyle spun around, unslung the Tikka and scanned with his eyes just above the scope. A bright green racer-type bike carrying two men came into view.

Doesn't look like any of the ones we saw earlier. He brought the rifle's muzzle down, still keeping a firm grip on the weapon. If this bike didn't belong, Jeanie—the former big city cop that had devoted more than a fair share of her time to guard duty—would already have been lighting it up with Kyle's AR or her SIG.

The bike came to a stop twenty yards from him. "Hey, bro!" his brother called as Greg killed the engine and flicked out the kickstand. "Forget about, 'never point a weapon at anything you do not intend to shoot?'"

"I didn't forget," Kyle yelled back. "Just a bit on edge right now. What's the situation at Cushman?"

Matt and Greg both hopped off the Kawasaki. "Eh.

Well," Matt began, "that same gang put a hurt on them pretty good but they drove them off a few days ago. Things are . . . *strange* . . . there but I think we can count on some help."

"You can fill me in shortly. Right now though, can you guys do me a favor?"

"What do you need?" Greg responded.

"Go around and gather everyone up for another fireside chat. This one's important."

The covered picnic area was once again the choice due to the on and off drizzle. Kyle sat atop one of the tables at the edge. This would be the first all-hands gathering since he'd made his Ayn Rand speech here a few weeks ago.

"Thanks for taking some time to hear me out." He scanned the crowd. The beards and tighter belts weren't the only changes he saw. Many more of the Sunshiners openly carried weapons now. Things had definitely graduated from the 'extended unplanned vacation' feel and were well into 'armed refugee camp' territory.

"Some of you may have heard that we have some new guests as of yesterday. They lived nearby, down near the Canal in Rembrandt Village, and had carried on in much the same way as we have up here. Yesterday, a marauder gang attacked and wiped Rembrandt Village off of the face of the Earth."

Kyle paused to let that sink in. He saw some solemn nods and heard several whispered curses. "This gang had attacked Lake Cushman a couple of days before, but they were pushed back. Both sides lost several people. While Greg and Matt were reconnoitering Cushman, I headed down to Rembrandt Village with one of the survivors, Malachi, mainly to ascertain if this gang could be a threat to us here. The answer is an unequivocal 'yes.'

"We set up an observation post several hundred yards

from where the gang is currently holed up. Most of you are familiar with the store and the bar along 101 there. I want to recount what we saw, but first I'd like Abigail, along with some of the older children, to take the little ones down to the dock area and wait until we're done. This isn't for their ears."

Kyle waited as the children shuffled out with Abigail in the lead. "This is . . . hard . . . to recount so bear with me, please." He took a deep breath, let it out, and continued. "Through my spotting scope I could see several bodies left out to rot. Three were strung up with rope on power poles nearby. If I had to guess, it was whoever had been staying put in those two buildings before the gang showed up. There was a single lookout posted between the bar and store, out of sight of anyone approaching along the highway. At about ten in the morning, four more men, each with a gun in one hand and a bottle of booze in the other, came out of the bar. They, along with the lookout, used those bodies for target practice for the better part of an hour. Several others eventually joined in. Later, around noon, we could hear faint screams that lasted for ten minutes or so. A few minutes later, two of the gang carried a body by its arms and legs outside and pitched it into the dirt. It was so bloody and beaten I couldn't tell if it was a man or a woman. I saw several of these... *animals*... urinate on the corpse of this person.

"At about one in the afternoon, a single small white sedan approached from the north. I didn't mention it before, but the gang has set up a homemade spike strip in the road, with the ditch on one side and their vehicles blocking the parking lot for the bar on the other. This sedan approached, stopped, saw the strip, then started to do a three-point when five of the gang came running out of the store with guns out and shot at it. The side windows shattered and the front windshield was a mass of holes and spider cracks. The car stopped accelerating but kept rolling backward and went into the far ditch. The five approached, pulled out the passengers and proceeded to loot the vehicle. When they finished they pushed it out behind the store, obviously to keep their trap working for next time.

"If there is still doubt in anyone's mind that these are evil men . . . they pulled a small child, alive, from the rear passenger seat and . . . I'm sorry, I just can't . . ."

Kyle stopped, shaking with tears forming in his eyes. He'd seen some gruesome things during his time in Iraq. Dead people lying beside dirt roads, limbs curled in rigor mortis and covered in fine dust. Burning vehicles . . . Kyle would never forget the smell of burning gasoline mixed with human bodies. But he'd been able to collect himself and remember that these were not his people; that they put a different standard on human life than he did, and he could look forward to the fact that he'd eventually return home to a much more sane existence. What he'd seen earlier that day was different. These were his fellow Americans, men that could have been his neighbors five weeks ago, waving back at Kyle as he mowed his fenced two acres perched on his Craftsman. Men that could have sat next to him and his family at church. He shuddered at this last thought.

He collected himself, took a deep breath, and continued. "I've come up with a plan but I want to bounce it off of all of you, then go into particulars in a smaller group. In short, I want to go down there and preemptively attack. Catch these pieces of human garbage by surprise and Wipe. Them. Out."

"Why not just wait here and build some kind of . . . defensive position?" a thin older man wearing a Seattle Seahawks ski hat asked from one of the tables in front. "Pardon my ignorance, I'm not a military man, but isn't it easier to defend rather than attack?" Kyle didn't recall his name but knew he was staying next to the Klein cabin, in #15.

"That's a good question and you have a point, but you're thinking strategically rather than tactically. Strategic is for big armies pounding away at one another. You're more vulnerable on the move than in an emplacement and there are small concerns like supply lines with food, gas, and ammo to contend with that make it hard to go on the offensive. But this is *tactical*. A small group of people that know what they're doing can easily take on a much larger force, especially if they catch the defenders with their pants down. Plus, the attacker gets to choose the time and the circumstances. If we go on the defensive we'll have to maintain a heavy guard until we're absolutely sure these guys are gone, and if they attack us unsuccessfully they can simply withdraw and go on to the next place. Or regroup and come at us again at their leisure. I don't want that to happen. We can't maintain a sizeable reaction force that's ready to go at a moment's notice *and* take care of ourselves indefinitely.

"This all leads to the big issue—we only have five or six people that know what they are about when the bullets start flying. There's no way I'm going down there undergunned. We're going to need twenty fighters, minimum, plus a support team of drivers and whatever we can scrape together for a medical team."

That prompted most of the Sunshiners to turn and look at their neighbors. Kyle could read their thoughts: *There are about eighty people here. Assuming that no women will be asked to fight, that brings it down to about forty. Out of those, about ten are very elderly or infirm, and another five or six are boys under the age of fifteen. This Kyle character is, in effect, asking every available male of fighting age to come forward.*

"What about the Cushman people? That's a big lake. Lots of people there for sure. They must want some payback too, right?" a woman called from the back.

Kyle looked at Matt and gestured at him with his right hand.

Matt cleared his throat. "Not as many as you might think. A lot of people there have already left for the refugee camps, and even more now after the attack. I think we can count on maybe four to six, coming up and helping out, but not stationed here as guards, no. They'll want to take care of business and head home, like my brother said."

Kyle gave a single nod toward Matt and continued. "I hope it's been pretty clear since the beginning that I'm not in charge—and have no interest in being in charge—of anyone but my own immediate family. I can't and won't order anybody to take part. When the bullets start flying I don't want to look to my left or my right and see someone who's only there because they were coerced. Just as none of us can vote on one another's possessions, we can't vote on someone else's participation. It's not right for people to send others to do their fighting for them. One way or another we're going to need a lot more warriors to either bulk up our defenses or lay those scumbags out.

"So, I'm going to ask for initial volunteers to fight. The current security team will also have to actively choose to put their names in the hat. You don't need to decide immediately, talk it over with your families, make sure it's the right choice, but keep in mind this door might close soon because if we decide to attack it'll be in the very near future. Clear?"

Kyle saw the nods and furtive glances back and forth. He wondered who would raise a hand here, if anyone. Greg's hand shot up simultaneously with Matt's, followed by his young friend Timothy, then Malachi, then Greg's new cabinmate Lenny. After some whispered words back and forth with his father, mother, and wife, Mike Klein put his big hand in the air.

"Thank you men for volunteering," Kyle said over the quieting din. "Let's meet immediately after this gathering. To everyone else, keep thinking about it. And, if you think you can help in some other way, let me know."

With that, the crowd started to break up and walk off into the dying light. That older man in the Seahawks hat that had spoken up earlier approached Kyle along with the six volunteers.

"Hi, I'm Norris, down in fifteen. I don't think I can

help much in a fight but I do have some guns you might want to use."

Kyle perked up. They were still desperately short of combat-worthy weapons.

"My father was a colonel in the Army back in World War Two," Norris began. "He was able to bring back some nice European military arms and he added on to that collection until he passed away. I inherited them and I have kept them up. They're not wall hangers; they all work."

Kyle tried not to frown. He'd briefly imagined a trove of high quality modern weapons. Eighty-year-old guns were probably not going to be a huge help. "What kind of weapons? I'm pretty knowledgeable. I know model numbers and such. Guns are one of my hobbies too."

"Well, there's the handguns, three P-38s and two Lugers. One's a Navy and the other is a standard model. Plus a Finnish Lahti and a Polish Radom."

All were 9mms, Kyle recalled, and he had ammo for them. But in a raid like he'd envisioned they'd need rifles. "Okay. Seeing as real machineguns are illegal in Washington State I'm guessing you're not hiding away a belt-fed MG34 or 42. But if you are, that sure would be nice. I won't turn you in to the feds, *wink wink*."

"Don't I wish," Norris said with a chuckle. "Dad did have a StG44,"—he pronounced the 'StG' as 'stig'—"that he picked up in Belgium in the last couple of months of the war. But he sold it back in the early eighties, not long before he passed away, and right before the moratorium on new machineguns. Some lucky schmuck had a fifty thousand dollar gun on his hands before . . . all this." The StG44 was the first true assault rifle, Kyle knew. Thirty rounds of full-auto firepower, even out of a museum piece, would have been great for the psychological effect if nothing else.

"But," Norris continued, "I do have three German Mausers—one is a scoped sniper model, a real one at that. Another is a 'Stalingrad Rifle' captured by the Soviets. Some G.I.

brought it back from Vietnam of all places as a war trophy and my dad snapped it up at a gun show. The other is a regular issue rifle, but in perfect condition. I also have a scoped Swedish Mauser and a Finnish-made Mosin-Nagant sniper rifle." Mausers and Mosins were bolt action and each held five shots. Excellent rifles and built with superb craftsmanship —especially the sniper models—but not really meant for ambushes where volume of fire was critical. Plus, sniper and rifle were a matched set. You couldn't simply hand a 'sniper rifle' to someone and expect anything to magically happen. It usually took months, even years, to develop that partnership between man and weapon, time they didn't have.

"Not sure we have much need for bolt actions," Kyle said. "I'm not really envisioning a sniper fest down there. Beggars can't be choosers though. What else do you have?"

"Well . . . I *do* have two semis. A German G43 and a Russian SVT-40. I should mention I have some ammo for all of these, but not a whole lot, maybe a hundred 8mm, a couple of boxes of twenty of the Swede 6.5, and about the same for the Mosin. About a hundred 9mm." Kyle racked his gun knowledge on those rifles. He knew that the G43 took the same 8mm as the German Mausers, something he didn't have, and one hundred rounds went quick in a battle.

"I think that SVT-40, if it's in good shape, is going to be the most useful," Kyle said. The SVT-40 took the same ammo as his shorty Vepr, a nice bit of luck as Kyle had almost a thousand rounds in that caliber, mostly inexpensive Russian surplus. "The bolt action rifles, not as much. No offense, but a good modern hunting rifle with a quality scope is going to equal or exceed those in application. I'll get back with you about the handguns, but we're probably okay there as well." For the combat vets, having a handgun as a backup would be a nice addition, but Kyle knew he simply didn't have the time to train a neophyte on how to use a handgun— the type of gun that was hardest to aim and hit with the least power—in combat.

"Okay then. So . . . I'll be around, in my cabin or helping with the work details. Just let me know."

Kyle nodded and turned to his small group. He noticed that Timothy was embroiled in a heated discussion with his parents. "So, my merry men, looks like we're it, at least for now."

"Taking on the role of Robin Hood now are you?" Matt joked.

"Weak attempt at humor, sorry. All I can manage right now, guys. Had what you might call a 'bad day' and now am planning another one. Probably worse."

"So, what's the deal?" Mike blurted. "We going to go down there tomorrow and take care of those assholes?"

Lenny spoke up. "Son, if you knew what combat was like you wouldn't be in such a hurry. I'm only here because I wouldn't be able to look these fellas square in the face if I sat this out. God willing, I got one more fight in me, bad eyes or no." The quiet man did wear some seriously thick Coke-bottle lenses but he was mentally as tough as they came. Kyle had gotten to know him over the course of several long guard shifts. Lenny had spent most of his tour in and around the A Shau Valley—part of the infamous Ho Chi Minh Trail. He had arrived not long after the Battle of Hamburger Hill to a unit bled white by the North Vietnamese and had seen some action. Even so, Kyle wondered if the old man really had one more fight in him; he had to be around seventy. Lenny had admitted that before this month he hadn't touched a rifle in fifty years.

"Here's my plan, but don't get me wrong, I'm not married to it," Kyle began. "Speak up if something doesn't seem quite right. Tomorrow, two of us are going to drive down there and—"

"Wait, what? Drive down into that trap?" Matt interrupted.

Kyle pointed a finger at his brother. "Hear me out. I'm not an idiot. I'm not going down there for a 'meet and greet' with a plate full of brownies. Tomorrow we'll go door-to-door, here at the lake, to gather up all the booze that's left. We'll take it down there, play like we see the spike strip, then run off and leave the vehicle and the hooch. I'm willing to sacrifice my Durango. Just don't tell Amber until it's done."

There were a couple of chuckles at that. "Shoot," Lenny said, "if'n you need a rig to sacrifice, my old Ranger barely got me here. That sucker has over two hundred grand on the odometer and a bum transmission. If one of you promises to haul me out of here if and when the time comes —"

"I got your back, bud, don't worry," Greg said.

"Okay, great," Kyle said, relieved he'd keep his SUV after all. "Just need to get all the booze. We'll have a note in the vehicle that says something to the effect that we're making a delivery and being paid in guns and ammo. My hope is it'll give them an incentive to pull up stakes and go there. The 'there' on the note will be someplace far, far from here."

"Hey, wait," Matt cried, indignant. "I thought the idea was to wipe these guys out. That's what you said at the meeting. Remember?"

"I did say that, yes, only because I didn't want to divulge every piece of my plan. I'm not a big fan of kicking the can down the road, but our number one goal is to all stay alive. If I can find a way to get them to leave without putting our lives on the line, I'm going to do it."

"Send 'em to Indian Island," Lenny offered.

"Indian Island?" Matt asked.

"It's up north of here a bit, near Port Townsend. I have ... had ... some friends up that way. There's a big Navy weapons and ammo dump there. Guarded even before this mess, probably locked down tighter'n a bull's tail end in fly time right now. Send 'em there and let the Navy and Marines take care of them."

"Not a bad idea," Kyle said.

"What happens if they don't fall for it?" Matt asked.

"Then, hopefully our enemy will be sauced up right before we go down there to fight 'em. Once we deliver the booze, we'll grab our two man team and come back to prepare for the next day. That's when we'll head down there under the cover of darkness and attack at dawn."

"Classic," Matt said, smiling.

"But I don't want to just show up guns blazing," Kyle added. "That bar and store would both make pretty good defensive positions. I don't want us out in the open. I want to draw them out into an ambush."

"How do you plan on making that happen?" Greg asked. "Gonna be tough to get them to all just walk outside and get shot at."

"Yeah, that's the part I'm nailing down in my mind. Best I can think of is to create a ruckus, draw some out, then hightail it away. They follow and we blast them."

"L-shaped ambush," Matt added.

Kyle nodded. "You *do* have a bit of experience with that one, brother. I was thinking the same thing."

"What's that?" Malachi asked.

"It's a pretty standard ambush layout," Kyle replied. "The long part of the 'L' consists of most of your close range firepower. The short part of the 'L' is usually your support weapons or snipers. You get the targets to go parallel to the long part of the 'L' but not too close to the short part."

"Why not just surround them?" Mike asked.

"Because," Matt said, "you'd end up shooting your own people in the confusion. This way, you shoot what's directly in front of you with no risk that your guys are on the receiving end."

"Exactly," Kyle said. "So a three or four man mobile team to draw them out, a short leg team, and at least two separate teams along the long leg."

"Looks like we need about, oh, twenty more guys," Greg observed.

"Yup," said Kyle. "We'll get some of these folks tomorrow when we go around begging for their booze. Greg, are you willing to head up one of those close range teams?"

"Absolutely, boss," Greg replied.

"What about training?" Matt asked. "This isn't something we can just discuss and throw out there on the battlefield."

"Of course not," Kyle said. "We'll take the crew west, behind the next ridge, and do a little target practice and familiarization. We'll practice hand signals, how the ambush will be laid out, assign to squads, all of that stuff. Let's not delve into minutiae too hard right now. We'll have time enough for that tomorrow."

"Excuse me, Kyle?" It was a woman's voice, high pitched but pleasant. "I wanted to talk with you."

Kyle recognized her. Kathy Rex, an older lady of about seventy. She volunteered often to help watch children so others could do grunt work. A younger man wearing a red ski jacket trailed behind.

"Sure, Kathy, what's up?"

"Well, during the meeting you mentioned something about a needing a medical team."

"Absolutely! You two volunteering?"

Kathy shook her head. "No, but my daughter Melissa's an Army field surgeon at Fort Lewis." Kathy used the old name for JBLM.

"Do you know how to get in touch with her? Or know if she's even still there? I know the government has moved around a lot of military personnel."

The younger man spoke up. Kyle had not seen him around before. "I'm Jerry, Kathy's son-in-law. Last Wednesday, we stopped right by the refugee camp and quickly found out the base was locked down, but one of their runners found Melissa and she sent us a note. She was glad to hear from us but apologized as she could not leave the base under any circumstances."

"What makes you think she'll be able to leave if she's forbidden by her command and we go down and ask for her? I'm not exactly seeing a track record of success here," Kyle said point-blank.

Jerry just shrugged.

Kyle frowned. "No, if we do this, it'll be total honesty. We're in mortal danger, we're going into battle, and we sure could use some help. If she can't come, that's just the way it is."

"If you decide to go, let me know," said Jerry. "I figure this is the best way I can help since I'm not a soldier." He turned to leave.

Kyle put his hand up. "Hold on for a second, Jerry. We're going to decide right now. If someone is going to go down there with Jerry and find Melissa, it must be done tonight before the curfew hits. That's the only way the timeline works, otherwise we're stretching it out a day and that just makes it more likely the marauders decide to pay us a visit."

"I'll go," Greg said. "It's worth a try."

Jerry pointed at Greg. "You have a NID?"

"A what?" Greg replied.

Jerry patted his back pocket. "Y'know, the new orange ID card."

Greg shook his head.

"That's not going to work," Jerry said. "You get caught without one, Peace Enforcement is going to detain you and force you to get one. You get picked up tonight and you're stuck until at least tomorrow. Maybe a lot longer if something trips in their system. And don't think you can just walk around looking like you blend in. Most of these guys have a scanner that confirms you have a card on you and reveals all your personal info. It's freakin' spooky to have some dude walk up to you and say, 'Hi Mr. Goodridge, I'm with Peace Enforcement, and I'm going to conduct a search of your person. Hands behind your head.'"

"I have an orange card," Matt said. "I'll go."

Kyle looked at his brother and shook his head slightly. "Matt, you've been through more than any of us. You're barely past recovering from your trip up here."

Plus, Des will kill me if you don't come back.

"I'm fine, bro. I'm the only one standing here with a new ID. Your choices are limited. Me or no one."

"Well this is going to throw a bit of a wrench in things," Kyle said. "I figured I'd be leaning on you heavy for the training portion. You two get down there right now, do what you have to do, and come back before dark tomorrow. With or without Melissa."

CHAPTER THIRTY-TWO

Tuesday, Fourth Week in November

Matt cracked the door open to the bedroom he shared with Des. He wasn't sure if his brother had noticed her absence at the meeting earlier. Matt certainly had. She lay there in the dark, a pillow over the top of her head. He lit the candle on the dresser with a wand lighter.

"Matt?" she croaked. "What's going on?"

No sense in beating around the bush. "I need to pack up and head out, princess. I'll be back tomorrow."

She sat up quickly, wide-eyed, and the pillow hit the floor. "What? Where in the *hell* are you going this time?"

He grabbed a box from the small closet that held the business casual attire he'd been wearing when he'd arrived. Jerry had mentioned it would be best to not stick out down in the camp. It was essential to look like real refugees. The feds were apparently starting to press veterans into involuntary service; wearing a closetful of surplus camo would be an invitation to determine if you'd slipped through the cracks. The torn and stained business wear Matt had worn up from California would be perfect. He pulled out the gray slacks and white shirt, along with the ski jacket, and started to change.

"Jerry Goodridge and I are running down to JBLM to find his sister-in-law. She's a doctor and she may be able to help us. We're going to hit that gang in a couple of days, Des. They're a real threat to us here. If we don't take them out on our terms, they might show up here anytime. You should have been there for Kyle's report. Those are some stone evil bastards down there." Matt took off the duty belt and set it on the dresser by the candle. To his dismay, he had to leave it there.

"You're driving all the way there, now, in the dark? Why you? *Why?* Why does it always have to be you? Eighty people up here and it's always *my* husband doing all the dirty work! I want a reason why someone else can't go!"

"Look, Des, sweetie, calm down. Truth is, we needed someone with one of the new IDs since the refugee camp is crawling with graysuits. Anyone without one would just get detained."

"Seriously?" she howled. "There must be twenty people up here with one of those. *I* have one. Naturally, *of course*, your paranoid brother doesn't have one. *He* gets to stay here with his family. How convenient. I bet this is all his idea. Right?"

Matt shook his head. "No, princess . . . look . . . *I volunteered*. It needs to be done by someone experienced in recon. And don't tear down Kyle, please. Without him we'd really be in trouble. We all gladly eat his food, drink his purified water, watch movies fed by his batteries, and listen to broadcasts on his radio."

"Yeah, your brother sure is a *swell* guy," Des replied, voice thick with sarcasm. "Y'know something, it turns out that my mother was right about you. Before the wedding, she told me, 'Des I love you, and I know you love your fiancé, but watch out, these people are right wing nuts. Every man in the family is trying to live out some sort of macho fantasy. His brother is one of those Bible-thumping survivalist bitter-clinger types. And here we are. You're like a little clone of your brother, running around with a gun on one adventure or another while your wife is stuck scared to death in her dark, cold room, expected to play *madrastra* to five stray kids. That's not who I married, Matt. You were different. You were better. And I stuck up for you."

It occurred to Matt just then that Des didn't like him. She possibly never had. She was in love with what they were *together*, the companionship, the shared experiences, but strip away all the fancy dinners, cocktail parties, shopping jaunts, and trips to Hawaii or Cabo, and to Des that left nothing. She would never be content with *just Matt*. And it hurt. A lot.

Matt finished packing the knapsack, fought the tightness in his throat, and left without another word.

They hit the road in Jerry's car, its broken driver's side window adding just a bit to their cover as haggard holdouts finally seeking the refugee camp and the promise of Uncle Sugar's sweet handouts.

"You look kinda like Al Pacino in that old cop movie," Jerry said as they headed south on Highway 101 toward Olympia. Although it was over two hours until curfew, it was completely dark. Not even the car provided any relief; in an effort to stave off any unwanted attention they'd pulled the fuses for all exterior and interior lights on the car.

Al Pacino. He didn't know old movies too well. But Matt was part Italian. He'd seen *The Godfather*. It was pretty much an ethnic requirement. "Old, you mean like in *The Godfather*? He was the opposite of a cop in that."

"No," Jerry replied, "he was a cop and he narced on the other cops taking bribes. *Serpico*, that's it. Hard to remember this stuff without the Internet, you know?"

Matt nodded and checked himself in the rearview mirror. His hair had gone wavy, very 1970s, and his beard was as thick as those his Italian great uncles had sported back in their days. All he was missing was the distressed leather jacket and a pair of gold-rimmed Aviators. Jerry, on the other hand, was slender, quite pale, and had reddish-brown hair. He looked like he'd only given up shaving about a week ago.

"What did you do before?" Jerry asked.

"I was a regional sales rep for a medical supply company. You?"

"Systems analyst for a regional health care group. Hey, we might know some of the same people."

"It's possible. I usually dealt with purchasing managers day-to-day. The big dogs when it came time to negotiate the next contract. Most of my job was just putting out fires, though. Missed delivery, need to return some equipment, that sort of thing."

Jerry smiled knowingly. "My job was to help keep the EHR system humming along. Juggling different balls every day. I'm not in love with the current situation, don't get me wrong, but I'm in no hurry to get back to my desk."

"Amen to that," Matt said. "So, you just came from Seattle. What's it like there now? Just one big ZOC?"

"Heck no. It's about fifteen little ones spread all over the city. People are all huddled up around those. Maybe seventy-five percent of Seattle's been left to rot. Gangs, arson, individual psychos going around killing people, armed looters everywhere."

"Is that why you left?"

"No, a lot more basic than that. The food handouts started to get really spotty. Well, spotty isn't the right term. The amount of food they hand out just isn't enough to live on. Government people, especially those Auxiliary types, were starting to act a lot like the gangs on the outside. It was time to go, and even then we'd waited too long."

They continued in silence, taking the interchange with Interstate 5 north up to the base. It was 8:15—less than an hour before curfew—when Jerry pulled off to the side of the road about a mile from the camp proper.

"Here?" Matt asked. "You said you parked right up next to it last time ... and ... oh. Right."

"No danger of it getting busted into again, true, but I'm more worried someone will drain the fuel and strand us."

"It's becoming an essential skill."

They started walking in the near pitch darkness. After about ten minutes, Matt heard the sound of helicopters approaching directly overhead from the west. He looked up to see two sets of green and red lights pass overhead.

"Blackhawks," Matt said. It had been a long time since they'd seen an active aircraft of any kind. "Maybe things are getting pieced together. Takes a lot of fuel and support to keep them in the air."

"Don't kid yourself," Jerry scoffed. "From what I've seen, the military and the government never came apart. They just *reorganized*. It's everything else that fell apart. I saw more than a few helos like that around Seattle, and some jets land at Boeing Field. I live ... *lived* right near there on Beacon Hill."

The pair crested a small rise. Before them was the former Eagles Pride Golf course across from the base. Dozens, no, hundreds of small fires crackled, illuminating tents ranging from the finest four-season adventurer models down to makeshift A-frames made of tarps and expedient poles. Most were closer to the latter. Ringing the edge and back in the trees were those better off in actual trailers or motorhomes. Even here, they could hear the faint cries of small children and the barking of several dogs. Figures using high-intensity LED flashlights walked slowly through the camp. They were almost certainly Peace Enforcement. Matt guessed that there were at least fifty thousand people occupying the eighteen hole course and the area around it.

"So, how does this work with the curfew?" Matt asked. "It's not exactly 'staying in your home' when you're out here in a tent."

"The understanding is that you'll stay in the camp and in your little area. Already there's a real estate battle going on. The prime territory is near the food distros—there are three of them—but not so close that you have a line of people right next to your tent. And if the size of this place impresses you, remember most of the refugees lived and got stopped *north* of the base. There's two camps on that end that are each even bigger than this one."

"How is it even sanitary?"

"Matt, c'mon, it's a *refugee camp*. It's *not* sanitary. They don't even bother to try anymore. A bucket that you take out into the trees or sand traps when full is pretty much the standard. From what I've heard, there's a more formal FEMA camp on the inside of the base that has actual facilities. That's for people with special skills. The dregs that the government doesn't want live out here. Unskilled hands. Like us."

"Hey now," Matt said, "How do you know I don't have any skills?"

"Because the gray goons would have pulled you out of a chow line already and put you on a white bus, that's how."

It didn't take long to find a place to bed down. They simply located a plot of dirt that hadn't been used as a latrine or otherwise covered with human effluents. Since they hadn't brought a tent, just a small tarp for each of them along with a wool blanket, they didn't take up much room. A small fire crackled nearby. Unfortunately, it reeked of burning wet garbage, smoky and unpleasant. Several people, some in camping chairs but most on the wet ground, were chatting, just indistinctly enough that Matt couldn't pick up the conversation.

As Matt watched, two figures brought more wood to the fire, and the conversation stopped. A man coughed nearby, wet and hacking. A little farther away, a man spewed obscenities. There was a single gunshot, well off in the distance. No one seemed to give any of it special attention.

"Not these two again," said a gruff voice as all of the original neighbors suddenly got up to leave. Curious, Matt walked over and sat down. Jerry joined him a few moments later.

"Well hello," called one of the two newcomers, a shorter bearded man in a baseball cap. It was hard to tell ages in the firelight but he looked to be about fifty. Beside him sat the man he'd walked up with: taller, maybe six foot two, surprisingly clean shaven, narrow-faced, and appeared to be about forty.

"Hello back," Matt replied. "Looks like you guys have a ... *reputation*."

The younger one shrugged. "Ehh, I'm tired of us too," he said in a polished New York City accent. "It happens. Look around. We're all pretty tired of one another."

"Understand completely," said Jerry from the other side of the fire. "I was here a week ago. Had my fill in one day."

"And yet here you are again," said the older man in a folksy tone, an affable Midwestern accent peeking through. To Matt he sounded like someone who might narrate a children's cartoon. By the looks of his shirt and clothes, he had been a good thirty pounds heavier in the recent past. *Come to think of it*, Matt mused, *that describes just about everyone*.

"We're trying to find someone on the base," Jerry said, getting right to the point. "Know anyone who can get on in the morning? A runner?"

"They congregate near the gate during the daytime. Pretty hard to miss. They don't work for free though," replied the older man.

"Of course," Matt said. "We brought payment. Like to be discrete about it. No offense."

"None taken," said the older one with a slight, wry smile. "And with whom do we have the pleasure of sharing our fire?"

Matt introduced himself and Jerry in turn. "Nice to meet you both," replied the older man. "A couple of months ago I was Dr. Reed, now I'm just Paul. My somewhat more... *taciturn* friend here is, was, Dr. Schlesinger. Simply Aaron now, I suppose. No one cares much for fancy titles anymore."

Matt perked up and he noticed Jerry did as well. "You guys are doctors?" Matt asked, trying to contain his excitement. "We're actually trying to link up with a doctor who can help—"

Paul held up his right hand. "Now hold up there. Matt, we're almost certainly *not* the type of doctors you're looking for. We were professors up in Seattle at one of the smaller colleges. History for me, specifically of the American variety."

"I taught economics and finance," Aaron added.

"So, even with PhDs the FEMA folks don't have you on their list?" Jerry asked. "I thought they're rounding up everyone with special skills."

Aaron snorted, a bit derisive. "Whoever is pulling the economic strings, it's *waaaay* above FEMA. Above the White House, above everything this side of Heaven. They definitely don't need a washed up trader turned professor."

"Not much calling for history either," said Paul. "You can't eat it, spend it, shoot it, or drink it."

"What do you mean, 'above everything'?" Jerry asked. "Do you guys know what actually happened?"

Aaron smiled a bit, his still-white teeth shining yellow in the firelight. He glanced at Paul. "Now you're hitting on why those schmoes got up and left. They've heard it from us already. Or maybe some secondhand version of it and didn't want another dose. It's not a happy tale. You sure you want to hear this?"

"Yeah, absolutely," Jerry replied. Matt just nodded.

The Tale of Two Professors

AARON: It would help to have a little background on Paul and I. Résumés. Whatever. I grew up in Brooklyn, son of a shopkeeper, last kid of five. Saw dad lose his store. Supposedly for tax reasons. I didn't get a free ride to college like my older brothers and sister. My oldest brother, Seth, Mr. Ivy League MBA, worked for one of the big firms on Wall Street and got me an "in" on the ground floor as a trader. I worked my way through college and busted my hump for *six years*. New York is the worst city in the world to work well over forty a week plus classes ... there is *always* something fun begging for your attention. But I did it.

Oh, did I mention I got in there a year before the tech bubble burst? That was my first taste of how fragile everything is and how it's *all* just numbers in a computer. People used their numbers to buy up other numbers which got erased in a few weeks. Then came 2008. That was far worse for those of us on Wall Street. The tech bust was like someone chopping off a branch of the tree. In 2008 we were faced with someone sawing it off at the trunk. But, people moved some numbers around and called it good. I won't bore you by going into petty details and insider jargon. That's all it really was ... moving numbers. None of it really *meant* anything, at least at that first level. But the ripples in the pond were real enough. Changing those numbers destroyed some people and made others rich. Not just "nice house in the suburbs" rich. I mean "private plane and three legit *mansions*" rich.

After that I realized the gig was up, at least for me. Seth *retired* off of that crash. Him and my sister-in-law got a big house up in the Catskills and became jeans and sandals multi-millionaires. That's not supposed to happen ... call me an idealist I guess. Maybe it was the fact that I worked my way through school, but I realized that there was no actual *value* in what I was doing. Sure, you can talk about wealth generation all you want but I never *saw* it. It was always just numbers. And the crazy thing is you could take those numbers and get something *real* with them, like a house or a sports car. Even with a master's in finance I just couldn't buy into the concept. I also knew that it was just a matter of time before it all came crashing down. The average Joe was leveraged to the hilt and there just wasn't anything more to squeeze. I sure as hell didn't want to be stuck in a Manhattan high rise with a couple of days of food and a few bottles of Perrier as "survival supplies."

So I got out. I wanted deeply to figure out the 'why' behind what I saw. If finance is like physics—the movement of money—then economics is the mathematics, the underpinning of it all. I knew there was no way I could afford my place as a graduate assistant working my way toward a PhD, so I packed up and moved out to Oklahoma. Yeah, the New York Jew in hayseed Oklahoma, I've heard all the jokes, thanks. Along the way to my doctorate I fell in with a handful of professors who opened my eyes to the Austrian school of economics.

MATT: I've heard of that. Not sure where. I was a business major, maybe it was in one of the economics classes. Actually, no. It was one of the blogs my brother turned me on to.

AARON: Well, just by knowing its name you have infinitely more knowledge about it than ninety-nine point nine nine percent of people out there. It got about the same treatment in most schools' econ departments that young Earth creationism got with the biology profs.

JERRY: What's wrong with it then?

AARON: There's nothing *wrong* with it. It just takes the power out of the hands of the government, investment banks, and big businesses and puts it in the hands of individuals. The competing economic view is the Keynesian school which dominates economic policy among all the meaningful players.

Heh. You're both about to ask me what the differences are. Fundamentally, the Keynesian model is about steady inflation, spending, and the accumulation of debt to keep an economy humming along. Austrian economics is about letting the market determine inflation or deflation, a high level of individual savings, and an emphasis on personal choice—real free markets—versus a planned economy.

We've all seen the real-world results of Keynesian economics in our lifetimes. Real inflation—the purchasing power of your Federal Reserve Notes, I call them 'ferns' just for kicks—outpaces your raises at work and any return you're going to see from a bank. This has been the way of life in America for decades. Saving is for chumps. So what do you do? You spend it. You fill your house up with stuff. You take trips. You buy a car, probably financed because, 'why not?' You're doing fine with a nine percent interest rate when real world inflation is really close to that. If you're a bigshot, you buy equities. Stocks. They deliver a return higher than inflation, right? Until they don't.

PAUL: Another part of Keynesian economics is using big government projects to spur the economy. This was the really attractive part about it back during the Great Depression. Huge capital projects that put chickens in workers' pots. Of course, this took financing. Lots of debt.

JERRY: So, again, what's wrong with that? With financing? I mean, if I can't afford a car, in cash, I finance it. The bank is happy, they get a little extra. The car manufacturer is happy. I get a car... I'm happy.

AARON: This actually works fine with your example. But you as an individual keep doing something that adds or produces value to someone else—your job—and that allows you to pay your debts. The problem is, the government doesn't have a 'job' that keeps producing value. All it can do is require other entities—individuals, companies, corporations, et cetera—to pay their due. And when the payments outstrip the borrowing, that's the ongoing debt. As of last year, it was ten times bigger than yearly tax revenue and growing.

MATT: So . . . who's loaning all that money? And why . . . if it's just going to keep stacking up?

AARON: <snorts> Look around, I think you have your answer! All the big players decided to end the game. To answer the first part though, it's the Federal Reserve and a polyglot of foreign governments. Like the car loan, they're happy to take their interest payments. Well, they *were* happy enough until about five weeks ago.

The boat has been headed for the proverbial iceberg for a long time now. But instead of just letting it crash, the big players made the choice to scuttle the ship beforehand . . . but not before telling their friends to head to the lifeboats. The continuous tinkering with financial markets, pumping up certain areas with money imagined out of thin air, just wasn't sustainable forever. You can hold off reality for only so long.

PAUL: I don't think Aaron is going back quite far enough. It would probably help if I filled in some blanks here. And oh, by the way, my personal history isn't nearly as interesting. Started school up in Minnesota and worked my way south to Iowa for graduate school. Every so often I peeked out at the real world and went right back to school. This was the early nineties, right before the tech boom. Job market stunk and I had the misfortune of pursuing degrees in history and English literature. Great for trivia games but doesn't exactly light up the HR department at a for-profit company. I came out to Seattle to follow a job offer as a lecturer. Aaron came through the doors a few years later. I noticed he didn't really fit in, didn't have the same bumper stickers as most of the faculty, that sort of thing. Which described me pretty well so we sort of fell into hanging out together.

Aaron mentioned the Federal Reserve. Unless we're just going to go as deep as, 'the big guys decided to end the game,' we're going to have to dig into the Federal Reserve.

MATT: Isn't that what it is though? The federal government's reserve of money. Their bank. The President appoints their leadership ... the chairman, right?

PAUL: I wish it were all that simple. Now, bear with me, none of this is tin foil hat stuff. No dark muttering of the Freemasons or the Illuminati here. No plots where the Scientologists team up with ancient aliens to rule Earth. I don't need to get daytime TV nutty ... there's plenty of juicy stuff that's public record. The Federal Reserve is a private banking cartel established way back in 1913. It is *not* a government agency and has successfully fought that definition in court. For example, you cannot, as an American citizen, demand information using the Freedom of Information Act from the Federal Reserve as you could from, say, the IRS. The U.S. government owns exactly *zero percent* of the Federal Reserve. Shocked? You should be! It's all owned by a group of private banks. When the U.S. Treasury needs money —Aaron's 'ferns'—the Federal Reserve just creates it. But it's debt to someone, often the Federal Reserve itself—wrap your brain around that one—but also foreign governments and immensely wealthy individuals. That's the 'note' part of Federal Reserve Note ... but Aaron's probably better at explaining all of that.

Since 1913 it's all worked to plan. A dollar in 1913 was pretty valuable. Twenty of them and you had a troy ounce of gold. Ninety nine percent of that value was gone by last summer.

JERRY: But you could have put it in a bank. Or invested it.

PAUL: Again, too simple. You're forgetting about inheritance taxes. Stock crashes. The recent 'bail-ins' a.k.a. legalized theft. The point is, the private banks that created

Michael Zargona

this system are completely immune to all of that *and* they get their interest payments. It's always a win for them and *always* a loss for the American taxpayers.

MATT: I think I have a general picture of the history. What about what happened in October?

AARON: You have a hot date waiting, boss? I get it. No offense, Paul, but history is just never quite as fun as current events, am I right?

I think most people by now have figured out what happened with the previous bank holiday, the hiccups here and there. Smoke out the crazies, make them look stupid, and get everyone to cry wolf when the real deal came around. You remember the huge line of folks streaming out of Seattle the day the banks locked up last month?

MATT: Uhh...

AARON: Exactly. Just about everyone stayed put to wait for the "all clear" signal. There's still some people who believe that signal is coming any day now. Most of us with a functioning brain figured it out in a week or so. But, by then we'd had a lot of time to think about our options and for most of us they stunk.

I saw the writing on the wall years ago. Not long after getting established here I bought a nice little cabin up in the mountains. On the Monday after the bank holiday, a week into it, I packed up and drove out there with my girlfriend, Claire. Found it was already occupied by some men with guns. They were kind enough to let us leave with our stuff and our lives. When we got back, a few days later my girl went down on her own to get food from the new distros and I never saw her again. Claire was an analyst for a government agency. My heart tells me she got conscripted. My head... well, no evidence one way or another.

But I digress once again. Again, this all boils down to money. And politics. Where there's enough of one you'll always find the other, guaranteed. If you wake up tomorrow and forget everything we talked about, remember that point.

The American dollar has ruled the worldwide currency scene since 1945. Undisputed *fact*. The only way to wrest political power away from the United States was... is... to kill the dollar and replace it with something else. Something more global. Remember those big banks I mentioned. They don't care about the dollar *per se*. Money, yes, but as long as they have control of money they don't care what it's called or whose faces appear on the bills.

Not long ago they came up with something called an SDR, or Special Drawing Rights. Not a real sexy name for a currency. It was a pool of several different currencies in widespread use worldwide. An important first step but... not the destination.

Sorry... yes, back to killing the dollar. In the simplest terms I can think of, there was a gigantic, coordinated call on all American government debt. They all saw the machinations of both inflation and capital controls and decided to take action. There wasn't nearly enough money—electronic or otherwise—to cover our debts. So they went after what they could. There were only two meaningful sources of wealth that could be scooped up immediately. Twenty five trillion, give or take, in retirement accounts and ten trillion in individual bank accounts.

JERRY: I don't claim to know a lot about this kind of stuff, but weren't most retirement accounts invested in securities? Like you said, that's not "real" money in the strict sense. When everything fell apart, wouldn't most of those companies cease to exist and take that wealth with them into oblivion?

AARON: Sure, if it was done slowly. But the Federal Reserve, the banks that comprise the Federal Reserve, and the United States government... and heck, probably some other international players pressed the pause button and made it all happen before anyone could blink. Some of the bigshots may have taken a haircut, but so what? Wealth is relative. Jerry, if you have a thousand dollars when just about everyone else has a hundred, you're doing pretty darn well. Change the scenario a bit. Now, you've taken a fifty percent reduction in wealth. You now have five hundred dollars. But everyone else sustained a massive crash and have, on average, five bucks. You have fewer digits in the bank but the pool of money available to everyone is much, much lower. You're actually much wealthier in relative purchasing power than you were before. You saw this phenomenon all the time in the Third World. Now it's our turn.

So they replaced those SDRs—and the American dollar, maybe even other currencies that were heavily pegged to the dollar—with *bancors*. Which is kind of a funny, in a dark way. Keynes coined the concept and clearly someone thought it was a good enough name for a global currency. Or has a pretty twisted sense of humor. Or maybe both. The joke is sort of an inside one. Keynes believed in debt above all. Now, we have no private debt.

MATT: What do you mean?

AARON: Go try and get a loan in bancors. Or finance a month's worth of food at the distro table. Won't happen. The debt ride is over for the little people. No credit for the serfs.

JERRY: So ... no debt? That's our future? Just accepting those few bits that get dropped on to our cards every month?

AARON: That's the future for people like us, sure. There are probably massive transactions among the big players. Remember, they still have plenty of money to play with.

It's like a huge Texas Hold 'Em poker table. For decades we all came to the table. We knew there were some real high rollers out there but we all played with the same chips. We had our tables and the rich people had theirs. Last month we all had our chips arbitrarily taken, given to others, and it's just that comparatively tiny group of high rollers now. We, the general public, can still stare in and look at the game but we have no way to buy back in. It's a spectator sport for everyone else at this point.

JERRY: But that doesn't make any sense. There's no industry. No stock market. Nothing to buy. What good is all the money in the world if you can't buy anything?

PAUL: <produces something small from his front pants pocket> Take a look at this.

MATT: My brother has some of those. It's a one ounce round of silver bullion.

PAUL: Exactly. And tomorrow I could turn it in and get a few more bancors put on my card and perhaps a little more food. Where do you think it goes from here?

MATT: Some storage facility? I really don't know.

PAUL: Well, someone has bancors and is willing to pay for this silver. Pretty soon you're going to see the buying up of land. Real estate. Guys like me see these formative stages for what they are. A return to old school tangible assets. We're deleveraging from a capitalist system to neofeudalism at an incredible pace.

JERRY: Feudalism? I don't understand. Like ... knights and dukes and what not?

PAUL: You're thinking of *medieval feudalism* or the *manorial model*. No, this is a different flavor. Actually, the warning signs are a lot older than just a few weeks. You two have probably heard about rich people buying up big chunks of land in the Rocky Mountain states and the Midwest over the last twenty or thirty years. Definitely a deviation from the norm. In the past, for their personal use, wealthy people typically bought high value real estate like a plot in the Hamptons or Beverly Hills. Not ten thousand acres of scrub prairie in Wyoming or North Dakota. Purchases like that are going to seem tiny by comparison. The polarization of wealth is so great right now that certain people are going to buy up *millions* of acres at a time. Aaron's example wasn't extreme enough. It's like you and I and almost everyone else has one dollar and there's a handful of millionaires and billionaires that we'll never see or meet. But from here on out they run the show.

MATT: So some people are going to make out. I mean, if you already own a bit of that land those mega rich will have to pay you for it. The wealth will start to spread back out.

PAUL: Not with this financial reset. You don't *own* a thing. It's all been wiped clean.

JERRY: But wait . . . they can't do that, right? Not legally. I own equity on my house. I *own* that. It's mine.

AARON: Yeah. And the government says you don't anymore. All your equity was on a bank's books and got poured into that dollar sinkhole and is gone now. Kaput.

MATT: Well, what about, say, my family's cabin? It's bought and paid for.

AARON: That's nice. In normal times, what would have happened if you hadn't paid your property taxes? Someone from the government would have come and kicked you off of "your" land. What are you going to do? Whine that the government can't do that? Take them to court with the money you don't have? That's a pretty big part of the point Paul and I have been trying to make here. You don't *own* anything you don't have in your hand and can protect. Paul owns that silver round, but he sure as hell doesn't own his house in Seattle anymore. Or the money in his account. Or his 401(k). IRA. It's all gone for good.

PAUL: Sad, but Aaron's right. It's not like it hasn't happened before. The Soviet Revolution. One day it was yours and the next it belonged to "the people" i.e. the commissars. Even here in the U.S. of A. the federal government confiscated all the meaningful chunks of gold back in the 1930s. One day it was yours, the next day it wasn't. Sure, you got compensated for it . . . in paper money. It's like that now—but for *everything* of value. Due to the threat of starvation everyone is being coerced into selling permanent stores of value just to survive. The frog in the pot method wasn't working. People, well smart people at least, were driving hard into tangibles like gold and silver even though there were all kinds of roadblocks being thrown up.

This is where neofeudalism comes in. You're going to have owners and tenants. Feudalism with a central economy. Two sets of rules. It's already been there in the background for years, it's just out in the open now. In the past some have coined it the *Deep State.* Ever wonder why nothing ever seemed to change politically at the national level? Democrat, Republican, didn't matter. Everyone that paid any attention saw they were all just crooks being fed money. Sure, both teams often got it from different sources but they got it just the same. Their strings were being pulled but—usually—we never saw the actors. Now, we still can't see them in the flesh but their presence is far more obvious. Like it or not, they're in charge now.

MATT: I don't know. I know quite a few people who would resist that. With force, if it came to it.

PAUL: A Second American Revolution? Listen ... the Founding Fathers had the means to fight because they had autonomy or *autarky*. They didn't need England, but England legitimately needed the Colonies to help pay debts. Those early patriots could support themselves just fine on their own. Farms, industry, you name it. The current situation is *much* different. Nearly everyone needs the system that the government has created in order to keep their bellies full, the lights on, and gas in their tanks. You could fight the new order, but what are you fighting? Are you going to march down to the distro and start shooting up the place in the name of freedom? You're going to get killed. And if you resist in any other way, you're going to get killed. If it comes about, a revolution, it'll look a lot more like the French than the American. All the aggrieved and heavily armed among us could come out from under their rocks and make things interesting for a while, but they're not going to overthrow the system. No chance.

MATT: So about all that. What will happen with guns? They ... the government ... don't seem to be too concerned. They'll confiscate them if you're running around with one but that seems to be it. My brother always thought that would be pretty early in the agenda, to go out and round them up.

PAUL: Well we know, and they know, that they can't get them all. Heck, they couldn't manage it in the UK or Australia with far fewer weapons in civilian hands. But really, why should they—the government I mean—even care that a bunch of scattered individuals have guns? It's not like there is an organized militia trying to wrest power from Washington, D.C. You have to look at this from a political power perspective and not one of personal self-defense. The federal government *doesn't care* right now if you can defend yourself or not. When you pen in a group of wild pigs to domesticate them, you don't care if the boars still have their tusks —they're behind the fence, dependent on you for food, and won't hurt the meal ticket. Eventually they'll start tying things back together and maybe then there will be some flare ups. If anyone has formed some sort of sovereign entity —armed with civilian weapons—they'll just crush it with military firepower. They're going to be far more worried about armed groups glomming together into something that can challenge their power and authority. Millions of disparate individuals armed with handheld weapons can't do that—as long as they stay that way. Honestly, with a government monopoly on modern communication methods I don't see how it will come about. A national-scale organized resistance, that is.

Sorry to be so blunt, but look ... Aaron and I are pretty pragmatic about all of this. Neither history nor economics has room for happy idealism. Something either *is*, or *is not*. Everything else can be fodder for a nice story, but if it doesn't jive, it's irrelevant.

MATT: Pretty depressing when you put it that way.

Everything you two have brought up is depressing, actually. What is the endgame here? Just that ... neofeudalism ... system? The ultra rich as overlords?

PAUL: That's clearly the plan that's been put in place. The Orwellian boot on the face of humanity ... forever. But plans and schemes that dramatic and far reaching almost never survive the test of the real world intact. Anything ... and I mean *anything* ... could be in store. Other players coming in and pushing for a change. Right now they appear to be in lockstep, but these are extremely craven people with their own schemes and motivations. History is pretty clear; give one person or a small group absolute power and they'll start to make some truly terrifying *diktats*. They may decide tomorrow that the world population needs to be quickly reduced by a factor of ten. World War Three. Invasions. Plagues. Only time will tell.

CHAPTER THIRTY-THREE

Wednesday, Fourth Week in November

Major Melissa Rex sat on her cot, exhausted, and it wasn't even quite ten in the morning yet. She put her head in her hands, still pink from thoroughly scrubbing off blood and gore. A young Forcer, just twenty, had been shot in the wee hours of the morning, what folks in the military termed "oh dark hundred," in nearby Tillicum, a typical off-base town that a few weeks before had been filled with sketchy pawn shops, tattoo parlors, and check cashing joints that did an impressive job of draining the pockets of young Army and Air Force shaveheads. Now it was an absolute no-go zone that abutted the base and the larger ZOC that contained it.

Whoever did the shooting had executed an effective plan. The Forcer had separated from his team for the most basic of reasons—a hasty squat to take a dump—and been shot through the right hip, probably a powerful handgun judging by the wound. The strategically aimed shot preserved the body armor he'd worn. Past tense. His armor, M4, seven full magazines, and SpyPhone—the feature-packed device that had suspiciously become available only a couple of weeks after the financial crash—had all been taken before his comrades arrived. Everyone knew SpyPhones were easily trackable. While it wasn't her job to ponder such things, she wondered if perhaps the attacker might use the device to set an ambush for any pursuers.

Melissa chuckled softly. She hadn't had a chance to ponder much besides sleep and fixing broken bodies—and not nearly enough of the former—these last few weeks. She'd joined the Army almost ten years ago, right after returning from a church medical mission in Haiti after the devastating earthquake there. The thrill of being in the middle of exciting times and making a difference was tough to forget. Plus, the more pragmatic reason of student loan forgiveness had led her to the Army Medical Corps. After two tours in Afghanistan, she'd returned to civilian life and had reverted to reserve status. She'd fallen into a comfortable lifestyle as a Nurse Practitioner with a Seattle medical group.

The day after the bank holiday had been announced, she'd received an email requiring her to report to any military installation within the next 24 hours. By opening it she'd started the clock ticking. Failure to report would make her a deserter and result in extremely harsh disciplinary action. Without a base within Seattle's city limits, she'd packed up and headed for JBLM. They had quickly put her to work and her time since averaged sixteen hours a day on duty.

There was a soft knock on the door to the converted office. "Major Rex?" The voice was that of one of her medical assistants.

"Yes?"

"There's a message here for you. A runner brought it in while you were in surgery."

She stood, checked herself with a small hand held mirror, and opened the door. "How is Private Daniels? Any update?" She was confident the young man would live despite a significant loss of blood but would have a limp for the rest of his life.

355

"No change. Still out of it. Here's the note." Major Rex took the folded piece of college ruled notebook paper.

It was written in ballpoint pen. In her mother's handwriting.

Melissa,

I hope this reaches you in good spirits and health. I sent Jerry to deliver this note. We're all staying up at the lake. Time is short! A violent gang has already attacked Rembrandt Village down by the highway. Some of the men here did some snooping and it looks like we might be their next target.

If you can bring help, maybe some soldiers, please do so! If nothing else, come and help patch up the men here after they take on that gang. We don't have any doctors or nurses up here. And your sister and I want to see you again!

Love, Mom

In different handwriting, down below, she read:

I'm in the camp on the golf course outside of the gate. Wearing a dark green jacket. Near the edge right by the freeway. I have a friend with me named Matt. He's a bit taller than me with a dark beard and a teal coat. We can only stay until about 7pm tonite and then need to head back. Come if you can and bring lots of medical supplies. -Jerry

Melissa furrowed her brow. She wasn't aware of any medical personnel being granted leave for any reason. Heck... *no one* in federal service got as much as a half day off to rest and recoup. It was a national state of emergency after all, and never a shortage of work. But, of course, she could always ask. All her new CO could do was say no.

She barely knew the man, Lt. Colonel Conger, who had been put in charge of the hastily assembled medical group on this end of the base, completely separate from the large base hospital to the northeast. Normally, field surgeons like her reported to the CO of the unit, a non-physician. With her unit disbanded and spread out among the new Peace Enforcement teams, she had been assigned to a medical team simply called "JBLM Field Medical Operation-South." Bureaucratic-sounding numerical designations and cool shoulder patches took a back seat during emergencies such as this one, at least for the medical folks.

"Colonel Conger?" she asked from just outside the door to his office.

"Yes? Oh. Melissa, what can I do for you?"

Melissa took the open chair in front of the man's immaculately clean and organized desk. The term 'OCD' had been bandied about around the proverbial water cooler. "Colonel, this is going to sound highly unusual, but I need to request a short leave. Off base."

"Absolutely not," he shot back. "You're not the first to ask. The stress is building for all of us and people are reaching a breaking point. Everyone seems to suddenly have business off post for one reason or another. I'm not worried about you specifically, but the desertion rate among the enlisted and junior officers has been extremely high."

She was taken aback. With the new NIDs it was effectively impossible to remain a deserter for very long. Not only would you get plucked right out of any food line you stumbled into, the Forcers wielding SpyPhones would nab you sooner or later. You'd have to abandon your NID and live off the land, away from the ZOCs, and essentially become a *nonperson*. "How high does that go, sir?"

The man sat silent. Melissa took that as a good sign. If it was a base order given by the commanding general there would be no wiggle room at all. So, COs like Conger down the line might have the authority to make exceptions. "Look, my mother is in serious trouble. There was a runner earlier —"

He nodded tersely. "Yes. I know."

She continued. "She and the rest of my family are

being threatened by a gang that's already wiped out a nearby town. I *really* need to get out and help her." Melissa was doing her best to maintain her composure and not raise her voice. It wasn't easy.

"That's what Peace Enforcement is for. Right?"

Tears began to well in the corners of her eyes. She could have fought them back but didn't. At this point she really didn't have anything to lose. "Colonel Conger, sir, *listen*. I may never see my mother again. If not this threat, then it may be another one. She has a bad heart and is almost certainly running out of meds. Diseases we haven't seen in seventy years are cropping up along with the new ones. She's almost eighty years old and her day could come at any time. *Please let me go.* Just for a few days. You have my word I'll be back. I don't have much, but whatever collateral you need, I'll give it."

The slender, bookish man sighed and rubbed his brow with his left hand. "Melissa, you're asking me to put my credibility—*and my career*—on the line here. You don't come back—deserter, dead, whatever—and I get to tell the full birds and flag officers above me that I let an experienced medical officer walk out the gate with my go-ahead. I understand your concern and your situation, but *we all* are experiencing that in one way or another. My daughter is an undergrad at Washington State University. Two hundred miles from here. I have no idea how she's doing. I'd love to go find out. But ... I can't."

Melissa wiped her eyes with a Kleenex off the colonel's desk. "I'm sorry to hear that, sir, but I *do* know what's going on with my mom and I'd like your permission to find out. I'm no warrior. I'm not going to get in a firefight or put myself in any unnecessary risk. Four days. That's all I need."

The man sighed again and nodded. "Word is you're the best, more consistent field surgeon we have here. Three days. We need you back in one piece. The seventy two hours start at noon. Report to me by noon in three days or ... you know what will happen."

Ten minutes to noon and she was all packed and ready to head out. She took one last look around and checked the drawers of her secretary once again. The half-empty bottle of Wild Turkey that had helped her through a few tough nights, just to take the edge off enough to help her sleep, stared back at her from the bottom left drawer. "I'm leaving you here, buddy-o. I won't need you for a few days," she whispered.

She slung her Blackhawk S.T.O.M.P. medical bag over her right shoulder*.

In her left hand was a smaller bag containing some civilian clothes, a toiletry bag, and five MREs.

Unfortunately, heading to the armory and checking out a weapon was impossible. A base order had come down in response to several suicides in the span of just a few days. And, as her role was strictly inside the fence, she had no body armor to speak of. She'd be completely dependent on Jerry and the others at the lake for protection.

She did one last visual scan and headed for the door.

*a complete inventory of Major Rex's medical bag can be found in Appendix B.

CHAPTER THIRTY-FOUR

Wednesday, Fourth Week in November

"Costello, this is Abbott. Do you copy?" Kyle had been calling over to Lake Cushman on the agreed frequency once every half hour since seven in the morning. It was now nine thirty and he was convinced they weren't listening. Not having the five or more people they'd promised would seriously limit his strategy. They'd have to shorten their line and by extension, the number of bad guys they could realistically get inside the kill box. That was the most crucial part of his plan; if they couldn't take out a majority of the bastards by surprise they were in big trouble.

Greg walked up, clutching his cross body slung HK91. "No answer, huh?"

"Nope. Well, the silver lining is that you guys got some good intel on the raiders' M.O. Maybe that wannabe mayor put the kibosh on your Ranger bud. Who knows?"

Greg simply shrugged. "Ready to get back to it?"

Kyle turned to the semicircle of men and boys behind him. *Too few. Far too few.* Each man was in the kneeling position he'd taught them earlier and sighting in on the small black stick figures he'd drawn on a piece of plywood with a permanent marker. Earlier that morning, well before dawn, he, Malachi, Greg, and Lenny had gone in opposite directions to wake up their other volunteers, beg for help from the others, and shake everyone down for the booze they needed for their plan. It was a calculated approach; he'd wanted to catch people in their cabins asleep and unprepared to argue.

Bill Klein had complained about his chronic bad back and had scratched himself as a volunteer. Kyle, honestly, wasn't too disappointed. On the positive side, Bill had given up a half-full twenty four pack of cheap beer and two open bottles of bourbon, each about a third full. All told, from every cabin, they'd been able to collect eighteen bottles of liquor—most of them open and partially empty—plus eleven bottles of wine or champagne and forty-six assorted cans and bottles of beer. Kyle wondered if it would be enough to get twenty or thirty "experienced drinkers" drunk enough to make a difference tomorrow.

Jeanie had been on duty guarding the gate. She'd told Kyle she'd be willing to volunteer. He'd declined, pointing out that she was perfect as a "stay behind" in case something went wrong with the ambush. It wasn't chivalry or male chauvinism—Kyle had a real job for her in mind. She'd be in charge of rallying whomever was left that could fight. He'd considered her for the medical crew as she had quite a bit of first aid training owing to her time in blue, but with no real medical supplies beyond bandages and gauze she was more valuable here.

The original volunteers from the night before (minus his brother of course) had been joined by:

Norris McGwire, the older bookish man with all the ancient guns. He shouldered his Russian SVT-40 rifle.

Timothy's brother-in-law, Rod Burkett, an angry-looking young man in an MMA-themed sweatshirt who'd been apprenticing as an electrician before the crash. At the moment he held Matt's AR. Kyle wasn't sure what to give him once Matt returned. *If he returned...*

Jeff Morrison down in cabin #18 had reluctantly volunteered though he'd never held a weapon before. As a southpaw he seemed a natural fit for Kyle's left-handed Tikka. Kyle planned on keeping the young father of three as far back from the thick of things as he could.

Kyle's friendly neighbors in cabin #12, three generations of Gautiers—Mel, Travis, and Jake—had come forward. Mel, a fifty-something Boeing machinist, had brought a nice wood stocked pump shotgun, a Remington 870, plus an older Smith and Wesson 9mm automatic, the great granddad to Kyle's Shield. Travis, a day route truck driver, had Kyle's Vepr .308. Jake was only sixteen but had been helping out from time to time on the security team. He'd ended up with Norris's German G43, not Kyle's preference due to its scarce ammo supply and questionable reliability after lying dormant for decades, but it was the best they had.

The original crew was set up pretty well. Greg Samuels with his .308 and Timothy Benson with Kyle's stubby 7.62x54R Vepr rifle. Mike Klein had brought his bargain-bin hunting rifle but Kyle had instead "issued" him his Mossberg 930 semiautomatic shotgun. The rifle had a blind magazine —meaning it had to be reloaded through the top of the rifle through the narrow ejection port—that would be very difficult to reload in the stress of combat. The Mossberg, on the other hand, was designed specifically for a firefight.

Lenny Jones, despite his Vietnam experience with the M16, had ended up with Kyle's other Mossberg shotgun, the five shot Model 500. Initially Kyle had given the man his Bushmaster, very similar to an M16, but his seventy-year-old eyes just couldn't make heads or tails of its ACOG optic which was designed for fast firing with both eyes open. The shotgun, aimed with a simple brass bead at the end of the barrel, seemed like a better choice.

Kyle had handed the AR off to Malachi—much to his pleasure. It was strange to watch someone work a weapon he'd never held but was highly familiar with. Kyle had to tell the boy to keep to the basics, take it slow, and real world competence—not video game "skill"—would develop.

They were immensely short on skill. Kyle, Matt, and Lenny were the only ones present who had fired shots in combat. Greg was the sole other man trained for warfare and was almost three decades removed from his last days in uniform. Travis Gautier had gone to Navy boot twenty years ago but had broken his leg and washed out long before even the cursory small arms training seaman recruits received. Mike—when sober—and Timothy were good hunters and competent marksmen, but neither had ever been asked to put crosshairs on a fellow human being. The rest were complete tenderfoots.

"Okay men, switch to a prone position," Kyle said. "Watch your muzzles! Just because this is practice and we've confirmed the guns are empty doesn't mean we get into bad habits. Now, for the attack some of you will be in this position and some in the kneeling. Get used to these positions because we'll have to hold them for however long it takes to draw the Bee Gees out." Bee Gee—BG—was simply code for Bad Guy.

"Now," Kyle continued, "it's my job to teach you as much as I can today. Just *one day*. So all we're going to focus on right now and up over the hill later is hitting a target right in front of you. We simply don't have the time to get more complex than that. You all are going to get certified at 'bad breath range' meaning out to a hundred yards or so for the rifles and twenty-five for the shotguns. At that range it's all just line up the sights and shoot. That's the easy part. The tough part is the psychology behind it. I want each of you to engage in a little exercise with me.

"Take a mental snapshot of that plywood target and your sights or reticle. Now, close your eyes. Replace the plywood with a human being. Not someone you know . . . just imagine some stranger holding a gun and he's pointing it right at you. Got the picture in your mind?

"I won't recite the entire Marine Corps Rifleman's Creed for you all. Partly because I don't remember the whole thing verbatim. Greg... no smiling. Concentrate. But here's the relevant part:

I must shoot straighter than my enemy who is trying to kill me. I must shoot him before he shoots me. I will.

"That enemy will kill you, everyone else here, and our friends and families here at Sunshine if *you* don't kill him first. *Can you do it? Can you line up on his chest and pull the trigger?* Now... it's all right—healthy, really—to be uncomfortable thinking about it. You shouldn't *want* to kill other people no matter how horrible they are. But listen... if you really did this mental exercise, you took is seriously, and you just can't imagine shooting another person, talk to me. It's okay. Like Gideon, I'd rather go down there with fewer men who are prepared to do what's necessary than a larger group who will yank their trigger or simply freeze up during the heat of battle. In the Marines they make dang sure they've drilled that mentality into you—kill or be killed—but it takes a lot of recruits time to adjust those thought patterns. We don't have months... we have *hours*."

The radio behind him on the table squawked. "*Abbott, this is Costello. Do you read me, over?*"

Kyle grabbed the handheld. "This is Abbott. Good to finally hear from you, over."

"*Ehh... long story. Over.*"

Kyle pulled the code book from his left cargo pocket. It and its twin down at Cushman consisted of seven sheets from a small spiral notepad. He and Greg had whipped them up two nights ago. In their experience, often those responsible for creating code books—usually officers—got too cute. Like, say, assigning different species of birds for each number from one to ten. While it looked neat on paper and could act as an easy mnemonic, it was less secure than creating a completely random code book. For example, their code for 'one' was 'Cessna' while 'two' was 'Artichoke.'

"Costello, you ready for message, over?" Kyle transmitted.

"Send it, over."

"Stand by. Crayon . . . Rucksack . . . Fireplace. Read back, over." 'Crayon' stood for 'the attack is a go.' 'Rucksack' meant 'tomorrow' while 'Fireplace' meant 'come to my position immediately.' As these were all likely parts of the scenario, they each had warranted their own code. The code book had a letter substitution section, but while a code book cipher was for all intents and purposes impossible to break, letter substitution was very easy to break, particularly with longer messages. The computing power found in a common smartphone could crack that in seconds. While Kyle doubted very much the scumbags holed up near Rembrandt Village had a crypto team—or were even listening to their transmissions—it was simply safer not to let anyone get insight into what was going on.

"Roger, solid copy. Crayon. Rucksack. Fireplace. Over."

"What is your status, over?" Kyle called. At this point, he assumed he was talking to the ex-Ranger there and didn't see the need to remind the man to respond in code.

"Fireplace is . . . Maple. I repeat, Maple. Bringing Awning, I repeat, bringing Awning. How copy, over?"

'Maple' was code for 'affirmative' while 'Awning' stood for 'five.' They were coming right away, along the back roads to avoid the gang, and bringing a total of five effectives. "Solid copy, Costello. Abbott out."

"Hey Kyle," called Greg, "can I stop imagining I'm drawing down on a Bee Gee now?"

Kyle snapped back to the dozen on their stomachs in the damp grass. "Umm . . . yeah. Go ahead and break out of that little roleplay, everyone. We need to hang tight here until the guys from Cushman arrive."

Michael Zargona

They'd been at the hill to the west of the lake for about three hours and it was almost time to head back and prep for the next stage. It had gone well, the weapon familiarization and live fire, but there had been a few hiccups. Norris had lined up to sight in his ancient SVT-40 but the rifle had refused to fire. Something was likely gumming up the firing pin, but Kyle had zero knowledge of the rifle itself and how to take it apart. The last time Norris had disassembled it, calendars still started with "19" and he didn't quite recall the process. Norris had taken one of the trucks back and grabbed his sniper-grade Swedish Mauser. It didn't have the ammo supply of his Mosin, but was more accurate and had a much better scope. They could do a lot worse. As the scoped rifle wasn't great in close quarters, Norris had brought his Lahti 9mm pistol, just in case.

While everyone save Kyle had done some shooting thus far, he and Greg had spent most of their time working with the inexperienced shooters. Jeff Morrison had been able to hit a #10 can at two hundred yards from a prone position with Kyle's Tikka and, at least in Kyle's eyes, passed. Jeff had taken one of Norris's Walther P-38 pistols as had both Travis and Jake Gautier. While not as *cool* as the Lugers, they were much simpler and more reliable. The Gautiers both had a steep learning curve with the Vepr and the G43, especially the latter with only a hundred rounds available. Jake had shot a single ten round magazine worth, putting those big 8mm slugs into a 12" pie plate at about a hundred yards—more than sufficient.

Malachi and Rod had been able to get up to speed quickly with the light recoiling ARs, especially aided with their high end optics. Malachi's young eyes had picked up the ACOG just fine.

The shotgunners ... Kyle just wanted to make sure

they could hit targets at close range, reload quickly, and fire on the move. They wouldn't have the benefit of sitting back and sniping. Mike Klein and Mel Gautier had done fine. Lenny ... not so much.

Greg Samuels sauntered up, his pants and boots covered in mud. "Hey, Kyle, I need to talk to you."

"What's up?" Kyle answered.

"It's Lenny. I . . . just . . . I just don't think he is going to be much use on this lil' escapade tomorrow. He's already really sore, and, well . . . ."

"He's half blind and mostly deaf? And can't run?" Kyle said, finishing Greg's train of thought.

Greg nodded and let out a breath. "Yeah. All that. He asked me if we have something that kicks less than that shotgun you gave him. He's pretty bony. His right shoulder has a nice purple bruise on it just from the five practice shells."

"Hmm. I'll talk with him. Go ahead and tell Jeanie when we get back. He can help her on the rear party." It was a disappointment for sure. Lenny was a combat veteran and a truly tough son of a gun. Kyle had envisioned him as sort of a modern day Caleb, aged but vigorous and ready to take on the hill tribes *mano y mano*. But he was, in reality, an old man with arthritis, bad knees, and severely diminished senses.

"Will do," Greg replied.

Just then, they heard the rumble of engines to the south and east, coming down the logging road they'd used to get to the clearing. Kyle turned and brought his Marlin to his shoulder and at the low ready. It was the only rifle he hadn't loaned out—besides his feeble 10/22—and while it was incredibly unlikely any deer or elk would saunter into the long clearing with all the two-legged critters present, Kyle would have cried if one slipped away because he'd had his hands in his pockets.

It turned out to be a single silver pickup, a big Ford quad cab that rolled toward their group of four parked vehicles. A big man with a thick red beard rode shotgun; the driver was an equally large dark skinned man in a boonie hat. Both were decked out in U.S. Army Multicam/Scorpion camouflage uniforms.

"Outback and Roadblock ... these your G.I. Joe buds, Greg?" Kyle jibed.

Greg turned and spat on the tall grass. "Heh. I'm going to tell them you said that. Yeah, that's Terry up front. Never seen the driver but then again I only met four people when I was up there."

Kyle took the butt of the rifle out of his shoulder and held it pointed to the ground in his left hand, waving with his right. The truck came to a stop beside his Dodge. In the back were three more men, all with old school wood-stocked hunting rifles. Kyle kept an even expression but was mildly disappointed. He'd hoped they would bring weapons that could lay down some sustained fire. Two of them, men in their late 20s or early 30s, wore quality hunting camouflage and, judging by their almost albino white hair, were related. The other man, quite a bit older with a reddish-brown complexion and a thick black mustache, had on dark blue jeans, a black denim jacket, and a dark brown cowboy hat. All five men wasted no time getting out of the truck.

"I'm Kyle. You must be Terry," Kyle greeted with his hand extended.

Terry cautiously limped over and shook his hand. "You got it. This is my friend DeSean," he said, motioning to the driver who just nodded. "Over there are Paul, Erik, and Edgar."

Kyle saw Terry had a very nice AR coated in Flat Dark Earth paint and sporting an Aimpoint Micro red dot sight. In his left hand was a black nylon rifle case. "I brought my haji gun, an AK," Terry said. "I offered it to my guys here," he added, motioning to the three that had ridden up in the back, "but they'd rather stick with the deer blasters they know best. Figured it might come in handy. Got some ammo in the back seat, too."

"Definitely," Kyle said. "When my brother gets back we'll be a rifle short." Terry motioned with the case and Kyle took it in his right hand. The driver's side rear door opened and DeSean pulled out a very long black Pelican hard case, set it on the ground, and meticulously worked the latches one at a time until it was fully unlocked. The big man lifted the lid. Inside was a long, heavy-barreled bolt action rifle with a thick adjustable stock in a forest green color that Kyle normally associated with European guns. Underneath was a folded Harris bipod, and mounted on top was an enormously expensive—and very high quality—Nightforce scope with long sunshade that looked to be a 3.5-15x or even a 5.5-22x magnification model. A thick suppressor that threaded on the end of the barrel was detached and buried in a perfectly sized cutout of the case's foam lining. Four small black magazines sat nestled together side by side in another cutout. Also inside were five boxes of ammunition. Kyle saw on the side that they were each 20 round boxes of 175 grain match .308 made by Black Hills.

Greg whistled in appreciation. "Man, how did you afford *that* sucker?"

"Hey," DeSean began, "all you good taxpayers chipped in for it. Fifty percent disability." He held up his right hand. Kyle hadn't noticed it before. DeSean was missing his middle and pinky fingers and his ring finger's tip was missing. "And a few months of eating ramen. It's a Sako." He pronounced it 'SAH-ko.' "TRG-22. Don't laugh, but I bought it because it was on *clearance*. I wasn't looking for it but it sure found me. The other stuff like the scope and the can,"—he was referring to the suppressor—"were, ah, not quite as good a deal. But it's one hell of a rifle. It'll hit a six inch steel plate at a thousand yards if I do my part."

Kyle looked up at Terry. "Well . . . I think it's pretty clear you Cushman guys are going to be the short leg on the ambush. You shouldn't have to move much but will have to take the longer, tougher shots. Seems you're well suited for that. We have a couple of guys here with *lesser* scoped rifles who will be on your immediate flank."

"L-shape?" Terry asked and waited for Kyle's nod. "Hmm. I kind of figured DeSean would hole up on his own, maybe with a spotter. Probably me, actually. Provide overwatch."

"I've scouted the area out pretty well," Kyle said. "There's really no place to set up within, say, five or six hundred yards and still be near and within sight of the rest of us. Without absolutely reliable comms we'll have to keep together. It'll be a little close for a rifle like that, but doable. Just need this to go as planned."

"Yeah, so," Terry said, "what *is* your plan?"

"*RUN!*" Kyle yelled as he swung the door open and leaped out of the still running truck. Two hundred yards away, three men were sprinting toward them, screaming obscenities.

Malachi, who was only weighed down by Kyle's Glock in a shoulder holster, quickly outpaced him in their race to the wood line. Kyle had to contend with his Bushmaster, Interceptor body armor, and a full loadout of ammo. They'd tried Matt's purloined SWAT armor on the teenager, but Malachi had decided to take his chances rather than lug around the oversized, heavy, and unfamiliar vest.

Lenny's clapped-out Ranger had barely gotten them down to the highway. To keep up the ruse that they were heading north, they'd taken some soft, muddy Forest Service roads in order to come out south of Rembrandt Village. Bad roads plus a leaky coolant system and what sounded like a totally shot front wheel bearing had made for a white-knuckle trip.

But ... not as dangerous as three heavily armed roadside butchers.

A shot boomed. Shotgun. Pretty dang optimistic given the range but it still caused him to tense up. Kyle watched as Malachi leaped across the ditch with a throaty yell and into the trees.

The urge to turn around and fire on their pursuers was intense. Kyle knew he could take one or more of them with a few quick shots and join his partner in retreat. But that would create some problems downstream. He wanted these human vermin to celebrate an easy victory tonight, not mourn the loss of their pals. It was far more important for them to take the bait today than for Kyle to cut one or two out of action for tomorrow.

Kyle leaped, just barely missing the ditch, and entered the darkness of the woods.

Malachi and Kyle ran about a quarter mile down an old game trail toward the same gravel road that they'd traveled earlier in the now-captured Ranger. Kyle stopped, looked back and listened to confirm for sure that no one was following, and pulled out the small hunting radio from his chest pouch.

"Albatross, this is Penguin, come in Albatross."

There was a crackle of static. *"Penguin, this is Albatross, go ahead."* It was Greg's voice coming back. He had staged himself in Kyle's Durango about a mile down the road.

"Roger. Proceed east, we'll be waiting."

"Roger that. Albatross out."

A couple of minutes went by and the vehicle, looking almost black in the gloom, rumbled into view. They clambered in quickly and, after a careful three point turn, headed back to the lake.

"Good to go?" Greg asked expectantly.

"Oh yeah," Kyle said. "No sweat. Well, a lot of sweat under this armor. But they took the bait. We'll see tomorrow if it was worth all the hassle."

As they approached his cabin, Kyle saw Jerry's beat up car in front of the Flanigan cabin. *Looks like they made it back OK*. Greg parked and the three of them hopped out.

Kyle opened the door and saw that his living room was beyond full capacity. The five from Cushman sat on the far side of the room. Amber, Loren, and his brother, who looked no worse for wear, sat on the nearest sofa while Jerry sat next to a newcomer on the other. She was on the short side, plump-faced with short brown hair and wore the standard Army combat uniform. On her right breast read "REX", on the left, "U.S. Army", and in the middle was the embroidered gold oak leaf of a major.

"You must be Melissa. Glad you could join us. I'm Kyle."

She shrugged. "Heard a little about you and the overall plan on the way here. So we all set for tomorrow? Hooch delivered?"

"We're good to go," Kyle replied. "Let's get the rest of the crew together, whip up some food, and go over some last minute planning."

"So what if they run back to the buildings?" Rod Burkett asked between spoonfuls of soup.

Kyle finished chewing his bite of salmon. He was well aware of the advice—go into combat on a long-empty stomach in case of a gut wound—but felt a good hot meal would be best. The team needed to get some rest before making their way down to the lake in the middle of the night, and it was hard to sleep with a growling stomach.

"Shoot them in the back," he said, loud enough for everyone to hear. "If they reach cover, hold your position and let the marksmen take them out. Whatever you do, don't give chase. Not only are you running out in front of a bunch of shooters, you're leaving what should be a pretty decent defensive position. That's the whole point of a planned ambush, to have all the advantages of the attacker *and* the defender. If you abandon your position, stand up, and run around, we'll lose a great deal of those advantages."

"What about all those vehicles? If they hole up in the building, and we're not going to chase them, are we shooting out the tires or what?" Jerry Goodridge asked from across the room. Seeing that he'd be one of the few able bodied men left at the lake, he had opted to join in on the attack and had ended up with the Mossberg that Kyle had originally pegged for Lenny. There wasn't enough time or daylight to train him on one of the rifles.

"Heck no. We don't want to strand them just a few miles from us. And if the Bee Gees make for their trucks and bikes, shoot them! They have to stand up and expose themselves in order to get in or get on a vehicle. Once it's moving, that's different. Don't bother shooting out the tires or the radiator. That's movie chase scene stuff. It takes a rad way too long to overheat and lots of vehicles have run-flats these days. On a civilian vehicle, your best target is the driver. If the driver ducks down, just shoot lower. If he gets so low he can't see, you're winning. If there's a passenger shooting at you and you're not in immediate danger of getting run over, that's where you switch from the driver to the threat."

"I heard some military guys on chat talking about 'OODA loops' or something, how it's important to maintain those." Malachi said. "What's that about?"

Kyle shot a glance at Terry who just smiled. "Don't worry about 'OODA loops'. That's just officer jargon for 'keep punching them in the mouth so they can't think straight.' Unless something goes completely south we're going to be awake, prepared, alert, and have a plan in place. They are going to be groggy, still half-drunk, and wondering what the heck is going on. There's your 'OODA loop.'

"Look, I'll skip all the fancy mnemonics and acronyms. There's only seven really important elements to a firefight. Firepower—how hard can you hit. Mobility—how fast and easily can you move. Range—how far away can you hit something. Communication—can you effectively talk with all those in the fight. Logistics—do you have enough ammo, food, batteries, bandages, water, et cetera. Intelligence—do you know what the heck you're up against. Training or the mental aspect—can you execute the plan well.

"Most of you guys like football. Now, don't get me wrong, football is *not* combat but I'm using it as an example. When you plan to play another team, you go after their weaknesses and lean on your strengths, right? If the other team relies on their depth on defense, you go no-huddle and keep their same guys on the field. If they're weak against the pass, you pass more. Pretty simple. No different here. So, breaking these down, based on what we know—the intelligence we've gathered—we're probably pretty equal on firepower. Unless you guys are holding out on me, or Major Rex pilfered a box of grenades and didn't tell me, we're basically even. We're actually *less* mobile, but that's okay in this instance since it's an ambush. We have the range advantage with DeSean's monster rifle plus a few other nice scoped guns . . . based on our intel the Bee Gees seem to go for up close and personal type weapons."

"Kyle's right," Terry said. "That's how we chased them off. We started sniping them from the trees. Fighting them in close quarters didn't go well for us. They don't hesitate and they're brutal . . . that's their comfort zone for sure."

"Communication is as good as we can make it," Kyle continued. "A couple of us will have radios to call back to the lake or to the medical team. It would be more important if we had separate elements or we could call for support. Logistics aren't as good as I'd like. We're pretty light on ammo for several of our weapons.

"Our intelligence is good. Not great though, it would have been ideal to leave an OP . . . someone down there to monitor the area. We could walk down tomorrow and find that they've ridden off somewhere else. Training, well . . . I wish I had a month to get us razor sharp. We don't have that. So we have a very simple plan. But I believe in my heart it's enough. One of the reasons I'm gung ho about going down there is we'll have the upper hand in all the likely scenarios. I've talked with the other combat vets here in this room—my brother, Terry, Greg, DeSean, plus Lenny—and we all agree that the Bee Gees are only likely to have three reactions. Yes, it's possible they'll do something unexpected, but it's far more likely they'll either chase after me and my team and fall right into the prepared ambush, or they'll hole up in the buildings and we use our range advantage and maneuverability. Or, they'll make for their vehicles and bug out. While this is the worst of the three, given the fact that they'll be alive and could come back to haunt us later, it's still a win for us."

"But do you think we have enough, y'know, guys to pull this off?" Malachi asked. "You just said it, there's like four of us who actually know what's up in a real fight. I mean, to make it a sure thing, what would you need? Or want?"

Kyle chuckled. "What would I *want*? Heck, as long as we're dreaming here, give me my old gun truck with a fifty-cal up top. And another one with a Mark Nineteen. Dump half a can of grenades each into both buildings and mop up whatever came out with the Ma Deuce."

"Don't forget about the SEAL Team coming out of Hood Canal in full battle rattle," Matt added, smiling.

"And a platoon of Rangers parachuting in on top of them," Terry said, "with knives in their teeth."

"Hey now," Malachi shot back defensively, reacting to their chuckles and sardonic smiles. "I was just . . . sayin'."

After a few minutes of more light-hearted discussion, the meal wound down. Kyle called for the squad leaders to meet him outside. He, Matt, Greg, and Terry walked toward the lake in the dull moonlight.

"I'm going to take Timothy, Malachi, and Rod in my squad," Kyle said. "I need some young guys who can run. Matt, Rod's pretty familiar with your AR so I'd like him to take it. Terry brought an AK with him as a spare. You willing to swap?"

"It's a straight shooter," Terry said. "Nice little red dot on the handguard. Never had a problem with it or else I wouldn't have lugged it up here."

"Sure," Matt said.

"Okay," Kyle said. "Bro, you take Jeff Morrison and the two younger Gautiers. You're going to be on the bottom of the 'L' next to Terry and his guys. Greg, Mike Klein, Mel Gautier, Norris, and Jerry Goodridge will be in your squad. You'll be at the top of the 'L' with most of the close range firepower. Terry, as I mentioned earlier today you five will make up the short leg as the sniper section. We'll do our best to keep them from getting too close."

"So, Kyle . . . what do you think? Are we ready?" Matt asked.

Kyle frowned. "If we catch them with their pants around their ankles and still half-drunk from the night before, we should be fine. But if it comes down to those professional murderers versus our desk jockeys and teenage boys tête-à-tête we're going to be in big trouble."

CHAPTER THIRTY-FIVE

**Thursday, Fourth Week in November
Thanksgiving**

Kyle stepped back inside the cabin after completing the rounds of waking his people. Amber and Loren looked up as he entered.

It was more than a mere send-off that had caused them to get up at two in the morning. Melissa had asked them both to assist her today despite their lack of medical training. They would do the simple grunt work so Melissa could apply her expertise as efficiently as possible. They would also act as ambulance drivers.

Amber had obviously gone out to the trailer and brewed a pot of fresh coffee using battery power while he'd been out and about. Kyle was already plenty keyed up with no help from caffeine but did not refuse the steaming mug that Amber nudged toward him.

From the other bedroom he heard an anxious voice —Des—although he couldn't make out the words. Then his brother's voice in a more conciliatory tone followed by sobbing. Kyle glanced at Amber who just shook her head.

"She's pretty close to the breaking point," Amber said in a low voice. She looked over at Loren and cocked an eyebrow, as if to say, *This is between us and us alone.* Loren picked up on the cue and nodded. Amber continued. "Besides the obvious, she doesn't want to take a chance at losing Matt, the overarching issue is that she is taking all this much harder than most of us. I mean, yes, it's bad for everyone, but especially for her. She told me that next year was finally the time she'd leave the rat race and start a family—kids, I mean—and move out the suburbs, get a dog and a lawnmower, that whole thing. Put her career on hold. It's a big deal for her. She's been locked into a career track to become a lawyer after having been a paralegal for several years to avoid the law school requirement. That's her dream, to have a couple of kids, work from home, do pro bono or discounted legal work for people who can't afford it. Matt continuing to run around, advancing his sales career. The crash coming along blew that plan all away."

"Well gosh, having kids and living in the woods is one of the few options that is still available," Kyle said. The look on their faces let him know his attempt to lighten the mood had fallen flat.

Loren had scrunched her nose. "That's just ... *selfish*," she said. "I'm a ... well, I *was* a junior in high school. I have my whole life in front of me. I haven't done *squat* yet. And if this is like you have been saying these last couple of days, that it's pretty much the end of America as we know it, I'll miss out on so much. On everything. I'll never go to college, or take a vacation, or buy that big house out in the suburbs. That's all gone to me now. I've lost my entire family. At least she's got you all and Matt. She got a chance to experience the good life and, y'know, make her own life decisions for a while."

"You're right, Loren, it *is* selfish," Kyle said. "Not to get all psychological, but she's gone from denial to anger to lashing out. Like a lot of us she's built this future in her mind and it's crashing down around her. Trust me, I've listened to these stories from my customers. They've lost their house in a forest fire, or a hurricane, or maybe the California earthquake a couple years back. One day they're plugging away at their career and the next they're rebuilding their house with the insurance money. Sometimes they're doing it with fewer members of their family than before."

"But you guys are so different," Loren said. "You don't seem worried about any of this. I mean, well, you two *do* have way more stuff than most people right now."

"That peace you see ... it's not about the stuff, really," Kyle replied evenly. "It's about faith and obedience in God. We've been blessed to be able to steward all this stuff for a while. But like anything it'll run out, or break, or just fall apart over time. I'll admit, it can be tough to see from the outside, but we've pinned our future to Christ, not to a pile of dried food, guns, and some neat gadgets. There are plenty of preparedness gurus who don't know Christ. I've met some of them. Right now, they don't have peace. Arrogance, sure, but not *real* peace. Our lack of worry is faith, plain and simple, that God will take care of us."

Loren frowned. "I don't know. Not trying to offend you, but I didn't see God showing up to stop those killers. Some of the people there believe ... believed, I mean, like you do."

"That's part of a big lie. Giving your life to Christ doesn't make everything safe and easy," Amber said. "Loren, following Jesus is *dangerous*. If you're authentic, you're going to do things that will set you back in the world or even get you killed. Out of the twelve Disciples—throwing out Judas and adding in Stephen—you know how many died of old age?"

Loren shrugged. "No idea. I don't know much Bible stuff."

"Just one," Amber answered. "John. The rest were put to death for their faith. That pretty much blows away the whole, 'nothing but good times' Christian philosophy. Our reward lies in eternity with Christ, not a good comfortable life here on Earth."

"Wow. I won't pretend I understand everything you just said, but it sounds pretty heavy," Loren said.

At that, the bedroom door opened and Matt emerged in full battle rattle. Terry Graham's well-accessorized AK was slung on his right shoulder. He wore the cop vest he'd brought back from his long journey plus the belt, pistol mags, and Glock similar to Kyle's own. Underneath was simple black clothing to match the police gear.

Kyle, in contrast, had donned his Swiss camo along with the decidedly non-matching Interceptor armor. While he lacked a helmet, he was wearing his dark green electronic ear muffs. These blocked out much of a gun's report but more importantly could be turned up to amplify natural hearing by a factor of about four. Along the barrel and magazine tube of the Marlin lever gun, he'd wrapped camouflage cloth tape both to break up its outline and provide a handy wrap or bandage if needed. Over the wooden handguard and along the chamber was a dark brown leather piece, wrapped tight, that held four cartridges in individual loops. Here Kyle had put his massive bronze solid rounds just in case he needed to punch through something substantial. The matching leather buttstock cover held seven of the more mundane plastic-tipped hunting rounds. Even this wasn't enough for a real extended firefight. He had forty more cartridges—two boxes—in a pouch. For his S&W .357, he had three speedloaders in individual pouches as well as a spare box of twenty five hollow points.

"You ready to head out?" Kyle asked his brother.

Matt took a deep breath. "Ready as I'll ever be."

They stepped outside into almost complete darkness. There was no moon and very little starlight punched through the low cloud cover. Kyle could just barely make out the men assembled on the road in front of the cabin. Other than a few murmurs, it was dead quiet. He was pleased to see no glow of white cloth—socks, undershirts, et cetera—that he'd specifically banned for the event.

"Listen up," Kyle began in a conversational tone. "We're going to head down there in what's known as a Ranger file. Grab onto the person in front of you and someone will grab onto your back. That way we won't lose anybody. If any of you brought flashlights, stow them on my porch. This ain't snipe hunting. Set off your light accidentally once we get close and this whole plan is blown.

"On the way down there I'll establish a rally point where you need to go if you get separated. Don't try to be a hero and crash through the woods looking for us. Once we get there, we'll set up into our positions one by one. It will take a while but if we all do it at the same time, we stand the risk of raising enough racket for someone to notice. Once you're in place, that's it. No movement or sound. If you picked an anthill to lie on, tough luck. You need to take a leak, lean over and take care of business.

"If this goes to plan, my team will be up there stirring up as many of them to chase us as possible. This will probably involve some shooting. That *doesn't* mean that the fighting is on and any of you have the authority to start the ambush. We need to get as many of them in the kill zone as we can for this plan to work. None of the enemy should have any reason to come directly at your positions unless you reveal yourselves beforehand ... so don't do it. With all that said, if things break down and one of the them starts engaging anyone in position for the ambush, and you're *one hundred percent* certain it's not one of us, by all means fire back. None of you has to martyr yourself over a rule. Greg, Matt, Terry, or DeSean should be the ones to kick this off. Once it's started, don't hesitate. Shoot the nearest Bee Gee right in front of you and then move on to the next. After the initial contact the team leaders will direct fire and movement. Remember the hand signals we covered today.

"Once that initial ambush is over, if you get legit hurt —shot or otherwise badly injured—and cannot fight, just yell, 'Medic!' as loud as you can. You see someone else in that state, do the same. Once the firefight begins, Major Rex and her team will move close to be accessible. We are *not* exposing Major Rex to enemy fire so you need to either get to her or someone needs to get you there. I don't have a better plan than that. As soon as you can disengage to get help, do so.

"Now, let's give today over to God. Bow your heads please. LORD God, please keep us safe today as we travel into that valley of the shadow of death Your servant David described. You are with us even there in the midst of mortal danger. Heavenly Father, I ask for a miracle today, that we will return to our friends and families safe and sound. And yes, we even pray for our enemies. May there be a better outcome than the shedding of blood today. I pray this in Your Son Jesus' name, Amen."

"Amen."

"Okay men, mount up. Double check everything. Once we leave, that's it. We're going down in squad order."

Dawn started to creep over the landscape and revealed that the marauder gang had indeed stayed put for the night. With the ambush in place and quiet to the rear, Kyle scanned the buildings with his Steiners. While he'd had a brief chance to peek from this angle yesterday, now he had nothing but time to take it all in. He and his squad faced northeast, toward the two buildings, the bar and the store. Both were on the Canal side of Highway 101 which ran north and south along this stretch. The bar was closest, just to the south of the store. They shared a parking lot that met up with the freeway across its entire length, a "turn in anywhere" lot, which was still full of vehicles. The bar was pretty typical of the sort out here in the sticks, with only a couple of high windows filled with extinguished neon beer signs. While it would be tough for the Bee Gees to fight from the bar, they could hole up in there and stay completely out of sight. The store had bigger windows on the side facing the highway but nothing along the other three sides. Out back was the usual assortment of dumpsters and loose garbage, along with a back door.

Kyle counted seven full sized trucks and fourteen motorcycles. Lenny's little white truck was not in sight. For that matter, neither was the sedan from two days before. Clearly the Bee Gees were smart enough to clear their trap using a winch and one of their trucks.

Kyle lay in prone, tucked into the brush alongside the freeway, with Timothy to his right. A little farther to the right were Malachi and Rod Burkett close together. Both Kyle and Matt had assigned "battle buddies" within their four man teams. Each man was directly responsible for another person.

"There's no one on guard," Timothy whispered. Kyle had noticed that as well. From their angle they could see the spot where the guard or lookout had set up two days before. And the spike strip had definitely been pulled away.

"The curfew, I think," replied Kyle softly. "They probably figure anyone running around then is either military or just nuts. Not someone to tangle with. You rip up the tires of one of those graysuit convoys and there'll be hell to pay."

"But it's after six, right?" Timothy asked.

"Yes, almost seven. Who knows? Maybe our little gambit paid off. Maybe they're all drunk as skunks."

As if on cue, a scraggly-bearded man in a dark sweatshirt and blue jeans stumbled out of the bar, turned to the left, walked to the corner of the building, and unzipped his pants.

"How far do you think he is?" Kyle whispered to Timothy.

"Hmm, maybe two hundred yards?"

"I think it's more like two-fifty," Kyle said. He brought the Marlin to shoulder, flicked the hammer to full cock—it was already off safe—and looked through the red dot scope.

"You need to sight in too," Kyle said. "If I miss, you need to take the shot." Kyle gave him a moment to prepare. Weak Bladder didn't look like he was in a particularly big hurry to finish his nature call.

The big, slow .45/70 bullets weren't great at longer ranges. They didn't move fast and didn't cut through the air as well as the smaller, sleeker, more modern projectiles. Even at this relatively modest range for a rifle—about double the full length of a football field—he'd have to account for the bullet drop, which Kyle knew from experience would be about twenty inches below the glowing red dot. At three hundred yards it would be more like forty inches and beyond that the trajectory started to look more like a rainbow. Aim too low and you'd shoot right between the target's legs or simply hit dirt.

Kyle put the dot directly on the man's face and noticed he was just about finished.

This is it. The early worm gets the bird.

While he'd been in some scrapes in Iraq, he'd never actually had to draw down his sights directly at another human being. It was possible he'd taken lives with his fifty cal, but given the long engagement ranges and with the fog of war he would never know this side of Heaven. This was a different animal entirely. Kyle didn't want to kill these men in spite of their past and future crimes and sins. But he also wasn't willing to sit back and let them hit Sunshine like they'd hit Cushman and God only knew how many other small communities.

Just as Weak Bladder started to turn, Kyle eased his left index finger back on the trigger. The rifle bucked and Kyle rode the recoil back. The report was attenuated by his earmuffs but Kyle knew it was plenty loud enough to get everyone's attention.

As he snapped the rifle back down, chambering a fresh cartridge along the way, Kyle saw that Weak Bladder had pitched face first on to the asphalt. Kyle let out a breath. The bar door swung open again and a tall man in black motorcycle leathers stepped out, a pistol in his right hand, looking back and forth. "What the . . ." he exclaimed, seeing the first man's body on the ground.

Kyle placed the dot at Biker's scalp and slowly pulled the trigger once again.

"You got him too!" Timothy barked, a little too loud. Kyle saw that the man had fallen over to the right of the door, which had started to swing shut owing to a mechanical spring but had caught on his boot.

No way it's going to be this easy much longer. He pulled two fresh cartridges from the Marlin's buttstock and fed them into its loading gate.

A tense couple of minutes went by in silence. Kyle snuck a glace over to Timothy and saw a line of sweat crossing the teenager's temple despite the forty degree weather.

Kyle snapped his eyes back to the bar and store just to see several figures rush from between the two buildings and toward the mass of parked vehicles. "Going for the vehicles!" Kyle yelled. "Light 'em up!"

The three rifles to his right fired on the six or seven men. Kyle saw the ricochets but to little effect. He frowned slightly. He'd hoped these three could do a little better against exposed targets, albeit running ones.

One man hopped onto a big black cruiser bike and kicked the engine over. Kyle tensed, his dream of two nights before flashing in his mind. A powerful bike like that could cover two hundred fifty yards in just a couple of seconds. Taking a tire to the face at fifty miles an hour was pretty low on Kyle's list of preferred ways to kick the bucket.

The bike spun, laying a crescent-shaped patch of burnt rubber, and sped off north, wobbling somewhat. Another biker performed a similar maneuver and followed his comrade. A truck door swung open, attracting fire from Malachi and Rod. Timothy, hampered by the Vepr's ten-round magazines, was busy slapping another one in and working the rifle's bolt handle.

Looking over his optic, Kyle aligned the rifle with the truck and snapped his left eye back down, sighting in. The truck engine turned over as three of the marauders hopped on the back, grabbing on to bits of loot to steady themselves. Kyle aimed just over the driver's side half of the cab and fired. The windshield starred closer to the middle. With his adrenaline now up he'd pulled the shot a bit.

Need to calm down. The truck lurched to the rear, braked hard, and turned to follow the two motorcycles, throwing a thick cloud of black exhaust.

There's six out of the fight . . . if I'd hit the driver those guys would still be here. Best to just let 'em go.

A bullet zip-cracked over his head and to the right, cutting between his position and Timothy's, followed by the report a split second later. Way too close. Kyle scanned but couldn't see the shooter. It wouldn't take long for him to get their range and start putting bullets on them.

Another rifle shot tore at the brush about two feet in front of his face. "Get up! Retreat! Retreat!" Kyle yelled, sweeping his head to the right. Per their training yesterday, the retreat call was merely to kick off the next phase of the ambush. If he had called, "Bug out!" his team would know to get to the rally point and call off the attack.

Kyle and his men took off down the edge of highway. Armed men streamed out of both the bar and the store. They weren't moving very fast.

Unlike yesterday, taking easy shots was definitely part of the plan. Kyle stopped, brought the Marlin to his shoulder, and snapped off a shot at the unwisely bunched up raiders. One of them stumbled and fell with a pained scream. Return fire came, all unaimed, but Kyle wasn't willing to try his luck any further. He spun and rushed after his team.

Another four hundred yards ahead was the small road off Highway 101 they'd picked for the ambush. There were better spots further south but they were simply too far away. No one would run a mile in pursuit if he could ride. Their pursuers were likely already running that idea through their half-drunk minds. It was the riskiest part of the plan. If the Bee Gees got to their trucks and bikes and ran them down before they could get to the ambush point, they'd most likely be killed. That thought bubbling up caused Kyle to increase his stride to a near-sprint.

Fire blossomed in his right leg and Kyle stumbled with a sharp yelp. *Hamstring.* Timothy turned, wide eyed, as Kyle nearly fell to one knee. Greg's guys were still a hundred yards away near the corner of the road. The obscenity-laced screaming from the rear reached a new level. Kyle could almost feel the muzzles of their weapons drawing down on him.

Timothy grabbed his armor near the left armpit and pulled. *Hard.* Kyle stumbled and hopped past Greg's squad and then over where Matt had set up with his crew. Kyle made a conscious effort to not look toward the wood line and possibly give away their positions.

Shots rang out from the rear. Up ahead was a bend in the road to the left. This was where the Cushman crew had set up, back off the road, in order to fire along its length for maximum effect.

A ricochet skipped off the asphalt at their feet. "C'mon!" Timothy yelled, dragging Kyle to the right and off the pavement. There was a *whang* sound from Kyle's back as they crossed into the brush by the roadside and crashed to the ground. The pain shot quickly from just to the right of his spine as wetness spread over the back of his legs.

❖ ❖ ❖

Matt sat behind a sturdy-looking cottonwood and stared down the road to the left. Having poor comms stunk. Radios without a reliable squelch were a no-go on an ambush. One hot mic and the whole shebang was toast. It meant he had to sit and be uber-vigilant in case something went against the plan.

He tensed as a scraggly-bearded figure clutching a rifle in both hands rounded the corner. In the dim early dawn light he couldn't quite make him out. A couple of seconds later, a shorter, smooth-faced young man joined him.

"Rod . . . Malachi," Matt whispered as he recognized them.

Where's Kyle and Timothy?

Several long seconds later he saw Timothy's bulky frame come into view. He . . . he was *pulling* Kyle along at barely a walking pace, his brother hopping along on his left leg.

No!

Rod and Malachi sprinted past his position, heading for the gap between his team and Terry's per the plan. Matt kept his eyes down the road. The first of their targets tore around the corner, followed closely by . . . a dozen more men. As they fired on the run, Matt tensed with each shot, expecting both Timothy and Kyle to crash to the ground.

Wait. Not in the kill zone yet. Don't blow it!

The pair stumbled past his position, the dead center point of the long leg of the ambush, turned, and crashed into the woods amidst increasing fire.

Now. The nearest BG was a slender man, pale with long black hair; he pointed a pistol straight out with his right hand. Matt felt his vision narrow through the forward mounted optic as its red dot found the man's chest. Matt squeezed once, twice, quickly, then looked over the sights and assessed. *Man down.* He shifted to the next man, darker skinned and heavier built, wide eyed and waving a shotgun wildly. Before Matt could sight in, that foe was cut down. He felt his ears, to this point essentially deaf, open a bit and heard that curious snarling sound of massed single shots reminiscent of Afghanistan. Matt stared over the optic, scanning for the next target, and spotted one running for the far side of the road. He put the dot on his back, squeezed the trigger twice, and saw him tumble into the ditch.

"Is . . . is that it?" said a voice to his left. No one had moved yet. Then, several shots rang out near the intersection with the highway.

"Shift up! Toward 101!" Matt cried. Several of their crew stood, weapons at the ready. Terry and his guys emerged from down the road, DeSean slapping a fresh magazine into that huge rifle of his. Matt looked back and to his right, searching for his brother, but saw no one.

◆ ◆ ◆

Kyle rolled over onto his stomach. "I'm hit!" he cried. His legs were soaked clear down to his boot socks. It felt as if a broomstick had been jabbed hard into his back. He'd never actually been shot before.

"You're . . . wet!" Timothy cried. Kyle felt the boy's hands exploring, trying to find the wound. "Can you move?"

"Yeah," Kyle croaked, followed by several coughs.

"Umm . . . I think your Camelbak is toast," Timothy said.

The Camelbak, Kyle realized. *I'm . . . just wet.* The hardened steel rear plate would stop anything short of an armor piercing rifle round. The plastic Camelbak, sitting on the outside, wouldn't stop a pocketknife.

Even so, it still hurt to move. There was no getting around physics: bullets hit hard. While the plate had stopped it from penetrating his flesh, all that energy had to go somewhere.

At that moment, the air erupted with the sounds of gunfire as the ambush opened up on their pursuers. Kyle got to his knees and grabbed his Marlin. He pointed toward the highway, back the way they came. Timothy nodded and they started out, Timothy's left arm wrapped around his back and pushing him along.

They were halfway back to the highway when the fire slacked, then stopped. Kyle's team was supposed to wheel back and support Greg's team. Rod and Malachi were nowhere to be seen. Kyle frowned, angry at their comm situation and inability to coordinate on the fly.

More shots rang out and Kyle heard the rumbling of engines and shouted battle cries. "Let's go!" he shouted, increasing what little stride he could manage. They came to the tree line facing the southbound lane. A gray truck was accelerating in their direction, the passenger hanging halfway out of the window, firing a pistol in a two-handed grip.

◆ ◆ ◆

A motorcycle barely made the corner, righted itself, and sped Matt's way, the rider firing a revolver with his left hand. Matt didn't even get a shot. There were several reports from the rear courtesy of the Cushman crew, and the bike lost control, hit a sturdy cedar next to the road with a loud *SMASH*, and threw the rider into the woods and out of sight.

Another big bike appeared and was cut down. Matt glanced back, counting heads. The younger Gautiers were running his way with Jeff Morrison pulling up the rear, breathing hard, slightly behind the Cushman team.

"C'mon!" Matt yelled. "We need to get up there!" His guys picked up the pace but the Cushman team started to lag. DeSean and one of the tow-headed brothers flanked Terry and helped him along as best they could.

That could be my brother's future, Matt feared. He motioned to his team to slow up. No sense in running out there piecemeal and getting picked off one by one. "How you holding up?" he asked Terry as he neared, huffing and puffing.

"Eh. I think I remember sayin' something about 'no

offensive maneuvers.' Guess it's just change step and go, like always."

"Pretty much. Even though they didn't all take the bait, I think we got about half of them. Should be no sweat to take out the rest. You see my brother or his sidekick?"

Terry shook his head. "Not since he went into the trees well short of the planned spot. Can't say as I blame him with all those tangos nippin' at his heels. Haven't seen the other two that ran in right before either. We'll round them up in a bit. First things though . . . take those buildings and make sure we're clear. Don't need some dirtbag biker roaring in while we're all high-fiving and what not."

"Amen to that. Let's go," DeSean said.

Matt nodded and they approached the intersection at a trot.

◆ ◆ ◆

The first shot struck the windshield as the truck sped by, then braked hard and fishtailed to face them once again, its passenger still firing wildly. Kyle slipped one of the bronze heavyweight cartridges from the Marlin's handguard ammo carrier, slid it into the loading gate with his right thumb, and worked the action briskly with his left hand. Timothy started firing from beside and slightly behind, the concussion of the muzzle blast buffeting Kyle's face and right arm. Kyle sighted in on the driver, who had a rictus grin across his brown-bearded face, and pulled the trigger.

The recoil rocked Kyle back, almost knocking him over. Fortunately, his good left leg planted well in the soft grass by the ditch. The truck swerved to Kyle's left, back toward the bar, and started drifting down the road.

The slender, black clad passenger sped out on foot, heading for the opposite tree line. Kyle, holding the Marlin in his left hand, drew his big .357 with his right and began firing at the fleeing figure. Others behind him joined in, shots ringing out, and their assailant slumped to the ground.

"Rod! Malachi!" Kyle called out.

"Yeah!" came a cry to the left. "We're here!"

Kyle heard a cry to his right and turned. Timothy lay there on his back, wincing, grabbing his left thigh. Blood ran between his fingers.

◆ ◆ ◆

Noise issued from ahead, into the trees, followed by several shots. "Left! Contact left!" Matt cried out as he raised the AK, scanning. Two BGs ran out into the street, saw Matt's nine armed guys, and quickly retreated, firing their rifles from the shoulder. Matt fired at the closest of the pair, a big man with an AK much like his except it belched long flames to either side when fired. Gunfire was exchanged and the opposing pair went down, one on his face and the other tumbling into the ditch and out of sight.

Matt wiped sweat from his brow and mechanically swapped his partially spent magazine for a fresh one.

"*Erik!*"

The cry was to Matt's right. He turned and saw one of the blond brothers hovering over the other, their matching camouflage making it tough to make out where one man stopped and the other began. Even in the still-dim light he could see blood pooling on the asphalt.

Terry waved Matt and his guys back. "You don't want to see this. Erik's ... *gone.*" Terry tapped his face with his left hand and turned back to his team. "C'mon," he said softly. "We need to finish this. Nothing more to be done here. Let's go, Paul. We'll come back for your brother. I promise."

Paul stood, tears running down his cheeks, and nodded curtly.

◆ ◆ ◆

"Rod! Malachi! Come to me!" Kyle called as he unslung the perforated hydration pack. Its side pouches held what little first aid gear he knew he could use during combat.

"*It . . . burns!*" Timothy cried. "I'm . . . I'm getting cold..."

Kyle saw the boy's face grow pale as he shivered. "You're going to be okay, all right? You're going into shock. Don't worry . . . that's totally normal. Now, let me get a bandage on you." Kyle tore the plastic wrapping off one of the Israeli-style bandages that had come standard with all of Bene Praepara's survival packages. "I have to move your leg to wrap it around, okay? It's going to hurt." Timothy nodded.

He heard the jostle of weapons and gear behind him and turned, his hand on his big Smith and Wesson back in its hip holster. It was just Malachi and Rod trotting up. "You need to cover us. Timothy's hurt." Their eyes grew wide when they saw Timothy lying in the wet grass.

"Did . . . did you call the medic?" Malachi stuttered out.

Kyle shook his head. "Move your hand," he told Timothy calmly. The wound was right through the meat of the thigh. The bleeding was significant but not what Kyle would expect from the femoral artery—that would be a death sentence even with Major Rex's help. He put the bandage over the wound and started to wrap it around the boy's thigh. "I think it's clean through. I need to grab another bandage for the exit wound." Kyle finished wrapping as gunshots rang out in the distance, back toward the ambush site. Another series followed as he wrapped the second bandage around.

"Thanks for taking out that one earlier. The guy who jumped from the truck," Kyle said as he worked.

"Uh, Kyle?" Malachi replied, still keeping his eyes on the road. "That wasn't a guy. I got a . . . a, uh, pretty good look with your ACOG. Did you mean to, ah . . . shoot the driver? Back at the lake, you said—"

"Yeah, I know what I said, Malachi," said Kyle, on edge. "I was more *concerned* with getting run over by that truck. Split second decision."

Timothy moaned, weaker now, as Kyle tightened down the second bandage. They all heard shuffling and footsteps from the highway, from the south.

"It's us! Our team!" Malachi cried.

Kyle stood and looked down the road, counting heads. Matt, pretty much in the middle, with his three plus three of Greg's—Jerry Goodridge, Norris McGwire, and the oldest Gautier, Mel. But no Greg Samuels and no Mike Klein. On the left were ... four of the Cushman crew. One missing. Kyle waved and his brother waved back.

"Where's Greg and Mike?" Kyle asked Matt as he approached.

Matt shrugged. "I don't know. We need to secure the ... is he—"

"Yeah. He'll be fine. Lost some blood though. I need to get our doc on the horn. I'm assuming everything's clear behind us?"

"As sure as I can be," Matt replied. "I'm glad to see you're upright, bro. You get tagged? I saw you come down pretty hard—"

Kyle shook his head, then nodded once. "Pulled a hammy. Then I got hit in the back. Thank God for AR500 steel."

"We're headed up to clear those buildings. You staying with him?" Matt asked.

Kyle took a step. The entire back of his right leg was still on fire. "Yeah. Definitely staying put. Rod, Malachi ... get a fresh mag in those rifles and stick close to my brother."

CHAPTER THIRTY-SIX
**Thursday, Fourth Week in November
Thanksgiving**

The trio carefully lifted Timothy's makeshift tarp and plastic conduit stretcher into the back of the Excursion. Melissa climbed in and shut the rear doors to keep in the heat. She heard the driver door open. Amber crawled in behind the wheel as Loren, popped in via the rear passenger door.

"How long did Kyle say? Five minutes?" Melissa asked the teenage girl.

"Yes. Five minutes since he was shot."

Taking her scissors from her bag, Melissa cut away the bloody pant leg and set it aside. She pulled the C-A-T® from her uniform sleeve, wrapped the tube around Timothy's bare thigh near his hip, and cranked down with the stick, locking it into place. The boy writhed and moaned. "Timothy? Listen, you need to be strong. I need to check out your wound. A little pain now is a lot better than losing your leg later because we were lazy and let it get infected."

Kyle had been right. Textbook entry and exit wounds, right through the middle of the left thigh. Definitely looked like a pistol-caliber GSW. Both wounds still oozed dark blood.

"I need to check to make sure your femur isn't broken. This ... will hurt." She grabbed his leg with both hands and twisted. Timothy yelled loud enough to hurt her ears. She glanced up. Loren was wide-eyed and her already pale complexion was completely blanched. She reached down and grabbed the boy's hand.

"Good news. Not broken. Now . . . I need to take off those bandages and clean those wounds."

Timothy nodded weakly. Melissa unwrapped both bandages, essentially identical to those she carried in her bag. "Distilled water," she said to Loren. The girl handed her a sealed plastic jug. Melissa unscrewed the top and irrigated the relatively clean entrance wound.

"Lift his leg, please," Melissa said. Loren nodded as she put her hand behind his knee and lifted. Melissa repeated the process on the much dirtier exit wound. She then bandaged both wounds with fresh ones from her bag, eased off the tourniquet, and checked for bleeding. Satisfied that the pressure dressings were working properly, she grabbed a space blanket borrowed from Kyle's surprisingly deep pile of supplies and laid it over the young man. Even though the truck was well-heated, it was easy to get cold with that kind of blood loss.

"Time for the IV. Loren, hold his left arm steady."

◆ ◆ ◆

DeSean Hupp cradled the big Sako in the crook of his right arm and helped his friend along with his left. He and Terry were falling behind. But that was fine. Neither was really set up to run through those two buildings up close and personal. They had a different task.

"Here," he said, dropping down to the soft dirt alongside the freeway. Both buildings were visible from an angle, not far from where the boy had been tagged just a couple of minutes ago and carted off. DeSean pushed out the legs of the bipod and got behind the scope. The Nightforce model he'd splurged on sported a Horus reticle that, to the untrained eye, looked like an incomprehensible 'Christmas tree' of lines and tiny dots. To a trained sniper, it allowed on-target adjustments, or 'dope', within the reticle itself—regardless of range, wind, or elevation—versus the slower, more traditional process of changing the point of aim with the scope's adjustment knobs.

His sniper training had come late in his career. DeSean had gone into the Navy straight out of high school when most of his buddies had joined the Army or Marines. He'd been razzed pretty hard for that but had enjoyed the faster promotions and the opportunity to see the world without eating mud and dust. Always a good athlete, he'd made petty officer and had earned a spot as a SEAL candidate. DeSean had easily passed all but the grueling swim test, something he'd always struggled at, and was sent back to his ship. Bored and more than a bit bitter at failing, he'd transferred over to the Army and quickly found himself in jump school and then on to the Rangers. Several years, and many schools and deployments later, he'd be blessed to officially become a sniper.

"Terry," DeSean called, "you're spotting me, right?"

"No ... I have some binos in my pack. Give me a min—"

"No ... get mine. I have my Vortex in there."

DeSean felt Terry rooting through his pack as he dialed in on the front windows of the store and the assortment of vehicles left in the lot. The bar's windows were blacked out. "Those store windows. Estimated height?"

Terry paused and looked as he adjusted the spotting scope. "I'd say three feet. A meter."

"Roger that." said. In DeSean's particular reticle, a standing man-sized target fit neatly between the solid lines at two hundred meters, and the window was less than half that. *So we're talking three hundred and fifty meters out.* He didn't need to check his supersonic range card—taped to the side of the stock next to its subsonic brother. It was just shy of two mils of adjustment in the scope.

"I got eyes on one," Terry whispered. "Behind the far corner of the store."

It was a clean shaven man with long, dark hair, clutching a small rifle. DeSean shifted slightly, aimed in, and fired. The rifle cracked, the supersonic bullet heading downrange, though the loud boom normally heard out of a high-powered rifle was absent, soaked up by the long titanium-bodied suppressor.

"Hit and down," Terry said, workmanlike. They had both done this before. "Got a runner . . . heading for the bikes."

DeSean worked the bolt quickly, the spent case rolling into the bottom of the ditch. He aimed and applied the appropriate lead on the reticle to account for the running of the man, who was clutching a pistol in one hand and some kind of bag or pack in the other, and squeezed the trigger again.

"Hit . . . although I think he's getting back up. Tough mother," Terry said.

DeSean chambered a fresh round and sighted in again but it wasn't necessary. Mr. Manbag had attracted the attention of the good guys moving in and they'd started to pop off shots. Some struck home.

"Looks like our guys are moving in to sweep," Terry said. "Let's keep our eyes peeled . . . bad guys might try and wheel back behind."

"Well, sir, we'll have none of that," DeSean deadpanned as he removed the Sako's magazine, handed it to Terry to reload, and slapped in a fresh one.

❖ ❖ ❖

They found Greg Samuels face down near the corner with the freeway, exactly where he would have set up for the ambush, shot through the upper back. Kyle turned away, the emotions of the day starting to crash down. Mike Klein, Greg's battle buddy, was nowhere in sight.

"How in the hell?" Matt spat angrily as he walked up. "Klein right there at his side . . . you guys securing the area around the freeway . . . I don't get it."

"Well, we were slow getting up there," Kyle said. "Still . . . to have someone slip in like that. I don't know."

"Wait a second," Matt said. "Those two we wasted that popped out the woods? They came right out from this spot. Wait here." Matt crashed off toward the side road.

"How many?" Kyle asked Terry Graham, who was crouched down with an unlit cigar in his mouth. Terry, DeSean, and Matt had volunteered for the gruesome task of counting the BG dead and gathering up and salvageable weapons and gear. All three had agreed it was best to spare the others those visuals.

"Twenty seven," he replied through clenched teeth. "No friendlies in either building. Very little booze or food left. They woulda taken off today or tomorrow for sure. Good timing on your part. Hell, I might have trained or done recon for another day. Marines . . . always in a hurry, right?"

Kyle raised his eyebrows. "I suppose. I probably would have done the same if you and your crew hadn't pitched in. I'm sorry about—"

"Erik? Yeah. Paul is pretty tore up. So am I. Erik was a good dude. You think that leg wound, that kid—"

"Timothy."

"Yeah. He gonna be okay?"

Kyle shrugged. "I hope so. His parents . . ." Kyle wasn't mentally prepared to broach that quite yet. "First things. We need to get Greg back to the lake and do what's right. Proper burial. And I need to figure out what in the heck happened to our friend Mr. Klein."

"Why did you come *here*?" Kyle demanded, trying to contain his emotions. They'd found the younger Klein sitting at the rally point, a half mile away from the action, eating a piece of deer jerky.

Mike shrugged. "I got separated in the battle. You said to come here if anything like that happened."

Matt, red-faced, began to open his mouth, and shut it.

Kyle shook his head. "Yeah, *en route* to the ambush. Once the shooting starts you can't just ... run away!"

"Like I said, I didn't know what to do. I didn't see any of you guys around."

"Did you hear the gunshots?" Matt asked sarcastically.

"Look," Kyle began, "Greg Samuels is dead. Shot in the back. He was *your* battle buddy. Do you have any idea how this looks from our perspective? Were you even there when he got shot?"

Mike turned his head away, staring off into the distance. "No. I'm ... I'm sorry."

"We're headed back down there. You ... go home and turn my shotgun in to Jeanie by the truck gate. We'll deal with this ... *situation* ... later."

They elected to draw numbers for the looted weapons. Kyle argued that the Cushman crew should get first crack, but both Terry and DeSean nixed the idea stating that everyone had put their life on the line equally. Kyle, already flush with weapons, opted out of the draw, though he managed to get Timothy a SIG .45 pistol with his pick—the one that had most likely shot him.

The vehicles themselves would be split up. Of six trucks, two would go to the Cushman team and four to Sunshine along with all contents. The inoperable seventh truck would get stripped down and divvied up equally.

Matt had come away from the draw with a 5.45x39mm model wire stocked AK that a few hours ago had been pointed at him in anger, along with a can and a half of rare Russian import ammo. As it was likely the weapon that had killed Erik, he'd offered it to Paul, who had refused, not wanting a constant reminder of what had killed his brother. Matt could relate.

After everyone had picked, there were still over twenty weapons remaining, mostly .22s and shotguns. Matt took a Ruger .22 pistol that he thought might make a good gift for one of the kids.

They piled into their new trucks. Kyle manned his Durango as Matt rode shotgun. The short drive back to Sunshine Lake was very quiet.

Kyle picked at his plate of slow cooked elk roast covered in drippings, a couple of bits of roast Canada goose, mashed potatoes with a dollop of canned butter, rehydrated fruit cocktail, and some pickled green beans. Despite the battle—or perhaps in spite of it—those that had stayed behind had prepared a reasonable facsimile of a Thanksgiving meal. Kyle lacked the appetite to truly enjoy it. Looking around the picnic area he saw he was not alone. The images, smells, and sounds of the firefight were far too fresh.

Several of the children were smiling and laughing, which cheered him considerably. This was the warrior's reward, to see your loved ones safe and happy. It certainly wasn't the thrill of victory. Victory was not the same as winning. Kyle didn't feel as though they'd won anything. Friends had died and innocence had been lost. Young people had given up a little bit of their humanity, temporarily taking on some of the characteristics of evil people in order to do what needed to be done. They would have memories... flashbacks... nightmares. For some, just days. For others, a lifetime.

Lenny had been heartbroken to learn of Greg's death. Kyle had not mentioned the circumstances. He suspected that if he did, he would have to prevent Lenny from confronting the Kleins, who were conspicuously absent from the festivities.

Kyle frowned. What would the Sunshiners do if today's heroics were needed again in a week? A month? They wouldn't be able to fend off serious trouble indefinitely. Ammunition and simple manpower would grind down to nothing. *Heck*, Kyle thought, *it was dumb luck that we had any heads up at all. A gang that size could roll up to the gate anytime.*

He finished eating, listening to the idle banter and watching the back-slapping, all given by the stay-behinds. Kyle turned to Amber, seated at his left. "I'm going to head back to the cabin and clean myself up."

She smiled. "Okay honey. I'm almost done too. Then I think I'll head over to spell Melissa a bit. Her sister brought her some food a bit ago, but she really needs a break. Timothy's still drugged up and nauseous."

Kyle stood and shuffled back toward the cabin, his leg still very sore. As he passed Greg's cabin, Kyle stopped and just stared for about half a minute. He'd only known the man a few weeks, yet Kyle felt as if an important piece of his life had been ripped away.

The next cabin, between his and Greg's, was the one that had been locked and vacant. That is, until a couple of hours ago. Melissa had felt it would be the best place to put a field hospital. Kyle had been less than thrilled—it simply wasn't theirs to use—but the logic was sound. The fact that there had been little or nothing of use inside had circumvented any more moral challenges.

Kyle knocked slightly. After a few seconds, Melissa opened the door. She'd changed from her Army uniform into comfortable civilian clothes. "Hey, Kyle. Here to see my patient?"

"Yeah. He asleep?" Kyle peeked in and could only make out half of the young man in the dim light. He was still.

Melissa nodded. "Are *you* okay? I heard about your leg. Seems to be the theme."

Kyle shrugged. "Hamstring. I'll be fine."

Melissa pursed her lips. "Don't just brush that off. If it's not healed in a few weeks, you'll probably need surgery to get right again. So take it easy."

"Doctor's orders?"

"Something like that."

"Got it. Well, Amber should be along in a bit. I'll check in on him again tomorrow."

Stepping off and turning his eyes to his own porch, Kyle spied something glint in the late afternoon shadows. He paused, hand going to the .357 still on his hip. There was movement and a figure appeared holding a scoped rifle.

It was Bill Klein. He was flushed and looked distraught. "Evening, Bill," Kyle called cautiously.

Bill narrowed his eyes. "My son told me about what happened. About how you chased him down and kicked him down the road."

"Now, Bill—"

The older man held a hand up. "Shut up. Don't try to sweet-talk me now. I know what's up here. We're not buds, never were. You need us to help with the dirty work, but once something doesn't go just the way you want, you push us aside. I came to tell you we're *done*. We ain't leaving . . . we're just *done* taking orders from *you*." To accentuate his point, he cocked his head and spat on Kyle's porch.

"That's your call, Bill. I laid out a system where we'd all help one another. You're not required to—"

"Spare me the explanation, chuck. Oh, and Mike's keeping that shotgun. You cut him out of his take from today. I figure that poop-colored gun will have to do."

Kyle gritted his teeth. "Your . . . son . . . *ran away* from the fight, Bill. There is no sharing in the spoils for cowards.

Mike was . . . is . . . a *coward*. End of story."

Bill twitched slightly. Kyle clutched the smooth wooden grip of his revolver a bit tighter.

"If I had any respect for you I'd—" Bill sputtered. "You and your brother both. Playing soldier and getting to pretend you're know-it-all bigshots to us poor bums who didn't have mommy's money to buy toys."

"You're . . . entitled to your opinion, Bill," Kyle forced out. "I advise you and Mike to not cross paths with me and my family from now on. And when you need something I have, and it will come up eventually, you'd better bring my Mossberg *plus* something else to trade. Now . . . *get off my porch*."

Kyle heard footsteps behind him but was unwilling to break his staredown. "Everything okay here?" Matt said, coming aside.

"Yeah. I was just heading out," Bill said as he slung his rifle and walked away.

"What was that all about?" his brother asked.

"The Kleins are going solo. They're off the charity list and the Flanigans are to have zero contact with them. Mike stole my shotgun. Just another day in paradise."

"Hmm. Can't say as I'll miss them much." Matt paused, clearly thinking. "We need to get back into our regular routine. Security posture, I mean. Jeanie and Lenny have been on duty all day. Don't worry—they got some grub."

"Okay, good."

"I thought we'd cover the evening, let them rest, and then figure out the early morning. I'll ask Jerry if he can help out. He's no warrior but he's smart and, well, can stay awake and alert. About all we can ask for at this point."

"I'll talk to Rod and Malachi. If you're willing, I'd like you to head up the team now. Even though Melissa told me to take it easy, with the Kleins going at it alone and Timothy laid up, I'm the only one to go get meat to put in the pot. I'll have to take on a couple of apprentices."

Kyle opened the door to the trailer. He wanted to call Jeanie at the gate to let her know they were on the way.

The scanner showed activity on several channels. "That's weird," Kyle said, stopping it at a strong signal.

"-ank you for that introduction. Ladies and gentlemen, fellow Americans. Thank you for your patience and understanding during these last few weeks. My security advisors have thought it best that I remain silent at this undisclosed, yet secure location. I have made the decision to end this silence today. Nearly four hundred Thanksgiving celebrations have passed since the survivors of the Mayflower landing. As colonies and as a nation we Americans have faced—and overcome—many challenges and hardships. I do not believe it is hyperbole to say we are currently in our greatest challenge in our nearly two-hundred-and-fifty-year history."

As the President spoke, Kyle grabbed the tablet off the counter, turned it on, and started the voice recorder.

"By our estimation, we have lost thirty million of our countrymen and women since the mass disruption of our economy and way of life. Disease outbreaks have been contained but this has only served to reduce the loss of life, not eliminate it. Many Americans, disappointingly, have chosen to act beyond the law and have taken lives for selfish gain. And, sadly, many have passed at their own hand, unable to cope with the dramatic changes we have experienced.

"You elected me on a platform of promised change and social justice and I see no reason to alter my stance now. Out of this immense tragedy, I see a unique opportunity to enact many of these long-needed changes. Changes like reversing the polarization of wealth in this country, where a CEO makes ten or twenty thousand times the income of the mail clerk or janitor in the same building. With federal government control of financial resources—something I intend to continue indefinitely—we can right those kind of wrongs. This new system will also destroy corruption and the outright purchasing of political support via campaign contributions and other means.

"All will have access to the same resources—food, water, healthcare, housing, power, and employment opportunities. Over time, it is my wish that some of these... aspects... will be re-privatized, albeit with heavy controls to avoid the abuse and greed that have led us to where we are today. We simply cannot allow Wall Street and our financial system to have this much control over our lives ever again."

"So our wonderful, all-knowing *government* will have that much control instead!" Kyle barked. "Private industries under strong government control has already been tried... it's called *fascism*."

"Shh, I want to hear this," Matt said.

"My Department of Homeland Security and specifically the Federal Emergency Management Agency have done an admirable job of restoring order and distributing food, clean water, vaccines, and other necessities of survival over these last several weeks. In the upcoming months, they will transition more into the supervision of national rebuilding efforts. We will all work—alongside one another, hand in hand—to restore this nation into something greater than it was. A better America for all of us.

"I ask that everyone cooperate with the authorities in their efforts. Those that selfishly work only to their own ends stand in the way of progress. Peace Enforcement, the Auxiliaries in particular, will act to uncover these... traitors to this new American experiment, and either bring them back into the fold or ensure they will not slow our progress.

"Some of you will receive international help as well. The United States has played a key role in giving international aid for decades and now it is our turn to receive. Fellow Americans, I require that you show international aid workers and soldiers the same respect and obedience you would of our own."

"God help us," Kyle said softly. "We're going to be invaded."

"At this time, I will turn the podium over to my Director of the Department of Homeland Security, H.M. Donaldson."

There was a pause of several seconds, then the familiar deep voice came in contrast to the President's much softer one.

"Thank you, Ms. President. I have a couple of announcements to the American people. First off, I must remind everyone listening that the national identification card program is mandatory and the cutoff date remains December 31st. After that date, those found without ID will be detained, investigated, and given an ID that denotes it was issued involuntarily. This ID will be yellow. As has been announced previously, Americans and residents with yellow ID will, for an indefinite period of time, only be eligible for the most basic of services.

"There have been many rumors regarding the Peace Enforcement program. It was born out of a cooperative memorandum between the Departments of Defense and Homeland Security along with select federal, state, and local police agencies. Peace Enforcement has the very difficult task of confronting lawbreakers without the traditional network of support. The President has green-lit directives to search suspects, confiscate weapons, and repossess obviously hoarded or stolen goods. Our network of Auxiliaries act as their eyes and ears."

"Spies. Brownshirts," Kyle said flatly.

"A number of inaccuracies surrounding the DHS must be addressed as well. The rumors of huge government holding camps tucked away in rural areas are completely unfounded. We do have a program in many areas where affected residents can opt to go on federal work details, and often this involves boarding a government bus to get there and back. Many have chosen to stay and continue to earn more—either in the form of bancors or future benefits. Others simply walk away. Some have joined the Auxiliaries. Others have critical skills and fall under the national service system.

"I know you are all concerned for our future. We've never faced anything like what we're going through right now. Now I, uh, don't have the President's gift with words. What I can say is yes, there is a plan in place to restore order. Some things will definitely be different moving forward. I can't guarantee everyone will be happy but we—the President, her staff, and her advisors—are working toward the greatest good for the greatest number of people.

"As most of you are listening to this address on public loudspeakers at one of our many ZOCs, you'll find that the DHS has made a heroic effort to serve a real Thanksgiving meal today. I'll be spending the holiday with my family giving thanks and, despite the circumstances, I hope you all will too. Good day and God bless America."

The broadcast cut to a man with a classic radio voice. "You've been listening to the President's Thanksgiving address. In case you missed it, it will repeat at the top of the hour throughout the weekend. Standard news updates will commence in thirty seconds."

Kyle let out a breath. "Wow. Well. Looks like we're sticking to the lake for the foreseeable future."

"What? You don't want to run down to Olympia for some turkey and stuffing?" Matt joked.

"Har har."

"Hey . . . scanner's picking up another signal. It's weaker . . . a lot weaker, but someone else is transmitting," Matt said.

"Let's hear it."

"—of you who have been listening to our dear President and her unelected crony, Donaldson, I have my own message. As this broadcast is being triangulated, I must keep it short. My name is Randy Barnhall. Yes, that's my real name—I refuse to hide behind a pseudonym. The man whose name I bear immigrated to this great nation to escape the Irish potato famine. His son fought for the Union in the Civil War. His grandson, my great grandfather, fought in Belleau Wood in France. My grandfather fought—and lost his life—in the Pacific. My father was in Vietnam and I got the so-called Global War on Terror. I know when it's time to fight. It's in my blood. So I'm risking my life rather than standing by while our nation dies before our eyes.

"I'm calling for mass insurrection against this illegal and

patently unconstitutional system of government. No less than a real coup d'état has occurred right here under our collective noses. Sure, some of the faces are the same, but don't be fooled. When an elected official claims they must have absolute power in order to overcome a crisis, let's call a spade a spade—that's a dictator. Julius Caesar. Napoleon Bonaparte. Adolf Hitler. All were elected. All later claimed total power and did not willingly relinquish it. Do any of you honestly believe our President will simply hand back the reins and drift into history? Of course not. There will always be a new crisis, another event that will require her power and control to overcome. Bet on it.

"This is exactly the circumstance the founders of this country envisioned when they included the Second Amendment in our Bill of Rights. As I've told friends, coworkers and family for years, it's not about hunting and shooting tin cans in the backyard. It provides the means to counter an overreaching government that rips away power from the public. The President that rules rather than serves. Government agencies that disregard law and human rights. Our once-trusted military has been converted into a murderous police force.

"We Americans must refuse this new totalitarian system. Your new, mandatory ID tracks your every move. You cannot leave your home without the threat of search and seizure, yet you must submit if you want to eat. If ordered, you must leave your family and place yourself at the government's whim—indefinitely. Your new 'Peace Enforcement' masters have no rules, only goals. They want to crush you and foster fear. Make you fear that your neighbor will rat you out for having some spare fuel, or some extra cans of food, or—Heaven forbid—arms to defend yourself.

"Those in power have miscalculated. After decades of trying—and failing—to disarm us, they believe we'll all simply get in line for our daily scraps, that we'll never bite the hand that feeds us. But I know better. My followers and I are set to start biting.

"Ready yourselves. On December First, you'll discover how serious my followers and I are. And then, just maybe, you'll

Michael Zargona

join us. That is all."

CHAPTER THIRTY-SEVEN

Friday, Fourth Week in November

Melissa had kept Timothy's wounds clean over the past day, packed with Iodoform gauze, and the leg was immobilized with a splint. Nevertheless, the boy's leg continued to swell.

"What is wrong with him?" Loren asked, face tight. She'd made a very good trainee, such as it was. Amber, with her dietitian education and experience brought a better understanding of the body's processes, but she'd been pulled away to take care of her family and, it seemed, half the camp as well. Loren had pulled an all-nighter with Melissa, slept for a few hours, and now was back at Timothy's side. Melissa had heard her story during the wee hours of the night. She could only imagine what the girl was going through.

"It's called *compartment syndrome*. In his case, one or more of the muscles in his leg are swelling and putting pressure on his tissues. Probably a blood clot from internal bleeding. It's more common in muscular people. Kyle told me Tim was a football player in school and lifted a lot of weights."

"So . . . he's going to just *blow up*? I don't get it."

Melissa shook her head. "No . . . not quite like that. But

it will get worse if we don't deal with it."

"What . . . what could happen? Is it serious?"

"Well, he could lose the use of his leg. Necrosis. Or die. So yes, it's serious. Let's get him prepped for surgery."

This involved removing the splint, administering morphine, and disinfecting Timothy's thigh. Once complete, Melissa made several long incisions with a scalpel—a *fasciotomy*—and removed a small amount of the connective tissue—the *fascia*—to allow the swollen muscles more room and relieve the pressure. The entire process took about an hour and a half. Without modern monitoring equipment, Melissa had tasked Loren with manually checking his pulse and blood pressure periodically. It was a simple surgery, but also quite rare, even for a military field surgeon accustomed to injuries like Timothy's.

"You did that like you'd done it before," Loren said as they washed off outside.

Melissa nodded. "Yes I have. In Afghanistan, about six years ago."

"So . . . what if it comes back? That swelling. I mean, you're leaving tomorrow morning. Right?"

"That's right."

"But . . . your family is here. And we *really* need you up here. We both know Timothy won't be the last to get hurt."

"Tucked up here by the lake it might feel like you're riding out the end of the world, but this all will get pieced back together before too long," Melissa countered, remaining calm. "I don't know what the future will look like, but I'd much rather experience it as Major Rex, United States Army than as Inmate Rex, convicted deserter. I am honor bound to do my duty. As much as it pains me to leave, after tomorrow morning you will all have to cope without me."

◆ ◆ ◆

They laid Greg Samuels to rest in a small clearing to the south of the lake, dug deep to thwart the mountain lions, bears, coyotes, and other denizens of the hill country. Kyle said a few words, paying his respects, and read Psalm 23 followed by Matthew 5:4.

"Blessed are those who mourn, for they will be comforted."

Others joined in with their memories of the man. During those long nights pulling security, Greg had mentioned he had little in the way of family or friends before the collapse. Had he died two months before, his passing would have been unremarkable and memorial lightly attended. However, it was clear that he would be missed greatly by his new family in the Sunshiners. Greg Samuels had done much and asked for little in return.

Lenny cried and Matt saw that his brother was close to tears as well. Isabella dutifully recorded the memorial with the family tablet computer.

Des stood at Matt's side, which caused Matt to raise an eyebrow. He would not have been surprised in the least if she'd opted to stay back at the cabin, pillow over her eyes. She still seemed dour, but then again, it was a memorial service.

As they walked back, she reached out and clutched his hand. Matt turned and raised an eyebrow, and Des gave a slight smile.

"Something you want to tell me?" Matt asked.

"I've had a lot of time to think," she began. "And, talking with Amber a bit over the last day or so. Trying to make sense of things."

"And?"

"I told her how angry I was. Everything we've worked for and everything your family had invested, gone in an instant. About being alone and scared. Your blind commitment to duty. You running off to fight. But, Amber made a couple of really valid points.

"One, if I didn't care, I wouldn't be angry. Two, you came back. And not because of the cabin, or because of Kyle, but because of *me*. Both points really struck me hard. At the end, I think I figured it all out. It seems stupid, but I was mad at myself for being mad at you. Dumb, right? I said some pretty hurtful things, didn't I?"

Now the tears came. "Uh ... yeah. You did. I doubted if you ever even really loved me. Made me feel like I was just a guy you picked out of the crowd who met your requirements in a husband. I mean, you brought up *your mother* for crying out loud. We both know how she feels about me."

Des started to tear up as well. "I have been pretty selfish. But I don't want to be one of those people who just crumbles under pressure. Coal or diamonds, right? I want better than that ... for both of us. So ... do you forgive me?"

Matt stopped and embraced her. "Of course."

◆ ◆ ◆

Before he side hilled to the left, Mike Klein looked down to the south and spied the memorial for Greg breaking up in the meadow beyond the lake. He turned, adjusted his rifle sling, took a few steps, and Sunshine Lake was out of sight.

"Idiots," he muttered as he scanned for game in the valley below with his scope cranked to nine power. *Especially Kyle. While he's busy playing minister, I'm heading to the prime hunting spot he shared with Dad and me. Might just get another deer out of here today.* It was tough to keep the first one—a nice big doe—a secret, curing the meat over the small fireplace in the cabin, but it meant they had their own family reserve of food. And if Kyle kept giving away all of his grub like a chump, just to get everyone to put up with him in charge, pretty soon they would have more than anyone and really be set for the winter. Kyle couldn't hunt and fish for eighty people. Especially not on a bad leg.

It was about time Kyle and his spoiled family started sharing. All those years of showing up to the lake with a new truck, or a new Bimmer for Matt's prissy wife, or silver spoon Mommy and her matching silver Porsche convertible. Slumming it with all the people who actually had to work for a living, pretending they were in their shoes, while at the same time looking down their noses at them. Then getting ticked off when their neighbors actually had some fun on the lake instead of just sitting and staring at it while sipping iced tea and filling their cakeholes with hors d'oeuvres.

Mike moved slowly down the hill toward the creek below. Unlike most that flowed quickly down the steep hillsides in tight draws, this one ran through a relatively flat marshy meadow that deer and elk couldn't seem to resist even in broad daylight. It wasn't perfect—it was a quarter mile from the nearest Forest Service road—but he and his old man had come up with a system. Dad had taken his truck out the western logging road, made his way around the hill, and sat to listen for the shot. Kyle and his brother weren't the only sharpshooters up at the lake. Mike didn't miss. Once the animal was down they'd dress it and bring it back. Canopy with tinted windows kept it all out of sight. Too easy.

Mike settled down in the money spot that looked down the length of the meadow. When game bent down to drink, they presented perfect flank shots from this vantage point. He sat, breathing periodically into his hands to keep them warm. About an hour passed before a smaller buck—two points on both sides of the rack—came into view from the left. It scanned the meadow and gingerly stepped toward the burbling stream. Mike slowly raised his .30-06 to his shoulder, clicked off the safety, put the crosshairs above the animal's foreleg for a heart and lung shot, and pulled the trigger.

The buck jerked, stumbled several yards, and went down in a heap. Mike smiled, slung his rifle, and walked toward his kill. *This is where Kyle would make up some meaningless prayer.* Confirming the animal was dead, he got to the dirty work of dressing it, hoping his old man was on his way to help with the drag out.

He had both hands inside the buck's belly, cutting the lungs loose when he heard the snap of a branch behind him. *Another deer? No matter . . . can't drag two out.*

"Don't move!" It was an angry shout in a voice Mike didn't recognize. He couldn't resist a glance to the rear. A dirty-faced middle-aged man, with the all-too-common six-week growth, wearing jeans and a black-and-white plaid flannel shirt, advanced holding a small rifle at his hip.

"I said don't move! Get your hands where I can see them!"

Mike exhaled, pulled his bloody hands free, and placed them, palms out, above his head. "Okay . . . okay. It's your deer, bro. Just don't . . . don't kill me."

"Shut up. Step away. Toward the woods. Don't even think about grabbing that rifle. You ain't quick enough. Bro."

Mike *had* thought of it, but remembered the chamber contained the spent case. Even if he was fast enough, or the man tripped, it would take a second or two for him to cycle the bolt. This man would never grant him that kind of time.

But Mike had an ace in the hole. Yesterday in the ditch, on his way to the rally point, he'd run across a raider who had clearly been caught in the ambush and had crawled away from the road before dying in a pool of his own blood. Mike had lifted a big revolver, a matte black .44 Magnum snub nose with rubber grips, along with a couple of full speedloaders, from the still-warm corpse, and had tucked it into his belt. Too uncomfortable to hike against his body, it rode in the left side pocket of his black sweatshirt. Mike was right handed, but in the right pocket it banged against the stock of his rifle when slung.

"Are you stupid, son? Get walkin'!" A slight breeze

kicked up and Mike caught wind of the man's stink, like a campfire made with wet wood mixed with the sour smell of old sweat.

Mike backed away, keeping his eyes on the muzzle of the man's rifle. He saw it dip as his assailant turned his eyes toward the buck.

No one takes what is mine. Mike whipped his left hand down and into his pocket. The older man's eyes went wide as he shifted to bring his rifle in line with Mike's torso.

Fingers still slick with the buck's blood, Mike fumbled with the rubber grip for a split second. A shot roared and burning sensation erupted through his right side as the breath in his lungs was forced out of his mouth. He brought the .44 up, trying to put the silhouette of its orange front sight on that dirty plaid shirt.

Why does it feel so ... heavy?

Another shot boomed. Mike pulled that too-heavy trigger and the gun almost flew from his hand, only catching on his index finger. He stumbled backward, vision swimming. Pain. A wave of it, radiating from near his stomach. His eyes snapped back to his attacker. Holding his rifle by the barrel, raising it above his head like a club. Mike gripped the pistol, tighter this time, and fired again.

◆ ◆ ◆

"Well well well! Welcome back," Loren said as she looked up from her notepad and saw Timothy stir. He'd been asleep for several hours. Still in serious condition, but stable. His mother, Jennifer, had just left a few minutes before.

"Whuh . . . my leg. On fire," Timothy whispered, barely audible. "So ... thirsty."

Loren reached for a glass of water, tipped it to his lips, and let a little trickle in. Some ran down his chin and ended up on the blankets.

"We . . . well, Melissa really, had to operate on your leg," Loren said. "Com . . . *compartment syndrome*. You were swelling up. You should be okay now, though. Just more cuts and more bandages. Melissa is going to stitch you up before she heads back. You'll have to take it real easy for at least a couple of months." Speaking of Melissa, she was certainly taking her time getting some late lunch.

Timothy groaned slightly and tilted his head to the side, eyes still closed.

"What you and the others did yesterday was so brave," Loren said. "I can't thank you enough. None of us can."

"Got . . . even . . . for you and . . . Malachi."

"That's not really how it was going down and we *both* know it. They were probably going to stop up here next. Pure survival."

Timothy opened his eyes, taking a few moments to focus. "What . . . what are you writing?" he asked, referencing the notepad she had on her lap.

"Oh, nothing special. A poem. I have lots. I mean, I've written a lot of them."

"Read me one."

Loren shrugged. "I can't promise much. I'm kind of a quantity over quality type. But here's what I was just working on.

> "By the water's edge so clear so deep,
> Lies her heart too dear to keep.
> Not knowing whence love does derive,
> Assured only that in her it can survive."

Timothy cracked a slight smile. "I . . . like it. Is . . . is . . . that all?"

"Erm. Well, I'm working on a second part. I don't think much of it.

*"Paths to the soul flow like streams,
Conscious above and below the fold.
Past present future glued like dreams,
Fuzzy shapes for her to behold."*

"I . . . don't know about . . . fuzzy. Maybe . . . try . . . hazy?" Timothy croaked.

"Hazy. Yeah. That works better. Thanks. No one up here bothered to bring a thesaurus. Y'know, the book kind."

Loren reached over, tipping the water glass once again to his lips with her right hand while grasping Timothy's open right hand with her left.

◆ ◆ ◆

"Foxtrot One, this is Foxtrot Two, come in, over." Kyle glanced down at the radio clipped to his belt. Foxtrot Two was his brother. He wasn't set to be on duty for a couple of hours.

"This is Foxtrot One. Send it."

"You better get up here. Cabin ten. Mike Klein's—"

Kyle keyed his radio. "Enough, I'll be up there in a bit." He didn't like leaving the "truck gate" unmanned but despite Matt's poor radio discipline, he was wise enough not to call unless it was a real emergency. *Why would Mike Klein be in cabin ten? Come to apologize?*

He started limping that way and saw Bill's burnt orange rig parked right in the middle of road. Hackles went up a bit and he glanced down at his Bushmaster, the image of a livid and armed Bill on his porch still fresh.

Matt sat on one of the Adirondack chairs on the porch, hand to his forehead. "So . . . what's up?" Kyle asked.

His brother looked up, eyes bloodshot and very tired-looking. "Just head inside."

"Wait," Kyle said. "Is it Timothy?"

Matt shook his head. "No. Mike Klein."

Kyle opened the door and peeked inside. Mike's wife and his mother embraced in the kitchen area, both sobbing. Beside Timothy's bed sat another, clearly occupied, with an IV bag clipped to the headboard. Bill Klein was pacing, staring at the floor, but looked up as Kyle scanned the room.

"Hey! You get your ass out of here!" Bill cried.

Melissa, a pained look on her face, stepped out from the shadows. "For God's sake keep your voice down. This is *my* field hospital and I'll determine who can and cannot be here. Kyle, let's speak outside."

They stepped out back into the cool late day air. "What happened?" Kyle asked.

"He was out hunting north of the lake. Someone shot him. Wound looks like a rifle bullet, hollow or soft point. Not at all a clean pass-through like Timothy's. Tore a big chunk out of his liver and, while it missed the really large blood vessels, it struck some smaller ones and he's lost a great deal of blood. It's a miracle he was able to stumble to the road where his father found him. Another couple inches to the right and it would have bruised or severed his spinal cord."

"Obviously working your honey hole up that way," Matt added.

Kyle glanced at his brother and shook his head. "You got him hooked up to one of those special IVs," Kyle said. "But...Melissa...I sense you're not real optimistic."

Melissa nodded twice, slowly. She too looked very tired. "Timothy's GSW was about the limit of what I can confidently handle with what I brought with me. Mike's is...far worse. Honestly, with his blood loss, shock, and tissue damage I'd give him about a five percent chance of survival past tomorrow."

"What about taking him with you? Back to JBLM?" Kyle offered.

"I doubt that would do any good. What little we have

in the way of blood supply is reserved for government use. Peace Enforcement mostly, of course, but secondarily anyone pressed into federal service. Since the young Mr. Klein isn't either one he'd still be without what he needs . . . a transfusion in the next twelve hours."

CHAPTER THIRTY-EIGHT

Friday, Third Week in December

Marshall Cross's briefing had been straightforward. A small group of about thirty ODTs—Overt Domestic Terrorists—had been discovered holing up several miles northwest of Battle Creek, Michigan. They were assumed part of the newly infamous "Randyite" faction that had brought everyone with a bone to pick with the government out into the open. The same Randyites that had, as promised, conducted over two dozen highly coordinated attacks on the first of December, three weeks ago today. Several generals and their staffs were killed in those attacks, along with at least three state governors and two Congressmen. An enormous amount of weapons, ammunition, and other war materiel were also stolen, almost certainly with inside help.

According to their intelligence report, the group's weapons should have included the usual assortment of civilian grade guns one might expect in rural deer hunting country.

The intel boys had messed up.

Three days ago, then-Lieutenant Cross had been on the mend in Chicago after having been struck by a ricochet.

The bullet, bent in half by a brick wall, had taken a nice chunk out of his left shoulder before heading again on its merry way. It had been fired by one of his own trigger-happy Forcers during yet another raid on the local organized gangs there. He'd been pulled away, trucked up to Michigan, promoted to captain, and assigned to lead an infantry company as part of a hastily-organized battalion. Outside of the cities, Peace Enforcement dropped the ridiculous "Direct Action Team" nomenclature and units used a more traditional military TOE—Table of Organization and Equipment.

But the equipment part still wasn't up to snuff. Most armored vehicles and aircraft required a tremendous amount of fuel and ongoing maintenance. Fuel was hard to come by right now, and many of the maintenance personnel had been converted to FEMA chow line guards and DHS door kickers by the President's command. Humvees and other simple wheeled vehicles including the new JLTV—Joint Light Tactical Vehicle—had come off the bench but could never match the punch or protection of, say, an Abrams tank or Apache helicopter.

Another mortar bomb exploded off in the distance, about a klick in front of them. Captain Cross tensed as he continued to scan with his binoculars through the passenger side window, the biting cold breeze striking his face as leafless trees whizzed by. The four ex-National Guard armored Humvees they brought as a mobile strike element would have been plenty—had the intel been accurate. Another eighty or so Peace Enforcers had been trucked in and, to the rear a couple of klicks, awaited the order to push forward on foot under the cover fire of Cross's gun trucks. Cross was not about to send threescore and ten men into a mortar kill zone with interlocking fields of machinegun fire.

Though his vehicle had its own machinegun up top

in the turret, a M240, it could only match what was coming from the insurgents in terms of range. Their one weapon capable of standing them off beyond their effective range, a similar Humvee mounting a Mk19 automatic grenade launcher, had been taken out by an almost perfect mortar strike about three minutes ago. Another vehicle had retreated—against his orders—and the fourth Humvee was stranded, inoperable and taking heavy fire.

Their destination.

"Driver! To the left! Left! You're taking us into the kill zone!" Marshall did not remember the young man's name. He did know he wasn't even supposed to be in uniform—he'd been waiting to leave for Army basic training when the crash happened and been pulled out of line at a distro since he was on file with the DoD. Many veterans, even those well past their obligations, had received the same treatment, but Marshall hadn't encountered another like this untrained teenager.

The young man grunted and pulled the wheel hard. Too hard. Cross's turret man, Sgt. Nelson, yelped, barely hanging on to the M240's black pistol grip with a tan gloved hand.

"Get to that rise!" Cross yelled. "I should be able to see them from there. Slow down a bit when you get there, but whatever you do, don't stop." Speed had rendered them a tough target to hit—their only real protection.

The radio mounted beside Cross crackled to life on their company freq. A machinegun chattered in the background. *"Is anyone coming? Help! HELP!"*

Marshall grabbed the mic. "Blue Three, this is Black Six actual en route to your position to extract. Hold tight for two mikes. Black Six out."

"We'll be dead by then! Call for support!"

Cross slowly shook his head. Ever since he could remember, The Good Guys were accustomed to absolute air support and most of the time could call for indirect fire—artillery or mortars. If things got too serious, you fell back and called for the big hitters.

Not today. The Humvees *were* the big hitters. He peered through the binoculars again. "Got 'em. About seven hundred meters ahead and slightly to the right." Cross didn't share that the vehicle was practically shredded with holes and the turret gunner lay slumped to the side. That left four possible Peace Enforcers against at least thirty well-armed, well-trained men. Obviously the attackers had a lot of military experience to run those mortars and walk controlled machinegun bursts in from several hundred yards. Deserters, almost certainly. Desertion had become a much bigger problem than combat casualties since the Randyite attacks.

"Whu... what do you want me to do... sir?" his driver asked, so scared he was shaking.

Marshall pointed with a gloved hand. "Private, get up there behind the vehicle, but not too close. Say a hundred yards or so. You hear that, Sergeant? Be ready to open up if we take fire."

"Yessir!"

The Humvee wasn't really set up for rescue, but in an emergency one could stack up troops like cordwood in the back, or they could ride up top and hold onto the machinegun as a last resort.

They were about five hundred yards behind the immobile Humvee when Marshall heard the distant boom and long whistle of another incoming mortar bomb. "Nelson! Get out of the turret!" he screamed.

It impacted about ten yards to the front and left of their destination, rocking the already nearly destroyed vehicle, fragments shredding it even further. His driver started to decelerate.

"Whatever you do, *don't stop*," Cross said. "Keep rolling up."

"They got the range now, Cap'n," said Nelson, down from the turret and squatting right behind Cross's left ear.

His breath was surprisingly hot. "We go up there, we get us blowed up too."

To punctuate the point, three more bombs whistled in—what mortar boys called a 'fire for effect'—and practically landed on the roof of the Humvee ahead of them. Three of its four doors flew off their hinges as shards of the vehicle's aluminum body caromed in all directions.

"Them boys is dead, sir," Nelson concluded. Cross did not disagree.

"Private, head back to the hardtop. Sergeant, get back into that turret and keep your eyes open."

Both men complied, the driver putting the vehicle in reverse and cranking the wheel to execute a three-point turn. There was a hard *thunk*, a splash of water, and then the whine of spinning tires. The ice in the low, marshy areas wouldn't support a heavy vehicle like this Hummer. Cross glared at his driver as he reached over and slipped the selector lever into 4H. "Hit the gas!"

The engine roared and they started to inch forward out of the mud. A loud thud vibrated the truck slightly, followed by several sharp cracks. Then another hit. A hole big enough to fit Cross's index finger appeared in the frame directly to Cross's right, matching up with a ragged opening through the vehicle's radio and out the driver's side door. It had passed only inches underneath the boy's arms.

That's a big hole . . . fifty cal at least. "We're getting sniped! C'mon, let's move private! Nelson, you have eyes on the sniper?"

"No sir!"

"Suppress that tree line while we get out of this hole!"

The teenager behind the wheel, white as a sheet, was pounding on the steering wheel with tears running down his face. He looked over at Cross, eyes wide, flipped the door latch, and jumped out.

"Get back here, Private!" Cross yelled over the stuttering din of the M240. The boy just kept sprinting away.

Another bomb exploded. Cross crawled behind the wheel and pressed on the gas.

Steam shot from out of the front of the hood as the engine screeched. Another *thud* sounded as something struck the far side of the vehicle. But Humvees were designed to take quite a bit of punishment before failing altogether. Cross pressed on the pedal and felt the tires spin, but not a lot of power was getting there.

A bomb detonated on his side, about a hundred meters away.

We're getting bracketed. These guys move quick.

"Sergeant Nelson! Abandon the vehicle! Let's go!" Cross called as he swung the driver's door open and leaped out. He turned, looked up, and saw the Peace Enforcer slumped over the machinegun, still. His upper back had a rough hole through the black plate carrier. Dark blood stained his gray uniform below.

"Ah, damn." Cross grabbed his driver's abandoned M16A2 and began running and weaving, closely following the boy's fresh footsteps leading to the rear.

He found him sobbing about a half a klick away with blood coming from his mouth. "I ... I can't *move!*"

"What's wrong? You get shot?" Cross asked, trying to contain his disdain.

"No! I ... I sprained my ankle and fell on my face!"

Cross couldn't expect much out of someone totally untrained for combat. But he expected more than this. "Get up. I ain't carrying you three klicks. Now let's go."

Inside the converted office building that served as the battalion HQ and officer quarters, Captain Cross opened the door to his "room"—formerly the space of a real estate agent—and sat down on his cot, rubbing his sore shoulder.

The debriefing was somber. After several minutes

without word from Cross, the battalion commander, Lt. Colonel Slaski, had ordered Cross's XO, Lieutenant Pappas, to take the infantry in and mop up anyway. The result was thirty eight confirmed KIA and forty-two wounded, many of whom were not expected to survive. Nearly eighty percent of the unit was out of action including Lt. Pappas plus several other officers and senior NCOs. Enemy losses were unconfirmed and anecdotal as they'd left no man behind.

Their HUMINT—human intelligence—that had come forward four days ago turned out to be local man who'd up and disappeared soon after spilling his guts to a Peace Enforcement Auxiliary who was probably hungry for a hot lead. Their 'source' was now assumed to be operating for the ODTs and had almost certainly led Cross and his men into the trap.

Even so, Captain Cross couldn't bring himself to hate those men on the other side of the marshy clearing. A few short weeks ago they could have been his neighbors or even fellow Marines. *This must be how the Union soldier must have felt, lining up to volley fire against Johnny Reb.* Despite their terrorist designation, Cross knew better. There were no good guys, no shining heroes on either team. One man's terrorist was another's freedom fighter, so the saying went.

There was a soft knock at his door. "Yes?"

"Colonel Slaski. You got a moment?"

Cross admitted the pot-bellied, silver-haired man, who'd likely been retired for years before being pulled off his couch to lead a battalion. "Of course, sir. You have news? Lieutenant Pappas? My driver?" *I still don't know his name.*

The older man shook his head. "No clue about your driver. Gary, though, will be fine. Doc says he'll keep his arm, maybe suffer some nerve damage and such. No, I need to discuss the future. Your future. I got word via our neighborhood DHS liaison officer that we're going to stand down for a week, rebuild your company, and prep for a new assignment."

A week? We need months to train up to the level where we could face the insurgents. "Sir, who's joining up? More discharged vets and never-beens?"

His CO shrugged off the jab. "That's what's available. We're spread incredibly thin, Marshall. I hear some units are being augmented with yellow carders. Not just a couple here and there. Whole battalions." *Yellow cards. Criminals drafted into fighting, like the old days. But back in the old days, a sergeant could punch an ex-jailbird private in the mouth if he got out of line.*

Cross held his tongue and Slaski continued. "What happened earlier today . . . That informant, when we catch him, is going to pay dearly for this."

"Sir, if I may, why did you go ahead with the assault? Everyone back there could hear the mortars. They knew they were marching into a beaten zone." Cross, not wanting to embarrass his commanding officer, had left the question unasked during the debriefing.

"I had my orders, Captain. We needed your cover fire and, well, we still had to take the ODTs out. The mission hasn't changed. We'll get them later."

Doubtful. Those guys were all back home with their weapons secreted away.

Colonel Slaski looked up at the ceiling. "There's, ah, something else I needed to talk to you about. Tell you, actually. This morning we received some news about your parents."

Cross's eyebrows shot up. "What . . . what happened?" he asked. News was never good.

"I don't know a good way to break news like this, Marshall, so I'll just . . . well . . . your parents both passed away earlier this week. Hemorrhagic fever. I'm so sorry."

Hemorrhagic fever? Ebola? Marshall was floored. His vision swam and he felt light headed. He reached up and pinched the bridge of his nose with his thumb and forefinger. "I . . . I don't understand. Sir. *The vaccines* . . ."

"There's a new strain. Ravaging the South and Midwest. It's not good. Quarantine's being established but the outbreak's too big to manage. But enough about that. Take the rest of the day and tomorrow off. If you're inclined, I have a couple bottles of scotch—"

Cross sunk into his chair. "Thank you, sir, but they won't be needed. I'll ... I'll be all right."

CHAPTER THIRTY-NINE

Friday, Third Week in December

"Hey," said Malachi, tapping him on the shoulder. "Your radio."

"Thanks," Kyle replied. The rechargeable batteries in his electronic earmuffs must have gone dead again. They were starting to show fatigue. He slipped them off.

"Foxtrot One this is Sierra Two. You got your ears on?" It was Jeanie's voice.

"This is Foxtrot One, go ahead." Even in the middle of the day, Kyle could see his own breath.

"Roger. Situation back here. Come A-S-A-P."

Kyle looked at his young companion, shrugged, and keyed the mic. "Details please, Sierra Two."

"It's . . . Bravo One." Timothy's code name. While not nearly back to normal, the young man had been on his feet for a week hobbling around on crutches. Kyle was a bit ahead of him, just needing a walking stick most of the time.

"He's arguing with his parents. They are heading out and he's staying put."

Malachi snorted. "It's because of Loren. So typ. The cheerleader and the jock."

Kyle frowned. Timothy would be eighteen in a couple

of months. He was, for all intents and purposes a man and was starting to act like one. It was clear to everyone that Timothy preferred to associate with the Flanigans versus his own parents. Kyle had mixed feelings on the matter. Tom and Jennifer Benson were good people, but they'd marginalized their son. Timothy liked to hunt, fish, and live in the woods. Not surprisingly, he also liked their pretty poet laureate, Loren. He would have none of that with his parents, struggling on the fringes of a ZOC.

"Roger. It's going to be a while, maybe three hours. Locate Foxtrot Two and hold them up as best you can." Kyle considered asking Matt to pick him up but even with the gas they'd acquired from the raiders' stock, they'd had to cut their short back-and-forth trips to a minimum. An elk or deer was worth it. A family squabble was not.

"He's already here. Negotiations are failing."

"Roger that. I'm en route. Foxtrot One out."

Kyle shook his head. Two people, police-trained in how to deescalate tense situations, and they expected Kyle to be the one to make it all better. He rose to his feet, right leg still tight, slung his Tikka and pushed hard on his alder walking stick. Malachi rose considerably quicker, his warbooty Ruger Mini-30 rifle in his gloved hands.

Three weeks had passed since Mike Klein had been shot about two hundred yards in front of this very spot. He'd passed on just hours after Jerry Goodridge and Matt had taken Melissa Rex back to JBLM. Naturally, Bill had held Kyle responsible in some way, though Kyle still wasn't sure what that could possibly be. The next day, the Kleins had put together a small memorial and laid Mike to rest in a different meadow, this one at the west end of the lake. Kyle and his family hadn't been invited. Bill, despite the fact Sunshine Lake should have been drained of all alcoholic beverages, had found a way to get stinking drunk that night and had yelled epithets, with Kyle and his family name salted in liberally, into the night from his porch.

A couple of days later, Bill, along with Mel and Travis Gautier, had gone up to the meadow to find out what had happened. The dead buck looked to Mel like it had had a few big chunks cut away with a knife, but it was tough to tell as the animal had been ravaged by scavengers. They never found any assailants or weapons, though Mel did find a cartridge casing that he'd shown to Kyle the following day. It was a .30 Carbine case, which matched up pretty well with Melissa Rex's diagnosis. Soft point bullets in that caliber produced messy wounds at close range.

Mel Gautier had let Kyle know that Bill, his wife, and widowed daughter-in-law were quite aware of the fact that they couldn't make it on their own through the winter. The two women had tried to work a bargain, using Mel as a messenger/go-between, where Kyle would help the women behind Bill's back. Kyle had politely refused and, again through Mel had let them know he was glad to help but there was still the matter of his stolen property. Pride being what it was, they'd opted to pull up stakes. Jeanie and Matt had blocked off the two roads leading back to civilization. They'd tried to bully their way past Jeanie at the main entrance. It had been tense. Bill had brandished a large snub nose revolver and Jeanie had trained Kyle's AR at him from her hip. A minute or so later, Matt had run over with his own rifle. Finding the standoff untenable, Bill had finally relented, with no small amount of cursing and wishing painful death, and had returned Kyle's shotgun. As to where he'd picked up that big six shooter, it had sparked a memory in Matt from the firefight. They'd found one of the raiders with an empty holster and speedloader pouches and had been unable to locate a matching weapon. It was almost certain that Mike had made off with it during his "retreat."

The Kleins were just the start to the deluge of folks leaving the lake. Part of it was absolutely due to the looming deadline imposed by the government. Some was definitely Kyle's fault, he freely admitted. He'd shown, pretty brazenly, that his charity wasn't without limits and he—not them—set those boundaries. But the main tipping point had been Melissa Rex. She'd talked at length with Timothy's parents, there in the hospital cabin, about how things weren't all that terrible in the camps by the base. They had food, clean water, and in some cases medical care. At the very least, no gangs would roll up and take over the place with thousands of twitchy-fingered Peace Enforcers and regular military personnel nearby. Word had spread quickly from there and people had made their choices. Many families, including the Rexes (who had graciously offered the use of their cabin to Matt, Des, Abby, and Kaleb), the McGwires, Gautiers, Morrisons, plus Rod Burkett and his wife had all left in those next few days. Nearly all the healthy manpower from the battle. Now, having waited for their son to heal, it appeared that the Bensons were going as well. Most of those remaining were in Kyle's immediate circle or were infirm and felt safer with the status quo here than the uncertainty of the camps.

A week ago, Matt and Malachi had made the weekly delivery to Louise, the elderly widow on Hood Canal who owned the fishing boat they'd been using/leasing these past several weeks. They'd found her in her bed, lifeless, with an open and empty pill bottle next to her bed. It was unclear what had happened. From his conversations with the woman—some quite long as she was lonely—Kyle had never suspected that she was the type to take her own life. Perhaps she'd simply run out of the medication she needed to live.

The radio had delivered the news about the Randyite blitz on the first of the month, both the government controlled media version and the one from "Uriah's Update"—Uriah ostensibly being some kind of official mouthpiece for Randy Barnhall and his pals. In response, DHS had announced that anyone found in public with a weapon—the exact definition of 'weapon' was not clear—would be arrested and detained indefinitely as a suspected domestic terrorist. Anyone *brandishing* a weapon would simply be shot. Blanket search warrants had been announced at the ZOCs and a shifting array of AOCs—Areas of Concern. Peace Enforcement had been granted unfettered access to private residences. According to Uriah and the short radio bursts from others around the country, most people's first clue they were in an AOC was a convoy of Peacers showing up armed to the teeth and shouting commands. Shootouts had been frequent. The American people, by and large, were fine with the government handing out food in times of crisis. Most were even fine with the new ID cards despite the loss of privacy. They were *not* fine with other Americans knocking down their doors and ransacking their homes just because someone said it was necessary for their collective safety.

Kyle wasn't sure what to make of this Randy character. Kyle was certainly not the type to lick his master's boots, but to actively seek out and kill generals and government officials ran contrary to his beliefs. He just wanted to be left alone, although he was well aware that state was likely temporary. Sooner or later, the government would extend its tendrils up here. Electricity and running water would be welcome, but if the price became subjugation and disarmament he'd choose to do without. The problem was they couldn't realistically fight the government as they had the marauders. Ambush and wipe out a Peace Enforcement patrol and someone would retaliate. In the event of a government takeover, running would be the only option. With that in mind, Kyle had scouted out an even smaller lake deep into Olympic National Park to act as a fallback, but it would be pretty much inaccessible until spring. They had to hold in place until then.

The pair slowly made their way downhill in silence. They didn't have much to say to one another. Malachi had turned sullen and depressed after the battle. He had washed out of the security team after having been found sleeping—twice—while manning the truck gate during the wee hours. They were shorthanded but had to draw the line at sleeping on post. Kyle hoped getting him more involved with hunting, fishing, and other tasks would improve his morale. While Timothy had responded well to the challenge of growing up, Malachi seemed to resent it.

When they reached the asphalt near cabin #20, Matt was there to meet them. "What's the scoop?" Kyle called.

"Timothy locked himself in his cabin." The boy had moved into #10 during his recovery and it had become a catch-all for storage and a play area for the kids. "His parents are taking turns yelling at his closed door or at me and Amber. Loren's holed up in our cabin. They accused her of some pretty nasty stuff."

"Yeah, they had to notice all the time they've been spending together, and not just 'nurse-patient' either," Kyle said. "But I looked Timothy in the eye some time ago and told him he'd better be a gentleman with Loren, and he agreed to do so. So nothing beyond some hand holding and a hug here and there. I trust him."

They passed their cabin and Loren emerged and joined them wordlessly. Amber, standing between the cabins in the woods and looking on, walked up as well.

"Kyle!" came the cry from the adjoining cabin. It was Tom Benson. "I'm trying to talk some sense into my son. I see those guns. I really hope you don't think you're going to intimidate me like you did Bill."

"What, this?" Kyle asked, tapping the stock of his rifle. "No. No...this isn't to force you to do what I want. We were out hunting, that's all. As for Bill Klein, he stole from me, end of story. I don't have any beef with you, Tom." The tall, lanky, mustachioed man was joined by his dark-haired wife. Kyle approached, trying to get into actual conversation range versus yelling from a hundred feet away. His entourage held their position.

"Yeah, well, you're stealing from *us*," Jennifer snapped. "Timothy is choosing you over Tom and me, *his own parents!* You've filled his brain with all your end-of-the-world nonsense, making it seem all fun and games to hide out in the middle of nowhere like some guerrilla fighter in a movie!"

"They're shooting people like you," Tom barked. "We both know it's just a matter of time before the authorities show up here. You're dooming yourselves by refusing to get with the program, stashing weapons, hoarding. We won't let our son do the same, no matter what you've told him."

"And then there's that *slut* you brought here," Jennifer spat, pointing.

Kyle put his hand up. "That's enough right there. I can take your shots, but leave Loren out of this. She doesn't deserve your insults. Now, with Timothy, what would you have me to do? Tell him he *has* to go with you? I don't think that's going to work. He's gone from being a kid to manhood these last couple of months. You're right—he looks up to me. But that only goes so far. I'm as in control of his actions as you are."

Tom crossed his arms. "I want you to go in there and talk with him."

Kyle matched the older man's stance. "I will not. He's made his choice. No one here can force him to go."

"Yeah, because you gave him a bunch of guns," Jennifer added.

Kyle couldn't argue with that. He had semi-permanently given the seventeen-year-old a rifle—his short barreled Vepr—plus the handgun Kyle had selected with his lot. "You're right, Jennifer, before the collapse what I did would have been out of bounds. But your son has been doing a man's work and even put his life on the line for you, Tom, and everyone else up here. I can't treat him like a man one day and a boy the next. I think you're either stuck here waiting for him to change his mind or heading out. I'm not negotiating for you. Mainly because I'm not even close to being impartial. Any argument I make for leaving will make me sound like a hypocrite. I'm staying here because I don't want to put myself at the mercy of the government and the camps. My brother told me plenty about what he's witnessed. I'll take my chances here and it looks like Timothy has come to the same conclusion."

Jennifer wasn't going to let it go. "You're killing my son. *My youngest child!* He's going to just ... die up here. And it will be *your* fault."

Tom just shook his head and headed toward his truck, loaded surprisingly light. Putting her head into her hands, Jennifer joined him, sobbing. Kyle watched as the truck roared to life, Jeanie opened the 'gate', and they drove away.

Amber walked up and put her arm around his waist. "They're all just lashing out, honey. Des, Bill, and now the Bensons. We're all stressed by what's going on," Amber said.

"Yeah, well, I just wish every time someone has to lash out, it wasn't directed at *me*."

CHAPTER FORTY
Monday, Fourth Week in December

Robert Overberg watched his housemate put the finishing touches on his sad little Christmas tree. It wasn't even a proper pine or fir—such trees being hard to come by in central Kansas—but was some hardy bush that had kept most of its leaves despite the harsh winter. He wondered why John bothered. It wasn't as if there would be any gifts.

They'd rolled up almost six weeks ago, right after their roadway firefight with the Auxiliaries, to the dark house Rob had once rented. Rob had resorted to popping the lock on the back door facing the lake with a tire iron. While the cupboards had been bare and the power out, it had proved to be a good spot to laager for the winter. Though it was even more remote than his place in Missouri, they'd been very careful to present a low profile. They only burned the woodstove at night to warm the house and to boil water for drinking and reconstituting Rob's stock of freeze-dried food. Rob had taken a decent buck the day before Thanksgiving; they'd had fried liver and onions to celebrate and were still eating the strips of jerky and occasional steak from the cooler they'd buried in the snow. Even during his early morning deer hunts, Rob saw very little evidence of others around the lake. There were no vehicles, no generators running, and no tall columns of smoke.

Michael Zargona

Rob knew he had been edgy and grumpier than usual. He'd finally run out of booze the week before. "I thought all of you hardcore Bible thumpers hated all the Christmas hullabaloo anyway. Black Friday was kind of a bust this year, I suppose. Good news for the Jesus freaks, right? Commercialism finally lost to solemn celebration and Gregorian chants."

John sighed but didn't look like he was taking the bait. "I like the tree. Don't you like it?"

"I don't believe in holidays," Rob answered. "When I get up in the morning, my body tells me what kind of day I'm going to have. Not a calendar."

"That's a shame. I missed a lot of holidays, back when I was on tour or on the speaking gigs. You might say I'm trying to catch up."

John had slowly leaked out the details of his past in dribs and drabs. There wasn't much else to do; they didn't have anything interesting to read, so beyond food prep and the occasional chore they spent most of their time bundled up, swapping stories. Like Rob, John had grown up in the Midwest and, after dropping out of high school, had co-founded a rock n' roll band in the wake of Woodstock. According to John, they'd opened for bigtime acts like Deep Purple and KISS in the early 1970s. They'd lingered on, never quite pushing into the mainstream, before breaking up in the latter part of the decade when most of the B-list arena rock bands flamed out. John had spiraled down into drugs and booze only to be rescued by his rock-solid Christian older sister. That's when he'd gone over to the Jesus team and become a preacher. No surprise, he'd relapsed and, after a run-in with the boys in blue, had found himself behind bars for seven years. After that, no church would even consider him for leadership so John had—successfully—tried his hand at public speaking and had finally hung up that gig just a few years ago.

"Well . . . I don't have anything to put under the tree. Nothing you'd want, anyway," Rob said.

"Don't worry about it. It's Jesus's birthday. He's our gift. That's the whole point. It's not about the material things. It never was."

Rob rolled his eyes. He'd gotten a progressively heavier dose of this from his nephew Kyle over the last few years. Now he'd gone and rescued the biggest Jesus lover in America. "Enough with the preaching already! I was dragged to church as a kid. It's nothing but nonsense and fairy tales. But at least those church people kept it to themselves the rest of the week. Even the minister... unless you beat down his door he didn't go out of his way to barrage you with 'Jesus this' and 'Jesus that' all the time."

John took a seat in the rocking chair near the wood stove. "This is probably best explained with a story I used to tell to certain crowds. Picture this scene. You're out walking one day and come across a set of railroad tracks. Off in the distance is a freight train coming in at thirty or forty miles an hour. On the tracks is a small boy of maybe three or four. He's completely oblivious to the inbound train.

"So what do you do? You've got about twenty seconds until the train hits the boy and you could easily get there at a dead run in ten. Do you say to yourself, 'Well, it's not *really* any of my business. It's not *my* child. I'm not *really* responsible for him, am I?' Surely he has parents to take care of this sort of thing...where are they? Or, do you break into a sprint, pull the boy off the tracks, and carry him off to safety?

"*This* demonstrates how I see the unsaved. They have no idea they are in mortal danger. It is actually even worse than this fictional example. The boy would lose his earthly life. Those that refuse salvation lose their *eternal life*. It is my job and the responsibility of every believer to spread this message."

Rob frowned. "So this is, in your way of looking at things, kind of like a big ol' chain letter. Pass it along or else bad luck will come your way. Sounds more like what we called F.U.D.—fear, uncertainty, and doubt."

John shook his head. "We are right to fear God in the fatherly sense. No one wants to face Dad's discipline as a child. But there is absolutely no uncertainty or doubt. That's *religion*. Religion says you need to do more to measure up, to work your way up the ladder. But there is no ladder. It is a figment of your imagination. It is your mind saying, 'It can't possibly be that simple.' But it is. Romans chapter ten, verse nine reads:

"If you confess with your mouth that Jesus is Lord and believe in your heart that God raised him from the dead, you will be saved.

"That is it. Everything else past that is building a relationship with Jesus Christ and discovering what He would have you do during your allotted time here on Planet Earth."

"I don't follow," said Rob. "How in the hell can you 'build a relationship' with Jesus? I don't have many friends but I'm pretty clear how it works. You hang out, throw back a few brews here and there, take 'em out in the boat fishing or head out to bag some pheasants. How you going to do any of that with a long dead Jewish guy?"

John paused and looked him in the eye. "That is a bit harder to explain. But, it appears we have plenty of time to kill, so I will do my best."

Rob had taken to making progressively larger circles around the house in search of game. He had probably scared off every deer within ten miles and was obliged to take a break so they'd forget about the bearded two-legged critter that was always chasing them around.

It was just as well that he was out of the house more—he and John had cabin fever. They were at odds and had been since the New Year had turned the calendar over a few weeks ago. They had long run out of things they wanted to discuss and were tired of playing card games.

Turn Red Tomorrow

He stumbled through the snow, no longer caring much that he left tracks. Footprints in the snow were impossible to hide—short of a fresh powder to cover them up—but they had to eat. Rob felt it didn't matter. He hadn't seen a soul since they'd arrived here four months before.

Rob continued trudging west, making his way back to the house under clear skies. He'd just passed a large barn when he heard a low rumble from behind. He quickly dove behind the halfway open barn door about a hundred yards from the house and peeked out.

A truck. A real, actual moving vehicle. It was white shot through with brown, dirty snow streaks and sounded like a big diesel. Texas plate up front. It came to a slow, careful stop, turned into the half moon driveway that faced the road, and stopped. After about five seconds, the driver emerged, a middle-aged man with shoulder-length brown hair popping out of a Texas Rangers baseball hat. He lumbered slowly through eight inches of snow to open the passenger side door. Rob couldn't see what was going on with the big door in his line of sight, but it seemed like the driver was helping someone get out. Finally, the man carried a short, dark haired woman to the front door. She looked wounded... or perhaps just very weak.

The man knocked several times over the course of about a minute and a half. There was no response.

No kidding. This whole county is empty except for two old coots.

To Rob's surprise, the man lifted a specific flowerpot on the porch, produced a key, and opened the door.

Rob was definitely starved for company but there were better first impressions to be made. He'd clean up a bit and come by soon.

Really? Something *was* different. Six months ago, he'd been perfectly content to avoid any human contact. Pick up some grub and booze, nod at the cashier, and get back to his life. Why the sudden desire to greet the new neighbors with warm cookies?

He made his way out the back of the barn and hiked the remaining couple miles home, huffing hard. The low calorie diet these last few months hadn't done his stamina any favors.

Rob entered the house and took off his boots. John was lying in his chair, eyes closed and face tight. He was very pale and appeared to be in some pain.

"You all right there, pardner?"

John nodded slightly, then shook his head, eyes and brow tightening. "Give ... a ... minute ... please."

Rob, acceding to his wishes, walked into the kitchen and got a glass of water from the pot, boiled the night before. When he returned he saw his reluctant companion breathing slowly, each breath deliberate.

"I ... I have something I need to get off my chest," John began. "I'm dying, Rob."

"Dying? Right now? Of what?" Rob demanded.

"Not ... at this very moment, no. But yes, I'm dying. Cancer. Started on my left lung and it had spread out. I had ... some drugs to fight it but ... they ran out about three weeks ago. I can ... feel ... it growing. It hurts like a ... a son of a gun."

This was the closest Rob had heard John come to cursing in their time together.

"Well, shi-... shoot, John. What can I do? Anything?"

John opened his eyes and looked up. "There is one thing you can do, actually. *Pray*."

Rob shrugged. "John ... what in the ... I mean, what is *that* going to do?"

"What can it hurt? You have the time. Time is something we are pretty rich in right now."

"But ... I don't believe in any of that stuff. What you believe."

"I state again . . . what could it hurt? Listen, Rob ...there's three possibilities. One, there is no God and faith is wasted energy. Two, there is a god but it's not the God of the Bible, and he, she, or it doesn't care one bit about us. Or three, the God of the Bible *does* exist and He's always listening. I can find nothing in the Bible that states that God will not answer the prayers of those who do not believe in Him."

"That doesn't make much sense to me. Don't join the club but still get the benefits?"

John smiled weakly. "You are forgetting something. *I* am the one trying to benefit here. Remember our discussions. An *experienced* Christ follower doesn't necessarily have more pull with God than someone who's never prayed before. Another belief not supported by Scripture."

"So ... we pray ... and ... wait and see what happens? Is there some way you believe works better than another way?"

John wagged a finger. "No. You cannot 'game' God with some special method or technique. Honest, from-the-heart prayer. And often."

"But no guarantees."

"Of course not. Pray and see what happens."

Rob chuckled. "Well doesn't sound like it's worth much. You pray, you die anyway, everyone just says that's how it was supposed to turn out. God's will or what have you. If you miraculously get better, we're all in awe of your recovery. Sounds like hedging your bets."

John coughed, then nodded slightly. "I agree it can appear that way. But there are a few things to keep in mind. One, no one can so much as lift a finger against God's will. Two, we are *all* going to go sometime. It's not through lack or prayer or faith that we eventually pass on. Three, I believe all the work I have been called to do is finished. Though, I could be wrong ... but I don't think so. So, no matter what happens, I am content. My prayer is this: 'God, if it is Your will to grant me more time here on Earth, let it be fruitful and for Your purposes. But if it is Your will to call me home, let it be without pain or burden to my friend Rob. In your Son's name, Amen.'"

Michael Zargona

Now that spring had finally come, the snowpack had begun to melt off in the last couple of weeks but a crunchy inch or two still lingered in shaded areas. The improving weather had emboldened Rob to pursue game a little further. Today he'd ranged several miles to the south and east. The sparse snow made it harder to track but easier to move —a double-edged sword.

Rob crested a low rise. Ahead and several hundred yards distant was an enormous fenced enclosure. He immediately went prone, bringing the Weatherby's scope up to his eye. There were yellow signs every hundred yards or so up and down the fence with black lettering that read:

**WARNING
ALARMED
ELECTRIC FENCE
10,000 VOLTS**

As he watched, a gate along the east fence line—to his left—opened up and admitted two large white buses with tall, blacked-out windows along each side. Both came to a stop and disgorged dozens of people, hatless with heads shorn clean, each dressed in a drab green coverall. *Prisoners.*

A hill obscured the back half of the facility, but what Rob could see awed him. There were three rows of long Quonset huts—the half-cylinder buildings most often associated with aircraft hangars. These clearly housed people. There was a four by five block of white trailers near the northwest corner to his right. At the top of the hill was a two story building with dull gray metal siding, pretty much identical to ones Rob recalled seeing all over military installations in his day. A mass of antennas sprouted from its roof. A few people in gray milled about along with a couple of groups dressed in that dowdy green outfit. Those dressed in green lacked the distinctive hats and thick coats of the ones in gray. A small white truck with a single flashing amber light on top patrolled a perimeter road outside the fence line.

This truck stopped directly in line with Rob's position and the passenger window slowly came down. A pair of binoculars popped into view, clearly looking straight at him.

Time to go. There weren't many hiding places on the Kansas prairie. If they decided to run him down it would be a short getaway. But he wouldn't go down without a fight.

Rob stood and loped off down the low hill and up the next one, heading straight north. Every thirty seconds or so he spun, checked his six, and continued across a patch of fallow grassland.

Before long, a white truck hummed into view along a dirt track at least eight hundred yards away. Rob kneeled, bringing the long-barreled Weatherby to his shoulder, and sighted in. Looked to be at least eight hundred yards away. He held way over the truck and squeezed off a shot. The truck slowed, made a three point turn, and headed back the other direction.

They're probably not going to let me get away with that. Still five miles from home. But the farmhouse was only a mile from here, if that. I never did get over there to say hello. Rob stood and jogged in that direction.

As he approached the house, he clearly heard more engines behind him. At least one big diesel rumbled with what sounded like a gas burner or two. The white Texas truck he'd seen previously in the driveway was long gone; even the tracks were just two indistinct lines of mud. Rob tried the door. *Locked. Wait—the flower pot.* Sure enough, the key was right there. Popping inside, he quickly scuttled to the long bay window that faced the road and crouched down, scanning.

A couple of minutes passed as the engine noises steadily grew. A late model gray Suburban appeared, running point for what looked like an eight-wheeled Stryker APC. Up top of the APC sat a small remote turret with a machinegun —probably a fifty cal by the profile of the barrel—and an elaborate optic and sensor suite.

Thermals! Rob hit the floor and commando crawled into the kitchen, putting two walls in between him and the road. It wouldn't do squat versus a fifty cal—that could punch through three farmhouses and out the other side —but might be enough to block his heat signature. They wouldn't shoot what they couldn't see.

The engine noise slowly faded away. Rob waited, trying not to shiver in the chill of the abandoned house. His pursuers would definitely come back along this route, for no other reason than to return to that prison camp. He had to wait for that to happen before exposing himself and heading back. This part of Kansas was all open and, once spotted, that eight wheeler would run him down in seconds.

In the dim light he could make out that it was a pretty typical farm house, with folksy knick-knacks lining the walls. In the dining room hung several oil paintings of Plains Indian chiefs or scenes of cowboys on horseback. The theme continued on the end tables with bronze cowboy-on-horseback lamps. The furniture didn't match but seemed as if it had been collected over decades of roaming yard sales and second hand stores.

Rob stood and brushed himself off.

A single sheet of paper sat on and contrasted with the otherwise clean counter. Rob picked it up and moved closer to the back window to pick up some light.

Mom, Dad,
We hoped to find you here. We're heading to Aunt Peg and Uncle Dave's next.
We had to get out of DFW. It's quarantined but even the

government can't block every dirt track in Texas. Luisa is really sick. It's not hemorrhagic fever. It seems like typhus. It's been a long time since I've thought about diseases like that. Podiatrists don't keep up on that sort of thing. I know it's treatable with antibiotics but there isn't a pill to be found here. I begged the medical liaison at our ZOC who simply said nothing was available.

Because of our plates we had to be pretty creative with our trip here. Everything south of the Panhandle is locked down and the Okies definitely want to know where you're from . . . they are scared as hell of Ebola and I don't blame them one bit. I'll drive to Uncle Dave's at night on remote roads or dirt tracks with my lights off. One stop where they find our we're from Plano and I've got a sick wife in the passenger seat and it's game over. Dad, thanks for recommending I get a truck with four wheel drive and a winch . . . it got us out of a couple spots on muddy roads in the middle of nowhere.

I really hope you get this and can make your way to meet us.

Love,

Dustin

Rob set the paper down and stared at his hands. *What in the world is* typhus? *Sounds like typhoid . . . and that is ridiculously easy to spread.* He'd had those vaccine shots in the Army but that was over twenty years ago. Trying to remain calm, he opened the cupboards under the sink. *Cleaning wipes.* He opened the cylinder and pulled out several. Starting with his hands, he began wiping himself down, then his rifle.

Getting darker out there. Maybe two hours of good light. Rob didn't want to get caught in the dark too far from the lake. There were no landmarks to go by in the pitch black. He tried to remember what kind of moon they'd have tonight. *A waning crescent . . . no help until nearly dawn.*

Those vehicles hadn't come back, but if he didn't

Michael Zargona

leave now and make good time he'd be better off staying put. In a cold and possibly biologically contaminated stranger's home. Easy decision.

Rob picked up his rifle and headed out.

He got the front door open by feel alone. It was cold inside. "John?" He hadn't been getting around well the last several days but still had found the strength to fire up the wood stove at dusk. *Maybe a good thing with those thermals out there scanning the neighborhood.* But still...

"John?" he called again. Still no answer. Rob walked into the small living room and saw his companion in his chair, head down. *Taking a nap.* He reached out, touched John's right hand, and recoiled. It was as cold as the rest of the house. Rob dropped his head. The drain of the day suddenly sank in. *Well friend, though I hardly knew ye... it appears we're at the end of the road.*

I know what I'm doing in the morning.

It was done. The grave was as deep as Rob could manage. The exercise was cathartic. It took his mind off the fact that life was short and John was just a bit ahead of him in the flow of time.

With a small run of baling wire, Rob tied two pieces of scrap lumber in the shape of a cross, and with his pocket knife he spent about fifteen minutes carving J-O-H-N into the horizontal piece. It seemed right. Silly waste of time, perhaps, but faith had been deeply important to the man.

He'd found John's Bible on the kitchen table earlier this morning. The red page marker was in the middle, in Psalms. It sparked a long-forgotten memory from Sunday school, almost sixty years ago.

Psalm 23. Rob had always liked that one. It had a distinct martial feel. The valley of the shadow of death. He had no idea what that really meant but it sure sounded like a righteously ruthless place.

Rob cleared his throat and read it aloud.

"Goodbye, friend." He stared down for another few seconds and turned.

Time to get back to work.

He'd had far longer than just the last several hours to think over this next step. The time had come to pull up stakes again. Susan's cabin was the only sensible destination. Every week or so, Rob had gone out to run both vehicles and make sure their batteries didn't run flat in the cold of winter. Doing so had burned a gallon or two of gas from both tanks which weren't all that full to begin with. In a perfect scenario he'd take John's RV, but it had a big ten cylinder engine that averaged about eight or nine miles a gallon. His Dodge could double that—if he left the boat behind.

Even with the RV's gas transferred over to the Dodge, he'd be struggling to make it as far as Cheyenne. But clearly *some* fuel was flowing—those vehicles he witnessed yesterday didn't run on rainbows and wishes. He figured he'd just have to wing it and see what happened.

First, he confirmed the Dodge would turn over and let the truck idle while he gathered up his fuel transfer gear. In his boat kit there was an inexpensive bulb-type siphon hose along with an almost full bottle of fuel stabilizer. Modern gas with ethanol added went bad quickly. . .and it was at least six months old. Rob moved the Dodge next to John's RV, shut it down, and got the siphon to work.

Hands now sore and stiff, Rob started to move his gear from the house. Not much remained of the storage food though he did still have about a pound of deer jerky. He placed the long guns in the two boxes that ran along the side of the bed.

Except the AR with the thermal sight. Rob frowned,

imagining losing that to a search by one of those lanyard punks. The hunting guns would be a big loss but nothing like seven grand worth of rifle and optics. He broke the rifle down into upper and lower, wrapping each in plastic and securing the bundles with clear packing tape. Rob made a third bundle containing the rifle's ammunition, magazines, and batteries for the scope. All three went into a plastic bin inside the lockable bed toolbox butted against the cabin.

Rob thought for a second and did the same with his scoped Ruger .44, his only other handgun. If searchers found one they'd find both, no doubt. Thinking ahead, he hid the key for the box under the driver's seat in between the upholstery and the cushion.

His other effects didn't take long to pack up. Rob traveled light. Expecting some foul weather, he tarped up the boxes and such in the bed and held it all down with bungees. Rob set John's Bible on the passenger seat, turned over the big Hemi engine, and headed out.

CHAPTER FORTY-ONE

Friday, First Week in April

Major Marshall Cross and his young second lieutenant picked their way through the rubble of what had once been an office building on the outskirts of a small Rust Belt industrial city. Occasional, staccato bursts of gunfire or screams disrupted the silence. Most often, the latter followed the former.

"Major!" When Lieutenant Samuel Williams had checked into Second Battalion a week ago, it took only a short conversation to convince Marshall to make him his personal aide and not a platoon commander. Williams'd likely get fragged by his own men otherwise. Not many in Marshall's unit cared for poshly educated kids. Or any upper one-percenters for that matter. Sam had been granted his lieutenant's bars due to his time in ROTC but that was the extent of his military experience.

Cross halted and his eyebrows involuntarily pursed. Normally, his appreciably less excitable sergeant major would have accompanied him, but he had lost most of his left hand last week from an ODT booby-trap. After the debacle in Michigan last December, Cross had worked hard to rebuild his company but pickings were slim; mostly teenagers, surly veterans who deeply resented being forced back into uniform, and criminals. The previous February, Cross had been promoted to battalion operations officer, the third in command. Six weeks ago, both Lt. Colonel Slaski and his XO, a Major Fritz, had checked out a vehicle, went over the wire, and had not returned. Marshall had been frocked to major and put in charge.

The entire division had migrated south into Ohio and Indiana where they'd been primarily tasked with sweeping Areas of Concern so they could be repurposed or resettled. Most of the Forcers simply called the forays *loot and shoots*. Even the officers were guilty of this mentality. He'd been made aware that one of his captains had a foot locker full of looted handguns. A lieutenant in Charlie Company focused on hoarding jewelry. Marshall had cracked down as hard as he could without inciting an all-out mutiny. It had earned him the nickname "Marshall Law".

Marshall's primary responsibility in the field was to guide his company and platoon commanders; listen in on their radio traffic and interject when they were about to do something stupid or illegal. Unfortunately, this was a well-known fact and the radio was almost always silent. For all intents and purposes, once they hit the sweep zone, it was every man for himself.

"Yes, Lieutenant?"

His aide pointed at a nearby building. "I saw something move in a—a window up there. You need me to call for —"

Marshall put up his hand. First Battalion was to the west and Third was on the eastern flank. "No, Sam. We're here. Let's take a quick look." He noticed the lieutenant gulp. The man had never been on a sweep before. Heck, he'd never been on anything before today. Marshall looked down and realized his M17 pistol was out of its holster and in his right hand, pointed forward. Lieutenant Williams took the hint and struggled briefly to unsling his carbine.

The office building in question was like any other in this neighborhood. Every window on the first story was broken, as were most on the second and third. Pockmarks from bullets and carbon-black scorched areas from Molotov cocktails marred its concrete exterior. Pigeons flittered in and out uncontested.

The new owners of this neighborhood, a Saudi Arabian holding company, had tendered a contract for a military security force. Cash. The American bid had won. It could have been a French, British, or even German unit doing the work. They were all in-country and open for business; Marshall had seen all three in action though they didn't mingle. He had heard that in some areas the UN not the federal government—even employed units from Nigeria and Pakistan. However, in this instance the Saudi owners had arranged financial compensation to the U.S. Treasury for their services—up front.

Even the federal government wasn't so heartless as to raze occupied buildings, so they'd *graciously* given a two week grace period to those in the target AOC. Vehicles had driven through with loudspeakers and pamphlets had been dropped. That was two weeks ago. Some still fluttered along when the breeze kicked up.

"Where was the movement? First floor?" Marshall inquired as they made their way carefully toward what had once been the main entrance. While there was little fear of snipers, being careful had kept Marshall alive and he wasn't about to start getting complacent. There were old warriors, and there were bold warriors, but there were very few old, bold warriors.

Lieutenant Williams cleared his throat. "Ah, yeah."

They knelt down in front of the building and Marshall scanned each window with his pistol and his aide repeated it with his carbine. Nothing moved. He started to reach for his SpyPhone to scan for NIDs. Most squatters had them. Most insurgents did not.

"Peace Enforcement! Yo, down there, identify yourselves or get shot!"

Marshall looked up at the source of the voice. The barrel of a rifle stuck out of a second story window.

"Major Cross, battalion commander! Show yourself!"

Two heads poked out. It was only Privates Sloan and Coolbaugh, attached directly to HQ. Marshall's headhunters.

Cross and his aide made their way through the building, noting the peeling wallpaper and desks moved to create communal sleeping areas. A pile of plastic FEMA ration wrappers lay on the floor, their insides licked clean by hungry tongues.

Sloan and Coolbaugh barely acknowledged Marshall's presence in the room as they opened drawers and cabinets. Sloan's thin face bore two tear tattoos below his left eye and a pattern of five dots under his right; the outmoded practice was still commonplace in the maximum security prisons of the Southwest, which was exactly where Sloan had come from. His dark eyes darted back and forth in a feral manner, continuously taking in his surroundings. A casual observer might think he had a nervous tick, but Marshall knew it to be a symptom of the man's upbringing on the streets.

Coolbaugh, nearly three hundred pounds, towered over his swarthy comrade, a Celtic giant of freckles and chronic acne. Bald with a wrestler's mangled ears, he'd served with the old Army in lieu of jail, went back to civilian life, became a bouncer, punched a guy into a coma, went back to jail, and had ended up in a Peace Enforcement uniform against his will.

Both were armed to the teeth, Sloan with the M4 he'd pointed at Marshall earlier, Coolbaugh with a non-regulation pistol grip shotgun. Both also carried assorted knives, saps, zip-cuffs, stunguns, brass knuckles, clubs, perhaps even an unauthorized pistol or two. And both knew that as long as they did exactly what Marshall told them to do, they could continue to bend—but not publicly break—the rules.

Cross kept both of them in his small headquarters detail, mainly so he could keep an eye on them, but also because they were useful—if dangerous—men. In a unit mostly comprised of uneducated teenagers and ex-desk jockeys, these two and others like them possessed the kind of street smarts that would keep them alive. And maybe, if Cross was lucky, him too.

"So, what's the story? Taking a breather?" he asked.

Sloan and Coolbaugh shrugged in unison. "Naw, Maj. Thought we heard something up here," Coolbaugh replied.

Cross nodded. "We heard it too. A minute ago I thought it was you two. Finished sweeping the building?"

"Yeah," Coolbaugh answered.

Cross pointed at the stairs. "Well, let's get a move on then. You know how I feel about those that fall behind the main body." He meant they were taking too much time to dig for treasures. They were here to sweep for people, not loot. But the headhunters swapped those priorities whenever they could.

Cross had come to think that whatever Hell was, in some way it must constitute leading draftees.

The two privates led the way out of the decrepit building, taking care not to trip on the collected debris of a dead city.

Cross pointed to the next building up the street. "You two know the drill. Check it out and radio me."

They certainly did know the drill, and stacked on the doorway, with Sloan checking for any tripwires or pressure switches. Marshall watched as the two criminals-turned-soldiers entered and began their sweep.

"Echo One Sierra to Black Six," squawked Marshall's radio into his ear.

Marshall keyed the headset. "This is Black Six, go."

Michael Zargona

"I...I think I found a cache. We'll be check—"

The blast blew out what little glass remained in the windows of the squat maintenance building, along with plastic wrappers, pieces of old dirty newspaper, chunks of insulation, and wood splinters.

Marshall threw Lieutenant Williams down to the weathered concrete as the concussion hit them, blowing over like a very firm, pressing hand.

He waited several seconds and helped his aide to his feet. "You all right?" Marshall asked.

"Those tuh-tuh-two..." Williams' words trailed off.

"Yeah... they're dead," he replied tiredly. The tally was now eighty-eight KIAs under his command since November. "Let's go, Lieutenant." As if to remove any doubt in either man's mind, the back wall of the building collapsed inward, toward the explosion, sending a secondary cloud of concrete dust and burning fragments into the air.

The radio broke in. *"Black Six, this is Red Two. Heard a blast behind us, you all right, over?"*

"Black Six to all units, two K-I-A, Coolbaugh and Sloan, headquarters detachment. Watch for traps. I'm fine."

- - - - -

Cross and Williams continued to walk, keeping well back from the main body lest a jumpy soldier confuse them with adversaries as the now-dead Sloan had almost done. After a few minutes, Cross heard men talking loudly and carrying on up ahead behind a short wall. He motioned with his finger at Lieutenant Williams to *wait here*.

"---rty tonight when we get back?"

Laughter. "You know it! Still got that stash back in the barracks from last time!"

A third voice. "Solid! Sit back an' enjoy the show gents, we'll be home free and *really free* before long!"

Three of his privates were sitting, backs to him

against the wall, casually puffing on low-grade marijuana rolled in onionskin paper, probably from a Bible. Most people who cared to classify such things called it "Two Bit Jane."

Peace Enforcement had a lot of gray areas. Drug use wasn't one of them. Cross came around the edge of the wall, hands on his hips. "Just what in the *hell* do you think you're doing! What company are you with?"

They stared at him sullenly. "Who are you to lecture me, you decrepit old fart?" the nearest one demanded.

Marshall was livid. *"On your feet NOW!"*

None of them stirred. "Man, you crazy. Who's gonna make me? You?"

Reaching down, Cross swiftly put his hand under the shoulder flap of the younger man's body armor and pulled mightily. The smaller private literally left the ground for an instant and was planted firmly on his feet.

"You jest wishin' to die!"

Three men, all armed, all high as could be, against a very angry commanding officer, who outweighed any of the three by at least thirty pounds, and who *wasn't* high as could be. Cross liked his odds.

One of the privates must have been thinking the same thing, and got up to run. The one that Cross had pulled to his feet was wheeling back for a haymaker.

Fifteen years ago, Cross had been about the age of these three. But instead of smoking dope on patrol in Indiana, he had been a Marine stationed in Okinawa, Japan. Okinawa had been one of those many polarizing locales for a young, single, American serviceman. Invariably, one either fell into alcohol, religion, or exercise.

Plenty of the exercise fanatics were into martial arts. Cross had sought out Sensei Higa. The elderly Japanese man had confessed he missed teaching real-deal Okinawan Karate, even to *gaijin*. Cross spent the next two years of his downtime in a *gi*.

The private's fist never landed. Marshall reached out, grabbed the man's wrist, and with a rapid turn of his hips and upper body flung the private over his shoulder.

It was at this time that Lieutenant Williams made his entrance, flying over the wall, carbine in hand. The remaining private had gotten upright and as the lieutenant landed, swung his rifle up in a tight arc. Cross watched helplessly as the end of the rifle's buttstock struck his aide under the chin with a sharp crack, knocking him out instantly.

Cross quickly stepped close to the rifle-wielding private, denying him effective use of his weapon, and delivered a sharp hook with the palm of his right hand to the side of the man's head.

He dropped as if he'd been shot. Marshall whipped around. Haymaker was slow getting on his feet. The sudden and unexpected impact of Marshall's left foot in his solar plexus made his attempt considerably slower. The private rolled over, groaning and retching.

Marshall checked in on his prostrate lieutenant. A little fast, but a good pulse, and breathing raggedly. A couple more privates ran up.

"Don't let these two move. Give aid to my lieutenant if he needs it. Got it?"

"Yessir!"

Cross left the hubbub of the scene, and keyed his headset. "Delta Bravo Two, this is Black Six."

It took several moments longer than Marshall would have liked, but the static-filled reply came. "*This is Delta Bravo Two. Go Black Six.*"

"I need casevac. And detention for a couple of privates. Stand by for coordinates." Marshall read the GPS coordinates off his wristwatch into the tiny pickup.

"*Copy that Black Six. En route.*"

"Black Six out."

It could be a long wait for a casevac truck. The telltale scuff of a shoe or sandal on dusty concrete made Cross jerk around. A young woman, no, a girl of perhaps seventeen, dressed in filthy rags, clutched an infant to her chest. Her eyes flared wide when she spotted him.

Their gazes locked. In her eyes was something that went beyond words or language. All of the woman's lost hopes, fears, and anguish poured into Cross in the blink of an eye along that gossamer link.

Why did this happen to me?
Why now?
Why?

The image engraved itself on Cross's memory.

"Major, you *killed* a man under your command!"

Marshall faced Colonel Armstrong, who'd been career Army before the Peace Enforcement takeover. "Yes, sir. An act of self-defense."

"I don't *care* about that!" he barked. "You know you're getting sent up, right? Lieutenant Williams in the hospital with his jaw wired shut, one private assaulted, another dead! Word travels fast, Major. Even if you weasel your way out of this, you're never going to get another command."

Marshall tensed. "I was ordered to take charge of this battalion and I followed that order. I never *wanted* a command. Sir."

His commanding officer sneered. "Well, by God you've solved that little problem, hmm?"

Marshall lost it. Months of pent-up emotion spilled forth. "Who are we kidding? We're taking the dregs of society, throwing them into uniforms, giving them weapons, to act like thugs and mercenaries for *private businesses*? This isn't the military *I* joined, sir. Not by a long shot."

The portly colonel slammed his fist into the desk and narrowed his eyes, staring daggers at Marshall. "Are you calling me and my men *thugs*, Major?"

Marshall only stared.

"It doesn't matter. *You* don't matter. We'll see what *you're* called when you're busy making big rocks into smaller ones for the next twenty or so years. You're confined to quarters until further notice. Dismissed."

Marshall snapped to attention, saluted in the Army manner and walked out.

Worrying was a waste of time. Peace Enforcement existed in a gray zone between the military and its cut-and-dry UCMJ—the Uniform Code of Military Justice—and federal law enforcement, which nominally would fall under a completely different set of rules. Cross wasn't quite sure how the proceedings would go but he figured if he plead no contest he'd simply be released from service, exchange his gray military ID for a civilian orange one, and head off into the same uncertainty everyone else faced.

What were his subordinates up to?

What would happen to him?

What about that girl and her baby?

Marshall Cross's sleep was fitful. When he did close his eyes, he saw *her* again.

Having to wait felt like the calm before the storm: the air was charged but the first lightning strike was unpredictable. It was late on the second day when there was a soft knock on his door. Too early to be dinner chow.

"Major, sir?"

Marshall got up and answered the door. It was a young female sergeant. Normally command would query him via his SpyPhone—a lot easier than sending runners. But that had been confiscated when he'd been confined to his room. "Yes?"

"Sir, please come with me. Your tribunal is ready."

Tribunal. Those only exist to try members of enemy

forces. Marshall hoped it was simply semantics or an honest mistake.

He was led into to a large, sparsely-decorated office. At the front of the room sat three men behind a large desk. On the right was Colonel Armstrong. In the center was unfamiliar man, skin dark like Marshall's, but he wore the single star of a brigadier general. On the left was a tall, distinguished man in a dark suit with a salt-and-pepper mustache, and hair neatly shaved down to the scalp. Something tickled in Marshall's brain. He had seen this civilian before.

"Report," the general ordered.

Marshall saluted. "Sir, Major Marshall Aaron Cross reports."

The general returned his salute. "Remain at attention. My name is General Andross. You know Colonel Armstrong. To my right is our division DHS liaison, Mr. Braithwhite."

Braithwhite. I know that name ... but from where?

General Andross continued. "We are in a technical state of war and as such can dispense with the pageantry and courtroom nonsense, Major. As this is a tribunal, you are not permitted to enter a plea or secure counsel. You are accused of a single count of homicide of a subordinate under your command, two counts of aggravated assault of a subordinate under your command, dereliction of duty, and conduct unbecoming an officer and a gentleman. We have Lieutenant Williams's written testimony as well as eyewitness accounts from no less than six others. Do you have anything to say, Major?"

Marshall cleared his throat. "No, *sir*." He just wanted this over with.

"Very well. Henceforth you are stripped of your rank and removed from federal service. All accrued time for purposes of retirement or other benefits is hereby rendered null and void. After these proceedings, you will be placed under the authority of the Department of Homeland Security for such a period of time as they deem necessary."

The civilian—Braithwhite—raised a finger. "General. I realize this is a bit unusual, but I'd like *Mister* Cross to be released directly into my custody. I have a special project brewing for which I believe he'd be a perfect fit." He spoke as if Marshall was not in the room, standing tall no more than ten feet from him.

Colonel Armstrong snorted derisively.

"If you want him, be my guest," General Andross said. "He's no longer the concern of Peace Enforcement. Mr. Cross, you're dismissed."

Marshall's arm twitched to salute, but his mind stopped it short. It was no longer necessary and the men before him didn't merit his respect.

The two uniformed men stood and left the room. "You probably have some questions, Marshall," Braithwhite began, voice calm. "Let's meet up in ten by the front doors and we'll take a drive. You need to get out of that uniform...it's not yours to wear anymore."

They sped away from the makeshift HQ and down an isolated country road. Braithwhite had donned a pair of Aviator sunglasses to fight off the glare on the wet road. The black SUV, armored with thick glass and heavy doors, was surprisingly nimble.

"So...where do I know you from? It's been ticking my mind since I walked into that..."

"Kangaroo court? It's okay. I'm on your side here. You probably knew me as Colonel Braithwhite, briefly XO of 2nd MEB in Afghanistan. You were on staff with one of the infantry battalions. Ten years ago now."

Yes. "I remember that. You left pretty suddenly, right? Details are a bit fuzzy. I was a brand new warrant back then. Didn't exactly move in the same circles as the senior brass."

"I left in the dark of night because I was offered a rather lofty role within the DIA."

Defense Intelligence Agency. Marshall was in the presence of a spy.

"Yeah... I've been a spook since. Nothing I can elaborate upon. You understand." To accentuate his point, Braithwhite slipped his SpyPhone out of his pocket and wiggled it, smiling. Although... Marshall wasn't entirely sure that's what it was. For one thing, it was larger than the one he'd carried for the past six months, and it was a satin silver color, not rubberized matte black.

Braithwhite pulled off to the side of the road and killed the engine. There were no houses in sight, just an open fallow field with a few distant deciduous trees sprouting fresh green leaves. Marshall felt the hairs on the back of his neck stand up. If the plan was to take care of him—permanently—this would be an ideal spot. Just because this man was a fellow Marine did not mean Marshall could trust him. These days you couldn't fully trust anyone.

"We needed some privacy. You'll see. Let's take a walk." As he stepped out, Braithwhite tossed his phone into his seat. The tall ex-colonel started off on a muddy track toward the horizon. Marshall got out and joined him.

"Apologies for the subterfuge," Braithwhite began. "But you'll realize in a few minutes that it is necessary. I'm going to present you with two–and only two—options, and you'll have until we reach the end of this dirt road to make your choice." Braithwhite smiled, then continued.

"I am a fairly high level player in a faction within the Department of Homeland Security in particular, and the federal government in general, that is working to undo the 'continuity of government' *coup* orchestrated by the President, her inner circle, and her international backers. I'm always on the hunt for those I feel have the skills, talents, mindset, and most importantly shared vision to bring into the fold.

"One reason your tribunal was delayed was that I needed to interview your subordinate officers. Yes, for official purposes... but also for my own. Your officers all hated your *guts*, Marshall."

"I noticed."

"But they're all corrupt. Everyone in the new order is as happy as a clam at high tide but it's just a massive, fraudulent mess at every level. The fact that you ran your battalion cleanly, your prior record, and lack of personal entanglements like family led me to believe you might be an excellent candidate."

"So I'd be a double agent? Working against the existing leadership?"

"Precisely. Instead, you'd be serving our country in accordance with the tenets of our Constitution. In the near term, you'd assist me in both my official and *unofficial* duties. We get in the car, I tap a message to the DHS operations center about twenty miles from here, they get you in the system. We stop in, gather up a few things, and we're off and running. Later, you'll get spun off to create your own cell once your *apprenticeship* is over."

Marshall was stunned, but ... intrigued. "So, what's the second option?"

"Behind door number two, well, that's where you say no, I take you down to the same center under custody, and you become a yellow carder and get assigned to whatever FEMA work detail is in the queue. Most likely a chain gang somewhere. If that's your decision, don't bother trying to throw me under the bus. I'm still clean. You're a dishonorably discharged Forcer. No regulatory body exists to help you right now, much less anyone who will take you at your word. It's the Wild Wild West out there. That plays to the advantage of me and my people."

Marshall coughed. "Not much of a choice, Mr. Braithwhite."

"Call me Jonathan, please. Although I have you at a big disadvantage here, I'm not going to railroad you into treason. Because that's what it is. Treason."

"*Hang from the neck until dead treason,*" Marshall confirmed.

"Yes, from day one forward. There's no opportunity to head back to the other side of the fence if you stick with me. It's just not possible. You want to live a long life, you're better off with FEMA. The reality is, our chances of success in the long run aren't great. The UN keeps flying in troops to bolster any Peace Enforcement losses. We don't have that pipeline of manpower. If we're snuffed out, only the Bubbas in the hills with grandpappy's ol' huntin' gun will be left to oppose tyranny."

"I wouldn't discount the 'Bubbas'. Some of them are pretty effective in the field." Marshall had a sudden moment of clarity. "So ... the Randyites. December 1st. That's *you*."

Jonathan shook his head. "I see what you're thinking, but no. Randy Barnhall and his followers have no ties to us." The taller man stopped and looked Marshall in the eye. "Now we're starting to get into the nitty gritty. Does this mean you're in? End of the road is right here."

"Yes. I'm in."

Jonathan smiled and extended his hand, which Marshall cautiously grasped. "Welcome aboard, Marshall. Get ready to drink from the fire hose."

"Thanks?"

"It should go without saying that we'll never speak of any of this in public or within reach of listening devices. First time I'll laugh and play it off. Second time and you're off the reservation."

"Noted."

"This is not a threat—I believe we're going to become close friends in the near future—but I must impress upon you the extremely serious nature of what we're involved in here. If I go down, I am connected to far too many links in the chain. Most cell leaders don't know my real name but unfortunately I know theirs. Trust me ... the enemy will employ irresistible means if they wish to extract information."

"I understand."

Braithwhite nodded. "Now, about Barnhall. There are two possibilities. He's either what he says he is—a folksy good ol' boy revolutionary who, before the crash, built a network of operatives—or he's an instrument of the government. We believe the latter is far more likely. Let me explain.

"The list of congresscritters, governors, and generals that were targeted for assassination wasn't random. These were all men—and a woman—who had opposed the President at some point in her long political past or had been earmarked as potential *future* adversaries. I know this because two of the targets are formative members of our group. One assassination was, unfortunately, successful."

"I always thought it was strange that a supposedly-underground group would have so broad an intelligence network that they could pinpoint the location of over two dozen protected VIPs on the same day."

"That's our question. The targets would have taken the Barnhall threat seriously and made themselves scarce on December First, but they were all located and attacked anyway."

They were now making their way back to the SUV. A flock of crows danced in the cold, clear sky. It was quiet enough that Marshall could hear their wingbeats.

Another lightbulb went off. "Wait . . . you've had a hand in directing Peace Enforcement over the better part of two states for several months. If you're gunning hard for the Randyites as probable foes, why has every Peace Enforcement operation been a total and complete failure? You're not sabotaging our efforts, right? Or . . ."

Jonathan nodded. "Or . . . are we? No. Randy Barnhall is probably a front, but the hundreds of thousands of people who have answered his call are not. The Bubbas, the ODTs, they *aren't* our enemy. But Peace Enforcement doesn't need any nudging to be incompetent and useless. It's that *by design."*

Marshall raised an eyebrow. "I don't follow."

"This was all game-planned a long time ago."

"Why did they—the President, DHS, DoD—create it then?"

"Think about it: in the event of a crisis, you have hundreds of thousands of active and reserve service members neatly organized into distinct units. Naturally, these would be a lot more effective—under any circumstances—than the fractured units that were whipped up from scratch."

"You got that right."

"So organized units could easily crush a Randyite-type revolution and all would be well. Sounds straightforward, right?"

"Yeah."

"Problem is, the *unit* desertion rate would be in the thirty percent range. Or more. Particularly the combat units. So right away, half the combat capability is lost and now the Peace Enforcement troops must fight organized, well-led units as well as any partisans. The war could go on for years.

"Now take the current scenario. Break up the combat units, leave the desk jockey units intact. Individuals are thrown in a pile and then reconstituted into units under direct civilian command. If they're wiped out or they desert, who cares? If they succeed and stave off the insurgent threat, great. If they fail, the feds turn to the United Nations and our 'allies' for help. The UN boys don't want to tussle with entire brigades comprised of experienced deserters but they're fine tackling small cells."

They were almost back at the vehicle, which would put an end to their frank discussion. "So, is this . . . secret revolt . . . the special project you wanted me for?" Marshall asked.

"Actually, no. This is an above-ground project. I've already been tapped for a new assignment. Heading out in

Michael Zargona

a few days to the Pacific Northwest to a deputy director post. I won't be tied down to a unit in the field, I'll have all of Washington and parts of both Oregon and Idaho as my playground. Those areas are thick with potential recruits. I know of a handful of retired officers I'll reach out to. I've confirmed through the national ID system that they're alive and kicking. Some of them, anyway."

"That's...interesting," Marshall said. "I have an old friend out that way. Survivalist type, we went to Iraq on the same boat. He's someone we'll want to reach out to. If he's still alive."

CHAPTER FORTY-TWO

Friday, First Week in April

It felt strange, being behind the wheel after so many months. It felt good. Liberating even. Rob let the radio scan for several minutes but wasn't exactly surprised when there was nothing to be found. Even in normal times, there weren't many stations in this part of the country.

He kept to the smaller highways once again, avoiding the I-80 and I-70, and zig-zagged north and west. There were no vehicles out and about. Every once in a while, Rob would catch a glimpse of what may have been a person—a curtain shifting in a window, a shadow that moved. *What are people hiding from?*

Somewhere in the Prairie Lakes region of Nebraska, the sun set in front of him. He had some time before the curfew . . . if that was still even enforced. For all Rob knew, just being out of his house was a capital offense. It certainly seemed possible.

Should stop anyway. Headlights will act like a beacon.

He spotted an old barn up ahead, its wood gone gray from age and exposure, but still standing tall. Rob slowed, scanning for anything resembling a road that led to the structure, but came up empty. He stopped the truck along the side of the highway, killed the engine, and spent a couple of minutes testing the ground with his foot. If he mired the truck in mud, that would be it.

Satisfied with the consistency of the ground, Rob pulled the truck up to the barn and stopped short at the doors. He exited the truck and peeked inside, checking for anything that could be a problem. Once again convinced it was safe, Rob backed the truck in, turned off the engine, and went to sleep.

He encountered the first vehicle besides his own about thirty miles east of Cheyenne. An older beige sedan, rear almost dragging on the pavement and stuffed with well-bundled people, headed in the opposite direction. Several more followed as he approached the city proper and the road widened to four lanes.

Things can't be too bad. Just needed to get closer to civilization to see it.

Vehicles ahead...in the road...no stoplights. Beyond that, a large white truck parked in the left lane with some kind of boom arm over the other lane. Two men in gray toted rifles. Rob swore under his breath.

Checkpoint. Hell of a lot more elaborate than that last one.

A minute went by with no movement. *Definitely not a peek and a wave through type of deal. Whatever is happening up there, it's thorough.* Now he realized why the eight or nine vehicles in front of his had turned back. This was going to be a long wait.

A truck pulled up behind, a black Ford single cab. Just as the engine died, the driver's door opened and a fiftyish man with a jowly face, Denver Broncos cap, and bulky green coat stepped out and approached Rob's Dodge. Rob pushed the window open.

"Missouri, huh? You get hit by that quake last month?"

He seemed friendly enough. Rob realized at that moment he had not talked to another human being—except for John—in six months. "Quake?"

"Yeah, 'round St. Louis, along that old fault. I heard the announcement while in line. Not real big, they said, but shook up the area pretty good. Not like there was much to destroy, right? I think half of St. Louis had already burned to the ground. So I hear. You didn't feel it, huh? You must have been on the other side of the state."

"I wintered in central Kansas," Rob said. "Gang of looters sort of forced me to relocate. What's the story with the checkpoint up there? Taking their sweet time."

The stranger raised an eyebrow. "Same time as always. Have ... have you been through one?"

Rob shook his head. "No." He wasn't about to mention the run in with the lanyard boys.

"Well, see, they're searching for contraband. Smugglers. Folks supporting the rebels."

"Rebels?"

The man chuckled. "Wow, guy, you sure have been out of the loop. You even have ID?"

"You mean that new card people were talking about last fall? No. Didn't get one."

His new friend rolled his eyes. "Shoot ... you're in a bit of a tight one then. You're about three months late. Those fellas up there are going to make you get one. Plus a bunch of vaccines and what not. Hope you're not in any real hurry. Do you have any *weapons*?"

Rob shrugged, grasping the butt of the .357 in his pocket. "Why?"

The man shifted slightly and produced a small two-tone pistol, pointing it at Rob's face. With his other he pulled out an encased brown badge on a lanyard, hidden by his coat.

Rob swore under his breath again.

"Don't move." He let the badge flop and pulled out

what looked like a cellphone and started to tap with his left thumb, still keeping an eye on Rob.

Not thirty seconds had passed before the red and blue glow of headlights blazed the checkpoint.

"You're an easy mark with those plates. Just about everyone who's traveled a few states is moving something they're not supposed to have. You've just paid for my dinner tonight."

God, we haven't had a chat in a long time, but I sure would appreciate it if you could see me out of this one.

The police vehicle, a black Ford SUV, one of the small crossover types, came to a stop.

"*Stay in your vehicle! You are under arrest!*"

Two angry looking guys in gray with black tactical vests hopped out and approached with a shotgun and an AR-15 leveled at his windshield. Pudgy Lanyard Guy holstered his pistol and stepped aside.

"Now," Shotgun Cop began in a stern voice, "when I say to do so, open your door and step out, *slowly*, with both hands in the air. So much as a twitch and you're dead. Got it? Do it *now*."

Rob nodded and complied. Everything was completely out of his control at this point. AR Cop kept back a bit, continuing to point at him, while Shotgun started to pat him down.

"*Weapon!*"

AR Cop stepped closer, finger on the trigger, while his compatriot removed Rob's Smith & Wesson from the large side pocket of his jacket.

"You're either one of those hermit types who didn't get the memo," Shotgun said, "or the dumbest Randyite in the state, rolling up on an established checkpoint with a freakin' magnum in your pocket. Pretty sweet truck for hermit though. Ah, nice pocketknife. I'll be taking that too. Got anything else?"

Rob merely shrugged. *What in the hell is a Randyite?*

"Lemme guess. No card either?"

"If you mean those new cards, no. Sir."

Shotgun looked back at his partner. "Joe, arrange for someone to take this truck back to impound." Then he snapped back to Rob. "Turn around, meathead."

Shotgun roughly grabbed Rob's hands and stuck them in the small of his back. Rob felt the sharp plastic of a zip tie around his wrists. "Get in the rig. Let's go."

- - - - -

They took him to a squat National Guard armory that had clearly been converted into some sort of local HQ and processing center. Shotgun roughly brought him to an open area with a large, south facing window, several desks and chairs, and sat him down at one. On the table was a vaccine jet injector much like the ones Rob got intimate with in the Army. A new-style flat computer connected by a thin black wire to a black box with a slot in the top also sat on the table. Rob watched as Shotgun approached an older cop-type with that gruff "I'm in charge" look. They whispered to one another in hushed but anxious tones. They didn't look his way.

A short, pale, black-haired woman of about forty walked in and sat across from Rob. She wore the same gray uniform. Without a tactical vest, he could clearly see the three chevrons of a sergeant in the middle of her chest. The name "HOLLEY" graced the nametape along her right breast. He had to admire the graysuit operation's forethought. Simple things like hiding rank insignia in combat were important when confronting those who pay attention to details like that. Unless snipers were present—always the primary target to take out—guerillas tended to shoot officers *first*.

"Standard procedure for card issuance is to take fingerprints, a retinal scan, a full head scan, and confirm identity documents. We have your state driver's license and military ID which suffice as documents. Can you confirm your Social Security number for me, please?"

He saw no reason not to and complied.

"Thank you." There was a low rumble that rattled the table slightly. Sgt. Holley glanced up at the two cops; Shotgun raised his eyebrows while Gruff Guy just examined the bottom of his coffee cup.

She took a minute and inputted the information from his license. There was another rumble, this one either smaller or farther away.

"Duncan, can you clip his tie so I can get prints?"

Shotgun/Duncan came over, whipped out a folding knife, and went to cut the zip tie holding Rob. "Don't try anything stupid, meathead. I've buttstroked about ten of you Randyites right here in this room since your little insurrection kicked off. If you want to eat through a straw for six months, by all means *try* something. Please."

Holley visibly perked up. "He's a Randyite?"

"'Fraid it's the only logical conclusion. Rolling around with a truck crammed full of guns and ammo. If it quacks like a duck and all that. Not sure where he was headed since he was about flat out of gas. Wouldn't have made it ten miles out of town. Most the Barnhall Bandit Boys are still out past Laramie somewhere, hiding in the mountains."

Must have found the guns in the side boxes. That was probably what they were whispering on about.

Holley scowled at Rob, her face now red. *Definitely some history there. Denying it won't help.*

He gave up his prints one by one. Duncan zip tied him again and retreated back to his corner. Holley scanned his eyes and each side of his head, then grabbed the jet injector as Duncan roughly rolled up his left sleeve. She quickly squeezed off the injection into his shoulder.

The black box started to hum just as a loud explosion went off outside, shaking the building. The large south facing window developed a long wavy crack running from the top left corner down to the bottom right, then branched in a couple of directions as he watched.

"What the hell?" the guy in charge spat.

"Fellas," Rob began in a level voice, "if my opinion means anything I'd say we're being *mortared*. And I ain't talkin' bricks."

"Shut up, *Randyite*," Holley barked. "Hey, now. Don't leave me alone with this guy!"

Rob angled his head back and saw the pair of cop-types heading for the door.

"We just need to check things out. We'll be back in a minute. Keep him in the chair, will ya?"

Rob turned back to the black box, which had stopped buzzing. On top lay a yellow card, a bit thicker than his driver's license.

"What's with the card?" Rob asked calmly. "Your friend Duncan mentioned something about an orange card. That one's yellow."

His disarming tone worked. Holley's face faded from angry to more of an ashen, worried look. "Yellow card ... you really *don't* know anything, do you?"

"I've been holed up for months, taking care of a sick friend," Rob replied.

She visibly relaxed. "Everyone was supposed to apply for cards before Christmas. The holdouts have been assumed to be rebels and they only qualify for one of these now. With it, you're locked out of most working parties, special benefits, and your bancor allotment is half of a regular civilian. Now, look ... I really don't have the time or the inclination to go through all this with you—"

Rob shook his head. "No problem. Just curious." *Bancor?*

Another blast, this one so close it blew out the far window and sent a shock wave through the room that blew the jet injector clear off the table. Papers fluttered. There was a brand new hole about the size of a fist on the near wall. *Shrapnel.*

Holley glanced back and forth. "Now . . . Robert . . . you stay *right there* while I go . . . find some help. Don't try anything stupid. You run off you're going to be in even more trouble. I'll be right back." She ran out the far door leading outside.

Rob didn't believe for a second she was coming 'right back'.

There was a loud *krrup* sound, then another. *Something bigger, maybe 155mm howitzers this time.* Whatever was going on, Rob wasn't going to stick around and wait for a chunk of a shell casing to take his head off or the roof to come crashing down on top of him. He got up—his wrists were tied but not to the chair—and started for the door leading outside.

Wrists. Let's take care of that little detail first. Breaking a zip-tie just required a little pressure in the right direction.

Hands freed, he walked back into the lobby and grabbed his card. Rob stared at it, then looked back at the tablet. An idea ran through his head. He grabbed the tablet and, as Sergeant Holley had done, tapped it to turn it on. It displayed a full keyboard, clearly requiring a password.

Damn. Rob set it down and went back into the hallway, searching offices as more shells impacted nearby, some shaking the building slightly. Big diesel engines gunned outside as well.

Here we go. Owing to the framed picture on the desk of her and a young boy, it was obviously Sgt. Holley's office. A yellow note was taped to the monitor of her computer.

PW: jonesy2016%

Rob had no way of knowing if it was just for the computer or would work with the tablet. He walked back to find out. After tapping it in, he pressed the Submit icon and was given the "wait circle". After about five seconds, the tablet splashed a screen with several app icons.

"Here we go." He was no computer guru but it all seemed pretty intuitive. He selected *Options* and saw that he could view history. He clicked on the record at the top—his, naturally—and it opened up with his information once again. At the bottom of the screen was a drop-down menu of card types, currently set to "04-Yellow". The other options were, in order, "01-Orange", "02-Gray," and "03-Blue". Rob had no idea what the other colors were for, so he selected "01-Orange" and pressed the "Resubmit Data" button. This popped up with the same password entry as the lockout screen.

With nothing else to try, Rob simply typed in the same password. It worked. It took him to a screen that prompted him to print or cancel; Rob pressed "Print". About ten seconds went by and the black box, a little dusty from the explosions at this point, hummed and spit out a card identical to the first one save the color.

He picked up both cards, then remembered something he'd seen in the recruiter's office. Rob went back, fired up the shredder, and slid the yellow card in. It chattered angrily but did its job.

Yet another impact, this one close, rattling the small window and metal blinds. A marker fell from the whiteboard, followed by one of the ceiling tiles which fell on the desk and bounced off, hitting Rob's left boot.

Time to get out of Dodge ... er ... Cheyenne.

- - - - -

Rob stumbled across the impound lot by accident. He'd been heading out of town on foot, every muscle aching from the rough treatment by the cops combined with all the running around he'd been doing these past couple of days.

It was obvious Cheyenne was under a real-deal combined arms attack, not just some lobbed mortar bombs. Twice he'd thrown his hands up as men with weapons

Michael Zargona

passed by. The first time it was the now-familiar graysuits. The second time . . . the other team, dressed mostly in various hunting camo or military patterns. *Partisans.* Rob watched them as they ran off.

Never thought I'd live to see a civil war.

Gunfire chattered. Smoke trails rose in the distance. The cool spring air smelled heavily of burnt plastic, rubber, and wet wood. *Panama.* Except for the temperature, the situation resembled Rob's only real taste of a war zone over a twenty year career. Even that had been a support role, handing out gear to the soldiers in his unit.

Amongst about fifty vehicles, he could see his distinctive black Dodge parked beside a white panel van, fresh mud adorning its flanks. No one seemed to be paying attention. Rob approached the unguarded shack near the locked gate; its faded green door hung wide open. Entering, he saw a large board of keys and began to hunt for his set. Twenty seconds later, Rob had his keys in hand along with the gate key, which was conveniently attached to a plunger handle with the word "GATE" scrawled in red permanent marker.

It didn't take long to ascertain that the guns and gear in the side boxes were long gone. His clothes and personal affects remained in the cab—along with John's Bible—but what little food he'd brought was gone as well. The bed box showed some evidence of tampering but had held up. Rob thought that maybe the graysuits were hard at work on it when the arty started to drop and the day job took a back seat to simple survival.

Well now. Rob spied a double column of five gallon gas cans beside the shack, at least fifteen. He walked over, opened the first one, confirmed it was gasoline, and got to work getting it into his truck's tank. He returned, thought about putting another in, and thought better of it. While the artillery had slacked, there was no telling where the next target would be. Five gallons would get him plenty far from Cheyenne. Rob pulled the Dodge up to the shack and tossed in the remaining thirteen cans, his muscles starting to give out near the end. Once finished, he unlocked the padlock to the gate, swung it wide, and threw the lock into the open field on the other side of the street.

With no food, no water, the Rocky Mountains in his way and just maybe enough gas to get clear to Western Washington, Rob got behind the steering wheel and pulled out.

He was about twenty miles west of Laramie, starting to get into the hills, when he spotted several very well armed men in front of a couple of full sized trucks that were parked perpendicular to the road. It was well-planned; the interstate, normally four lanes together, split here with a rocky median that few road-going vehicles would be able to manage. The hillside had blocked his view until he was almost right on top of them. Behind him, another truck came into view.

Damn.

He slammed on the brakes and saw a couple of the men bring their weapons up, well within range. Rob put the Dodge in park and stepped out, hands up.

An older man approached, looking every bit like a ranch hand who'd seen a lot of hard winters. Only a little white fuzz peeked out from underneath a brown cowboy hat, matching his thick white mustache. He had a stainless hunting rifle in his hands.

"My scout says you come up from Cheyenne?" His voice was authoritative and just a little raspy.

"Yes sir. Just left."

Mustache Man eyed his front plate. "Missouri huh? Long ways from home. You're about thirty minutes ahead of a Peace Enforcement convoy comin' up for some payback." He pulled out what looked like a small tablet or large cellphone. "Hmm. Let me see your ID."

"You too? You're not one of those lanyard clowns—"

Cowboy Hat smiled and exhaled through his nose. "You takin' me for one of them peabrains? C'mon now. I need to check somethin'."

Rob pulled out his wallet and handed it over.

"You wanna explain to me why you have an ID with an issue date of *today* ... Robert?"

"If I start telling the story behind it, I might not get done before that convoy gets here. I'm going to take a stab and guess they're coming this way because some of your ... associates tore Cheyenne a new one earlier. You guys must be those Randyites everyone keeps going on about."

The old cowboy's face darkened as several of the other men shifted or spat on the ground. "That's a word I'd just a soon prefer you not utter again, friend. The government likes to lump us all into one batch but it's just a wee bit more complex than that.

"No, I ask about your ID because in some parts the Peace Enforcement boys have taken to using civilian scouts. They know we can tell blue from orange, and they know we have lil' toys like this thing here," Cowboy said, holding up the tablet, "so they end run that with men like *you*. It's just a mite *suspicious* when a nice truck with about a hunnerd gallons of gas just rolls on up on us, and the driver has an ID that's still warm from the printer."

"Yeah," Rob began, "I can see where you're coming from. Look, I was in Kansas yesterday. Buried a friend of mine that morning. Been holed up all winter, eating out of cans plus a couple of deer. Rolled into Cheyenne to look for gas, anything to get farther out west, and got zip-tied by those guys in gray. Hell, those clowns thought I was one of *you*. Took my guns, food, almost everything. Only reason I got away is because you guys nearly blew up the building I was in. And that's the truth."

Cowboy turned to his crew. "What do you all think? Rob here all right?"

Most of them nodded. Cowboy turned back. "Forgive me for not introducing myself, we're not real big on names. You can just call me James. Now, until this all goes down you'll need to stick close to us. We see you tryin' to work a SpyPhone or a radio, you're gonna have a lot of explain' to do. Right now you have the benefit of the doubt. Don't spoil that."

Rob just nodded. Over the next few minutes, they got the vehicles off the road and out of sight. Rob watched in fascination as three men set up a tripod, locked in a fifty caliber machinegun receiver, and screwed in the barrel, checking headspace with a gauge set. He also caught a pair of AT-4s—disposable single-use antitank rockets—being handed out. He turned to James and whispered, "You guys aren't messing around. You really expect that convoy to just waltz into this ambush?"

"Yes I do, 'cause they do it all the time. They're cocky. Though we don't bring out our big guns too often . . . it just might start to *sink in* that we're a bit more than a bunch of dumb toothless hicks."

Rob was stunned. "Are they *that* dense? You guys brought down *arty* on the state capital!"

"You'll see."

He did. Ten minutes later, just as the chill really began to sink in, the first vehicle came into view. Just a plain jane Humvee with Army markings, followed by one of those eight wheeled Stryker APCs—not unlike the one he saw two days ago except it was Army green and lacked a turret, a couple of five ton trucks, and another Stryker bringing up the rear. Rob tensed, expecting that Ma Deuce to open up. Instead it was the tremendous *BOOM* of one of the AT-4s, shattering the rear Stryker with a hit over the second tire from the front. Snow and dirt kicked up by the backblast hung in the air for a second and came raining down just as the fifty cal and several personal weapons opened up, targeting the lead Humvee, which tailed off into the far guardrail.

The remaining APC revved and looked like it was going to make a run for it, abandoning who or whatever was in the nearly defenseless five ton trucks. The second AT-4 fired but struck short, creating a man-sized hole in the interstate but doing little more than scratching the green paint on the Stryker. A trooper in gray appeared up top, attempted to grab the spade grips on the top mounted machinegun, and was cut down by fire. The fifty caliber machinegun stitched holes along its flank. It began to smoke heavily and came to a stop, its engine screeching and throwing black oil all over the road. Water vapor mixed with the thick smoke, partially obscuring Rob's view.

Muzzles stuck out from underneath the cargo cover and winked, completely unaimed and not particularly wise. Rob watched as the fire converged on that truck and riddled the cover with no less than fifty holes in just a few seconds. The big fifty-cal hammered away at the engine compartment as the driver bailed. Several of the troops were doing the same, running for the other side of the interstate, the eastbound lanes. Most were cut down before they dove down the embankment and disappeared.

"Woof. Never seen anything like that with my own eyes," Rob puffed.

James turned and smiled. He had rattled off a couple of shots at the outset but since had simply watched along with Rob. He wasn't even breathing hard. "I'm just glad it wasn't the Indians."

"You mean the ... Shoshone? Or some other tribe?"

James just stared, a quizzical look on his face. Then he broke into another smile, this one wider than the last. "Shucks, no ... I mean real *Indians*, like worshippin' cattle an' all that. Some unit pulled from Pakistan come out here, stationed in company-size elements all over the northern Rockies. Unlike our boys, these Indians have been fighting as a unit for a long time. They're a tough bunch and know how to fight in bad conditions and high elevations. I'm guessing you know a little about serving, I saw that retired military ID in your wallet."

"Twenty in the Army," Rob replied.

"Ah. I did twenty-two."

"Doing...?" Rob asked

"Ate a few snakes, if you catch my drift."

Special Forces.

James went on. "Don't get offended if I'm, well, a little close to the chest with details. You're catch and release. Don't want a bunch of rumors to start floating around."

A younger man walked up. "Some pretty good loot in the other truck. Four more AT-4s, two more Ma Deuces, four M240s, about twenty thousand rounds of ammo, grenades, MREs, batteries. The usual for a three day raid by these knuckleheads."

James smiled again. "Well that's pretty doggone efficient. Shoot two AT-4s to get four more. Okay, load it up and let's scoot. Make sure and scan for those check-in devices. Dig 'em out if you can."

James turned to Rob and explained. "They've taken to putting GPS-type devices in vehicles and the bigger guns, the machineguns and whatnot. They check-in every so often with a radio signal, maybe picked up by the cell towers, not sure. Not a lot of range but all it takes is one pop and they got you. We don't want to take them home like that, you understand."

James stuck out his gloved hand and Rob grasped it, giving it a firm shake though he sensed he couldn't match the strength of the old rancher. "Rob, good luck out there. I take it you're crossin' the state on I-80?"

"Uh ... yes. Planned on it. You all know where I can get some gas? And some food? They took it all when they searched my truck."

"Plenty of diesel tanked up right there in the road. Gasoline, that's a bit tougher. FEMA boys are rationing that real hard, even for those folks stupid enough to trade in their gold for more of their newfangled money made out of thin air. Food's pretty easy ... about four hundred MREs in the truck there. I think we can spare us a couple or three."

Rob nodded. He wasn't sure if these were the good guys ... but he wasn't going to turn down the offer.

James continued. "Be careful as you cross the southwest part of the state and into Idaho. No federal control out there at all. They've all pulled back to Jackson Hole and the zillionaires up that way. Anyone running around is probably up to no good. You see *Road Warrior* back in the day?"

Rob nodded.

"Yeah, kinda like that. My free advice, and worth every penny, is to travel at night with your lights off. Go slow. Old guys like you an' me don't have night peepers like we used to, right?"

"Too true. Funny you should mention it ... I know of at least one other person who drove at night to avoid trouble."

"Everyone who's still not under the traitor government's thumb does it. Don't try it near the cities and the bases. Lots of those traitor Auxiliaries poking around looking for a score. Vehicles and helicopters with thermals will pick you out at ten miles or more. Can't hide a hot engine from FLIR. They keep an AO of about that around the bigger ZOCs."

Rob noticed the rancher accent dropped off as James slipped into military lingo. "Noted. I got a taste of those back in Kansas. Well, I'll gladly take what you can give me and I suppose I'll hole up until dark. Speaking of helicopters though ... can't those people in control of Cheyenne send a couple out here to check up on the convoy?"

James smiled again. "What do you think our prime number one target was this morning? We got nothin' to worry about."

He followed James' no-cost advice, waiting until dark to head out and taking it slowly and carefully. The remainder of the journey was a lot less eventful. Rob ended losing his Ruger .44 in a trade at a farm outside Pocatello, but got a very decent hot meal plus twenty gallons of gasoline in return. That put him well over the top of what he needed and allowed him to take the roundabout way to avoid going near any large cities or military bases.

The last day, he decided to continue to push on after sunrise. It was midmorning when he turned off Highway 101 up to Sunshine Lake. Below the regular sign was a hand-painted one, obviously another metal sign that had been turned around and bolted on, that read:

SUNSHINE LAKE AREA IS
FULL - ONLY LEGITIMATE
PROPERTY OWNERS AND
THEIR GUESTS MAY ENTER

The makeshift sign had several bullet holes in it. There were three or four thick smoke trails up ahead, toward the lake.

CHAPTER FORTY-THREE

Monday, Second Week in April

Dillon Traylor extinguished the butt of his cigarette on the asphalt with his new, shiny black combat boot and casually walked back to where the other trainees were congregating.

"Okay, lissen up!" Dillon's training officer for the past several days shouted. "Time to get paired up with your FTO! Dixon, you're with Marquette. Traylor!"

Dillon looked up. "You're with Riggs," the officer barked, pointing at a tall, thin Auxiliary leaning up against a newer black Chevy SUV with big off-road tires and lights.

Peace Enforcement Auxiliary Officer Traylor ambled up to the man, who stood with arms crossed, eyes occluded by mirrored sunglasses. Riggs was almost a foot taller than the five-foot-seven Dillon, but couldn't weigh more than one-ninety soaking wet. He had a mortician's face, with deep-set eyes, sunken cheeks, and a long chin that came to a point. To Dillon, Riggs' black, bristly hair made him look vaguely Mexican.

Dillon didn't like Mexicans.

Actually, Dillon didn't like Africans, Asians, Indians, Arabs, Euros, women, gays, Bible-beaters, the rich, the educated, old people, the handicapped, or children much either.

Dillon Traylor really didn't care for anyone. And until just recently, he hadn't cared much for cops either, but seeing as he had officially become one just an hour before, that line of thinking would have to change.

"I'm Lewiston Riggs. Everyone just calls me Lew. Dillon Traylor, hmm? Funny name, you get teased a lot as a kid?"

Hey, it's Traylor trash!

If Dilly's family goes campin' in the woods, does it make it a Traylor park?

Whaddya callit when Dilly walks around town? A mobile home!

Dillon shook his head, trying to block his surfacing thoughts. "No. Naw, man. Nothing like that."

"All right, chief." Lew put his hands up in mock self-defense. "So, I'm your FTO for the next couple of months, and you'd better be able to take a little proddin' here an' there, bud."

Dillon shrugged. "What the hell does FTO mean?"

Lew stared. "Didn't you pay any attention? I'm you're field training officer. You need to take what you learned in there," he said, pointing to the squat, whitewashed building where Dillon had spent the last four days in a cold classroom, "and apply it out in the real world. I'm here to make sure you have your head screwed on straight." Lew pointed at Dillon's chest. "But it boils down to just a few rules, really. First Commandment : Don't dare hassle anyone with a blue card. Second Commandment: Don't get in the way of the graysuits. Third Commandment: Get results or get lost."

Lew opened the driver's door. "Let's hit the road. We need to sync up with a Forcer assault group in about an hour."

Dillon climbed in as Lew turned the key. "This yours?" Traylor asked.

Lew nodded. "You got it, Traylor buddy. Had to put in

my time as a foot soldier first. You're lucky you're with me. A lot of those other RTOs are still hoofing it everywhere."

They began to cruise down the blacktop, passing mostly-closed down storefronts and gas stations. It was too far from a ZOC, way out here, which meant zero people would be milling around.

As long as they didn't come anywhere near the FEMA holding facility out near the Tri Cities, anywhere was fine with him. Four and a half months of handcuffs, prisoner greens, and a tight rubber necklace that held his old yellow card made his new job look like bliss.

Lew pulled out a pack of cigarettes. "Smoke?"

"Yeah, sure. Got anything a lil' stronger?"

"Not on duty, man."

The taller man flicked his wrist in a practiced manner, and a single cigarette fell into Dillon's hand. It was new production, generic, like everything else these days.

"Lighter's there," Lew said, motioning to the dash.

◆ ◆ ◆

Lew tried to contain his excitement as they arrived. It was something new, tagging along with the Peace Enforcement boys as they did their work. It felt good, being on the other side of the legal line. He shivered as they stepped out, his thin coat not doing much to stave off the chill here in the mountains. His new companion swore under his breath as he shut the passenger door.

Being here was a small reward for having discovered this small band of holdouts a couple of days before. At the very least they were basic lawbreakers who refused to get with the program. A twenty man team of men armed to the teeth stood in front of him. They'd brought two of those eight wheeled armored monsters, each with a belt-fed machinegun up on top. The holdouts wouldn't stand a chance.

It beat his initial Auxiliary gig, where there really was only one sure play: unannounced body searches. Lots of them. Those first few months in the Auxiliary had been tough. When his face got noticed and people started walking the other way, he'd move to a new area. Even the guys with a good network of informants were struggling; too many idiots had divulged what Auxiliaries earned for various *activities*. Snitches were always after a bigger slice of the take.

A couple of months back, Lew got tasked with assisting the local remnant of the BATFE—Bureau of Alcohol, Tobacco, and Firearms—in tracking down known gun owners. When those running the scanners at the ZOCs got a positive hit, they let him know via a simple hand signal—and he'd tail the suspect home. From there, using his Auxiliary-issue SpyPhone, he'd call in a squad of Peace Enforcement dudes who'd run a search. About nine times out of ten they'd find weapons. It was way too easy.

But people who'd refused to comply and get ID completely avoided the food handouts, so catching them required a different approach. He'd do his own vehicle patrols in the decidedly non-government looking, almost brand new Chevy SUV he'd scored, searching for little villages like this one. Lew wasn't alone in his strategy. Most of the well-known spots—campgrounds, RV parks, and resorts—had already been searched. One either had to go a little further out or a little further up, deeper into the mountains, to find a good target.

"Come out and stand with your hands in the air!" a megaphone blared. "Each building will be searched thoroughly. Anyone who does not comply will be assumed to be an aggressor and will be shot."

Several shots rang out, a couple ricocheting off the vehicles. Reflexively, Lew ducked behind the nearest one and grabbed at his holster, drawing his new-to-him 9mm, a CZ-75. He'd confiscated it during a routine search about three weeks earlier. After the initial few shots, all hell broke loose as the Peace Enforcement team opened up on the buildings. "Loan me a gun!" the Traylor kid pestered once again.

"Find your own."

A minute went by and the fire slacked. Nothing moved. In teams of four, they bounded ahead and began the hard work of combing through each and every house. One of the drivers of the eight-wheelers, clearly bored, sauntered over.

"How *dumb* do you have to be?" Traylor said, taking a drag off his cigarette. "Turn down free food, free *money* fer cryin' out loud, just to live like *this* out in the middle of nowhere? I think we're doing the gene pool a favor by wiping these idiots out."

"Definitely," Lew said. He turned to the Forcer beside them. "You seen much of this out there already?"

"Oh yeah, all the time. None of them put up much of a fight. I saw a captain get tagged at about six hundred meters so there's a few who can shoot. But most of them are just these antisocial retards who dream about fighting The Man but can barely tie their boots. Once we apply some firepower on 'em they either just dip or throw their hands up crying."

"Dip?" Traylor asked.

"Sorry. I forget most of you Auxies aren't military. D-I-P. Die In Place. What are you scoring for finding these morons?"

Lew bit his lip. It really wasn't much. The government made it impossible to get comfortably wealthy. He'd socked away far more in goods he'd, ah, *failed to report* than he'd ever see deposited into his account. Most other Auxiliaries were in the same situation.

There was a loud explosion, then another. Fire shot into the sky from a couple of houses.

"What was *that*?" Lew asked excitedly. "That us?"

His smoking buddy shook his head. "Could be anything. Propane tank rigged to blow. One of the boys with a grenade. Just sit tight and enjoy the show."

❖ ❖ ❖

David Levi looked up from his tablet and saw a familiar face. Uziel, the lead project manager was old enough to be his father. That described just about everyone here outside of a junior assistant role, actually. Behind Uziel trailed a tall, striking woman of about thirty, her heels clacking on the floor. She had long dark wavy hair, wore a black pantsuit, and was beautifully out of place in David's cluttered, messy work area.

She looked like a...

"I'm not a reporter," she said in a professional tone, in Hebrew. *Mind reader.* "My name is Meira Peretz. I'm with the Chief of Staff's office. As you're probably figuring at this moment, I am here to check up on the progress of the Defender project. In person."

"She's cleared to hear and see anything and everything," Uziel added in his gruff tone.

"I've sent over extensive updates and reports," David informed her.

Meira took off her glasses and rubbed one lens with her finger. "And we've read and evaluated them all. David, I know you're new to this process, but by now you should know how things work. Every once in a while, people—*generals*—want to have assurance of actual progress. Thanks to recent political developments, the Chief of Staff and our investors want to *accelerate* the completion of initial prototypes, conduct field testing, and begin series production no later than the end of the year."

David exhaled slowly through his mouth. That timeline was amazingly optimistic for such a complex, revolutionary project. And Israel wasn't the old U.S., or Russia, or

493

China. There wasn't an adequate industrial base to begin manufacturing machines of this nature in a hurry.

Uziel coughed slightly. "I have some other duties to attend. Ms. Peretz, call if you need anything else from me."

David motioned toward the far door and escorted his guest down a long hallway.

"So, I understand you're the youngest member of the Defender team," she began. "It's quite an achievement. You were valedictorian at the Technion?"

"Yes, ma'am. I'm still technically part of the school, here doing graduate research."

"Call me Meira, please."

"I do have *one* question... Meira. Why not have Uziel show you the prototypes? I'm involved in only a small portion of the project. He oversees the entire thing."

Meira exhaled sharply through her nose. "Uziel is very good at what he does, but he answers to a lot of important people. He's far too... politically motivated. He'll give politically correct answers when the straightforward variety is needed. No, the heart of this *machine* is based on your ideas and research at the Technion. That's what I want to see."

David swiped his card and watched the reader's light go from red to amber. He then pressed his right thumb against the glass and after a second, the light turned green and the door clicked. They entered a large open bay occupied by peripheral banks of equipment, tool cabinets, and terminals. The four Defenders dominated the center of the room. Today, Defender I was deadlined, awaiting a new battery array after a catastrophic failure during stress testing; Defender II was the closest thing they had to a runner; Defender III, the test pig was hooked up to diagnostic equipment; and Defender IV was simply incomplete, missing its right track and turret. It was understandably quiet here, the day after the end of *Pesach*—Passover. David didn't observe the traditional Jewish holidays. He'd been working nonstop for six weeks. He'd only taken the occasional day off since being assigned to the project in mid-December.

He and the attractive *attaché* were alone.

"So, David, go ahead and walk me through. Assume I know nothing and I haven't read any of those reports."

David was starting to piece things together. Uziel, or perhaps someone above his head, had probably edited David's reports before sending them off. But to what end? To make it seem like the project was farther away from completion, to get them more time? With events in the Muslim world coming to a head, and Russia getting more involved, any and every weapon system project was being accelerated. So it probably wasn't that. It also wasn't likely that David's superiors had claimed they were *closer* to completion than they actually were. They'd appear foolish when a deadline was missed. Project managers were always loathe to go down that road even under heavy pressure. It ruined their professional credibility.

David approached the Defender II prototype. "Meira, how good is your English? Explaining technical aspects would be easier. My Hebrew is coming along but I still have a ways to go." It was true. David had only been in Israel for five years—he'd grown up in Toronto. His parents had emigrated for a number of reasons. In retrospect they seemed very wise. North America was not the place to be at present.

"That's fine," she replied in English with a faint British accent.

"Okay. Well, to begin with, the Defender project is designed to—"

Meira held up a hand. "Not quite *that* basic. Explain the power system."

"Certainly. As you know—"

"And don't use that phrase," she interrupted. "I *don't* know, remember?"

"Right. So, anyway, the heart of the Defender, the truly revolutionary concept is that the primary armor of the vehicle also serves as its power storage system. The armor is a one-atom-thick graphene grid separated at each layer with a similar thickness of high-tensile strength ceramic. Graphene is a pretty fantastic armor substance but has its weaknesses; the ceramic takes up the slack. It's not my side of the house, but those materials guys call it *ceramalloy*. There's a similar material used in the internals called *plasalloy*. Polymers and metals."

"Each layer? Just an atom wide?"

"No, sorry. Each layer is about a millimeter wide. Each of the graphene layers is interconnected to the rest of the vehicle and holds the substantial amount of electrical charge needed to conduct extended operations in the field. The juice feeds into one of four controllers—redundancy—which can feed the drive motor in the front, move the turret, power the main gun, targeting, heating, cooling, you name it. Since graphene is far lighter than steel, and there is no separate battery or fuel compartment, it means the Defender can be far lighter than previous designs. If I remember right the fighting weight is about thirty-five tons compared to about sixty tons for a modern tank."

"What happens when a layer becomes inoperable? Enemy fire, simple failure, et cetera," Meira asked.

"Not much other than the loss of that power. Each body panel is highly compartmentalized. Even taking a solid hit from another tank or antitank missile will at most cause the loss of, oh, five percent of power capacity. The grid, by default, drains at the same rate all around, though the crew can choose a different profile. Expecting contact from the front? Just start draining the front-facing armor panels, for example."

Meira pointed to the remote turret. It was considerably smaller than the traditional manned turret and merely housed the weapon systems, sensors, and ammunition. "So, the main gun. Rail gun?" She referenced the three meter long tube protruding from the front.

"Correct. The magnetic rails push out a long fin-stabilized dart, forty millimeters wide and about three hundred and fifty long, to about two thousand meters per second—almost six times the speed of sound. The dart is a sandwich of tungsten, ceramics, and nickel steel. It'll defeat any existing or projected armored vehicle, even frontal armor hits, out to seven or eight *thousand* meters."

"Impressive."

David nodded. "The coaxial machinegun is also new. The design team ditched the traditional cartridge-firing machinegun in favor of another railgun. This one spits out seven hundred, eight millimeter wide darts per minute from a ten thousand round hopper. No tracers are necessary; the arcs are tracked by the gunnery computer and those are visible to the crew inside. Each of those little darts will punch through more steel plate than a standard twenty-five millimeter cannon. Neither the main gun nor the coaxial gun have any explosive effect. We still need to add an area effect weapon to the side of the turret. We're currently testing a couple of different rocket systems. We would prefer one with some kind of anti-aircraft capability but that seems to be out of scope. The Defender will be an amazing fighting vehicle but it can't do everything."

Meira looked impressed. "You certainly know a lot about its expected tactical employment. Did you serve in the IDF? Armored Corps perhaps?"

Israel Defense Force. "I was placed in special studies and did my required short basic training three years ago. That's it. My knowledge of armored warfare is nearly all academic. Due to my work, I've been excused from further uniformed military service. This project is my service, actually."

"Let's open it up. I'd like to peek inside."

David went to the rear and pulled a large lever. A standoff shield, there to protect against shaped charges to the much more vulnerable rear, lifted up and out of the way.

For decades, Israeli tankers had been victimized by foes who simply waited for them to pass by and then fired RPGs or other antitank weapons at their backsides. There were two doors beneath the shield, a smaller one on the left and a larger one on the right. Larger was relative as either would be a tight squeeze for most crew members. Prominent handles and step-ups bracketed each door. David turned the handle for the larger door followed by the smallest.

Meira peered in the larger hatch, then carefully climbed up and slid into the commander's seat on the right. "This reclines more than I would have expected."

"That's a common complaint." To keep the Defender as low as possible, each crew member practically had to lie down inside. The seats were almost too comfortable. "In tests, drivers have been known to nod off, so by design, most of the controls are wired. Even if the driver fell asleep, the vehicle commander or the gunner could take over, albeit through a less intuitive interface."

"Interesting."

David stepped up and slid into the gunner's position, almost in the centerline of the hull. The remote turret was directly overhead and the ammunition loading hatches were visible. To the left was the driver's position. Up ahead the crew compartment abruptly ended where the main drive motor began, a design concept that would be familiar to current Israeli tankers and their Merkavas. Most tank designs had the driver up front with the engine in the back. There was also a secondary motor that the team called the "Crawler" as it wasn't connected to the transmission and could move the vehicle at only fifteen kilometers per hour. It was there only if the main motor was damaged or inoperative and to give the crew a chance to move away from trouble.

"Can we turn it on? Does this one . . . work?" Meira asked, clearly hopeful.

"Press that large orange button to your right," David

replied.

There was no rumble of a diesel engine, no spinning up of a turbine. Screens came to life, requesting authentication like a modern PC or smartphone. David tapped in his credentials and up popped an icon interface. He glanced over and saw Meira poking and playing with her touchscreen.

"This is incredible," she said. "Is everything done through the screen?"

"No. Movement of the turret and the tank itself is still done via stick. Still easier that way. Though the reticle, ranging, and target info is all displayed on the screen. Standard optical, thermal, or if you want an overlay of both can be displayed. Based on the active profile, it will also outline targets with different colors. Red for an enemy that can be engaged, orange for out of range, green for friendly. If the information on friendlies is available, it will display unit info as well. The tank commander can click on a friendly and communicate via standard encrypted radio signals. They're still working on the microwave frequency line of sight communicator from what I understand."

"Ranging by laser?"

"Not anymore," David replied. "Too many detection and jamming systems out there. The Defender is all passive—ranging is done via software and an automatic coincidence rangefinder—using parallax to determine range. It's not quite as exact as a laser but there is nothing emitted for the enemy to detect or try to spoof. Being off by a few meters won't affect weapon accuracy, these rail guns shoot incredibly flat. Move the reticle around and the vehicle will automatically give you a range with about a half-second delay. Lock on to a target and it will keep the selected weapon system ready to fire and hit at the correct range. It requires some fairly sensitive, twitchy optics which we've put behind a small corundum bubble on top of the turret."

"*Corundum?*" Meira had a genuine look of curiosity

this time.

"Aluminum oxide. White sapphire. Diamond would be better ... but we're not quite at the point where we can craft an artificial diamond of that size and shape. With or without good optical clarity."

"So, David, does this prototype *run*? I mean, beyond just turning on. Is it ready to *fight*?"

David thought for a few seconds. "Give me a half hour and I could have this one checked out and ready to roll. Give me a couple of hours, let me make some calls, and we could arrange for live fire. I'll warn you though, no prototype has gone more than a few hours in the field without some bug or problem surfacing that would take it out of action in a combat setting. So they're not ready for war just yet."

Meira smiled tightly. "Well, David, that's the thing. You and the team need to hurry. Time is running short."

◆ ◆ ◆

The GeU-44 was an incredible aircraft. Sergei Kostadinov banked hard, insuring that he didn't leave Russian airspace, and pulled back on the stick again, shooting from just under the speed of sound to Mach 1.8 in less than a minute. He'd pushed it only once, hitting two and a half times the speed of sound, but that was a very special test run. Sergei needed to keep it under Mach 2 today.

Some on the committee disapproved of the design, particularly the old guard that still held fond memories of the Cold War, when the Soviet Union had to come up with designs on its own. The new consortium that had designed, and would build the GeU-44 was highly international. Many American engineers and other staff had accepted contract positions with the firm, and later accepted a free trip for their families out of the utter brutality and confusion that was most of the United States right now.

The fighter definitely had a strong American influence. Sergei thought that, if you squinted a bit, it looked a bit like a two-thirds scale SR-71, the now-ancient American supersonic reconnaissance aircraft. But SR-71s didn't have long range millimeter-wave radar and passive thermal detection systems, or hypervelocity air-to-air missiles —a necessity on a jet this fast—or a solid state laser under the cockpit that could either engage other aircraft at short range or stave off incoming antiaircraft missiles.

The GeU-44 was actually an older program than Russia's most modern fighter in service, the T-50, but had been shrouded in secrecy reminiscent of the old American "Skunk Works." Staying dark, of course, was easier back in the days before ubiquitous cameras and the ability to fit gigabytes of technical data and photos on the head of a pin. While every major nation saw the need for a multirole fighter jet that used stealth technology, only Russia had been seriously working on a dedicated interceptor that essentially ignored stealth and paid only cursory attention to low speed maneuverability. The GeU-44 did not conduct secretive nighttime bombing raids at low altitude or engage in cannon battles at "feel the heat of the jetwash" range. No, it had one purpose. Enter the targeted airspace at relatively high altitude, use powerful detection gear to find enemy aircraft at extreme range, and fire missiles that could reach Mach 7 while outrunning slower munitions. Its speed and a powerful laser could defeat ground-based anti-air systems.

Sergei let out a breath. The last six months had been a complete whirlwind. After returning to Moscow, a major from the Russian Air Force ordered him to report for duty. His fun, mostly casual time as a student in America was over. To his surprise, he was not ordered back into an Su-27 squadron. Despite his tarnished record, the same innate piloting skills that had led to his ignominious stint with the Russian Knights got him shuffled off to the GeU-44 test team.

Then there was the matter of Lyudmila, for whom

he'd developed strong feelings. Sergei had met her three months ago. She was the daughter of an influential colonel who was, thankfully, not in his chain of command ... though an angry colonel could cause a lot of trouble for him, hot shot pilot skills not withstanding. Sergei and Lyudmila weren't alone. It seemed like a growing number of people had been shaken out of a cycle of casual relationships. Something big was looming. Maybe even World War Three. With the United States taken off the world stage, the power vacuum was tremendous and a clear successor had not yet come to the fore. China, Russia, or the European Union seemed the best bets to emerge on top. Then there was the weird coalition consisting of Brazil, South Africa, and India. There were rumors that Australia, some Southeast Asian nations, Taiwan, South Korea, and Japan were working on their own coalition to deter China and North Korea. Sergei didn't give that alliance much of a chance. They didn't have much firepower, especially without American logistical support.

The dark horse would be the newly announced Islamic Caliphate. Through both agreements and war, the Caliphate had absorbed Iraq, Iran, Syria, and Turkey, and now had hold of what was left of Saudi Arabia and the smaller Persian Gulf states. Sergei had heard that the fighting around Damascus had been horrific and the ancient city was for all intents and purposes destroyed. Jordan would succumb soon. The missing royal family was presumed to be somewhere in America. Next to amalgamate would likely be Northern Africa.

Sergei continued south at close to Mach 2. Sochi, the site of the Winter Olympics several years before was visible when he looked at the visuals feeding into his flight helmet's external cameras. Snow still barely covered the tops of some of the larger mountains to the east. His orders were to land at a secret airfield in eastern Turkey and begin his new assignment: training Caliphate pilots on both Su-27s and, strangely enough, GeU-44s. As little as two years ago a Russian fighter pilot would have been very unwelcome in Turkey, but the Caliphate had prevailed there. The democracy had toppled with little violence and replaced by a regional theocrat. Sergei forgot what they were called. *An emir?* In any case, the Caliphate had chosen to ally with Russia, ostensibly for its help defeating the incumbent ISIS, which was never going to earn the endorsement of the world at large as a legitimate government.

Sergei tried not to think of the politics. But everything pointed in one direction. There was only one more significant stumbling block to complete Caliphate hegemony from Morocco to the Arabian Peninsula. *Israel.* And Russia was going to help move it aside.

CHAPTER FORTY-FOUR

Monday, Second Week in April

Robert Overberg edged the Dodge along at low speed, scanning. He thought about stopping and extricating the big-bore AR from its hiding place, but weighed the reassurance against the threat of being caught traveling with a weapon. Sunshine Lake could be firmly under the thumb of FEMA and the DHS by now. He didn't want a repeat of Cheyenne.

He neared the "T" next to the public park. Columns of smoke were prominent; one straight ahead. Several people were in proximity to bonfires, though none wore gray uniforms. That didn't mean much.

A tall young man of about twenty, dressed in a black and gold track suit, approached Rob's truck and locked eyes with him. He had a wooden baseball bat in his right hand, pointed at the ground.

"Yo, retard, you miss the sign?" Bat Boy called with forced bravado. "This area's full up."

"Well," Rob began, stopping just short of returning the favor with an epithet of his own, "I'm headed to my sister's cabin. But if that's not good enough for you, I'll see your *stick* there and raise you a six thousand pound truck with four hundred and twenty horses on tap." He revved the engine to make his point.

Bat Boy appeared to consider it for a second, then turned and jogged back into the crowd huddled near the large, smoky fire. Rob shrugged, turned left, and soon spotted Kyle's red Ram. A long black, silver and white toy hauler trailer was hitched to it.

He let out an audible sigh. *If I had come all this way...*

Rob pulled in behind it and was in no time surrounded by a small army of relatives and strangers. Des, Amber and her two little ones he knew well. Then there were a couple of teenagers—one clutching a baby—and a couple of younger kids. They made him feel slightly uncomfortable. Rob had never much cared for kids, and his time holed up away from the rest of humanity had not helped. But where were his nephews?

"Uncle Rob!" Kyle called, making his way slowly with the aid of a walking stick.

Matt trailed behind, smiling wide. "I can't believe you made it! Where in the world have you been?"

Wow . . . they both sure got skinny. And bearded. I probably look just about the same as I have for years. He embraced his nephews and was soon in a mass hug with everyone. "Long story. What I'd really like is to sit down on something besides the driver's seat of my truck. Take my boots off. Maybe . . . a hot plate of food? If it's not too much trouble and all."

"Sure thing," Kyle said. "We'll help you unpack."

"That'll take about sixty seconds," Rob joked. "Guys in gray stripped me pretty bare."

◆ ◆ ◆

Kyle poured hot water into the top of the French press. They were running out of whole bean coffee, but this was a special occasion. Uncle Rob sat at the head of the cabin's small kitchen table, with the adults filling the other chairs. Timothy and Loren sat on the counter while Abby kept the Gang of Four occupied in the living room. "So, Missouri? That great bass lake you're always bragging about?" Kyle asked. He'd meant to head out there sometime, catch up with his uncle, but his responsibilities had always conspired against such a trip. Now it was too late.

"Yeah. But it picked up a bad case of the raiders." Kyle listened as Rob recounted the two run-ins with looters, then the trip to Kansas, then Cheyenne.

"We picked up a case, too," Matt said. "But we managed to fight off the infection."

"This 'John' sounds really familiar," Kyle said. "I may have seen him speak, if not in person maybe online. Don't take this the wrong way, Rob, but I would have loved to be a fly on the wall while you two debated faith."

Rob lowered his gaze. "Kyle, I know you, you'd have wanted to join in right alongside the old coot. He used all your arguments, but he was smoother. More practiced. More stories and examples. But that's the difference between three decades and seven. John saw a lot in his life."

"He convince you of anything?" Amber asked good-naturedly.

Rob shook his head, then shrugged and nodded once. "Convince me there's a God who can all at once be involved in our every affair and give us free will, too? All the Jesus, 'I'm a man but God, too' stuff? No. But I'm convinced that it was what John needed. Maybe it's what you all need too, to get by. Sure, the odds were long I'd get here but here I sit, and no miracles or visions of Jacob's Ladder."

Kyle met Amber's eyes and smiled. "Well, if you need another improbable, borderline *miraculous* homecoming journey story, I'm sure my brother can help."

Rob looked at Matt. "Oh? What happened?"

Matt took a few minutes and quickly recounted his

journey up from California last fall.

Rob frowned. "Yeah. It sounds as though we both should be in a prison camp right now. Damn lucky."

"I can't call it luck," Kyle said.

"I need a favor right about now," Rob said, changing the subject. "Feed a man my age three cups of coffee and, well..."

"Say no more," Kyle said. "Bathrooms here are a no-go so we have public latrines. Though...the neighborhood isn't quite as friendly as it used to be." Kyle paused. "Give me a minute, I'm going to fetch something."

Rob had mentioned earlier that his collection of arms —once as great as Kyle's own—had been winnowed down to just a wild hog hunting AR with the big thermal sight up top. A lot to lug around while heading out to take a leak.

"Here," Kyle said, presenting his uncle a bundle of leather, hardwood, and stainless steel.

"Hey now," Rob said, cracking a smile. "I remember this one. My old .41 Mag!"

"Of course. It's yours until you feel like giving it back."

"You think I need a gun just to take a leak?"

Kyle nodded. "I'm afraid the lake isn't as friendly as it used to be."

"I think I know what you mean."

They pointed Uncle Rob in the right direction and Kyle watched as the faces around the table changed. It was one more mouth to feed. They'd already run out of most of the tasty food and were down to staples: wheat, beans, rice, some TVP, and the fresh meat and fish. Hardy vegetables rounded out the diet though keeping a close eye on their small garden was taxing.

Recent events had been a strange mix of action/reaction. After several long counseling sessions with Timothy and Loren, Kyle and Amber had given their blessing. The official engagement had been on Christmas Day. The following day, Malachi had stolen Greg's Ninja—no one even knew he could ride—and had taken off, almost certainly headed to the nearest ZOC to get plugged into the system. Loren admitted part of it had almost certainly been spurned love—Malachi hadn't been the best at voicing his feelings but the clues were there.

Around the New Year, a serious flu or pneumonia bug had made its way through the Sunshiners. Matt and his entire cabin had been hit hard, and Bella had picked it up as well. What was a difficult couple weeks for them and others had proved *fatal* for several of the older residents. Amber, Jeanie, and Lenny had, by virtue of their good health, become the burial team. Then, Lenny caught it bad and had, sadly, succumbed as well. Jeanie, in a fit of emotion, had taken off for good soon after they'd paid Lenny his respects.

Then came the refugees. First, a family of four crammed into a minivan that was barely running due to gasoline that was halfway to becoming varnish. Then, three days later, four more groups showed up, followed by several more over the next few weeks. They were running from graysuits, foreign troops, food shortages, riots, and rumors of plagues. Unlike the original wave of residents last fall, these people had brought *nothing* beyond the clothes on their backs. Kyle and Amber had explained the charity system they'd set up—though nearly all those it initially covered had since left—and helped them as they could. Kyle guessed about a hundred and twenty people had come, though some had moved on. Some had died. There were stranger diseases about than the flu these days, and in-fighting among the different groups had also claimed several.

As the cabins filled up—the refugees simply breaking in to take possession—Matt, Des, Abby, and Kaleb had wisely opted to move once again, occupying Greg Samuels' old cabin, #9, which had been kept clear—though not easily—by a group effort of Kyle, Amber, Timothy, and Loren. It created a small, much more easily defensible block. Up to that point, there hadn't been any outright threats, but there had definitely been opposition to the Flanigans claiming what the refugees considered to be 'public property'.

Finally, three weeks ago, a noticeably thinner Bill Klein had arrived one afternoon in his truck. Alone. Kyle had no idea where Bill's wife and daughter-in-law were and thought better than to ask. If anything, the man was more angry and reckless than he had been before. Oddly enough, it had been Bill who had made the "Area Full" sign and had bolted it up by the highway. Kyle still had no idea why.

Klein's arrival heralded the end of Kyle's cooperation with the newcomers. It had always been pretty shaky; they were all glad to accept his clean water and food and occasionally help here and there, though not with the same sense of community as before, and were wary of all the firepower Kyle and his 'clan' possessed. Nearly all of the refugees had either been disarmed by the post-Barnhall confiscation push or had never been in the first place. But the delicate balance of wary assistance crashed once Bill began to spread falsehoods about Kyle and his family: how they had killed his son and evicted him from the camp at gunpoint. That was somewhat ironic considering his first act upon returning had been to wave that big .44 and kick out the extended Asian immigrant family who had been squatting his cabin. He also told tales of the amazingly deep pile of food and other goodies Kyle had been hoarding, watching other families starve. Bill had brought about a third of the refugees under his wing, mostly the young and the angry. Kyle had won a handful of allies, particularly out of the initial arrivals when he was more charitable, but none he could really count on in a power struggle, and none who could physically stand up to Bill's thugs.

So, for the past two weeks plus, there had been an uneasy standoff in place. Bill's many versus Kyle's few. It was the kind of defensive standoff he'd managed to avoid with the marauders before. But his heart just wasn't in a preemptive strike. Kyle couldn't generate any hatred for the refugees and taking out Bill would merely confirm their prejudices. There was also the small detail that Bill hadn't done anything deserving of death. Kyle felt how easy it was to start justifying such actions. And he didn't like it.

◆ ◆ ◆

Rob walked back toward the cabin, watching the midday shadows for movement. Kyle believed there were goblins afoot and that was good enough for him. The chunky Smith and Wesson revolver, considerably larger than the one he'd lost in Cheyenne, was quite comforting.

Out of the corner of his left eye he spotted a man emerge from the trees. Tall, broad-chested, with chocolate brown skin covered up by a Multicam-pattern outfit. He had a scoped and suppressed bolt action rifle in his hands.

Rob grabbed at the grip of his pistol but the other man didn't even flinch. He looked exceedingly tired.

Maybe even more tired than I am.

"Hey there," the stranger called. "This is it, right? Sunshine Lake?"

Rob ignored the question. "Who are you?"

The big stranger sighed heavily. Rob now saw the sweat stains around his armpits. He'd been running hard for a long time. "Look, guy, I'm a friend of Kyle and Matt Flanigan. Brothers, about my age, white. You know them?"

Rob stayed cagey. "Hmm. . .maybe. Lots of people up here. Just give me your name and I'll ask around."

"DeSean Hupp."

"Okay. Wait here." Rob traced back to Kyle's cabin in a roundabout way and knocked on the door facing the lake. Amber opened it and Rob stepped back inside. "Hey Kyle . . . Matt . . . you two know a *DeSean Hupp?*"

"He's *here?*" Matt replied, perking up.

"Of course, knucklehead, how else would I know his name?"

Kyle and Matt both shot out the other door and returned a couple of minutes later, the visitor in tow.

"Looks like this is reunion day," Kyle noted.

DeSean leaned his rifle against the wall and sat down heavily on the padded chair near the door. Kyle handed him a tall glass of water and DeSean finished it in a single gulp. "I am ... *extremely* glad you all decided to stick around. I don't think I could have kept going much further."

"What in the heck happened?" Matt asked.

"The *United Nations* happened. Two days ago a platoon of—get this—*Libyans* ... with blue helmets just shows up and, through a grayouit interpreter demands we line up and come along with them, no questions asked. A bunch of us decided to split in a hurry, and quietly, but..."

The rest of the room was silent as DeSean gathered his thoughts. "During the house-to-house deal one of the Libyans starts getting grabby with one of the teenage girls. Girl's old man comes out with a shotgun and shoots off his d—" DeSean looked around the room, took note of the children, and continued. "Crotch. Well that starts a big ol' shootout and, well, we were going to come up short of that one. They had belt feds, armored vehicles, and while they were stinkin' terrible shots, as you guys know quantity *will* beat quality if you have enough of it. I got off a mag or two. Popped the guys dumb enough to climb up on their APCs to use the machineguns up top. Then they started to get a bead on us with a quick-fire cannon, a thirty mike-mike I think."

"Terry?" Kyle asked in a somber tone.

DeSean sunk his head, then after several seconds brought it back up. "Terry decided to cover our escape. I tried to talk him out of it ... but ... no. That's the last I saw of him. Me and a few other guys just started running. Most headed west, deeper into the mountains. I headed north, alone."

"You sleep since the firefight?" Matt asked. DeSean shook his head.

"Take the kids' room for right now," Kyle said. "We'll have some chow up shortly. I'm sure you're hungry."

"You bet," DeSean replied, rubbing his eyes. "Thanks."

They watched the big man stumble down the hall, the fatigue toxins clearly hitting hard. Then Matt turned to Kyle. "Looks like our time really is up. If they hit Cushman —"

Kyle held up a hand. "Let's look at our options. *All* of them."

"Well, we can't take on professional soldiers. Right?" Amber pleaded. "This isn't like Thanksgiving. Now we have, what, *five* people who can really fight? We're not going to get any help from the refugees out there, either."

"I've thought about that point quite a bit. Long before today," Kyle added. "You're right. If we're threatened by an organized military force we have to retreat. No question."

"Why is everyone assuming we have to either fight or run?" Des asked. "There must be a third option. We could, y'know, stay here and see what happens. It's not like they're lining up the people who submit and shooting them in the back of the head."

"Because when people put a gun in your back and load you on a bus, they ain't taking you to Disneyland to hang out with Mickey and the Clubhouse gang," Rob said bluntly. "Look, I've seen a DHS prison camp. I've seen the government troops up close. And I got to hang out with the insurgents—those so-called Randyites—for a short time. Des, honey, I hear what you're saying. Few people like to be on the fringe all the time. Trust me, I know. I thought I did. I thought I was this hardcore lone wolf who depended on no one. I've *really* been alone. I don't think I could do what those partisans did: ambush and slaughter fellow Americans who were simply following bad orders. But I got caught once. I'm *never* getting loaded up, disarmed and helpless, again.

The group continued to debate for about forty-five minutes, but couldn't come up with any other options. Amber got up to fetch more hot water for coffee. Someone pounded at the door. Those so equipped put hands on pistol grips. Rob glanced back as the teenage boy—Timothy—answered the door.

It was a familiar face. *Bat Boy*. And he still had the bat. No doubt it was the tool he'd used to get their attention.

"Yo," the young man began in a haughty tone, "Mr. Klein is calling an all-hands meeting. At the park. Ten minutes."

There were several murmurs and muttered curses at the table. "You tell Bill we're coming," Kyle said, voice level. Timothy shut the door and locked it.

"So . . . here's what's going to happen," Kyle began. "Uncle Rob and I will go . . . and *only* the two of us. Bill knows our M.O.s too well. So, I want a wild card. Having my uncle there might throw him off. The rest of you, arm up and get ready for *anything*. Matt, you're in charge here."

"Got it," Matt replied. "You want me to wake up DeSean?"

Kyle shook his head. "No, let him get some rest. If something starts up I'm sure he'll pop awake. For that matter, how long have *you* been up, Uncle Rob? You said you were driving all night and into the morning. It's almost noon."

"Oh, about twenty hours," Rob said. "But I'll be fine. What's the deal? You expecting some trouble from this Bill character?"

"Always," Kyle replied.

They walked down, loaded for bear, Kyle with a shotgun and Glock while Rob carried his Beowulf carbine with the big magnum on his hip. A group of about seventy had already gathered, clearly waiting for them. A few, mostly young men, grasped handguns and a couple of rifles. There was a fiftyish man in a green jacket and blue jeans with a flushed complexion standing on one of the tables, a black revolver in one hand.

"That your huckleberry?" Rob asked quietly as they walked up. Kyle merely nodded.

"Where's the rest of your little clan?" Bill called disdainfully.

"This is enough," Kyle shot back. "So what's up?"

Bill Klein crossed his arms. "Well, we've been talking, and we all think it's about time to get organized again. Like before."

"That's fine," Kyle said. "Matter of fact, I think it's a good idea."

"But I remember what you said when we all got together the first time," Bill said. "The whole *charity* as opposed to *commune* thing. You mind going over that again?"

"I suppose," Kyle replied, bringing his volume up to speak to the group. "Charity's where no one is in charge and we help one another as we can. Those that don't help out don't get much help back, unless they legitimately can't—the elderly, handicapped, and so on. Commune is where we pile everything together and dole it out equally. Like I said last fall, the problem with the commune is someone has to be the one to dole it out. That person or group is always the one that's in charge of everyone else."

Murmurs shot through the crowd. "That's pretty much how I remembered it," Bill said in a loud voice. "Well, we all decided on the *commune* deal. Obvious, now, the other system failed... everyone but you and your people, the ones with all the stuff, had to leave just to survive."

"That's not tr—" Kyle interrupted.

"*I have the floor!*" Bill yelled. "This is *my* meeting!" He continued in a more normal tone. "How else can you explain what happened here? No, we need to level the playing field this time. Make things equal. Right, everyone?" By now Bill Klein was grinning. There were more than a few cheers and claps from the crowd.

"What's the deal with this guy?" Rob whispered to his nephew.

"He's a big union honcho," Kyle whispered back without taking his eyes off the armed men. "Used to riling up a crowd for maximum impact. Just follow my lead, all right?

"Bill," Kyle boomed, "since you remember my first meeting so well, you'll also recall that I made it clear I would *never* be part of a commune system."

"Yeah, I remember ... because you have everything to *lose*," Bill interjected, still grinning wide.

"That may be true," Kyle continued. "But the fact remains that *none* of you can vote me out of what I own."

Rob noticed a few fingers stretching to rest on triggers, and he slowly clicked his rifle off safe. The setup wasn't great: him and Kyle against about seven visibly armed men on the other side of the covered area, and lots of unarmed people in between.

"I have an announcement," Kyle stated preemptively, turning his head to get the attention of everyone gathered. "We're leaving. Tomorrow morning. Vote and decide on whatever you like, but anyone who isn't a family member or friend who approaches our cabins—nine, ten, eleven, and twelve—tonight will be shot."

Rob tapped the thermal sight on his Beowulf. "Don't try it. Can't hide from this sucker. It's like Santa Claus, so be good, for goodness sake."

◆ ◆ ◆

The night passed without incident; nothing larger than a raccoon had come crawling anywhere near their block of cabins. Kyle glanced back at the convoy aimed toward the logging road to the west. His Durango would lead, with Timothy riding shotgun, as only they had spent any significant time out on these roads, and only Kyle had scoped out the upcountry lake he'd picked as their destination. Next came Matt and Des in their Bimmer wagon. In the middle was Amber, driving the red Dodge that pulled the well-laden fifth wheel. The big rig's cab was full of kids: Loren holding Max in the other front passenger seat with Bella in the middle, and Abigail, Cole, and Kaleb in the back. Rob and DeSean, both now well-rested, brought up the rear in Rob's black Ram. DeSean sat in the bed, looking back while clutching that huge rifle. Insurance against anyone stupid enough to try and follow them.

Kyle wondered, not for the first time, if his snap decision had been the right one. It meant abandoning not only the cabins and their dwindling stores of firewood, but also the boat on Hood Canal and that steady source of seafood. Without Kyle's—and others in their group's—help, Sunshine Lake would simply starve. Bill and the weak-minded people propping him up would never be able to hunt, fish, and farm enough to feed everyone. Some might crawl back and lick the boots of the oppressors from whom they'd originally fled. But there simply were no good options. Even for him, and he'd planned for this sort of situation for years.

"Mount up," Kyle yelled, scanning back and forth along the tree line. He wasn't ready to ignore the risk that Bill might take a literal parting shot. Satisfied, he planted his good left leg on the step up, got in, and turned the engine over. *Starting to run a little rough.* Unlike the truck, the Durango had a gas engine, and gasoline tended to degrade pretty quickly. They'd treated their fuel with stabilizer but that only delayed the inevitable. They also all had the issue of supply—none of the vehicles had more than a half of a tank by now, with nothing in spare cans.

They took the shortest route. Kyle had considered devising a more circuitous route to throw off any pursuers, but there was no hiding so many vehicles traveling on muddy roads. They concluded the forty-five minute drive without incident. The lake was less than half the size of Sunshine and had little more than a few cleared spaces for tent campers. They parked and got to work setting up Kyle's large but not particularly substantial ten man tent along with Matt's smaller dome one. Kyle kicked himself for about the five hundredth time for not investing in one of those large canvas tents with a wood stove inside, the kind popular with big hunting groups.

"We're going to live in *tents*? All the time?" Loren asked, looking him in the eye while patting a sleeping Max. Kyle read her thoughts. It still got plenty cold at night—snow graced the peaks around them—and a baby would be tough to keep happy and content.

"Some of us, for now," Kyle replied. "You, Max, and the kids will stay in the trailer. It'll be a bit warmer in there." The trailer's heater was most definitely *not* attached to the battery stack as it would drain it in short order.

Her lips turned down. No doubt she was wondering if she'd made the right choice, hitching her future to Kyle and his crew.

"Look, Loren, I know this isn't easy. But we'll either get through this together or go down together. Remember that, please."

She nodded. "I just wish there was . . . more . . . than that."

"There is," Kyle said, turning to face the others just finishing up on the dome tent. "I think it's a very good time to pray. Will you all join me?"

CHAPTER FORTY-FIVE

Tuesday, Second Week in April

It was aggravating to be unable to spit out questions as they came to mind. Less than a year ago, Marshall Cross had been working his way toward his next warrant officer rank and likely an instructor position to ride out the last couple of years of his Marine Corps career. Then, the meteoric rise to command a battalion of virtually untrained draftees, then crashing down to nothing, and now ... what? As they traveled west, a general feeling of *doubt* had begun to settle in. He still knew very little about what he'd gotten himself into. Ostensibly, to the public eye, he was Braithwhite's assistant-spear carrier-chauffeur. Jonathan had even found Marshall a dark suit that fit surprisingly well so he'd be able to pull off the stereotypical G-Man look.

The twenty-odd vehicle convoy had maintained a steady forty-five mile an hour pace since the day previous, with infrequent stops to accommodate the concerns of the forward scouts. The radio—actually, Braithwhite's silver phone—often chirped with known or likely ambush points. Today, Jonathan rode shotgun.

Their SUV was in the middle and slightly to the front. By that, and a few other clues, Marshall had picked up that

Braithwhite wasn't quite in VIP range—more like an 'IP'. Three SUVs—similar to theirs but longer and probably even better armored—were squarely in the center.

There be the unseen VIP.

"*Coming up on a recent ambush site. Keep your eyes peeled,*" one of the scouts said. As they rolled forward steadily, Marshall noticed the scorched pavement and had to swerve to avoid a couple of recent potholes . . . *impact craters* . . . that had filled with muddy water. It was a good place for an ambush: the road split and turned sharply.

The convoy headed on to the nearby mega-base, JBLM, that had spilled out from its original borders into a sort of gigantic ZOC. There were still some holes to fill but it more or less extended north clear into Seattle and on to the Navy shipyard north of there in Everett. Marshall and Braithwhite continued on toward an open-air market in that semi-controlled area that had been given over to the UN. Or taken over by the UN. It wasn't really clear.

"I need to find a couple of things," Braithwhite said as they walked toward the market tables. Marshall had gotten used to his generalizations. "Things" obviously meant something that he couldn't expand upon within range of his SpyPhone.

"Anything I should look out for?" Marshall asked. The whole area stunk like open sewage, unwashed bodies, and rotting garbage.

"Find a small lock box or safe," Jonathan whispered and stepped away, toward some E-Z-Ups that protected against the light spring drizzle coming down.

A pair of young men approached, lanyards just visible around their necks and holding small phones. They frowned at Marshall, then each other, and walked in the other direction. A few minutes later, the same thing happened with a middle aged woman holding a similar device.

They're avoiding me.

They also clearly avoided the uniformed UN troops.

Here, south of Seattle, their units were a hodgepodge of Pakistani, Indonesian, and South Africans with a few higher brass from various countries sprinkled in. As they'd ditched the blue helmets for regular camouflage headgear they were a bit tougher to spot. It was odd to see sellers—Americans—pandering to foreign soldiers. Marshall watched as one of the Pakistani officers pulled out a green colored card, tapped it against a pre-Crash regular smartphone held by a thin merchant woman with unkempt hair, and walked away with a pair of black leather boots. On the short Pakistani's hip, Marshall spied the wooden butt of a long barreled stainless steel revolver. One of his aides-de-camp carried a nickel-plated pump shotgun while the other had the usual Third World rifle, a folding-stock AK-47. Marshall had seen those by the hundreds in Iraq and Afghanistan. Not for the first time, he felt naked without a weapon. Jonathan had said he'd been unable to get him one. Marshall read between the lines: he would remain on probation until it was determined he was fully on board with Braithwhite's conspiracy.

At that same stand, Marshall spotted a black metal box with a small, bright circle at one end. A brass key was stuck inside.

Perfect. He approached, picked it up, and read the tag:

฿15

What is that? A letter 'B'?

"Fifteen *bancors*," the woman said, seeing Marshall's confusion. She sounded like she was recovering from pneumonia. "You want it or not?"

Not quite as polite to fellow Americans. "Sure." Marshall produced his new blue NID, which caused the woman to raise her eyebrows and break into a greedy grin.

"You want something else, too? Ten percent discount for you. Anything you want."

He took a quick glance back and forth. It looked like the stuff typically found at a yard sale—knick-knacks he would have passed up without a thought last summer. It occurred to Marshall, just then, that this *was* just a giant glorified yard sale, where everyone was trying to offload their worldly possessions just to get by. "No, thank you. Just the box."

"Real popular, these, among you government types."

Marshall shrugged. He really had no idea why Braithwhite wanted one. He swiped his card as he'd seen the Pakistani do, trusting that Braithwhite had disbursed some funds at some point. The woman raised no objections as Marshall took his card back and turned, tiny safe in hand.

"Ah, good job," Jonathan said as he approached. "Let's head back to the vehicle."

Jonathan took the safe from Marshall and slipped his SpyPhone inside. After locking it, he turned to face Marshall. "This will act as a Faraday cage to prevent the worst of the snooping. The vehicle is still a problem as it's synced up. I managed to get us a small truck we can use for the time being."

"What about our IDs?" Marshall asked. "We can't avoid the checkpoints."

"We might run into some of those, sure. There will always be a general snapshot of where we go. It's impossible to hide from that any longer. But I'm trying to avoid providing exact coordinates on anything."

They were walking away from the armored SUV. "We're leaving the Chevy *here*? This doesn't look like a great spot to leave *anything* that you want to get back."

"It'll be fine. I had a *chat* with a couple of local brown badgers. No one will mess with a vehicle with government plates."

They headed east, back the way they'd come.

"My first stop is out near Lake Chelan, over the mountains from here," Jonathan explained. "A man named Colliers. My first battalion commander... a Vietnam vet, Silver Star, Purple Heart... real deal infantry officer. He's plugged into that group of retired officers I told you about."

"Sounds like he's been out of it for a while," Marshall noted.

"Oh, he's still plenty useful," Braithwhite shot back. "He's pretty old, around eighty I'm guessing. But this isn't a quantity play. I'd rather have ten old, wise, *experienced* men than a hundred wide-eyed troopies. I don't turn away the young guys, but so few of them have any skills I need... or a track record I can look at and come away impressed."

"Navy SEALs. Force Recon. D-Boys." *Delta Force... the elite unit the Army won't admit exists, but does.*

Jonathan chuckled. "Seriously? I *never* approach those guys. Even a former one with a chip on his shoulder. If the government wanted to infiltrate this network, the chalk play would be to send a high-speed-low-drag guy like that our way, someone we'd just *love* to have. This is about ninety-nine percent keeping your mouth shut and one percent pulling triggers. I need people I trust more than I need razor-sharp operator skills."

"Those UN boys back there," Marshall began, changing the subject. "It was odd. What about the Chinese? Surprised they haven't dropped in a regiment or twenty in our laps. They definitely have the manpower. I figured they'd be first in line."

Jonathan glanced his way. "The Chinese? They've been too busy invading Taiwan. Hear it's just about wrapped up. They took those little disputed islands in the South China Sea too, the ones the Philippines claimed. Now word is they've moved into Mongolia. As you said, it's not like they lack the troops. Had to wait 'til the snow cleared there. After that's done, they'll probably target the Senkaku and Ryuku islands, including Okinawa. Or the Philippines proper. No, I don't think we're going to see the Chinese here anytime soon. Owing to the Taiwan deal, we've technically been at war with China—but no shooting quite yet—for about five weeks now."

War with China. Marshall exhaled as it sunk in. His whole life, he'd figured World War Three would begin in an instant, not this slow slide into oblivion.

Marshall was surprised by the strength in the old man's grip. "Cyrus Colliers. But everyone your age just calls me 'Codge'." He was stocky, bald, and clean shaven, with thick bifocals. He looked more like a greeter at the local big box store than an old-school Marine Corps warrior, but Marshall wouldn't underestimate him.

"What have you been up to, Colonel?" Braithwhite asked as they took seats around the man's kitchen table. Codge remained standing and turned on the stove to boil some water. He had electricity here.

"I've been out of coffee since Christmas," Codge explained. "Got some tea, though. To answer your question, Jonathan, I've been sitting tight waiting for someone to show up. Honestly, I kind of figured it would be my son or my granddaughter, they're just down in Wenatchee. But no word since the phones went kaput. The neighbors who used my back forty for their cattle up and disappeared not long after everything went down the drain. Wolves and cougars started to pop up and killed about ten of them, then the two-legged sort of predator started to come by and cleaned the rest up. I managed to take one the easy way, a .45 to the brain, and butchered him up best I could." Codge caught their glances. "One of the steers, not the two-legged predators. They never got into pistol range. Guess that makes me a rustler, too. That, with the fruit trees and what I'd stored up kept me okay through the winter. Lost power for about two months but one day it just came back on. Grand Coulee Dam isn't too far from here, I figure we got our juice back before most people."

"But ... sir ... you have a new ID. That's how I tracked you down," Braithwhite told him.

"Oh sure, that stupid *card*," Codge replied with a wave of a hand. "I went into town to try and see if there were any authorities left. Ran right into the food handout fellas. I lined up for that exactly *once*. Just too far for me to go. And my guts can't handle those dadgum MREs anymore. I ate the one they gave me and didn't crap for three days!"

Marshall smiled and shot a glance at Jonathan, trying to give that look that said, *"This guy is your prized recruit we drove four hours to see?"*

Jonathan quieted him with a gesture and turned back to their host. "Any problems with raiders? Government types poking around?"

Codge shook his head. "Early December, there was a big gun battle. Probably about twenty shooters, maybe a quarter mile down the road. No idea how it shook out. There were some exchanges into the next day, sniping and what not. I sat right here with my M1A, scanning out that way, but it was beyond the ridge to the south. I'm too old to be very curious, gents."

"Understood. What are you going to do now, sir?" Jonathan asked. "Can't live on a slaughtered steer and cans of pears forever."

"Boy, you sure cut to it! What happened to that wide-eyed lieutenant, Jonathan? He had some *tact*."

Braithwhite smiled. "He grew up, sir."

There were a few moments of silence and Braithwhite continued. "I'm glad to see you're okay, sir. I did have another reason for coming all the way out here." Marshall sat, saying nothing, as Jonathan outlined a proposition to his former commanding officer. Not as a direct aide but more in a general assistance role.

The silence stretched. Then, Codge uttered one word. "No."

Braithwhite's left eyebrow arched. He wasn't used to being refused. "Ah . . . I know it's a lot to take in all at once. But take some time and—"

"No. I don't want to be a part of it," Codge replied. "I took an *oath*. Both of you men did as well. Trust me, gentlemen, I'm not pleased with the current state of things. But maybe I have a bit more perspective than you. Age will do that. My grandfather was a Marine officer too, back before World War Two. His description of most of America didn't differ much from what we're seeing right now. But people back then could take care of themselves better. Folks were a little more used to not running to a restaurant every time their tummy tickled.

"But I digress. He told me of the *Bonus Army*, an effort for veterans to get paid early on their certificates. Wrapped up in that was General Smedley Butler. Yeah, him, the one in the cadences. There were some big money fat cat types back then that tried to get General Butler to rile up those veterans and cause a coup, to kick out FDR. He refused. He looked at the bigger picture . . . and I'll do the same now. So, again, I must refuse."

There was no tension in the older man's voice. He was calm and level. And definitely wasn't changing his mind.

"So, where are we headed from here?" Marshall asked.

"There are a few others on my list. But Colliers was the crux. If they learn I tried and failed to get the Colonel on board, they'll drop away. That's why I came here first. I'll check in with the rest later. Let's go find your buddy. Then I'll need to report. I can't run around doing my own thing forever."

"Sounds good."

The next morning, they headed out to Kyle's house, using Braithwhite's lookup tools. Tools that also pointed out Kyle and his family never got IDs.

"Estimates are that ninety-eight percent of all eligible Americans got ID," Jonathan said. "Most in the first week."

"He's an independent sort," Marshall shot back. "Survival nut."

"Well, he may have skylined himself as an ODT. Or been killed. We'll see."

Kyle's Enumclaw home was a bust. It was empty and had clearly been broken into and looted thoroughly. His woodshed was completely empty, though not chopped apart for firewood. Next year, maybe.

"Sure are a lot more vehicles out this way," Marshall commented as they went by the line of cars near JBLM. They were in the far lane, reserved for government or VIP traffic, whizzing by the hundred vehicles or more that all sat still, waiting for their turn at the checkpoint. Most had turned their engines off and pushed their vehicles forward in neutral, clearly to save fuel. Marshall witnessed one of the few charitable acts he'd seen in months: people helping others push their vehicles along.

"Well, there's actually fuel available, for those who can afford it," Braithwhite explained. "The refinery up north is operational—under federal control of course—and there's money flowing in courtesy of the heavy UN and PE presence around here."

From there, they headed out toward the cabin, taxing Marshall's memory. Jonathan had access to a search service similar to those everyone used before the crash, but run by the government, which helped point them in the right direction.

They crawled up toward the public park. Several

young men and women were staving off the spring cold around an improvised fire pit. They were gaunt, filthy, and eyed the vehicle with suspicion. One lumbered off purposefully.

"You remember where his cabin is?" Jonathan asked, scanning out the thick windshield.

"Sure. Turn left."

Three young men, who looked cleaner and better fed than the rest, approached down the narrow road. One carried a crowbar, another a baseball bat. The third had his hands free but Marshall didn't believe for a second he was unarmed.

"Looks like the welcoming party found us," Jonathan quipped as he put down his window, other hand on his 9mm.

It made Marshall nervous. Not for their safety—the Chevy would take care of anything short of armor piercing rifle rounds—but because it was doubtful Kyle and roaming gangs of punks would coexist. They were walking right in front of his cabin and no vehicles were parked in front.

The guy with the bat walked forward. "Hey, you miss th—"

Jonathan nonchalantly flipped open his wallet in the youth's face, showing both his blue NID and DHS badge. "I'm looking for someone," Jonathan said calmly.

"Uh . . . what?" the youth mumbled.

Jonathan lowered the wallet. "Look, son, I don't have time for a long conversation. I'm looking for . . . Marshall? What's the name?"

"Kyle Flanigan."

"Right. Ring a bell?"

"Uh, yeah . . . you really need to talk to the boss, though."

"Who? Kyle? Kyle is the boss?" Braithwhite asked.

The young man just shook his head and walked off.

Five minutes passed. About twenty people had gathered, gawking at a distance. Out of the crowd, a lone man approached. Older, with a white beard, and a big pistol in his right hand.

"My guy says you're looking for *Kyle Flanigan?*" He practically spit out the name.

Braithwhite nodded. "Yeah. This is his cabin here, right?"

The old man spat on the ground. "Wait . . . you all are government people. You trying to find him to arrest him?"

Jonathan shrugged. "What's it to you?"

"Yeah . . . that's what this is," the bearded man said, ignoring Braithwhite's jab. "Well, you just missed him. Him and his whole clique took off oh, about two weeks ago. Headed up further into the mountains on the forest service road behind me. No idea where. He sure as hell wasn't going to tell me."

Not saying another word, Braithwhite put up the window and started out. "That guy sure was eager to tell me all about your friend once he believed we were there to arrest him."

"Yeah," Marshall said. "But we'll take help any way we can get it."

Jonathan stopped the vehicle once they hit dirt and gravel. "I don't mind a long, romantic drive in the mountains but you're the wrong gender, Marshall. I'd rather let technology do the work." He spent about a minute tapping his SpyPhone. "Looks like there was a satellite pass about a day ago. Let me zoom in and . . . here we go. Collection of vehicles, a trailer, a tent. Bingo."

CHAPTER FORTY-SIX

Monday, Third Week in April

Matt glanced back and watched as Des and Abby hung laundry along an OD Green paracord line strung between the trailer and Uncle Rob's Dodge. The younger kids were gathered around the tablet in the trailer, watching a movie. His brother, sister-in-law, and the teenage lovebirds were down by the water. DeSean was out scouting the woods to the west. Matt smiled.

Life is good. For now, at least.

With that thought, the smile turned down. They were running out of food. Kyle had given away three quarters of his storage food during their time at Sunshine Lake. And for what? Ungrateful people who had either left the community or had conspired to steal the rest of it via majority rule. Rations that could comfortably last a group their size for months had been reduced to a small pile in the back of Kyle's trailer. They had maybe another two weeks left. Efforts to supplement it hadn't been very successful. The fish out of this lake were even smaller than the trout in Sunshine. Hunting was much tougher up here. According to Kyle, it was still a bit too cold—deer and elk would stick to the lower hills for another month or two. With the garden and better access to game, Sunshine might have been viable long after the last #10 can was empty. Here, at this remote glacial melt pond, no chance. They had clean water, plenty of fresh air, and little else.

No one had any clue what to do once the food ran out. Head back to civilization? Uncle Rob told everyone what the checkpoints were like for those without ID. Kyle, Amber, and the teenagers would all be in trouble. There had been some idle talk of splitting up, leaving them here, but it didn't go anywhere. Matt and his uncle had both worked far too hard to make it up here, to reunite as a family, to just break it up at the first sign of hardship.

Matt heard the low rumble of an engine and his eyes snapped up. He brought his AR to his shoulder and flicked the selector to FIRE.

A dark SUV rolled slowly into view. Looking over the red dot, he continued to gaze, scanning for more vehicles. Not that a single vehicle full of six or seven well-trained and well-armed men wouldn't be enough to force their hand.

But none followed. The lone vehicle—Matt could now make out the white government plates—stopped at a safe distance and both front doors opened simultaneously. Two men emerged, both in dark suits wearing sunglasses. The driver was rangy and bald while the passenger was dark skinned and stockier. Both walked forward confidently, as if they belonged there. Matt lowered his weapon. It might not be a friendly social call, but this definitely wasn't a raid.

"Hello!" Matt called. The shorter man waved. He could see now that the passenger wasn't really short—he was Matt's six foot one or better—it was just that the driver was an easy six foot five.

"State your business, please," Matt said, assertive.

"I'm looking for a friend of mine," the shorter man said as he approached. "Kyle Flanigan."

Matt's heart spiked. He didn't know how to reply. He couldn't think of a good reason why two G-Men would be looking for his brother. But it wasn't as if he could pull off a lie with Kyle likely only a couple of hundred yards away, down by the lakeside. "I'm his brother," Matt began. "How do you know Kyle?"

"I served with him in the Marines," the shorter man replied. "Name's Marshall. Marshall Cross. This is my boss, Jonathan Braithwhite."

Matt had heard Cross's name come up before. "All right. Apologize for being cautious, but—"

"Cross! How in the world did you find me?" It was Kyle's voice, full of excitement. Matt turned and saw his brother with a huge grin, holding a fishing pole.

"Lep!" Cross cried as they embraced.

"Lep?" Matt said, confused.

Kyle turned his way. "It's kind of a long story."

"Not *too* long," Cross said. "See, we were on the same boat—LHA—heading out to the Gulf for the initial invasion. We would get together, play cards, shoot the breeze, whatever. This new guy joined us one time..."

"Simmons," Kyle added.

"Yeah, Simmons. I introduced him to Kyle and he says, 'Flanigan, what kind of name is *that*?'"

"To which I said, 'Irish,'" Kyle said.

"And Simmons says, 'Irish? What, you mean like a leprechaun?'" Cross added. "We tried calling him 'Leprechaun' but it was too long."

"And then, later, while in-country we found out we had a different connection," Kyle began.

"Yeah. My dad worked in one of your grandpa's drug stores, out in Oklahoma. It was his first job after high school," Cross said.

"Small world," Matt added.

While they'd been talking, the older ones in their little camp had gathered around—Amber, Des, Timothy, and Loren—while the children kept their distance. "Marshall gave you high praise, Kyle," Braithwhite said, clearing his throat. "I know... the fed plates on the rig will put the hairs on the back of your neck up a bit. We're here as friends."

"Braithwhite and I are, well, on a *recruitment drive*,"

Marshall said. "I'll let him explain."

And he did, going into the details of their cause. Matt was still cautious, but he saw that Kyle truly trusted his friend. Matt took his cues. If Kyle wasn't asking the hard questions, Matt wasn't going to play bad cop.

"So . . . what do you want from us?" Kyle asked. "Personally I'd like to throw in with you . . . but as you can see I have a family. What are they supposed to do?"

"I hear you," Jonathan said. "There's a system we've put in place in other parts of the country. Something I had looked to build out in the Midwest, but I received orders to head out here. Honestly, I think it will work a lot better here than out there."

The silence of anticipation hung in the air as Braithwhite continued. "There are a lot of flea markets and bazaars popping up everywhere, mostly catering to the government employees and foreigners with money. People are selling off their own stuff or, yes, scavenging and flat out looting for more. But I think there's a better approach. I plan on setting up a salvage business to front our efforts here. Through DHS I'll have no problem setting up some contacts downstream who will be eager to buy. Based on condition and value, we'll either break items down or sell them as-is. Like it or not, there's a river of electronics, valuables, et cetera flowing out of the country right now. It's the easiest way to make money. Later, once that dies down, we'll have to figure something else out. We probably have a year or two with that as a viable business."

It sounded pretty solid to Matt, the salesman thought-track coming back. "What about the kids? You have somewhere for all of us to stay?"

"Leave that to me," Braithwhite said. "Kyle, we went by your house, it's a total loss. I'm sorry. But I like that area in general. I think it'll be perfect. It's pretty much in the middle of everything without being in the city itself. I'll have to be pretty hands-off though. I figure Marshall here and a few of you will run it day-to-day. The proceeds will keep you better off than the majority of people right now, and we can use that to recruit more people. Most won't have much insight as to what's going on at a high level. Can't have too many people with that sort of knowledge."

Matt accelerated away from the checkpoint and merged with traffic.

It had been two months since they'd left the unnamed lake with Braithwhite and Cross. Braithwhite had used his authority to get them through no less than three checkpoints before reaching the first halfway house. Kyle and his circle—to include Timothy, Loren, and Max—had set up there, dropping their trailer inside the long horse barn and hiding the vehicles behind it, under tarps. Next stop was another remote house, this one about a mile away outside the town of Buckley. This would end up being his home along with his wife, Abby, and Kaleb. It turned out the older couple that owned the spread, the Van Horns, had been contacted by Braithwhite on their way back from the mountains. They were somehow part of that network he'd talked about. Matt learned a few days later that Marshall, Uncle Rob, and DeSean had been set up with an apartment nearby.

Little time had been wasted getting the front business off the ground. Braithwhite, using Marshall as his proxy, had set up White River Enterprises in a light industrial park just down the road. He'd procured a couple of abandoned trucks for them to use. The business model was simple and straightforward. They hung out near the food lines during handout time with a big sign on the truck and put out feelers on anything useful. For the most part, they required people to bring everything to them. It was too risky to wander out somewhere they might get bushwhacked. At first, the original crew sorted the goods out and a panel truck came by a couple of times a week to cart it all away. They'd grown to four trucks working at the same time and had to hire on several eager employees—none in on Braithwhite's conspiracy, yet—to stay back at the warehouse and solely sort and break down salvage. Even with all the work and success of the new business, they hadn't seen much personal economic benefit, particularly since they had to subsidize Kyle and his family completely. It was a complete one-eighty from six months before, when Kyle was their benefactor.

Matt glanced out the side window as several matte black vehicles whizzed by. Out this way, a Middle Eastern unit was in charge—possibly the same one that had attacked Lake Cushman. He'd spotted some of them milling about in their tan uniforms, smoking and cajoling anyone who passed by.

Later on, after dark, these same UN "troops" would likely be found at a local brothel or getting drugs on the street. Those were sure-fire moneymakers in the UN-controlled areas; providing officers with room and board was another way people got their hands on precious extra *bancors*.

It kind of surprised Matt to see Arab or North African troops here in America given what was happening in the Middle East. The TV was solid propaganda and of no use, but through Jonathan they'd learned that the new Caliphate, with their new ally Russia, was gearing up to take on Israel and completely consolidate power in the area. Elsewhere, China had finished taking Taiwan and Mongolia. Word on the street was that an American sub had sunk a brand-new Chinese sub of the hunter-killer variety near Hawaii a couple of weeks before. War was on the horizon.

Matt saw two Auxiliaries, one holding a pistol and scanner, pat-searching a woman while her little boy and girl looked on. They made him think of Abby and Kaleb, both back at the house. Through Braithwhite, Matt had learned that their grandmother they'd been heading to find in Medford all those months ago had passed on. Their parents had never applied for IDs and were presumed dead, though Matt, after breaking the hard news to both children, had reminded them that Kyle and Amber weren't on that list either and were alive and well, so there was hope.

Matt checked the address on the small piece of paper in his hand—literally ready to eat it should that prove necessary. He was meeting a contact who supposedly had a fully unlocked and private SpyPhone, a full Peace Enforcement model, not the limited one issued to Auxiliaries. Sitting around talking one night, Uncle Rob had told them about the old Green Beret in Wyoming who'd had one. Something like that would be one heck of a powerful tool, useful in a myriad of ways. They all did their best to innocently inquire about them as they went about their business. Eventually, DeSean had struck paydirt.

Matt knocked twice, then three times more. The door cracked open slightly. "Yeah, what?" came a raspy voice. Warm air reeking of tobacco smoke and body odor drifted out.

"Here to see Davis. I'm a buyer."

The door opened further. The man standing there was short, stoop-shouldered, and gray haired. "Well, c'mon in already. Need to check you out first."

He led Matt to a small room and closed the door. Matt stood there for about a minute, heard a faint *hum*, and the door across the room opened to show a bespectacled younger man, about Matt's own age, standing there.

"Checking to see if I was clean?" Matt asked.

"Exactly. Way easier than the manual method."

Matt stepped into the next room, filled floor to ceiling with various tools and electronic equipment. There were no less than four work areas holding different devices in various states of disassembly. The air smelled of solder, ozone, and burnt plastic and there was electronic music pumping at a low volume.

535

He saw the SpyPhone on the far workbench. "Mind if I test it out first? The price is pretty steep, after all." Matt wasn't too worried after seeing Davis's setup. If the device didn't work, they knew where to find him.

Davis shrugged. Matt picked it up and turned it on. After adding a password, he navigated to ACTIVE SCAN. Holding it flat, he turned it toward Davis and saw no change.

"Stainless steel mesh wallet, buddy boy. Try your own."

Ah. Matt pulled out his own wallet, placed it on the nearest bench, and kept scanning. An orange dot popped up and he clicked it. All of the information on his card popped up along with a MORE icon. Curious, Matt clicked on it.

Wow. Matt scrolled, seeing notes detailing his military experience, work history, and his past addresses, but most eye-opening was a detailed history of where and when his badge was scanned, dating all the way back to when it was issued down in California. He frowned when he saw the notes on his record:

HIGH PROBABILITY (80) OF INSURGENCY / INSURGENT SUPPORT BASED ON SCAN HISTORY (ALGORITHM: MAIN CORE)

WAS ASKING SOME OF THE VENDERS HERE ABOUT UNLOKED SPYPHONES AND WARE TO GET ONE (J. MARTINEZ - OPEA) **DATE/TIME/LOCATION INFO**

LOITERING AROUND THE DISTRO ASKING ABOUT SALVAGABLE ITEMS. SAID HES PART OF SOME NEW COMPANY THAT IS PAYING FOR JUNK. NEVER HEARD OF THE OUTFIT. STAY ALERT FOR THIS GUY. (SGT P. REDMAN - OPE) **DATE/TIME/LOCATION INFO**

Matt remembered that last encounter from a couple of weeks ago. Word was starting to get around about White River, and Peace Enforcement didn't hassle him anymore.

Matter of fact, they were a pretty good source of leads.

"So, what's the secret?" Matt asked. "How am not going to get tracked and arrested with this thing?"

Davis, arms akimbo, gave him a wan smile. "You get caught with it, you're in deep doo-doo, bud. But tracked? No. I turned that off when I flashed it. I had to undo the voice recording capabilities the hard way, by taking apart the case and disabling the hardware."

"So what keeps the government from figuring out my SpyPhone isn't legit?"

"Let me explain. The login password was really easy to crack. It's just to get into the device itself. There's not much functionality if you can't get on to the government network. The network authentication works on a shared encryption key plus the device's MAC address. The encryption key is two hundred and fifty six bit. That's way too stout to break. But as long as your device is whitelisted by MAC address, even if the encryption key gets changed you're good to go."

"Can I get kicked off that whitelist?"

"No. That's the hole in their setup. When I flashed the firmware, it included a *spoofer* and about two dozen other MAC addresses that I know are good to go. Every time you boot up, it picks a different one. One, this makes it ridiculously difficult for you to be tracked by usage alone. Two, even if several of the MAC addresses are taken out of commission, you still have a usable device. The bad ones get erased from the device automatically. Down the road, if things tighten up and you're only down to a couple of valid MAC addresses, come back and see me and we'll reflash. Satisfied?"

"Yeah." Matt took off one shoe, then the other, and pulled on the heel of each one. "Here you go. Four ounces of gold." That had been the difficult part, negotiating with Kyle and convincing him to part with one-tenth of his small pile of gold. But he had eventually seen the value in having an off-

Michael Zargona

grid SpyPhone as well.

CHAPTER FORTY-SEVEN

Wednesday, Second Week in June

Kyle closed his Bible. "Besides the usual, are there any prayer requests?" He and several others sat in the living room of the country home where Matt and his crew had been holing up. They'd done their best to continue the Bible studies and discussions they'd held up at Sunshine, but geography was now an issue. Though it felt good to go out occasionally, there was always a risk of being caught, even using the quiet country roads between the two houses. Amber had stayed back this time though both Timothy and Loren had elected to tag along. Each of them was armed with a concealed pistol; getting picked up with no ID was essentially a one-way ticket to a FEMA camp—or worse.

Roger Van Horn, their host, held up his hand. The stocky, balding man had been an easy convert for Braithwhite's people. He'd had all of his cattle and chickens confiscated without compensation. All had almost certainly been slaughtered immediately, the best cuts destined for the Feds themselves. "Some of you may have already heard, but the daughter of some folks down the street, the McBrides, went missing two days ago. Her name is Amy. They fear the worst."

Kyle nodded and bowed his head. Young women were

going missing. It had become a local epidemic. He had no doubt it was due to the UN troops and the more diabolical of the Peace Enforcers.

"Kyle," Loren interjected. "You've always said, 'If you're able to help with a need, you shouldn't just pray, you should *help*.' Maybe *you're* the one who God is going to use. Like all those people up at the lake. I remember that whole 'we're blessed to help others' chat you gave me when I showed up. The whole time there you went hunting and fishing to help keep them fed. You didn't just pray for food to fall from the sky. There *has* to be something we can do. I mean, we're not helpless."

"If you mean fight the UN and American government directly, no, I'm always against that," Kyle said. "My opinion hasn't changed." It had been somewhat of a standoff between him and Braithwhite. Kyle's trust in the man stemmed from Marshall, but he was less enthusiastic about the aims of whatever organization they were a part of. Kyle had agreed to render support where he could but had drawn the line at fighting the authorities directly.

"C'mon, Kyle, you took out half of that gang last fall by yourself," Matt chimed in. He attended their studies for the conversation but remained obstinately agnostic. "Now you're going conscientious objector on us? This is a legitimate threat. No different, really."

"Yeah," Timothy said. "I remember our study of Romans, up at the lake. Don't fight the authorities because they're established by God. But we're not talking about fighting the police who are just doing their jobs. These are rapists and murderers."

Kyle nodded. "You have a point. I take a pretty strict interpretation of that verse, partly because it's safer, but also because I don't want to skyline us. What would the occupation forces do if some of *their* people went missing for a change?"

"I'll go," Loren piped. "I mean, I'll be the bait. Y'know,

so we can draw them out."

"No way!" Timothy cried.

"I dunno..." Matt mumbled.

Kyle touched his chin. "I don' t like it, but it's probably the only way to get to the actual perpetrators."

"No. Use *me* instead." It was the high-pitched but surprisingly powerful voice of the youngest one in the room, Abigail. "Think about it, guys. Loren is a mom. Max *needs* her. And Timothy would go nuts if something happened to her. If I get hurt, so what? Who cares? I'm just some random orphan."

"You're not an orphan to *me*," Matt exclaimed, red-faced. "*Everyone* in this room cares about you, Abby. Don't think for a minute you wouldn't be missed if something happened to you."

Kyle's eyes stung with admiration at her courage. What a sad world, where girls felt the need to become *rape-bait* in order to bring about justice. Horrified, he realized Abby, at twelve, would be just as enticing a target for those monsters as seventeen-year-old Loren.

"No, Abby," Kyle began, "there's *no way* we will let you do that. I can hardly believe I'd even consider putting Loren in that kind of danger, but I can't think of a better way to draw the worst of them out and send a clear message. You all *do* realize that their reaction might be to flood this area with troops and tear it apart, right? The whole 'nail sticking up gets hammered down' routine. And that's if we don't get shot up in the process, or they don't roll up in a bulletproof APC to snatch Loren."

"I get the risks," Loren said flatly. "I'm all for *where* and *when*."

It was nearly dark. Kyle leaned over and whispered to his uncle. "See anything?"

541

"Nope."

That thermal sight was a nice boon for night work. Kyle sat, on his knees in the ditch, clutching his Bushmaster AR while scanning both approaches. He would have liked one of the harder-hitting rifles, just in case they ran up against body armor or vehicles, but he also needed an optic he could see in near darkness. Not only did the AR have an illuminated sight, it had an LED flashlight mounted in front of the handguards, once surprise was no longer needed.

"Headlights, coming our way," Marshall called out in a harsh whisper. Kyle had given his old friend Greg Samuels' small gun collection. This evening, Marshall was using the man's HK91 rifle.

Loren stood, trying to look bored, at the bus stop on the corner. She was wearing a form fitting dress, one of the many outfits they'd scavenged courtesy of their salvaging operations. The plan was simple. If anyone came by and tried to lay hands on Loren, they'd pop up and demand their surrender. It was a concession they'd agreed on, both for Kyle's conscience and Loren's safety. If guns started blazing she'd be caught in a crossfire. This way, they'd capture some much-needed weapons plus some uniforms that may or may not come in handy down the road. And probably a vehicle, too.

An open-topped drab green vehicle, with four soldiers inside, slowed. Kyle had seen ones like these before, while in the Marines. The Recon guys used them...they were made by Mercedes. Last time he'd seen his Uncle Rich, he'd bragged he'd bought one, the luxury civilian version.

"Hey! You, girl! You par-tee?" the driver yelled. The accent sounded German.

Loren shook her head. "I'm waiting for a friend."

"No. . .you par-tee!" shouted one of the laughing young soldiers in the back seat. "You come with us and par-tee!"

"No thanks."

"Not asking, telling," the front passenger chimed in. "You get in."

Loren stepped back from the road. The soldier in back, nearest to the road, hopped out. While they clearly had rifles in the vehicle, none were in their hands. They were comfortable—probably a bit drunk or stoned—and their guard was all the way down. Kyle knew that wouldn't be the case in the future if they pulled this off. He held, waiting, until the soldier grabbed Loren by the arm and tried to drag her back.

"Let *go* of me!" she hollered.

Kyle staggered upright and pointed his AR right at the driver. He didn't have to glance around to know that Uncle Rob, Marshall, Matt, DeSean, and Timothy had done the same to each other soldier. Even Loren had gotten into it, shoving the barrel of Matt's scavenged .38 revolver into the ribs of her would-be kidnapper.

"Surrender!" Kyle shouted. "Put your hands up!"

All the men, wide-eyed with fear, immediately complied. What would terrify them more, the idea of retaliation, or what their command would do to them when they returned? *If* they returned.

"*Steigen Sie eines, idioten,*" Uncle Rob bellowed. Kyle had forgotten that he'd spent years serving in Germany. It had to be surreal for him to see the *Bundeswehr* operating in the U.S.

"*Herr, erbarme dich unser!*" one of the men moaned.

"Step out of the G-wagon and strip down to your *unterwäsche. Schnell!*"

◆ ◆ ◆

Rob drove the captured Mercedes to a nearby abandoned house, opened the garage, and simply parked it inside. They all holed up at the Rosenberg's place that night.

543

Now, mid-morning, it was plenty safe to hit the road back to the apartment. Marshall and DeSean loaded their gear into the lockbox. Unfortunately, none of those German M4-type rifles were coming along. To be prudent, they'd split the four up between the country homes. It would be bad enough if their apartment were ever raided. Captured military weapons would bump the consequences into another category altogether.

Rob turned in at the prominent wooden sign that had once read *Heron Park*. At some point, some enterprising screwhead had carved an "i" in between the "O" and "N" of "Heron".

"That was about the *easiest* operation I've ever done," DeSean quipped from the back seat.

"Yeah, well, it ain't gonna be like that *next* time," Rob reminded him. "Their behinds'll be puckered a lot tighter around here for a while."

"If it makes them think twice before plucking girls off the road, that's fine with me," Marshall said.

They got out, leaving their weapons locked up in the truck. There were far too many prying eyes around, even with cased weapons. They'd wait 'til dark.

"I think I'm gonna crash," DeSean said as Rob opened the door to their apartment. The young man had pulled watch through most of the night.

"All right. I'm gonna check the news," Rob said.

He saw Marshall raise an eyebrow. "You think we made the news?"

Rob shook his head. "No chance in hell. Way bigger things cookin' out there. Plus, they'd be too embarrassed to report that some random guys stripped down UN soldiers and took their guns. It might give people *ideas*."

The TV they'd taken home from work, one of the fancy models with a white, curved bezel and Ultra HD screen, came alive. It was the President, giving an outdoor speech with a crowd of seated dignitaries and other VIPs behind her.

"—*mise that we will restore elections next year. And furthermore...*"

"Wait," Rob whispered, rubbing his eyes. "It can't be..."

There, behind the President of the United States of America and to the left, seated in the front row, was *Susan*. His big sister.

CHAPTER FORTY-EIGHT

Monday, First Week in July

The troop transport van bounced noisily down the country road, causing some of the PE troops in the back to curse and complain. Lew Riggs, sitting in the front passenger seat, just smiled. If this place proved to be an insurgent hideout, it would almost certainly push him up into Permanent class. Permanent, as in he'd no longer have a monthly quota to maintain. No more training schlubs like Traylor, who was on a detail at the north JBLM refugee camp today, searching for insurgents. Permanent class would open the door to training positions, desk jobs, even supervisor roles within the Auxiliaries. Once Riggs was Permanent, he'd be home free.

"You go out on the raids much?" his driver, a middle aged Forcer with dark hair and olive skin, asked. "I mean, most Auxies don't wanna be anywhere close once the shooting starts."

"Oh yeah," Lew replied. "I like to see the job done, that's all."

"Man, I hear you. I know all about gettin' your hands dirty."

Lew turned to face the man. "Yeah?"

"You know it. When this all went down, I was out in Florida, right? Fresh out of the pen. My best friend had taken over my business. I got together some old compadres and we started to jump from place to place, hittin' the soft targets and such. Have to be careful, down there. The 'hoods full of gun-totin' rednecks look just like the ones full of retirees if you don't know what to look for. Know what I'm sayin'?"

"Sure thing, chief."

"Craziest thing I ever saw happened right around that time. Me and my boys rolled this whole rich 'hood. Most gave up easy, a few didn't. One guy, though, get this—I'm about to blow him away for lying to me, and he just seizes up and dies right there. My jaw hit the floor, y'know?"

"That's savage," Lew said. "Florida, huh? You're a long way from home, brother."

"Right? Things got bad. I mean, there was nothin' left to take from people. So we ended up just jumping people leaving the food lines." The older man chuckled. "That didn't last long. I got picked up and the choice was the work camps or *this*." He tugged at his uniform shirt. "My unit got moved out to Texas, for the *quar-an-tine*. Did nothin' but sling body bags for two months. None of us trusted the vaccine to work, y'know? Eventually, a few of us got shuttled up here."

"Damn. That is quite the trip."

"So, my man, how'd you find out about this place we're goin' to?"

"Kinda different. We got a tip, not even one of my contacts. My supe asked me to keep an eye out around curfew. There was a lot of coming and going from a few houses. I kept watch, bided my time, and got to know their patterns. Then, a few days ago, I struck gold. Spotted a couple of guys with rifles moving through the woods, trying to stay out of sight. They would have got away with it if I wasn't right there. Took some pictures and here we are."

"Randyites?" the driver asked.

"Probably."

Lew watched as the lead vehicle in his convoy, a dark SUV, pulled into the long driveway up to the house. Two small children were playing in the front yard, oblivious.

◆ ◆ ◆

Amber Flanigan placed the last clean plate on the rack to dry and pulled the plug, draining the sink. Making the move down from the lake hadn't been all roses, but running water and electricity were a blessing. The Rosenbergs had gone to nearby Orting for a few days to help their son and daughter-in-law repair the roof of their house. Amber intended to reward their hospitality by thoroughly cleaning the house. Kyle was out at Matt's. There was some important meeting that included Marshall and the other salvage guys in the "inner circle".

She heard the crunch of gravel and peered through the open window over the sink. It appeared Braithwhite was paying them a visit.

But . . . odd . . . Kyle had mentioned he was heading over to the Van Horns' specifically to meet with the man and the rest of the inner circle. Change of plans?

Then she saw the large gray van with two long whip antennas and her breath caught in her throat. She focused closer, to the yard.

Bella. Cole.

Both kids had dropped whatever they were doing and were watching the two . . . no . . . three vehicles enter their yard.

"Timothy! Loren! Emergency!" she bellowed as she pulled the German army rifle from the closet. Timothy came crashing down with its twin in hand. Loren, holding her nephew, was right behind.

"The kids!" Amber shouted. "They're outside!"

Amber swung the front door open but was too late. Four men in gray with body armor and helmets were already out of that first SUV, and several more spilled from the back of the van. All held rifles.

"Kids! Run!" Amber screamed.

But one of Enforcers was faster, grabbing her daughter by the arm and then Cole by the collar of his shirt. "Got 'em!" he yelled triumphantly.

"Get down on the ground, now!" one of the Forcers shouted, weapon leveled at the doorway. Amber slammed the door shut and dove to the side. There were several sharp *cracks* as half a dozen new holes appeared in the door and surrounding wall.

"Hold your fire, idiot! We're here to take them in!" came an assertive voice from the outside. "Come out with your hands up! Don't do anything stupid! We have your children!"

Max was screaming, scared by the gunfire. "You three need to get out of here," Amber ordered. "The tunnel."

"No... we can't leave you!" Timothy growled, his face a crimson mask.

"Amber," Loren said, voice level. "Come with us."

"No," Amber whispered. "You've got to get to Kyle. I'm not leaving Bella and Cole behind. Don't die for my sake. Get going. Now."

❖ ❖ ❖

Timothy looked his fiancée in the eyes. "I'm not leaving. We *have* to fight! *Bella and Cole...*"

Loren shook her head. "She's right...if we stay, we're history. We surrender...and we'll never see each other again. Ever." She tugged at his arm, leading them downstairs. "She's made her choice," Loren said, "and she wants us to *live*. So let's *go*."

549

They ran down the carpeted stairs, into the basement, and through the open door into the large guest bedroom. Along the far wall was an inconspicuous closet. Timothy slid open the door and revealed wooden panels about two feet in diameter.

The Rosenbergs had discovered it. The passage only led to the horse shed and no further. Kyle had guessed it might have been for a moonshine or smuggling operation of some sort, back during Prohibition. The house was about that old. It wouldn't put them very far from the house, but it would give them a head start.

Timothy pulled aside the wooden hatch and set it aside. "You have a flashlight?"

Loren shook her head.

"Okay. Hand me Max and go through," Timothy asked.

His love complied and slid through. Handing the now merely blubbering one year old back, he slid the closet door closed, went through, pulled the panel back into place and by feel grabbed the rifle.

They heard a faint *crack* from above, then an avalanche of them all at once.

"Amber," Loren whispered anxiously.

"Yes. Let's keep moving," Timothy said, trying to keep his voice from wavering. He'd known this day might come. He'd envisioned being shoulder to shoulder with Kyle and other members of his family, though. Running away, leaving Amber alone, it seemed... *cowardly*. The temptation to turn back was very strong. *What will I tell Kyle?*

The truth.

"How far is it?" Loren asked as they felt their way along in the pitch blackness. A *thud* sounded above. An explosion.

"The barn," Timothy began, "is maybe a hundred yards from the house. Not far. Just keep moving, Loren."

There was another *thud*, then another, before they

reached the rebar rungs that led up to the floor of the barn. Timothy went first, sliding the hatch on this end to the side. Old hay and dirt fell into his face, forcing him to spit on his hand and wipe his eyes. The faint light in the barn hit him like noon sunshine and he squinted, hard, as he rose out of the hole.

"Okay. The barn should shield us from view . . . if they've stayed put. We're going to head out the far side. Gather your breath, we're going to be running hard. If we get separated, just make it to the Van Horns. Any way you can."

"You . . . you think, maybe, we could just hide *here*? Until dark?" Loren said as she crawled out.

Timothy shook his head. "Think about it. They're going to find that tunnel. Or just search the whole property. Are you going to trust Max to keep quiet?"

Loren looked away, agreeing but not pleased. Fresh tears ran down her already well-streaked cheeks. Timothy didn't blame her. She had grown tired of running away a long time ago.

"Okay. Here we go."

Timothy threw the door open and motioned for Loren to go first, clutching her nephew. He followed at a dead run, his bad leg complaining from the effort. Glancing back, he saw a dark column of smoke rising skyward where the house would be.

They broke out into the open now, heading for the forest which was at least five hundred long yards away. Just then, Timothy heard the angry *whizz-crack* of bullets followed by their matching reports off in the distance. They'd been spotted.

He turned, took a knee, and put the rifle to his shoulder. Flicking the selector up, he peered into the sight and put the crosshairs just over a Forcer standing still, rattling off a burst of fire. Timothy squeezed once, dropped the reticle on target again, and squeezed again.

Looking again, he didn't see his target. But the return

fire was getting fierce. He stood and started to zig-zag toward Loren, now a good hundred yards ahead. Through the din he heard the unmistakable growl of a big engine. Turning again, he saw a long, dark SUV tearing through the muddy field, headed straight toward him.

He flicked the selector all the way over to full auto. Pushing the rifle hard into his shoulder, Timothy pressed the trigger for a couple of seconds, peppering the vehicle with about half of the thirty round magazine. The windshield starred and the big machine swerved hard in the mud, hit a small rise, and flipped over onto its hood. The wheels kept spinning lazily.

Timothy snapped back to the moment. More *cracks* sounded around him. He turned and headed for the trees once again.

◆ ◆ ◆

Lew and his cohorts fanned out to search the property. The house was a total loss. One of the stupid Forcers had fired what was supposed to have been a CS grenade—tear gas—to smoke out any insurgents inside but had turned out to be high explosive. Then the return fire from the house started and all hell broke loose.

Whoever had been in there, they could shoot. The one holding the children had sprouted a new hole in his neck. Next, the commander, who'd ridden up in the lead vehicle, had taken a round right beside his nose, dropping him like a sack of rocks.

Then those two runners had emerged from the big barn out back. No one had caught up to them so far although there were a few on their tail. Lew tried the big swinging doors up front but they were locked or braced somehow. He strode around back and through the open side door of the barn.

"Hey, check this out," his companion called. "A big trailer." The shorter man was already working on the trailer's door, clearly locked, with a large knife. A long fifth-wheel job, real nice.

He looked to the side and saw a dark square in the floor. "I think I know how those two escaped, look at this here."

"Hnnh. Find a pipe or crowbar, will ya?" the Forcer demanded.

Lew started looking around when he heard a loud *pop*. The door to the trailer swung open.

Stepping inside, Lew saw a motherlode of radio gear on the table. Not something he could fence very readily. They started opening doors, drawers, anything that might contain something valuable.

Lew picked up the seat cushion by the table with the radio gear. Underneath was a storage cubby full of clothes. He threw them out and started to explore with his hands.

The near wall of the booth was unusually thick. Lew felt around the edge, got his finger around what felt like a loose piece of veneer, and pulled it aside. Something hit his hand and fell to the floor with a *plop*.

He picked it up. It was a small dark blue binder, fairly heavy. Plastic sleeve pages poked out from the edges. He set it on the table and flipped it open.

Gold. Big, round, glorious coins. More than he'd ever seen in his life.

The Forcer had stepped up next to him, and once he glimpsed the contents he inhaled sharply. They stood there, admiring the haul for a few seconds. *Jackpot!*

Lew caught a *glint* out of the corner of his eye and reflexively threw himself backward, toward the front of the trailer. The tip of the huge knife just missed driving deep into his stomach.

Lew stepped back again, quickly, as the man lunged forward, murder in his eyes. Lew's height and reach were an advantage, even in the tight confines of the trailer. Lew lashed out with his right foot and connected with the crazed Forcer's shin.

Stunned with pain for only for a split second, the determined Forcer advanced forward slowly, knife pointed straight out, guarding against another quick kick. Lew smiled, smoothly produced his CZ-75 from small of his back, and shot the man once, right at the base of his neck.

Working fast, Lew dragged his assailant out of the trailer and into the square hole, pushing the cover back into place. There was a trail of blood that he started to rub with the tip of his boot.

"Hey! We heard a shot! Everything all right?"

A wide-eyed Forcer stood by the door. "Had to blow the lock to the trailer," Lew said, thinking on the fly. "Got to check it out. Might be insurgents hiding in there."

"Good call," the curious one said and left.

Lew re-entered the trailer, gathered up the binder, and tucked it into his pants opposite his holster.

◆ ◆ ◆

"Answer is still no," Kyle said firmly. The all-hands meeting had stretched to almost dusk. If they didn't hurry, he'd have to stay put for the night. Lately the neighborhood had been crawling with both Auxiliaries and armed vehicle patrols, no doubt owing to their little raid three weeks ago. It wasn't the time to risk heading out. Heck, just a few hours before they heard what sounded like a small war off in the distance.

"Look, Kyle, be reasonable," Braithwhite pleaded. "This is our window to really make a difference. You think that street corner robbery you guys pulled off on your own amounts to a hill of beans in the big picture? What I'm talking about is striking to the *core*. I need everyone to cash in their chips for this one. And it looks like everyone else is in except you. Why?" Braithwhite swept his open palm to the side, fanning the others: Uncle Rob, Matt, DeSean, and Marshall.

"Sorry, Jonathan, I disagree completely that it will make any difference at all. Capturing or killing a bureaucrat, even a high level one, won't do a thing in the long run. They'll just replace him and move on. He's a cog in the machine. We can't take down the whole machine, all we can do is promote his deputy."

Braithwhite had become aware of an upcoming unofficial visit by Donaldson, the head honcho of the entire DHS, the man who'd done the radio and TV announcements they'd grown to despise. Braithwhite had already met with the commander of the security detail to "complement his efforts with local elements" and had mapped the entire route from wheels down at Boeing Field clear into downtown Seattle and the DHS regional headquarters.

The plan was to hit the convoy not long after it left the private airfield. It didn't even require that much subterfuge. DeSean would be the overwatch sniper, perched up high somewhere. The rest would be down on street level and inside now-abandoned buildings. Jonathan had been working down in Oregon for the last couple of weeks and was bringing up some extra muscle just for the occasion. The only thing they'd have to keep out of sight would be the three AT-4 man portable rockets Braithwhite had appropriated. Even the toughest wheeled vehicle armor would be no match for those. He also was providing a few grenades as backup. They wouldn't punch armor nearly as well but could definitely disable a vehicle.

It was a good plan, Kyle had to admit. They were on the inside and no one would expect a double cross this grand, this *audacious*. But he also felt his logic for staying out of it was sound. It was an assassination, plain and simple, and of someone who'd never directly done a thing to Kyle or his family.

"Uncle Rob, you told us a while back that you saw Mom on TV, clearly on the President's staff," Kyle said. "Will she be a target, too?" His uncle turned away, squirming in his seat.

"But wait a second," Matt interjected, "what about last Thanksgiving? You were chomping at the bit to go down and wipe out those scumbags, to go on the offensive. How is this any different?"

"Those *scumbags* were almost certainly about to head up and kill us first. Donaldson and his staff *aren't*. And, if you search your memory a little better, you'll remember I really tried to get those marauders to simply leave. I know it's hard for you all to believe, but I just want peace. I just want to be left alone to live my life as I see fit.

"Here's a quote for you all that's been on my mind lately. I've always liked it." Kyle flipped to a page in his green notebook.

"'*Returning violence for violence multiplies violence, adding a deeper darkness to a night already devoid of stars. Darkness cannot drive out darkness, only love can do that. Hate cannot drive out hate, only love can do that.*' The Reverend Martin Luther King, Jr. said that. Right along the lines with Jesus's words in Matthew chapter five. Jonathan, I have a lot of respect for you, but I can't be a part of this."

Braithwhite frowned. Clearly the former Marine Corps officer and senior DIA counterintelligence spook wasn't accustomed to being flat-out told, 'no'. "Marshall chatted you up as a great infantry Marine, a real straight shooter. When *I* agreed to get you away from that end-of-the-road lake, *you* in turn agreed to help as needed. Like I said before, I'm calling in that help. And as I've mentioned before, we're doing this because we need to send a message. Not just to the criminals running the show, but also to those sympathetic to our cause. We'll be able to say, "*We're* the ones who took out Donaldson. *We're* a credible force to rally behind. The Barnhall supporters go after pawns; we're after the queens and kings."

There was a hard knock at the front door. Kyle, thankful for the interruption, stood and peered out the peephole.

It was Timothy, with one of the ex-German 416s slung across his chest along with Loren holding Max. They were all covered in mud, grime, and scratches. Kyle quickly opened the door and got them inside and out of sight. "What in the world happened?"

"The house . . . got attacked. Raided," Timothy sputtered. The young man looked exhausted.

"But where is . . . Amber . . . and . . ." Kyle trailed off.

Timothy just slowly shook his head, not meeting his eye.

CHAPTER FORTY-NINE

Thursday, Third Week in June

Kyle scanned the immediate area with Matt's hacked SpyPhone. One of the features of the device was the ability to ping for others in the vicinity. It was a double-edged sword; when not in use, it required them to turn it off and remove the battery to block the signal.

Satisfied that they were in the clear, Kyle did just that, tucking the phone and battery into his pack.

Kyle was still numb . . . didn't know what to feel exactly. Neither Timothy nor Loren had actually witnessed his wife or children die. His mind told him they were gone. His heart held out hope they had been captured, taken away by their Peace Enforcement assailants. Timothy had said the children were outside when it all went down. Braithwhite had kept his ear to the ground but had heard nothing about the outcome. Unfortunately, what had happened three days ago was now all too common.

"This is it," Timothy whispered. "This is where we looped around and..."

"Doubled back," Kyle finished, remembering his recount of the escape. "Good move."

They continued down the trail and before long

popped out into the muddy field. The barn partially obscured the house, but from what he could see, it was a total loss. Very little remained, with several pieces of the yellow-painted siding scattered in the grass, blown out by an explosion.

Kyle moved closer, trying to look as if he belonged there while still checking the surroundings. Just because they were reasonably certain the authorities weren't present, that didn't mean there couldn't be an informant eyeballing the property from afar, looking for some kickback for ratting them out. The SpyPhone could scan or 'ping' for nearby NIDs, but the range wasn't that far, maybe fifty yards. He could plainly see no strangers were within that circle.

"I need to look. I need to make sure," Kyle said to Timothy, who trailed by a few steps. The house no longer smoldered but probably had some hot spots. He picked his way around the perimeter, trying to peer in. Some of the outer walls remained standing, but most of the roof had collapsed in whether by fire or explosion. They'd need something stronger than their two backs to move the debris and truly uncover anything.

If Kyle Flanigan was looking for some closure, it escaped him.

He kneeled, overcome suddenly with emotion. Kyle had done his best to tamp it down, to put on a strong front, but grief still bumbled underneath.

"LORD," Kyle began, head down. "I'm lost. I don't know what to ask for. I want my family back, God. Please lead me back to them. Please show me the way. In your Son's name, Amen."

Kyle stood, pressing the knuckles of his thumbs into his stinging eyes. Timothy stood next to him, clearly at a loss for words.

"Okay," Kyle said after half a minute. "Let's see what's left in the trailer."

They entered the barn and immediately Kyle saw the

door had been forced open. He swiftly drew his Glock and saw Timothy get his big SIG .45 out to match. Just inside, Kyle saw a brownish-red smear with half of a boot print in the middle.

"Blood," Kyle whispered as he pointed with his left hand. *Maybe someone Timothy hit during his escape. Or Amber, for that matter. Despite not being a gun nut she was a good shot.*

Looking to the left, he saw the cushion overturned. "Gold's gone."

But everything else seemed in order. Whoever had searched the place had seemingly boogied after discovering the coin binder. Kyle understood the reasoning—it was a considerable haul in any age—but was merely a significant fraction of what Kyle had kept out here. The additional hiding spots, including the big ones in the dividing walls, were intact. He still had his few hundred ounces of silver along with several of the guns. It didn't surprise Kyle that all the valuable communications gear remained. None of it was compatible with the secure, cellular communications network mandated for federal use.

Kyle picked up two of the heavy ammo cans and trudged out to his Dodge. Timothy followed, carrying one of Kyle's Vepr rifles in each hand.

"Matt says you're reconsidering going on that raid," Timothy said.

Kyle nodded. "Yes. I am. More than just reconsidering. I'm going."

"Because of all this? What happened?"

"This may surprise you, but no. It isn't about revenge and it isn't about getting justice for Amber, Bella, and Cole. Because there's no satisfaction to be had there. Not for me."

"That's sort of what Loren said," Timothy said solemnly. "About Thanksgiving. She didn't feel any better knowing the killers were dead. It didn't change the fact that her family was still..." Timothy trailed off.

Kyle nodded, acknowledging he knew that the young

man was just trying to be polite. "And I'm not going because our friend Mr. Braithwhite suddenly convinced me of his cause. It's still not clear who exactly steps into the massive power vacuum they'd create if . . . *when* they're successful. Who's to say the next guy will be any better? I don't like the thought of being a pawn in something I don't understand.

"But to answer your question, I'm doing it because I want to do what I can to make sure I don't lose more people than I already have. If I sat out and something happened to my family and friends, something I could have maybe prevented, I don't know where I'd be."

"What about me?" Timothy asked as they walked back for the next load.

They hadn't shared many details of the plan with him for a very specific reason. Kyle stopped, looking the young man in the eye. "Timothy, you're not going. End of story."

"Hey, I can decide for myself," the teenager huffed.

"*No*," Kyle began, "it's *our* team and *we* get to decide who is coming along. Point number one: you have zero military experience. This is a relatively slick military operation with many more separate moving parts than the ambush last year. Point number two: you have a lot more of your life ahead of you than the rest of us. You have Loren. And, I know we've discussed this to death, you're the only father Max has. He loves you."

Timothy snorted. He really did love Max, but probably never figured Kyle would come at him from that angle.

"It isn't just my choice," Kyle continued. "The team is set. Just remember, if things go horribly wrong and we don't come back, you're in charge."

❖ ❖ ❖

Getting down there should be the easy part, Rob Overberg reasoned. There were several routes that avoided the permanent checkpoints—that part was straightforward enough. But running into an ad-hoc one, or simply being routinely stopped by an Auxiliary with a vehicle full of armed men would spell disaster for this exercise.

So they called the "bringing in the captives" play. Kyle and Matt had come over to the apartment yesterday; Matt in his BMW and Kyle carefully making his way on foot using the SpyPhone to ensure a clear path. Earlier that week, they had procured a large white van through the salvage business, which would make great cover once mated up with some U.S. Government plates off a vehicle destined for scrap. Cross took the driver's seat, with DeSean acting as his assistant on the passenger side; Rob and his nephews sat in the back, wrists held fast by zip-ties. They hid the weapons—including Braithwhite's heavy hitters—in long, green military shipping containers in the back.

This all hinged on the magic of Marshall's blue federal service NID. No one would expect that someone with that sort of guaranteed meal ticket would risk throwing it away for any reason. The common belief was that while a small handful of those in Peace Enforcement were insurgent sympathizers, blue carders never were. That, along with the official-looking plates, meant they were essentially immune from being searched.

I wonder what we're really getting into here. It wasn't the first time Rob had had doubts. This Braithwhite cat seemed sharp enough not to get embroiled in a futile cause. But Rob had been around the block more than a few times. He'd known of CIA field ops types who had gone to Afghanistan in the 1980s to train the *mujahideen* only to have their sons get shot at by the descendants of those former allies twenty five or thirty years later. In war, particularly of the civil variety, there were no good guys or bad guys. There was only "my team" and "their team". Or, sometimes, multiple "their teams" if things got fractured enough. Like his nephew Kyle, Rob wasn't in love with the idea of pinning his future to this cause. But it appeared to be theirs, for better or worse.

He glanced to the right. Kyle's expression seemed focused and stern. Rob hadn't mentioned his loss since that night. It hurt him, too. Rob had never felt grief like this, this particular flavor of loss, before. When he'd lost his parents, ten years apart, it was different; they had lived full, mostly happy lives. Same with his friend John. But not here. Amber had been a fine lady in every respect. While Rob would probably never be much for small children, the knowledge that he'd never again see his mother's namesake, Bella, or the curious and clever Cole, cut deep.

They crossed over Interstate 5 into the industrial area immediately south of downtown Seattle. When Rob had lived up this way, twenty years ago now, he hadn't spent much time in the city proper and it was completely unfamiliar to him now. What looked to be battered one hundred year old warehouses shared blocks with nearly brand new loft-space type buildings constructed for New Economy twentysomethings. Of course, there were no warehouse workers or computer engineers in sight today. Far from population centers, the food distros, and the enveloping ZOCs, they'd passed a couple of destitute-looking men, one slowly pushing a shopping cart, the other simply walking with an overstuffed backpack.

"Scavengers," Marshall remarked from the front seat. They knew the type; lots of them came by White River.

"Maybe I'm paranoid," Matt said, "but couldn't they be, y'know, informants? Watching over the area?"

"Anyone could be," Marshall answered. "We just need to act natural and look like we belong here. We can also use the bureaucracy to our advantage. It's going to take a while for an informant's suspicions to reach the convoy."

Marshall turned onto a dead end street, then slowly backed into one of the loading docks of the abandoned warehouse personally scouted by Braithwhite a couple of weeks prior. Keeping to the ruse, he and DeSean led Rob, Matt, and

Kyle inside and promptly cut their bonds. Both men left and, after a minute carried in one of the long storage boxes between them.

"Okay. Take your positions, facing the street," Marshall instructed. "Remember, these are the newer 'confined space' variant of the AT-4, and this warehouse is pretty open, but naturally be aware of who and what is behind you. DeSean and I will be up top, across the street and a less than a block north. Recap: hit the center vehicle first. Fire one rocket, ensure the center vehicle is destroyed, then hit the next best target. Obviously if it's not taken out, you have one more so make it count. We'll have the last rocket up top just in case.

"Hit them hard and *immediately* radio the signal and come to us. If we leave at the same time, we should all run into one another at the van in the alley. We'll scoot home from there. Braithwhite's Oregon crew should be here any minute. They'll cover us and mop up the scene before the area gets cordoned off."

With that, Marshall and DeSean left to move the van and get into position. Rob knew they'd make a good sniper team. They'd been rehearsing nearly non-stop after work for several days. Marshall, a trained Marine Corps rifleman and combat veteran, had already been nine-tenths of the way there. DeSean had merely added into the gaps in his knowledge of ranging and calling shots.

Kyle cracked open the box and the trio started to suit up. Rob donned an older, woodland-pattern Load Bearing Vest that they'd picked up through salvage. It held six loaded rifle magazines and they'd rather artfully sewn on the holster for the big .41 Magnum snub Kyle had returned to him. The design was obsolete, lacking spots to put plates; out of the three, he'd be the only one without body armor. Next, Rob picked up one of the two German rifles, the other slotted for Kyle. Matt had, after some complaining about it being bad luck, opted to bring the AR he'd picked up in California.

This way they all had rifles that took the same magazines and ammunition in case they needed to supply one another. It wasn't a hard decision to leave his big bore AR behind; it fired a completely different round and its thermal sight was not designed to lay down heavy fire in broad daylight. Marshall would have the remaining rifle captured from the Germans while DeSean would naturally have his slick sniper rig. Each man had two of the supplied hand grenades, the regular ol' round green fragmentation variety.

Satisfied he was ready, he looked up at Kyle, who had finished putting on his brown body armor and was checking his rifle. His nephews would be the rocket gunners; they'd actually fired the shoot and throw-away AT-4s before. Rob had only seen them in action, out in Wyoming.

"You guys ready?" Kyle asked. Rob nodded and saw Matt do the same. They took positions by the chest-high windows along the street, Rob the closest to the loading dock and furthest from the direction of approach. Fortunately for them, vandals had broken out most of the windows, making it a lot easier to just point and shoot as necessary. A window suddenly busting out would be a dead giveaway.

Time ticked by. Rob had the best view of Braithwhite and his team's planned approach route, but so far they were a no-show.

He checked his watch. *Ten minutes to go.*

Wait. A distant vehicle was approaching from the north, from the direction of downtown. But something was wrong. He dug into the front pocket of his Gore-Tex and produced his small set of binoculars.

It was one of those dull gray eight-wheeled APCs, nearly identical to the one he'd seen out in Kansas. But this one had a bigger turret, with *two* big barrels sprouting from the front, one fat and short, the other longer and more slender. As Rob watched, another appeared right behind it, rumbling in their direction. Its turret, different than the first, sported a ... *Gatling gun.* Both turrets scanned slowly back and forth at street level.

It didn't make any sense. If Braithwhite had so much pull that he could get a couple of *those*, he sure as hell didn't need their ambush crew. He could just roll up, blast the convoy with heavy machinegun fire, and drive off.

"Boys," Rob shouted, "unless Braithwhite is a lot crazier than I think he is, we're in big, big trouble."

◆ ◆ ◆

"Damn, look at *those*," Marshall whispered.

"Yeah, eyes on," DeSean said, right eye peering through the scope of his rifle. He'd swiveled it and his body when he'd heard the engines. "Braithwhite?"

"If Jonathan had those, he would have told me. No, this is either a coincidence, a bad one, or we're about to—"

As Marshall spoke, both vehicles had slowed to crawl. There was a distinctive *PUM PUM PUM* sound. Instantly, the near corner of the warehouse—where their other team was set up—exploded in a mass of concrete fragments.

Marshall whipped his handheld up and keyed the mic. "Bug out! Bug out!"

A muffled shot rang in his ears. DeSean was working the bolt.

Time to bring out the big guy.

He rolled away from the edge and came up to one knee. The AT-4 was unpacked and ready to go. Marshall picked it up, worked the tiny cocking lever, and made his way over to the edge.

Easily four hundred yards. It was a long shot for the unguided weapon. Hit or miss. Marshall took aim at the lead vehicle, which was still crawling forward and pumping grenades into the warehouse.

Now. Marshall fired, the backblast slapping his backside and kicking up a cloud of wet debris. He tossed the empty tube off the building and looked down.

There was a fresh crater in the street, about ten feet in front of the lead vehicle, which had stopped. The rear vehicle, scanning, stopped suddenly and whipped its gun up in their direction.

"DeSean! Move!" he yelled.

Time seemed to slow then. The turret of the rear APC winked with bright light, and Marshall heard a *whine* just as the three story office building shook slightly. Glass shattered below. Then another *whine*. To his left, DeSean slid to his knees and then fell backward. There was a piercing, pained scream.

"DeSean!" Marshall grabbed the bigger man by his camouflage shirt and dragged him away from the edge. Explosions sounded below and the building shook, harder this time. He looked down at his companion. Teeth clenched, eyes closed. A dark patch was starting to spread from his upper left chest, near the collarbone.

"Brother, let's go! I'll carry you!" Marshall cried.

The former soldier shook his head and held out his right hand, the one with the missing fingers. "I . . . can . . . walk . . ."

Marshall grabbed it and hauled DeSean to his feet. The man winced, obviously in great pain.

"My rifle . . ." DeSean sputtered, eyes now open.

Marshall shook his head. It was only fifteen feet away but it may as well have been on the other side of the moon. The cracks of machinegun bullets whizzing over their heads made it clear that approaching the edge of the building was not survivable. "No. Let's *go*. Rifle's gone. We need to get out of here and get you patched up. If you're still alive now, you'll survive," Marshall said, but it felt hollow. *How in the hell are we going to get away?*

❖ ❖ ❖

The wall exploded, missing Matt with the biggest fragments but covering his uncle, twenty feet away, with light gray dust. Matt ran over to him. "Uncle Rob! You okay?"

More explosions jarred the building. Matt heard his uncle cough several times. "Yeah! I'm just peachy! Hit those bastards with the rockets! Now!"

Matt ran back, picked up the heavy tube, and slid it just slightly out the window. He looked back. Kyle was farther down along the wall. At this angle he'd be somewhat behind Matt and about fifty yards to his left. "Kyle! Going hot!"

"Go!" his brother yelled. Matt could see he was lining up a shot as well. He turned and looked out the shattered frame. There was a loud *CLAP* and the ground in front of the lead vehicle exploded with a resonating *BOOM!* Asphalt chunks were thrown all over the street, but the lead APC remained intact.

CLAP! BOOM! Kyle fired, his rocket sailing over and impacting a building behind. They were well beyond the effective range of the weapon. . .several hundred yards. Matt held his fire, waiting for the vehicle to come closer.

But it held position in front of the crater, still firing. The wall above and between he and Kyle shattered, sending more chunks of concrete earthward. A smaller one, about the size of a cue ball, struck Matt in the left shoulder, stinging despite the padding provided by the armored SWAT vest.

"We need to bug out!" Kyle yelled. "Send that rocket!"

Matt aimed in at the lead vehicle, held over for the extreme range, and pressed the firing stud. Nothing happened. Stunned, he reworked the charging handle and sighted in again. Still nothing.

"Matt!" Kyle shouted.

Matt examined the outside frantically, looking for anything he might have missed. It took a few steps to make the rocket ready, and he'd clearly done each one. "It's a dud! Misfire!"

"Throw it out the window!"

Matt obliged, tossing it like a spear, then, peered through the window once more. Two more vehicles—large vans in the same color scheme as the upgraded Strykers—had pulled up and just behind the lead vehicle. They had already disgorged a few men each. Each wore the standard PE gray with those black tactical vests and matching balaclavas with gray helmets.

Rifle fire rang out in his uncle's direction, three short bursts from his weapon. Kyle chimed in as well with three of his own. There were several long bursts of return fire, the thrumming of a heavy machinegun, then the far corner of the building, next to the empty storage box, gave way completely with a massive *CRASH*!

Uncle Rob came up beside Matt in the still-settling cloud. His bearded face was a grayish mask of caked concrete dust held fast by sweat. "Let's *di di mau*, boys!"

Matt hurried over to his brother, who was lying flat on his back, hands out at his sides.

No!

"Kyle! What happened? *Are you hit?*"

But Matt could see what had happened, even in the poor light inside the warehouse. The right side of his Interceptor armor, near the ribs, was gouged out badly. Something had struck the edge of his steel SAPI plate and penetrated his side. Kyle's breathing was ragged and his eyes fluttered.

"We need to go, *now!*" his uncle cried. "Let's get him up! C'mon!"

"No, I'll take him!" Matt shouted back. "Get to the front of the building, up by the offices! Clear it out and get to the street! Go!"

Uncle Rob raised his eyebrows, nodded, and scurried away.

Matt threw his brother's arm over his shoulder, grabbed his midsection, and with a mighty heave picked

Kyle up in a classic fireman's carry.

He turned toward the door, which still swung slightly from Uncle Rob's passing just moments before. Already laboring hard, Matt trudged toward the door, and turned sideways to get through.

An intensely bright flash.

BOOOM!

Matt stumbled into the tight linoleum-tiled hallway, mostly deafened by the flash-bang. Losing his night vision was of little consequence; the passageway was pitch black once the door automatically swung shut.

Commotion—to the rear, by the entrance to the warehouse. Voices.

"Search the room! You three, come with me!" It was a surly man's voice, clearly in no mood to negotiate.

There was a dim sliver of light up ahead. Around a doorway. Matt pressed forward, willing his fatigued legs to keep pumping. No matter what though, their unburdened pursuers would catch up very soon. He pushed open the not-quite-latched door and discovered a lunchroom.

Sunlight streamed through more broken windows. Not a great room in which to set up an ambush. They'd probably throw another flash-bang in here anyway. The one in the warehouse had been sixty plus yards away and had still stunned him a bit . . . this room wasn't even fifteen yards wide.

"Hang in there, bro," Matt whispered. Kyle answered with a faint grunt.

Matt stumbled over to the far side of the room, set his AR against the wall, and opened the door. Another long hallway, but better lit than the first owing to the open office doors along its length, stretched about twenty yards and turned to the left.

At the floor, Matt spied a gray plastic doorstop. He kicked it into the hallway, grabbed his rifle, shut the door, and blocked it with several hard kicks from his booted foot.

It wouldn't hold those chasing them for very long, but Matt could and would use any advantage presented.

He lurched around the corner. The hallway simply doglegged again to the right. At the end of this longer stretch hung a useless white and green "EXIT" sign, long out of battery power in this electrical dead zone. Though it was much dimmer than the first part, Matt could make out a door handle below the sign and to the right.

"Okay, Kyle, let's get out of here."

Matt lurched forward and was almost to the end when he heard the pounding from behind, from the blocked door.

"Matt..." Kyle croaked.

"What, bro?"

"Put...me...down."

Matt paused. The Enforcers would be on them in just a few moments. He couldn't fight with Kyle on his back. Here, at the end of the hallway, would have to do.

"Okay," Matt whispered as he pushed the door open.

"No...here. In...the hallway."

"No way, bro. This area's gonna get hot in a hurry." He squatted and set his brother down inside the doorway. Now, open to the air, Matt could feel the sticky wetness on his neck and the back of his head.

His brother's blood.

Kyle tilted his head to look him in the eye. It seemed to take tremendous effort on his part. "Matt...just go. I'll... I'll cover you. Go."

Matt looked at his brother's face. It seemed impossibly calm, though blood ringed his lips, mixing with the concrete dust. Kyle already had his Glock in one hand and one of the frag grenades in the other. *He's serious!*

"No. We do this together. I'm not leaving you!"

"God be with you, brother," Kyle whispered. "Take care of your family. *All of them.*"

There was a *thud* and something knocked around the

hallway. Quicker than Matt thought possible, Kyle pulled the pin on his frag and threw it with a snap of his right arm. It bounced off the wall on the right and around the corner.

Matt rolled back, tucking into a fetal position as his world exploded in light and thunder.

CHAPTER FIFTY
Friday, Third Week in June

Marshall Cross led a hastily-bandaged DeSean down the roof access ladder and into the building proper. They made it to the pitch black stairs and began to descend slowly by pure feel, every step down causing his companion to grunt with pain.

They were on the second story landing when Marshall heard the door open below and saw a flashlight beam pierce the darkness. Tucking the stock of the HK into his shoulder one-handed, Marshall waited until he could see the source of the beam, put the reticle just to the right, and pressed the trigger, sending a burst of four rounds down the stairwell.

The flashlight—almost certainly attached to the man's weapon—went tumbling away. When it came to a stop, it lit up the far wall.

There were voices, muffled by the closed door. *"In here!"*

Marshall leaned down and, as gently as he could manage, sat DeSean down against the wall. "Going to get loud. Plug your ears, brother." He dug into a cargo pocket and produced one of the frags. With a simple 'grab-twist-pull' he armed the grenade, milked it for just a second, tossed it down, and covered his ears with his hands.

The explosion was still near-deafening in the tight stairwell. Marshall opened his eyes. The flashlight had been extinguished but a new, much softer light pierced the dust and smoke. The door to the sun-lit lobby had been blown clean off its hinges.

Marshall looked down at DeSean, who still held his eyes closed tight. "Wait here. I'm going to clear the lobby. Here's the radio. Try and bring Kyle and them up, all right?"

DeSean nodded, face strained, as he took the handheld in his right hand. Maybe it was just the light and the dust, but DeSean looked like he was turning a shade of gray.

Cross patted him gently on his good shoulder, turned, and advanced, carbine straight forward and sweeping back and forth. The same adrenaline rush. Familiar smell of gunpowder, explosive, dust, and sweat.

Fallujah. Where he'd picked up his lone Purple Heart. And memories, nightmares, that had only just started to fade in the last couple of years.

If I make it out of this . . . I'll have another ten years' worth. Maybe more.

There was a dead Forcer by the doorway and two more beyond. Marshall looked down at their shattered bodies, deeply saddened. *I wore that uniform, albeit under duress.* Deep down, he'd known once he pinned his fortunes to Braithwhite and his Cause that it would eventually come to this . . . fighting his own countrymen.

Braithwhite. Where in the hell was he, anyway?

A helmeted figure appeared in the lobby entryway. Marshall instinctively put the dot on his chest and fired another short burst. The Forcer collapsed to the marble tiled floor. Marshall quickly clambered behind the reception desk and looked out for another minute or so. Nothing moved.

Walking backward, he re-entered the stairwell and found DeSean lying on his right side, taking labored breaths. The radio lay in his right hand, completely silent. Marshall put an index finger on the man's neck. His pulse was fast and very weak.

"C'mon, DeSean, hang in there. We're going for the

van."

Marshall put his arm around the taller man and got him to his feet. While DeSean was conscious, moaning with pain, there was very little strength in his legs.

◆ ◆ ◆

Rob scanned the street from the lobby window. About three minutes before, the APCs had stopped firing, obviously because their own people were inside the building. Soon after, he'd heard a *thud*. Then nothing.

A squad of five had approached the other building. From his spot, Rob had zeroed in on one of them and put a well-aimed single shot in his side. The vehicles had held their fire, but not the troopies. Automatic fire had poured in. Holding his position, he'd tagged another one. For his diligence, Rob had earned a bloody line across his left cheek. A piece of the wall had been blown off and had sliced past him. It was a good trade.

THUD. BOOOM . . . BOOOM! Grenades. Behind him, further inside the building. Rob swiveled, covering the double doors leading into the myriad of offices, storage closets, and bathrooms that he'd passed through minutes before.

The doors burst open and Rob tensed, finger on the trigger.

It was *Matt*. Alone. Rob raised an eyebrow. His nephew looked like he'd had a bomb dropped on him. He'd lost his boonie hat, tan and black shemagh, and was covered in grime.

"Where's Kyle, kid?"

Matt looked up and coughed. "He . . . he got wounded. We got separated. They're not far behind!"

"You gotta be kidding, right? You *left* him in there?"

Matt stumbled over to him and fell heavily on to his back about six feet away. The doors swung open again and two masked Forcers brazenly busted through; right into Rob's line of fire. He dumped about fifteen rounds in a long burst, sending both men sprawling. Reaching into the vest, he pulled out a fresh magazine and slapped it home.

"So, again, where *exactly* did you leave Kyle?" Rob huffed. "If you're not going back for him, I sure am. You tell me right now. Is he alive?"

Matt coughed again. "I . . . I don't know. He took more of the blast than I did."

"Well, son, get up. We're going back in there."

Rob took the lead, walking cautiously. His body was already fatiguing. North of sixty, once you blew your initial burst of energy there just wasn't a second wind to gain.

Drained or no, he wasn't leaving his nephew.

Matt stopped right by a door. Beyond, inside the hallway, was nothing but shattered walls, bits of concrete everywhere. An 'EXIT' sign hung by one wire. "Here. Right here. But—"

"But what?" Rob barked. It was then he noticed a bloody smear on the floor, half in and half out of the doorway.

"He's not here. This is where I last saw him. There was so much dust . . . smoke . . . I grabbed for him after the explosions but couldn't find him. Then I saw the beams . . . the weapon lights. I ran . . . I ran until I found you."

Rob perked up, hearing the distinct sound of boots on a hard floor. "More coming our way. Let's go."

They scrambled back to the lobby. Rob looked out the window once again. The APCs had not moved an inch.

"All right," Rob began, "we're going to make our way to the office building, try and link up with the others. You can run, right?"

Matt nodded.

"Good, 'cause I barely can. Push me if you have to." With that he burst out into the street, not even glancing toward the armored vehicles. About halfway across, Rob heard the heavy machinegun open up on them. He could *feel* the huge projectiles passing through the air above him, buffeting his head and face. Despite his head start, Rob barely beat his much faster nephew across the street and into the alley.

Three launched grenades detonated behind them, in the street, nearly slamming Rob to the ground as he ran.

"Ahh!" came a yell from behind. Rob turned and saw Matt clutching his right arm with a black gloved left hand. "Got hit!"

"Keep moving! You're fine!" Rob shouted back.

"Hey! Over here!" It was a new voice. Rob turned back, starting down the alley.

Marshall. The van!

"Get in!" Marshall yelled.

They stumbled down the alley and tossed themselves into the back seat. Rob sat up just as Marshall hit the gas. DeSean was slumped in the passenger seat, eyes closed and barely breathing. His color looked...off.

"Where's Lep? *Where is he?*" Marshall asked anxiously.

"He...we got separated," Matt said. "We went back to find him, but..."

"But what?" Marshall growled.

"He's *gone*," Matt said with finality.

"Uh oh," Marshall said after a short pause, straight-faced. Rob had seen this out of combat vets, the ability to compartmentalize under stress. Grieving for Kyle would have to wait. "We're being pursued. One of the gray vans. One of you needs to get to the back and slow them down."

Rob nodded, crawled over the seat, and opened one of the back doors. The Forcer van started to swerve slightly, slowing them somewhat. He brought up the German AR and fired a couple of quick bursts. The van swerved harder, lost control and skidded to a stop right in front of a power pole.

"We've got more company," Rob said. "Drone."

"Can you hit it?" Marshall asked.

Rob looked up. It was at least several hundred yards

577

away. And way up in the air. "Maybe." He sighted in and dumped the rest of the magazine, about twenty rounds, in two long bursts. He was rewarded; while the drone didn't fall from the sky, it fell back and faded into the distance, headed elsewhere.

Satisfied, he returned to his seat next to Matt, who had his head in his hands, exhaling deeply. His nephew looked up, eyes red and puffy.

Rob felt his anger build. He didn't try to stop it. He'd trusted Matt to carry his brother out of there. Live or die, that was his one responsibility. And he'd failed. "Don't think you can just come cry on *my* shoulder, son. A fellow soldier would be bad enough, but your own brother? Matt, you broke the *code*."

◆ ◆ ◆

"Yeah. We're burned here," Marshall said as he dropped the binos. Their route back had taken them right by the salvage yard. Seeing some activity there, he'd parked a few blocks away to observe.

"Burned . . . like . . . ?" Rob asked from the back seat. They'd stopped briefly to rearrange and see to DeSean. The big man was now spread across the back seat in an effort to keep a good blood supply to his brain. Rob was doing what he could, keeping pressure on his wound. Nevertheless, he was fading.

"Burned like, there's an Enforcer van here, too."

"How?" Matt blurted from the passenger seat.

"Only one thing makes sense," Marshall said solemnly. "Someone got to Braithwhite. Probably earlier today. If it had been yesterday, or earlier this week, they would have just arrested us at our desks right here at work."

"Or Braithwhite double-crossed us," Matt opined.

Now it was Cross's turn to get angry. He trusted Jonathan. The man had delivered him from the work camps. Marshall could think of no reason why his friend would sacrifice them. "That just doesn't fit. Somehow, they got to him. They re-routed our target and hurried out some assets to take care of us. They knew we had some heavy hitters so they stayed back and out of range. Since White River is in Braithwhite's name, it was straightforward to come here and search the place."

"Well, that means our apartment is next," Rob stated. It, too, was technically Braithwhite's. "If they're not there already."

"Yeah," Marshall said. "Let's go."

◆ ◆ ◆

The apartment complex was clear. Marshall and Matt spent about twenty minutes loading up essentials while Rob played medic and lookout.

They'd finished up with the first few loads when Marshall spotted a speck in the sky, off to the northwest. "I think our drone friend is back," he quipped, bringing the binos up. That confirmed it; it was one of those four-rotor surveillance drones. He'd seen them flying around before, particularly within the established ZOCs. Unlike the military models he was more familiar with, these designs weren't very fast. They were built for surveillance, not pursuit.

"We can outrun that sucker," Marshall said, looking at Matt. "Hop in."

Matt complied and they sped off, heading east. Marshall had to temper his desire to simply floor it with the knowledge that would skyline them and invite more trouble.

"Still there," Matt said, looking back.

"We were losing it! What happened?" Cross asked.

"I saw the same thing. But here it is," Matt replied.

Must be a second one. Maybe this is the third one. They really want to keep eyes on us.

"The G-wagon," Rob quipped from the back. "That place isn't far from here. Speed up, get out of sight of this one, and we'll pull in the garage. There's enough space for both rigs. Unless someone took over the place."

"So . . . then we wait and take the Mercedes back?" Matt asked. "Do you not think *maybe* driving a stolen military vehicle in broad daylight might attract even *more* attention?"

"Open to a better idea," Rob shot back, glaring at his nephew. "And it doesn't have to be broad daylight. I say we wait a while, let things cool off. They aren't going to dedicate hundreds of men to cordon off the area. If they do, no plan is going to work."

"I'm going to give it a try," Marshall said.

CHAPTER FIFTY-ONE

Friday, Third Week in June

They lost DeSean just after they'd pulled in and sealed the garage again. He had faded without so much as a whimper. There had been nothing more they could have done.

Matt, still quite emotionally stunned, had worked to transfer their gear over to the G-wagon and put the stowed olive green soft top in place. Uncle Rob had barely looked his way, much less spoke with him. Marshall had not been much better. They'd simply waited until dark and drove back to the Van Horn's house. There hadn't been any heightened PE presence he could detect.

The vehicle lurched to a stop just off the country road. Matt gathered up his rifle and opened the door.

"Matt," Marshall called from the driver's seat. "Take care of yourself. And your family."

Matt nodded back. "Where . . . where are you two going to go?"

"Braithwhite knew some retired officers around here," said Marshall. "We even met with one of them, out over the mountains. But with checkpoints and what not there's zero chance we'll make it that far if there's a flag on our NIDs, which I'm sure by now is so. One of those officers had a cabin, a real nice modern one, well off the beaten path but on this side of the Cascades. Jonathan went up there, about a month ago. I have the directions in my gear. I think we'll head there first and lay low."

Uncle Rob didn't even so much as turn his head to acknowledge him. Matt watched as they drove off.

More people I'll probably never see again. Too long of a list.

Roger opened the door, a pistol in his right hand. "Hurry. Inside."

Des embraced him tightly, face wet with tears. "I—I thought..." she whispered hoarsely.

Matt looked over her shoulder into the small living room. Roger's wife, Cynthia, a waifish older woman with long, wavy gray hair, sat on the couch. Timothy and Loren sat together on the matching green loveseat. All three had long faces and red, bloodshot eyes. They'd been crying, too.

"It was on the news," Roger began softly. "A battle between Peace Enforcement and insurgents in Seattle. The report said all the terrorists had been killed. Was... was that—"

"Yeah," Matt said tiredly. "That was us."

Roger frowned. "Kyle." It was not a question.

Matt nodded once. All but Roger broke into fresh sobbing, and the old farmer put his head into his left palm.

"I don't think there is any question we—Marshall, Uncle Rob, and I—are going to be hunted down after what happened today," Matt said somberly. "Peace Enforcers were searching the salvage yard earlier. I'm sure we're on some list by now. Timothy, Loren, I think you need to take the kids and stay out in the barn for a while. Put together some packs. Take what's left of the MREs and storage food. If they come for me, well..." He didn't need to finish. The two had seen firsthand what happened when the Enforcers came looking for trouble.

Des broke her embrace and stepped back. "Jonathan. He needs to fix this. Is... is he even still..."

"Don't know," Matt said. "He and his crew never showed. Marshall thinks he was captured somehow, spilled his guts about the ambush."

"You don't sound so sure," Roger noted.

Matt shrugged. "It could be that. It probably was, really. But I never trusted him one hundred percent like Cross did."

"You mean he set you up? Possibly?" Roger said. "But ... what in the world would he gain? I don't see it."

"I don't either," Matt said. "But it's all academic unless I run into him and get his side. Which seems highly unlikely at this point."

He winced as he rolled over, arm expertly bandaged and disinfected by Loren but still raw. Matt, exhausted by the day, still struggled to sleep.

He's gone.

Did I really leave him? Did I abandon my own brother?

God ... I'm still not convinced You're out there, listening to me. Watching over me. Us. If so, why would You take the best among us? The ones who followed You the closest. I don't understand ... if all things are in Your power, how could You let this happen?

More to the moment, what is going to happen to Des and the rest? The income from White River had paid for the extra food they needed for all the kids. Even if both Matt and Des collected their maximum free handout, that alone would barely keep both of them fed. He'd talk with Timothy and Loren in the morning. It just might be best if they turned themselves in. It would mean their strange glommed-together family would disintegrate. While Timothy was an adult, the other kids were all orphaned minors and would become wards of the state. But that was better than slowly starving to death.

He felt the covers move as his wife slid in next to him. Earlier, she'd volunteered for first watch. Starting with

583

Greg's memorial last fall and even more so since leaving Sunshine Lake, Des had resigned herself to their present reality and had become more... helpful.

"Still up?" she asked.

"Yeah. Can't sleep."

"I understand," she began. "We'll get through this, honey. Let's just get to tomorrow."

"I wish I shared your optimism, sweetheart," Matt said, turning over to face her in the near pitch-black room.

"Matt, listen," Des said. "There's, ah, something I need to tell you. To share with you. I wish the timing was better, but..."

But what?

"I'm pregnant."

Matt exhaled loudly. "Whoa. I didn't see that coming." *How am I supposed to feel right now? I just finished justifying how I could give up all responsibility for the kids. And now, this.* "How long have you known, Des?"

"About a week. I didn't want to tell you before... today. I knew you needed to focus."

"Does... does anyone else know?"

Des started crying softly. "I only told one other person before you. I hope you'll understand why. A few days ago, I told Kyle."

◆ ◆ ◆

They'd sent two gray vans, identical to the ones Timothy had seen during the assault on the Rosenberg's property. *Possibly even the same ones.* He watched with the captured rifle's red dot, the 3x magnifier flipped into place. Among the hay bales in the loft they'd camped out for the night, but Timothy slept light and had been woken by the sound of the van's engines. The sun wasn't quite up but the pre-dawn light was plenty bright to see what was going on.

Loren crawled over on her hands and knees. "Timothy... don't shoot, okay? It's not worth it," she whispered.

"If they shoot first, it's on," he whispered back. "But everything is pretty calm. For now."

He watched, teeth clenched, as one of the Forcers led Matt out, wrists zip-tied, followed by Roger, Cynthia, a sobbing Des, and a couple more graysuits. One held Matt's SWAT vest and belt, while the other had a rifle in each hand: Matt's cop AR and the AK he'd picked up after the Thanksgiving firefight.

"You need to go and make sure Max keeps quiet," Timothy muttered. *That was a little sharper than intended.* "Please."

Her spot was quickly occupied by Abby and Kaleb. "What's going on? Are they arresting Matt and Des?" Abby asked, voice uncomfortably just above a whisper.

Timothy put a finger to his lips. "Yes," he said under his breath. "All of them. Keep quiet unless you'd like us all to join them."

There was a slam of the van door. *That's it. Our supposed 'last stand'. With me lying here doing jack squat.*

A pair of the Forcers broke off, one with a rifle in hand, the other a SpyPhone identical to the hacked one residing in Timothy's backpack.

Abby looked at him. "Wha—"

He put his finger to his lips again. "He's scanning. For ID cards... but maybe anything else. Heat signature. Stay still." The gap between the bales was tiny, barely enough to fit the front end of the rifle through, and the gap in loft door was equally small.

They were close enough now that Timothy could hear their conversation.

"—really one of the Seattle terrorists, the ones on the news?"

"Yeah, that's the word. Last of them, supposedly. A detachment from Thirty-Six raided the place they worked, some scummy front business. Heard that from McGregor... if you can believe that mouth-breather."

There was chuckling. "Better check out the inside while we're here."

"No pingbacks. Sure it's worth it?"

"You know Braddock. He'll ask. No point in lying when we can just open up, shine a light, and call it done."

Just below where they lay, the pair opened the main doors. A weapon light stabbed at the darkness for about ten seconds. There was a small squeak, behind him. *Max.*

"You hear that?"

"Yeah. Prolly a mouse or something."

"Forget it. Let's get back and hit the rack for a few hours. These early AM raids are a pain in my ass."

Timothy kept his rifle trained on the pair as they walked back, got in the second van, and both vehicles crawled away.

They waited a couple of minutes, just to be sure. "Okay. Let's get moving," Timothy said, at normal volume this time. He walked over and hefted his overstuffed pack. Inside was a change of clothes, some personal effects, half of Kyle's silver bullion (the other half split between Loren and Abby's packs), four water bottles, Kyle's two-way radio with the hand crank, a couple of spare boxes of ammunition for the SIG .45, about two hundred rounds for the captured German rifle, and Matt's remaining hand grenade. He broke the rifle down, wrapped it in his spare sweatshirt, and stuck the bundle into the pack.

"Hey, Matt did that. With his gun, when we came up from Cali," Abby noted, smiling. Then, the girl looked away, smile fading.

"No sense in alarming everyone we run across," Timothy said. "I'll still have a pistol handy. So will Loren."

His fiancée sat there on a nearby bale, holding Max, who was saying 'En' over and over, what he called his aunt. Timothy was, for now, 'Em.'

"Don't forget...I will too," Abby said, holding up the blue and silver aluminum framed Ruger .22 pistol Matt had given her. She smiled as she wiggled the looted gun.

"Maybe so," Timothy said. "But don't start thinking you're some kind of warrior all of a sudden. It's a last resort. It's probably best if you and your brother just run from any real trouble."

Timothy caught the girl's scowl as she turned away. If her fight actually matched her body, she'd be a giant.

They moved the packs down the ladder and attached them to the four bikes—Matt and Des's expensive road-race models and the two that Abby and Kaleb had recently acquired through the salvage business. Max, bundled against the cold, would ride in a toddler pack that Timothy and Loren would hand off as needed. It was too bad Matt and Des never had kids. A baby carrier on the back of one of the bikes would have been much appreciated.

"So...decided on where we're going?" Abby asked.

Timothy shrugged. "No. But I know what Kyle would do next."

"What's that?" Kaleb asked, clutching his blue and orange single-speed.

"Pray."

❖ ❖ ❖

Susan Overberg stared at the wrench on her desk, incongruous among the two LCD screens, keyboard, mouse, and neat stacks of bureaucratically indispensable paperwork. Just a standard stainless steel one, nothing special, half inch on one end and five-eighths on the other.

It was there as a reminder of her last conversation with her good friend Erin.

We are all just tools.

Susan had survived the assault last fall with little

Michael Zargona

more than some scrapes and a minor concussion. Erin had not been so fortunate. Most there that day had not. It had the beginning to a long, strange journey to her current station. Stepping into Erin's shoes, she'd taken over the distribution management of that particular ZOC, then replaced the intensely unlikeable Shandra after the woman took a promotion out in Texas. From there, Susan had replaced the regional director in charge of the states of Illinois, Indiana, Michigan, and Wisconsin. He'd disappeared without a trace right after the rise of the Barnhall insurgency. Only three months later, she had been tapped to fill a deputy director role within the now enormously unwieldy FEMA organization chart.

Ostensibly, she was to plan and execute the food distribution plan for the entire country. What she found, in reality, was that she had nearly zero control of the actual process. Susan, working with her team, would present a plan that would invariably either be vetoed or simply never considered by anyone; a passive-aggressive approach familiar to anyone who'd followed politics for more than fifteen minutes. Those who actually pulled the strings would route the distribution as they saw fit. Trucks, entire trains would go missing. Employees disappeared without a trace. Actual deliveries of X quantity of wheat, corn, or soybeans would fall far below promised levels. Those that made the promises faced no consequences for their faulty projections, but the intended recipients went hungry. No one had yet found a way to make an I.O.U. fill a belly.

It was strange, but coming to D.C. had been the path of least resistance. Most of the younger, hungrier, and more determined wanted to stay well away from the center of power. Out in the rest of the country, a director-level federal employee was akin to God and could run their affairs as they saw fit. Here, under the umbrella of the *real* power brokers, even a director had to watch his or her steps closely.

But it's all an illusion, brought on by blind greed and a

quest for power. There are no distant princedoms. For those that desire to know, one's every move can be tracked.

And now the shakeup had struck at the very top, right under the President. Director Donaldson had been assassinated. By one of his own security team, a bullet to the back of the head, if reports were to be believed. Without a word, his assassin had then turned the gun on himself.

There was a soft knock on the door.

"Come in."

It was Deirdre, her young assistant. As she was most every day, her dark blonde hair was done up in a tight French braid and she wore a sensible dark blue pantsuit. A tablet was in her left hand and tucked into her side.

"Director Overberg, I'm out in front of some news I need to share with you."

"More on Donaldson?"

She shook her as the door swung shut. "No, ma'am. It's about your family. Your sons."

Susan breathed in sharply. She'd known her youngest and Des had gotten into the national system, that much was easy to check. Both of her brothers as well. But Kyle and Amber had not. She'd tried not to think about why.

"Matthew was arrested by Peace Enforcement this morning. He was in possession of several proscribed weapons."

"Just out walking around?"

"Umm . . . no, ma'am. At his temporary residence. PE believes he was involved in an insurgent attack in Seattle that killed eight of their men."

Susan felt the blood drain from her face. Her vision swam, then returned. "What . . . what will happen next? To my son?"

Deirdre looked away. "Ma'am, I'm afraid the standard penalty with these charges would be capital. Execution in no more than thirty days unless there is a reason for a trial. There very rarely is. I'm so sorry, Director. And there's news about your daughter-in-law, Desirée. She was detained as well, though her charges aren't as dire. More of the conspiracy variety. According to the officer's notes, she's pregnant."

"Very well. I think I need to make a call, Deirdre. Thank you." Susan fought to keep her composure, to maintain that professional face despite her boiling emotions.

She'd been prodding those two since they got married to not wait until their lives were in order to start a family —sometimes that sense of order, of the right timing never happened.

But... not like this.

Susan casually picked up the wrench with her right hand and stared at it again, slowly spinning it with her fingers.

Whose tool did you become, Matt?

Susan put the wrench down, placed her hand on her mouse, and went to her contact directory. She didn't have many that owed her any favors, but there were a few within DHS and Peace Enforcement she could lean on.

Then she remembered. Deirdre had specifically said, "your sons."

Kyle.

Susan looked up, but the door had already shut.

TO BE CONTINUED

CAST OF CHARACTERS (IN ORDER OF APPEARANCE)

John: Retired public speaker.

Matthew Flanigan: Territory account manager for Dynamix Medical. Former U.S. Army MP (military policeman). Son of Roger Flanigan and Susan Overberg. Married to Desirée Flanigan.

Edward Vasquez: Regional Vice President for Dynamix Medical. Married to Samantha Vasquez.

Desirée Flanigan: Paralegal. Married to Matthew Flanigan.

Sergei Kostadinov: Engineering student, University of New Mexico. Former Russian Air Force fighter pilot.

David Levi: Postgraduate student/researcher, Technion (Israel). Child prodigy.

Samantha Vasquez: Housewife and charity volunteer. Married to Edward Vasquez.

Kyle Flanigan: Owner of Bene Praepara Supply. Son of Roger Flanigan and Susan Overberg. Married to Amber Flanigan. Father of Isabella and Cole.

H. M. Donaldson: Director of the Department of Homeland Security.

Amber Flanigan: Homemaker. Married to Kyle Flanigan. Mother of Isabella and Cole.

Isabella Flanigan: Daughter of Kyle and Amber.

Cole Flanigan: Son of Kyle and Amber.

Robert Overberg: Retired Military (U.S. Army). Brother of Susan and Richard. Uncle of Kyle and Matt Flanigan.

Abigail Thompson: From the Eureka area. Parents missing. Sister of Kaleb.

Kaleb Thompson: From the Eureka area. Parents missing. Brother of Abigail.

Susan Overberg: Semi-retired social worker. Sister of Robert and Richard Overberg. Mother of Kyle and Matt Flanigan.

Erin Young: Director of the Society for a New America (SNA).

Shandra Williams: Homeland Security liaison for the north side of Chicago.

CWO3 Marshall Cross: United States Marine Corps CBRN Officer. Friend of Kyle Flanigan.

Bill Klein: Union boss (longshoreman). Father of Mike Klein. Resident of Sunshine Lake.

Mike Klein: Longshoreman. Son of Bill Klein. Resident of Sunshine Lake.

Greg Samuels: Marine Corps veteran. Resident of Sunshine Lake.

Dillon Traylor: High school dropout. Living near Sunnyside, WA.

Richard Overberg: Retired financial analyst and broker. Residing in Tarpon Springs, Florida. Married to Dot (Dorothy). Brother of Susan and Robert. Uncle of Kyle and Matt Flanigan.

Kevin Biemal: Marina employee in Eureka, CA.

Lewiston Riggs: Gang member from the Spokane, WA area.

Andy Peterson: Resident of Astoria, OR. Friend of Kevin Biemal. Husband of Yuki.

Yuki Peterson: Resident of Astoria, OR. Wife of Andy.

Timothy Benson: Senior in high school. Resident of Sunshine Lake. Son of Tom and Jennifer.

Loren Pearce: Junior in high school. Resident of Rembrandt Village. Aunt of Maximillian.

Maximillian: Infant nephew of Loren Pearce.

Malachi Hayden: Junior in high school. Resident of Rembrandt Village.

Kent Lawson: Administrative leader of the Lake Cushman residents.

Terry Graham: Medically retired U.S. Army Ranger. Resident of Lake Cushman.

Jeanie Suarez: Former Houston police officer. Resident of Sunshine Lake.

Lenny Jones: Vietnam veteran, U.S. Army. Resident of Sunshine Lake.

Norris McGwire: WWII firearms collector. Resident of Sunshine Lake.

Jerry Goodridge: Healthcare systems analyst. Son in law of Kathy Rex. Brother-in-law of Melissa Rex. Resident of Sunshine Lake.

Dr. Aaron Schlesinger: Economics professor. Resident of the southern JBLM refugee camp.

Dr. Paul Reed: History professor. Resident of the southern JBLM refugee camp.

Major Melissa Rex: Field surgeon, U.S. Army. Daughter of Kathy Rex. Sister-in-law of Jerry Goodridge. Stationed at JBLM.

Rod Burkett: Electrician. Brother-in-law to Timothy Benson. Resident of Sunshine Lake.

Jeff Morrison: Resident of Sunshine Lake.

Mel Gautier: Father of Travis and grandfather of Jake. Resident of Sunshine Lake.

Travis Gautier: Son of Mel and father of Jake. Resident of Sunshine Lake.

Jake Gautier: Son of Travis and grandson of Mel. Resident of Sunshine Lake.

DeSean Hupp: Medically retired U.S. Army Ranger. Resident of Lake Cushman.

Randy Barnhall: Head of an insurrection movement. Whereabouts unknown.

Jonathan Braithwhite: Retired Marine Colonel and DIA employee. Homeland Security liaison for a Peace Enforcement field division.

Cyrus "Codge" Colliers: Retired Marine Colonel. Friend of Jonathan Braithwhite. Resident of open country east of Chelan, WA.

Roger Van Horn: Associate of Jonathan Braithwhite. Resident of Buckley, WA. Husband to Cynthia.

Cynthia Van Horn: Associate of Jonathan Brathwhite. Residen of Buckley, WA. Wife of Roger.

Michael Zargona

GLOSSARY OF TERMS

1911: In the context of the book, denotes any handgun based on the original military 1911 or 1911A1 pattern. Most often chambered in .45 ACP though available in a bewildering variety of cartridges. Standard U.S military pistol from 1911 until 1985.

ACOG: Stands for Advanced Combat Optical Gunsight and is manufactured by the American company Trijicon. There are dozens of variants of this optic produced since its inception in 1987, but most feature low magnification and a battery and/or tritium illuminated reticle.

AK: Stands for *Avtomat Kalashnikova* or "Kalashnikov's Automatic Rifle" after the designer, Soviet Gen. Kalashnikov. A rugged design that became the basis for the most produced military rifle in human history, the AK-47. Others based on the design include the AK-74, RPK, and dozens of former Communist Bloc variations along with their civilian counterparts.

AO: Area of Operation. Used in military planning to give control of specified areas to individual units, enhancing control and accountability.

AOC: Area of Concern. Fictional term for a designated area outside of formal ZOCs where temporary control is established to meet specific goals e.g. the eradication of an insurgent group.

APC: Acronym for Armored Personnel Carrier. A military vehicle intended to deliver troops to the battlefield while providing protection against small arms fire and artillery fragments, but not enough to withstand direct fire from a tank or anti-tank weapon systems.

AR: Stands for Armalite Rifle, not "Assault Rifle" as many assume. Alludes to the AR-15, the civilian semi-automatic version of the U.S. military M16, though has come to be a general label for any weapon based on the original design.

AT-4: A single-use anti-tank unguided rocket consisting of a disposable tube/flip-up sights/trigger and the contained rocket.

Bancor: A fictional monetary unit denoted by the symbol ฿. Created by an unknown global agency as a new fiat currency i.e. not backed by tangible assets.

Blackhawk: The standard light transport helicopter of the U.S. Army and successor to the UH-1 Huey.

BPS: Abbreviation of the fictional Bene Praepara Supply, Kyle Flanigan's package-focused preparedness company out of Enumclaw, WA.

Bullpup: A firearms design in which the ammunition is fed behind the grip/trigger. Often denoted by the weapon's magazine behind the firing grip. Results in a more compact weapon.

Bushmaster: An American firearm manufacturer best known for their inexpensive AR-pattern rifles.

Camp Lejeune: A Marine Corps base located just east of the city of Jacksonville, NC and home to the 2nd Marine Division.

CASEVAC: Short for casualty evacuation. Unlike MEDEVAC, it involves the use of non-dedicated vehicles/means of transport.

CB (Citizen's Band): A personal and business use AM radio communications band created in 1958 and most often associated with older "walkie-talkies" and vehicle-mounted systems.

CBRN: Acronym for Chemical, Biological, Radiological, Nuclear. Most often used in relation to disposal or mitigation measures e.g. *CBRN defense*.

Colt: An iconic American firearms manufacturer best known for their handguns with civilian and military appeal (the Single Action Army and 1911) and more recently with M16/AR-15 rifle family.

CS: The chemical compound o-chlorobenzylidene malononitrile, usually referred to as *CS gas* or *tear gas* though it is actually a solid. The name is an acronym of the two discoverers' last names. Causes irritation of the eyes, lungs, and mucus membranes and usually used in riot control.

Daedalus Systems: A fictional company specializing in high-end custom safes and security systems.

DAT: Acronym for Direct Action Team, a fictitious organization of ten to several dozen Peace Enforcement personnel, typically used for urban operations.

DHS: Acronym for the Department of Homeland Security, created in 2002 after the 9/11/01 terror attacks, and includes FEMA, the U.S. Coast Guard, the Secret Service, and other agencies.

Ebola: Name of a strain of often-fatal hemorrhagic fever. Fictionally spread in *Turn Red Tomorrow* via airborne and other means.

Eureka: A small city located in the northwest corner of California along the Pacific Ocean. Heading north along the coast, the last significant metropolitan area for several hundred miles.

Executive Order 13603: A very real-life Executive Order signed by then-President Obama that updates older, similar orders and allows for near total federal takeover of food production, transportation, healthcare, and forced labor in the event of a national emergency.

FEMA: Acronym for the Federal Emergency Management Agency, created in 1979 by executive order, and primarily tasked with dealing with emergencies too large for local and state agencies to handle. Fell under the Department of Homeland Security in 2003.

FLIR: Acronym for Forward Looking Infrared. A form of thermal optics typically used on aircraft, ships, and combat vehicles.

FRS (Family Radio Service): A personal-use FM radio communications band created in 1996 and most often associated with inexpensive "walkie-talkies" made after that time.

Fully-Automatic: A firearms term denoting a weapon that will continue to fire as long as the trigger is depressed and ammunition is available. Contrary to popular belief, such weapons are very difficult for civilians to obtain in the United States.

Glock: An Austrian firearms manufacturer with significant manufacturing in the U.S., and best known for their extremely popular line of polymer-framed semi-automatic pistols.

GSW: Acronym for Gun Shot Wound.

H&K: Sometimes written simply as "HK" and standing for Heckler and Koch, a German firearms manufacturer best known for their rugged designs intended for the military and law enforcement markets.

Hood Canal: A natural body of salt water (technically a fjord) in Western Washington State between the Olympic Peninsula to the west and the Kitsap Peninsula to the east.

Jarhead: Slang for a U.S. Marine.

JBLM (Joint Base Lewis-McChord): A large joint Army/Air Force base located southwest of Tacoma, WA and home to the Army's I Corps and the Air Force's 62d Airlift Wing.

KA-BAR: While the name of a knife manufacturer, the term is most often attributed to the USMC blade design that dates back to WWII.

Lake Cushman: A lake (reservoir) located west of Hoodsport and partially surrounded by Olympic National Park.

M16: Standard U.S. military rifle from the early 1960s and only recently supplanted by the M4 Carbine. The A1 variant, most often associated with the Vietnam War, was fully-automatic and sported a thin 20" barrel, while the later A2 had only a three-round burst and had a thicker 20" barrel. The A3 brought back the full-auto setting, while the final variant, the A4, was essentially an A2 with an optic rail instead of a carrying handle.

M240: Standard general-purpose machinegun for all U.S. (and many foreign) military branches. Belt fed, 7.62x51mm, accepts optics, highly reliable.

M2HB: Standard heavy machinegun for all U.S. (and many foreign) military branches. Belt fed, .50BMG, tripod or vehicle mounted.

M4 Carbine: The standard issue rifle of all U.S. military branches, distinguished from earlier rifles by its short 14.5" barrel and railed receiver to aid in the mounting of an optic. The M4 has a 3-round burst setting while the M4A1 is fully automatic.

Marlin: A firearms manufacturer formerly based in New Haven, CT (now in Ilion, NY) and best known for their lever-action rifles.

MEDEVAC: Short for medical evacuation.

Mk19: Standard U.S. military fully-automatic grenade launcher. Fires 40mm grenades over 2000m (1.25 miles).

M.O.: Acronym for the Latin *Modus Operandi* or Mode of Operations. Simply put, how things are done.

Mossberg: A firearms manufacturer based in New Haven, CT and best known for their rugged and inexpensive shotguns.

MRE: Acronym for Meal, Ready to Eat. Standard military field ration that includes a main meal, sides, toilet paper, spices, chewing gum, and a water-activated heater. Civilian versions exist, usually with less food/fewer calories.

National Identification Card (NID): A fictitious chip-enabled photo ID card issued to all U.S. residents. Blue for civilian government employees, gray for military personnel, yellow for prisoners, and orange for everyone else.

OODA Loop: OODA stands for Observe, Orient, Decide, Act; the process naturally "loops" back based on feedback from each step. A concept developed by USAF Col. John Boyd. In a military context, most units/assets have a specific part to play in the decision-making process, and the goal of training is to enhance the speed and precision of each step to gain an advantage over the opposing force.

Olympic Mountains: A non-volcanic mountain range located in Washington State on the peninsula of the same name. Best known for its temperate rain forests and diverse wildlife.

Peace Enforcement: A fictional organization created within the DHS hierarchy and staffed by shifting nearly all military personnel within the United States into its framework, ostensibly to create a massive federal law enforcement agency, but possibly for other unknown reasons as well.

Peace Enforcement Auxiliary: A fictional organization, also created under DHS, but staffed by civilian volunteers. While they have no authority to arrest, they have wide latitude to detain suspects and confiscate a long list of items including weapons, fuel, and precious metals.

Pogue: American military slang for anyone serving in a support or rear-echelon role (versus combat roles like infantry or armor).

Posse Comitatus: In general usage, refers to citizens assisting law enforcement. The *Posse Comitatus Act* prohibits American civilian authorities from using military personnel in a law enforcement capacity.

Randall: A knife maker out of Orlando, FL that achieved fame during WWII and is best known for their high-end production military and sporting designs.

Rapture: A Christian concept derived from the Greek *harpazo*, meaning to "snatch up" or "seize." An event where all believers are brought to Heaven preceding the Second Coming of Jesus Christ.

Rembrandt Village: A fictional community just north of the real town of Lilliwaup, WA along Highway 101, and consisting of little more than a large mobile home park, gas station, and bar.

RFID: Acronym for Radio Frequency Identification, a modern system utilizing smart labels, tags, or microchips that provide stored data to radio-wave readers.

ROE: Acronym for Rules of Engagement. Military term for blanket rules defining how and when force can be applied.

Ruger: A firearms manufacturer based in Southport, CT and best known for their rugged and inexpensive designs.

Sako: A firearms manufacturer out of Finland best known for their fine bolt action rifles.

SAW: Acronym for Squad Automatic Weapon. In the U.S. military, this is the M249, a belt-fed light machinegun with an uneven record for reliability.

Semi-Automatic: A firearm term that means one and only one shot is fired per pull of the trigger, and the force of firing re-loads the firearm as long as there are cartridges in the magazine or belt.

SIG Sauer: Originally a partnership between two firearms manufacturers, SIG of Switzerland and Sauer of West Germany and best known for their high-quality semiautomatic pistols.

Siskiyou Mountains: A group of mountains straddling the Oregon and California border from the Pacific Ocean inland about 100 miles. Known for their variety of conifer trees, heavy precipitation, and lack of natural passes/long valleys.

Smith and Wesson: Abbreviated as S&W. Firearms and police equipment manufacturer based in Springfield, MA and best known for their many revolver and semi-automatic pistol designs.

SNA: Acronym for the fictitious Society for a New America, loosely based on several real-life progressive political and community action groups.

Spyphone: A colloquialism of the fictional government issued cellphones used by several characters in *Turn Red Tomorrow*. These phones have RFID and data access capabilities beyond commonly available civilian models.

Stryker: An eight-wheeled APC in use by the U.S. Army.

Sunshine Lake: A fictional small lake on the Olympic Peninsula located several miles northwest of the real town of Lilliwaup, WA.

Tarpon Springs: A beachside community along the Gulf of Mexico northwest of Tampa, FL.

Taurus: A firearm manufacturer out of Brazil best known for their copies/near copies of Beretta, Colt, and S&W designs.

Ten Scale: Referred to several times by Kyle Flanigan. An easy system of classifying knowledge and/or experience. A zero means no frame of reference — a Roman centurion holding a modern pistol would have no idea what it was or what it might be used for. A one means recognition but no experience — a teenager who has consumed modern American entertainment knows what a pistol is and that bullets leave the muzzle when the trigger is pulled. The levels progress from there to ten — a true master and typically a category reserved for the top 100 practitioners in the world. E.g. when first introduced, Malachi Hayden is a level one rifle shooter, Kyle Flanigan is a level seven, and DeScan Hupp is a borderline nine.

Tikka: The budget line of Sako rifles made in Finland.

Thermals: Colloquial term for any optical device using thermal imaging or thermography to form an image. Such devices detect infrared radiation below visible red light and represent in such as way to be visible to the human eye. Uses include night navigation, firefighting, and of course military targeting and detection applications.

TOC: Acronym for Tactical Operations Center. Military and law enforcement term for a centralized post to real-time observe and guide a mission or operation.

Vepr: A series of AK-derived rifles and pistols made by Molot in Russia. Pertaining to *Turn Red Tomorrow*, refers to fictional rifles made in the U.S. using the same design (manufacturer not stated).

Weatherby: An American firearms manufacturer best known for their sporting rifles in Weatherby-specific high velocity chamberings.

Zero: Referring to the process of calibrating a given firearm or weapon system to strike a target at an exact range e.g. Kyle's Marlin is zeroed to 100 yards.

ZOC: Zone of Control, colloquially "zock." Fictional term for an area designated by FEMA and/or the DHS for food distri-

Michael Zargona

bution and other relief measures, along with strict enforcement of government mandates.

APPENDIX A – SUNSHINE LAKE RESIDENTS (BY CABIN)

#1: Not stated
#2: Not stated
#3: Rex/Goodridge
#4: Benson/Burkett
#5: Not stated
#6: Jeanie Suarez + family
#7: Not stated
#8: Rufus + Wife
#9: Greg Samuels + Lenny
#10: Empty
#11: Flanigan
#12: Gautier
#13: Not stated
#14: Klein
#15: McGwire
#16: Not stated
#17: Not stated
#18: Morrison
#19: Not stated
#20: Not stated

APPENDIX B – MAJOR REX'S FIELD SURGEON BAG

Five C-A-T®s - Combat Application Tourniquets. These were each a complete kit: band, stick, and white strip to write the time the tourniquet was applied. They were a huge step up from the Cold War era "find a stick, a piece of rope, and grease pencil the time on the patient's forehead" field expedient methods taught to the ground pounders. Melissa carried two more of these in her sleeve pocket.

Three Hextend IVs. These were newer and another major step up from what came before. IVs were great but, on a patient with significant blood loss, could lead to problems as they thinned an already reduced blood supply. Hextend IVs actually drew out red blood cells and worked to prevent this. In the field it wasn't feasible to carry blood so this was the next best thing.

Eight "Israeli" battle dressings, named for those that developed them in the first place. Each was six inches wide and nearly six feet in length and were the standard compression bandage to help stop bleeding and cover open wounds.

Two chest seals, the newer style with a bubble in the middle. These were special bandages for open pneumothorax—more commonly known as a sucking chest wound. Simply sealing up the wound was contraindicative and would lead to air being trapped in the chest cavity as the victim inhaled. Purpose-built chest seals kept blood in, dirt out, and allowed air to escape.

Four 14 gauge Quick Caths for needle chest decompression.

Six vacuum-sealed "Combat Gauze" bandages impregnated with a coagulant chemical to stop bleeding.

Two eye dressings. Also special bandages, these were specifically for eye injuries that protected and kept pressure off the eye.

Several rolls each of gauze, Ace wraps, and two inch medical tape.

A box of smaller bandages e.g. Band-Aids.

A box of nitrile gloves.

Scissors.

Combat Casualty Cards.

A smaller kit containing morphine, several kinds of antibiotics, Ondansetron (to counter morphine's nausea-inducing side effects), and atropine (most commonly for those affected by nerve agents).

A standard 100oz hydration bladder for personal use (not sterile).

ABOUT THE AUTHOR

Michael Zargona is a Christian, military veteran, family man, honors college graduate, and small business owner who both grew up and currently lives in the Pacific Northwest with his wife and children. Unsurprisingly, Michael enjoys hunting, sport shooting, hiking, and tinkering with computers, home projects, and firearms. And, when there's time, writing.

He can be reached at michaelzargona@gmail.com